2

英语语境语法 2

教师参考用书

（第四版）

Grammar in Context

TEACHER'S ANNOTATED EDITION

4TH EDITION

SANDRA N. ELBAUM

HILARY GRANT

北京大学出版社
PEKING UNIVERSITY PRESS

著作权合同登记　图字：01-2006-4115号

图书在版编目（CIP）数据

英语语境语法 2 教师参考用书（第四版）= Grammar in Context 2 Teacher's Annotated Edition (Fourth Edition)/桑德拉·艾尔鲍姆（Sandra N. Elbaum），希拉里·格兰特（Hilary Grant）．—影印本．—北京：北京大学出版社，2006.8

（英语语境语法系列丛书）

ISBN 7-301-11037-5

Ⅰ.英…　Ⅱ.①桑…　②希…　Ⅲ.英语-语法-高等学校-教学参考资料　Ⅳ.H314

中国版本图书馆 CIP 数据核字（2006）第 103711 号

SANDRA N. ELBAUM/HILARY GRANT

Grammar in Context 2 Teacher's Annotated Edition (Fourth Edition)

EISBN: 1-4130-0747-3

978-981-4195-50-8

Thomson Learning (A division of Thomson Asia Pte Ltd)
5 Shenton Way, #01-01 UIC Building Singapore 068808

书　　名：英语语境语法 2 教师参考用书（第四版）
Grammar in Context 2 Teacher's Annotated Edition (Fourth Edition)
著作责任者：桑德拉·艾尔鲍姆（Sandra N. Elbaum）希拉里·格兰特（Hilary Grant）
责 任 编 辑：胡 娜
标 准 书 号：ISBN 7-301-11037-5/H · 1683
出 版 发 行：北京大学出版社
地　　址：北京市海淀区成府路 205 号　100871
网　　址：http://www.pup.cn
电　　话：邮购部 62752015　发行部 62750672　编辑部 62767347　出版部 62754962
电 子 邮 箱：zbing@pup.pku.edu.cn
印 刷 者：北京大学印刷厂
经 销 者：新华书店
889 毫米×1194 毫米　16 开本　33.25 印张　840 千字
2006 年 8 月第 1 版　2006 年 8 月第 1 次印刷
定　　价：66.00元

导 言

北京大学英语系教授 王逢鑫

一

语言由语音、词汇和语法三个要素组成。学习一门外语,必须掌握这三个要素,缺一不可。有人认为只要记住单词,能读出音来,就行了,而语法可有可无。其实这是一种误解。语法是组词造句的法则,十分重要。传统英语语法细分为词法(morphology)和句法(syntax)。词法解释词分为哪些种类,即词类;告诉人们每个词类有什么特点,即词性;说明一个词与别的什么词可以联系在一起使用,即在句子里起什么作用。英语词汇形态与汉语有很大的区别。例如,名词有单、复数之分,还有可数与不可数之分。人称代词有主格、宾格和所有格之分。动词有现在式、过去式和过去分词三种不同形式;还有不定式、现在分词、过去分词和动名词等非谓语动词形式。形容词有原级、比较级和最高级三种形式。数词有基数词和序数词之分。以上词类大都是规则变化,但是也有很多不规则变化的例外情况。例如英语有一百来个不规则动词,其中多数是常用动词。介词后面跟人称代词要用宾格,跟动词要用动名词形式。英语的冠词更是难学。有人学了多年英语,还是弄不清楚什么时候用定冠词,什么时候用不定冠词,什么时候不用任何冠词。虽然不定冠词仅有 a 和 an 两种形式, 但是有人把 an hour 写成 a hour, 把 a university 写成 an university。这些繁杂的内容都是初学者必须掌握的,使用不当就要犯错误。

英语句法分析句子的种类、结构和功能。英语句法比汉语复杂。英语有各种各样的时态,每种时态有自己固定的形式,不能用错。句法规则繁多,几乎没有什么道理可讲。例如,在一般现在时里,单数第三人称的动词要加-s。情态动词和助动词后面要跟原形动词。英语句子讲究人称和时态前后呼应,左右照顾。诸如此类的条条框框都是初学者的"拦路虎"。

国内外的语言学家和英语教师,曾经尝试使用各种各样的方法来教英语语法。时代不同,学习目的不同,教学对象不同,教材不同,学习方法不同,使得人们很难找到学习英语语法的一个最佳方案。但是,我们了解一下国内外英语语法教学的来龙去脉,或许有助于我们吸取教训,总结经验,寻找有效的学习英语语法的途径。

传统法(traditional method)强调以语法为纲,以语法为教学中心。学生按部就班学习语法规则,先是死记硬背条条框框,然后做大量的机械性(mechanical)练习,基本上是没有上下文的单句翻译、语法填空和造句练习。追求的是语法形式正确无误,而不管在什么情况下使用语言。学习语法,不是为了交际,而是为了阅读内容艰深的文章,分析复杂的句法结构。我国解放前和解放初期的英语专业大学生,是通过传统法学习英语语法的,虽然有一些弊端,例如引导学生重视阅读和笔译,而忽视口头表达能力的培养。但是这种方法也并非一无是处。学生中不乏精通英语的成功者。传统法强调阅读小说、诗歌、戏剧和散文等文学作品,认为文学语言是最好的语言。通过对语句和篇章细致的句法分析,学生获得对语句和篇章结构，尤其是繁杂结构的精确理解。今天我们强调学习语言是为了交流思想，重视口头表达能力，传统法是难当此任的。

听说法(audio-visual method)将英语分成许多基本句型(sentence pattern)，将语法教学与句型教学结合在一起。要求学生熟练掌握句型，反复口头练习，达到不假思索，脱口而出的程度。掌握了句型，就等于掌握了语法。20 世纪 60 年代初，听说法引入我国，在当时的英语专业大学生中间曾经奏效。学生反复练习没有上下文的基本句型，虽然枯燥无味，但是在当时的历史环境下，多数学生能够不厌其烦地做大量的机械性口头练习，而取得较好的学习效果。现在的学生要求在学习过程中有更多的独立自主，对死记硬背基本句型不太感兴趣。利用听说法学习英语语法似乎不太合乎时宜了。

语言学家和英语教师总是想方设法改进语法教学。他们先是将以单句练习为主的机械性句型练习，扩充为共有两句话的二人对话，构成一个简单的情景，使所练习的句型变得有意义。再往后，进一步将二人对话扩大为围绕一个主题的、有上下文的情景会话(situational conversation)。这样，学生可以在一定的语境(context)之中通过句型学习英语语法。最初的语境是为了练习某个语言点，或为了掌握某种意念功能而编造的，具有人为的成分。20 世纪 80 年代初，国内外兴起交际法(communicative method)。这种教学法的目标是让学生不仅学会听、说、读、写的语言能力 (linguistic competence)，还要掌握交际能力(communicative competence)。交际法从交流的目的出发，既要求语法正确(correct in grammar)，更要求语用得体(appropriate in use)。因而在教学中引进了社会与文化因素。学习内容不再是干巴巴的基本句型，而是人们关注的社会问题和文化现象。学生不再为学习语法而学习语法，而是为了交际来学习语法。他们希望能够使用语法正确、语用得体的语言，就人们关注的社会问题和文化现象进行交流。这样就需要在一定的社会环境和文化语境里学习语言，包括学习语法。在学习语言的同时，必须了解英语国家的文化背景，以及中外文化差异。只有学习了相关的文化背景知识，才能更好地掌握语言。这套名为 *Grammar in Context* (《英语语境语法》)的教材，在上述背景下应运而生。

二

这套《英语语境语法》的编者 Sandra N. Elbaum 女士，是美国的一位英语教师，专门教授从世界各地到美国的移民，他们是以英语为第二语言的学生。Elbaum 女士幼年随父母由波兰移民到美国，语言差异和文化差异经常使她的父母感到困惑。Elbaum 女士在移民聚居的社区中成长，深知一个外国移民在美国生存，不仅要逾越语言障碍，更要克服文化差异。她有一个信念，就是通过语境学习语法。她不但在教学中身体力行，通过语境教英语语法，而且亲自编写教材，体现这一理念。

这套英语教材名曰《英语语境语法》，实际上是教给学生通过语境学习英语语言。这套教材的宗旨是：让学习者在语境中学习语法，以便学到更多东西，记住更多东西，更加有效地运用语言。

这套教材有如下突出特点：

1. 教给学生进行口头交流和书面交流所必需的语法知识。按照循序渐进原则安排语法点，讲解后面的语法内容都联系和复习前面的语法内容，使整个语法系统构成一个有机的整体。解释每个语法点，都使用形象的语法图表(grammar chart)，一目了然。每个语法图表提供有语境的精选例句，并给出清晰的解释，还配以语言提示(language note)，增强学习者对所学语法结构的理解。每个语法点还以图表方式解释其形式、用途、语序、主语、相关结构、描述与定义、所需介词搭配、肯定句、否定句和疑问句及回答等项目。每个项目都配有大量的口头和笔头练习。

2. 不是为教语法而教语法，而是通过语法教学，给学习者提供有用的(useful)、有意义的(meaningful)技能和基本文化知识。在课堂上，教师不是局限于让学生做机械性练习，而是让他们通过二人对话、小组活动、游戏、讨论等多种形式的扩展活动(expansion activity)，互相启发，互相帮助，学以致用。通过阅读、作文、独立思考的练习等方式，学习者拓展自己的语言知识和交际能力，最终达到既能有效使用语言，又有信心正确使用语言进行交流的双重目的。

3. 教材将英语语法学习和美国文化语境结合起来。全套教材分为1、2、3三级，每级又分为两个分册，共有1A、1B、2A、2B、3A、3B等6个分册。1级和2级各有14课；3级有10课。每课内容，包括语法讲解和练习、阅读课文和扩展活动，都围绕美国社会的一个热门话题，构成一个语境。从语言学习角度，涉及一个语法点；从文化学习角度，涉及一个话题。二者巧妙结合。1级有学校生活、美国政府、美国节日、美国人及其住宅、家庭与姓名、美国人生活方式、婚礼、飞行、购物、营养与健康、伟大女性、美国地理、约会与婚姻、实习等14个话题。2级有宠物、老年生活、改善生活、婚礼、感恩节与印第安人、健康、移民、租房、上网搜索、找工作、交友、体育、法律、货币等14个话题。3级有工作、好莱坞、灾难与悲剧、消费者警告、肯尼迪家族、计算机与互联网、帮助他人、来到美国、关爱儿童、科学与科幻小说等10个话题。这些语境概括了美国社会的方方面面，是了解美国文化和在美国生存所必需的基本知识。这些语境有助于学习者掌握必需的文化背景知识，使他们懂得美国文化在语言、信仰和日常生活情景等方面的重要作用。

这是一套通过语境学习英语的好教材。使用这套教材，学习者不仅可以熟练掌握英语语法，运用英语语言；而且可以学习美国文化背景知识，在语境中学习英语，在语境中使用英语。希望学习者喜欢这套教材，并通过学习这套教材学好英语。

Contents

Appendices

In loving memory of
Roberto Garrido Alfaro

Acknowledgments

Many thanks to Dennis Hogan, Jim Brown, Sherrise Roehr, Yeny Kim, and Sally Giangrande from Thomson Heinle for their ongoing support of the *Grammar in Context* series. I would especially like to thank my editor, Charlotte Sturdy, for her keen eye to detail and invaluable suggestions.

And many thanks to my students at Truman College, who have increased my understanding of my own language and taught me to see life from another point of view. By sharing their observations, questions, and life stories, they have enriched my life enormously.—*Sandra N. Elbaum*

Heinle would like to thank the following people for their contributions:

Marki Alexander
Oklahoma State University
Stillwater, OK

Joan M. Amore
Triton College
River Grove, IL

Edina Pingleton Bagley
Nassau Community College
Garden City, NY

Judith A. G. Benka
Normandale Community College
Bloomington, MN

Judith Book-Ehrlichman
Bergen Community College
Paramus, NJ

Lyn Buchheit
Community College of Philadelphia
Philadelphia, PA

Charlotte M. Calobrisi
Northern Virginia Community College
Annandale, VA

Sarah A. Carpenter
Normandale Community College
Bloomington, MN

Jeanette Clement
Duquesne University
Pittsburgh, PA

Allis Cole
Shoreline Community College
Shoreline, WA

Jacqueline M. Cunningham
Triton College
River Grove, IL

Lisa DePaoli
Sierra College
Rocklin, CA

Maha Edlbi
Sierra College
Rocklin, CA

Rhonda J. Farley
Cosumnes River College
Sacramento, CA

Jennifer Farnell
University of Connecticut American Language Program
Stamford, CT

Abigail-Marie Fiattarone
Mesa Community College
Mesa, AZ

Marcia Gethin-Jones
University of Connecticut American Language Program
Storrs, CT

Linda Harlow
Santa Rosa Junior College
Santa Rosa, CA

Suha R. Hattab
Triton College
River Grove, IL

Bill Keniston
Normandale Community College
Bloomington, MN

Walton King
Arkansas State University
Jonesboro, AR

Kathleen Krokar
Truman College
Chicago, IL

John Larkin
NVCC-Community and Workforce Development
Annandale, VA

Michael Larsen
American River College
Sacramento, CA

Bea C. Lawn
Gavilan College
Gilroy, CA

Rob Lee
Pasadena City College
Pasadena, CA

Oranit Limmaneeprasert
American River College
Sacramento, CA

Gennell Lockwood
Shoreline Community College
Shoreline, WA

Linda Louie
Highline Community College
Des Moines, WA

Melanie A. Majeski
Naugatuck Valley Community College
Waterbury, CT

Maria Marin
De Anza College
Cupertino, CA

Karen Miceli
Cosumnes River College
Sacramento, CA

Jeanie Pavichevich
Triton College
River Grove, IL

Herbert Pierson
St. John's University
New York City, NY

Dina Poggi
De Anza College
Cupertino, CA

Mark Rau
American River College
Sacramento, CA

John W. Roberts
Shoreline Community College
Shoreline, WA

Azize R. Ruttler
Bergen Community College
Paramus, NJ

Ann Salzmann
University of Illinois,
Urbana, IL

Eva Teagarden
Yuba College
Marysville, CA

Susan Wilson
San Jose City College
San Jose, CA

Martha Yeager-Tobar
Cerritos College
Norwalk, CA

A word from the author

It seems that I was born to be an ESL teacher. My parents immigrated to the U.S. from Poland as adults and were confused not only by the English language but by American culture as well. Born in the U.S., I often had the task as a child to explain the intricacies of the language and allay my parents' fears about the culture. It is no wonder to me that I became an ESL teacher, and later, an ESL writer who focuses on explanations of American culture in order to illustrate grammar. My life growing up in an immigrant neighborhood was very similar to the lives of my students, so I have a feel for what confuses them and what they need to know about American life.

ESL teachers often find themselves explaining confusing customs and providing practical information about life in the U.S. Often, teachers are a student's only source of information about American life. With ***Grammar in Context, Fourth Edition,*** I enjoy sharing my experiences with you.

Grammar in Context, Fourth Edition connects grammar with American cultural context, providing learners of English with a useful and meaningful skill and knowledge base. Students learn the grammar necessary to communicate verbally and in writing, and learn how American culture plays a role in language, beliefs, and everyday situations.

Enjoy the new edition of ***Grammar in Context!***

Sandra N. Elbaum

Grammar in Context

Students learn more, remember more, and use language more effectively when they learn grammar in context.

Learning a language through meaningful themes and practicing it in a contextualized setting promote both linguistic and cognitive development. In ***Grammar in Context,*** grammar is presented in interesting and culturally informative readings, and the language and context are subsequently practiced throughout the chapter.

New to this edition

- **New and updated readings** on current American topics such as Instant Messaging and eBay.
- **Updated grammar charts** that now include essential language notes.
- **Updated exercises and activities** that provide contextualized practice using a variety of exercise types, as well as additional practice for more difficult structures.
- **New lower-level *Grammar in Context Basic*** for beginning level students.
- **New wrap-around Teacher's Annotated Edition** with page-by-page, point-of-use teaching suggestions.
- **Expanded Assessment CD-ROM** with *ExamView® Pro* Test Generator now contains more question types and assessment options to easily allow teachers to create tests and quizzes.

Distinctive Features of *Grammar in Context*

Students are prepared for academic assignments and everyday language tasks.

Discussions, readings, compositions, and exercises involving higher-level critical thinking skills develop overall language and communication skills.

Students expand their knowledge of American topics and culture.

The readings in ***Grammar in Context*** help students gain insight into and enrich their knowledge of American culture and history. Students gain ample exposure to the practicalities of American life, such as writing a résumé, dealing with telemarketers, junk mail, and getting student internships. Their new knowledge helps them adapt to everyday life in the U.S.

Students learn to use their new skills to communicate.

The exercises and Expansion Activities in ***Grammar in Context*** help students learn English while practicing their writing and speaking skills. Students work together in pairs and groups to find more information about topics, to make presentations, to play games, and to role-play. Their confidence in using English increases, as does their ability to communicate effectively.

Grammar in Context Student Book Supplements

Audio Program

- Audio CDs and Audio Tapes allow students to listen to every reading in the book as well as selected dialogs.

***More Grammar Practice* Workbooks**

- Workbooks can be used with *Grammar in Context* or any skills text to learn and review the essential grammar.
- Great for in-class practice or homework.
- Includes practice on all grammar points in *Grammar in Context.*

Teacher's Annotated Edition

- New component offers page-by-page answers and teaching suggestions.

Assessment CD-ROM with *ExamView® Pro* Test Generator

- Test Generator allows teachers to create tests and quizzes quickly and easily.

Interactive CD-ROM

- CD-ROM allows for supplemental interactive practice on grammar points from *Grammar in Context.*

Split Editions

- Split Editions provide options for short courses.

Instructional Video/DVD

- Video/DVD offers teaching suggestions and advice on how to use *Grammar in Context.*

Web Site

- Web site gives access to additional activities and promotes the use of the Internet.

Welcome to *Grammar in Context, Fourth Edition*

Students learn more, remember more, and use language more effectively when they learn grammar in context.

Grammar in Context, Fourth Edition connects grammar with rich, American cultural context, providing learners of English with a useful and meaningful skill and knowledge base.

An **Audio Program** allows students to hear the readings and dialogs, and provides an opportunity to practice their listening skills.

Readings on American topics such as Google, Internet Matchmaking, and Jury Duty present and illustrate the grammatical structure in an informative and meaningful context.

Grammar charts offer clear explanations and provide contextualized examples of the structure.

Language Notes refine students' understanding of the target structure.

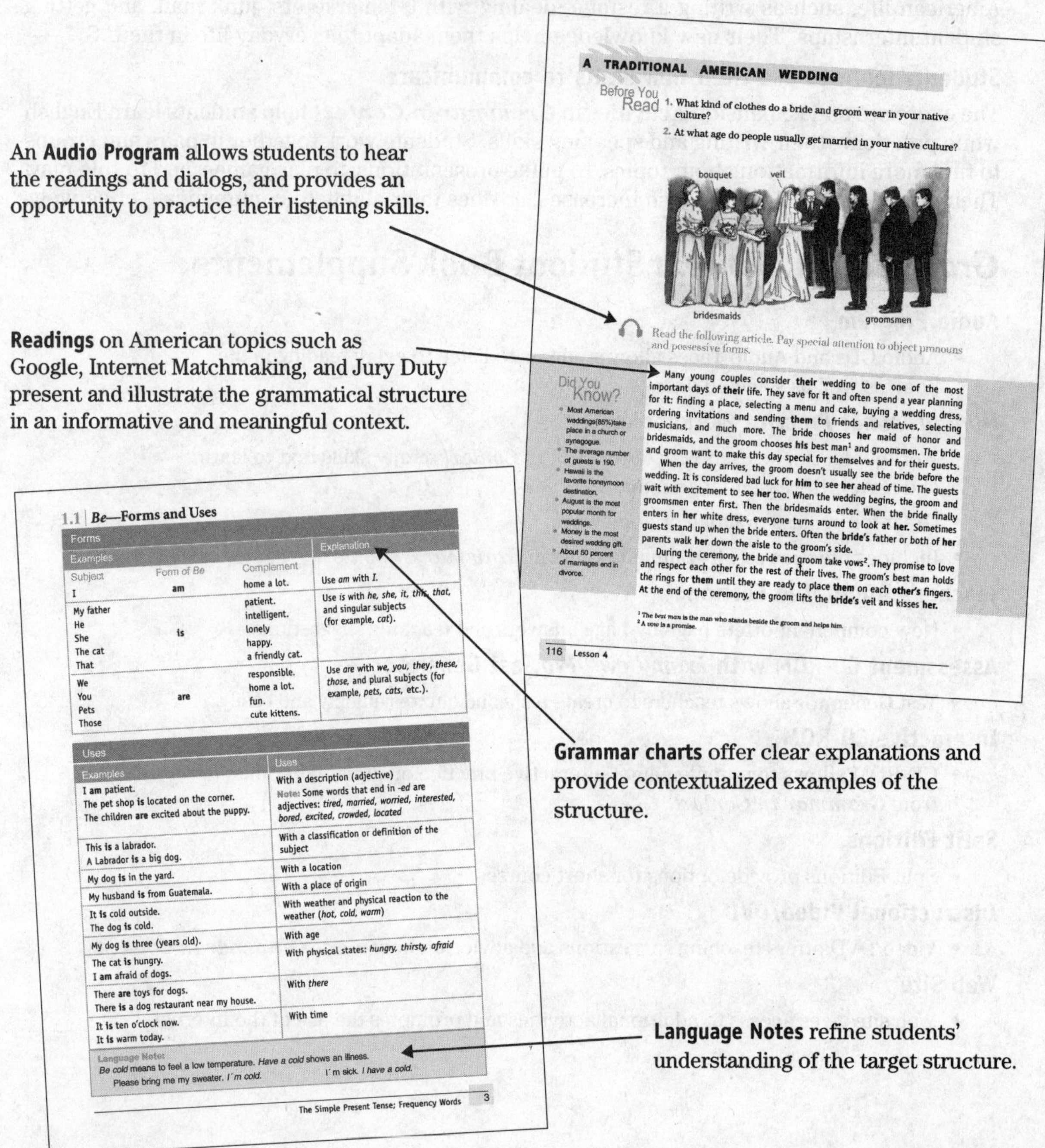

A TRADITIONAL AMERICAN WEDDING

Before You Read

1. What kind of clothes do a bride and groom wear in your native culture?
2. At what age do people usually get married in your native culture?

Read the following article. Pay special attention to object pronouns and possessive forms.

Did You Know?

- Most American weddings(85%)take place in a church or synagogue.
- The average number of guests is 190.
- Hawaii is the favorite honeymoon destination.
- August is the most popular month for weddings.
- Money is the most desired wedding gift.
- About 50 percent of marriages end in divorce.

Many young couples consider **their** wedding to be one of the most important days of **their** life. They save for **it** and often spend a year planning for **it**: finding a place, selecting a menu and cake, buying a wedding dress, ordering invitations and sending **them** to friends and relatives, selecting musicians, and much more. The bride chooses **her** maid of honor and bridesmaids, and the groom chooses **his** best man[1] and groomsmen. The bride and groom want to make this day special for themselves and for their guests.

When the day arrives, the groom doesn't usually see the bride before the wedding. It is considered bad luck for **him** to see **her** ahead of time. The guests wait with excitement to see **her** too. When the wedding begins, the groom and groomsmen enter first. Then the bridesmaids enter. When the bride finally enters in **her** white dress, everyone turns around to look at **her.** Sometimes guests stand up when the bride enters. Often the **bride's** father or both of **her** parents walk **her** down the aisle to the groom's side.

During the ceremony, the bride and groom take vows[2]. They promise to love and respect each other for the rest of their lives. The groom's best man holds the rings for **them** until they are ready to place **them** on each **other's** fingers. At the end of the ceremony, the groom lifts the **bride's** veil and kisses **her.**

[1] The *best man* is the man who stands beside the groom and helps him.
[2] A *vow* is a promise.

116 Lesson 4

1.1 | *Be*—Forms and Uses

Forms

Subject	Form of Be	Complement	Explanation
I	**am**	home a lot.	Use *am* with *I*.
My father He She The cat That	**is**	patient. intelligent. lonely happy. a friendly cat.	Use *is* with *he, she, it, this, that,* and singular subjects (for example, *cat*).
We You Pets Those	**are**	responsible. home a lot. fun. cute kittens.	Use *are* with *we, you, they, these, those,* and plural subjects (for example, *pets, cats,* etc.).

Uses

Examples	Uses
I **am** patient. The pet shop **is** located on the corner. The children **are** excited about the puppy.	With a description (adjective) **Note:** Some words that end in *-ed* are adjectives: *tired, married, worried, interested, bored, excited, crowded, located*
This **is** a labrador. A Labrador **is** a big dog.	With a classification or definition of the subject
My dog **is** in the yard.	With a location
My husband **is** from Guatemala.	With a place of origin
It **is** cold outside. The dog **is** cold.	With weather and physical reaction to the weather (*hot, cold, warm*)
My dog **is** three (years old).	With age
The cat **is** hungry. I **am** afraid of dogs.	With physical states: *hungry, thirsty, afraid*
There **are** toys for dogs. There **is** a dog restaurant near my house.	With *there*
It **is** ten o'clock now. It **is** warm today.	With time

Language Note:
Be cold means to feel a low temperature. *Have a cold* shows an illness.
Please bring me my sweater. *I´m cold.* I´m sick. *I have a cold.*

The Simple Present Tense; Frequency Words 3

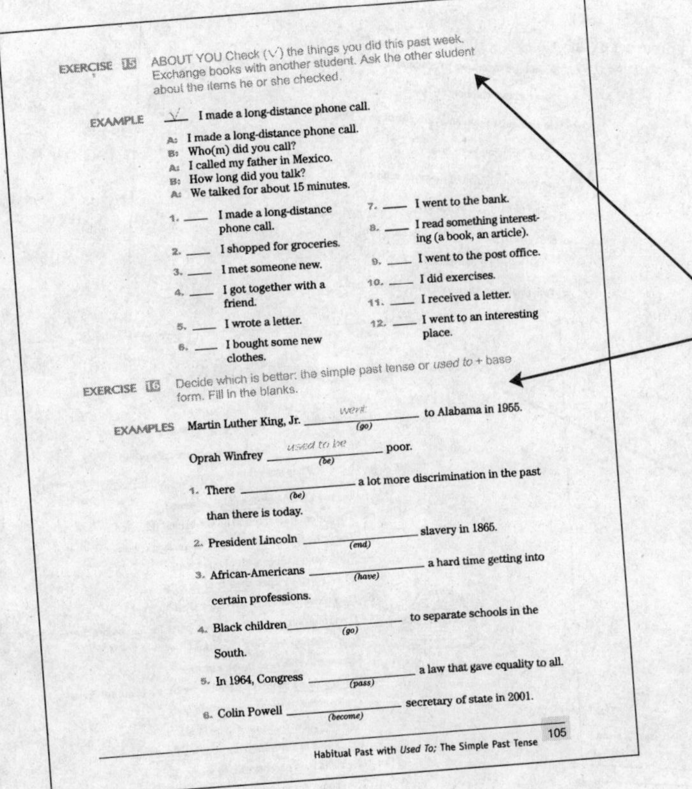

EXERCISE 15 ABOUT YOU Check (✓) the things you did this past week. Exchange books with another student. Ask the other student about the items he or she checked.

EXAMPLE ✓ I made a long-distance phone call.

A: I made a long-distance phone call.
B: Who(m) did you call?
A: I called my father in Mexico.
B: How long did you talk?
A: We talked for about 15 minutes.

1. ____ I made a long-distance phone call.
2. ____ I shopped for groceries.
3. ____ I met someone new.
4. ____ I got together with a friend.
5. ____ I wrote a letter.
6. ____ I bought some new clothes.
7. ____ I went to the bank.
8. ____ I read something interesting (a book, an article).
9. ____ I went to the post office.
10. ____ I did exercises.
11. ____ I received a letter.
12. ____ I went to an interesting place.

EXERCISE 16 Decide which is better: the simple past tense or *used to* + base form. Fill in the blanks.

EXAMPLES Martin Luther King, Jr. *went* (go) to Alabama in 1955.

Oprah Winfrey *used to be* (be) poor.

1. There ________ (be) a lot more discrimination in the past than there is today.
2. President Lincoln ________ (end) slavery in 1865.
3. African-Americans ________ (have) a hard time getting into certain professions.
4. Black children ________ (go) to separate schools in the South.
5. In 1964, Congress ________ (pass) a law that gave equality to all.
6. Colin Powell ________ (become) secretary of state in 2001.

Habitual Past with *Used To;* The Simple Past Tense 105

A variety of contextualized activities keeps the classroom lively and targets different learning styles.

A **Summary** provides the lesson's essential grammar in an easy-to-reference format.

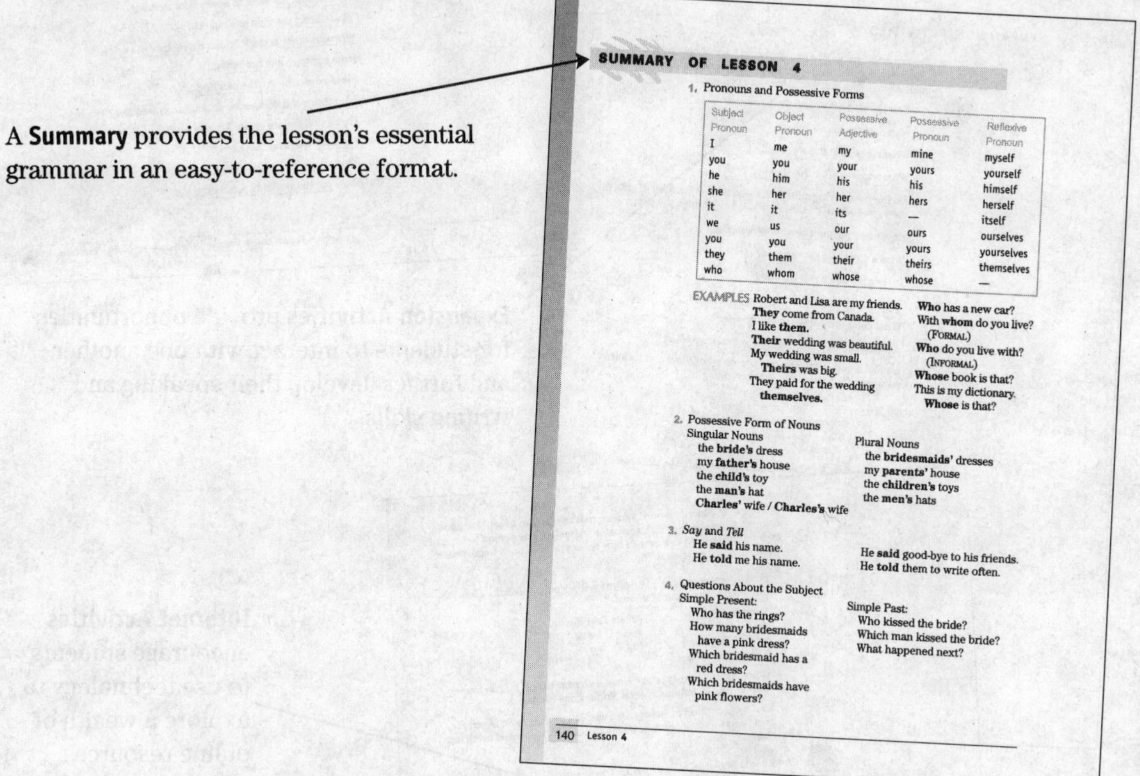

SUMMARY OF LESSON 4

1. Pronouns and Possessive Forms

Subject Pronoun	Object Pronoun	Possessive Adjective	Possessive Pronoun	Reflexive Pronoun
I	me	my	mine	myself
you	you	your	yours	yourself
he	him	his	his	himself
she	her	her	hers	herself
it	it	its	—	itself
we	us	our	ours	ourselves
you	you	your	yours	yourselves
they	them	their	theirs	themselves
who	whom	whose	whose	—

EXAMPLES Robert and Lisa are my friends. **They** come from Canada.
I like **them.**
Their wedding was beautiful.
My wedding was small.
Theirs was big.
They paid for the wedding **themselves.**

Who has a new car?
With **whom** do you live? (FORMAL)
Who do you live with? (INFORMAL)
Whose book is that?
This is my dictionary.
Whose is that?

2. Possessive Form of Nouns

Singular Nouns
the **bride's** dress
my **father's** house
the **child's** toy
the **man's** hat
Charles' wife / **Charles's** wife

Plural Nouns
the **bridesmaids'** dresses
my **parents'** house
the **children's** toys
the **men's** hats

3. *Say* and *Tell*

He **said** his name.
He **told** me his name.
He **said** good-bye to his friends.
He **told** them to write often.

4. Questions About the Subject

Simple Present:
Who has the rings?
How many bridesmaids have a pink dress?
Which bridesmaid has a red dress?
Which bridesmaids have pink flowers?

Simple Past:
Who kissed the bride?
Which man kissed the bride?
What happened next?

140 Lesson 4

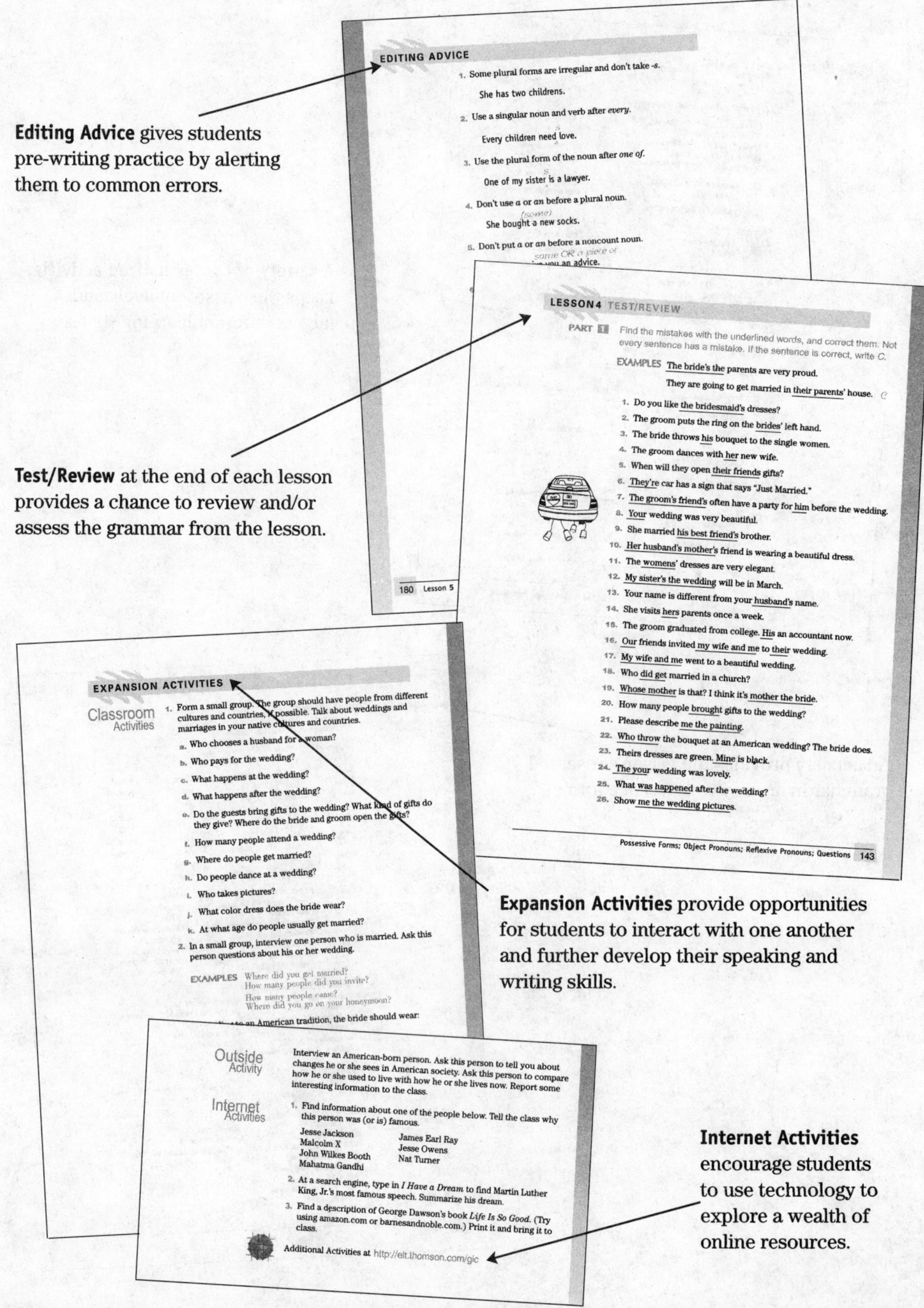

EDITING ADVICE

1. Some plural forms are irregular and don't take -*s*.
   She has two childrens.
2. Use a singular noun and verb after *every*.
   Every children need love.
3. Use the plural form of the noun after *one of*.
   One of my sister is a lawyer.
4. Don't use *a* or *an* before a plural noun.
   She bought a new socks.
5. Don't put *a* or *an* before a noncount noun.

180 Lesson 5

LESSON4 TEST/REVIEW

PART 1 Find the mistakes with the underlined words, and correct them. Not every sentence has a mistake. If the sentence is correct, write *C*.

EXAMPLES The bride's the parents are very proud.
They are going to get married in their parents' house. *C*

1. Do you like the bridesmaid's dresses?
2. The groom puts the ring on the brides' left hand.
3. The bride throws his bouquet to the single women.
4. The groom dances with her new wife.
5. When will they open their friends gifts?
6. They're car has a sign that says "Just Married."
7. The groom's friend's often have a party for him before the wedding.
8. Your wedding was very beautiful.
9. She married his best friend's brother.
10. Her husband's mother's friend is wearing a beautiful dress.
11. The womens' dresses are very elegant.
12. My sister's the wedding will be in March.
13. Your name is different from your husband's name.
14. She visits hers parents once a week.
15. The groom graduated from college. His an accountant now.
16. Our friends invited my wife and me to their wedding.
17. My wife and me went to a beautiful wedding.
18. Who did get married in a church?
19. Whose mother is that? I think it's mother the bride.
20. How many people brought gifts to the wedding?
21. Please describe me the painting.
22. Who throw the bouquet at an American wedding? The bride does.
23. Theirs dresses are green. Mine is black.
24. The your wedding was lovely.
25. What was happened after the wedding?
26. Show me the wedding pictures.

Possessive Forms; Object Pronouns; Reflexive Pronouns; Questions 143

EXPANSION ACTIVITIES

Classroom Activities

1. Form a small group. The group should have people from different cultures and countries, if possible. Talk about weddings and marriages in your native cultures and countries.
   a. Who chooses a husband for a woman?
   b. Who pays for the wedding?
   c. What happens at the wedding?
   d. What happens after the wedding?
   e. Do the guests bring gifts to the wedding? What kind of gifts do they give? Where do the bride and groom open the gifts?
   f. How many people attend a wedding?
   g. Where do people get married?
   h. Do people dance at a wedding?
   i. Who takes pictures?
   j. What color dress does the bride wear?
   k. At what age do people usually get married?
2. In a small group, interview one person who is married. Ask this person questions about his or her wedding.

EXAMPLES Where did you get married?
How many people did you invite?
How many people came?
Where did you go on your honeymoon?

Outside Activity

Interview an American-born person. Ask this person to tell you about changes he or she sees in American society. Ask this person to compare how he or she used to live with how he or she lives now. Report some interesting information to the class.

Internet Activities

1. Find information about one of the people below. Tell the class why this person was (or is) famous.
   Jesse Jackson, Malcolm X, John Wilkes Booth, Mahatma Gandhi, James Earl Ray, Jesse Owens, Nat Turner
2. At a search engine, type in *I Have a Dream* to find Martin Luther King, Jr.'s most famous speech. Summarize his dream.
3. Find a description of George Dawson's book *Life Is So Good*. (Try using amazon.com or barnesandnoble.com.) Print it and bring it to class.

Additional Activities at http://elt.thomson.com/gic

Editing Advice gives students pre-writing practice by alerting them to common errors.

Test/Review at the end of each lesson provides a chance to review and/or assess the grammar from the lesson.

Expansion Activities provide opportunities for students to interact with one another and further develop their speaking and writing skills.

Internet Activities encourage students to use technology to explore a wealth of online resources.

Frequently Asked Questions About Teaching with *Grammar in Context*

1. "What role do the readings play in teaching grammar? How much time do I spend on the readings? Should students read them for homework? Should they be read with the audio? What is most effective for grammar students?"

The readings are important in introducing the grammar in context. The readings should not be skipped. They can be done as either readings or listening activities. To save class time, the reading/listening can be done at home. The reading level is low enough that classroom instruction on "how to" read should not be necessary. The readings are not meant to challenge and improve one's reading skills; they are meant to illustrate the grammar in a stimulating context. In class, you can ask if there are any questions about the readings or the vocabulary within. There can be a short discussion on the "Before You Read" questions, if time allows. If there is sufficient class time, it is a good idea to have students listen to the audio and answer some comprehension questions as well. But this is not necessary in a grammar class. If there is a speech component in your program, the speech teacher can handle the listening activity.

2. "There is so much material. Do I have to do all of the exercises? If not, which ones do I cut, and which ones do I focus on?"

There is a lot of material, but you, as a teacher, are not required or expected to cover everything in a lesson. It would simply be impossible to do so in most ESL programs. If your program focuses on interactive oral communication, do the ABOUT YOU exercises. If your students attend another class for speech and conversation, these exercises can be skipped. These exercises are fun to do, and, if you find your students' attention waning, you can insert one of these activities. The other exercises can be split into classroom exercises and homework exercises. The simpler exercises can be done in class, leaving the more challenging combination exercises for home. Or, you can do half of an exercise in class, leaving the other half to be done at home.

One way to find out how much practice your students need is to give them the Lesson Test/Review at the *beginning* of the lesson. If you find that most of your students can do this with relatively few errors, then you can skip the lesson altogether or focus only on the sticking points. It may be enough to only do the editing exercise, as this will reveal typical mistakes students make; they may just need to be reminded of these mistakes rather than being taught the entire lesson. For example, most students in levels two and three "know" that they have to use the *-s* ending for third person singular, but many still leave it out. There's no point in *teaching* the base form and the *-s* form when a simple reminder may be enough.

In some cases, a section of a lesson can be omitted altogether or assigned for self-study extra credit to save class time. For example, in the lesson on adjective clauses in Book 2, a teacher can skip the part about the nonrestrictive clauses altogether. Or it may be enough to teach contrary-to-fact clauses in the present without getting into the past or mixed tenses. Let your curriculum guide you on what is absolutely necessary. Some lessons can probably be skipped altogether if your program teaches the grammar point in a higher or lower level.

3. "If my students need more writing practice, what should I do?"

In addition to the "Write About it" activities, any of the "Talk About it" questions can be used as a writing activity if more writing practice is needed in paragraph or essay writing. If students need help at a sentence level of writing, the ABOUT YOU exercises can be assigned for writing. The Internet Activities, which suggest that the students look up some information on a Web site, can be used for summary writing. (Write a summary of the information you found on the Web site.) There are also additional writing activities on the Web site (http://elt.thomson.com/gic).

4. "I have students from the UAE (or other country), and they always have trouble with this grammar point. How can I help them specifically?"

If you know a lot about the student's native language and the grammar mistakes the student is likely to make because of L1 interference, you can focus in on the editing activities that correct for that particular mistake. For example, if you have eastern Europeans (Russians, Poles, etc.) in your class, you will want to do a lot of work with articles. They also have confusion with *that* and *what* in noun clauses: *I know what you like pizza.* If you have students who speak Ethiopian languages, they are likely to make mistakes in past tenses by using the verb *be: He was go* instead of *He went.* Near-native speakers who learned English by ear rather than through grammar classes are likely to leave off endings and leave out words: *I am concern about my health. I been here for two hours.* The focus should be less on grammatical terms and categories for them and more on error correction.

It is not necessary to be a native speaker of your students' languages to know what kind of interference is likely to occur; if you have a large number of students from one language background, over time you will learn the consistent mistakes that are made. When I do the editing activity, I always call on the student who is most likely to make that particular mistake. In some cases, almost all students are likely to make a mistake; subject/verb reversal in dependent clauses is a common mistake for almost all students: *When arrived the teacher, the class began.*

5. "Any tips for doing the Expansion Activities?"

The Expansion Activities at the end of lessons are fun, but time is limited. Ideally, there is a speech component in your program that can pick up on the oral activities here. If not, try to choose the activity that seems the most enjoyable. Students are likely to remember the lesson better if there is a fun element.

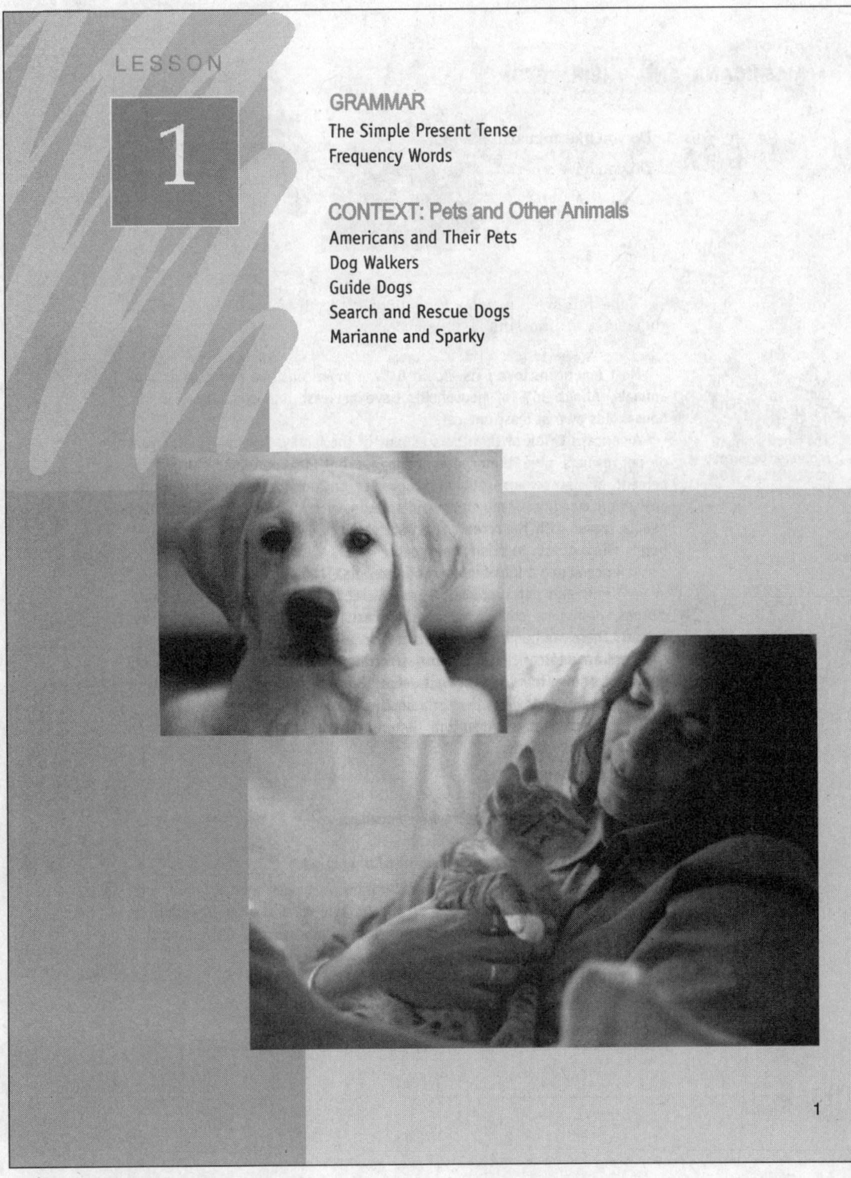

Lesson | 1

Lesson Overview

GRAMMAR

Ask: *What tense will we study in this lesson?* (the simple present tense) *What are some examples of the simple present tense?* Write the examples on the board. *What else will we study?* (frequency words) *Do you know any frequency words?* (*always, sometimes, often,* etc.) Have students give examples. Write the examples on the board.

CONTEXT

1. Ask: *What will we learn about in this lesson?* (pets, other animals, working dogs) If you have a pet, share information about your pet with the class.
2. Activate students' prior knowledge. Ask: *Do any of you have pets?* Have students share information about their pets.

Photo

1. Direct students' attention to the photos. Ask: *Do you know what kind of dog this is?* (probably a Labrador retriever) *How do you think this woman feels about her cat? How do you know?*
2. Ask students: *How do you feel about your pets?*

To save class time, have students do the Test/Review at the end of the lesson, or administer a lesson test generated from the Assessment CD-ROM with *ExamView® Pro.* Skip sections of the lesson that students have already mastered. You may also assign some sections for self-study for extra credit.

Expansion

Theme The topic for this lesson can be enhanced with the following ideas:

1. Books on pets
2. Ads for pet supply stores
3. Pictures of your pet

Americans and Their Pets (Reading)

1. Have students look at the pictures. Ask: *What are the pets doing?* (riding a motorcycle and sleeping with their owners) *Do people from your culture treat their pets like this?*
2. Have students look at the title of the reading. Ask: *What is the reading about?* Have students use the title and pictures to make predictions about the reading.
3. Preteach any vocabulary words your students may not know, such as *allow*, *cemetery*, and *attention*.

BEFORE YOU READ

1. Have students discuss the questions in pairs.
2. Ask for a few volunteers to share their answers with the class.

To save class time, skip "Before You Read" or have students prepare answers for homework ahead of time.

Reading CD 1, Track 1

1. Have students first read the text silently. Tell them to pay special attention to the verb *be* and other verbs in the simple present tense. Then play the audio and have students read along silently.
2. Check students' comprehension. Ask questions such as: *How do Americans feel about pets?* (They love them.) *Do more Americans own dogs or cats?* (dogs) *How do they treat their pets?* (like members of the family) Do Americans spend a lot of money on their pets? (yes) *Why are pets good for people?* (Pets are fun; contact with pets can be good for your health; pets keep lonely people company; etc.)

To save class time, have students do the reading for homework ahead of time.

DID YOU KNOW?

The Top Ten Dog Breeds in the U.S.

Labrador Retriever
Golden Retriever
German Shepherd
Beagle
Dachshund
Yorkshire Terrier
Boxer
Poodle
Chihuahua
Shih Tzu

AMERICANS AND THEIR PETS

Before You Read

1. Do you like animals?
2. Do you have a pet?

Read the following article. Pay special attention to the verb *be* and other verbs in the simple present tense.

Did You Know? The most common registered breed of dog in the U.S. is the Labrador retriever.

Most Americans **love** pets. About 64% of Americans **live** with one or more animals. About 36% of households **have** at least one dog. Three in ten households **own** at least one cat.

Americans **think** of their pets as part of the family. Seventy-nine percent of pet owners **give** their pets holiday or birthday presents. Thirty-three percent of pet owners **talk** to their pets on the phone or through the answering machine. Many pet owners **sleep** with their dogs or cats. Many people **travel** with their pets. (It **costs** about $50 to fly with a pet.) Some hotels **allow** guests to bring their pets.

Americans **pay** a lot of money to keep pets. They **spend** $12 billion a year in vet[1] bills and pet supplies. There **are** schools, toys, hotels, restaurants, clothes, perfumes, and cemeteries for pets. There **are** magazines for pet owners. There **are** hundreds of Web sites for pet owners.

Pets **are** a lot of fun. They **are** affectionate[2] too. People who **are** lonely **get** a lot of love from their animals. Medical research **shows** that contact with a dog or a cat can lower a person's blood pressure.

Pets **need** a lot of attention. Before you **buy** a pet, it **is** important to answer these questions:

- **Are** you patient?
- **Are** you home a lot?
- If you **have** children, **are** they responsible?
- **Are** pets allowed where you live?
- **Do** you **have** money for medical bills for your pet?

Unfortunately, some people **don't realize** that pets need a lot of care. Some people **see** a cute puppy or kitten, **buy** it, and later **abandon**[3] it because they **don't want** to take care of it. It **is** important to understand that a pet is a long-term responsibility.

[1] *Vet* is short for *veterinarian*. This is an animal doctor.
[2] *Affectionate* means loving.
[3] *To abandon* means to leave something. When people abandon a pet, they leave it on the street.

2 Lesson 1

Reading Variation

To practice listening skills, have students first listen to the audio alone. Ask a few comprehension questions. Repeat the audio if necessary. Then have them open their books and read along as they listen to the audio.

Reading Glossary

allow: let; permit
attention: work; care
cemetery: a burial place for the dead; graveyard

1.1 *Be*—Forms and Uses

Forms

Subject	Form of Be	Complement	Explanation
I	**am**	home a lot.	Use *am* with *I*.
My father He She The cat That	**is**	patient. intelligent. lonely happy. a friendly cat.	Use *is* with *he, she, it, this, that,* and singular subjects (for example, *cat*).
We You Pets Those	**are**	responsible. home a lot. fun. cute kittens.	Use *are* with *we, you, they, these, those,* and plural subjects (for example, *pets, cats,* etc.).

Uses

Examples	Uses
I **am** patient. The pet shop **is** located on the corner. The children **are** excited about the puppy.	With a description (adjective) **Note:** Some words that end in *-ed* are adjectives: *tired, married, worried, interested, bored, excited, crowded, located*
This **is** a labrador. A Labrador **is** a big dog.	With a classification or definition of the subject
My dog **is** in the yard.	With a location
My husband **is** from Guatemala.	With a place of origin
It **is** cold outside. The dog **is** cold.	With weather and physical reaction to the weather (*hot, cold, warm*)
My dog **is** three (years old).	With age
The cat **is** hungry. I **am** afraid of dogs.	With physical states: *hungry, thirsty, afraid*
There **are** toys for dogs. There **is** a dog restaurant near my house.	With *there*
It **is** ten o'clock now. It **is** warm today.	With time

Language Note:
Be cold means to feel a low temperature. *Have a cold* shows an illness.
Please bring me my sweater. *I'm cold.* I'm sick. *I have a cold.*

The Simple Present Tense; Frequency Words 3

1.1 *Be*—Forms and Uses

1. Have students cover up grammar chart **1.1** on page 3. Activate students' prior knowledge. Write the uses of the verb *be* on the board. Ask volunteers to go up to the board and write examples. Or have students write examples in pairs and go over them as a class. For example, write:
   1. descriptions
   2. classification or definition
   3. location
   etc.
2. Have students look at grammar chart **1.1.** Ask students to compare their sentences with the example sentences. Check that students were able to provide an example for each use. Go over trouble spots with the whole class. Review the example sentences in the grammar chart.
3. Point out that to *be cold* and to *have a cold* have different meanings. *Be cold* means to feel a low temperature. *Have a cold* shows an illness.

Grammar Variation

Write example sentences for each use and have students decide what the use is. For example, write: *I am patient.* Students say: *description.* If students have difficulty, write the list of uses on the board.

EXERCISE 1

1. Have students read the direction line. Ask: *What words do we use here?* (*is, are, am*) Go over the example in the book. Then do #1 with the class. Ask: *What form of* be *goes here?* (*are*)
2. Have students complete Exercise 1 individually. Then have them check their answers in pairs. Circulate and observe the pair work. Check the answers as a class.
3. If necessary, review grammar chart **1.1** on page 3.

EXERCISE 1 Fill in the blanks with the correct form of *be*.

EXAMPLE My dog __is__ very small.

1. You take care of your dog. You __are__ responsible.
2. Pet ownership __is__ a big responsibility.
3. My cat __is__ soft.
4. Dogs __are__ great pets because they __are__ affectionate. They __are__ also good protection for a house.
5. My dog __is__ a member of my family.
6. Some cats __are__ very affectionate. Other cats __are__ very independent.
7. It __is__ a big responsibility to own a pet.
8. Kittens and puppies __are__ cute.
9. We __are__ ready to get a pet.
10. Some people __are__ lonely.
11. My kitten __is__ very sweet.
12. The dog __is__ cold.

1.2 | Contractions with *Be*

A *contraction* combines two words. We put an apostrophe(') in place of the missing letter.

Examples		Explanation
I am You are She is He is It is We are They are	**I'm** responsible. **You're** patient. **She's** happy. **He's** kind. **It's** necessary to walk a dog. **We're** busy. **They're** cute.	We can make a contraction with the subject pronoun (*I, you, she,* etc.) and *am, is, are.*
There is That is	**There's** a cat on the computer. **That's** a friendly cat.	We can make a contraction with *there is.* We can make a contraction with *that is.*
My **grandmother's** lonely. Your **dog's** cute.		We can make a contraction with most nouns and *is.*
A fox is a relative of a dog. A mouse is a small animal. This is a cute cat.	fox	We don't make a contraction with *is* if the noun ends in *s, se, ce, ze, sh, ch,* or *x.*
Pet **products are** expensive. **Dogs are** popular pets. **There are** hotels for pets.		In writing, don't make a contraction with a plural noun and *are* or with *there are.*
The owner **is not** home now. She **isn't** home in the day. You **are not** ready for a pet. You **aren't** patient.		To make a negative with *be,* put *not* after a form of *be.* The negative contractions are *isn't* and *aren't.* There is no contraction for *am not.*

EXERCISE 2 Which of the sentences in Exercise 1 can use a contraction?
1, 2, 3, 4, 5, 7, 9, 11, 12

EXERCISE 3 Fill in the blank with the correct form of *be.* Then fill in the second blank with a negative form. Use contractions wherever possible.

EXAMPLE Today *'s* my daughter's birthday. It *isn't* a holiday.

Answers will vary.

1. My daughter and I *are* at the pet shop. We *aren't* at home.
2. My husband *'s* at work now. He *isn't* with me.
3. I *'m* patient. My husband *isn't* patient.
4. This puppy *'s* for my daughter. It *isn't* for my son.

The Simple Present Tense; Frequency Words 5

1.2 | Contractions with *Be*

1. Have students cover up grammar chart **1.2** in their books. Write the list of pronouns and *be* from the grammar chart on the board. Have volunteers make sentences. Say: *Make a sentence. Use contractions such as* I'm.
2. Then write: *My grandmother's lonely.* Ask: *Is this contraction correct?* (yes) Continue with: *A fox's a relative of a dog.* Ask: *Is this contraction correct?* (no) *Why can't we use a contraction here? Does anyone remember?* (We don't make contractions with nouns that end in *s, se, ce, ze, sh, ch,* or *x*.) Then write: *Dogs're popular pets.* Ask: *Is this contraction correct?* (no) *Why can't we use a contraction here?* (In writing, we don't make a contraction with a plural noun and *are*.) Ask: *Is there a contraction for* am not? (no)
3. Have students look at grammar chart **1.2.** Say: *Compare our list with the list in the chart.*
4. Review the example sentences and explanations in the grammar chart.

EXERCISE 2

1. Have students read the direction line. Point out that students need to go back to Exercise 1 on page 4.
2. Have students complete Exercise 2 in pairs. Then check the answers as a class.
3. If necessary, review grammar chart **1.2** on page 5.

EXERCISE 3

1. Have students read the direction line. Ask: *What goes in the second blank?* (the negative form) Go over the example in the book.
2. Have students complete the rest of Exercise 3 individually. Then have them compare their answers in pairs. Circulate to observe pair work. Give help as needed.
3. If necessary, review grammar chart **1.2** on page 5.

Grammar Variation

Write five mixed-up sentences from the reading on the board. Tell students they have two minutes to put them in the correct order. Then elicit the rule for sentence order.

Expansion

Exercise 2 Go back to grammar chart **1.1** on page 3. Review the example sentences. Ask: *Which sentences can use a contraction?*

EXERCISE 4

1. Have students read the direction line. Say: *Fill in the blanks with the correct form of* be. Go over the example in the book. Then do #1 with the class. Ask a volunteer to give answers.
2. Have students complete Exercise 4 individually. Have them compare their answers in pairs. Circulate to observe pair work. Give help as needed.
3. If necessary, review grammar chart **1.2** on page 5.

To save class time, have students do half of the exercise in class and complete the other half for homework.

5. My daughter _'s_ responsible. My son _isn't_ responsible.
6. Dogs _are_ good for protection. Cats _aren't_ good for protection.
7. My daughter _'s_ excited. She _isn't_ bored.
8. I _'m_ afraid of big dogs. I _'m not_ afraid of small dogs.
9. This _is_ a Chihuahua. It _isn't_ a big dog.

EXERCISE 4 Fill in the blanks.

My dog _'s_ hungry. He wants to eat.

1. My cat _'s_ near the window.
2. My aunt _isn't_ (not) married. Her dog _'s_ her only companion.
3. In the U.S., there _are_ cemeteries for pets.
4. Some cats _are_ very affectionate.
5. My dog _'s_ thirsty. Put water in his dish.
6. This _is_ a kitten. It _'s_ only two weeks _old_.
7. Don't leave your dog in the car. _It's_ hot today.
8. My dog _'s_ cold in the winter. She needs a sweater.
9. My vet's office _is_ located about two miles from my house.
10. _This_ is a picture of my dog.
11. I _'m_ worried about my dog because she _'s_ sick.
12. Your son _isn't_ (not) responsible because he _'s_ only four years _old_.

6 Lesson 1

Expansion

Exercise 4 Have students work in pairs to write five to eight sentences about their own families and pets with the verb *be*. Ask students to use contractions.

DOG WALKERS

Before You Read

1. Do working people have problems taking care of their pets?
2. Are some animals easier to take care of than others?

Read the following conversation. Pay special attention to questions with the verb *be*.

A: Your dog is beautiful. What kind of a dog **is it?**
B: It's a Dalmatian.
A: How old **is he?**
B: It's a *she*. She's two years old.
A: **What's her name?**
B: Her name is Missy.
A: **Are we** neighbors? **Are you** new in the neighborhood?
B: I don't live here. Missy isn't my dog. I'm a dog walker.
A: A dog walker? What**'s that?**
B: I walk other people's dogs when they're at work or on vacation.
A: **Are you** a friend of the family?
B: No. I'm from an agency.
A: What agency **are you** from?
B: It's a professional dog-walking service.
A: **Are you** serious?
B: Of course, I'm serious.
A: **Is the pay** good?
B: It's OK. But I love my job for other reasons. My "customers" are always happy to see me. Also, I'm outside all day.
A: Cool! **Are the owners** happy too?
B: Yes, they are. When they go to work, they're worried that their dogs can be lonely or bored. Some people even leave the TV on for their pets. But when they use a dog-walking service, they are happy because their dogs are happy too.
A: **Are there** jobs at your agency?
B: Yes, there are. **Are you** interested in becoming a dog walker too?
A: Yes. It sounds like fun.
B: Here's my card. The agency's phone number is on the card.
A: Thanks!

Dog Walkers (Reading)

1. Have students look at the picture. Ask: *What are the people doing?* (walking a dog) *Who are the people?* (*dog walkers*)
2. Have students look at the title of the reading. Ask: *What is the reading about?* Have students make predictions.
3. Preteach any vocabulary words your students may not know, such as *agency, customer,* and *Dalmation.*

BEFORE YOU READ

1. Have students discuss the questions in pairs.
2. Ask for a few volunteers to share their answers with the class.

To save class time, skip "Before You Read" or have students prepare answers for homework ahead of time.

Reading *CD 1, Track 2*

1. Have students first read the text silently. Tell them to pay special attention to questions with *be*. Then play the audio and have students read along silently.
2. Check students' comprehension. Ask questions such as: *What's a dog walker?* (Someone who walks other people's dogs.) *Why does person B like her job?* (Her customers are always happy to see her, and she likes working outside.) *Who is person B talking about when she says "customers"?* (the dogs she walks) *Does person A want to become a dog walker?* (yes)

To save class time, have students do the reading for homework ahead of time.

Expansion

Theme The topic for this lesson can be enhanced with the following ideas:

1. Funny pictures of dog walkers in New York with lots of dogs
2. Newspaper ads for dog walkers

Reading Variation

To practice listening skills, have students first listen to the audio alone. Ask a few comprehension questions. Repeat the audio if necessary. Then have them open their books and read along as they listen to the audio.

Reading Glossary

agency: a type of business that helps people do something
customer: person or business that buys from another person or business; client
Dalmatian: a white dog with black spots often kept as a pet by firefighters

1.3 | Questions with *Be*

1. Have students cover up grammar chart **1.3** on page 8. Activate prior knowledge. Write the statements from the grammar chart on the board. Have volunteers go to the board to write questions and short answers, or have students write questions and answers in pairs. Say: *Write* yes/no *questions and short answers for these statements.* Remind students to use contractions whenever possible.
2. Then write the statements from the second chart on the board. Have students write *wh-* questions for each statement. Ask volunteers to write the questions on the board or have students work in pairs.
3. Have students look at grammar chart **1.3.** Say: *Now compare your work with the chart.* Go over any trouble spots with the class. Review the example sentences and explanations in the grammar chart.

1.3 | Questions with *Be*

Compare statement word order and word order in *yes/no* questions.

Statement Word Order	*Yes/No* Question	Short Answer	Explanation
I am responsible.	**Am I** responsible with pets?	Yes, you are.	In a *yes/no* question, we put *am, is, are* before the subject.
You are a dog walker.	**Are you** a friend of the family?	No, I'm not.	
The owner is busy.	**Is the owner** at home?	No, she isn't.	
The pay is important.	**Is the pay** good?	No, it isn't.	We usually answer a *yes/no* question with a short answer. A short answer contains a pronoun (*he, it, we, they,* etc.).
The dog is a female.	**Is the dog** young?	Yes, she is.	
It is a big dog.	**Is it** a Labrador?	No, it isn't.	
We are new here.	**Are we** neighbors?	No, we aren't.	
The owners are at work.	**Are the owners** happy?	Yes, they are.	We don't use a contraction for a short *yes* answer. We usually use a contraction for a short *no* answer.
They are out.	**Are they** at work?	Yes, they are.	
There are interesting jobs.	**Are there** jobs at your agency?	Yes, there are.	
That is a cute dog.	**Is that** your dog?	No, it isn't.	
It isn't a big dog.	**Isn't it** a puppy?	No, it isn't.	

Pronunciation Note:
We usually end a *yes/no* question with rising intonation. Listen to your teacher pronounce the questions above.

Compare statement word order and word order in *Wh-* questions.

Statement Word Order	*Wh-* Question	Explanation
I am lost. **You are** from an agency. **That is** a nice dog. **The dog is** old. **That is** a strange pet. **Her name is** long. **You are** here. **There are** a lot of dog walkers.	Where **am I?** What agency **are you** from? What kind of dog **is that?** How old **is the dog?** What **is that?** What **is her name?** Why **are you** here? How many dog walkers **are there** in your agency?	We put *am, is, are* before the subject.
The owner isn't home. The dogs **aren't bored.** **You aren't** at work.	Why **isn't the owner** at home? Why **aren't the dogs** bored? Why **aren't you** at work?	Notice the word order in negative *wh-* questions.

8 Lesson 1

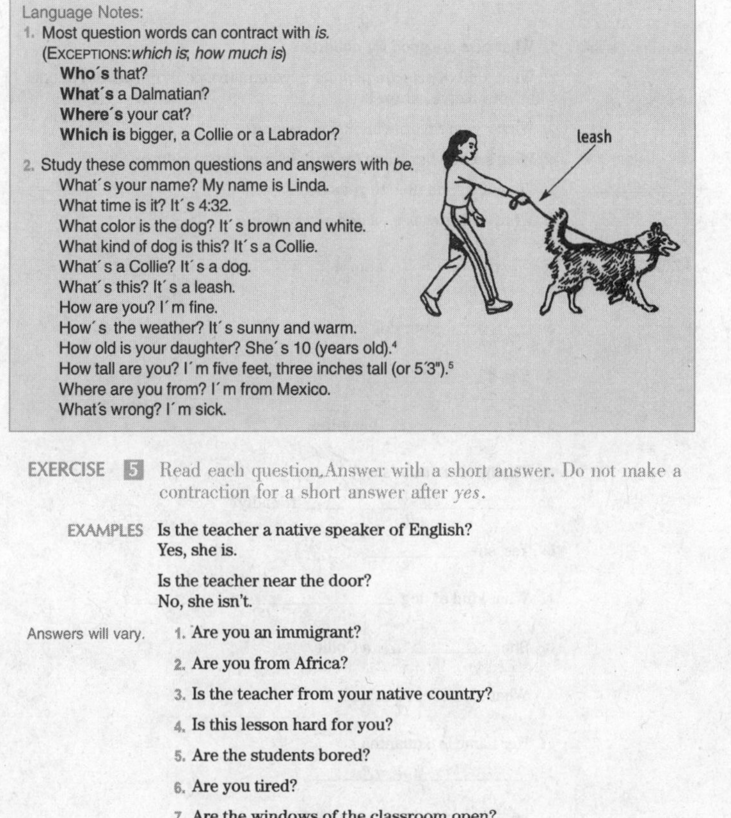

Language Notes:

1. Most question words can contract with *is*.
   (EXCEPTIONS: *which is*; *how much is*)
   Who's that?
   What's a Dalmatian?
   Where's your cat?
   Which is bigger, a Collie or a Labrador?
2. Study these common questions and answers with *be*.
   What's your name? My name is Linda.
   What time is it? It's 4:32.
   What color is the dog? It's brown and white.
   What kind of dog is this? It's a Collie.
   What's a Collie? It's a dog.
   What's this? It's a leash.
   How are you? I'm fine.
   How's the weather? It's sunny and warm.
   How old is your daughter? She's 10 (years old).[4]
   How tall are you? I'm five feet, three inches tall (or 5'3").[5]
   Where are you from? I'm from Mexico.
   What's wrong? I'm sick.

EXERCISE 5 Read each question. Answer with a short answer. Do not make a contraction for a short answer after *yes*.

EXAMPLES Is the teacher a native speaker of English?
Yes, she is.

Is the teacher near the door?
No, she isn't.

Answers will vary.

1. Are you an immigrant?
2. Are you from Africa?
3. Is the teacher from your native country?
4. Is this lesson hard for you?
5. Are the students bored?
6. Are you tired?
7. Are the windows of the classroom open?
8. Is the door open?
9. Is it warm in the classroom?
10. Is there a map in the classroom?
11. Is the school located near your house?

[4] It is not polite to ask an adult American about his or her age.
[5] For conversion to the metric system, see Appendix D.

The Simple Present Tense; Frequency Words 9

1.3 | Questions with *Be* (*cont.*)

4. Direct students to the Language Notes. Point out that most question words, except for *which* and *how much*, can contract with *is*. Review the list of common questions with *be*.

EXERCISE 5

1. Tell students that this exercise is about the class and the classroom. Have students read the direction line. Ask: *What kind of questions are we going to ask?* (*yes/no* questions) *What kind of answers are we going to give?* (short answers) *Do we always make contractions in short answers?* (No. Not with affirmative short answers.) Go over the examples in the book. Have students model the examples.
2. Have students complete Exercise 5 individually. Then have students take turns asking and answering the questions in pairs. Circulate to observe pair work. Give help as needed.
3. If necessary, review grammar chart **1.3** on pages 8–9.

Expansion

Grammar Create two rings of students. Have half of the students stand in an outer ring around the classroom. Have the other half stand in an inner ring, facing the outer ring. Instruct students to ask and answer questions from the Language Notes on page 9. Say: *Ask your partner common questions from the list in the grammar chart.* Call out "turn" every minute or so. Students in the inner ring should move one space clockwise. Students now ask and answer with their new partners. Make sure students look at each other when they're speaking.

Expansion

Exercise 5 Have students write three more *yes/no* questions about the class or classroom. Then have students ask and answer their questions in pairs.

EXERCISE 6

1. Have students read the direction line. Say: *Answer the questions in complete sentences.* Model #1: *Gerbils are good pets for children.*
2. Have students complete Exercise 6 individually. Then have students ask and answer the questions in pairs. Circulate to observe pair work. Give help as needed.
3. If necessary, review grammar chart **1.3** on pages 8–9.

To save class time, have students do the exercise in writing for homework.

EXERCISE 7

CD 1, Track 3

1. Have students read the direction line. Go over the example.
2. Have students complete Exercise 7 individually. Check answers as a class.
3. If necessary, review grammar charts **1.1** on page 3, **1.2** on page 5, and **1.3** on pages 8–9.

To save class time, have students do half of the exercise in class and complete the other half for homework. Or assign the entire exercise for homework.

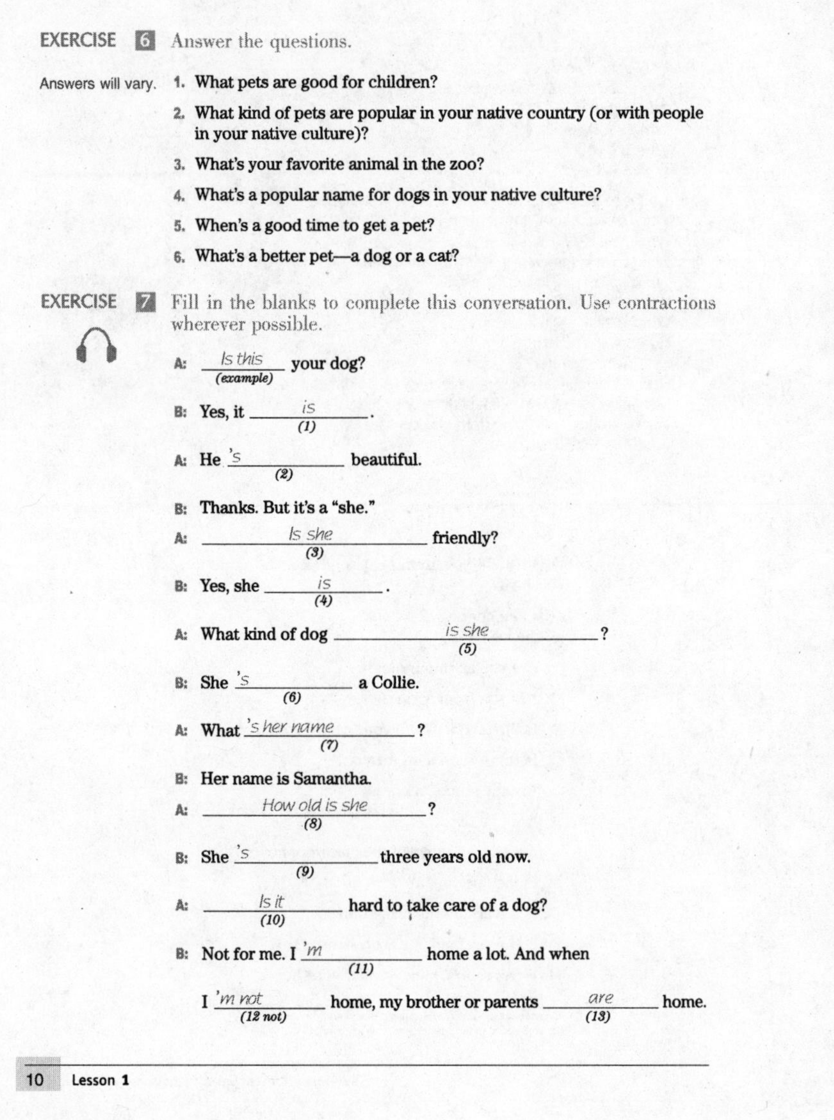

EXERCISE 6 Answer the questions.

Answers will vary.

1. What pets are good for children?
2. What kind of pets are popular in your native country (or with people in your native culture)?
3. What's your favorite animal in the zoo?
4. What's a popular name for dogs in your native culture?
5. When's a good time to get a pet?
6. What's a better pet—a dog or a cat?

EXERCISE 7 Fill in the blanks to complete this conversation. Use contractions wherever possible.

A: *Is this* (example) your dog?

B: Yes, it *is* (1).

A: He *'s* (2) beautiful.

B: Thanks. But it's a "she."

A: *Is she* (3) friendly?

B: Yes, she *is* (4).

A: What kind of dog *is she* (5)?

B: She *'s* (6) a Collie.

A: What *'s her name* (7)?

B: Her name is Samantha.

A: *How old is she* (8)?

B: She *'s* (9) three years old now.

A: *Is it* (10) hard to take care of a dog?

B: Not for me. I *'m* (11) home a lot. And when I *'m not* (12 not) home, my brother or parents *are* (13) home.

10 Lesson 1

Expansion

Exercise 6 Have students discuss the questions in groups and report their results to the class. Take a class survey about pets and animals.

Exercise 7 Variation

To provide practice with listening skills, have students close their books and listen to the audio. Repeat the audio as needed. Ask comprehension questions, such as: *Is the dog male or female?* (female) *How old is the dog?* (three years old) *Why is the grandmother lonely?* (because nobody is home all day; everyone is at work) Then have students open their books and complete Exercise 7.

A: I love dogs, but I'm not (14 not) home very much, so that's a problem.

B: Why aren't you home (15) a lot?

A: Because I'm a nurse. I work eight hours a day. I want to get a dog for my grandmother.

B: Why?

A: Because she's (16) lonely.

B: Why is she (17) lonely?

A: Because nobody's (18) home all day. We're (19) all at work.

B: I think that's (20) a good idea.

EXERCISE 8 Fill in the blanks in the following cell phone conversation.

A: Hello?

B: Hi. This is (example) Betty.

A: Hi, Betty. How are you (1)?

B: I'm fine. How are you (2)?

A: I'm fine. But the cat's (3) sick. I'm not (4 not) home now. I'm (5) at the animal hospital.

B: What's (6) wrong?

A: Fluffy's not (7 not) hungry or thirsty. He's (8) tired all the time.

B: It's (9) so hot today. Maybe the heat is (10) the problem.

A: I don't think so. The house is (11) air-conditioned.

B: How old is he (12)?

A: He's (13) only four years old (14).

B: Are you (15) alone?

A: No, I'm not.

The Simple Present Tense; Frequency Words 11

EXERCISE 8

CD 1, Track 4

1. Have students read the direction line. Go over the example.
2. Have students complete Exercise 8 individually. Check answers as a class.
3. If necessary, review grammar charts **1.1** on page 3, **1.2** on page 5, and **1.3** on pages 8–9.

To save class time, have students do half of the exercise in class and complete the other half for homework.

Expansion

Exercise 7 Have students practice the conversation in pairs. Have volunteers act out the conversation for the class.

Exercise 8 Variation

To provide practice with listening skills, have students close their books and listen to the audio. Repeat the audio as needed. Ask comprehension questions, such as: *Who made the call?* (Betty) *What's wrong with the cat?* (He's sick; he isn't hungry or thirsty; he's tired all the time.) Then have students open their books and complete Exercise 8.

EXERCISE 9

CD 1, Track 5

1. Have students read the direction line. Go over the example. Remind students to use contractions whenever possible.
2. Have students complete Exercise 9 individually. Check answers as a class.
3. If necessary, review grammar charts **1.1** on page 3, **1.2** on page 5, and **1.3** on pages 8–9.

To save class time, have students do half of the exercise in class and complete the other half for homework. Or assign the entire exercise for homework.

B: *Who's* (16) with you?

A: My daughter *'s* (17) with me. We *'re* (18) in the waiting room.

B: Why *isn't she* (19) at school?

A: She *'s* (20) on spring break now. I think the doctor *'s* (21) ready to see us now.

B: Call me when you get home. Let me know if I can help.

A: Thanks. *You're* (22) a good friend.

EXERCISE 9 Fill in the blanks in the following conversation.

A: Look at the dog. What kind of dog *is it* (example)?

B: I think it *'s* (1) a mutt.

A: What *'s* (2) a mutt?

B: It *'s* (3) a mixed breed dog. Look, it *'s* (4) so friendly with those children.

A: My daughter's birthday is next week. She wants a dog. But dogs *are* (5) so expensive.

B: A purebred[6] dog, like a Labrador, is expensive, but a mutt *isn't* (6 not) so expensive. In fact, there *are* (7) animal shelters that can give you a dog for free or for a very low price.

A: What *'s* (8) an animal shelter?

B: It's an organization that takes unwanted pets and tries to find homes for them.

A: But *are they* (9) healthy?

B: Yes, they are. The shelter's doctors check an animal's health before giving it to a family.

A: Why *are there* (10) so many unwanted pets?

[6] A *purebred* dog is one breed (race) only. It is not mixed with other breeds.

12 Lesson 1

Expansion

Exercise 8 Have students practice the conversation in pairs. Have volunteers act out the conversation for the class.

Exercise 9 Variation

To provide practice with listening skills, have students close their books and listen to the audio. Repeat the audio as needed. Ask comprehension questions, such as: *What's a mutt?* (a mixed breed dog) *Are mutts expensive?* (no) *Are the animals at shelters healthy?* (yes) *How do you know?* (The shelter's doctors check an animal's health before giving it to a family.) Then have students open their books and complete Exercise 9.

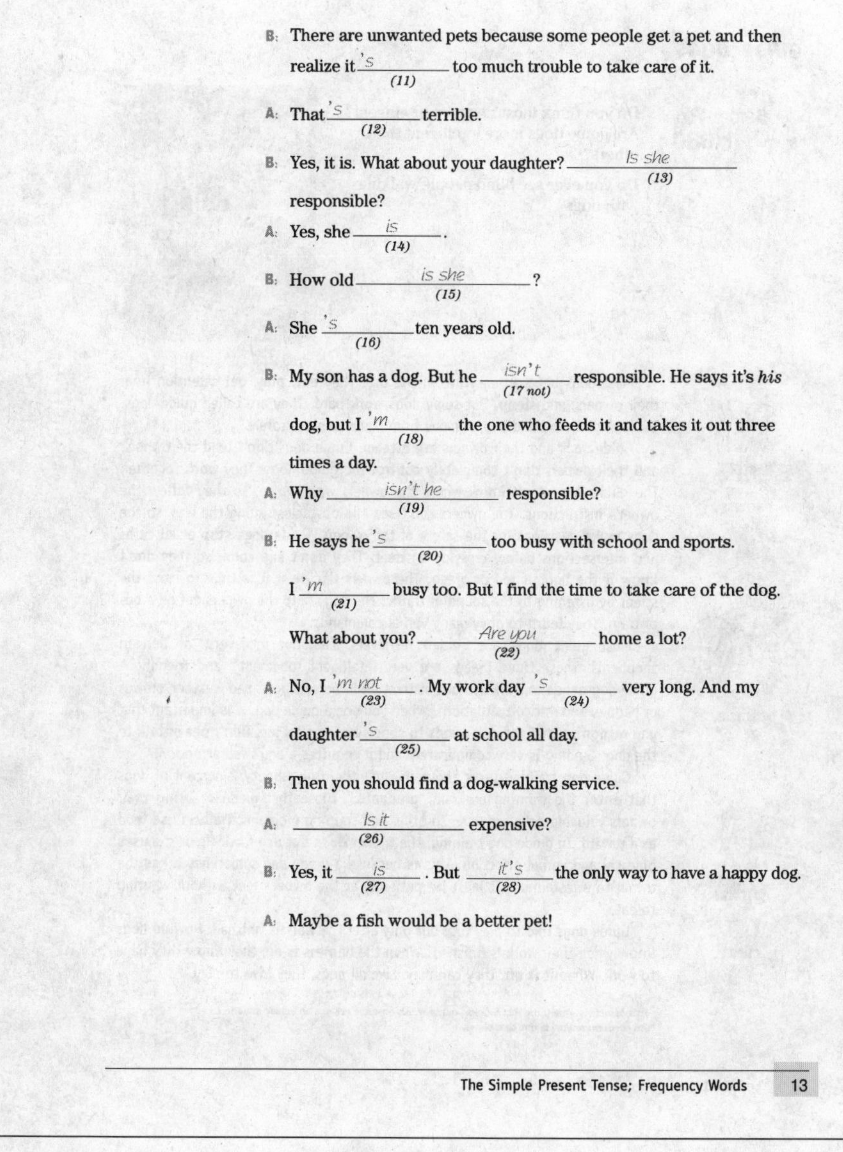

B: There are unwanted pets because some people get a pet and then realize it _'s_ (11) too much trouble to take care of it.

A: That _'s_ (12) terrible.

B: Yes, it is. What about your daughter? _Is she_ (13) responsible?

A: Yes, she _is_ (14).

B: How old _is she_ (15)?

A: She _'s_ (16) ten years old.

B: My son has a dog. But he _isn't_ (17 not) responsible. He says it's *his* dog, but I _'m_ (18) the one who feeds it and takes it out three times a day.

A: Why _isn't he_ (19) responsible?

B: He says he _'s_ (20) too busy with school and sports. I _'m_ (21) busy too. But I find the time to take care of the dog. What about you? _Are you_ (22) home a lot?

A: No, I _'m not_ (23). My work day _'s_ (24) very long. And my daughter _'s_ (25) at school all day.

B: Then you should find a dog-walking service.

A: _Is it_ (26) expensive?

B: Yes, it _is_ (27). But _it's_ (28) the only way to have a happy dog.

A: Maybe a fish would be a better pet!

The Simple Present Tense; Frequency Words 13

Expansion

Exercise 9 Have students practice the conversation in pairs. Have volunteers act out the conversation for the class.

Guide Dogs (Reading)

1. Have students look at the photo. Ask: *What's happening in the photo?* (A visually impaired person is walking in a crowd with her guide dog.)
2. Have students look at the title of the reading. Ask: *What is the reading about?* Have students make predictions.
3. Preteach any vocabulary words your students may not know, such as *curb, intersection, distraction,* and *harness.* Point out the pictures of *harness, obstacle,* and *curb.*

BEFORE YOU READ

1. Have students discuss the questions in pairs.
2. Ask for a few volunteers to share their answers with the class.

To save class time, skip "Before You Read" or have students prepare answers for homework ahead of time.

Reading CD 1, Track 6

1. Have students first read the text silently. Tell them to pay special attention to simple present tense verbs. Then play the audio and have students read along silently.
2. Check students' comprehension. Ask questions such as: *Do guide dogs work alone?* (No. They work as a team with their owner.) *What do guide dogs do at all intersections?* (Stop and wait.) *Should you pet guide dogs when you see them?* (No. They are working and need to concentrate.) *How do trainers reward their dogs?* (with physical and verbal affection) *When do guide dogs know they can play?* (when their harnesses are off)

To save class time, have students do the reading for homework ahead of time.

GUIDE DOGS

Before You Read

1. Do you think most dogs are intelligent? Are some dogs more intelligent than others?
2. Do you ever see blind people walking with dogs?

Read the following article. Pay special attention to simple present tense verbs.

harness

obstacle

curb

Most dogs **have** an easy life in the U.S. They **eat, play, get** attention from their owners, and **sleep.** But some dogs **work** hard. They **are** called guide dogs. Guide dogs **help** blind people move from place to place safely.

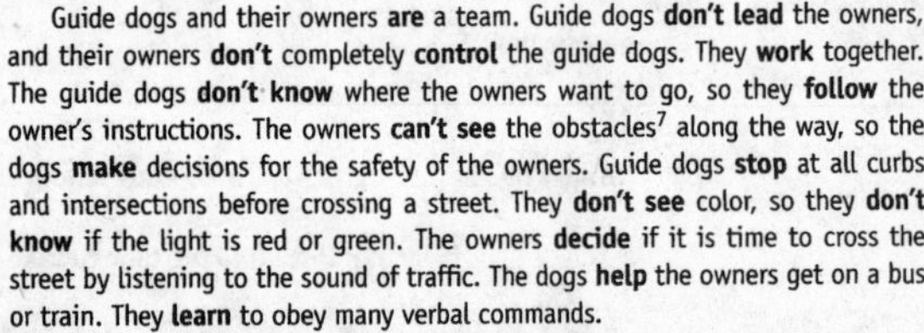

Guide dogs and their owners **are** a team. Guide dogs **don't lead** the owners, and their owners **don't** completely **control** the guide dogs. They **work** together. The guide dogs **don't know** where the owners want to go, so they **follow** the owner's instructions. The owners **can't see** the obstacles[7] along the way, so the dogs **make** decisions for the safety of the owners. Guide dogs **stop** at all curbs and intersections before crossing a street. They **don't see** color, so they **don't know** if the light is red or green. The owners **decide** if it is time to cross the street by listening to the sound of traffic. The dogs **help** the owners get on a bus or train. They **learn** to obey many verbal commands.

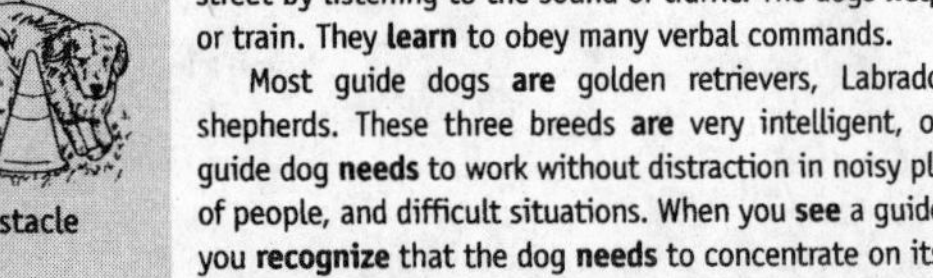

Most guide dogs **are** golden retrievers, Labrador retrievers, or German shepherds. These three breeds **are** very intelligent, obedient[8], and friendly. A guide dog **needs** to work without distraction in noisy places, bad weather, crowds of people, and difficult situations. When you **see** a guide dog, it **is** important that you **recognize** that the dog **needs** to concentrate on its job. **Don't pet** or **talk** to the dog. Guiding **is** very complicated, and it **requires** a dog's full attention.

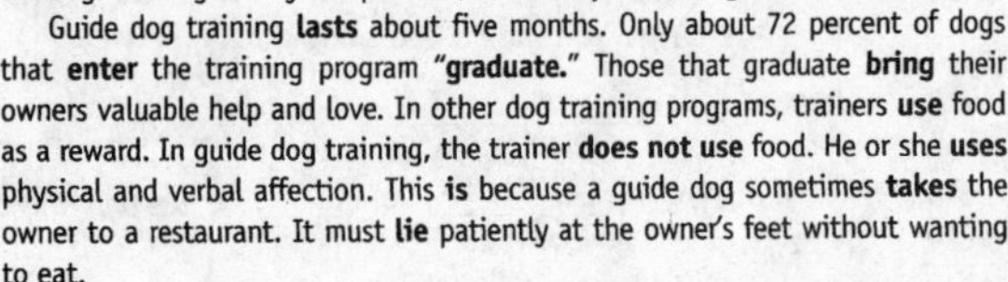

Guide dog training **lasts** about five months. Only about 72 percent of dogs that **enter** the training program **"graduate."** Those that graduate **bring** their owners valuable help and love. In other dog training programs, trainers **use** food as a reward. In guide dog training, the trainer **does not use** food. He or she **uses** physical and verbal affection. This **is** because a guide dog sometimes **takes** the owner to a restaurant. It must **lie** patiently at the owner's feet without wanting to eat.

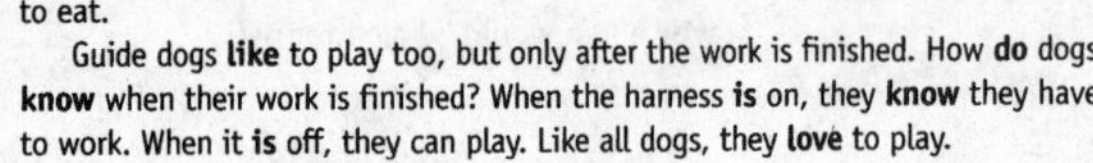

Guide dogs **like** to play too, but only after the work is finished. How **do** dogs **know** when their work is finished? When the harness **is** on, they **know** they have to work. When it **is** off, they can play. Like all dogs, they **love** to play.

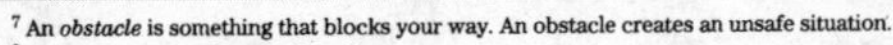

[7] An *obstacle* is something that blocks your way. An obstacle creates an unsafe situation.
[8] An *obedient* animal is one that obeys.

14 Lesson 1

Reading Variation

To practice listening skills, have students first listen to the audio alone. Ask a few comprehension questions. Repeat the audio if necessary. Then have them open their books and read along as they listen to the audio.

Reading Glossary

curb: the edge and border area of a sidewalk; a curbstone
distraction: something that interrupts; a disturbance
harness: straps and a collar that horses and other animals wear to pull loads
intersection: a crossing of roads

Culture Note

In addition to guide dogs, there are many other kinds of service dogs trained to assist people with various disabilities. There are hearing dogs that alert their owners to sounds, there are mobility dogs that may pull wheelchairs or physically support their owners. There are even seizure alert dogs that help their owners get to a safe place when they sense a seizure coming on.

1.4 | The Simple Present Tense—Affirmative Statements

Form	
A simple present tense verb has two forms: the base form and the -*s* form.[9]	
Examples	**Explanation**
Subject / Base Form / Complement I You We **work** hard. They Guide dogs	We use the base form when the subject is *I, you, we, they,* or a plural noun.
Subject / -*s* Form / Complement He She It **works** hard. The dog	We use the -*s* form when the subject is *he, she, it,* or a singular noun.
My family **has** three cats. Everyone in the shelter **likes** animals. No one **wants** the new kittens.	We use the -*s* form with *family, everyone, everybody, no one, nobody,* and *nothing.*
I **have** a pet dog. My friend **has** a guide dog. I **go** out without my dog. My friend **goes** everywhere with his dog. I **do** a lot of work. A guide dog **does** a lot of work too.	Three verbs have an irregular -*s* form: have → has (pronunciation /hæz/) go → goes do → does (pronunciation /dəz/)

Use	
Examples	**Uses**
Dogs **give** people love. Guide dogs **help** people. Most dogs **have** an easy life. Americans **love** pets.	With general truths, to show that something is consistently true
Many pet owners **sleep** with their dogs or cats. Some pet owners **buy** presents for their pets. Owners **walk** dogs on a leash.	With customs
He **walks** his dog three times a day. He **feeds** his cat every morning and every night.	To show regular activity (a habit) or repeated action
I **come** from Bosnia. He **comes** from Pakistan.	To show place of origin

[9] For the spelling of the -*s* form, see Appendix A.

1.4 | The Simple Present Tense—Affirmative Statements

1. Have students go back to the reading on page 14. Say: *Circle three examples of the base form and three examples of the -s form in the simple present tense. Look at the subject. When do you use the base form? When do you use the -s form?* Write students' examples on the board.
2. Review the examples and explanations of the simple present tense in the grammar chart on page 15. Go over when to use the base form (with *I, you, we, they,* or plural nouns). Go over when to use the -*s* form (with *he, she, it,* or a singular noun). Point out that the -*s* form is used with *family, everyone, everybody, no one, nobody,* and *nothing.*
3. Point out the verbs that have irregular -*s* forms.
4. Review the uses of the simple present tense. Go over the examples and explanations in the chart. Then have students go back to the reading on page 14. Say: *Find an example of one or two of the uses.* Write students' examples on the board.

Expansion

Grammar Have students go back to the reading on page 2 (*Americans and Their Pets*). Say: *Circle three verbs in the simple present tense base form and one verb in the -s form.*

EXERCISE 10

1. Have students read the direction line. Go over the examples in the book.
2. Have students complete the exercise individually. Check the answers as a class.
3. If necessary, review grammar chart **1.4** on page 15.

To save class time, do this exercise as a class or have students do half of this exercise for homework.

EXERCISE 10 Fill in the blanks with the base form or the *-s* form.

EXAMPLES Americans *love* (love) pets.

My son *loves* (love) his new kitten.

1. Most dogs *have* (have) an easy life.
2. My dog *sleeps* (sleep) all day.
3. Guide dogs *learn* (learn) to obey many commands.
4. A guide dog *makes* (make) safety decisions.
5. Trainers *work* (work) with a dog for five months.
6. Most guide dogs *graduate* (graduate) from the training program.
7. My girlfriend *gives* (give) her dog a present on his birthday.
8. People *get* (get) affection from animals.
9. Everyone *needs* (need) affection.
10. It *costs* (cost) a lot of money to have a pet.
11. Some pet owners *talk* (talk) to their pets on the phone.
12. My daughter *wants* (want) a puppy for her birthday.
13. My neighbor's dog *barks* (bark) all the time.
14. Some people *travel* (travel) with their dogs.
15. Forty percent of Americans *have* (have) at least one dog.
16. My brother *has* (have) three dogs.
17. Dogs *protect* (protect) their owners.
18. My family *loves* (love) animals.
19. Nobody *knows* (know) the dog's age.
20. Everybody *thinks* (think) that puppies and kittens are cute.

16 Lesson 1

Exercise 10 Variation

Have students work in pairs to complete the exercise orally. Say: *The first partner covers up the exercise. The second partner reads the first ten sentences out loud. The first partner fills in the blank* (e.g., Partner 1: Love. My brother BLANK pets. Partner 2: Loves.)

1.5 | Negative Statements with the Simple Present Tense

Examples	Explanation
The owner **knows** the destination. The dog **doesn't know** the destination. The dog **stops** at a curb. It **doesn't stop** because of a red light.	Use *doesn't* + the base form with *he, she, it,* or a singular noun. Compare: knows → doesn't **know** stops → doesn't **stop** *Doesn't* is the contraction for *does not.*
Some trainers **use** food to reward a dog. Guide dog trainers **don't use** food. Guide dogs **work** when the harness is on. They **don't work** when the harness is off. You **have** a cat. You **don't have** a dog.	Use *don't* + the base form with *I, you, we, they,* or a plural noun. Compare: use → don't **use** work → don't **work** *Don't* is the contraction for *do not.*

Usage Note:
American English and British English use different grammar to form the negative of *have*.
Compare:
American: He *doesn't have* a dog.
British: He *hasn't* a dog. OR He *hasn't got* a dog.

EXERCISE 11 Fill in the blanks with the negative form of the underlined verb.

EXAMPLE A guide dog needs a lot of training. A pet dog *doesn't need* a lot of training.

1. Most dogs play a lot. Guide dogs *don't play* a lot.
2. Obedience trainers use food to teach dogs. Guide dog trainers *don't use* food.
3. A guide dog works hard. A pet dog *doesn't work* hard.
4. People see colors. Dogs *don't see* colors.
5. A guide dog goes on public transportation. A pet dog *doesn't go* on public transportation.
6. My cats eat special food. They *don't eat* food from our table.
7. My cats like fish. They *don't like* chicken.
8. One cat sleeps on my bed. She *doesn't sleep* alone.
9. My landlord allows cats. He *doesn't allow* dogs.
10. My cats need attention. They *don't need* a lot of my time.
11. We have cats. We *don't have* fish.
12. I like cats. My sister *doesn't like* cats.

The Simple Present Tense; Frequency Words 17

1.5 | Negative Statements with the Simple Present Tense

1. Have students cover up grammar chart **1.5.** Write the following statements on the board:
   1. *The owner knows the destination.*
   2. *Some trainers use food to reward a dog.*
   3. *You have a cat.*
   4. *The dog stops at a curb.*
   5. *He has a dog.*
   6. *Guide dogs work when the harness is on.*

   Ask students to write a negative statement for each sentence.
2. Have students look at grammar chart **1.5.** Say: *Check your work.* Go over trouble spots with the whole class. Review the example sentences and explanations in the grammar chart.

EXERCISE 11

1. Have students read the direction line. Ask: *What will we put in the blanks?* (the negative of the underlined verb) Remind students that they should use contractions whenever possible. Go over the example in the book.
2. Have students complete the exercise individually. Check the answers as a class.
3. If necessary, review grammar chart **1.5** on page 17.

Grammar Variation

Have students go back to the reading on page 14. Ask students to find all the examples of negative statements from the reading. Write them on the board (*Guide dogs don't lead the owners; Their owners don't completely control the guide dogs,* etc.). Have volunteers explain the rules for forming negative statements in the simple present tense. Write the rules on the board.

Search and Rescue Dogs (Reading)

1. Have students look at the photo. Ask: *What's going on in the photo?* (A rescue dog and his handler are searching for someone in the woods.)
2. Have students look at the title of the reading. Ask: *What is the reading about?* Have students make predictions.
3. Preteach any vocabulary words your students may not know, such as *disaster, earthquake,* and *flood.*

BEFORE YOU READ

1. Have students discuss the questions in pairs.
2. Ask for a few volunteers to share their answers with the class.

To save class time, skip Before You Read or have students prepare answers for homework ahead of time.

Reading *CD 1, Track 7*

1. Have students first read the text silently. Tell them to pay special attention to questions with the simple present tense. Then play the audio and have students read along silently. Point out that *SAR* stands for *search and rescue.*
2. Check students' comprehension. Ask questions such as: *What do search and rescue dogs do?* (They help find missing people in disasters like earthquakes.) *How do they find people?* (by smelling them) *What kind of dogs are usually search and rescue dogs?* (large dogs like Labrador retrievers and golden retrievers)

To save class time, have students do the reading for homework ahead of time.

SEARCH AND RESCUE DOGS

Before you Read

1. Besides helping blind people, do you know of any other ways that dogs work?
2. Do dogs have some qualities that humans don't have?

Read the following conversation. Pay special attention to questions with the simple present tense.

A: There's a program on TV tonight about search and rescue dogs. **Do** you **want** to watch it with me?
B: I know about guide dogs. But I don't know anything about search and rescue dogs. What **does** "search" **mean?** What **does** "rescue" **mean?**
A: Search means "look for." Rescue means "to help someone in a dangerous situation."
B: What **do** these dogs **do?**
A: When there is a disaster, like an earthquake or a flood, they help the workers find missing people. They save people's lives.
B: How **do** they **do** that?
A: They have a great sense of smell. They can find things that people can't.
B: **Do** they **need** a lot of training?
A: I think they need at least one year of training.
B: What kind of dogs **do** they **use** as search and rescue dogs?
A: They usually use large, strong dogs. Labrador retrievers or golden retrievers are often SAR dogs. Let's watch the program together tonight.
B: What time **does** it **begin?**
A: At 9 p.m.
B: **Does** your dog **want** to watch the program with us?
A: My dog is a lazy, spoiled Chihuahua. She just wants to eat, play, and sleep.

18 Lesson 1

Reading Variation

To practice listening skills, have students first listen to the audio alone. Ask a few comprehension questions. Repeat the audio if necessary. Then have them open their books and read along as they listen to the audio.

Reading Glossary

disaster: a sudden great act of destruction and loss
earthquake: sudden, violent movements of the earth's surface
flood: covering of dry land with water; an overflow

Culture Note

Approximately 300 dogs and their handlers participated in search and rescue efforts after the World Trade Center disaster on September 11, 2001. Dogs representing 19 states together with all the police canine units from New York worked together to find victims in the debris and rubble. In addition, a number of canine search and rescue teams from all over the world also volunteered their services.

1.6 | Questions with the Simple Present Tense

Compare statements and *yes/no* questions

Do	Subject	Verb	Complement	Short Answer	Explanation
	Guide dogs	need	training.		For questions with *I, we, you, they*, or a plural noun, use:
Do	rescue dogs	need	training?	Yes, they do.	
	You	like	dogs.		*Do* + subject + base form + complement
Do	you	like	cats?	No, I don't.	
Does	**Subject**	**Verb**	**Complement**	**Short Answer**	**Explanation**
	Jamie	trains	rescue dogs.		For questions with *he, she, it*, or a singular subject, use:
Does	Jamie	train	guide dogs?	No, she doesn't.	
	My dog	plays	a lot.		*Does* + subject + base form + complement
Does	a rescue dog	play	a lot?	No, it doesn't.	

Compare statements and *wh-* questions

Wh- Word	*do*	Subject	Verb	Complement	Explanation
		Rescue dogs	need	training.	For questions with *I, we, you, they*, or a plural noun, use:
How much training	do	they	need?		
		You	prefer	cats.	*Wh-* word + *do* + subject + base form + complement
Why	do	you	prefer	cats?	
Wh- Word	***does***	**Subject**	**Verb**	**Complement**	**Explanation**
		The program	begins	soon.	For questions with *he, she, it*, or a singular noun, use:
What time	does	the program	begin?		
		My dog	sleeps	a lot.	*Wh-* word + *does* + subject + base form + complement
Where	does	your dog	sleep?		

Compare negative statements and *why* questions

Why	*don't/doesn't*	Subject	Negative Verb	Complement
		I	don't like	cats.
Why	don't	you	like	cats?
		My dog	doesn't sleep	in his bed.
Why	doesn't	he	sleep	in his bed?

Language Note:
Compare questions with be to other simple present tense questions:
Is the dog friendly? Yes,it **is**.
Does the dog **have** a sweater? Yes, it **does**.
Where is your dog?
What kind of dog **do** you **have?**

The Simple Present Tense; Frequency Words 19

1.6 | Questions with the Simple Present Tense

1. Have students cover up grammar chart **1.6** on page 19. Ask students to find examples of *yes/no* questions in the reading. Write them on the board. Make sure students find examples with both *do* and *does*.
2. Have students look at grammar chart **1.6** on page 19. Review the example sentences and explanations in the grammar chart.
3. Then have students go back to the reading on page 18. Say: *Find all the different kinds of* wh- *questions in the reading.* Write students' examples on the board (e.g., *What does* search *mean? What do these dogs do?*).
4. Have students look at grammar chart **1.6** on page 19. Review the example sentences and explanations in the grammar chart. Ask: *What* wh- *questions in the chart are not in the reading?* (*where* and *why*)
5. Review negative questions with *why*. Go over the examples in the chart and have students ask you questions about the class (e.g., *Why don't you stop class at 7:00? Why don't we have a break?*).
6. Direct students to the Language Note. Compare questions with *be* to questions with other verbs. Go over the examples in the chart. Then have students write *yes/no* and *wh-* questions about the class.

Expansion

Grammar Have students go back to the reading on page 14 (*Guide Dogs*). Ask students to work in pairs to write ten questions. Say: *Write* yes/no, wh-, *and negative questions.* Then have one pair exchange questions with another pair.

EXERCISE 12

CD 1, Track 8

1. Have students read the direction line. Go over the example. Remind students to use contractions whenever possible.
2. Have students complete Exercise 12 individually. Check answers as a class.
3. If necessary, review grammar chart **1.6** on page 19.

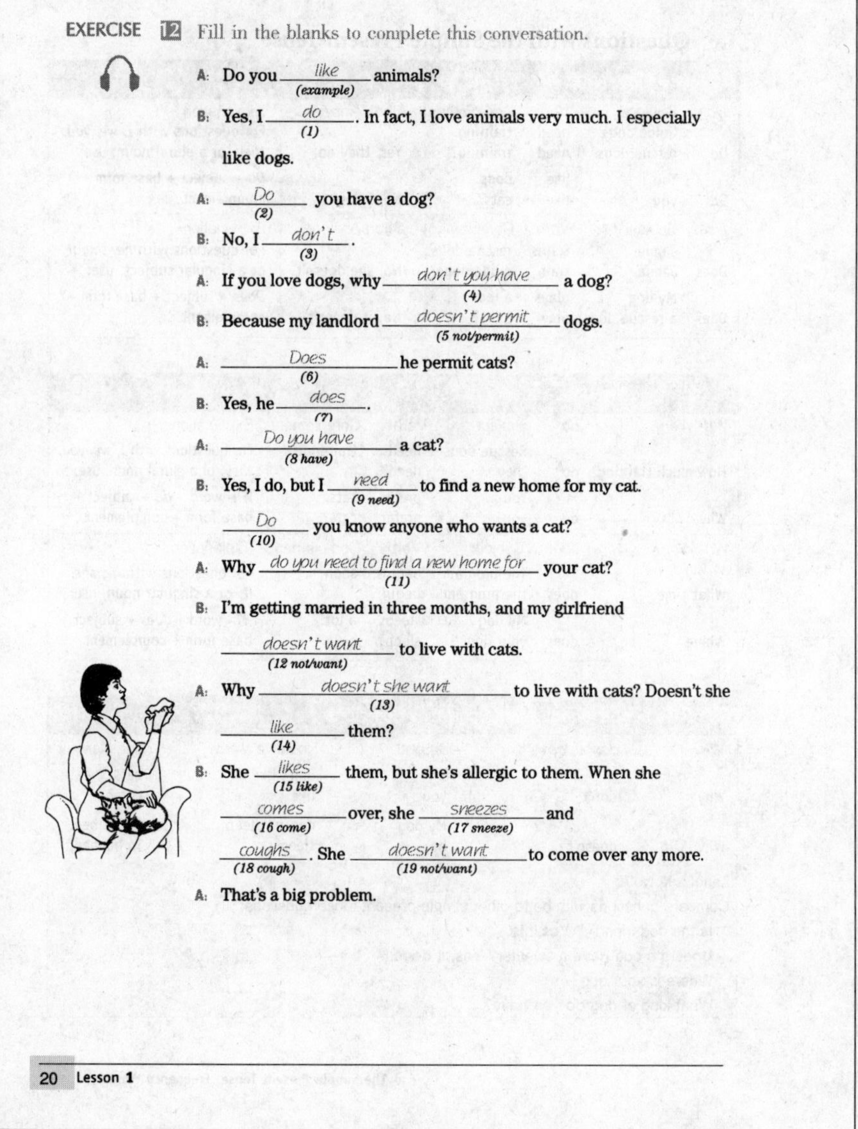

EXERCISE 12 Fill in the blanks to complete this conversation.

A: Do you *like* (example) animals?

B: Yes, I *do* (1). In fact, I love animals very much. I especially like dogs.

A: *Do* (2) you have a dog?

B: No, I *don't* (3).

A: If you love dogs, why *don't you have* (4) a dog?

B: Because my landlord *doesn't permit* (5 not/permit) dogs.

A: *Does* (6) he permit cats?

B: Yes, he *does* (7).

A: *Do you have* (8 have) a cat?

B: Yes, I do, but I *need* (9 need) to find a new home for my cat. *Do* (10) you know anyone who wants a cat?

A: Why *do you need to find a new home for* (11) your cat?

B: I'm getting married in three months, and my girlfriend *doesn't want* (12 not/want) to live with cats.

A: Why *doesn't she want* (13) to live with cats? Doesn't she *like* (14) them?

B: She *likes* (15 like) them, but she's allergic to them. When she *comes* (16 come) over, she *sneezes* (17 sneeze) and *coughs* (18 cough). She *doesn't want* (19 not/want) to come over any more.

A: That's a big problem.

20 Lesson 1

Exercise 12 Variation

To provide practice with listening skills, have students close their books and listen to the audio. Repeat the audio as needed. Ask comprehension questions, such as: *What kind of pet does the landlord permit?* (cats) *What is the cat owner doing in three months?* (getting married) *What does he have to do before then?* (find a new home for his cat) *Why?* (because his girlfriend is allergic to cats) Then have students open their books and complete Exercise 12.

Expansion

Exercise 12 Have students practice the conversation in pairs. Ask volunteers to act out the conversation for the class.

EXERCISE 13 Part 1: Use the words below to interview a student with a dog.

EXAMPLES

your dog / big
A: Is your dog big?
B: Yes, she is.

your dog / sleep a lot (how many hours)
A: Does your dog sleep a lot?
B: Yes, she does.
A: How many hours does she sleep?
B: She sleeps about 15 hours a day.

1. how old / your dog
How old is your dog?
2. what / your dog's name
What's your dog's name?
3. it / a male or a female
Is it a male or a female?
4. what / your dog / eat
What does your dog eat?
5. how often / you / take your dog out
How often do you take your dog out?
6. your dog / do tricks (what kind)
What kind of tricks does your dog do?
7. your dog / have toys (what kind)
What kind of toys does your dog have?
8. your dog / friendly
Is your dog friendly?
9. your dog / bark a lot
Does your dog bark a lot?
10. why / you / like dogs
Why do you like dogs?

Part 2: Use the words below to interview a student with a cat.

1. how old / your cat
How old is your cat?
2. what / your cat's name
What's your cat's name?
3. it / a male or a female
Is it a male or a female?
4. your cat / catch mice
Does your cat catch mice?
5. your cat / friendly
Is your cat friendly?
6. your cat / sit on your lap a lot
Does your cat sit on your lap a lot?
7. your cat / have toys (what kind)
What kind of toys does your cat have?
8. why / you / like cats
Why do you like cats?

lap

1.7 | *Wh-* Questions with a Preposition

Examples	Explanation
What does she talk **about?** She talks about her cats. What does your cat sleep **on?** She sleeps on a pillow.	In conversation, most people put the preposition at the end of the sentence.
Formal: **With whom** does the dog sleep? Informal: **Who** does the dog sleep **with?**	Putting the preposition before a question word is very formal. When the preposition comes at the beginning, we use *whom*, not *who*.
Where do you come **from?** I come from Mexico. Where are you **from?** I'm from Mexico.	For country of origin, you can use *be from* or *come from*.
What time does the program begin? It begins at 9 p.m.	Omit *at* in a question about time.

EXERCISE 13

1. Tell students that in Part 1 they will have to interview a student who has a dog. Part 2 is for interviewing a student with a cat. Identify dog owners and cat owners in the classroom. Ask: *Who owns a dog? Who owns a cat?* Go over the examples. Have volunteers model the examples.
2. Have students complete the exercise in pairs. Circulate to observe pair work. Give help as needed.
3. If necessary, review grammar chart **1.6** on page 19.

To save class time, have students write the interview questions for homework and conduct the interview in class.

1.7 | *Wh-* Questions with a Preposition

1. Have students cover up grammar chart **1.7** on page 21. Write the following on the board:
   1. What does she talk ______?
   2. What does your cat sleep ______?
   3. Who does the dog sleep ______?
   4. Where do you come ______?
   5. Where are you ______?
   Activate students' prior knowledge. Say: *Fill in the blanks with the missing words.*
2. Have students look at grammar chart **1.7**. Say: *Now compare your sentences with the chart.* Review the example sentences in the grammar chart.
3. Point out the formal *with whom*. Review questions and answers with time (e.g., *What time does the class begin? At 7:00.*).

Expansion

Exercise 13 Do a class survey with the information from the interviews. Have students discuss their information in groups (people with dogs and people with cats) and then have them report their findings to the class.

EXERCISE 14

1. Tell students that they will be answering questions about themselves. Have students read the direction line. Ask: *What kind of question do we ask first?* (a *yes/no* question) Say: *Then ask a* wh-*question, if possible.* Go over the example in the book. Model the example with a volunteer. Answer "no" to the question.
2. Have students complete Exercise 14 in pairs. Circulate and observe the pair work. Go over any trouble spots with the class.
3. If necessary, review grammar chart **1.7** on page 21.

EXERCISE 15

CD 1, Track 9

1. Have students read the direction line. Go over the example. Do #1 with the class.
2. Have students complete Exercise 15 individually. Check answers as a class.
3. If necessary, review grammar charts **1.6** on page 19 and **1.7** on page 21.

To save class time, have students do half of the exercise in class and complete the other half for homework. Or assign the entire exercise for homework.

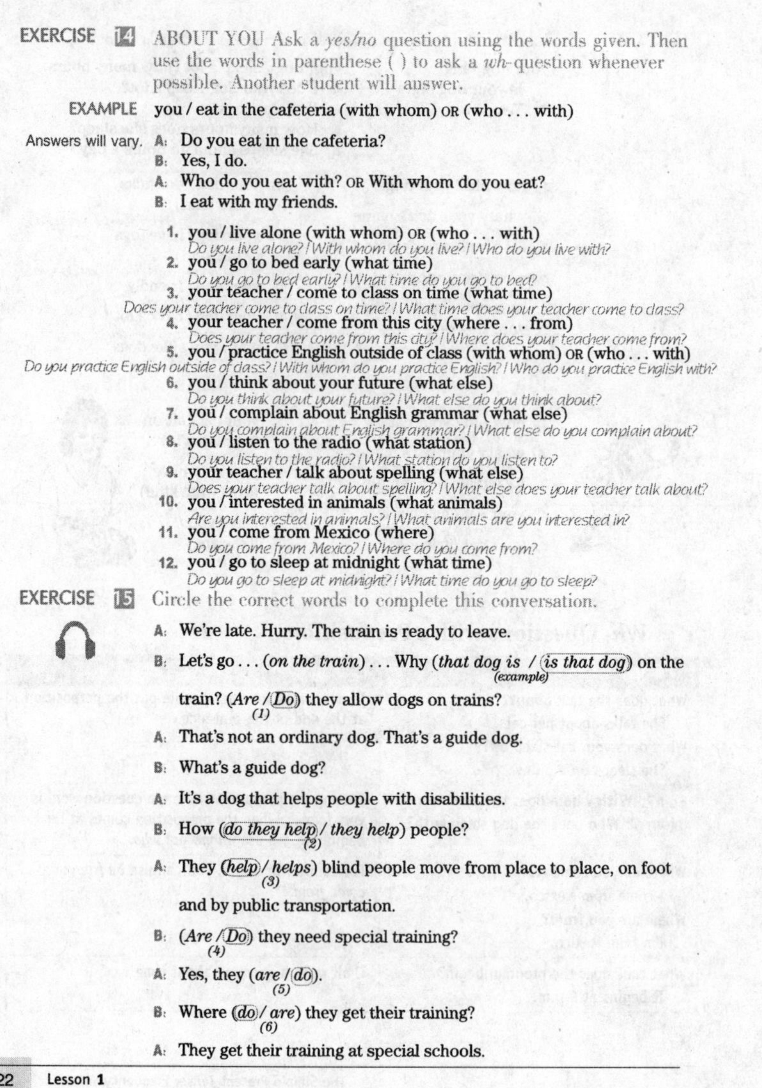

EXERCISE 14 ABOUT YOU Ask a *yes/no* question using the words given. Then use the words in parenthese ( ) to ask a *wh*-question whenever possible. Another student will answer.

EXAMPLE you / eat in the cafeteria (with whom) OR (who . . . with)

Answers will vary.
A: Do you eat in the cafeteria?
B: Yes, I do.
A: Who do you eat with? OR With whom do you eat?
B: I eat with my friends.

1. you / live alone (with whom) OR (who . . . with)
Do you live alone? / With whom do you live? / Who do you live with?
2. you / go to bed early (what time)
Do you go to bed early? / What time do you go to bed?
3. your teacher / come to class on time (what time)
Does your teacher come to class on time? / What time does your teacher come to class?
4. your teacher / come from this city (where . . . from)
Does your teacher come from this city? / Where does your teacher come from?
5. you / practice English outside of class (with whom) OR (who . . . with)
Do you practice English outside of class? / With whom do you practice English? / Who do you practice English with?
6. you / think about your future (what else)
Do you think about your future? / What else do you think about?
7. you / complain about English grammar (what else)
Do you complain about English grammar? / What else do you complain about?
8. you / listen to the radio (what station)
Do you listen to the radio? / What station do you listen to?
9. your teacher / talk about spelling (what else)
Does your teacher talk about spelling? / What else does your teacher talk about?
10. you / interested in animals (what animals)
Are you interested in animals? / What animals are you interested in?
11. you / come from Mexico (where)
Do you come from Mexico? / Where do you come from?
12. you / go to sleep at midnight (what time)
Do you go to sleep at midnight? / What time do you go to sleep?

EXERCISE 15 Circle the correct words to complete this conversation.

A: We're late. Hurry. The train is ready to leave.
B: Let's go . . . (*on the train*) . . . Why (*that dog is* / *is that dog*) on the train? (*Are* / *Do*) they allow dogs on trains?
(example) (1)
A: That's not an ordinary dog. That's a guide dog.
B: What's a guide dog?
A: It's a dog that helps people with disabilities.
B: How (*do they help* / *they help*) people?
(2)
A: They (*help* / *helps*) blind people move from place to place, on foot and by public transportation.
(3)
B: (*Are* / *Do*) they need special training?
(4)
A: Yes, they (*are* / *do*).
(5)
B: Where (*do* / *are*) they get their training?
(6)
A: They get their training at special schools.

22 Lesson 1

Expansion

Exercise 14 Do a class survey with the information from the interviews. Write the results on the board (e.g., Do you live alone? Yes: 5 No: 7).

Exercise 15 Variation

To provide practice with listening skills, have students close their books and listen to the audio. Repeat the audio as needed. Ask comprehension questions, such as: *What do guide dogs do?* (help people with disabilities; help blind people move from place to place, on foot and by public transportation) *What kind of people do guide dogs help?* (blind people, deaf people, people in wheelchairs) *When do guide dogs play?* (when the owner takes off the dog's harness) Then have students open their books and complete Exercise 15.

B: Are they only for blind people?

A: No. Guide dogs help people with other disabilities too. There are guide dogs for the deaf[10] and for people in wheelchairs.

B: Why (are you / you are) such an expert on guide dogs? (7)

A: My cousin is blind. He has a guide dog.

B: Let's play with the dog.

A: No. (It's not / It doesn't) good to distract a guide dog. A guide dog (8) (need / needs) to concentrate. (9)

B: When (are / do) they play? (10)

A: They (play / plays) when the owner (takes / take) off the dog's harness. (11) (12)

B: What (do / does) they eat? (13)

A: They eat the same thing other dogs eat.

B: It's amazing what a dog can do.

1.8 | Questions About Meaning, Spelling, and Cost

Wh- Word	Do/ Does	Subject	Verb (Base form)	Complement	Explanation
What	does	"kitten"	mean?		*Mean, spell, say,* and *cost* are verbs and should be in the verb position of a question. Use the base form in the question.
How	do	you	spell	"kitten"?	
How	do	you	say	"kitten" in your language?	
How much	does	a kitten	cost?		

EXERCISE 16 Fill in the blanks to complete the conversation.

A: *Do you have* (example) a pet?

B: Yes. I have a new kitten.

A: I don't know the word "kitten." What *does it mean* (1)?

B: Kitten means baby cat.

A: Oh. What's his name?

B: Romeo.

A: How *do you spell it* (2)?

[10] A *deaf* person cannot hear.

The Simple Present Tense; Frequency Words 23

1.8 | Questions About Meaning, Spelling, and Cost

1. Have students look at grammar chart **1.8** on page 23. Review the questions and explanations in the chart.
2. Then ask students to work in pairs to create three sentences with *mean, spell,* and *say* to ask you, the teacher. Have volunteers ask you questions.

EXERCISE 16

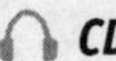 **CD 1, Track 10**

1. Tell students that in this exercise they will be completing the questions. Go over the example.
2. Have students complete Exercise 16 individually. Check answers as a class.
3. If necessary, review grammar chart **1.8** on page 23.

Exercise 16 Variation

To provide practice with listening skills, have students close their books and listen to the audio. Repeat the audio as needed. Ask comprehension questions, such as: *What does* kitten *mean?* (baby cat) *How much do parrots usually cost?* (between $175 and $1,000) *What does Chico eat?* (fruit, vegetables, rice, nuts, and seeds) Then have students open their books and complete Exercise 16.

B: R-O-M-E-O.

A: Where ___does he sleep___ (3) ?

B: He sleeps with me, of course. ___Do you have___ (4) any pets?

A: Yes, I do.

B: What kind of pet ___do you have___ (5) ?

A: I have a bird that talks. I don't know the word in English. How ___do you say___ (6) "perico" in English?

B: Parrot. So you have a parrot. What ___'s his name___ (7) ?

A: His name is Chico.

B: How old ___is he___ (8) ?

A: He's almost 20 years old.

B: Wow! How long ___do they live___ (9) ?

A: They live a long time. Some live up to 80 years.

B: Are parrots expensive? How much ___do they cost___ (10) ?

A: It depends on what kind you get. But they usually cost between $175 and $1,000.

B: ___Are___ (11) parrots affectionate?

A: Oh, yes. They're very affectionate. Chico sits on my shoulder all the time.

B: What ___does he eat___ (12) ?

A: He eats fruit, vegetables, rice, nuts, and seeds.

B: ___Does he talk___ (13) ?

A: Yes. He talks a lot.

B: What ___does he say___ (14) ?

A: He says, "Good-bye," "Hello," "I love you," and many more things. He speaks Spanish and English.

B: Maybe he speaks English better than we do!

Expansion

Exercise 16 Have students practice the conversation in pairs. Ask volunteers to act out the conversation for the class.

EXERCISE 17 Fill in the blanks to complete the conversation.

A: I know you love dogs. _Do you have_ (example) a dog now?

B: No, I _don't_ (1). But I have two cats. I don't have time for a dog.

A: Why _don't you have_ (2) a dog?

B: Because I'm not at home very much.

A: Why _not/aren't you home very much_ (3)?

B: Because I work eight hours a day, and at night, I take classes. Dogs need a lot of attention. I _don't_ (4) have enough time right now.

A: What about your cats? _Do they_ (5) need attention too?

B: Not as much as dogs. What about you? _Do you have_ (6) any pets?

A: I have several tropical fish.[11]

B: _Are they_ (7) expensive?

A: Some of them are very expensive.

B: How much _do they cost_ (8)?

A: Some of them cost over $100.

B: Wow! That's a lot of money for a boring pet.

A: Fish _aren't_ (9) boring. It _'s_ (10) fun to look at them. And when I go to work, they _don't_ (11) get lonely, like dogs and cats.

B: Yes, but they _aren't_ (12) affectionate like dogs and cats.

A: They _don't_ (13) make noise like dogs do, so neighbors never complain about fish.

B: How many fish _do you have_ (14)?

A: I have about 14 or 15. My favorite is my Oranda.

B: How _do you spell_ (15) "Oranda"?

A: O-R-A-N-D-A. It's a kind of a goldfish. When you have time, come and see my fish tank.

[11] *Fish* can be singular or plural. In this case, *fish* is plural.

The Simple Present Tense; Frequency Words 25

EXERCISE 17

CD 1, Track 11

1. Have students read the directions. Go over the example. Remind students to use contractions whenever possible.
2. Have students complete Exercise 17 individually. Check answers as a class.
3. If necessary, review grammar charts **1.6** on page 19, **1.7** on page 21, and **1.8** on page 23.

To save class time, have students do half of the exercise in class and complete the other half for homework. Or assign the entire exercise for homework.

Exercise 17 Variation

To provide practice with listening skills, have students close their books and listen to the audio. Repeat the audio as needed. Ask comprehension questions, such as: *Do you need a lot of time to own a dog?* (Yes, dogs need a lot of attention.) *How much do some tropical fish cost?* (over $100) *What kind of fish is an Oranda?* (a kind of goldfish) Then have students open their books and complete Exercise 17.

Expansion

Exercise 17 Have students practice the conversation in pairs. Instruct students to create their own conversations about their pets. Then have volunteers role-play their conversations in front of the class.

Marianne and Sparky (Reading)

1. Have students look at the photo. Ask: *What is the woman doing to the dog?* (fixing his bow)
2. Have students look at the title of the reading. Ask: *What is the reading about?* Have students make predictions.
3. Preteach any vocabulary words your students may not know, such as *dog groomer* and *kennel.*

BEFORE YOU READ

1. Have students discuss the questions in pairs.
2. Ask for a few volunteers to share their answers with the class.

To save class time, skip "Before You Read" or have students prepare answers for homework ahead of time.

Reading *CD 1, Track 12*

1. Have students first read the text silently. Tell them to pay special attention to frequency words. Then play the audio and have students read along silently.
2. Check students' comprehension. Ask questions such as: *Who is Marianne?* (a friend of Elena's) *Who is Sparky?* (Marianne's dog) *Does Marianne call her dog on the telephone?* (Yes. She talks to him through the answering machine.) *Who takes care of her dog when she's at work?* (a dog walker) *Where does Marianne like to go with Sparky when the weather is nice?* (to a beach for dogs and their owners) *Does Elena think Marianne and other Americans should treat their pets the way they do?* (probably not)

To save class time, have students do the reading for homework ahead of time.

MARIANNE AND SPARKY

Before You Read

Do people in your native culture treat pets the same way Americans do?

What kinds of animals or pets do people prefer in your native culture?

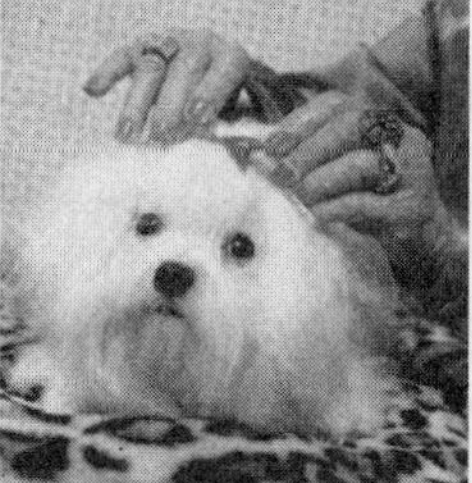

Read the following letter from Elena in the U.S. to her friend Sofia in Russia. Pay special attention to frequency words.

Dear Sofia,

I want to tell you about one aspect of American life that seems strange to me—how Americans treat their pets. I have a new American friend, Marianne. She lives alone, but she has a dog, Sparky. Marianne treats him like a child. She **always** carries a picture of Sparky in her wallet. She **often** buys toys for him, especially on his birthday. She **often** calls him on the telephone when she's not home and talks into the answering machine. Sparky **always** sleeps in bed with her.

When she goes to work, she uses a dog walking service. **Twice a day,** someone comes to her house to play with Sparky and take him for a walk. She says that he gets lonely if he's home alone all day. She **always** leaves the TV on when she goes to work to keep Sparky entertained.

Once a month, she takes him to a dog groomer. The groomer gives him a bath and cuts and paints his nails. When she travels, she **usually** takes him with her, but **sometimes** she puts him in a kennel[12] or pet hotel. All of these dog services cost a lot of money. But Marianne doesn't care. Nothing is too expensive when it comes to Sparky.

There's a small beach near her house that is just for dogs and their owners. She takes Sparky there **whenever** the weather is nice so that he can play with other dogs. While the dogs play together, the dog owners talk to each other. She **always** cleans up after her dog.

In winter, she **always** puts a coat on Sparky. In fact, Sparky has about four different winter coats. **Whenever** it rains, Sparky wears his bright yellow raincoat.

Sometimes I think American dogs live better than most people in the world.

Your good friend,
Elena

[12] A *kennel* is a place where pets are kept while their owners are away.

26 Lesson 1

Reading Variation

To practice listening skills, have students first listen to the audio alone. Ask a few comprehension questions. Repeat the audio if necessary. Then have them open their books and read along as they listen to the audio.

Reading Glossary

dog groomer: a person who makes dogs look neat and clean
kennel: a place where dogs are kept, usually while their owners are away

1.9 | Simple Present Tense with Frequency Words

Examples	Explanation
Marianne **often** calls her dog on the phone. Sparky **always** sleeps in bed with her. When she travels, she **usually** takes Sparky with her.	We use the simple present tense with frequency words to show a regular activity. Frequency words are: *always, usually, often, sometimes, rarely, seldom,* and *never.*
Whenever the weather is nice, she takes her dog to the beach. Sparky wears a raincoat **whenever** it rains.	*Whenever* shows a regular activity. It means "any time."
Once a month, she takes her dog to a groomer. Someone comes to her house to walk the dog **twice a day.**	Expressions that show frequency are: • every day (week, month, year) • every other day (week, month, year) • once a day (week, month, year) • from time to time • once in a while
Frequency Words: always usually/generally often/frequently sometimes/occasionally rarely/seldom/hardly ever never/not ever	100% ↕ 0%

EXERCISE 18 Fill in the blanks with an appropriate verb.

EXAMPLE Marianne always ___puts___ a coat on Sparky when the weather is cold.

1. Elena sometimes ___writes___ a letter to her friend Sofia.
2. Marianne ___is___ always worried about her dog.
3. The dog ___is___ always happy to see Marianne when she comes home.
4. Marianne often ___buys___ toys for her dog.
5. The TV ___is___ always on when Marianne is at work.
6. Sparky always ___sleeps___ in bed with Marianne.
7. Marianne usually ___travels___ with her dog when she goes on vacation.

EXERCISE 19 ABOUT YOU Fill in the blanks with an appropriate frequency word.

EXAMPLE I ___rarely___ use a public telephone.

Answers will vary.

1. I ____________ say, "How are you?" when I meet a friend.
2. I'm ________________ confused about American customs.

Expansion

Exercise 19 Say: *What do you do in the United States that you don't do in your native country? Write comparisons. Use frequency-words* (e.g., *Here I eat in fast-food restaurants once a week. In Colombia, I never eat in fast-food restaurants.*).

1.9 | Simple Present Tense With Frequency Words

1. Have students cover up grammar chart **1.9.** Write the following frequency words on the board in random order:
   rarely/seldom/hardly ever
   usually/generally
   always
   never/not ever
   often/frequently
   sometimes/occasionally
   Draw a 0%–100% scale on the board. Ask volunteers to place the frequency words on the scale.
2. Have students look at grammar chart **1.9.** Say: *Check our scale on the board with the scale in the book.* Review the example sentences in the grammar chart.
3. Explain to students that frequency words are used with the simple present tense to show regular activity.
4. Review frequency expressions such as *every day, once a week, from time to time,* etc.

EXERCISE 18

1. Tell students that this exercise is based on the reading. Have students read the direction line. Go over the example.
2. Have students complete the rest of the exercise individually. Go over the answers as a class.
3. If necessary, review grammar chart **1.9** on page 27.

EXERCISE 19

1. Say: *Complete the sentences based on what's true for you.* Have students read the direction line. Go over the example in the book.
2. Have students complete the exercise individually. Then have students compare answers with a partner.
3. If necessary, review grammar chart **1.9** on page 27.

To save class time, have students do half of the exercise in class and complete the other half for homework.

EXERCISE 20

1. Tell students that this exercise is about customs and habits in their native culture. Have students read the direction line. Go over the example in the book.
2. Have students complete the exercise individually. Then have students compare answers in pairs or groups.
3. If necessary, review grammar chart **1.9** on page 27.

To save class time, have students do half of the exercise in class and complete the other half for homework. Or assign the entire exercise for homework.

3. I ______________ smile when I pass someone I know.
4. I ______________ shake hands when I get together with a friend.
5. Americans ______________ ask me, "What country are you from?"
6. I ______________ celebrate my birthday in a restaurant.
7. I ______________ buy birthday presents for my good friends.
8. If I invite a friend to a restaurant, I ______________ pay for both of us.
9. I ______________ use a cell phone.
10. I ______________ eat in fast-food restaurants.
11. I ______________ leave my computer on overnight.

EXERCISE 20 Fill in the blanks with an appropriate frequency word. You may find a partner and compare your answers.

EXAMPLE People in my native culture ___*rarely*___ ask, "How are you?"

Answers will vary.

1. Dogs in my native culture ______________ sleep with their owners.
2. Dogs in my native culture are ______________ part of the family.
3. Cats in my native culture are ______________ part of the family.
4. People in my native culture ______________ feed pet food to cats and dogs.
5. People in my native culture ______________ travel with their pets.
6. Women in my native culture ______________ kiss their friends when they get together.
7. People in my native culture ______________ visit each other without calling first.
8. Men in my native culture ______________ do housework.
9. Married women in my native culture ______________ wear a wedding ring.
10. Married men in my native culture ______________ wear a wedding ring.
11. Women in my native culture ______________ wear shorts in the summer.
12. People in my native culture ______________ eat in restaurants.

28 Lesson 1

Expansion

Exercise 20 On the board, make a grid of the nationalities represented in the class and the item numbers (1–12) from Exercise 20. Write the frequency word under each nationality for each item of the exercise.

	El Salvador	Morocco	Saudi Arabia
1.	rarely	never	never
2.			
3.			

EXERCISE 21 In the sentences in Exercise 20, notice if the frequency word comes before or after the verb. Write *B* for *before* or *A* for *after*.

EXAMPLE People in my native culture ___rarely___ ask, "How are you?" B

1.10 | Position of Frequency Words and Expressions

Examples	Explanation
Sparky *is* (Verb) **always** happy to see Marianne. The TV *is* (Verb) **always** on in the day. Marianne *is* (Verb) **rarely** home during the day.	The frequency word comes **after** the verb *be*.
Marianne **often** *calls* (Verb) Sparky on the phone. She **usually** *travels* (Verb) with Sparky. She **always** *carries* (Verb) a picture of Sparky.	The frequency word comes **before** other verbs.
Sometimes she puts Sparky in a kennel. **Usually** she feeds Sparky dog food. **Often** Elena writes to her friend about American customs.	*Sometimes, usually,* and *often* can come at the beginning of the sentence too. Do not put *always, never, rarely,* and *seldom* at the beginning of the sentence. *Wrong: Always* she carries a picture of her dog.
Once a month, she travels. She travels **once a month.** **Every week,** she goes to the beach. She goes to the beach **every week.**	A frequency expression can come at the beginning or at the end of a sentence. When it comes at the beginning of the sentence, we sometimes separate it from the sentence with a comma.

EXERCISE 22 ABOUT YOU Add a frequency word to each sentence to make a **true** statement about yourself.

EXAMPLE I drink coffee at night.
I never drink coffee at night.

Answers will vary.

1. I talk to my neighbors.
2. I pay my rent on time.
3. I'm busy on Saturdays.
4. I receive e-mail from my friends.

Expansion

Exercise 22 Have students make questions from the statements in Exercise 22. Ask students to ask and answer questions with a partner.

EXERCISE 21

1. Have students read the direction line. Go over the example in the book.
2. Have students complete the exercise individually. Then go over answers with the class. Make two lists on the board: frequency words that go before the verb and frequency words that go after the verb.

To save class time, have students do half of the exercise in class and complete the other half for homework. Or assign the entire exercise for homework.

1.10 | Position of Frequency Words and Expressions

1. Have students look at grammar chart **1.10.** Have students compare the lists the class made on the board with the examples in the grammar chart.
2. Review the example sentences in the grammar chart. Point out that *sometimes, usually,* and *often* can come at the beginning of sentences. Tell students not to put *always, never, rarely,* and *seldom* at the beginning of the sentence.
3. Explain to students that frequency expressions can come at the beginning or at the end of a sentence. If a frequency expression comes at the beginning, you can use a comma to separate it from the rest of the sentence.

EXERCISE 22

1. Have students read the direction line. Ask: *What kind of word are we going to add to make the sentence true?* (a frequency word) Go over the example in the book.
2. Have students complete the exercise individually. Then have students compare answers in pairs. Circulate to observe pair work.
3. If necessary, review grammar chart **1.10** on page 29.

EXERCISE 23

1. Have students read the direction line. Model the example for the students and have a volunteer also model the example.
2. Have students complete the exercise individually. Then have students compare answers with a partner. Circulate to observe pair work. Give help as needed.
3. If necessary, review grammar charts **1.1** on page 3 and **1.9** on page 27.

To save class time, have students do half of the exercise as a class and complete the other half for homework.

5. I call my family in my native country.
6. I travel in the summer.
7. I speak English at home with my family.
8. I eat meat for dinner.
9. I go out of town.
10. I study in the library.
11. I eat cereal for breakfast.
12. I bring my dictionary to class.

EXERCISE 23 ABOUT YOU Add a verb (phrase) to make a **true** statement about yourself.

EXAMPLE **I / usually**

I usually drink coffee in the morning. OR

I'm usually afraid to go out at night.

1. I / rarely / on Sunday
   Answers will vary.
2. I / usually / on the weekend
3. I / hardly ever
4. I / sometimes / at night
5. people from my native culture / often
6. people from my native culture / seldom
7. My family / sometimes
8. My family / rarely
9. women from my native culture / hardly ever
10. men from my native culture / hardly ever

30 Lesson 1

Expansion

Exercise 23 Have students compare their answers from Exercise 23 in groups. If possible, put students from different cultures/nationalities in groups.

1.11 | Questions with *Ever*

We use *ever* in a question when we want an answer that has a frequency word.

Do/Does	Subject	*Ever*	Verb	Complement	Short Answer
Do	you	**ever**	sleep	with your cat?	Yes, I **sometimes** do.
Does	the teacher	**ever**	bring	her dog to school?	No, she **never** does.
Be	**Subject**	***Ever***		**Complement**	**Short Answer**
Are	dogs	**ever**		unhappy?	Yes, they **sometimes** are.
Is	Marianne	**ever**		home during the day?	No, she **never** is.

Language Notes:

1. In a short answer, the frequency word comes between the subject and the verb.
2. The verb after *never* is affirmative.
   Does your cat ever drink milk?
   No, she never **does.**

EXERCISE 24 ABOUT YOU Fill in the blanks with a frequency word to make a **true** statement about yourself. Then ask a question with *ever*. Another student will answer.

EXAMPLE I *rarely* eat breakfast in a restaurant.

Answers will vary. A: Do you ever eat breakfast in a restaurant?
B: No, I never do.

1. I __________ sleep with the light on.
2. I __________ watch TV in the morning.
3. I __________ take a bubble bath.
4. I __________ spend money on foolish things.
5. I'm __________ afraid to go out at night.
6. I'm __________ tired while I'm in class.
7. I __________ cry during a sad movie.
8. I __________ dream in English.
9. I __________ take off my shoes when I enter my house.
10. I __________ babysit for a member of my family.
11. I __________ eat fast food.
12. I __________ wear a watch.
13. I __________ use cologne or perfume.
14. I __________ fall asleep with the TV on.

1.11 | Questions with *Ever*

1. Have students look at grammar chart **1.11.** Say: *When we want an answer that has a frequency word, use* ever *in the question.* Go over the examples for *do/does.* Go around the room and ask students questions with *ever* (e.g., *Do you ever walk to school? Do you ever bring your lunch? Do they ever talk in class?*).
2. Say: *You can use* ever *in sentences with* be, *too.* Go over the examples. Go around the class asking questions with *be* and *ever* (e.g., *Are you ever sad? Are they ever quiet? Is he ever late?*).
3. Point out that in short answers the frequency word comes between the subject and the verb. Tell students that the verb after *never* is always affirmative. Go over the example in the chart.

EXERCISE 24

1. Tell students that this exercise is about their customs and habits. Have students read the direction line. Say: *Complete the statements for yourself. Then ask a partner.* Go over the example in the book. Model the example with a volunteer. Then have two volunteers model #1.
2. Have students complete the statements individually. Point out the picture of a bubble bath. Then have students take turns asking and answering questions. Circulate to observe pair work. Give help as needed.
3. If necessary, review grammar chart **1.11** on page 31.

1.12 | Questions with *How Often* and Answers with Frequency Expressions

1. Have students cover up grammar chart **1.12.** Write some frequency expressions on the board (e.g., *once a week, every day, every week,* and *twice a month*). Go around the room and ask questions with *How often?* (e.g., *How often do we come to class? How often do you visit your parents? How often do you call your grandmother? How often do you watch TV?*)
2. Now have students look at grammar chart **1.12.** Go over the examples and explanations. Point out that frequency expressions can come at the beginning or the end of the sentence.

EXERCISE 25

1. Tell students that they're going to ask their partners about their customs and habits. Go over the example. Have two volunteers model the example.
2. Have students complete the exercise in pairs. Circulate to observe pair work. Give help as needed.
3. If necessary, review grammar chart **1.12** on page 32.

15. I ____________ fall asleep in class.
16. I ____________ write personal letters to my friends and family.
17. I ____________ sit in the sun to get a suntan.
18. I ____________ carry a personal stereo.
19. I ____________ wear running shoes.
20. I ____________ discuss politics with my friends.
21. I ____________ wear sandals in warm weather.
22. I'm ____________ friendly with my neighbors.

1.12 | Questions with *How Often* and Answers with Frequency Expressions

Examples	Explanation
How often do you take your dog out? I take her out **three times a day.** **How often** does Marianne travel? She travels **every other month.** **How often** do you take your cat to the doctor? I take my cat to the doctor **twice a year.**	We use *how often* when we want to ask about the frequency of an activity.
Once a month, she takes her dog to a groomer. She takes her dog to a groomer **once a month.**	Frequency expressions can come at the beginning or the end of the sentence.

EXERCISE 25 ABOUT YOU Ask a question with "*How often do you . . .?*" and the words given. Another student will answer.

EXAMPLE eat in a restaurant

A: How often do you eat in a restaurant?
B: I eat in a restaurant once a week.

1. check your e-mail
How often do you check your e-mail?
2. shop for groceries
How often do you shop for groceries?
3. exercise
How often do you exercise?
4. get a haircut
How often do you get a haircut?
5. use your dictionary
How often do you use your dictionary?
6. use public transportation
How often do you use public transportation?
7. use the Internet
How often do you use the Internet?
8. go to the dentist
How often do you go to the dentist?
9. watch the news on TV
How often do you watch the news on TV?
10. go to the teacher's office
How often do you go to the teacher's office?

32 Lesson 1

Expansion

Exercise 25 Create two rings of students. Have half of the students stand in an outer ring around the classroom. Have the other half stand in an inner ring, facing the outer ring. Instruct students to ask and answer the questions from Exercise 25. Call out "turn" every minute or so. Students in the inner ring should move one space clockwise. Students now ask and answer with their new partners. Say: *Ask questions in random order.* Make sure students look at each other when they're speaking.

SUMMARY OF LESSON 1

1. Observe the simple present tense with the verb *be*.

   Your dog **is** beautiful.
   It **isn't** big.
   Is it a Collie? No, it **isn't.**
   What kind of dog **is** it?

   You **are** young.
   You **aren't** ready for a dog.
   Are you responsible? Yes, I **am.**
   Why **aren't** you ready for a dog?

2. Observe the simple present tense with other verbs.

Base Form	***-s* Form**
They **have** a dog.	She **likes** birds.
They **don't have** a cat.	She **doesn't like** cats.
Do they **have** a bird?	**Does** she **like** small birds?
No, they **don't.**	Yes, she **does.**
What kind of dog **do** they **have?**	Why **does** she **like** birds?
Why **don't** they **have** a cat?	Why **doesn't** she **like** cats?

3. Frequency words:

always	100%
usually / generally	↑
often / frequently	
sometimes / occasionally	
rarely / seldom / hardly ever	↓
never / not ever	0%

4. Questions with frequency words:

   Does he **ever** take his dog to the park? Yes, he **often** does.
   How often does he feed his dog? Twice a day.

EDITING ADVICE

1. Don't use a contraction in a short affirmative answer.

   Are you happy in the U.S.? Yes, ~~I'm~~. *I am*

2. Don't make a contraction with a word that ends with *s, se, ce, ze, sh, ch,* or *x*.

   English~~'s~~ a difficult language. *is*

3. Don't use *have* with age. Do not use *years* without *old*.

   My daughter ~~has~~ 10 years ^. *is* ... *old*

The Simple Present Tense; Frequency Words 33

Summary Variation

Item 3 Play a game. Create two scrambled scales on the board. Divide students into Team A and Team B. See which team can unscramble the scale first.

Summary of Lesson 1

1. **Simple present tense with *be***
   Review the examples. Then have students write their own sentences. Say: *Write the following with* is *and* are:
   1. affirmative statement
   2. negative statement
   3. yes/no *question*
   4. short answer
   5. wh- *question*
   6. negative question
   If necessary, have students review: **Lesson 1.**
2. **Simple present tense with other verbs**
   Review the examples. Then have students write their own sentences. Say: *Write the following with the base form and with the -s form:*
   1. affirmative statement
   2. negative statement
   3. yes/no *question*
   4. short answer
   5. wh- *question*
   6. negative question
   If necessary, have students review: **Lesson 1.**
3. **Frequency words**
   On the board write a scale with the frequency words in scrambled order. Have the students unscramble the scale. If necessary, have students review:
   1.9 Simple Present Tense with Frequency Words (p. 27)
   1.10 Position of Frequency Words and Expressions (p. 29).
4. **Questions with frequency words**
   Have students write five questions with *ever* and *how often* to ask their classmates. Let students mingle in the room as they ask their questions. Have volunteers share the information. If necessary, have students review:
   1.11 Questions with *Ever* (p. 31)
   1.12 Questions with *How Often* and Answers with Frequency Expressions (p. 32).

Editing Advice

Have students close their books. Write the example sentences without editing marks or corrections on the board. For example:

1. Are you happy in the U.S.? Yes, I'm.
2. English's a difficult language.

Editing Advice (*cont.*)

Ask students to correct each sentence and provide a rule or explanation for each correction. This activity can be done individually, in pairs, or as a class. After students have corrected each sentence, tell them to turn to pages 33–36. Say: *Now compare your work with the Editing Advice in the book.*

4. Don't use *have* with *hungry, thirsty, hot, cold,* or *afraid.*

   Please open the window. I ~~have~~ *am* hot.

5. Don't forget the subject *it* with time, weather, and impersonal expressions.

   It i~~Is~~ cold today.

   It i~~Is~~ important to know English.

6. Don't forget the verb *be*. Remember that some words that end in *-ed* are adjectives, not verbs.

   The college ^*is* located downtown.

   I ^*am* very tired.

7. Don't confuse *your* (possession) and *you're* (*you are*).

   ~~Your~~ *You're* a very good student.

8. Use correct word order in questions.

   Why ~~you are~~ *are you* late?

   Why ~~your sister doesn't~~ *doesn't your sister* drive?

9. In a contraction, be careful to put the apostrophe in place of the missing letter. Put the apostrophe above the line.

   The teacher ~~is'nt~~ *isn't* here today.

   He ~~doesn,t~~ *doesn't* know the answer.

10. There's no contraction for *am not.*

    ~~I amn't~~ *I'm not* sick today.

11. Don't repeat the subject with a pronoun.

    My brother ~~he~~ lives in Puerto Rico.

12. Don't use *be* with another present tense verb.

    I~~'m~~ come from Poland.

    We~~'re~~ have a new computer.

13. Use the *-s* form when the subject is ***he, she, it, everyone,*** or ***family.***

My father live^s in New York.

Everyone know^s the answer.

My family live^s in Egypt.

14. Use ***doesn't*** when the subject is ***he, she, it,*** or ***family.***

doesn't
He ~~don't~~ have a car.

doesn't
My family ~~don't~~ live here.

15. Use the base form after ***does.***

He doesn't speak~~s~~ English.

Where does he live~~s~~?

16. Don't forget to use ***do*** or ***does*** and the base form in the question.

does
Where ^ your father work~~s~~?

17. Use normal question formation for ***spell, mean,*** and ***cost.***

does "custom" mean?
What ~~means "custom"~~?

do you
How ^ spell "responsible"?

does *cost*
How much ~~costs~~ the newspaper ^?

18. Use the correct word order with frequency words.

sometimes goes
He ~~goes sometimes~~ to the zoo.

I never
~~Never I~~ eat in a restaurant.

am never
I ~~never am~~ late to class.

19. Don't put a frequency phrase between the subject and the verb.

all the time
She ~~all the time~~ talks on the phone ^.

Lesson 1 Test/Review

For additional practice, review, and assessment materials, see Assessment CD-ROM with *ExamView Pro, More Grammar Practice* Workbook 2, Interactive CD-ROM, and Web site http://elt.thomson.com/gic

PART 1

1. Part 1 may be used as an in-class test to assess student performance, in addition to the Assessment CD-ROM with *ExamView Pro.* Have students read the direction line. Ask: *Does every sentence have a mistake?* (no) Review the examples.
2. Collect for assessment.
3. If necessary, have students review: **Lesson 1.**

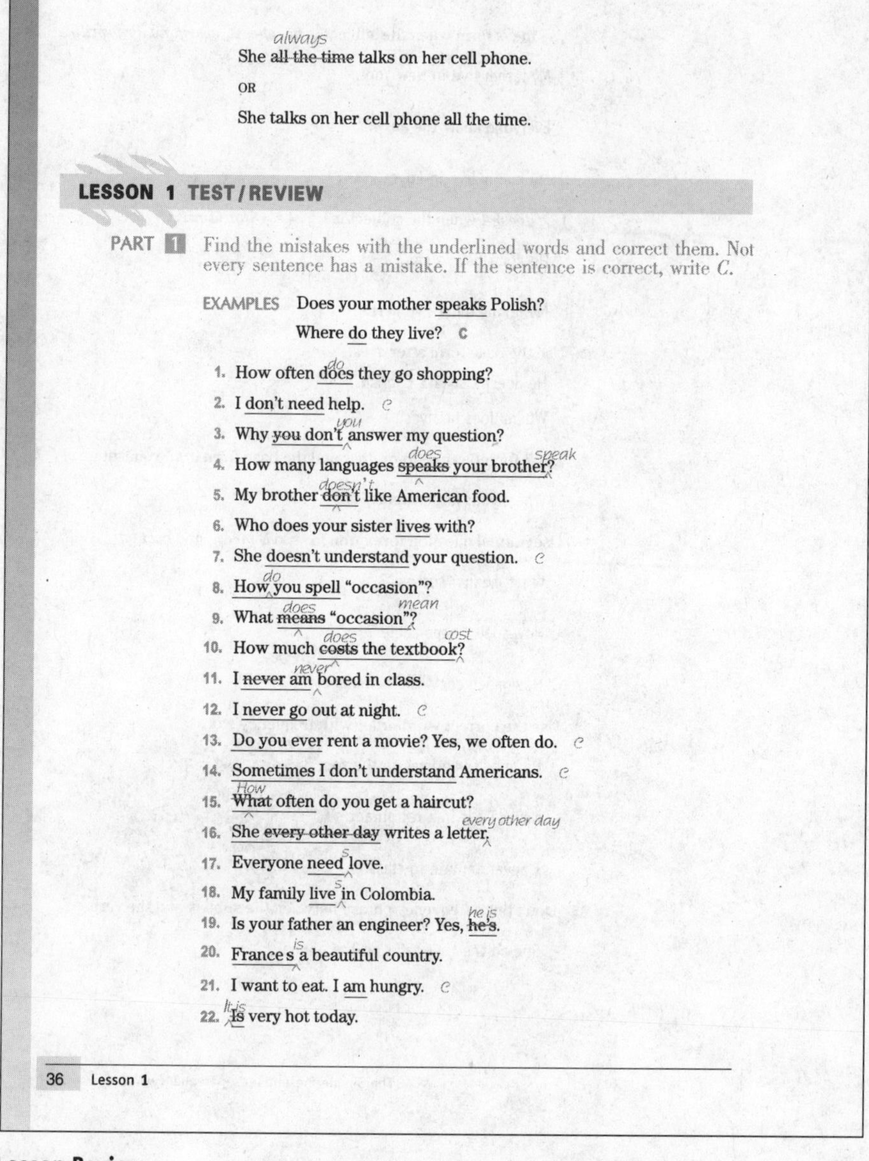

She all the time talks on her cell phone.

OR

She talks on her cell phone all the time.

LESSON 1 TEST/REVIEW

PART **1** Find the mistakes with the underlined words and correct them. Not every sentence has a mistake. If the sentence is correct, write *C.*

EXAMPLES Does your mother speaks Polish?

Where do they live? C

1. How often does they go shopping?
2. I don't need help.
3. Why you don't answer my question?
4. How many languages speaks your brother?
5. My brother don't like American food.
6. Who does your sister lives with?
7. She doesn't understand your question.
8. How you spell "occasion"?
9. What means "occasion"?
10. How much costs the textbook?
11. I never am bored in class.
12. I never go out at night.
13. Do you ever rent a movie? Yes, we often do.
14. Sometimes I don't understand Americans.
15. What often do you get a haircut?
16. She every other day writes a letter.
17. Everyone need love.
18. My family live in Colombia.
19. Is your father an engineer? Yes, he's.
20. France s a beautiful country.
21. I want to eat. I am hungry.
22. Is very hot today.

36 Lesson 1

Lesson Review

To use Part 1 as a review, assign it as homework or use it as an in-class activity to be completed individually or in pairs. Check answers and review errors as a class. Reteach grammar points that students haven't mastered. Then student learning may be assessed using a test generated from the Assessment CD-ROM with *ExamView Pro.*

23. The college is located on Main and Green.

24. You're my favorite teacher. C

25. Why isn't the teacher isn't here today?

26. My little brother is has 10 years old.

27. I 'm not don't interested in sports.

28. She doesn't have a cell phone. C

29. I have my sweater, so I 'm not amn't cold.

30. I have I'm have a new TV.

31. She's comes from Mexico.

PART 2 Fill in the blanks with the affirmative form of the verb in parentheses ( ). Then write the negative form of the verb.

EXAMPLES Elena wants (want) to write about strange American customs.

She doesn't want to write about the weather.

1. Marianne knows (know) Elena.

She doesn't know Sofia.

2. Marianne has (have) a dog.

Elena doesn't have a dog.

3. Elena lives (live) in the U.S.

Sofia doesn't live in the U.S.

4. Marianne is (be) American.

Elena isn't American.

5. You understand (understand) some American customs.

You don't understand all American customs.

6. American customs are (be) strange for Elena.

American customs aren't strange for Marianne.

7. I like (like) cats.

I don't like dogs.

The Simple Present Tense; Frequency Words 37

PART 2

1. Part 2 may also be used as an in-class test to assess student performance, in addition to the Assessment CD-ROM with *ExamView Pro*. Have students read the direction line. Go over the examples. Say: *Remember to use contractions.*
2. Have students complete the exercise individually. Collect for assessment.
3. If necessary, have students review:
   - **1.2** Contractions with *Be* (p. 5)
   - **1.4** The Simple Present Tense—Affirmative Statements (p. 15)
   - **1.5** Negative Statements with the Simple Present Tense (p. 17).

Lesson Review

To use Part 2 as a review, assign it as homework or use it as an in-class activity to be completed individually or in pairs. Check answers and review errors as a class. Reteach grammar points that students haven't mastered. Then student learning may be assessed using a test generated from the Assessment CD-ROM with *ExamView Pro*.

PART 3

1. Part 3 may also be used as an in-class test to assess student performance, in addition to the Assessment CD-ROM with *ExamView Pro*. Tell students that they will be writing *yes/no* questions and short answers. Have students read the direction line. Go over the example.
2. Have students complete individually. Collect for assessment.
3. If necessary, have students review:
   1.3 Questions with *Be* (p. 8)
   1.6 Questions with the Simple Present Tense (p. 19)
   1.11 Questions with *Ever* (p. 31).

PART 4

1. Part 4 may also be used as an in-class test to assess student performance, in addition to the Assessment CD-ROM with *ExamView Pro*. Have students read the direction line. Go over the example.
2. Have students complete the exercise individually. Collect for assessment.
3. If necessary, have students review:
   1.12 Questions with *How Often* and Answers with Frequency Expressions (p. 32).

8. Dogs ___*need*___ (need) a lot of attention.
   Cats ___*don't need*___ so much attention.
9. Almost everyone ___*loves*___ (love) kittens and puppies.
   Most people ___*don't like/love*___ snakes.

PART 3 Read each statement. Then write a *yes/no* question about the words in parentheses ( ). Write a short answer.

EXAMPLE Elena lives in the U.S. (Marianne)
Does Marianne live in the U.S.? Yes, she does.

1. Marianne has a dog. (Elena) (no)
   Does Elena have a dog? No, she doesn't.
2. Elena and Marianne live in the U.S. (Sofia) (no)
   Does Sofia live in the U.S.? No, she doesn't.
3. Elena has an American friend. (Sofia) (no)
   Does Sofia have an American friend? No, she doesn't.
4. Elena often writes letters. (you / ever) [Give a true answer about yourself.]
   Do you ever write letters?
5. You like animals. (you / ever / go to the zoo)
   Do you ever go to the zoo?
6. American customs are strange for Elena. (for Marianne) (no)
   Are American customs strange for Marianne? No, they aren't.

PART 4 Fill in the blanks to complete the question.

EXAMPLE Dogs like people.
Why ___*do dogs like people?*___

1. Marianne sometimes travels with her dog.
   How ___*often does Marianne travel*___ with her dog?
2. Sofia doesn't understand American customs.
   Why ___*doesn't she understand*___ American customs?
3. Elena writes to Sofia once a week.
   How often ___*does she write*___ to Elena?

38 Lesson 1

Lesson Review

To use Parts 3 and 4 as a review, assign them as homework or use them as in-class activities to be completed individually or in pairs. Check answers and review errors as a class. Reteach grammar points that students haven't mastered. Then student learning may be assessed using a test generated from the Assessment CD-ROM with *ExamView Pro*.

4. A dog service costs a lot of money.

How much ___does it / a dog service cost___?

5. Elena doesn't have a dog.

Why ___doesn't she have___ a dog?

6. Marianne carries a picture of Sparky in her wallet.

Why ___does she carry a picture of Sparky___ in her wallet?

7. Marianne walks her dog several times a day.

How often ___does she walk her dog___?

8. She takes her dog to the animal hospital.

How often ___does she take her dog___ to the animal hospital?

9. Guide dogs need a lot of training.

Why ___do they need___ a lot of training?

10. Rescue dogs save people's lives.

How ___do they save___ people's lives?

11. A purebred dog costs a lot of money.

How much ___does a purebred dog cost___?

PART 5 Write a question with the words given.

EXAMPLE What / a dog / eat
What does a dog eat?

1. How / spell / "kitten"
How do you spell "kitten"?
2. What / mean / "puppy"
What does "puppy" mean?
3. How / say / "cat" in Spanish
How do you say "cat" in Spanish?
4. How much / cost / a parrot
How much does a parrot cost?

EXPANSION ACTIVITIES

Classroom Activity

Customs Put a check (√) to indicate which of the following are typical customs in the U.S. and which are typical customs in your native culture. Discuss your answers in a small group or with the entire class.

The Simple Present Tense; Frequency Words 39

Lesson Review

To use Part 5 as a review, assign it as homework or use it as an in-class activity to be completed individually or in pairs. Check answers and review errors as a class. Reteach grammar points that students haven't mastered. Then student learning may be assessed using a test generated from the Assessment CD-ROM with *ExamView Pro*.

PART 5

1. Part 5 may also be used as an in-class test to assess student performance, in addition to the Assessment CD-ROM with *ExamView Pro*. Have students read the directions. Review the example.
2. Have students complete the questions individually. Collect for assessment.
3. If necessary, have students review:
   1.8 Questions About Meaning, Spelling, and Cost (p. 23).

Expansion Activities

These expansion activities provide opportunities for students to interact with one another and further develop their speaking and writing skills. Encourage students to use grammar from this lesson whenever possible.

To save class time, assign parts of the activities as homework. Then use class time for interaction and communication. If students do not need additional speaking practice, some of the activities may be assigned as writing activities for homework, or skipped altogether.

CLASSROOM ACTIVITY

Say: *This chart lists different customs. Which customs are practiced here in the U.S. and which are practiced in your native cultures?* Point out the pictures of the chopsticks and gym shoes. Have students complete the charts individually. Then put students in groups to compare.

Customs	In the U.S.	In my native culture
People walk their dogs on a leash.	√	
Dogs have jackets and other clothes.		
Supermarkets sell a lot of pet food.		
Students wear jeans to class.		
Students call their teachers by their first names.		
Students write in their textbooks.		
Teachers stand in class.		
People talk a lot about politics.		
People drink a lot of soft drinks.		
Children watch TV a lot.		
Friends get together in coffee houses.		
Women wear makeup.		
People eat some foods with their hands.		
People are friendly with their neighbors.		
People say, "How are you?"		
People use credit cards.		
Men open doors for women.		
People eat with chopsticks.		
People have a car.		
People wear gym shoes.		
People travel in the summer.		
People take off their shoes when they enter a house.		
Young adults live separately from their parents.		
People usually leave a tip in a restaurant.		
People know how to use a computer.		
People pay attention to the weather report.		
Students study a foreign language.		

40 Lesson 1

Talk About it

1. Do a lot of people you know have a pet? Do they treat their pet like a member of the family? Do you have a pet now? What kind?
2. Work with a partner or in a small group. Tell if you think this animal is a good pet. Why or why not?

a. A snake

b. A parakeet

c. A rabbit

d. A lizard

e. A turtle

f. A hamster

g. A cat

h. A dog

i. Tropical fish (**Note:** *Fish* can be singular or plural)

3. **Proverbs** The following proverbs mention animals. Discuss the meaning of each proverb. Do you have a similar proverb in your native language?

a. You can't teach an old dog new tricks.

b. While the cat's away, the mice will play.

c. Man's best friend is his dog.

d. Curiosity killed the cat.

e. The dog's bark is worse than his bite.

TALK ABOUT IT

1. Have students talk over the questions about pets in groups.
2. Have students discuss their opinions about the pets pictured in the book. Then take a survey of the class's opinions and write the results on the board. Encourage students to use the simple present tense and frequency words.
3. Have students discuss the proverbs in groups. Then go over the proverbs as a class.

TALK ABOUT IT (*cont.*)

4. Go over the joke as a class. Ask students to share animal jokes from their cultures.

WRITE ABOUT IT

1. Tell students they can use the list of customs on page 40 or use any of their own thoughts and ideas.
2. Brainstorm with the class a list of ways that Americans treat pets. Write them on the board.

OUTSIDE ACTIVITIES

1. Tell students that they should observe how owners behave with their dogs, what they do with them, how they treat them, and how they talk to them. Ask volunteers to share their observations with the rest of the class.
2. Have students interview English-speaking pet owners. Have students write their interview questions in class before the interview.
3. Have students discuss the movie in groups. Then take a class survey: Who liked the movie and who didn't?

INTERNET ACTIVITIES

1. Ask volunteers to share their findings with the rest of the class. Vote on the strangest pet product.
2. Have students create a poster on their favorite breed of dog or cat. Ask students to include a picture if possible. Display the posters around the class.
3. Discuss the animal shelter(s) in your area. What information did the students find?

4. **Joke** A woman is outside of her house. A dog is near her. A man walks by and is interested in the dog. He wants to pet the dog. He asks the woman, "Does your dog bite?" The woman answers no. The man pets the dog and the dog bites him. He says, "You told me that your dog doesn't bite." The woman answers, "This is not my dog. My dog is in the house."

Write About it

1. Write about three American customs that seem strange to you. Compare these customs to how people behave in your country or native culture.
2. Write about differences in how people treat pets in the U.S. and in another country you know about.

Outside Activities

1. Take a notebook and a pen / pencil and go to a park. Observe people with dogs. Write your observations. Bring your notebook to class and discuss your observations with your classmates.
2. Interview a friend or neighbor who has a pet. Find out five interesting things about this pet. Bring the results of your interview to the class.
3. Rent the movie *Best in Show*. Write a summary of the movie.

Internet Activities

1. At a search engine type in *pet*. Find a Web site that advertises pet supplies. Make a list of all the unusual things people buy for their pets.
2. Find information about a breed of dog that you like. (Try the Web site of the American Kennel Club or AKC.)
3. At a search engine, type in *animal shelter* and the name of the city where you live (or the nearest big city). Find information about what this shelter does.

Additional Activities at http://elt.thomson.com/gic

Talk About it Variation

Joke Have students create a dialogue based on the joke. Then have students practice role-playing the dialogue. Ask volunteers to perform the joke in front of the class.

Write About it Variation

Have students exchange first drafts with a partner. Ask students to help their partners edit their drafts. Refer students to the Editing Advice on pages 33–36.

Outside Activities Variation

Activity 2 As an alternative, you may invite a guest that has a pet (another teacher, an administrator at your school, etc.) and have students do a class interview. Students should prepare their interview questions ahead of time.

LESSON

2

GRAMMAR

The Present Continuous Tense[1]
Action and Nonaction Verbs
The Future Tense

CONTEXT: Getting older

Retirement Living
Life After Retirement
The Graying of America

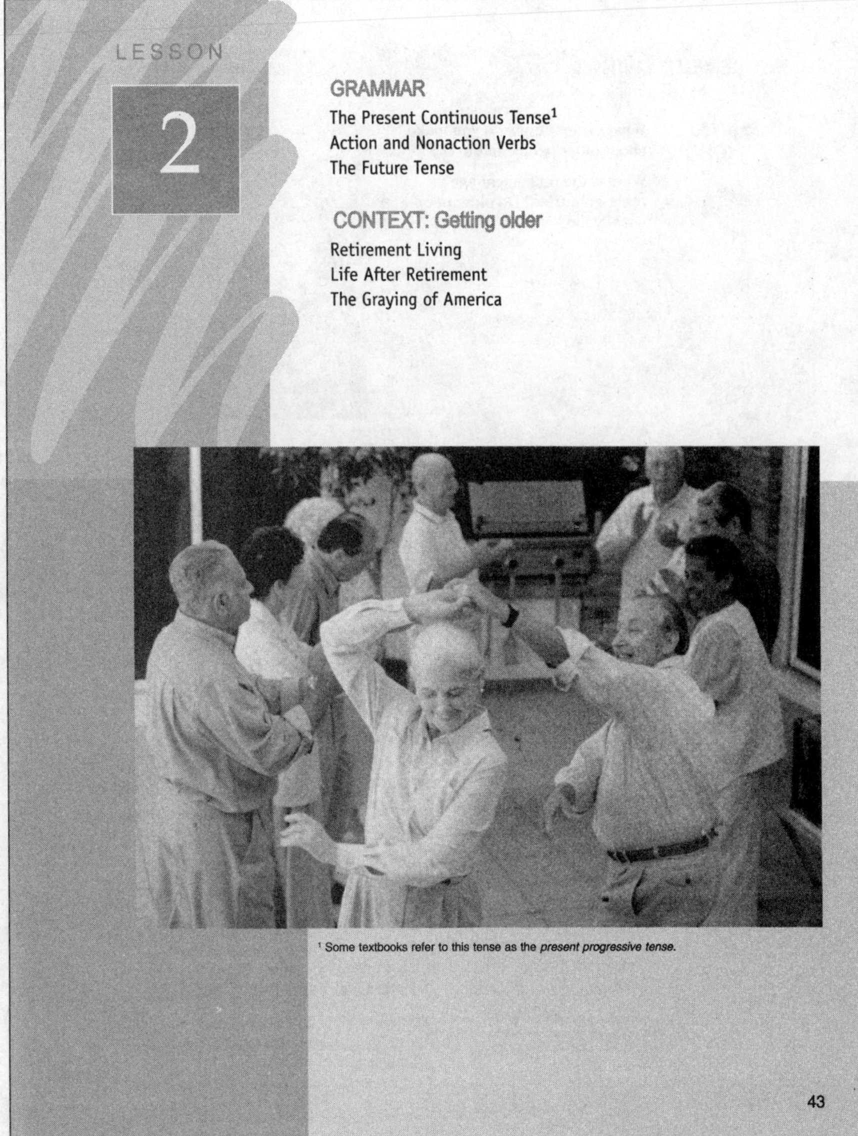

[1] Some textbooks refer to this tense as the *present progressive tense.*

43

Lesson 2

Lesson Overview

GRAMMAR

Ask: *What tense did we study in Lesson 1?* (the simple present tense) *What tenses will we study in this lesson?* (the present continuous and the future tense) Ask volunteers to give examples of the present continuous and the future. Write them on the board. Then ask: *Can anyone give examples of action and nonaction verbs?*

CONTEXT

1. Ask: *What will we learn about in this lesson?* (getting older and retirement) Activate students' prior knowledge. *What's life like for senior citizens in the U.S.? Is it different from your native countries?*
2. Have students share their knowledge and personal experiences.

Photo

Direct students' attention to the photo. Ask: *What's going on in this photo?* (Senior citizens are dancing.) Ask: *Do they look like they're having fun? Is this a typical image everyone has of older people?*

To save class time, have students do the Test/Review at the end of the lesson, or administer a lesson test generated from the Assessment CD-ROM with *ExamView® Pro.* Skip sections of the lesson that students have already mastered. You may also assign some sections for self-study for extra credit.

Expansion

Theme The topic for this lesson can be enhanced with the following ideas:

1. Brochures from retirement communities
2. Copies of AARP (American Association of Retired Persons) magazine

Retirement Living (Reading)

1. Have students look at the photo. Ask: *Can you do what this woman is doing? How old do you think she is?*
2. Have students look at the title of the reading. Ask: *What is the reading about?* Have students use the title and photo to make predictions about the reading.
3. Preteach any vocabulary words your students may not know, such as *village* and *widower.*

BEFORE YOU READ

1. Have students discuss the questions in pairs.
2. Ask for a few volunteers to share their answers with the class.

To save class time, skip "Before You Read" or have students prepare answers for homework ahead of time.

Reading  *CD 1, Track 13*

1. Have students first read the text silently. Explain that this is a conversation between Jack (a 62-year-old man who is taking a tour of a retirement village) and the manager of the retirement village. Tell students to pay special attention to present continuous tense verbs. Then play the audio and have students read along silently.
2. Check students' comprehension. Ask questions such as: *What kinds of houses do they have at the retirement village?* (single family homes, townhouses, and apartments) *Are there many activities at the village?* (yes) *What are people learning in the computer class?* (how to design Web pages) *Are there more men or more women at the retirement village?* (more women) *How often does the singles group meet?* (once a week)

To save class time, have students do the reading for homework ahead of time.

RETIREMENT LIVING

Before You Read

1. What observations do you make about older people in the U.S.?
2. What is the retirement age in other countries? Do older people usually have a good life?

As the U.S. population ages, many building developers **are building** homes for people over 55. Read the following conversation of a sixty-two-year-old man, Jack (J), taking a tour of a retirement village, and the manager of the retirement village (M). Pay special attention to present continuous tense verbs.

J: **I'm thinking** about moving to this retirement village. Can you give me some information?

M: This is a village for people over 55 years old. The people here are retired, but most are very active. There are different types of housing: single family homes, townhouses[2], and apartments. For those who need more help, we also have an assisted living section. Let me give you a tour. This is our fitness center. It has state-of-the-art equipment[3].

J: What **are** those people **doing**?

M: **They're doing** yoga. And that group over there **is lifting** weights. Another group **is doing** aerobics. Let's move on to the game room. Those people **are playing** chess. And that group **is playing** cards. Now let me take you to the pool area. In this area, people **are swimming** laps[4].

J: What **are** those people **doing?**

M: Those people **are taking** a water aerobics class. Let's go to the computer room now. That's the computer teacher. He's **teaching** that group how to design Web pages. Jerry, over there, **is putting** all his family pictures on his Web site. Marge, in the corner, **is designing** a Web site with her vacation pictures and stories about her interesting trips. She likes to travel all over the world. . . . Now let's look at the dance area.

[2] A *townhouse* is one of a series of houses attached to each other in a row.
[3] *State-of-the-art* equipment is the latest equipment.
[4] Swimming *laps* means swimming from one end of the pool to the other and back again, over and over.

44 Lesson 2

Reading Variation

To practice listening skills, have students first listen to the audio alone. Ask a few comprehension questions. Repeat the audio if necessary. Then have students open their books and read along as they listen to the audio.

Reading Glossary

village: a group of houses forming a settlement smaller than a town or city
widower: husband whose wife has died

Did You Know?

In 2000, there were 20.6 million older women and 14.4 million older men, or a ratio of 143 women for every 100 men. The female-to-male ratio increases with age, with 245 women for every 100 men in the 85 and over age group.

J: The band **is playing** a great song, and many of the people **are dancing.** This place is beautiful and certainly offers a lot of activities. But I don't know if it's right for me. I don't know how to dance, play chess, or design Web pages.

M: Don't worry. There are instructors here who will help you.

J: **Is** everybody **doing** something?

M: No. My wife is at home now. I think she'**s reading** or **watching** TV. Or maybe she'**s playing** with our grandchildren.

J: I notice that there are more women than men here.

M: Well, as you know, women live longer than men.

J: I'm a widower, you know. Maybe I can meet a woman here.

M: That's entirely possible. We have a singles group that meets once a week in the game room. Mary Dodge can give you information about the singles group. She'**s standing** over there. She'**s wearing** blue jeans and a red T-shirt.

J: How much does it cost to live here?

M: That depends on what kind of a house you choose. Come to my office and we'll look at the costs.

The Present Continuous Tense; Action and Nonaction Verbs; the Future Tense 45

DID YOU KNOW?

It seems that at least as far back as the 1500s, when the first reliable statistics on death and dying were kept, women have been outliving men. Lower death rates for women start as early as the womb. More female fetuses make it to birth than male fetuses. Many reasons are attributed to the longevity gap: hormones, genetics, and menopause might all play a role in the longer lifespan of women.

2.1 | Present Continuous Tense

1. Have students go back to the reading on pages 44–45. Say: *Find examples of the present continuous tense with* am, is, *and* are. Write students' sentences on the board.
2. Ask: *How do we form the present continuous?* (*be* + verb *-ing*) Write it on the board.
3. Ask: *When do we use the present continuous?* (to describe an action in progress at this moment; to describe a state or condition using *sit, stand, wear,* and *sleep*) Write students' responses on the board. Ask students to find an example of each use from the reading.
4. Ask students to explain how to form contractions. Have them find examples from the reading and write them on the board. Then write the following on the board:
   They are playing cards.
   Jack is taking a tour.
   He is asking questions.
   The manager is asking questions.
   Ask students to make contractions using the subject and verb.
5. Review how to form the negative. Have them find examples from the reading and write them on the board.
   Then write the following on the board:
   Jack is doing yoga.
   Most people are watching TV.
   I'm playing tennis.
   Have students make the sentences into negative statements.
6. Have students look at grammar chart **2.1** on page 46. Say: *Compare your work with the grammar chart.* Review the examples and explanations.
7. Point out that they shouldn't repeat the verb *be* after the connectors *or* and *and.*

2.1 | Present Continuous Tense

To form the present continuous tense, use a form of *be (is, am, are)* + verb *-ing*[5].

Examples	Explanation
Subj. *Be* Verb + *-ing* Complement I **am putting** my pictures on a Web site. Jack **is visiting** a retirement village. She **is teaching** Web design. They **are doing** yoga.	I → am He/She/It → is Singular Subject → is We/You/They → are Plural Subject → are (am / is / are) + verb *-ing*
a. Some people **are dancing** now. b. My wife **is watching** TV now.	In sentences (a) and (b), we use the present continuous tense to describe an action in progress at this moment.
c. Mary Dodge **is standing** over there. d. She **is wearing** blue jeans. e. A man **is sitting** in front of a computer.	In sentences (c), (d), and (e), we use the present continuous tense to describe a state or condition, using the following verbs: *sit, stand, wear,* and *sleep.* We can observe these things now.
They**'re playing** cards. **Jack's taking** a tour of the retirement village. He**'s asking** questions. The **manager's answering** his questions.	We can make a contraction with the subject pronoun and a form of *be*. Most nouns can also contract with *is*.[6]
Jack **isn't** doing yoga. Most people **aren't** watching TV. **I'm not** playing tennis.	To form the negative, put *not* after the verb *am/is/are.* Negative contractions: is not = isn't are not = aren't There is no contraction for *am not.*
Jerry **is designing** a Web site *and* **putting** his family pictures on it. They **are playing** cards *and* **laughing.** She**'s reading** *or* **watching** TV.	Do not repeat the *be* verb after these connectors: *and* *or*

[5] For a review of the spelling of the *-ing* form of the verb, see Appendix A.
[6] See Lesson 1, page 5 for exceptions.

46 Lesson 2

EXERCISE **1** Fill in the blanks with the present continuous form of the verb in parentheses( ). Use correct spelling.

EXAMPLE Jack *is visiting* (visit) a retirement village.

1. He *'s taking* (take) a tour.
2. He *'s looking* (look) at the different activities.
3. The manager of the village *is giving* (give) him information.
4. Some people *are dancing* (dance).
5. Some people *are using* (use) the exercise equipment.
6. One woman *is lifting* (lift) weights.
7. Those people *are playing* (play) chess.
8. Some people *are swimming* (swim).
9. Jerry *isn't reading* (not/read). He *'s putting* (put) his family pictures on his Web site.
10. The manager's wife is at home. She *'s reading* (read) or *watching* (watch) TV. She *isn't taking* (not/take) an aerobics class.
11. Some people *aren't doing* (not/do) anything.

EXERCISE **2** Fill in the blanks with an affirmative or negative verb to make a **true** statement about what is happening now.

EXAMPLES I *'m wearing* (wear) jeans now.

The teacher *isn't writing* (write) on the blackboard now.

1. The sun Answers may vary. (shine) now.
2. It ______ (rain) now.

The Present Continuous Tense; Action and Nonaction Verbs; the Future Tense 47

EXERCISE 1

1. Have students read the direction line. Go over the example in the book. Remind students to use contractions whenever possible.
2. Have students complete Exercise 1 individually. Check the answers as a class. If necessary, review grammar chart **2.1** on page 46.

EXERCISE 2

1. Have students read the direction line. Say: *You're going to make true statements for what's happening now in the class and outside.* Go over the examples in the book. Model the exercise with your own information.
2. Have students complete Exercise 2 individually. Then have students compare answers with a partner. Circulate to observe pair work. Give help as needed.
3. If necessary, review grammar chart **2.1** on page 46.

To save class time, have students do half of the exercise in class and complete the other half for homework.

Expansion

Exercise 1 Have students rewrite the sentences in Exercise 1 using the negative form of the verb.

Life After Retirement (Reading)

1. Have students look at the photo on page 49. Ask: *What are these people doing?* (The man is teaching or tutoring the child.)
2. Have students look at the title of the reading. Ask: *What is the reading about?* Have students use the title and photo to make predictions about the reading.
3. Preteach any vocabulary words your students may not know, such as *avenue, pension, volunteer, pantry,* and *hobby.*

BEFORE YOU READ

1. Have students discuss the questions in pairs.
2. Ask for a few volunteers to share their answers with the class.

To save class time, skip "Before You Read" or have students prepare answers for homework ahead of time.

Reading CD 1, Track 14

1. Have students first read the text silently. Tell them to pay special attention to present continuous tense verbs and simple present tense verbs. Then play the audio and have students read along silently.
2. Check students' comprehension. Ask questions such as: *What are more and more Americans doing after retirement?* (Many are starting new careers.) *What is Judy Pearlman doing now?* (making dolls) *What kind of classes is Charles Haskell taking?* (art classes) *What else are retirees doing in their free time?* (volunteering)

To save class time, have students do the reading for homework ahead of time.

3. I ______________ (write) my answers in my book.
4. I ______________ (use) a pencil to write this exercise.
5. We ______________ (do) this exercise together.
6. The teacher ______________ (help) the students with this exercise.
7. The teacher ______________ (wear) a watch.
8. I ______________ (use) my dictionary now.
9. We ______________ (practice) possessive forms now.
10. I ______________ (wear) jeans.
11. The teacher ______________ (stand).
12. I ______________ (sit) near the door.

LIFE AFTER RETIREMENT

Before You Read

1. Is anyone in your family retired? How does that person keep busy?
2. What observations do you make about older Americans?

Read the following article. Pay special attention to present continuous tense verbs and simple present tense verbs.

The U.S. population **is aging.** More and more Americans **are thinking** about retirement. But today, many people **are retiring** younger and healthier than ever before. People **are living** longer. But they **are not leaving** their jobs to spend their days at the beach or babysitting for their grandchildren. Most older people **prefer** to keep busy. Many healthy seniors **are starting** new careers. They **want** to explore new avenues in their lives.

Judy Pearlman is a 62-year-old retired school teacher from Chicago. After 35 years in education, she **is starting** a new career—making dolls. "Now I **have** time to do what I always dreamed about," she says. "**I'm having** more fun than ever before. **I'm meeting** new people, **traveling** in my new job, and **earning** money all at the same time. And **I'm** still **getting** my teacher pension. **I'm enjoying** every minute of it. I **think** this is the best time of my life."

48 Lesson 2

Expansion

Exercise 2 Have students work in pairs to write five more true statements about what's happening in the class right now.

Reading Variation

To practice listening skills, have students first listen to the audio alone. Ask a few comprehension questions. Repeat the audio if necessary. Then have students open their books and read along as they listen to the audio.

"After 33 years as an accountant, **I'm** now **taking** art classes," says Charles Haskell of Cleveland. "**I'm discovering** a new talent."

Some senior citizens decide not to retire at all. Frank Babbit of Milwaukee is a carpenter. He has his own business and **works** 50 hours a week. And he's almost 88 years old.

Many older women **are returning** to work after raising their children. "My kids are grown and **don't need** me now," says Miriam Orland of San Francisco. "So I **have** time for myself now. **I'm taking** courses at a community college. **I'm thinking** about a career in Web design."

Some retirees **are using** their free time to volunteer. "I retired as an accountant six months ago, and now I **volunteer** as a math tutor in a public library near my house. I **go** to the library twice a week to help students who **are having** trouble with math," says Ron Meyers of Miami. "I **work** in a food pantry and **feed** the homeless three times a week," says Linda Carlson of Washington, DC. "It **gives** me a lot of satisfaction."

Today healthy retirees **are exploring** many options, from relaxing to starting a new business or making a hobby into a new career. How do you see yourself as a retiree?

Did You Know?

Today 28 percent of retired people **are working.**

2.2 | Using the Present Continuous for Longer Actions

Examples	Explanation
Judy **is meeting** new people. She **is getting** her pension and **earning** money from her new job. She **is enjoying** her new career. My grandfather **is planning** to retire soon.	We use the present continuous tense to show a long-term action that is in progress. It may not be happening at this exact moment.
More and more retired Americans **are looking** for a second career. Some older people **are working** because of economic necessity. Americans **are living** longer. Many older women **are returning** to work after their children are grown.	We use the present continuous tense to describe a *trend*. A trend is a behavior that many people in society are doing at this time. It describes a change in behavior from an earlier time.

EXERCISE 3 Fill in the blanks with an appropriate verb. Answers may vary.

EXAMPLE More and more retired people *are working* these days.

1. Many people *are retiring* at a younger age.
2. They *'re not spending* (not) their time at the beach or babysitting for their grandchildren.

The Present Continuous Tense; Action and Nonaction Verbs; the Future Tense 49

Reading Glossary

hobby: an activity done for pleasure or relaxation
pantry: a small room next to the kitchen used to store food, dishes, and cooking equipment
pension: a regular payment made by a business or government to a person who has retired from a job
volunteer: to agree to do something of one's own free will rather than by necessity

DID YOU KNOW?

According to the AARP (the American Association of Retired Persons), 69% of older workers who were surveyed in 2002 said that they planned to work during the traditional retirement years.

2.2 | Using the Present Continuous for Longer Actions

1. Have students look at grammar chart **2.2** on page 49. Say: *We use the present continuous to describe actions that are happening now, but we also use it to describe long-term actions and trends.* Go over the examples and explanations in the chart.
2. Ask volunteers to make sentences that describe trends in the world now (e.g., *Women are having fewer babies. Children are watching more TV.*).

EXERCISE 3

1. Tell students that this exercise is based on the reading on pages 48–49. Have students read the direction line. Ask: *What do we write in the blanks?* (the present continuous tense) Go over the example in the book.
2. Have students complete Exercise 3 individually. Have students compare answers in pairs. Circulate to observe pair work.
3. If necessary, review grammar chart **2.2** on page 49.

EXERCISE 4

1. Tell students that they will be making three long-term statements about themselves. Say: *The statements have to be about your life as a student.* Have students read the direction line. Point out the list of verbs provided. Go over the examples in the book. Model three statements about your own life.
2. Have students complete Exercise 4 individually. Then have students compare sentences in groups. Circulate to observe group work. Have volunteers share some of their sentences with the class.
3. If necessary, review grammar chart **2.2** on page 49.

EXERCISE 5

1. Tell students that they will be making three long-term statements about things that are changing in their lives. Say: *Then you will ask your partner questions.* Have students read the direction line. Go over the examples in the book. Model three statements about your own life.
2. Have students write sentences individually. Then have students ask and answer questions in pairs. Circulate to observe pair work. Have volunteers share some of their sentences with the class.
3. If necessary, review grammar chart **2.2** on page 49.

To save class time, have students write the sentences for homework. Then have students ask a partner the questions in class.

EXERCISE 6

1. Have students read the direction line. Say: *Complete the activity for your native country or another country. You can write affirmative or negative sentences.* Model item 1 (e.g., *In the U.S., older people are not getting more respect than before.*).
2. Have students complete Exercise 6 in groups. If possible, have students from different countries work together. Circulate to observe group work. Give help as needed.
3. If necessary, review grammar chart **2.2** on page 49.

To save class time, have students decide where the trends are happening for homework. Then, if class time allows, discuss a few items in pairs, in small groups, or as a class.

---

3. They *'re starting* new careers.
4. People *are living* longer and healthier lives.
5. Some people *are discovering* new talents and abilities.
6. Some older women *are returning* to work after raising a family.

EXERCISE 4 ABOUT YOU Write three sentences about being a student. Tell what is happening in your life as a student. (You may share your sentences with the class.)

EXAMPLES *I'm taking five courses this semester.*

I'm staying with my sister this semester.

I'm majoring in math.

You may use these verbs: *learn, study, take courses, stay, live, major,* and *plan*.

Answers will vary.

1. ______
2. ______
3. ______

EXERCISE 5 ABOUT YOU Write three sentences to tell which things in your life are changing. Then find a partner and ask your partner if he or she is experiencing the same changes.

EXAMPLES *I'm gaining weight. Are you gaining weight?*

I'm planning to buy a house. Are you planning to buy a house?

My English pronunciation is improving. Is your pronunciation improving?

You may use the following verbs: *plan, get (become), learn, grow, gain, lose, improve, think about, change,* and *start*.

Answers will vary.

1. ______
2. ______
3. ______

EXERCISE 6 Tell if these things are happening at this point in time in the U.S., in the world, or in another country you know about. Discuss your answers.

Answers will vary.

1. **Older people are getting more respect than before.**
2. **People are living healthier lives.**
3. **People are living longer.**
4. **The world is becoming a more dangerous place.**

Expansion

Exercises 4 and 5 Have students write a letter or an e-mail to a friend in a different city about their lives now. Say: ***Use some of the statements from Exercises 4 and 5 and add new ones.***

5. The economy is getting better.
6. Medical science is advancing quickly.
7. A lot of people are losing their jobs.
8. People are working harder than before.
9. People are doing more and enjoying less.
10. The cost of a college education is going down.
11. The cost of computers is going down.
12. More and more people are using cell phones.
13. Cars are getting bigger.
14. Kids are growing up faster than before.

2.3 | Questions with the Present Continuous Tense

Affirmative Statements and Questions

Wh-Word	*Be*	Subject	*Be*	Verb + *-ing*	Complement	Short Answer
		Jerry	is	designing	something.	
	Is	he		designing	a house?	No, he isn't.
What	is	he		designing?		A Web site.
		They	are	taking	courses at college.	
	Are	they		taking	biology?	No, they aren't.
What courses	are	they		taking?		Computer courses.
		He	is	thinking	about a new career.	
	Is	he		thinking	about a career in computers?	No, he isn't.

Language Note:
1. We can leave a preposition at the end of a question.
   What kind of career is he thinking about?
2. When the question is "What . . . doing?" we usually answer with a different verb.
   What are they **doing?** They're **taking** an aerobics class.
   What are those people **doing?** They're **playing** chess.

Negative Statements and Questions

Wh-Word	*Be* + *n't*	Subject	*Be* + *n't*	Verb + *-ing*	Complement
		Mary	isn't	dancing.	
Why	isn't	she		dancing?	
		You	aren't	using	the computer.
Why	aren't	you		using	the computer?

Expansion

Exercise 6 Have a class debate about one of the statements from the exercise. Divide the class into two groups. Assign one side of the argument to each group. Have groups prepare their arguments and present them to the opposing group.

2.3 | Questions with the Present Continuous Tense

1. Have students cover up grammar chart **2.3.** Write the following two sentences on the board:
   Jerry is designing something.
   They are taking courses at college.
   Say: *For each sentence, write a* yes/no *question, a short answer, and a* wh- *question.*
2. Have students look at grammar chart **2.3.** Say: *Compare your sentences to the ones in the book.* Review the statements and questions. Go over any trouble spots.
3. Direct students to the Language Notes. Point out that a preposition can end a sentence (e.g., *What is he thinking about?*). Explain that we usually answer the question *What . . . doing?* with another verb (e.g., *What's she doing? She's watching TV.*).
4. Review the negative statements and questions in the chart. Have students go around the room making negative statements and questions. Say: *I'm going to make a negative statement. I want you to make a negative question.* Model the exercise with a volunteer (e.g., Teacher: *Sam isn't studying.* Student: *Why isn't Sam studying?*). Then instruct the volunteer to make a negative statement, and have another student ask a negative question. Continue the statement-question chain.

EXERCISE 7

1. Have students read the direction line. Go over the example in the book.
2. Have students complete Exercise 7 individually. Check the answers as a class.
3. If necessary, review grammar chart **2.3** on page 51.

EXERCISE 8

1. Have students read the direction line. Ask: *What kind of questions are we going to write here?* (*wh*-questions) Go over the example in the book. Remind students that they don't have to write an answer.
2. Have students complete Exercise 8 individually. Have students compare answers in pairs. Circulate to observe pair work.
3. If necessary, review grammar chart **2.3** on page 51.

To save class time, have students do half of the exercise as a class and complete the other half for homework.

EXERCISE 7 Fill in the blanks to make *yes/no* questions about the readings in this lesson.

EXAMPLE *Are those men playing* checkers? No, they aren't. Those men are playing chess.

1. *Are you considering* this retirement home? Yes, I am. I'm considering it now that my wife is gone.
2. *Is Marge designing* a Web site. Yes, she is. Marge is designing a Web site with pictures of her vacations.
3. *Is he taking* pictures now? No, he isn't taking pictures. He's putting his pictures on his Web site.
4. *Is everyone doing* something? No, not everyone is doing something. Some people are just relaxing.
5. *Are they taking* art classes? Yes, they are. Judy and Charles love art so they're taking a lot of classes.
6. *Am I asking* too many questions? No, you're not. You can ask as many questions as you want.

EXERCISE 8 Read each statement. Then write a question using the word in parentheses ( ). An answer is not necessary.

EXAMPLE Some retirees are discovering new interests. (how)
How are they discovering new interests?

Answers will vary.

1. Judy is having more fun now. (why)
Why is Judy having more fun now?
2. Judy is traveling to many new places. (where)
Where is she traveling?
3. I am starting a new career. (what kind of career)
What kind of career are you starting?
4. Some students are having trouble with math. (why)
Why are some students having trouble with math?
5. My father is thinking about retirement. (why)
Why is your father thinking about retirement?
6. My mother is looking for a new career. (what kind)
What kind of career is your mother looking for?
7. We're not planning to retire. (why)
Why aren't you planning to retire?

52 Lesson 2

Exercise 8 Variation

To provide speaking practice, have students use each item to create a short dialogue. Instruct students to make a *yes/no* question from the statement and ask a partner. The partner answers with a *yes* short answer. Then students ask the information question for the item, and the partner answers the question.
For example:
A: Is Judy having more fun now?
B: Yes, she is.
A: Why is Judy having more fun now?
B: Because she loves her new hobbies.
Then have students complete the written exercise.

8. People are living longer nowadays. (why)
Why are people living longer nowadays?

9. I'm doing things that interest me. (what kinds of things)
What kinds of things are you doing?

EXERCISE 9 Fill in the blanks to form *yes / no* questions about the reading on pages 44–45. Use the present continuous tense.

Jack (J) is talking to his neighbor, Alan (A).

A: What *are you doing* (example: you/do), Jack?

J: I *'m looking* (1 look) at some brochures.

A: What kind of brochures *are you looking at* (2 you/look at)?

J: They're from a retirement village.

A: So *are you thinking* (3 you/think) about moving?

J: Yes, I'm thinking about moving into a retirement village.

A: Why?

J: Now that Rose is gone, I feel lonely.

A: But you have a lot of good neighbors here.

J: Most of the people here are young. My neighbors to the north are never home. Right now they *'re working* (4 work). And my neighbors across the street are never home.

A: They're older people. *are they working* (5 work) too?

J: No. They *'re traveling* (6 travel) now. Right now they *'re taking* (7 take) a cruise[7] to Alaska.

[7] A *cruise* is a pleasure trip on a large passenger boat.

EXERCISE 9

CD 1, Track 15

1. Say: *A man (Jack) is talking to his neighbor (Alan) about moving to a retirement village.* Have students read the direction line. Go over the example in the book.
2. Have students complete Exercise 9 individually. Then have students compare answers in pairs. Circulate to observe pair work. Give help as needed.
3. If necessary, review grammar charts **2.1** on page 46, **2.2** on page 49, and **2.3** on page 51.

To save class time, have students do the exercise for homework.

Expansion

Exercise 8 Have students write five statements about themselves in the present continuous tense. Say: *Write about long-term actions.* Then have students exchange papers. Say: *Take turns asking and answering questions* (e.g., *I'm watching a lot of TV in the evening. Why are you watching a lot of TV? I'm bored.*).

Exercise 9 Variation

To provide practice with listening skills, have students close their books and listen to the audio. Repeat the audio as needed. Ask comprehension questions, such as: *What is Jack doing?* (looking at some brochures) *Where are the brochures from?* (a retirement village) *What is Jack thinking about doing?* (moving into a retirement village) Then have students open their books and complete Exercise 9.

EXERCISE 10

1. Have students read the direction line. Go over the example in the book. Do item 1 with the class.
2. Have students complete the rest of Exercise 10 individually. Then have partners practice the mini-dialogues and compare answers. Circulate to observe pair work. Give help as needed.
3. If necessary, review grammar chart **2.3** on page 51.

To save class time, have students do half of the exercise in class and complete the other half for homework. Or assign the entire exercise for homework.

A: But I'm here. I *'m watering* (8 water) my lawn, as usual. And my wife is inside. She *'s talking* (9 talk) on the phone, as usual.

J: I'm sorry I'm complaining so much.

A: You *'re not complaining* (10 not/complain). You *'re just looking* (11 just/look) for something to do.

J: There's a lot to do. I just don't want to do things alone.

A: But your daughter lives with you.

J: She's in her 20s. She doesn't want to do things with her dad. Right now she *'s watching* (12 watch) a movie with her friends.

A: What movie *are they watching* (13 they/watch)?

J: Who knows? Something for young people. Her movies don't interest me.

A: What retirement village *are you planning* (14 you/plan) to go to?

J: Sun Valley Senior Village seems nice.

A: What about your daughter?

J: She *'s planning* (15 plan) to move in with a friend of hers.

EXERCISE 10 Fill in the blanks to complete the questions. Answers may vary.

EXAMPLE A: Why *is your sister wearing* sunglasses? It's not sunny.

B: My sister's wearing sunglasses because she wants to look like a movie star.

1. A: What *are you reading*?

   B: I'm reading an article about older Americans.

   A: *Are you enjoying* the article?

   B: Oh, yes. I'm enjoying it very much.

2. A: Where *'s Grandma going* now?

   B: She's going to the park. Grandma always goes to the park on Sundays to jog.

   A: (not) *Isn't it raining* now?

   B: Yes, it's raining. But that doesn't matter. The park has an indoor track.

54 Lesson 2

Expansion

Exercise 9 Have students practice the conversation in pairs. Then ask volunteers to act out the conversation for the class.

3. A: Martha is on her cell phone. Who _'s she talking to_?

B: She's talking to her best friend.

A: Why _'s she talking_ on her cell phone?

Why _isn't she using_ her home phone?

B: Because her sister is using the home phone.

4. Student: _Is my accent improving_?

Teacher: Yes. You're accent is improving a lot.

Student: How _am I doing_ with my grammar?

Teacher: You're doing very well.

5. Wife: Something smells good. What _are you cooking_?

Husband: I'm cooking your favorite dinner—steak and potatoes.

(*A few minutes later . . .*)

Wife: _Is there_ something _burning_?

Husband: Uh, oh. The steaks are burning.

6. A: The kids are watching TV. What _are they watching_?

B: They're watching cartoons.

A: Why _aren't they doing_ their homework?

B: They're not doing their homework because they don't have homework today.

7. A: I'm leaving.

B: Where _are you going_?

A: I'm going to the library.

B: Why _are you going to the library_?

A: Because you're making too much noise. I have to study.

8. Dad: I'm planning to retire next year.

Son: You're so young. Why _are you retiring_?

Dad: First of all, I'm not so young. I'm almost 60. I'm planning to travel.

Son: _Are you planning to travel_ alone?

Dad: No, of course not. I_'m going_ with Mom.

Son: But she's still _working_.

Dad: She is now. But she's thinking about retiring too. She loves her work, but enough's enough. It's time to have fun.

Expansion

Exercise 10 Have students write additional lines to extend the mini-conversations. Then have volunteers role-play the mini-conversations in front of the class.

2.4 | Contrasting the Simple Present and the Present Continuous

1. Have students cover up grammar chart **2.4** in their books. Make a matching activity. Write the following sentences on the board:

   <u>Simple Present</u>
   1. Some singles belong to a singles group.
   2. Many people retire at age 65.
   3. Judy often travels.
   a. a general truth
   b. a habitual activity
   c. a custom

   <u>Present Continuous Tense</u>
   1. We are studying this grammar chart now.
   2. People are living longer these days.
   3. She's earning money at her hobby.
   a. an action that is in progress now
   b. a longer action in progress at this general time
   c. recent trends in society

   Say: *Match the examples to the explanations.*
2. Have students look at grammar chart **2.4.** Say: *Check your work.* Go over the rest of the example sentences.
3. Compare the two tenses. Review the verb *live* in the two tenses. Have volunteers make similar sentences with *live.* Repeat steps with the questions. Ask volunteers to create questions with the simple present and present continuous.

2.4 | Contrasting the Simple Present and the Present Continuous

Form

Simple Present Tense	Present Continuous Tense
He sometimes **travels** in the summer.	He **is planning** his vacation.
He **doesn't travel** in the winter.	He **isn't planning** his retirement.
Does he **travel** with his daughter?	**Is** he **planning** a trip to Hawaii?
No, he **doesn't.**	No, he **isn't.**
How often **does** he **travel?**	Where **is** he **planning** to go?
Why **doesn't** he **travel** with his daughter?	Why **isn't** he **planning** to retire?

Use

Examples	Explanation
a. Many people **retire** at age 65. a. Retirees **get** Social Security. a. People **like** to feel useful.	Use the **simple present tense** to talk about: a. a general truth
b. Jack *sometimes* **feels** lonely. b. He *rarely* **watches** movies with his daughter. b. Ron **volunteers** in a library *twice a week.* b. Judy *often* **travels.**	b. a habitual activity
c. Grown children **live** separatly from their parents. c. Parents **call** their grown children before they visit them. c. Some singles **belong** to a singles group.	c. a custom
a. Jack **is visiting** a retirement village now. a. We **are studying** this grammar chart now.	Use the **present continuous tense** for: a. an action that is in progress now
b. Judy **is meeting** a lot of new people at this time. b. She**'s earning** money at her hobby.	b. a longer action that is in progress at this general time
c. People **are living** longer these days. c. People **are retiring** earlier these days.	c. recent trends in society
Compare: a. My parents **live** in a retirement village. b. My sister **is living** in a dorm this semester.	a. *Live* in the simple present shows a person's home. b. *Live* in the present continuous shows a temporary, short-term residence.
Compare: a. **What does she do (for a living)?** She's a nurse. b. **What is she doing?** She's waiting for the bus.	Sentence (a) asks about a job or profession. It uses the simple present tense. Sentence (b) asks about an activity now. It uses the present continuous tense.

BUS STOP

56 Lesson 2

EXERCISE 11 Fill in the blanks with the simple present or the present continuous tense of the verb in parentheses ( ).

1. A: What *are you eating* (example: you/eat) ? Is that a hamburger?

   B: No, it isn't. It's a veggie burger. I never *eat* (1 eat) meat. Where's your lunch?

   A: I don't want to eat lunch. I *'m gaining* (2 gain) too much weight. I *'m trying* (3 try) to lose weight. I *eat* (4 eat) only twice a day—breakfast and dinner.

   B: But you *'re drinking* (5 drink) a soda now.

   A: It's a diet cola.

2. A: What *are you doing* (6 you/do)?

   B: I *'m filling* (7 fill) in the answers.

   A: Why *aren't you using/don't you use* (8 you/use) a pen? A pencil is better. What if you make a mistake?

   B: I never *make* (9 make) mistakes. My grammar is perfect!

   A: That's not true. We all *make* (10 make) mistakes. That's why we're in this class.

EXERCISE 10

CD 1, Track 16

1. Have students read the direction line. Say: *You have to decide between the simple present and present continuous.* Go over the example in the book. Do the next item with the class.
2. Have students complete the rest of Exercise 11 individually. Go over answers as a class.
3. If necessary, review grammar chart **2.4** on page 56.

Exercise 11 Variation

To provide practice with listening skills, have students close their books and listen to the audio. Repeat the audio as needed. Say: *In this selection, you will be listening to five short conversations.* Ask comprehension questions, such as: *In conversation 1, is person A eating a hamburger?* (no) *What's person A eating?* (a veggie burger) *Does person A eat meat?* (no) Then have students open their books and complete Exercise 11.

B: I'm just kidding. Of course I ___make___ (11 make) mistakes all the time.

3. A: What ___does your father do___ (12 your father/do) for a living?

B: He's a commercial artist. He ___works___ (13 work) for a big company downtown. But this week he's on vacation.

A: What ___'s he doing___ (14 he/do) this week?

B: He ___'s playing___ (15 play) golf with his friends.

A: Is your mom on vacation too?

B: No. She ___takes___ (16 take) a vacation every December.

4. A: Where ___'s the teacher going___ (17 the teacher/go)?

B: She ___'s going___ (18 go) to her office.

A: She ___'s carrying___ (19 carry) heavy books. Let's help her.

B: I'm late for my next class. My math teacher always ___starts___ (20 start) on time. He ___gets___ (21 get) angry if someone is late.

5. A: You ___'re sleeping___ (22 sleep), Daniel. Wake up.

B: I'm so tired. I never ___get___ (23 get) enough sleep.

A: How many hours ___do you sleep___ (24 you/sleep) a night?

B: Only about four or five.

A: That's not enough. You always ___fall___ (25 fall) asleep in class.

B: I know. But I ___'m taking___ (26 take) 18 credit hours this semester.

A: That's too much. I never ___take___ (27 take) more than 12.

58 Lesson 2

Expansion

Exercise 11 Have students practice the mini-conversation (or create similar conversations) in pairs. Ask volunteers to role-play the mini-conversation in front of the class.

2.5 | Action and Nonaction Verbs

Some verbs are action verbs. These verbs show physical or mental activity *(run, play, study, drive, eat,* etc.). Some verbs are nonaction verbs. These verbs describe a state, condition, or feeling, not an action.

Examples	Explanation
Miriam says, "My kids **don't need** me now. I **have** free time now." Judy says, "I **love** my second career now." My grandmother is old. She **needs** a lot of care now.	With nonaction verbs, we use the simple present tense, even when we talk about now. We do not usually use a continuous form with these verbs.
a. Jack **is watching** the dancers. b. He **sees** more women than men.	*Watch* is an action verb. *See* is a nonaction verb.
a. Some people **are listening** to music. b. Jack **hears** the music.	*Listen* is an action verb. *Hear* is a nonaction verb.
a. Judy **is meeting** new people. b. She **knows** a lot of people.	*Meet* is an action verb. *Know* is a nonaction verb.
a. Miriam is **thinking *about*** a career in Web design.	a. When you think *about* or *of* something, *think* is an action verb.
b. She **thinks *that*** Web design is interesting.	b. *Think that* shows an opinion about something. It is a nonaction verb.
a. Judy **is having** a lot of fun now. a. I **am having** a burger for lunch.	a. When *have* means to experience something or to eat or drink something, it is an action verb.
b. Miriam **has** free time now. b. I **have** three brothers. b. Ron **has** a fever now.	b. When *have* shows possession, relationship, or illness, it is a nonaction verb.
a. Jack **is looking** at the people in the swimming pool. a. Mary **is smelling** the flowers.	a. When the sense-perception verbs describe an action, they are action verbs.
b. The aerobics class **looks** interesting. b. The flowers **smell** nice.	b. When the sense-perception verbs describe a state, they are nonaction verbs.

Nonaction Verbs:

like	know	see	cost
love	believe	smell	own
hate	think (that)	hear	have (*for* possession)
want	care (about)	taste	matter
need	understand	feel	mean
prefer	remember	seem	

The Present Continuous Tense; Action and Nonaction Verbs; the Future Tense 59

2.5 | Action and Nonaction Verbs

1. Have students cover up grammar chart **2.5.** Write the following verbs on the board: *run, like, hate, need, play, drive, know, eat, understand, smell, walk, talk, feel,* and *cost.*
2. Say: *Some verbs are action verbs. They show mental or physical activity. Some verbs are nonaction verbs. They describe a state, condition, or a feeling. Look at the verbs on the board. Which ones are action verbs and which ones are nonaction verbs?* Ask students to create two lists in their notebooks. Give them a few minutes to sort through the verbs. Then go over the verbs with the class.
3. Review the pairs *watch/see; listen/hear;* and *meet/know.* Write the sentences from the chart on the board. Ask students to say whether the verbs are action or nonaction. Then review *think about* and *think that.* Write the sentences from the book on the board, and ask students to say in which instance *think* is an action or nonaction verb. Do the same with the rest of the verbs in the chart.
4. Finally, have students look at grammar chart **2.5.** Say: *We usually use the simple present tense with nonaction verbs.*

EXERCISE 12

CD 1, Track 17

1. Have students read the direction line. Say: *You have to decide between the simple present and present continuous.* Go over the example in the book.
2. Have students complete Exercise 12 individually. Go over the answers as a class.
3. If necessary, review grammar chart **2.5** on page 59.

To save class time, have students do half of the exercise in class and complete the other half for homework.

EXERCISE 12 Fill in the blanks with the simple present or the present continuous tense of the verb in parentheses ( ).

1. A: Grandpa volunteers his time. Twice a week he reads (example: read) for blind people.

   B: My grandmother works (1 work) part-time in a bookstore. She loves (2 love) books. She usually rides (3 ride) her bike to work. She likes (4 like) the exercise.

   A: Where is she now? Is she working (5 she/work) now?

   B: Now she's on vacation. She 's sailing (6 sail) in Florida.

2. A: Can I borrow your dictionary?

   B: I'm sorry. I 'm using (7 use) it now. Where's your dictionary?

   A: I never bring (8 bring) it to class. It's too heavy.

   B: Do you expect (9 expect) to use my dictionary all the time? You need (10 need) an electronic dictionary. It's very light.

3. A: What 's the teacher saying (11 the teacher/say)? She 's talking (12 talk) too fast, so I don't understand (13 not/understand) her now.

   B: I don't know. I 'm not listening (14 not/listen). I 'm thinking (15 think) about my girlfriend.

   A: I think (16 think) you are a very romantic guy.

   B: Yes. I 'm thinking (17 think) about asking her to marry me.

60 Lesson 2

Exercise 12 Variation

To provide practice with listening skills, have students close their books and listen to the audio. Say: *In this selection, you'll hear eight short conversations.* Repeat the audio as needed. Ask comprehension questions, such as: *In conversation 1, what does person A's grandfather do with his time?* (volunteers) *How often?* (twice a week) *Who does he help?* (blind people) Then have students open their books and complete Exercise 12.

4. A: What ___are you writing___? (18 you/write)

B: I ___'m writing___ a composition about (19 write)

my grandparents. I ___love___ them very much. (20 love)

A: ___Do they live___ with you? (21 they/live)

B: No, they don't. They live in Pakistan. They

___visit___ us once a year. (22 visit)

A: ___Do you ever send___ them e-mail? (23 you/ever/send)

B: Sometimes I do. But right now their computer ___isn't working___. (24 not/work)

Anyway, they ___prefer___ handwritten letters. (25 prefer)

A: I do too.

5. A: Look at that girl. Who is she?

B: She's in my math class. I ___know___ her pretty well. (26 know)

A: What ___'s she wearing___? (27 she/wear)

B: She ___'s wearing___ a dress and army boots. (28 wear)

A: She ___looks___ strange. ___Does she always wear___ (29 look) (30 she/always/wear)

a dress and army boots?

B: No, not always. Sometimes she ___wears___ sandals. (31 wear)

And sometimes she ___doesn't wear___ any shoes at all. (32 not/wear)

6. A: ___Do you see___ that guy over there? Who is he? (33 you/see)

B: That's my English teacher.

A: He ___'s wearing___ jeans and gym shoes. And he (34 wear)

___has___ an earring in his ear. He ___looks___ (35 have) (36 look)

like a student.

B: I ___know___. Everyone ___thinks___ (37 know) (38 think)

he's a student. But he's a very professional teacher.

A: What level ___does he teach___ (39 he/teach)?

B: He teaches level four. But now he ___'s looking___ (40 look) for another job because he ___doesn't have___ (41 not/have) a full-time job here. He ___wants___ (42 want) to work full-time.

7. A: What ___are you studying___ (43 you/study) this semester?

B: English, math, and biology.

A: ___Are you doing___ (44 you/do) well in all your courses?

B: I ___'m doing___ (45 do) well in English and math. But biology is hard for me. I ___need___ (46 need) to drop it. I ___don't understand___ (47 not/understand) the teacher very well. He ___talks___ (48 talk) too fast for me.

8. A: What ___does your mother do___ (49 your mother/do) for a living?

B: She's retired now.

A: ___Is she___ (50 be) old?

B: No, she's only 58.

A: What ___does she do___ (51 she/do) with her free time?

B: She does a lot of things. In fact, she ___doesn't have___ (52 not/have) any free time at all. She ___takes___ (53 take) two art courses at the art center this semester. Right now she ___'s painting___ (54 paint) a beautiful picture of me. She also ___volunteers___ (55 volunteer) at a hospital twice a week.

A: That's wonderful. A lot of retired people ___are volunteering___ (56 volunteer) these days.

62 Lesson 2

Expansion

Exercise 12 Have students practice the mini-conversations (or create similar conversations) in pairs. Have volunteers role-play the conversations in front of the class.

EXERCISE 13 This is a phone conversation between two friends, Patty (P) and Linda (L). Fill in the blanks with the missing words. Use the simple present or the present continuous tense.

P: Hello?

L: Hi, Patty. This is Linda.

P: Hi, Linda. What ___are you doing___ (example: you/do) now?

L: Not much. ___Do you want___ (1 you/want) to meet for coffee?

P: I can't. I ___'m cooking___ (2 cook). I ___have___ (3 have) dinner in the oven now, and I ___'m waiting___ (4 wait) for it to be finished. What ___are you doing___ (5 you/do)?

L: I ___'m studying___ (6 study) for a test. But I ___want___ (7 want) to take a break now. Besides, I ___need___ (8 need) to talk to someone. I usually ___talk___ (9 talk) to my roommate when I ___have___ (10 have) a problem, but she ___'s visiting___ (11 visit) some friends in New York now.

P: We can talk while I ___'m preparing___ (12 prepare) dinner. It ___sounds___ (13 sound) serious.

L: My parents ___are planning___ (14 plan) to put Grandma in a nursing home.

P: But why?

L: My mom ___thinks___ (15 think) she'll receive better care there.

P: I ___don't think___ (16 not/think) that's such a good idea. In my family, we ___never put___ (17 never/put) our parents and grandparents in a nursing home. We ___always take care___ (18 always/take care) of them at home.

The Present Continuous Tense; Action and Nonaction Verbs; the Future Tense 63

EXERCISE 13

CD 1, Track 18

1. Have students read the direction line. Say: *You have to decide between the simple present and present continuous.* Point out that this conversation is between two friends, Patty and Linda. Go over the example in the book.
2. Have students complete Exercise 13 individually. Point out the drawing of a walker and a cane on page 64. Go over the answers as a class.
3. If necessary, review grammar chart **2.5** on page 59.

To save class time, have students do the exercise for homework.

Exercise 13 Variation

To provide practice with listening skills, have students close their books and listen to the audio. Repeat the audio as needed. Ask comprehension questions, such as: *Can Patty meet Linda for coffee?* (no) *Why not?* (She's cooking dinner.) *What's Linda doing?* (studying for a test) Then have students open their books and complete Exercise 13.

The Graying of America (Reading)

1. Have students look at the title of the reading and the photos. Ask: *What is the reading about?* Have students use the title and the photos to make predictions about the reading.
2. Preteach any vocabulary words your students may not know, such as *shortage* and *influence.*

BEFORE YOU READ

1. Have students discuss the questions in pairs.
2. Ask for a few volunteers to share their answers with the class.

To save class time, skip "Before You Read" or have students prepare answers for homework ahead of time.

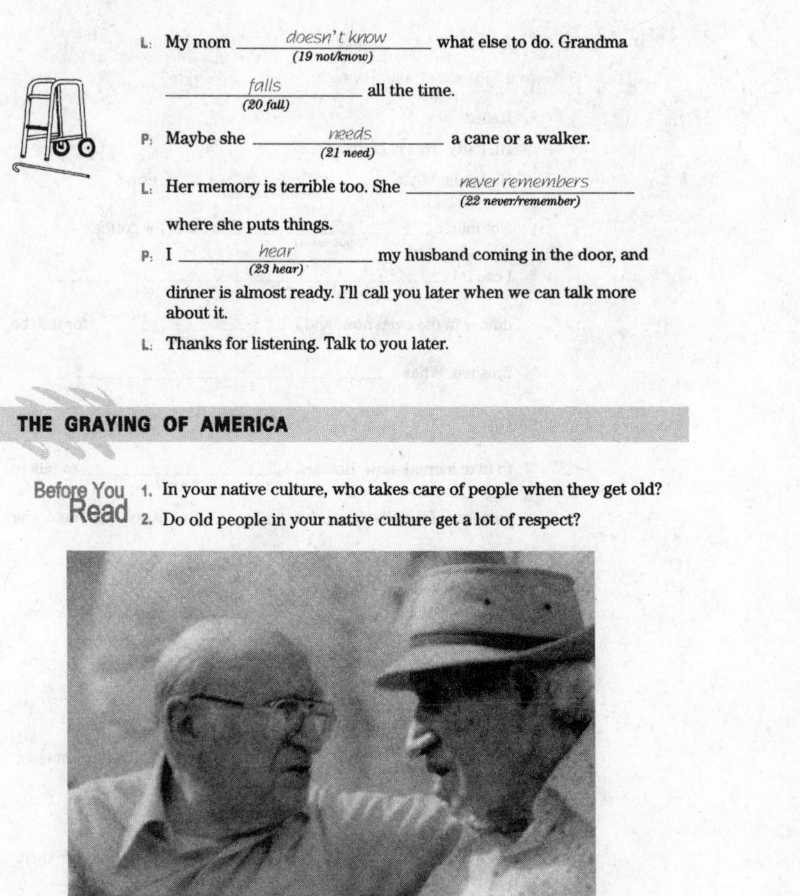

L: My mom doesn't know (19 not/know) what else to do. Grandma falls (20 fall) all the time.

P: Maybe she needs (21 need) a cane or a walker.

L: Her memory is terrible too. She never remembers (22 never/remember) where she puts things.

P: I hear (23 hear) my husband coming in the door, and dinner is almost ready. I'll call you later when we can talk more about it.

L: Thanks for listening. Talk to you later.

THE GRAYING OF AMERICA

Before You Read

1. In your native culture, who takes care of people when they get old?
2. Do old people in your native culture get a lot of respect?

64 Lesson 2

Expansion

Exercise 13 Have students practice the conversation in pairs. Then ask volunteers to act out the conversation for the class.

Read the following article. Pay special attention to future tense verbs.

The overall population of the U.S. is growing slowly. In the year 2004, the American population was 293 million. By the middle of this century, it **is going to be** 404 million. Even though this is not a big growth, one group is growing very fast—the elderly (65 years old and over). By 2030, twenty percent of the American population **will be** 65 or over. Today there are three million people 85 or older. In 2050, 28 million **will be** 85 or older.

There are two reasons for this sudden rise in the number of older Americans. First, life expectancy is increasing. In 1900, when the life expectancy was 47, 1 in 25 Americans was elderly. In 2000, with a life expectancy of 79.5 years for women and 74 for men, 1 in 8 was elderly. By 2050, 1 in 5 **will be** elderly.

The second reason for this growth is the aging of the "baby boomers." In the eighteen years after World War II, from 1946 to 1964, a large number of babies were born—75 million. The people born during this period, known as the baby boomers, are now middle-aged and **will** soon **be** elderly. The average age of the population is increasing as the baby boomers get older and live longer. The median age of Americans in 1970 was 28; in 2000 it was 35.3. By 2050, it **will be** 40.3.

What does this mean for America? First, there **will be** a labor shortage as the baby boomers retire. There are fewer younger people to take their place at work. For taxpayers, the aging of Americans means that they **are going to pay** more taxes as one-fifth of the population uses one-half of the resources. Also, the country **will see** an increase in the number of nursing homes and the need for people to work in them.

The housing market **will have** to respond to the needs of the baby boomers too. As their children grow up and move out, many baby boomers **will sell** their bigger houses and **move** to smaller ones. Others **will convert** extra bedrooms to offices and home gyms. Also, we **will see** more and more retirement villages for active seniors. Some seniors will move from the suburbs to the city. "We live in a suburb of Chicago now," says Paula Hoffman, 52, "because the schools for our teenage children are good. But when they go away to college, we **are going to move** back into the city. There's much more activity for us there."

Susan Brecht, a housing consultant in Philadelphia, Pennsylvania, says, "Baby boomers do not view retirement the way their parents and grandparents did. For starters, they're much more active. My 55 is not my mother's 55," Brecht stated. "I think there is a change in how different generations respond to the aging process. And, that's what we're seeing now and **will see** in a dramatic way for the next 10 to 20 years."

It **will be** interesting to see how the baby boomers **are going to continue** to influence the future of America.

The Present Continuous Tense; Action and Nonaction Verbs; the Future Tense 65

Reading *CD 1, Track 19*

1. Have students first read the text silently. Tell them to pay special attention to future tense verbs. Then play the audio and have students read along silently.
2. Check students' comprehension. Ask questions such as: *What part or segment of the population is growing fastest?* (the elderly) *What are the two reasons this is happening?* (Life expectancy is rising, and the baby boomers are getting older.) *Why are younger people going to pay more taxes?* (Fewer people will be working.) *Why will some people move from the suburbs to the city?* (Their children will be out of school, and there are more activities for older people in the cities.)

To save class time, have students do the reading for homework ahead of time.

Reading Variation

To practice listening skills, have students first listen to the audio alone. Ask a few comprehension questions. Repeat the audio if necessary. Then have students open their books and read along as they listen to the audio.

Reading Glossary

influence: the power to change or persuade others
shortage: a state of not having enough, a lack of something

Culture Note

When workers retire, they receive payments from Social Security based on the length of time they or their spouses worked. Social Security is funded through a tax on earnings. This payment is presently keeping 48% of retirees out of poverty. But in about 40 years, experts say that the funds in Social Security will not be able to cover the number of benefits needed. There are currently 35 million retired people. In 2050 there will be more than 85 million. The problem is that there aren't enough workers to pay into Social Security.

2.6 The Future Tense with *Will*

1. Have students look at grammar chart **2.6.** Go over the examples and the explanations in the grammar chart. Review how to form the future with *will* (*will* + base form), how to make contractions with the subject (subject pronoun + *'ll*), and how to form the negative (*will* + *not* + verb). Explain that *will not* contracts to *won't.*
2. Finally, review how to form questions (*will* + subject + verb or *wh-* word + *will* + subject + verb). Review how to form negative questions beginning with *why* (*why* + *won't* + subject + verb).
3. Have students write between three and five sentences in the future tense on any topic. Ask volunteers to share them with the class. Go over any trouble spots.

EXERCISE 14

1. Tell students that the information in the exercise is based on the reading on page 64. Have students read the direction line. Go over the example in the book.
2. Have students complete Exercise 14 individually. Check the answers as a class.
3. If necessary, review grammar chart **2.6** on page 66.

2.6 The Future Tense with *Will*

Examples	Explanation
We **will move** back to the city. You **will see** a big change in the next 10 to 20 years.	We use *will* + the base form for the future tense.
I *will* **always** *help* my parents. My parents *will* **never** *go* to a nursing home.	We can put a frequency word between *will* and the main verb.
I'll be 72 in 2050. **You'll** take care of your elderly parents.	We can contract *will* with the subject pronouns: *I'll, you'll, he'll, she'll, it'll, we'll,* and *they'll.*
The population **will not** go down. I **won't** live with my children.	To form the negative, put *not* after *will.* The contraction for *will not* is *won't.*

Compare affirmative statements and questions with *will.*

Wh- Word	*Will*	Subject	*Will*	Verb (Base Form)	Complement	Short Answer
		She	will	live	with her daughter.	
	Will	she		live	with her son?	No, she won't.
When	will	she		live	with her daughter?	Soon.

Compare negative statements and questions with *will.*

Wh- Word	*Won't*	Subject	*Won't*	Verb (Base Form)	Complement
		They	won't	need	a large house.
Why	won't	they		need	a large house?

EXERCISE 14 Fill in the blanks with an appropriate verb in the future tense. Use *will.* Answers may vary.

EXAMPLE In the future, people *will live* longer.

1. The population of old people *will grow* .
2. There *will be* more older people by 2050.
3. Where *will* you *go* when you are old?
4. *Will* your children *take* care of you?
5. How old *will* you *be* in 2050?
6. The baby boomers are middle-aged now. They *will* soon *be* elderly.

EXERCISE 15 A 30-year-old woman is saying good-bye to her 60-year-old parents. They are leaving on a trip in their recreational vehicle(RV). Fill in the blanks to complete this conversation. Use the future with *will*. Answers may vary.

A: I'm worried about you. You _will be_ (example) gone for a long time.

B: Don't worry. We _'ll_ (1) only _be_ (2) gone for the summer months.

A: You _'ll be_ (3) alone on the road.

B: We _won't be_ (4) on the road all the time.

We _'ll be_ (5) at campsites with lots of other RVs and campers.

A: How _will you wash_ (6) your clothes?

B: The RV has a washing machine.

A: Where _will you cook_ (7) your food?

B: We'll buy food at a supermarket on the way and cook it in the RV. The RV has everything—a stove, a microwave, a dishwasher. Sometimes we _'ll make_ (8) a fire and cook on the grill.

Other times we _'ll eat_ (9) out in restaurants.

A: Where _will you go_ (10) first?

B: First, we'll go to the Grand Canyon.

A: That's fabulous! _Will you send_ (11) me a postcard from there?

B: Of course, we _will_ (12). And we _'ll_ (13) send you e-mail too.

A: How _are you going to send_ (14) e-mail?

B: From our computer, of course. We _'ll have_ (15) it with us.

A: Where _will you get_ (16) electricity for all these things?

The Present Continuous Tense; Action and Nonaction Verbs; the Future Tense 67

EXERCISE 15

CD 1, Track 20

1. Say: *In this exercise, a daughter is saying goodbye to her 60-year-old parents who are taking a trip in their recreational vehicle.* Have students read the direction line. Go over the example in the book. Remind students that several answers may be correct.
2. Have students complete Exercise 15 individually. Point out the pictures on page 67 and the photo on page 68 of an RV. Then have students compare answers in pairs. Circulate to observe pair work. Give help as needed.
3. If necessary, review grammar chart **2.6** on page 66.

To save class time, have students do half of the exercise in class and complete the other half for homework. Or assign the entire exercise for homework.

Exercise 15 Variation

To provide practice with listening skills, have students close their books and listen to the audio. Say: *In this exercise, a daughter is saying goodbye to her 60-year-old parents who are taking a trip in their recreational vehicle.* Repeat the audio as needed. Ask comprehension questions, such as: *How long will the woman's parents be gone?* (for the summer months) *How will the parents wash their clothes?* (with a washing machine in the RV) *Does the RV have a microwave?* (yes) Then have students open their books and complete Exercise 15.

B: At the campsites, there are electrical hookups.

A: You *'ll have* (17) all the comforts of home. Why, then, are you leaving?

B: We can't see the Grand Canyon from our home.

A: *Will you take* (18) pictures?

B: Yes, we'll take a lot of pictures. We'll have our digital camera with us. There *will be* (19) a lot of beautiful things to take pictures of. We *'ll send* (20) them to you by e-mail.

A: Have a good time. I *'ll miss* (21) you.

B: We'll miss you too.

Expansion

Exercise 15 Have students practice the dialogue in pairs. Then have students create a skit or role-play the conversation. Ask volunteers to perform in front of the class.

2.7 | The Future Tense with *Be Going To*

Examples	Explanation
People **are going to live** longer. They **are going to need** help from their children. There **are going to be** more elderly people in 50 years.	We use a form of *be* + *going to* + the base form to form the future tense.
I'm not going to live with my children. He **isn't** going to retire.	To form the negative, put *not* after *am, is,* or *are*.
We're **going to go** on a long trip in the RV. We're **going** on a long trip in the RV.	We often shorten *going to go* to *going*.
We're going to return **in** two months. I'm going to retire **in** ten years.	We use the preposition *in* with the future tense to mean *after*.

Pronunciation Notes:

1. In informal speech, *going to* before another verb often sounds like "gonna." In formal English, we don't write "gonna." Listen to your teacher's pronunciation of *going to* in the following sentences.
   Where's he going to live? (Where's he "gonna" live?)
   He's going to live in a dorm. (He's "gonna" live in a dorm.)
2. Only *going to* before another verb sounds like "gonna." We don't pronounce "gonna" at the end of a sentence or before a noun.
   Where is he going?
   He's going to the bookstore.

Compare affirmative statements and questions with *be going to.*

Wh- Word	*Be*	Subject	*Be*	*Going to* + Verb (Base Form)	Complement	Short Answer
		They	are	going to sell	their house.	
	Are	they		going to sell	it soon?	Yes, they are.
Why	are	they		going to sell	it?	Because they don't need a big house.

Compare negative statements and questions with *be going to.*

Wh- Word	*Be + n't*	Subject	*Be + n't*	*Going to* + Verb(Base Form)	Complement
		She	isn't	going to retire	from her job.
Why	isn't	she		going to retire?	

2.7 | The Future Tense with *Be Going To*

1. Have students go back to the reading on pages 64–65. Say: *There's another way to express the future. Can you give me some examples from this reading?* Write the students' examples on the board. Ask: *How do we form the future with* be going to? (*be* + *going to* + verb) How do we form the negative? (*be* + *not* + *going to* + verb)
2. Have students look at grammar chart **2.7.** Go over the examples and explanations. Point out that *going to go* is usually shortened to *going.* Give examples (e.g., *We're going to go to New York tomorrow. We're going to New York tomorrow.*).
3. Explain that when *in* is used with the future, it means *after* (a period of time). Give examples (e.g., *We're going to take a break in 10 minutes.*).
4. Go over the Pronunciation Notes. Explain that *going to* is often pronounced by native speakers as *gonna.* Point out that although we say *gonna,* we don't use it in formal written English.

EXERCISE 16

1. Have students read the direction line. Ask: *What do we write on the blanks?* (the future with *be going to*) Go over the example in the book.
2. Have students complete Exercise 16 individually. Check the answers as a class.
3. If necessary, review grammar chart **2.7** on page 69.

EXERCISE 17

CD 1, Track 21

1. Say: *A man is talking to his coworker about retiring early.* Have students read the direction line. Go over the example in the book.
2. Have students complete Exercise 17 individually. Then have students compare answers in pairs. Circulate to observe pair work. Give help as needed.
3. If necessary, review grammar chart **2.7** on page 69.

To save class time, have students do the exercise as a class.

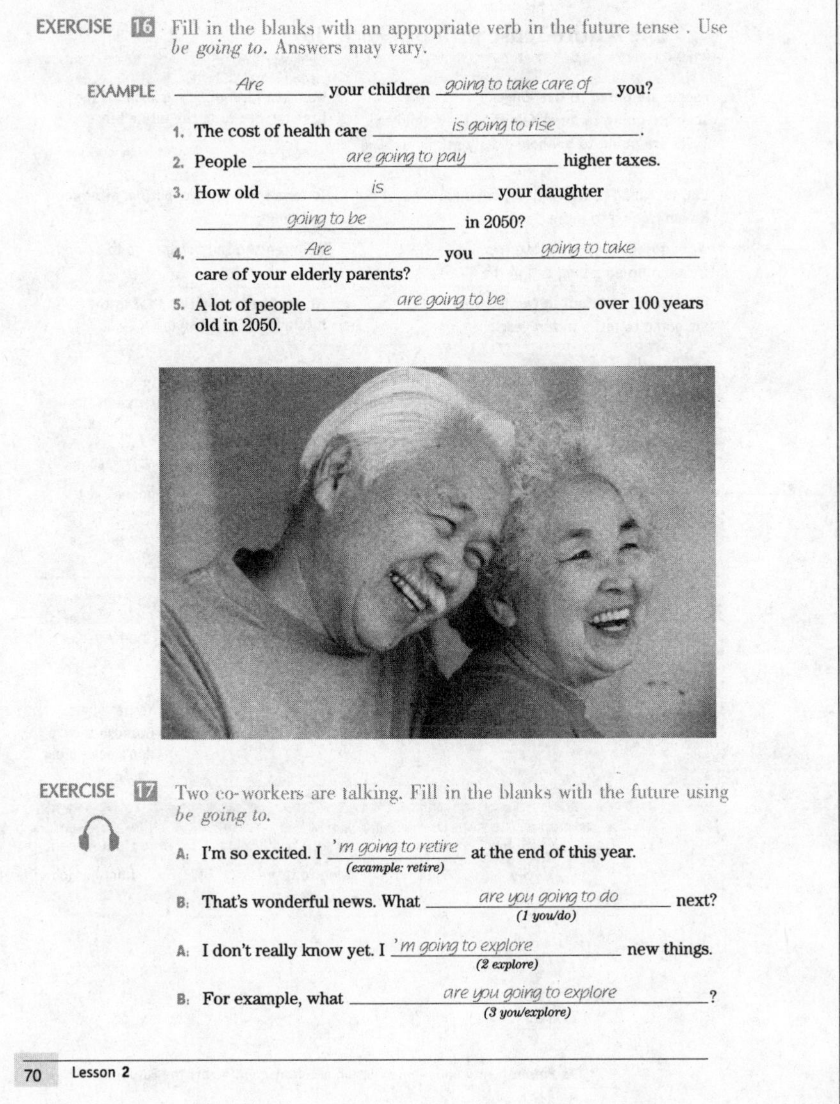

EXERCISE 16 Fill in the blanks with an appropriate verb in the future tense . Use *be going to*. Answers may vary.

EXAMPLE *Are* your children *going to take care of* you?

1. The cost of health care *is going to rise*.
2. People *are going to pay* higher taxes.
3. How old *is* your daughter *going to be* in 2050?
4. *Are* you *going to take* care of your elderly parents?
5. A lot of people *are going to be* over 100 years old in 2050.

EXERCISE 17 Two co-workers are talking. Fill in the blanks with the future using *be going to*.

A: I'm so excited. I *'m going to retire* (example: retire) at the end of this year.

B: That's wonderful news. What *are you going to do* (1 you/do) next?

A: I don't really know yet. I *'m going to explore* (2 explore) new things.

B: For example, what *are you going to explore* (3 you/explore)?

70 Lesson 2

Exercise 17 Variation

To provide practice with listening skills, have students close their books and listen to the audio. Say: *A man is talking to his coworker about retiring early.* Repeat the audio as needed. Ask comprehension questions, such as: *Why is person A excited?* (Person A is going to retire at the end of this year.) *What kind of classes is person A going to take?* (art classes) *Is person A going to work?* (no) Then have students open their books and complete Exercise 17.

A: I think I have a talent for art. I *'m going to take* (4 take) art classes.

B: *Are you going to work* (5 you/work) part time?

A: No way! I *'m going to do* (6 do) exactly what I want to do, when I want to do it.

B: Is your wife happy about your retirement?

A: Yes. She *'s going to retire* (7 retire) too.

B: But you're not that old.

A: I'm 58 and she's 56. Our children aren't going to need us much anymore.

B: Why *aren't they going to need* (8 not/need) you?

A: Our youngest son *is going to leave* (9 leave) for college in September. And the other two are already on their own. The oldest *is going to get* (10 get) married next year, and the middle one has her own apartment and a job.

B: I *'m going to miss* (11 miss) you at work.

A: I *'m going to miss* (12 miss) you too. But I *'m not going to miss* (13 not/miss) the boss and the long hours.

EXERCISE 18 Do you have questions for the teacher about this semester, next semester, or his or her life in general? Write three questions to ask the teacher about the near or distant future.

EXAMPLES *What time are you going to leave today?*
When are you going to give us a test?
Are you going to retire soon?

1. Answers will vary.
2.
3.

EXERCISE 18

1. Say: *Now you get to ask me anything you want!* Have students read the direction line. Say: *What tense will your questions be in?* (the future with *be going to*) Go over the examples in the book.
2. Have students complete Exercise 18 individually. Then answer questions from each of the students.
3. If necessary, review grammar chart **2.7** on page 69.

To save class time, have students write the questions for homework. Then have a few volunteers ask you questions in class.

Expansion

Exercise 17 Have students practice the conversation in pairs. Then have students create a new conversation in pairs. Ask volunteers to role-play their conversations in front of the class.

Exercise 18 Have students write three questions for three other people in the class. Have students take turns asking and answering questions. Ask volunteers to report anything interesting they learned about their classmates.

Culture Note

Some types of questions are considered too personal and, therefore, impolite in American culture. You shouldn't ask questions about age, earnings, the cost of clothing or other items, love relationships, or religion.

2.8 | *Will* vs. *Be Going To*

1. Have students cover up grammar chart **2.8** on page 72. Copy part of the chart from page 72 onto the board:

Uses	***Will***	***Be Going To***
Prediction		
Fact		
Scheduled event		

   Ask students to work in pairs to fill in the chart with example sentences using *will* and *be going to*. Remind students that sometimes you can use both *will* and *be going to*.
2. Have students look at grammar chart **2.8.** Say: *Compare your sentences with the sentences from the chart in the book.* Review the chart.
3. Direct students to the Language Note. Point out that we can use the present continuous to express the future. Review the example sentences in the chart.

EXERCISE 19

CD 1, Track 22

1. Say: *In this exercise, you'll choose to use* will *or* be going to. Have students read the direction line. Go over the example with the class. Have volunteers complete #1.
2. Have students complete Exercise 19 individually. Go over the answers as a class.
3. If necessary, review grammar chart **2.8** on page 72.

To save class time, have students do half of the exercise in class and complete the other half for homework.

2.8 | *Will* vs. *Be Going To*

In some cases, *will* is the better choice for the future tense. In some cases, *be going to* is the better choice. In some cases, both forms of the future work.

Uses	*Will*	*Be Going To*
Prediction	My father always exercises and eats well. I think he **will live** a long time.	I think my father **is going to live** a long time.
Fact	The sun **will set** at 6:43 tonight. The population of older people **will increase.**	The sun **is going to set** at 6:43 tonight. The population of older people **is going to increase.**
Scheduled event	The movie **will begin** at 8 o'clock.	The movie **is going to begin** at 8 o'clock.
Plan		My grandfather **is going to move** to Florida next year. **I am going to return** to my native country in three years.
Promise	I **will** always **take** care of you, Mom.	
Offer to help	A: This box is heavy. B: **I'll carry** it for you.	

Language Note:
We sometimes use the present continuous tense with a future meaning. We can do this with planned events in the near future. We do this especially with verbs of motion.
My grandmother **is moving** into a retirement home on Friday.
I'm helping her move on Friday.

EXERCISE 19 Choose *will* or *be going to* to fill in the blanks. In some cases, both are possible.

1. A: Where are you going?
   B: I'm going to the park this afternoon. I ___am going to meet___ *(example: meet)* my friend and play tennis with her. I have to return some videos to the video store, but I don't have time.
   A: Give them to me. I ___'m going to pass___ *(1 pass)* that way. I ___'ll return___ *(2 return)* them for you.

72 Lesson 2

Grammar Variation

Have students cover up grammar chart **2.8.** Write the example sentences on the board for both *will* and *be going to.* On another part of the board, write a list of the uses of the future in scrambled order. Ask students to read the sentences and match them with the appropriate uses.

2. A: I have to go to the airport. My sister's plane will arrive (3 arrive) at four o'clock this afternoon.

B: I 'll go (4 go) with you. I 'll stay (5 stay) in the car while you go into the airport. That way, you won't have to (6 not/have to) pay for parking.

3. A: My sister's birthday is next week.

B: Are you going to give (7 you/give) her a birthday present?

A: Of course, I will (8).

B: What are you going to give (9 you/give) her?

A: She loves the theater. I 'm going to buy (10 buy) her tickets to a play.

B: How old will she be/is she going to be (11 be)?

A: She 'll be/'s going to be (12 be) 21 years old.

4. Teacher: Next week we 're going to have (13 have) our midterm test.

Student: Will it be (14 it/be) hard?

Teacher: Yes, but I 'll help (15 help) you prepare for it.

5. Wife: I won't have time to pick up the children this afternoon. I have to work late.

Husband: Don't worry. I 'll pick (16 pick) them up.

Wife: I won't have time to cook either.

Husband: Just relax. I 'll prepare (17 prepare) dinner tonight.

Exercise 19 Variation

To provide practice with listening skills, have students close their books and listen to the audio. Say: *In this listening selection, you will hear eight short conversations.* Repeat the audio as needed. Ask comprehension questions, such as: In conversation 1, *where is person B going?* (to the park) *Why?* (to meet a friend and play tennis with her) *Who is going to pass by the video store?* (person A) Then have students open their books and complete Exercise 19.

6. Man: I want to marry you.

Woman: But we're only 19. We're too young.

Man: I _'ll be/'m going to be_ (18 be) 20 in April.

Woman: But you don't even have a job.

Man: I _'ll find_ (19 find) a job.

Woman: Let's wait a few years.

Man: I _'ll wait_ (20 wait) for you forever. I _'ll always love_ (21 always/love) you.

7. A: Do you want to watch the football game with me on Saturday?

B: I can't. My brother _is going to move_ (22 move).

I _'m going to help_ (23 help) him.

A: Do you need any help?

B: We need boxes. Do you have any?

A: No, but I _'m going to look_ (24 look) for boxes. I _'m going to go_ (25 go) to the supermarket this afternoon. I _'ll get_ (26 get) boxes there. I _'ll bring_ (27 bring) them to your house.

B: Thanks.

8. A: I'm so excited! I _'m going to get_ (28 get) a puppy.

B: That's a big responsibility. You're never home. How _will you take/are you going to take_ (29 take) care of it?

A: My cousin lives with me now. She doesn't have a job. She _'s going to help_ (30 help) me take care of the dog.

B: What about your landlord? Is it OK with him?

A: I _'m not going to tell_ (31 not/tell) him.

B: You have to tell him. He _'ll know/'s going to know_ (32 know) if you have a dog. You _'ll have to/'re going to have to_ (33 have to) take the dog out three times a day. And the dog _will bark/is going to bark_ (34 bark).

74 Lesson 2

Expansion

Exercise 19 Have students practice the mini-conversations in pairs. Ask volunteers to role-play the conversations in front of the class.

2.9 | Future Tense + Time/*If* Clause[8]

Some future sentences have two clauses: a main clause and a time or *if* clause.		
Time or *if* Clause (Simple Present Tense)	**Main Clause (Future Tense)**	**Explanation**
When the children **grow** up,	we **will move** back to the city.	We use the *future* only in the main clause; we use the *simple present tense* in the time/*if* clause.
If I **am** healthy,	I **will continue** to work for the rest of my life.	
Main Clause (Future Tense)	**Time or *If* Clause (Simple Present Tense)**	We can put the time/*if* clause before the main clause. Or we can put the main clause before the time/*if* clause.
He **will move** to a warm climate	as soon as he **retires**.	
My parents **are going to travel**	if they **take** an early retirement.	

Punctuation Note:
If the time/*if* clause comes before the main clause, we use a comma to separate the two parts of the sentence. If the main clause comes first, we don't use a comma.

EXERCISE 20 Connect the sentences using the word in parentheses ( ).

EXAMPLE **I will retire. I will play golf. (when)**
When I retire, I will play golf. OR *I will play golf when I retire.*

1. **I will retire. I'm not going to live with my children. (when)**
When I retire, I'm not going to live with my children.

2. **I will be old. I will take care of myself. (when)**
When I'm old, I'll take care of myself.

3. **My parents will need help. I'll take care of them. (if)**
If my parents need help, I'll take care of them.

4. **I won't be healthy. I'll live with my children. (if)**
If I'm not healthy, I'll live with my children.

5. **I won't have money. I will get help from the government. (if)**
If I don't have money, I'll get help from the government.

6. **My parents will die. I'll move to another city. (after)**
After my parents die, I'll move to another city.

[8] A *clause* is a group of words that has a subject and a verb. Some sentences have more than one clause.

2.9 | Future Tense + Time/*If* Clause

1. Have students cover up grammar chart **2.9.** Write several sentences from the grammar chart on the board. Point out that these sentences are made up of two clauses, the time clause and the main clause. Underline the time clause and double underline the main clause. Ask: *What tense is used in the time clause?* (simple present) *What tense is used in the main clause?* (future)
2. Have students look at grammar chart **2.9.** Review all of the examples and explanations.
3. Direct students to the Punctuation Note. Point out that the main clause can come before or after the time/*if* clause. Explain that when the time/*if* clause goes first they must use a comma. Go over the examples.

1. Say: *In this exercise, we will connect two sentences using the word in parentheses.* Have students read the direction line. Go over the example in the book. Remind students that if they write the time clause or *if* clause first, they must use a comma.
2. Have students complete the exercise individually. Check the answers as a class.
3. If necessary, review grammar chart **2.9** on page 75.

EXERCISE 21

1. Say: *In this exercise, you're going to write about your future.* Have students read the direction line. Go over the examples in the book. Model the exercise with your own examples.
2. Have students complete the exercise individually. Then have students compare answers in pairs. Circulate to observe pair work. Give help as needed.
3. If necessary, review grammar chart **2.9** on page 75.

To save class time, have students do the exercise for homework. Then students may compare answers with a partner in class.

EXERCISE 22

CD 1, Track 23

1. Say: *In this exercise, you'll choose to use* will *or* be going to. *Remember that in many cases, you can use both.* Have students read the direction line. Go over the example with the class.
2. Have students complete Exercise 22 individually. Then have students compare answers in pairs. Circulate to observe pair work. Give help as needed.
3. If necessary, review grammar charts **2.7** on page 69, **2.8** on page 72, and **2.9** on page 75.

To save class time, have students do half of the exercise as a class and complete the other half for homework.

7. **I will get a pension. I won't need to depend on my children. (if)**
   If I get a pension, I won't need to depend on my children.
8. **I'll retire. I'm going to save my money. (before)**
   Before I retire, I'm going to save my money.

EXERCISE 21 ABOUT YOU Think about a specific time in your future(when you graduate, when you get married, when you have children, when you find a job, when you return to your native country, when you are old, etc.). Write three sentences to tell what will happen at that time. Find a partner who is close to your age. Compare your answers to your partner's answers.

EXAMPLES
When I have children, I won't have as much free time as I do now.
When I have children, I'm going to have a lot more responsibilities.
When I have children, my parents will be very happy.

1. Answers will vary.
2. ______
3. ______

EXERCISE 22 A foreign student (F) is talking to an American (A) about getting old. Fill in the blanks with the correct form of the verb to complete this conversation. In many cases, you can use either *be going to* or *will.*

F: **How's your grandfather?**
A: **He's OK. I** *'m going to visit* **(example: visit) him this afternoon.**
F: **How's he doing?**
A: **He's in great health. Next week he** *'s going to go* **(1 go) to Hawaii to play golf.**
F: **How old is he?**
A: **He** *'ll be/'s going to be* **(2 be) 78 next month. Did I tell you? In June, he** *'s going to get* **(3 get) married to a widow he met in the retirement home.**
F: **That seems so strange to me. Why** *is he going to do* **(4 he/do) that?**
A: **Why not? They like each other, and they want to be together.**
F: **What** *are you going to do* **(5 you/do) when he's no longer able to take care of himself?**

76 Lesson 2

Expansion

Exercise 21 Have students write a letter or an e-mail to a friend in another city or country. Say: *Talk about your future plans. Use* will *and* be going to *and time/*if *clauses.*

Exercise 22 Variation

To provide practice with listening skills, have students close their books and listen to the audio. Say: *A foreign student is talking to an American about getting old.* Repeat the audio as needed. Ask comprehension questions, such as: *Who is the American going to visit this afternoon?* (the American's grandfather) *What is the grandfather going to do next week?* (go to Hawaii to play golf) *What is the grandfather going to do in June?* (get married) Then have students open their books and complete Exercise 22.

A: We never think about it. He's in such great shape that we think he 'll be/'s going to be (6 be) healthy forever. I think he 'll outlive/'s going to outlive (7 outlive) us all.

F: But he 'll probably need (8 probably/need) help as he gets older.

A: We 'll cross (9 cross) that bridge when we come to it. Do you have plans for your parents as they get older?

F: They're in their 50s now. But when they 're (10 be) older, they 're going to live (11 live) with me and my wife. In our country, it's an honor to take care of our parents.

A: That sounds like a great custom. But I think older people should be independent. I'm glad that Grandpa doesn't depend on us. And when I 'm (12 be) old, I 'll take (13 take) care of myself. I don't want to depend on anyone.

F: You 'll change/'re going to change (14 change) your mind when you 're (15 be) old.

A: Maybe. I have to catch my bus now. Grandpa is waiting for me. I 'll see (16 see) you later.

F: Wait. I have my car. I 'll drive (17 drive) you to your grandfather's place.

A: Thanks.

EXERCISE 23 This is a conversation between two co-workers. They are talking about retirement. Fill in the blanks with the correct form and tense of the verb in parentheses ( ).

A: I hear you're going to retire this year.

B: Yes. Isn't it wonderful? I will be (example: be) 65 in September.

A: What are you going to do (1 you/do) after you retire (2 retire)?

EXERCISE 23

CD 1, Track 24

1. Have students read the direction line. Explain that this is a conversation between two coworkers. Go over the example with the class.
2. Have students complete Exercise 23 individually. Then have students compare answers in pairs. Circulate to observe pair work. Give help as needed.
3. If necessary, review grammar charts **2.7** on page 69, **2.8** on page 72, and **2.9** on page 75.

To save class time, have students do the exercise for homework.

Expansion

Exercise 22 Have students practice the conversation in pairs. Then ask volunteers to act out the conversation for the class.

Exercise 23 Variation

To provide practice with listening skills, have students close their books and listen to the audio. Explain that this is a conversation between two coworkers. Repeat the audio as needed. Ask comprehension questions, such as: *What's person B going to do this year?* (retire) *When will person B turn 65 years old?* (in September) *Where does person B want to live?* (in Florida; in a condo) Then have students open their books and complete Exercise 23.

B: I'm trying to sell my house now. When I ___sell___ (3 sell) it, I ___'m going to move___ (4 move) to Florida and buy a condo.

A: What ___are you going to do___ (5 you/do) in Florida?

B: I ___'m going to buy___ (6 buy) a sailboat and spend most of my time on the water.

A: But a sailboat is expensive.

B: When I ___'m___ (7 be) 65, I ___'m going to start___ (8 start) to use my savings. Also, I ___'m going to get___ (9 get) a lot of money when I ___sell___ (10 sell) my house. What ___are you going to do___ (11 you/do) when you ___retire___ (12 retire)?

A: I'm only 45 years old. I have another 20 years until I ___retire___ (13 retire).

B: Now is the time to start thinking about retirement. If you ___save___ (14 save) your money for the next 20 years, you ___'ll have___ (15 have) a comfortable retirement. But if you ___don't think___ (16 not/think) about it until the time ___comes___ (17 come), you ___'re not going to have___ (18 not/have) enough money to live on.

A: I ___'ll worry___ (19 worry) about it when the time ___comes___ (20 come). I'm too young to worry about it now.

B: If you ___wait___ (21 wait) until you ___'re___ (22 be) 65 to think about it, you ___'ll be___ (23 be) a poor, old man. On Monday morning when we ___'re___ (24 be) at work,

78 Lesson 2

Expansion

Exercise 23 Have students practice the conversation in pairs. Then ask volunteers to act out the conversation for the class.

I *'ll introduce* (25 introduce) you to a woman who can explain the company's savings plan to you. After you *talk* (26 talk) to her, I'm sure you *'ll change* (27 change) your mind about when to worry about retirement.

SUMMARY OF LESSON 2

Uses of Tenses	
Simple Present Tense	
General truths, facts	Many people **retire** in their sixties. Retirees **get** Social Security.
Regular activities, habits, customs	Jack **plays** golf twice a week. I **always** visit my grandparents on the weekend.
Place of origin	My grandfather comes from Mexico. My grandmother **comes** from Peru.
In a time clause or in an *if* clause of a future statement	When she **retires**, she will enjoy life. If grandma **needs** help, she will live with her daughter.
With nonaction verbs	I **care** about my grandparents. Your grandfather **needs** help now. My grandfather **prefers** to live alone now.

Present Continuous (with action verbs only)	
Now	**We're comparing** verb tenses now. **I'm looking** at page 79 now.
A long-term action in progress at this general time	Judy **is earning** money by making dolls. Jack is retired now. He **is starting** a new career.
A trend in society	The population of the U.S. **is getting** older. Americans **are living** longer.
A plan in the near future	She **is retiring** next month. She **is going** on a long trip soon.
A descriptive state	Mary **is standing** over there. She **is wearing** blue jeans and a T-shirt.

Summary of Lesson 2

1. **Simple Present Tense** Have students cover up the first chart in the summary. Ask: *When do we use the simple present tense?* Write the students' answers on the board. Ask students to give example sentences. If necessary, have students review:
   2.4 Contrasting the Simple Present and the Present Continuous (p. 56).
2. **Present Continuous (with action verbs only)** Have students cover up the second chart in the summary. Ask: *When do we use the present continuous?* Write the students' answers on the board. Ask students to give example sentences. If necessary, have students review:
   2.1 Present Continuous Tense (p. 46)
   2.2 Using the Present Continuous for Longer Actions (p. 49)
   2.3 Questions with the Present Continuous Tense (p. 51)
   2.4 Contrasting the Simple Present and the Present Continuous (p. 56)
   2.5 Action and Nonaction Verbs (p. 59).

Expansion

Exercise 23 Have students create a conversation about retirement between two people they know, such as their parents.

Summary of Lesson 2 (*cont.*)

3. **Future** Have students cover up the third chart in the summary. Ask: *When do we use* will *and* be going to*?* Write the students' answers on the board. Ask students to give example sentences. If necessary, have students review:
   2.6 The Future Tense with *Will* (p. 66)
   2.7 The Future Tense with *Be Going To* (p. 69)
   2.8 *Will* vs. *Be Going To* (p. 72)
   2.9 Future Tense + Time/*If* Clause (p. 75).

Editing Advice

Have students close their books. Write the example sentences without editing marks or corrections on the board. For example:

1. She working now.
2. I am liking your new car.

Ask students to correct each sentence and provide a rule or explanation for each correction. This activity can be done individually, in pairs, or as a class. After students have corrected each sentence, tell them to turn to pages 80–81. Say: *Now compare your work with the Editing Advice in the book.*

Future	*will*	*be going to*
A plan		He **is going to retire** in two years.
A fact	The number of old people **will increase.**	The number of old people **is going to increase.**
A prediction	I think you **will enjoy** retirement.	I think you **are going to enjoy** retirement.
A promise	I **will** take care of you when you're old.	
An offer to help	Grandma, **I'll carry** your grocery bags for you.	
A scheduled event	Dance instruction **will begin** at 8 p.m. on Saturday.	Dance instruction **is going to begin** at 8 p.m. on Saturday.

EDITING ADVICE

1. Always include *be* in a present continuous tense verb.

   She ^*is* working now.

2. Don't use the present continuous tense with a nonaction verb.

   I ~~am~~ lik~~ing~~*e* your new car.

3. Don't use *be* with another verb for the future.

   I will ~~be~~ go back to my native country in five years.

4. Include *be* in a future sentence that has no other verb.

   He will ^*be* angry.

   There will ^*be* a party soon.

5. Don't combine *will* and *be going to.*

   He will ~~going to~~ leave. OR *He's going to leave.*

6. Use the future tense with an offer to help.

   The phone's ringing. I^*'ll* get it.

80 Lesson 2

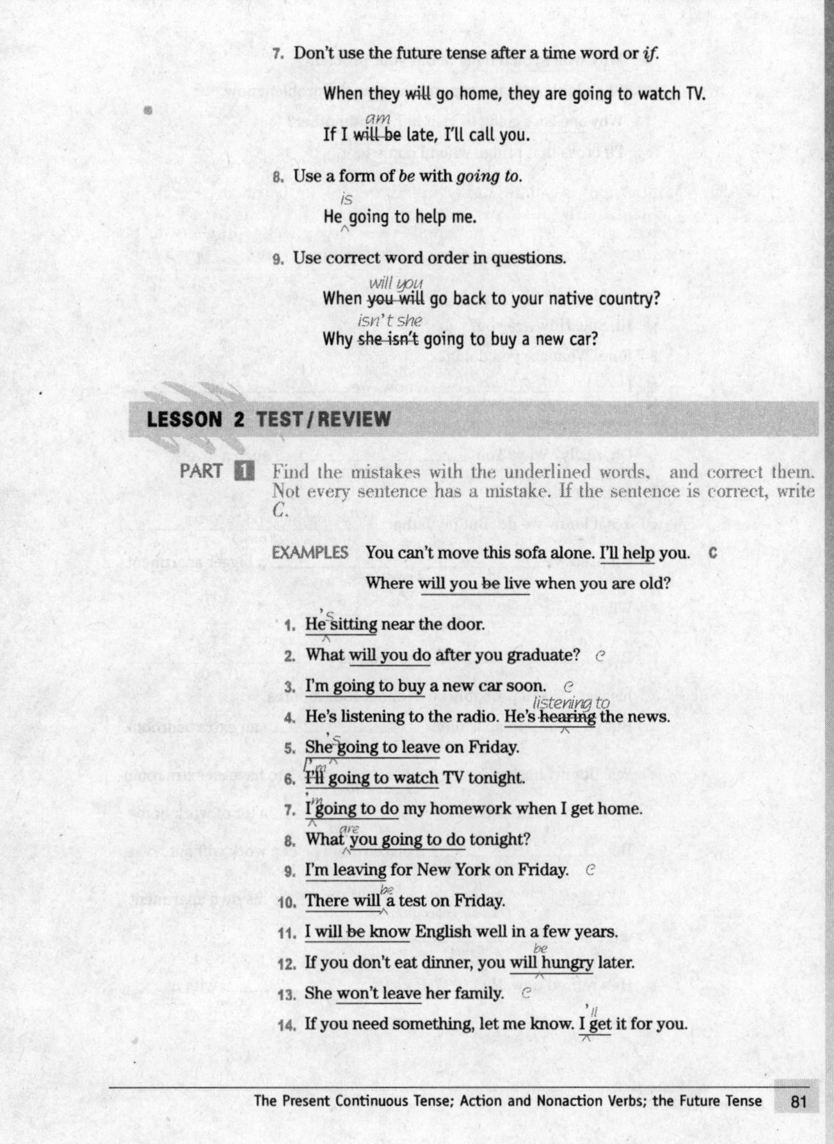

7. Don't use the future tense after a time word or *if*.

When they ~~will~~ go home, they are going to watch TV.

If I ~~will be~~ *am* late, I'll call you.

8. Use a form of *be* with *going to*.

He *is* going to help me.

9. Use correct word order in questions.

When ~~you will~~ *will you* go back to your native country?

Why ~~she isn't~~ *isn't she* going to buy a new car?

LESSON 2 TEST/REVIEW

PART 1 Find the mistakes with the underlined words, and correct them. Not every sentence has a mistake. If the sentence is correct, write *C*.

EXAMPLES You can't move this sofa alone. I'll help you. C

Where will you ~~be~~ live when you are old?

1. He*'s* sitting near the door.
2. What will you do after you graduate? *C*
3. I'm going to buy a new car soon. *C*
4. He's listening to the radio. He's ~~hearing~~ *listening to* the news.
5. She*'s* going to leave on Friday.
6. ~~I'll~~ *I'm* going to watch TV tonight.
7. I*'m* going to do my homework when I get home.
8. What *are* you going to do tonight?
9. I'm leaving for New York on Friday. *C*
10. There will *be* a test on Friday.
11. I will ~~be~~ know English well in a few years.
12. If you don't eat dinner, you will *be* hungry later.
13. She won't leave her family. *C*
14. If you need something, let me know. I*'ll* get it for you.

The Present Continuous Tense; Action and Nonaction Verbs; the Future Tense 81

Lesson 2 Test/Review

For additional practice, review, and assessment materials, see Assessment CD-ROM with *ExamView Pro*, *More Grammar Practice* Workbook 2, Interactive CD-ROM, and Web site http://elt.thomson.com/gic

PART 1

1. Part 1 may be used as an in-class test to assess student performance, in addition to the Assessment CD-ROM with *ExamView Pro*. Have students read the direction line. Ask: *Does every sentence have a mistake?* (no) Go over the examples with the class.
2. Have students complete the assignment individually. Collect for assessment.
3. If necessary, have students review: **Lesson 2.**

Lesson Review

To use Part 1 as a review, assign it as homework or use it as an in-class activity to be completed individually or in pairs. Check answers and review errors as a class. Reteach grammar points that students haven't mastered. Then student learning may be assessed using a test generated from the Assessment CD-ROM with *ExamView Pro*.

PART 2

1. Part 2 may also be used as an in-class test to assess student performance, in addition to the Assessment CD-ROM with *ExamView Pro*. Have students read the direction line. Point out that this exercise is a phone conversation between Mary and Sue. Go over the example with the class.
2. Have students complete the exercise individually. Collect for assessment.
3. If necessary, have students review: **Lesson 2.**

15. Why won't you tell me about your problem? C
16. She's looking at the report. She sees the problem now. C
17. Why ~~she isn't~~ isn't she going to visit her grandmother?
18. I'll cross that bridge when I come to it. C

PART 2 Mary (M) is talking to her friend Sue (S) on the phone. Fill in the blanks with the correct tense and form of the words in parentheses ( ). Use the simple present, present continuous, or future tenses. In some cases, more than one answer is possible.

S: Hi, Mary.

M: Hi, Sue. How are you?

S: Fine. What are you doing?

M: I *am packing* (example: pack) now. We *'re moving* (1 move) next Saturday.

S: Oh, really? Why? You *have* (2 have) such a lovely apartment now.

M: Yes, I know we do. But my father *'s coming/'s going to come* (3 come) soon, so we *need* (4 need) a bigger apartment.

S: When *is he coming/is he going to come* (5 come)?

M: He *'s going to come/'ll come* (6 come) as soon as he *gets* (7 get) his visa. That'll probably be in about four months.

S: But your present apartment *has* (8 have) an extra bedroom.

M: Yes. But my husband *always likes* (9 always/like) to have an extra room for an office. He usually *brings* (10 bring) a lot of work home. He *needs* (11 need) a place where he can work without noise.

S: *Will your father get/Is your father going to get* (12 your father/get) his own apartment after he *finds* (13 find) a job?

M: He's retired now. He *'s going to live* (14 live) with us. He *doesn't like* (15 not/like) to live alone.

82 Lesson 2

Lesson Review

To use Part 2 as a review, assign it as homework or use it as an in-class activity to be completed individually or in pairs. Check answers and review errors as a class. Reteach grammar points that students haven't mastered. Then student learning may be assessed using a test generated from the Assessment CD-ROM with *ExamView Pro*.

S: Do you need help with your packing?

M: Not really. Bill and I *are staying/are going to stay* (16 stay) home this week to finish the packing. And my sister *is helping* (17 help) me now too.

S: I *'ll come* (18 come) over next Saturday to help you move.

M: We *'re going to use* (19 use) professional movers on Saturday. We don't want to bother our friends.

S: It's no bother. I *want* (20 want) to help.

M: Thanks. There probably *will be* (21 be) a few things you can help me with on Saturday. I have to go now. I *hear* (22 hear) Bill. He *'s calling* (23 call) me. He *wants* (24 want) me to help him in the basement. I *'ll call* (25 call) you back later.

You don't have to call me back. I *'ll see* (26 see) you on Saturday. Bye.

PART 3 Fill in the blanks with the negative form of the underlined verb.

EXAMPLE Mary is busy. Sue *isn't* busy.

1. Sue is talking to Mary. She *isn't talking* to her husband.
2. Mary is going to move to a bigger apartment. She *isn't going to move* to a house.
3. Mary's husband needs an extra room. He *doesn't need* a big room.
4. Sue will go to Mary's house on Saturday. She *won't go* tomorrow.
5. Mary will move the small things. She *won't move* the furniture.
6. Her new apartment has an extra room. Her old apartment *doesn't have* an extra room.
7. Her father likes to live with family. He *doesn't like* to live alone.

PART 3

1. Part 3 may also be used as an in-class test to assess student performance, in addition to the Assessment CD-ROM with *ExamView Pro.* Have students read the direction line. Ask: *What do we write in the blanks?* (the negative form of the underlined verb) Go over the example with the class.
2. Have students complete the exercise individually. Collect for assessment.
3. If necessary, have students review:
   2.1 Present Continuous Tense (p. 46)
   2.6 The Future Tense with *Will* (p. 66)
   2.7 The Future Tense with *Be Going To* (p. 69).

Lesson Review

To use Part 3 as a review, assign it as homework or use it as an in-class activity to be completed individually or in pairs. Check answers and review errors as a class. Reteach grammar points that students haven't mastered. Then student learning may be assessed using a test generated from the Assessment CD-ROM with *ExamView Pro.*

PART 4

1. Part 4 may also be used as an in-class test to assess student performance, in addition to the Assessment CD-ROM with *ExamView Pro*. Have students read the direction line. Ask: ***What kind of questions do we write?*** (*yes/no* questions) Point out that the answers should be based on the conversation in Part 2. Go over the example with the class.
2. Have students complete the exercise individually. Collect for assessment.
3. If necessary, have students review:
   2.3 Questions with the Present Continuous Tense (p. 51)
   2.6 The Future Tense with *Will* (p. 66)
   2.7 The Future Tense with *Be Going To* (p. 69).

PART 5

1. Part 5 may also be used as an in-class test to assess student performance, in addition to the Assessment CD-ROM with *ExamView Pro*. Have students read the direction line. Ask: ***What kind of questions are you going to write?*** (*wh-* questions) Go over the examples with the class. Remind students that an answer isn't necessary.
2. Have students complete the exercise individually. Collect for assessment.
3. If necessary, have students review:
   2.3 Questions with the Present Continuous Tense (p. 51)
   2.6 The Future Tense with *Will* (p. 66)
   2.7 The Future Tense with *Be Going To* (p. 69).

PART 4 Write *a yes/no* question about the words in parentheses ( ). Then write a short answer based on the conversation in Part 2 on pages 82–83.

EXAMPLE **Sue is busy. (her husband)**
Is her husband busy? Yes, he is.

1. **Sue's husband is helping her pack. (her sister)**
   Is her sister helping her pack? No, she isn't.
2. **Her husband works in an office. (at home)**
   Does he work at home? Yes, he does.
3. **Her present apartment has an extra room for an office. (for her father)**
   Does her present apartment have an extra room for her father? No it doesn't.
4. **Professional movers will move the furniture. (her friends)**
   Will her friends move the furniture? No, they won't
5. **Mary is staying home this week. (her husband)**
   Is her husband staying home this week? Yes, he is.
6. **Mary's going to move. (Sue)**
   Is Sue going to move? No, she isn't.

PART 5 Write *a wh-* question about the words in parentheses ( ). An answer is not necessary.

EXAMPLE **Mary's packing now. (why)**
Why is Mary packing?

1. **They're going to move to a bigger apartment. (why)**
   Why are they going to move to a bigger apartment?
2. **Her husband needs an extra bedroom. (why)**
   Why does her husband need an extra bedroom?
3. **She doesn't want her friends to help her move. (why)**
   Why doesn't she want her friend to help her move?
4. **Her father is going to come soon. (when)**
   When is her father going to come?
5. **Bill is calling Mary now. (why)**
   Why is Bill calling Mary?
6. **They'll use professional movers. (when)**
   When will they use professional movers?

84 Lesson 2

Lesson Review

To use Parts 4 and 5 as a review, assign them as homework or use them as in-class activities to be completed individually or in pairs. Check answers and review errors as a class. Reteach grammar points that students haven't mastered. Then student learning may be assessed using a test generated from the Assessment CD-ROM with *ExamView Pro*.

EXPANSION ACTIVITIES

Classroom Activities

1. Check (√) your predictions about the future. Form a small group and discuss your predictions with your group. Give reasons for your beliefs.

a. ____ People are going to have fewer children than they do today.
b. ____ People will live longer.
c. ____ People will have a healthier life.
d. ____ People are going to be happier.
e. ____ People will be lonelier.
f. ____ People will be more educated.
g. ____ Everyone is going to have a computer.
h. ____ There will be a cure for cancer and other serious illnesses.
i. ____ There will be a cure for the common cold.

2. Check (√) the activities that you plan to do soon. Form a group of between five and seven students. Ask questions about the items another student checked.

EXAMPLE √ move
When are you going to move?
Why are you moving?
Are your friends going to help you?
Are you going to rent a truck?
Where are you going to move to?

a. ____ send an e-mail
b. ____ visit a friend
c. ____ invite guests to my house
d. ____ buy something new
e. ____ take a vacation
f. ____ celebrate a birthday or holiday
g. ____ go to a concert or sporting event
h. ____ transfer to another school
i. ____ move
j. ____ take the citizenship test
k. ____ start a new job
l. ____ have an out-of-town visitor
m. ____ get married

Expansion Activities

These expansion activities provide opportunities for students to interact with one another and further develop their speaking and writing skills. Encourage students to use grammar from this lesson whenever possible.

To save class time, assign parts of the activities as homework. Then use class time for interaction and communication. If students do not need additional speaking practice, some of the activities may be assigned as writing activities for homework, or skipped altogether.

CLASSROOM ACTIVITIES

1. Have students complete the checklist on their own. Then have students get into groups to discuss their predictions (e.g., *I think people are going to have fewer children than they do today. These days, both men and women work. They don't have time or money for big families. I agree/disagree.*). Circulate to observe pair work. Give help as needed.
2. Have students complete the checklist on their own. Then have students get into groups to ask and answer questions about their plans. Instruct students to ask *wh-* questions and *yes/no* questions. Encourage them to use the future tense. Circulate to observe pair work. Give help as needed.

WRITE ABOUT IT

1. Briefly model the activity with the class. Talk a little about what your life will be like in 10 years (e.g., *In 10 years, I will only work part-time. I will buy a house in Puerto Rico and live there during the winter.*). Collect for assessment and/or have students present their paragraphs to a group.
2. Help students brainstorm a list of activities and write them on the board (e.g., *eat, walk, read the newspaper, watch TV, volunteer at the hospital, take a nap*). Collect for assessment and/or have students present their paragraphs to a group.
3. Briefly model the activity with the class. Talk a little about what your life will be like when you retire (e.g., *I'm going to buy a house in Puerto Rico and live there during the winter. In the spring and the summer, I'm going to visit my sons, daughters and grandchildren.*). Collect for assessment and/or have students present their paragraphs to a group.

OUTSIDE ACTIVITIES

1. Have students discuss the results of their interviews in a group.
2. Have students discuss their observations in a group. Say: *Discuss behaviors you observed that are different from behaviors in your native country or culture.*

INTERNET ACTIVITIES

1. Say: *Find at least five products or services that you think would be very helpful for an elderly person.* Have volunteers talk about their findings. Vote on the most useful product or service.
2. Who's going to live the longest? Do a class survey.
3. Ask students to find short articles on baby boomers. Have students give a short oral summary of the articles they found.
4. Have students create a presentation of the retirement community they researched. Ask students to include information on cost, types of activities, and types of housing. Vote on the best place to live.

Write About it

1. Write a short composition telling how you think your life will be when you are ten years older than you are now. *Sample beginning*: I'm 25 years old now. When I'm 35 years old, I think I will . . .
2. Write a short composition describing the life of an old person you know—a family member, a friend, a neighbor, etc.
3. Write a short composition telling what you want your life to be like when you retire.

Outside Activities

1. Give the list from Classroom Activity 1 to a native speaker of English. Find out his or her predictions. Report to the class something interesting that the American told you.
2. Keep a small notebook and a pen with you at all times for a week. Write down all the behaviors of older people that seem strange to you. Observe food, clothes, shopping, recreation, relationships between parents and children, behaviors on public transportation, etc. Write what people are doing as you are observing.

EXAMPLE An old woman is standing on the bus. No one is giving her a seat.
An old man is jogging in the park.

Internet Activities

1. Find a Web site for the elderly. Find out what kinds of products and services are available for senior citizens. Search under *senior citizens* or try the *National Council of Senior Citizens* (NCSC) or *American Association of Retired Persons* (AARP).
2. Look for a life expectancy calculator on the Internet. Calculate how long you will probably live.
3. At a search engine, type in *baby boomers*. Find an article about the baby boomers and bring it to class.
4. Find information about a retirement community in the area where you live. Get information about the cost, types of activities, and types of housing.

Additional Activities at http://elt.thomson.com/gic

86 Lesson 2

Write About it Variation

Have students exchange first drafts with a partner. Ask students to help their partners edit their drafts. Refer students to the Editing Advice on pages 80–81.

LESSON 3

GRAMMAR

Habitual Past with *Used To*
The Simple Past Tense

CONTEXT: Working Towards a Better Life

Equal Rights for All
George Dawson—Life Is So Good

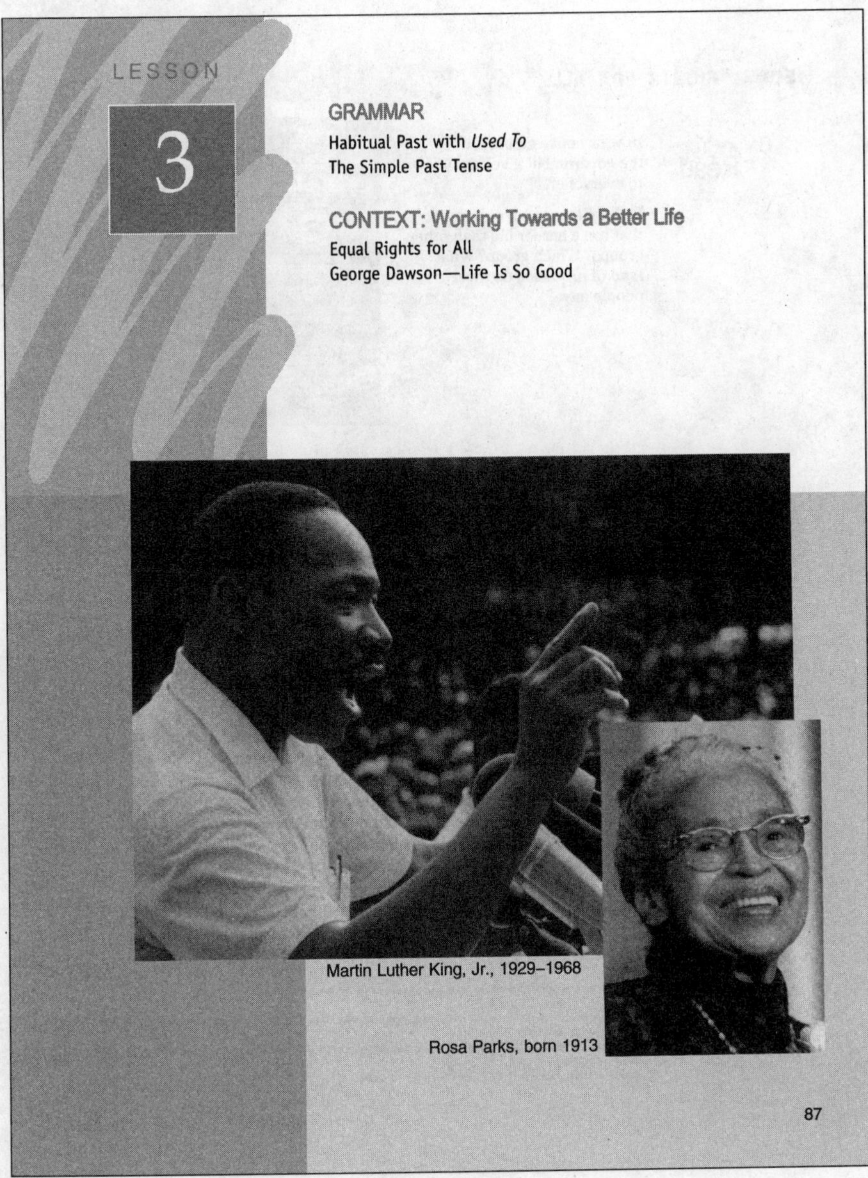

Martin Luther King, Jr., 1929–1968

Rosa Parks, born 1913

87

Lesson | 3

Lesson Overview

GRAMMAR

1. Briefly review other tenses students have learned. Ask: *What tense did we study in Lesson 1?* (simple present tense) *What tenses did we study in Lesson 2?* (present continuous and future)
2. Ask: *What will we study in this lesson?* (the habitual past with *used to* and the simple past tense) *Can anyone make a sentence with* used to? (e.g., *I used to go to the gym every day.*) Have students give examples. Write the examples on the board. Then ask volunteers for sentences in the simple past.

CONTEXT

1. Ask: *What will we learn about in this lesson?* (equal rights) Activate students' prior knowledge. Ask: *What are equal rights?*
2. Have students share their knowledge and personal experiences.

Photo

1. Direct students' attention to the photos. Ask: *Who are Martin Luther King, Jr., and Rosa Parks?* (leaders of the Civil Rights Movement)
2. Have students share their knowledge of Martin Luther King, Jr., and Rosa Parks.

To save class time, have students do the Test/Review at the end of the lesson, or administer a lesson test generated from the Assessment CD-ROM with *ExamView® Pro*. Skip sections of the lesson that students have already mastered. You may also assign some sections for self-study for extra credit.

Expansion

Theme The topic for this lesson can be enhanced with the following ideas:

1. A recording of the "I Have a Dream" speech by Martin Luther King, Jr.
2. Pictures of Dr. King and Rosa Parks
3. Pictures of Civil Rights marches, riots, etc.

Equal Rights for All (Reading)

1. Have students look at the photo. Ask: *What does the sign on the door say? What does it mean?*
2. Have students look at the title of the reading. Ask: *What is the reading about?* Have students use the title and photos to make predictions.
3. Preteach any vocabulary words your students may not know, such as *rights, inferior, reserve, arrest,* and *boycott.*

BEFORE YOU READ

1. Have students discuss the questions in pairs. Try to pair students of different cultures together.
2. Ask a few volunteers to share their answers with the class.

To save class time, skip "Before You Read" or have students prepare answers for homework ahead of time.

Reading CD 1, Track 25

1. Have students first read the text silently. Tell them to pay special attention to simple past tense verbs and *used to* + base form. Then play the audio and have students read along silently.
2. Check students' comprehension. Ask questions such as: *When did slavery end in the U.S.?* (in 1865) *In what ways did blacks continue to suffer discrimination even after slavery ended?* (Businesses and schools were segregated.) *Who refused to give her bus seat to white people?* (Rosa Parks)

To save class time, have students do the reading for homework ahead of time.

DID YOU KNOW ?

Mahatma Gandhi was born and raised in India and then later studied law in England. After his studies, he worked in South Africa where he witnessed first hand the terrible prejudices people of color faced. He worked to end the injustices immigrant Indian workers endured there and was often sent to jail. It was in South Africa where he began to develop his philosophy of passive resistance. Back in India, he took the lead in the struggle for independence from Britain. He often fasted to end the violence between the British, Hindu, ad Muslims. He was assassinated in 1948.

EQUAL RIGHTS FOR ALL

Before You Read

1. In your native country, does the government give equality to everyone?
2. Is there one group of people that has a harder life than other groups? Which group? What kind of problems do these people have?

Read the following article. Pay special attention to simple past tense verbs and *used to* + base form.

Today all people in the United States have equal rights under the law. But this **was** not always the case, especially for African-Americans[1]. Even though slavery in the U.S. **ended** in 1865, blacks **continued** to suffer discrimination[2] and segregation[3], especially in the South. Many hotels, schools, and restaurants **were** for whites only. Many businesses there **used to have** signs in their windows that **said:** "Blacks Not Allowed." Black children **used to go** to separate, and often inferior, schools. Many professions **were** for whites only. Even in sports, blacks could not join the major leagues; there **used to be** separate leagues for blacks.

In many places in the South, buses **used to reserve** the front seats for white people. One evening in December of 1955, a 42-year-old woman, Rosa Parks, **got** on a bus in Montgomery, Alabama, to go home from work. She **was** tired when she **sat** down. When some white people **got** on the crowded bus, the bus driver **ordered** Ms. Parks to stand up. Ms. Parks **refused** to leave her seat. The bus driver **called** the police, and they **came** and **arrested** Ms. Parks.

Martin Luther King, Jr.[4], a black minister living in Montgomery, Alabama, **wanted** to put an end to discrimination. When King **heard** about Ms. Park's arrest, he **told** African-Americans in Montgomery to boycott the bus company. People who **used to** ride the bus to work **decided** to walk instead. As a result of the boycott, the Supreme Court **outlawed**[5] discrimination on public transportation.

Did You Know?

Martin Luther King, Jr., was interested in the ideas of Mahatma Gandhi of India. He studied and used Gandhi's technique of nonviolent protest.

[1] *African-Americans,* whose ancestors came from Africa as slaves, are sometimes called "blacks." They used to be called "negroes" or "colored."
[2] *Discrimination* means giving some people unfair treatment, especially because of race, age, religion, etc.
[3] *Segregation* means separation of the races.
[4] When a father and son have the same name, the father uses *senior* (Sr.) after his name; the son puts *junior* (Jr.) after his name.
[5] *To outlaw* means to make an action illegal or against the law.

88 Lesson 3

Reading Variation

To practice listening skills, have students first listen to the audio alone. Ask a few comprehension questions. Repeat the audio if necessary. Then have them open their books and read along as they listen to the audio.

Reading Glossary

arrest: to seize or hold something by legal authority
boycott: a refusal for political reasons to buy certain products or do business with a certain store or company
inferior: lower in quality
reserve: to hold or keep for oneself
rights: permission to do something guaranteed by law

In 1964, about 100 years after the end of slavery, Congress **passed** a new law that officially **gave** equality to all Americans. This law **made** discrimination in employment and education illegal. King **won** the Nobel Peace Prize[6] for his work in creating a better world.

In 1968, a great tragedy **occurred.** Someone **shot** and **killed** King when he was only 39 years old.

In 1983, Martin Luther King's birthday (January 15) **became** a national holiday.

African-American Firsts	
1947	Jackie Robinson was the first African-American to play on a major league baseball team.
1983	Guion Bluford was the first African-American to go into space.
1989	Oprah Winfrey became the first African-American to own her own television and film production company.
1997	Tiger Woods, whose father is African-American and whose mother is Thai, became both the first African-American and the first Asian-American to win the Masters golf tournament.
2001	Halle Berry was the first African-American woman to win an Oscar for best actress.
2001	General Colin Powell became the first African-American secretary of state.
2005	Condoleezza Rice became the first female African-American secretary of state.

Tiger Woods

Halle Berry

[6] The *Nobel Peace Prize* is one of six international prizes given once a year for great work in literature, science, economics, and world peace.

Expansion

Theme Ask students about champions of civil rights from their native countries (e.g., Mahatma Gandhi, the students of Tiananmen Square, etc.) or of their own countries' "firsts."

3.1 | Habitual Past with *Used To*

1. Have students go through the reading on pages 88–89 and find examples of *used to*. Write students' examples on the board (e.g., *Many businesses there used to have signs in their windows that said: "Blacks Not Allowed."*). Ask: *How do you form the habitual past with* used to? (*used to* + base form) Ask students questions about the sentences, such as: *Do these businesses still have the signs? Are there still separate sports teams for blacks? Do buses still reserve front seats for whites?*
2. Have students look at grammar chart **3.1.** Say: Used to *shows a habit or custom from the past. The custom is no longer practiced.* Go through the examples. Point out that the negative is *didn't use to*.
3. Compare the use of the simple past (an event that happened once in the past) and *used to* (a custom that was followed over time in the past). Go over the examples in the Language Note.

EXERCISE 1

1. Tell students that this exercise is about the things they used to do as a child. Have students read the direction line. Go over the example in the book. Have a volunteer complete #1 for the class.
2. Have students complete Exercise 1 individually. Then have them compare their answers in pairs. Circulate to observe the pair work. If necessary, check the answers as a class.
3. If necessary, review grammar chart **3.1** on page 90.

3.1 | Habitual Past with *Used To*

Examples	Explanation
Black children **used to** have separate schools. Many professions **used to** be for white people only. There **used to** be special baseball teams for black people.	*Used to* + a base form shows a habit or custom over a past period of time. This custom no longer exists.
Some restaurants **didn't use to** serve African-Americans.	For negatives, omit the *d* in *used to*.

Language Note:
Used to is for past habits or customs. It is not for an action that happened once or a few times.
Many restaurants **used to** serve white people only. (This happened over a period of time.)
Rosa Parks **used to** ride the bus to work. (This happened over a period of time.)
In 1955, Rosa Parks **got** on the bus and **refused** to stand. (This happened one time.)
The bus driver **called** the police. (This happened one time.)

EXERCISE 1 ABOUT YOU Tell which of the following you used to do when you were a child.

EXAMPLE cry a lot
I used to cry a lot.
OR
I didn't use to cry a lot.

Answers will vary.

1. enjoy school
2. obey my parents
3. attend religious school
4. play with dolls
5. play soccer
6. fight with other children
7. draw pictures
8. have a pet
9. tell lies
10. read mystery stories
11. live on a farm
12. eat a lot of candy
13. live with my grandparents
14. believe in Santa Claus
15. watch a lot of TV
16. read comic books

90 Lesson 3

Expansion

Exercise 1 Review how to make a question with *used to*. Write on the board: *Did you use to cry a lot when you were a child?* Remind students that in questions, as in negatives, *use to* is written without the *d*. In pairs, have students ask each other questions from Exercise 1 and answer them (e.g., *Did you use to enjoy school when you were a child? Yes, I did.*).

EXERCISE 2 ABOUT YOU Name something. Practice *used to.*

EXAMPLE Name something you used to know when you were in elementary school.

I used to know the names of all the presidents (but I don't know them anymore).

Answers will vary.

1. Name something you used to do when you were a child.
2. Tell what kind of stories you used to enjoy when you were a child.
3. Name something you used to believe when you were a child.
4. Name something you used to like to eat when you were a child.
5. Tell about some things your parents, grandparents, or teachers used to tell you when you were a child.
6. Tell about some things you used to do when you were younger.

EXERCISE 3 ABOUT YOU Write sentences comparing the way you used to live with the way you live now. Share your sentences with a partner or with the entire class.

EXAMPLES *I used to live with my whole family. Now I live alone.*

I used to work in a restaurant. Now I'm a full-time student.

I didn't use to speak English at all. Now I speak English pretty well.

Ideas for sentences:
school job hobbies apartment / house family life friends

Answers will vary.

1. ______________________________
2. ______________________________
3. ______________________________
4. ______________________________
5. ______________________________

Habitual Past with *Used To;* The Simple Past Tense 91

EXERCISE 2

1. Have students read the direction line. Go over the example in the book. Say: *You will name something you used to do or know, etc., in the past but that you don't do or know now.* Model the example for the class. Have a volunteer model the example as well.
2. Have students complete Exercise 2 individually. Then have them compare their answers in pairs. Circulate to observe the pair work.
3. If necessary, review grammar chart **3.1** on page 90.

To save time, have students do this exercise for homework.

EXERCISE 3

1. Have students read the direction line. Say: *What did you use to do, and what do you do now? Use your own ideas or the ideas listed here.* Go over the examples in the book. Model the exercise for the class.
2. Have students complete Exercise 3 individually. Then have them compare their answers in pairs.
3. If necessary, review grammar chart **3.1** on page 90.

To save class time, have students do half of the exercise in class and complete the other half for homework. Or assign the entire exercise for homework.

Expansion

Exercise 2 Have students create a question for each item in Exercise 2 (e.g., *What did you use to do when you were a child? What kind of stories did you use to enjoy when you were a child?*). Then have students ask a new partner the questions.

Exercise 3 Say: *Find out something new from three of your classmates.* Have students mingle around the room asking and answering questions about the past (e.g., *Do you live in a house? I used to live in an apartment, but now I live in a house.*). Then have students report to the class the information they learned about the three classmates.

EXERCISE 4

1. Ask: *Do you think you're a different person now than you were in the past?* Have students read the direction line. Go over the example. Ask a volunteer to model the example.
2. Have students complete Exercise 4 individually. Then have them compare their answers in pairs.
3. If necessary, review grammar chart **3.1** on page 90.

To save class time, have students do half of the exercise as a class and complete the other half for homework.

George Dawson (Reading)

1. Have students look at the photo on page 93. Ask: *Who was George Dawson?* Have students make predictions.
2. Preteach any vocabulary words your students may not know, such as *witness, wonder,* and *trouble.*

BEFORE YOU READ

1. Have students discuss the questions in pairs. Try to pair students of different cultures together.
2. Ask for a few volunteers to share their answers with the class.

To save class time, have students do the reading for homework ahead of time.

Reading *CD 1, Track 26*

1. Have students first read the text silently. Tell them to pay special attention to the simple past tense. Then play the audio and have students read along silently.
2. Check students' comprehension. Ask questions such as: *How many centuries did Mr. Dawson live in?* (three) *Why did he have to go to work when he was four years old?* (His family was very poor.) *Where did he work most of the time when he was an adult?* (on a dairy farm) *When did he learn to write?* (when he was 98 years old) *Who helped him write his biography?* (an elementary school teacher) *What was the main message in his book?* (Life is good.)

To save class time, have students do the reading for homework ahead of time.

EXERCISE 4 A young man is comparing how his life used to be five years ago and how his life is now. Complete his statements. Answers may vary.

EXAMPLE I used to *be lazy*. Now I'm hard-working.

1. I used to *spend my money*. Now I save my money.
2. I used to *be a lazy student*. Now I'm a serious student.
3. I used to *live with my family*. Now I live alone.
4. I used to *watch TV all the time*. Now I almost never watch TV.
5. I used to *go out after work*. Now I come home after work and study.
6. I used to *have long hair*. Now I have short hair.
7. I used to *walk everywhere*. Now I have a car and drive everywhere.
8. I used to *weigh a lot*. Now I'm on a diet and I'm losing weight.
9. I used to *do what my parents told me*. Now I make my own decisions.
10. I used to *use cash*. Now I use my credit card for most of my purchases.

GEORGE DAWSON—LIFE IS SO GOOD

Before You Read

1. Is it necessary to know how to read in order to have a good life?
2. Is it hard for old people to learn new things?

Read the following article. Pay special attention to the simple past tense.

George Dawson **lived** in three centuries—the end of the nineteenth, all through the twentieth, and the start of the twenty-first. He **was** born in 1898 in Texas, the grandson of slaves. He **was** the oldest of five children. His family **was** very poor, so George **had** to go to work to help his family. He **started** working full-time for his father when he was four years old. As a result, he **didn't attend** school. He **worked at** many jobs during his lifetime: he **chopped** wood, **swept** floors, **helped** build the railroad, and **cleaned** houses. For most of his adult life, he **ran** farm machinery at a dairy farm[7].

[7] On a *dairy farm*, cows are used to produce milk and milk products.

Expansion

Exercise 4 Have students discuss their responses to Exercise 4 in groups. Ask: *Who has changed a lot? Who is still the same?*

Reading Variation

To practice listening skills, have students first listen to the audio alone. Ask a few comprehension questions. Repeat the audio if necessary. Then have them open their books and read along as they listen to the audio.

Reading Glossary

trouble: difficulty, distress, especially by accident
witness: to see, observe an incident
wonder: to express an interest in knowing

In his lifetime, great technological changes **occurred:** cars, television, airplanes, spaceships, and computers **came** into being. He **saw** several wars and political changes in the U.S. He **outlived**[8] four wives and two of his seven children.

He **lived** at a time when African-Americans **had** fewer opportunities than they do today. And he **lived** in the South, where there **was** a lot of discrimination against African-Americans; African-Americans **were** segregated from others, and job possibilities **were** limited. By the end of his life, he **saw** others have the opportunities that he didn't have when he **was** young. He **witnessed** the success of many African-Americans.

George Dawson (1898–2001)

Because he **didn't know** how to read or write, he **signed** his name with an X. Then, when he **was** 98 years old, Dawson **started** attending school. He **went** to adult literacy classes in Dallas County. The teacher **asked** him, "Do you know the alphabet?" He **answered,** "No." Over the next few years, his teacher, Carl Henry, **taught** Dawson to read and write. Dawson **said,** "Every morning I get up and I wonder what I might learn that day."

In 1998, an elementary school teacher, Richard Glaubman, **read** an article about Dawson in the newspaper. He **wanted** to meet Dawson. Together Glaubman and Dawson **wrote** a book about Dawson's life, called *Life Is So Good*. In this book, Dawson tells about what makes a person happy. Dawson **had** a close family and never **felt** lonely. He **learned** from his father to see the good things in life. His father **told** him, "We **were** born to die. You **didn't come** here to stay, and life is something to enjoy." He **taught** his children to see the richness in life. Dawson says in the book, "We make our own way. Trouble is out there, but a person can leave it alone and just do the right thing. Then, if trouble still finds you, you've done the best you can. . . . People worry too much. Life is good, just the way it is."

Excerpt from Dawson's book:
"My first day of school was January 4, 1996. I was ninety-eight years old and I'm still going. . . . I'm up by five-thirty to make my lunch, pack my books, and go over my schoolwork. Books was[9] something missing from my life for so long. . . . I learned to read my ABC's in two days—I was in a hurry. . . . Now I am a man that can read."

[8] *To outlive* means to live longer than others.
[9] These are Dawson's exact words. However, this sentence is not grammatically correct. The correct way is: Books *were* . . . .

3.2 | Past Tense of *Be*

1. Have students cover up grammar chart **3.2** on page 94. Activate prior knowledge. Ask: *What are the two forms of the past tense of* be? *(was, were)*
2. Write the following on the board:
   Life____hard for George Dawson.
   He____poor.
   His grandparents____slaves.
   There____discrimination in the South.
   There____many changes in the twentieth century.
   Dawson's life____(not) easy.
   Education and books____(not) available to Dawson as a child.
   Dawson____born in 1898.
   Dawson____married four times.
   Say: *Fill in the blanks with the correct verb.*
3. Have students look at grammar chart **3.2.** Say: *Check your work with the chart.* Review the examples and explanations in the grammar chart. Review the contractions for *was not (wasn't)* and *were not (weren't)*. Have students work in pairs to write sentences for the adjectives in the chart that end in *-ed*.
4. Compare the affirmative and negative statements and questions.

3.2 | Past Tense of *Be*

The past tense of *be* has two forms: *was* and *were.*

Examples	Explanation
Life **was** hard for George Dawson. He **was** poor. His grandparents **were** slaves.	The past of the verb *be* has two forms: *was* and *were*. I, he, she, it → was we, you, they → were
There **was** discrimination in the South. There **were** many changes in the twentieth century.	After *there*, use *was* or *were* depending on the noun that follows. Use *was* with a singular noun. Use *were* with a plural noun.
Dawson's life **wasn't** easy. Education and books **weren't** available to Dawson as a child.	To make a negative statement, put *not* after *was* or *were*. The contraction for *was not* is *wasn't*. The contraction for *were not* is *weren't*.
Dawson **was born** in 1898.	Always use a form of *be* with *born*.
Dawson **was** married four times. He **was** interested in reading at the age of 98.	Use *be* with adjectives that end in *-ed*: *crowded, tired, bored, interested, worried, married, divorced, allowed,* and *permitted.*

Compare statements and questions

Affirmative Statements and Questions

Wh- Word	*Was/Were* *Wasn't/Weren't*	Subject	*Was/Were* *Wasn't/Weren't*	Complement	Short Answer
		Dawson	**was**	poor.	
		He	**wasn't**	in school.	
	Was	he		a slave?	No, he **wasn't.**
Where	**was**	he		from?	
Why	**wasn't**	he		in school?	

Negative Statements and Questions

Wh- Word	*Wasn't/Weren't*	Subject	*Wasn't/Weren't*	Complement
		Dawson	**wasn't**	in school.
Why	**wasn't**	he		in school?
		There	**weren't**	many opportunities.
Why	**weren't**	there		many opportunities?

94 Lesson 3

EXERCISE 5 Fill in the blanks with an appropriate word. Answers may vary.

EXAMPLE George Dawson ___was___ poor.

1. Dawson was ___born___ in 1898.
2. At that time, there ___was___ a lot of discrimination.
3. His parents ___were___ poor.
4. Life for most African-Americans in the South was ___hard___.
5. Job possibilities for African-Americans ___were___ limited.
6. When he was ___98___, he learned how to read.
7. Dawson's father used to tell him, "We ___were___ born to die."
8. He was poor, but he wasn't ___unhappy___.

EXERCISE 6 Fill in the blanks with the correct word(s).

EXAMPLE Martin Luther King, Jr., ___was___ a great American.

1. Martin Luther King, Jr., ___was___ born in Georgia.
2. He (not) ___wasn't___ born in Alabama.
3. He and his father ___were___ ministers.
4. He ___was___ tired of discrimination toward African-Americans.
5. African-Americans (not) ___were not___ allowed to enter some restaurants in the South.
6. There ___was___ discrimination on public transportation.
7. ___Was there___ discrimination in employment? Yes, there ___was___.
8. Rosa Parks was a citizen of Montgomery, Alabama. ___Was she___ an African-American? Yes, she was.
9. She was tired and took a seat on the bus. Why ___was she___ tired?
10. African-Americans weren't allowed to sit down on a crowded bus in Montgomery. Why ___weren't they___ allowed to sit down?
11. How old ___was he___ when he was killed? He was 39.

EXERCISE 5

1. Tell students that this exercise is based on the reading on pages 92–93. Have students read the direction line. Go over the example in the book.
2. Have students complete the rest of Exercise 5 individually. Then have them compare their answers in pairs. Finally, check the answers as a class.
3. If necessary, review grammar chart **3.2** on page 94.

EXERCISE 6

1. Have students read the direction line. Go over the example in the book.
2. Have students complete the exercise individually. Go over the answers as a class.
3. If necessary, review grammar chart **3.2** on page 94.

To save class time, have students do half of the exercise in class and complete the other half for homework. Or assign the entire exercise for homework.

3.3 | The Simple Past Tense of Regular Verbs

1. Have students go back to the reading on pages 92 and 93. Say: *Find verbs in the past that end in -ed* (*lived, started, worked, chopped*, etc.). Write the verbs on the board. Then ask students to tell you the base form of the verbs. Write them next to the past tense (*live, start, work, chop*).
2. Have students look at grammar chart **3.3**. Explain that to form the simple past of regular verbs, we add *-ed*. If the verb ends in *-e*, add only *-d*. Review the examples in the chart. Remind students that the past forms are the same for all persons. If necessary, review the spelling and pronunciation rules for the past tense form in Appendix A.
3. Explain that verbs that come after *to* are in the infinitive form, not the past, so their endings do not change.

EXERCISE 7

1. Have students read the direction line. Ask: *What do we write in the blanks?* (the past tense of the verb) Go over the example.
2. Have students complete Exercise 7 individually. Then check the answers as a class.
3. If necessary, review grammar chart **3.3** on page 96.

EXERCISE 8

1. Have students read the direction line. Go over the example.
2. Have students complete the exercise individually. Check the answers as a class.
3. If necessary, review grammar chart **3.3** on page 96.

To save class time, have students do half of the exercise in class and complete the other half for homework. Or assign the entire exercise for homework.

3.3 | The Simple Past Tense of Regular Verbs

To form the simple past tense of regular verbs, add *-ed* to the base form.[10]

Examples	Explanation	
	Base Form	Past Form
Dawson **signed** his name with an X.	sign	**signed**
Dawson **learned** a lot from his father.	learn	**learned**
African-Americans **suffered** discrimination.	suffer	**suffered**
Dawson **lived** to be 103 years old.	live	**lived**
	If the verb ends in an *-e*, add only *-d*.[10] The past forms are the same for all persons.	
Dawson **learned** *to read and write*. A teacher **wanted** *to meet* Dawson.	The verb after *to* does **not** use the past form.	

EXERCISE 7 Fill in the blanks with the past tense of the verb in parentheses ( ).

EXAMPLE Dawson ___*learned*___ (learn) to read when he was 98.

1. He ___*lived*___ (live) many, many years.
2. He ___*signed*___ (sign) his name with an X.
3. He ___*outlived*___ (outlive) all his wives.
4. Many changes ___*occurred*___ (occur) during his long life.
5. He ___*attended*___ (attend) school when he was 98.
6. His teacher ___*asked*___ (ask), "Do you know the alphabet?"
7. Dawson ___*learned*___ (learn) from his father to enjoy life.
8. Richard Glaubman ___*wanted*___ (want) to meet Dawson.

EXERCISE 8 Fill in the blanks with the simple past tense of the verb in parentheses ( ).

EXAMPLE King ___*lived*___ (live) in the South.

1. Slavery ___*ended*___ (end) in 1865, but discrimination ___*continued*___ (continue).

[10] For a review of the spelling and pronunciation of the -ed past form, see Appendix A.

2. King *wanted* (want) equality for all people.

3. King *worked* (work) as a minister.

4. In many places, the law *separated* (separate) whites from blacks.

5. In 1968, a great tragedy *occurred* (occur). Someone *killed* (kill) King.

6. The bus driver *ordered* (order) Rosa Parks to stand up, but she *refused* (refuse).

7. The bus driver *called* (call) the police.

8. The police *arrested* (arrest) Ms. Parks.

9. King *organized* (organize) a peaceful protest.

10. In 1964, Congress *changed* (change) the law.

11. Black children *attended* (attend) separate schools.

Culture Note

Direct students to the photo. Ask: *Do you know what's going on here? What do the signs say?* In 1954, the Supreme Court declared separate but equal education unconstitutional. This landmark case is known as *Brown v. Board of Education.* After *Brown v. Board of Education*, the courts made most remaining forms of segregation illegal.

Expansion

Exercise 8 Have students prepare a short presentation about an event in U.S. history or in the history of their native countries. Have students create a timeline of their events. Brainstorm ideas with the class. Ask volunteers to talk about their events in front of the class.

3.4 | The Simple Past of Irregular Verbs

1. Have students cover up grammar chart **3.4** on page 98. Write the following sentences on the board:
   Dawson —— (have) a close family.
   He —— (go) to classes when he was 98.
   Carl Henry —— (teach) him to read.
   Say: *Fill in the blanks with the past of the verb in the parentheses.*
2. Then have students look at grammar chart **3.4.** Say: *Check your work with the grammar chart.* Explain that many past tense verbs are irregular and that their forms must be memorized. Point out the chart of irregular past tense verbs on page 98.
3. To help students memorize the simple past tense of irregular verbs, give students quizzes on the irregular forms. Group the verbs by spelling patterns, and space the quizzes as appropriate. Tell students that there is an alphabetical list of irregular verbs in Appendix M.

3.4 | The Simple Past Tense of Irregular Verbs[11]

Many past-tense verbs are irregular. They do not have a *-ed* ending.

Verbs with no change				Final *d* changes to *t*	
beat	fit	put	spit	bend—bent	send—sent
bet	hit	quit	split	build—built	spend—spent
cost	hurt	set	spread	lend—lent	
cut	let	shut			

Verbs with Vowel Changes			
feel—felt	mean—meant[12]	dig—dug	sting—stung
keep—kept	sleep—slept	hang—hung	strike—struck
leave—left	sweep—swept	spin—spun	swing—swung
lose—lost	weep—wept	stick—stuck	win—won
awake—awoke	speak—spoke	begin—began	sing—sang
break—broke	steal—stole	drink—drank	sink—sank
choose—chose	wake—woke	forbid—forbade	spring—sprang
freeze—froze		ring—rang	swim—swam
		shrink—shrank	
bring—brought	fight—fought	blow—blew	grow—grew
buy—bought	teach—taught	draw—drew	know—knew
catch—caught	think—thought	fly—flew	throw—threw
arise—arose	rise—rose	bleed—bled	meet—met
drive—drove	shine—shone	feed—fed	read—read[13]
ride—rode	write—wrote	flee—fled	speed—sped
		lead—led	
sell—sold	tell—told	find—found	wind—wound
mistake—mistook	take—took	lay—laid	say—said[14]
shake—shook		pay—paid	
swear—swore	wear—wore	bite—bit	light—lit
tear—tore		hide—hid	slide—slid
become—became		fall—fell	hold—held
come—came			
eat—ate			
forgive—forgave		run—ran	
give—gave		sit—sat	
lie—lay		see—saw	
forget—forgot	shoot—shot	stand—stood	
get—got		understand—understood	

Miscellaneous Changes		
be—was/were	go—went	hear—heard
do—did	have—had	make—made

[11] For an alphabetical list of irregular verbs, see Appendix M.

Language Note:
[12] There is a change in the vowel sound. *Meant* rhymes with *sent.*
[13] The past form of *read* is pronounced like the color *red.*
[14] *Said* rhymes with *bed.*

EXERCISE 9 Fill in the blanks with the past tense of the verb in parentheses ( ).

EXAMPLE Dawson *had* (have) a hard life.

1. His father was poor, so he *had* (have) to work.
2. He *began* (begin) to work for his father when he was four years old.
3. He *saw* (see) many changes in his lifetime.
4. He *became* (become) interested in reading when he was 98.
5. He *went* (go) to the adult literacy program in Dallas County.
6. His teacher *taught* (teach) him the alphabet.
7. Dawson *said* (say), "I wonder what I might learn today."

EXERCISE 10 Fill in the blanks with the past tense of the verb in parentheses ( ).

EXAMPLE King *fought* (fight) for the rights of all people.

1. King *was* (be) born in 1929.
2. King *became* (become) a minister.
3. He *got* (get) married in 1953.
4. He *found* (find) a job in a church in Montgomery, Alabama.

EXERCISE 9

1. Tell students that this exercise is about George Dawson. Have students read the direction line. Say: *If you don't know the past tense of these irregular verbs, find them on the chart on page 98.* Go over the example in the book.
2. Have students complete the exercise individually. Check the answers as a class.
3. If necessary, review grammar chart **3.4** on pages 98–99.

EXERCISE 10

1. Tell students that this exercise is about Martin Luther King, Jr. Have students read the direction line. Say: *If you don't know the past tense of these irregular verbs, find them on the chart on page 98.* Go over the example in the book.
2. Have students complete the exercise individually. Check the answers as a class.
3. If necessary, review grammar chart **3.4** on pages 98–99.

To save class time, have students do half of the exercise as a class and complete the other half for homework.

EXERCISE 11

CD 1, Track 27

1. Tell students that this exercise is about Oprah Winfrey, a famous TV personality in the U.S. Have students read the direction line. Go over the example in the book.
2. Have students complete Exercise 11 individually. Check answers as a class.
3. If necessary, review grammar charts **3.3** on page 96 and **3.4** on pages 98–99.

To save class time, have students do the exercise for homework.

5. Rosa Parks was tired and *sat* (sit) down on the bus.
6. Some white people *got* (get) on the bus.
7. The bus driver *told* (tell) Parks to stand up.
8. Police *came* (come) and arrested Parks.
9. King *heard* (hear) about her arrest.
10. In 1963, he *gave* (give) a beautiful speech in Washington, D.C.
11. Many people *went* (go) to see King in Washington in 1963.
12. King *won* (win) an important prize for his work.
13. A man *shot* (shoot) King in 1968.

EXERCISE 11 Fill in the blanks with the correct past tense form of the verb in parentheses ( ) in this short biography of Oprah Winfrey.

Oprah Winfrey, talk show host, publisher, and actress, is one of the richest women in the U.S. today. But she *came* (example: come) from a poor family. In fact, she *was* (1 be) born to unmarried teenage parents and *had* (2 have) a very difficult childhood. She *lived* (3 live) first with her grandmother, later with her mother, and when she was a teenager, she *went* (4 go) to live with her father. Her father *encouraged* (5 encourage) her to read a lot. She *entered* (6 enter) Tennessee State University in 1971 and *began* (7 begin) working as a reporter for a radio station at age 19. In 1976, Winfrey *moved* to

Oprah Winfrey

Exercise 11 Variation

To provide practice with listening skills, have students close their books and listen to the audio. Say: *In this listening selection, you will hear biographical information about Oprah Winfrey.* Repeat the audio as needed. Ask comprehension questions, such as: *Who is Oprah Winfrey?* (She's a talk show host, publisher, and actress.) *Was she always rich?* (No. She was born into a poor family.) *Did she attend university?* (yes) Then have students open their books and complete Exercise 11.

Baltimore and ___got___ (9 get) her own talk show on TV. It ___became___ (10 become) very popular.

In 1986, Oprah's show went national. By the end of its first year, the show ___brought___ (11 bring) in $125 million and Oprah ___earned___ (12 earn) $30 million. Around this time, Oprah ___began___ (13 begin) an acting career. In 2000, she ___started___ (14 start) publishing a magazine, *O: The Oprah Magazine*. Oprah ___went___ (15 go) from being a poor black farm girl from Mississippi to a national celebrity.

3.5 | Negative Statements

Compare affirmative (A) and negative (N) statements with past tense verbs.	
Examples	**Explanation**
A: Dawson **learned** to read when he was old. N: He **didn't learn** to read when he was a child.	For the negative past tense, we use *didn't* + base form for ALL verbs, regular and irregular.
A: Dawson **lived** in the South. N: He **didn't live** alone. A: He **knew** many things. N: He **didn't know** the alphabet. A: He **went** to school when he was old. N: He **didn't go** to school when he was young.	Compare: learned—didn't learn lived—didn't live knew—didn't know went—didn't go

Language Note:
Remember: Some past tense verbs are the same as the base form.
A. He **put** an X on the line.
N. He **didn't put** his name on the line.

3.5 | Negative Statements

1. Have students cover up grammar chart **3.5.** Ask students to go back to the reading on pages 92–93. Say: *Circle the negative verbs in the past tense.* Write students' examples on the board (*didn't attend* and *didn't know*).
2. Tell students to look at grammar chart **3.5.** Write on the board: *didn't* + base form. Explain that this is how the negative is formed for all verbs, regular and irregular.
3. Review all of the example sentences in the chart. Remind students that sometimes the base form and past form are the same for some irregular verbs. Go over the examples in the Language Note.

Expansion

Exercise 11 Have students write about a famous person from the U.S. or from their native country who overcame difficulties such as poverty and racism. Have students discuss the person they wrote about in small groups.

EXERCISE 12

1. Tell students that this exercise is about George Dawson. Have students read the direction line. Go over the example.
2. Have students complete the exercise individually. Then have them check answers in pairs.
3. If necessary, review grammar chart **3.5** on page 101.

EXERCISE 13

1. Tell students that this exercise is about Dr. Martin Luther King, Jr. Have students read the direction line. Go over the example in the book.
2. Have students complete the exercise individually. Then have students check answers in pairs.
3. If necessary, review grammar chart **3.5** on page 101.

To save class time, have students do half of the exercise in class and complete the other half for homework. Or assign the entire exercise for homework.

EXERCISE 12 Fill in the blanks with the negative form of the underlined word.

EXAMPLE **Dawson came from a poor family. He** *didn't come* **from a middle-class family.**

1. **He felt happy because he had a good family. He** *didn't feel* **lonely.**
2. **Children from families with money attended school. Dawson** *didn't attend* **school.**
3. **He went to school when he was old. He** *didn't go* **to school when he was young.**
4. **He learned to read when he was old. He** *didn't learn* **to read when he was a child.**
5. **He knew many things. He** *didn't know* **how to write or read.**
6. **Carl Henry taught Dawson. Richard Glaubman** *didn't teach* **Dawson.**

EXERCISE 13 Write the negative form of the underlined words.

EXAMPLE **Slavery ended in 1865. Discrimination** *didn't end***.**

1. **King lived in the South. He** *didn't live* **in the North.**
2. **King wanted equality for everyone. He** *didn't want* **separate schools for blacks and whites.**
3. **He thought about the future of his children. He** *didn't think* **about his own safety.**
4. **He believed in peace. He** *didn't believe* **in violence.**
5. **He became a minister. He** *didn't become* **a politician.**
6. **He was in jail for his protests. He** *wasn't* **in jail for a crime.**
7. **African-Americans had to stand on a crowded bus. White people** *didn't have* **to stand.**
8. **African-Americans rode the buses in Montgomery every day. They** *didn't ride* **the buses after the arrest of Rosa Parks.**
9. **King went to Memphis in 1968. His wife** *didn't go* **there.**
10. **He died violently. He** *didn't die* **peacefully.**

102 Lesson 3

Expansion

Exercise 12 Ask students if they know anyone like George Dawson. Have them discuss ordinary people who have achieved amazing things (e.g., ***My neighbor, David Goldberg, received a BA in history when he was 83 years old.***).

3.6 | Questions with the Simple Past Tense

Compare affirmative statements and questions

Wh- Word	*Did*	Subject	Verb	Complement	Short Answer
		Dawson	**learned**	to read.	
	Did	he	**learn**	to read when he was young?	No, he didn't.
When	**did**	he	**learn**	to read?	When he was 98.
		Dawson	**wrote**	a book.	
	Did	he	**write**	it alone?	No, he didn't.
Why	**did**	he	**write**	a book?	Because he wanted to tell his life story.

Language Note:
The base form is used in questions after *did.*

Compare negative statements and questions

Wh- Word	*Didn't*	Subject	Verb	Complement
		Dawson	**didn't learn** to read	when he was young.
Why	**didn't**	he	**learn** to read	when he was young?
		Dawson	**didn't go**	to school.
Why	**didn't**	he	**go**	to school?

EXERCISE 14 A student is interviewing her teacher about Martin Luther King, Jr. Fill in the blanks with the correct form of the verb.

S: Do you remember Martin Luther King, Jr.?

T: Of course I do. I ___saw___ *(example: see)* him on TV many times when I ___was___ *(1 be)* young.

S: ___Did you see___ *(2 see)* him on TV when he was in Washington, D.C.?

T: Yes, I ___did___ *(3)*. I remember his famous speech in Washington in 1963.

S: What ___did he speak___ *(4 speak)* about?

T: He ___spoke___ *(5 speak)* about equality for everyone.

Exercise 14 Variation

To provide practice with listening skills, have students close their books and listen to the audio. Say: *In this conversation, a student is interviewing her teacher about Martin Luther King, Jr.* Repeat the audio as needed. Ask comprehension questions, such as: *Where was Martin Luther King, Jr., when he made his famous speech in 1963?* (Washington, D.C.) *How many people were in Washington to hear his speech?* (250,000) *Who told the teacher's class about King's death?* (the high school principal) Then have students open their books and complete Exercise 14.

3.6 | Questions with the Simple Past Tense

1. Have students cover up grammar chart **3.6.** Write the following affirmative sentences on the board:
   Dawson learned to read.
   Dawson wrote a book.
   Say: *Write* yes/no *questions, short answers, and* wh- *questions for these two sentences.*
2. Then write the following negative sentences on the board:
   Dawson didn't learn to read when he was young.
   Dawson didn't go to school.
   Say: *Write negative questions with* why *for these two negative statements.*
3. Have students look at grammar chart **3.6.** Say: *Now compare your sentences with the sentences in the grammar chart.* Write on the board: Did + *subject* + *base form . . . ?* Explain that this is how *yes/no* questions are formed in the simple past for all verbs—regular and irregular. Review negative and affirmative short answers.
4. Now write on the board: Wh- *word* + did + *subject* + *base form . . . ?* Explain that this is how *wh-* questions are formed in the simple past for all verbs—regular and irregular.
5. Finally write: Why + didn't + *subject* + *base form . . . ?* Explain that this is how negative questions are formed in the simple past for all verbs—regular and irregular.

EXERCISE 14

CD 1, Track 28

1. Tell students that this exercise is a conversation between a student and her teacher. Have students read the direction line. Go over the example in the book.
2. Have students complete Exercise 14 individually. Then check the answers as a class.
3. If necessary, review grammar chart **3.6** on page 103.

S: ___Did a lot of people go___ (6 a lot of people/go) to Washington?

T: Oh, yes. 250,000 people ___went___ (7 go) to Washington.

S: Do you remember when he died?

T: I was in high school when he ___died___ (8 die). The principal ___came___ (9 come) to our class and ___told___ (10 tell) us the news.

S: What ___did you do___ (11 do) when you heard the news?

T: At first we ___didn't believe___ (12 not/believe) it. Then we all started to ___cry___ (13 cry). We ___went___ (14 go) home from school and ___watched___ (15 watch) the news on TV.

S: Where ___was___ (16 be) he when he died?

T: He ___was___ (17 be) on the balcony of a hotel in Memphis when a man ___came___ (18 come) and ___shot___ (19 shoot) him. It was terrible. But we should remember King for his life, not his death. We celebrate Martin Luther King, Jr.'s birthday.

S: Really? I ___didn't know___ (20 not/know) that. When is it?

T: He ___was___ (21 be) born on January 15. We don't have school on that date.

S: ___Did this date become___ (22 this date/become) a holiday right after he died?

T: No. It ___became___ (23 become) a holiday in 1983.

S: How do you remember so much about King?

T: I ___wrote___ (24 write) a paper on him when I was in college.

104 Lesson 3

Expansion

Exercise 14 Have students practice the conversation in pairs. Then ask volunteers to act out the conversation for the class, or have students ask you questions about an important historical event during your lifetime, such as 9/11.

EXERCISE 15 ABOUT YOU Check (√) the things you did this past week. Exchange books with another student. Ask the other student about the items he or she checked.

EXAMPLE √ I made a long-distance phone call.

A: I made a long-distance phone call.
B: Who(m) did you call?
A: I called my father in Mexico.
B: How long did you talk?
A: We talked for about 15 minutes.

Answers will vary.

1. ____ I made a long-distance phone call.
2. ____ I shopped for groceries.
3. ____ I met someone new.
4. ____ I got together with a friend.
5. ____ I wrote a letter.
6. ____ I bought some new clothes.
7. ____ I went to the bank.
8. ____ I read something interesting (a book, an article).
9. ____ I went to the post office.
10. ____ I did exercises.
11. ____ I received a letter.
12. ____ I went to an interesting place.

EXERCISE 16 Decide which is better: the simple past tense or *used to* + base form. Fill in the blanks.

EXAMPLES Martin Luther King, Jr. ___went___ (go) to Alabama in 1955.

Oprah Winfrey ___used to be___ (be) poor.

1. There ___used to be___ (be) a lot more discrimination in the past than there is today.
2. President Lincoln ___ended___ (end) slavery in 1865.
3. African-Americans ___used to have___ (have) a hard time getting into certain professions.
4. Black children ___used to go___ (go) to separate schools in the South.
5. In 1964, Congress ___passed___ (pass) a law that gave equality to all.
6. Colin Powell ___became___ (become) secretary of state in 2001.

EXERCISE 15

1. Have students read the direction line. Say: *Your partner will ask you questions about things you have done this past week.* Go over the example. Model #2 with another student.
2. Have students complete the checklist individually. Then have students exchange lists and ask and answer questions in pairs.
3. If necessary, review grammar chart **3.6** on page 103.

EXERCISE 16

1. Have students read the direction line. Review the difference between *used to* and the simple past. Say: Used to *describes habitual or customary activities done in the past but not done now. The simple past is used to describe something that happened once.* Go over the examples.
2. Have students complete Exercise 16 individually. Go over the answers with the class.
3. If necessary, review grammar charts **3.1** on page 90, **3.2** on page 94, **3.3** on page 96, and **3.4** on pages 98–99.

To save class time, have students do half of the exercise in class and complete the other half for homework. Or assign the entire exercise for homework.

Expansion

Exercise 15 Create two rings of students. Have half of the students stand in an outer ring around the classroom. Have the other half stand in an inner ring, facing the outer ring. Instruct students to ask each other *yes/no* questions in random order from Exercise 15 (e.g., *Did you make a long-distance phone call this week? Did you go to the post office this week?*). Call out "turn" every minute or so. Students in the inner ring should move one space clockwise. Students now interview their new partners. Make sure students look at each other when they're asking and answering questions.

Summary of Lesson 3

1. **Simple Past Tense** Have students cover up the summary. Write the following on the board:
   (be)
   1. Dawson____happy.
   2. He____rich.
   3. ____he from a large family?
   4. Yes, he____.
   5. Where____he born?
   6. Why____he in school?
   (live)
   1. Dawson____for 103 years.
   2. He____in the time of slavery.
   3. ____he____in the North?
   4. No, he____.
   5. Where____he____?
   6. Why____he____in the North?
   (feel)
   1. Dawson____happy.
   2. He____lonely.
   3. ____he____good when he learned to read?
   4. Yes, he____.
   5. How____he____about his life?
   6. Why____he____lonely?

   If necessary, have students review:
   3.2 Past Tense of *Be* (p. 94)
   3.3 The Simple Past Tense of Regular Verbs (p. 96)
   3.4 The Simple Past Tense of Irregular Verbs (pp. 98–99)
   3.5 Negative Statements (p. 101)
   3.6 Questions with the Simple Past Tense (p. 103).
2. **Habitual Past with *Used To*** Have students cover up the summary. Write the following on the board:
   1. Oprah____poor. Now she's rich.
   2. Black children and white children____to separate schools. Now schools are for all children.
   If necessary, have students review:
   3.1 Habitual Past with *Used To* (p. 90).

Editing Advice

Have students close their books. Write the example sentences without editing marks or corrections on the board. For example:

1. He born in Germany.
2. He was died two years ago.

Ask students to correct each sentence and provide a rule or explanation for each correction. This activity can be done individually, in pairs, or as a class. After students have corrected each sentence, tell them to turn to pages 106–107. Say: *Now compare your work with the Editing Advice in the book.*

SUMARY OF LESSON 3

1. Simple Past Tense

Be

Dawson **was** happy.
He **wasn't** rich.
Was he from a large family? Yes, he **was**.
Where **was** he born?
Why **wasn't** he in school?

Regular Verb

Dawson **lived** for 103 years.
He **didn't live** in the time of slavery.
Did he **live** in the North? No, he **didn't**.
Where **did** he **live?**
Why **didn't** he **live** in the North?

Irregular Verb

Dawson **felt** happy.
He **didn't feel** lonely.
Did he **feel** good when he learned to read? Yes, he **did**.
How **did** he **feel** about his life?
Why **didn't** he **feel** lonely?

2. Habitual Past with *Used To*

Oprah **used to** be poor. Now she's rich.
Black children and white children **used to** go to separate schools. Now schools are for all children.

EDITING ADVICE

1. Use *was / were* with *born.*

He ^was born in Germany.

2. Don't use *was / were* with *die.*

He was died two years ago.

3. Don't use a past form after *to.*

I decided to ~~left~~ *leave* early.

I wanted to go home and watched TV.

106 Lesson 3

Summary Variation

Have students write their own sentences with *be, live, feel,* and *used to.* Say: *Write affirmative statements,* yes/no *questions, short answers,* wh- *questions, and negative questions.*

4. Don't use *was* or *were* to form a simple past tense.

He ~~was go~~ went home yesterday.

5. Use *there* when a new subject is introduced.

There w ~~W~~as a big earthquake in 1906.

6. Use a form of *be* before an adjective. Remember, some *-ed* words are adjectives.

They ^were excited about their trip to America.

7. Don't use *did* with an adjective. Use *was / were.*

Why ~~did~~ were you afraid?

8. Use the correct word order in a question.

Why ~~you didn't~~ didn't you return?

9. Use *did* + the base form in a question.

What kind of car ^did you ~~bought~~ buy?

10. Use the base form after *didn't.*

He didn't worked yesterday.

11. Don't forget the *d* in *used to.*

She use^d to live in Miami.

12. Don't add the verb *be* before *used to* for habitual past.

I'~~m~~ used to play soccer in my country.

Lesson 3 Test/Review

For additional practice, review, and assessment materials, see Assessment CD-ROM with *ExamView Pro*, *More Grammar Practice* Workbook 2, Interactive CD-ROM, and Web site http://elt.thomson.com/gic

PART 1

1. Part 1 may be used as an in-class test to assess student performance, in addition to the Assessment CD-ROM with *ExamView Pro*. Have students read the direction line. Say: *Some verbs may be regular and some may be irregular.* Collect for assessment.
2. If necessary, have students review:
   3.3 The Simple Past Tense of Regular Verbs (p. 96)
   3.4 The Simple Past Tense of Irregular Verbs (pp. 98–99).

PART 2

1. Part 2 may also be used as an in-class test to assess student performance, in addition to the Assessment CD-ROM with *ExamView Pro*. Have students read the direction line. Ask: *Does every sentence have a mistake?* (no) Collect for assessment.
2. If necessary, have students review: **Lesson 3.**

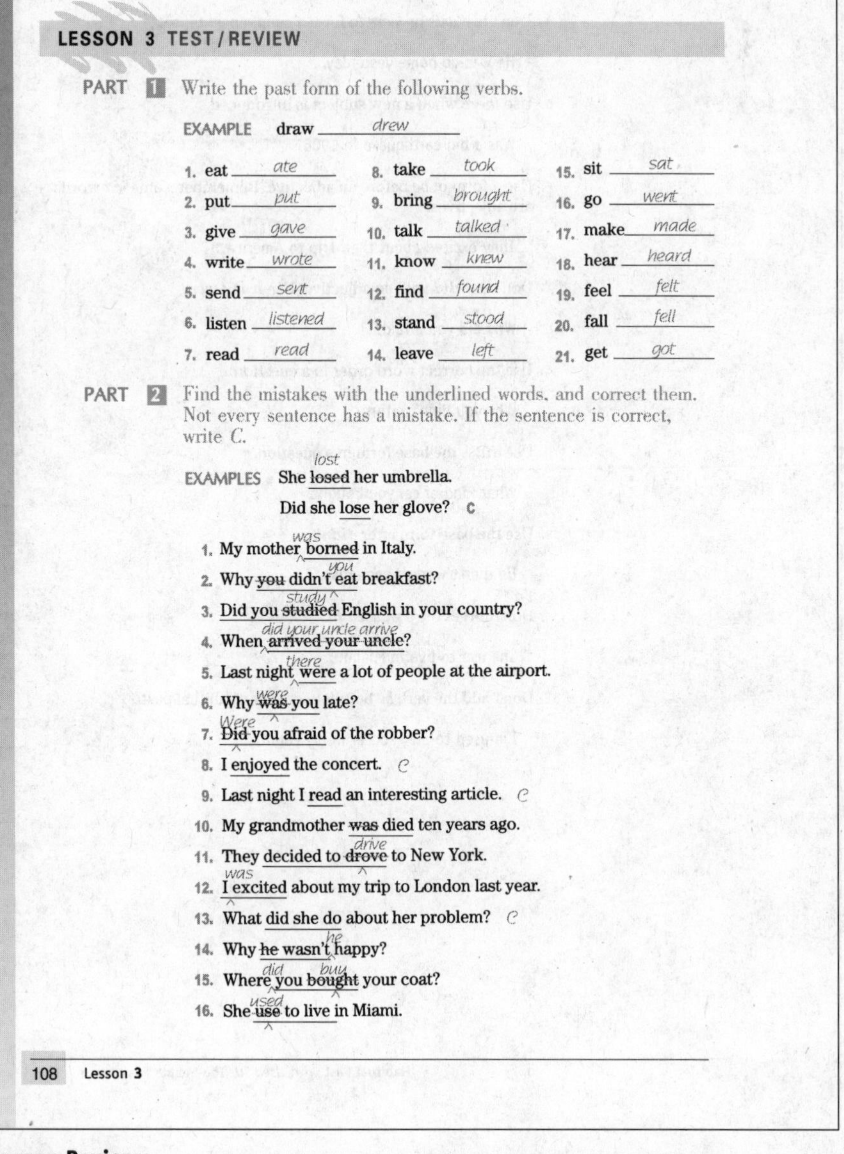

LESSON 3 TEST/REVIEW

PART 1 Write the past form of the following verbs.

EXAMPLE draw *drew*

1. eat *ate*	8. take *took*	15. sit *sat*
2. put *put*	9. bring *brought*	16. go *went*
3. give *gave*	10. talk *talked*	17. make *made*
4. write *wrote*	11. know *knew*	18. hear *heard*
5. send *sent*	12. find *found*	19. feel *felt*
6. listen *listened*	13. stand *stood*	20. fall *fell*
7. read *read*	14. leave *left*	21. get *got*

PART 2 Find the mistakes with the underlined words, and correct them. Not every sentence has a mistake. If the sentence is correct, write *C*.

EXAMPLES She losed her umbrella. *lost*
Did she lose her glove? C

1. My mother borned in Italy. *was born*
2. Why you didn't eat breakfast? *didn't you eat*
3. Did you studied English in your country? *study*
4. When arrived your uncle? *did your uncle arrive*
5. Last night were a lot of people at the airport. *there were*
6. Why was you late? *were*
7. Did you afraid of the robber? *Were*
8. I enjoyed the concert. *C*
9. Last night I read an interesting article. *C*
10. My grandmother was died ten years ago. *died*
11. They decided to drove to New York. *drive*
12. I excited about my trip to London last year. *was excited*
13. What did she do about her problem? *C*
14. Why he wasn't happy? *wasn't he*
15. Where you bought your coat? *did you buy*
16. She use to live in Miami. *used*

108 Lesson 3

Lesson Review

To use Parts 1 and 2 as a review, assign them as homework or use them as in-class activities to be completed individually or in pairs. Check answers and review errors as a class. Reteach grammar points that students haven't mastered. Then student learning may be assessed using a test generated from the Assessment CD-ROM with *ExamView Pro*.

PART 3 Write the negative form of the underlined word.

EXAMPLE Rosa Parks lived in Alabama. She *didn't live* in Washington.

1. She was tired when she got out of work. She *wasn't* sick.
2. She went to work by bus. She *didn't go* to work by car.
3. The bus driver told African-Americans to stand. He *didn't tell* white Americans to stand.
4. Some African-Americans stood up. Rosa Parks *didn't stand* up.
5. The police came to the bus. They *didn't come* to her house.
6. They took her to jail. They *didn't take* her to her house.
7. Martin Luther King, Jr., organized a protest. Rosa Parks *didn't organize* a protest.
8. Slavery ended in 1865. Discrimination *didn't end* in 1865.
9. King believed in peaceful protest. He *didn't believe* in violence.
10. King spoke about brotherhood. He *didn't speak* about violence.
11. Many people had the opportunity for education. George Dawson *didn't have* the opportunity for education.
12. George Dawson wrote a book. He *didn't write* it alone.

PART 3

1. Part 3 may also be used as an in-class test to assess student performance, in addition to the Assessment CD-ROM with *ExamView Pro*. Have students read the direction line. Review the example. Ask: ***What do we write in the blank?*** (the negative of the underlined word) Collect for assessment.
2. If necessary, have students review:
   - **3.1** Habitual Past with *Used To* (p. 90)
   - **3.2** Past Tense of *Be* (p. 94)
   - **3.5** Negative Statements (p. 101).

Lesson Review

To use Part 3 as a review, assign it as homework or use it as an in-class activity to be completed individually or in pairs. Check answers and review errors as a class. Reteach grammar points that students haven't mastered. Then student learning may be assessed using a test generated from the Assessment CD-ROM with *ExamView Pro*.

PART 4

1. Part 4 may also be used as an in-class test to assess student performance, in addition to the Assessment CD-ROM with *ExamView Pro*. Have students read the direction line. Go over the example. Remind students that they do not have to write an answer. Collect for assessment.
2. If necessary, have students review:
   3.6 Questions with the Simple Past (p. 103).

PART 4 Write a question beginning with the word given. An answer is not necessary.

EXAMPLE Martin Luther King, Jr., lived in the South.
Where *did he live?*

1. King became a minister.
   Why *did he become a minister?*
2. King was born in Georgia.
   When *was he born?*
3. King didn't like segregation.
   Why *didn't he like segregation?*
4. Black children went to separate schools.
   Why *did they go to separate schools?*
5. Some restaurants didn't permit black people to eat there.
   Why *didn't some restaurants permit black people to eat there?*
6. King was in jail many times because of his protests.
   How many times *was he in jail because of his protests?*
7. King won the Nobel Peace Prize.
   When *did he win the Nobel Peace Prize?*
8. Rosa Parks worked in Montgomery.
   Where *did she work?*
9. She was tired.
   Why *was she tired?*
10. She went home by bus.
    How many times *did she go home by bus?*
11. She lived in the South.
    Where *did she live?*
12. She didn't want to obey the law.
    Why *didn't she want to obey the law?*
13. The police took her to jail.
    Why *did the police take her to jail?*
14. George Dawson believed in the goodness of life.
    Why *did he believe in the goodness of life?*

110 Lesson 3

Lesson Review

To use Part 4 as a review, assign it as homework or use it as an in-class activity to be completed individually or in pairs. Check answers and review errors as a class. Reteach grammar points that students haven't mastered. Then student learning may be assessed using a test generated from the Assessment CD-ROM with *ExamView Pro*.

15. Dawson taught his children to see the richness in life.

How *did he teach his children to see the richness in life?*

15. Dawson didn't feel lonely.

Why *didn't he feel lonely?*

PART 5 Write two sentences with *used to* comparing your life ten years ago with your life today.

1. Answers will vary.
2.

EXPANSION ACTIVITIES

Classroom Activities

1. Check (✓) the sentences that are true for you. Find a partner and exchange books. Give each other more information about the things you checked. Ask each other questions about these activities.

(a) ____ I bought a CD in the past week.
(b) ____ I worked last Saturday.
(c) ____ I rode a bike this past week.
(d) ____ I went to a party last weekend.
(e) ____ I got a driver's license in the past year.
(f) ____ I took a trip in the past year.
(g) ____ I got married in the last two years.
(h) ____ I found a job this month.
(i) ____ I spent more than $50 today.
(j) ____ I received some money this week.
(k) ____ I ate pizza in the past month.
(l) ____ I bought a car in the past year.
(m) ____ I came to the U.S. alone.

2. Who did it?

Teacher: Pass out an index card to each student.

Students: Write something you did last weekend. It can be something unusual or something ordinary. (Examples: I went fishing. I baked a pie. I did my laundry.)

Teacher: Collect the cards. Pull out one card at a time and read the sentence to the class. The students have to guess who wrote the card.

Habitual Past with *Used To;* The Simple Past Tense 111

Classroom Activities Variation

Activity 1 Don't have students exchange books to read the checklists. Have students tell each other what they did and didn't do. Then have students discuss their activities (e.g., *What kind of CD did you buy? I bought a jazz CD.*). Circulate to observe pair work. Give help as needed.

Activity 2 On an index card, have students write a false statement about something they did in the past and two true statements about something they did (e.g., *I went to Disney World five times. I met the president of my country. I lived in the Amazon.*). Students should write their names on the card. Then read the statements, and have students guess which statement is false.

PART 5

1. Part 5 may also be used as an in-class test to assess student performance, in addition to the Assessment CD-ROM with *ExamView Pro*. Have students read the direction line. Say: *How is your life different? Write about two things that you used to do in the past that are different from what you do today.* Collect for assessment.
2. If necessary, have students review: **3.1** Habitual Past with *Used To* (p. 90).

Expansion Activities

These expansion activities provide opportunities for students to interact with one another and further develop their speaking and writing skills. Encourage students to use grammar from this lesson whenever possible.

To save class time, assign parts of the activities as homework. Then use class time for interaction and communication. If students do not need additional speaking practice, some of the activities may be assigned as writing activities for homework, or skipped altogether.

CLASSROOM ACTIVITIES

1. Have students complete the checklist on their own. Then have students get into pairs to discuss their activities (e.g., *What kind of CD did you buy? I bought a jazz CD.*). Circulate to observe pair work. Give help as needed.
2. Say: *Let's find out how well you know each other.* Tell students to write two or three things they did in the past week on the index card.

CLASSROOM ACTIVITIES (*cont.*)

3. Ask: *What do you know about your classmates' past?* Tell students to write two or three things they used to do on the index card.
4. This activity can be done with the whole class or in groups. Model the activity for the students. Bring in a picture of yourself when you were younger.
5. Model the activity for the class with your own information. If possible, try to put students together in groups from different cultures or countries.
6. Have students tell the class questions they would ask George Dawson.

TALK ABOUT IT

If possible, try to put students together in groups or pairs from different cultures or countries to talk about changes in their life or about changes in fashion.

WRITE ABOUT IT

Brainstorm ideas and vocabulary for the writing tasks with the class. For ideas about item number 3, draw two columns on the board: *single/married.* Ask students to think of things for each column (e.g., *eat out a lot/eat home-cooked meals*).

3. **Who used to do it?**

   Teacher: Pass out an index card to each student.

   Students: Think of some things you used to be, wear, do, etc. when you were younger. Think of things that other students would not guess about you. Write two or three of these things on the card.

   Teacher: Collect the cards. Pull out one card at a time and read the sentences to the class. The students have to guess who wrote the card.

   EXAMPLES I used to hate studying a foreign language.
   I used to have very long hair.
   I used to be a terrible student.

4. **Bring in a picture of yourself when you were younger. Describe how you were at that time and compare yourself to how you are now.**

   EXAMPLE I used to play soccer all day with my friends. Now I don't have time for it.

5. **Fill in the blank. Discuss your answers in a small group or with the entire class.**

   Before I came to the U.S., I used to believe that ______________ ______________, but now I know it's not true.

6. **With a partner, write a few questions to ask George Dawson.**

   EXAMPLES Why didn't you go to school?
   What kind of jobs did you have?
   What was the first book you read?

Talk About it

In a small group or with the entire class, discuss the following:

1. **Changes in daily life: Compare how life used to be when you were younger with how it is now.**
2. **Fashions: Talk about different styles or fashions in the past.**

   EXAMPLE In the 1960s, men used to wear their hair long.

Write About it

Choose one of the following topics to write a short composition.

1. **Write a paragraph or paragraphs telling about your childhood.**
2. **Write a paragraph or paragraphs telling about changes in your native country. Compare how life used to be with how it is now.**
3. **If you are married, write a paragraph or paragraphs comparing your life as a married person with your life as a single person.**

112 Lesson 3

Classroom Activities Variation

Activity 4 Have students make a poster of themselves when they were younger. Tell students to include pictures. Ask students not to include their names. Put the posters up around the class. Have students walk around to view the posters. Ask students to guess who is who and to make comparisons (e.g., *Jose used to wear glasses. Now he wears contacts.*).

Talk About it Variation

Item 1 Alternatively, ask students to describe how their partners' life used to be (e.g., *Miguel used to live with his whole family—parents, grandparents, and brothers and sisters. Now he lives alone.*).

Outside Activity

Interview an American-born person. Ask this person to tell you about changes he or she sees in American society. Ask this person to compare how he or she used to live with how he or she lives now. Report some interesting information to the class.

Internet Activities

1. Find information about one of the people below. Tell the class why this person was (or is) famous.

Jesse Jackson	James Earl Ray
Malcolm X	Jesse Owens
John Wilkes Booth	Nat Turner
Mahatma Gandhi	

2. At a search engine, type in *I Have a Dream* to find Martin Luther King, Jr.'s most famous speech. Summarize his dream.
3. Find a description of George Dawson's book *Life Is So Good.* (Try using amazon.com or barnesandnoble.com.) Print it and bring it to class.

Additional Activities at http://elt.thomson.com/gic

OUTSIDE ACTIVITY

With the class, brainstorm questions to ask an American-born person about how life has changed in the U.S. (e.g., *How did you use to call people? How did you use to get your information? How did you use to see movies?*).

INTERNET ACTIVITIES

1. Survey the class to see how many students know these people before beginning the research.
   Jesse Jackson—minister and politician; he became the first African American presidential candidate in 1988
   Malcolm X—an African American civil rights leader
   John Wilkes Booth—man who assassinated President Abraham Lincoln
   Mahatma Gandhi—Indian civil rights leader who promoted nonviolent protest
   James Earl Ray—man who assassinated Dr. Martin Luther King, Jr.
   Jesse Owens—African American track star; among his accomplishments are four gold medals won at the 1936 Olympic Games in Berlin
   Nat Turner—slave in Virginia who led a rebellion in 1821 against white slaver owners; he was eventually captured and then executed in 1831
2. If possible, have students listen to a recording of "I Have a Dream" before they begin their Internet searches.
3. Ask volunteers to describe the book to the whole class.

Outside Activity Variation

Invite an older American to the class for students to interview. If possible, brainstorm questions beforehand.

Internet Activities Variation

Remind students that if they don't have Internet access, they can use Internet facilities at a public library or they can use traditional research methods to find out information, including looking at encyclopedias, magazines, books, journals, and newspapers.

LESSON

4

GRAMMAR

Possessive Forms
Object Pronouns
Reflexive Pronouns
Questions

CONTEXT : Weddings

A Traditional American Wedding
New Wedding Trends
Economizing on a Wedding
Questions and Answers About an American Wedding

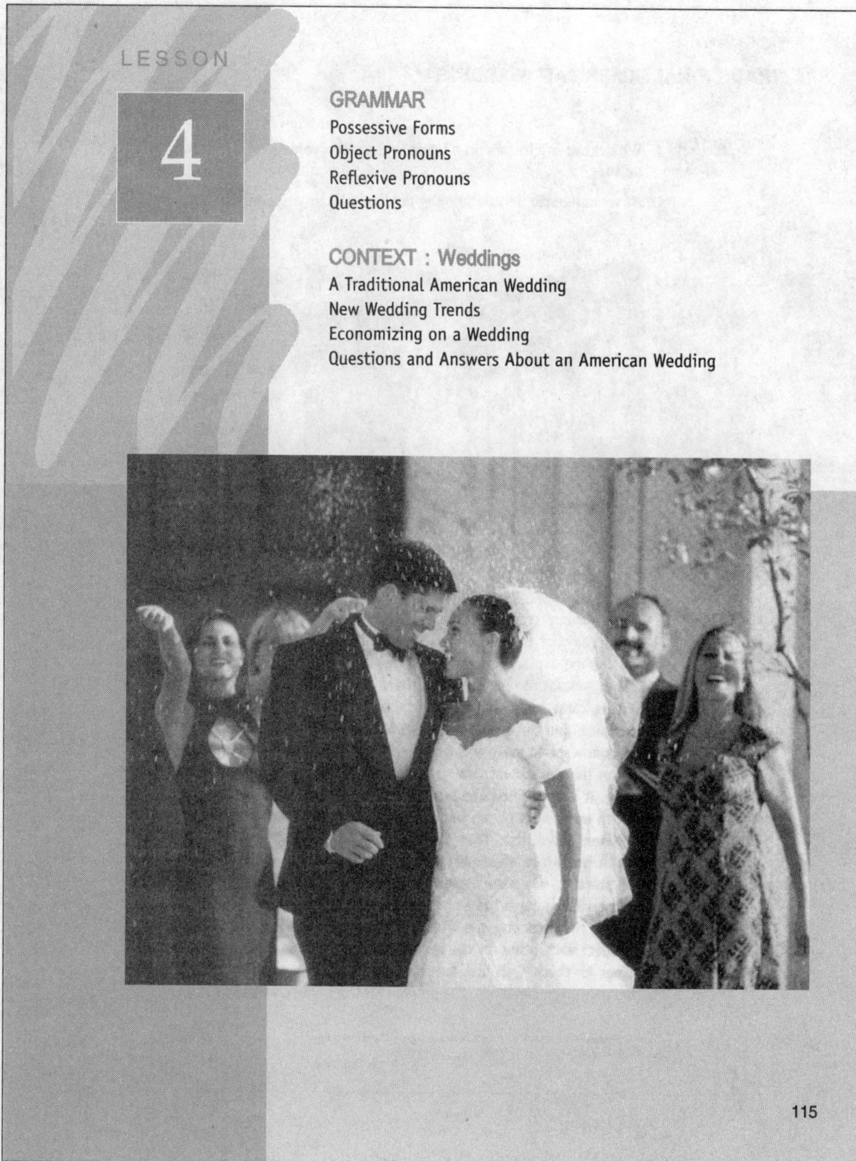

115

Lesson | 4

Lesson Overview

GRAMMAR

1. Briefly review what students learned in Lesson 3. Ask: *What did we study in Lesson 3?* (the habitual past with *used to* and the simple past tense)
2. Ask: *What are we going to study in this lesson?* (possessive forms, object pronouns, reflexive pronouns, and questions) *What are possessive forms?* (e.g., **Mary's** coat. **My** hat. It's **mine.**) Have students give examples. Write the examples on the board. Ask: *What are object pronouns?* (pronouns that are the object in a sentence, such as *He loves me*) *Give me some examples of reflexive pronouns.* (*myself, herself*)

CONTEXT

1. Ask: *What are we going to learn about in this lesson?* (weddings) Activate students' prior knowledge. Ask: *What do you know about American weddings?*
2. Have students share their knowledge and personal experiences.

Photo

1. Direct students' attention to the photo. Ask: *What's happening in this picture?* (A couple has just gotten married. Guests are throwing rice at them for good luck.)
2. Have students share their knowledge of American wedding traditions.

To save class time, have students do the Test/Review at the end of the lesson, or administer a lesson test generated from the Assessment CD-ROM with *ExamView® Pro.* Skip sections of the lesson that students have already mastered. You may also assign some sections for self-study for extra credit.

Expansion

Theme The topic for this lesson can be enhanced with the following ideas:

1. A wedding album (yours or someone else's)
2. Bridal and wedding magazines
3. A wedding planner book

A Traditional American Wedding (Reading)

1. Have students look at the illustration. Say: *This is a traditional bridal party. Who are these people? What's happening?*
2. Have students look at the title of the reading. Ask: *What is the reading about?* Have students use the title and picture to make predictions about the reading.
3. Preteach any vocabulary words your students may not know such as: *maid of honor, bridesmaid, groomsmen, ceremony,* and *bouquet.* Point out the illustrations of the bride and groom and the wedding party on page 116.

BEFORE YOU READ

1. Have students discuss the questions in pairs. Try to pair students of different cultures together.
2. Ask for a few volunteers to share their answers with the class.

To save class time, skip "Before You Read" or have students prepare answers for homework ahead of time.

Reading CD 2, Track 1

1. Have students first read the text silently. Tell them to pay special attention to object pronouns and possessive forms. Then play the audio and have students read along silently.
2. Check students' comprehension. Ask questions such as: *How long do couples spend planning for their weddings?* (one year) *Who chooses the maid of honor?* (the bride) *Why can't the groom see the bride before the wedding?* (It's bad luck.) *What happens when the bride enters?* (Everyone turns to look. Sometimes people stand.)

To save class time, have students do the reading for homework ahead of time.

DID YOU KNOW?

The least popular months for weddings are March, February, and January. Only 5.13% of weddings take place in January.

A TRADITIONAL AMERICAN WEDDING

Before You Read

1. What kind of clothes do a bride and groom wear in your native culture?
2. At what age do people usually get married in your native culture?

Read the following article. Pay special attention to object pronouns and possessive forms.

Did You Know?

- Most American weddings (85%) take place in a church or synagogue.
- The average number of guests in 190.
- Hawaii is the favorite honeymoon destination.
- August is the most popular month for weddings.
- Money is the most desired wedding gift.
- About 50 percent of marriages end in divorce.

Many young couples consider **their** wedding to be one of the most important days of **their** life. They save for **it** and often spend a year planning for **it**: finding a place, selecting a menu and cake, buying a wedding dress, ordering invitations and sending **them** to friends and relatives, selecting musicians, and much more. The bride chooses **her** maid of honor and bridesmaids, and the groom chooses **his** best man[1] and groomsmen. The bride and groom want to make this day special for themselves and for their guests.

When the day arrives, the groom doesn't usually see the bride before the wedding. It is considered bad luck for **him** to see **her** ahead of time. The guests wait with excitement to see **her** too. When the wedding begins, the groom and groomsmen enter first. Then the bridesmaids enter. When the bride finally enters in **her** white dress, everyone turns around to look at **her.** Sometimes guests stand up when the bride enters. Often the **bride's** father or both of **her** parents walk **her** down the aisle to the groom's side.

During the ceremony, the bride and groom take vows[2]. They promise to love and respect each other for the rest of their lives. The groom's best man holds the rings for **them** until they are ready to place **them** on each **other's** fingers. At the end of the ceremony, the groom lifts the **bride's** veil and kisses **her.**

[1] The *best man* is the man who stands beside the groom and helps him.
[2] A *vow* is a promise.

116 Lesson 4

Reading Variation

To practice listening skills, have students first listen to the audio alone. Ask a few comprehension questions. Repeat the audio if necessary. Then have them open their books and read along as they listen to the audio.

Reading Glossary

bouquet: a bunch of flowers
bridesmaid: a bride's attendant
ceremony: a formal event usually with rituals
groomsman: a man who is an attendant to the groom
maid of honor: a bride's main attendant at her wedding

Culture Note

It's a custom in American weddings for the bride to have "something old, something new, something borrowed, and something blue." Each item is a good-luck token. The old symbolizes a connection with the past (the bride's family), the new with the future (her life with her husband). The borrowed item from a happily married couple will bring the bride good luck, and the color blue in the past symbolized virtue and fidelity.

There is a party after the ceremony. People make toasts[3], eat dinner, and dance. The bride and groom usually dance the first dance alone. Then guests join **them.**

Before the bride and groom leave the party, the bride throws **her** bouquet over **her** head, and the single women try to catch **it**. It is believed that the woman who catches **it** will be the next one to get married.

The newlyweds[4] usually take a trip, called a honeymoon, immediately after the wedding.

4.1 Possessive Forms of Nouns

We use possessive forms to show ownership or relationship.

Noun	Ending	Examples
Singular noun: bride groom	Add apostrophe + *s*	The **bride's** dress is white. The **groom's** tuxedo is black.
Plural noun ending in *-s*: parents guests	Add apostrophe only	She got married in her **parents'** house. The **guests'** coats are in the coat room.
Irregular plural noun: men women	Add apostrophe + *s*	The **men's** suits are black. The **women's** dresses are beautiful.
Names that end in *-s*: Charles	Add apostrophe only OR Add apostrophe + *s*	Do you know **Charles'** wife? OR Do you know **Charles's** wife?
Inanimate objects: the church the dress	Use *"the _______ of _______."* Do not use apostrophe + *s*.	St. Peter's is **the name of the church.** **The front of the dress** has pearls.

[3] A *toast* is a wish for good luck, usually while holding a glass.
[4] For a short time after they are married, the bride and groom are called *newlyweds*.

4.1 | Possessive Forms of Nouns

1. Have students close their books. Say: *We use possessive forms to show ownership or relationship.* Give an example, such as *The teacher's desk is big.* Put students into pairs. Write grammar chart **4.1** on the board. Keep the middle column (*Ending*) empty. Say: *Study the nouns and the examples of possessives. Try to guess the rule for the ending.* Have volunteers write the rules on the board.
2. Then ask students to look at grammar chart **4.1** to compare their chart with the chart in the book.
3. Make sure to point out that possession by inanimate objects is expressed in the following way: "the ____ of ____."

EXERCISE 1

1. Have students read the direction line. Go over the example in the book. Have a volunteer do #1 for the class.
2. Have students complete Exercise 1 individually. Go over the answers as a class.
3. If necessary, review grammar chart **4.1** on page 117.

EXERCISE 2

1. Have students read the direction line. Go over the examples in the book. Ask: *When do you use the possessive form with apostrophe* + s? (with people or animals)
2. Have students complete Exercise 2 individually. Then have them compare their answers in pairs. Circulate to observe the pair work.
3. If necessary, review grammar chart **4.1** on page 117.

EXERCISE 1 Fill in the blanks to make the possessive form of the noun.

EXAMPLE The bride _'s_ grandfather looks very handsome.

1. The groom _'s_ mother is very nice.
2. The bride _'s_ flowers are beautiful.
3. The bridesmaids _'_ dresses are blue.
4. They invited many guests to the wedding. They didn't invite the guests _'_ children.
5. The women _'s_ dresses are very elegant.
6. Charles _'or's_ sister is a bridesmaid.
7. The newlyweds _'_ picture is in the newspaper.
8. Do you know the children _'s_ names?

EXERCISE 2 Fill in the blanks with the two nouns in parentheses( ). Put them in the correct order. Use the possessive form of one of the nouns, except with non-living things.

EXAMPLES The _bride's name_ (name/the bride) is Lisa.

I don't like the _color of your outfit_ (your outfit/color).

1. The _bride's grandmother_ (bride/grandmother) came to the wedding from London.
2. The _church's floor_ (church/floor) has a red carpet.
3. The _church's windows_ (windows /church) are very beautiful.
4. The _bride's mother_ (bride/mother) is crying.
5. The _church's name_ (church/name) is Saint Paul's.
6. The _men's tuxedos_ (men/tuxedos) are black.
7. The _limousine's color_ (limousine/color) is white.
8. The _girls' dresses_ (dresses/girls) are pretty.
9. Who chose the _color of the flowers_ (flowers/color)?
10. Some people get married in their _parents' house_ (house/parents).

Expansion

Exercise 1 Have students work in pairs to make ten sentences about the class and the classroom (e.g., *The door of the class is brown. Serena's jacket is pretty.*). Circulate to observe pair work.

Exercise 2 Divide students into small groups. Give each group a picture of a wedding party, a bride and groom, etc. Have groups make sentences about the pictures using the possessive form of nouns (e.g., *The color of the cake is white.*).

4.2 | Possessive Adjectives

Possessive adjectives show ownership or relationship.

Examples	Explanation	
	Subject Pronouns	Possessive Adjectives
My brother is getting married.	I	my
Your gift is wonderful.	you	your
The groom chooses **his** best man.	he	his
The bride chooses **her** bridesmaids.	she	her
The restaurant has **its** own reception hall.	it	its
Our cousins came from out of town.	we	our
The wedding is the most important day of **their** life.	they	their
My sister loves **her** husband. **My uncle** lives with **his** daughter.	Be careful not to confuse *his* and *her*. *Wrong:* My sister loves *his* husband. *Wrong:* My uncle lives with *her* daughter.	
The **bride's mother's** dress is blue.	We can use two possessive nouns together.	
My brother's wife did not attend the wedding.	We can use a possessive adjective (*my*) before a possessive noun (*brother's*).	

EXERCISE 3 Fill in the blanks with a possessive adjective.

EXAMPLE I love ___my___ parents.

1. I have one sister. ___My___ sister got married five years ago.
2. She loves ___her___ husband very much.
3. He's an accountant. He has ___his___ own business.
4. They have one child. ___Their___ son's name is Jason.
5. They bought a house last year. ___Their___ house isn't far from my house.
6. My sister and I visit ___our___ parents once a month. They live two hours away from us.
7. My sister said, "My car isn't working this week. Let's visit them in ___your___ car."

4.2 | Possessive Adjectives

1. Have students cover up grammar chart **4.2** in their books. Activate prior knowledge. Ask: *What are the subject pronouns?* (*I, you, he,* etc.) Write them on the board. Then ask: *Do you know what the possessive adjectives are for these pronouns?* (*my, your, his,* etc.) Write them on the board next to the subject pronouns.
2. Have students look at grammar chart **4.2.** Say: *Compare our lists with the grammar chart.* Go over any errors.
3. Review the examples in the chart. Point out that possessive adjectives must be followed by a noun (e.g., *Your gift is wonderful,* NOT *Your is wonderful.*).
4. Point out that English learners sometimes confuse *his* and *her.* Instruct students not to confuse *its* and *it's,* and *their* and *there.* Explain that although these words are pronounced the same, their spellings and meanings are different.

EXERCISE 3

1. Have students read the direction line. Go over the example in the book.
2. Have students complete Exercise 3 individually. Then have them compare their answers in pairs.
3. If necessary, review grammar chart **4.2** on page 119.

Expansion

Exercise 3 Say: *Write about your family and friends. Use Exercise 3 as a model.* Have students write five to seven sentences about their families using possessive adjectives. Then have students compare sentences in pairs.

EXERCISE 4

CD 2, Track 2

1. Tell students that this exercise is a conversation about a wedding. Have students read the direction line. Go over the example in the book.
2. Have students complete Exercise 4 individually. Point out the picture of the cottage on page 120. Check answers as a class.
3. If necessary, review grammar chart **4.2** on page 119.

4.3 | Possessive Pronouns

1. Have students cover up grammar chart **4.3** in their books. Activate prior knowledge. Say: *OK. Let's review. What are the subject pronouns?* Write them on the board. *What are the possessive adjectives?* (*my, your, his,* etc.) Write them on the board. Then ask: *Do you know what the possessive pronouns are?* (*mine, yours, his, hers,* etc.) Write them on the board next to the possessive adjectives.
2. Have students look at grammar chart **4.3** on pages 120–121. Say: *Compare our lists with the grammar chart.* Go over any errors.
3. Review the examples in the chart. Ask: *What does a pronoun take the place of?* (a noun) *What does a possessive pronoun take the place of?* (a possessive adjective + noun) Say: *We use possessive pronouns to avoid repetition of a noun.* Go over the examples in the chart. For example, say: *Her dress is white. Mine is blue. What does* mine *mean?* (my dress)
4. Explain that after a possessive noun, the noun can be omitted. Go over the example in the book.

EXERCISE 4 Fill in the blanks with a possessive adjective.

A: What are you going to wear to ___your___ (example) sister's wedding?

B: I'm going to wear ___my___ (1) new blue dress.

A: Did your sister buy a new dress for her wedding?

B: No. She's going to borrow ___her___ (2) best friend's dress.

A: Will the wedding be at your home?

B: Oh, no. We live in an apartment. ___Our___ (3) apartment is too small. We're going to invite over 200 guests. The wedding is going to be at a church. Afterwards, we're going to have a dinner in a restaurant. The restaurant has ___its___ (4) own reception hall.

A: Are the newlyweds going on a honeymoon after the wedding?

B: Yes. They have friends who have a cottage. They're going to stay at ___their___ (5) friends' cottage in the country for a week.

A: Is the groom's mother a nice woman?

B: I don't know ___his___ (6) mother. I'll meet her at the wedding for the first time.

4.3 | Possessive Pronouns

We can use possessive pronouns (*mine, yours, his, hers, ours, theirs*) to show ownership or relationship.

Possessive Adjective	Possessive Pronoun	Explanation
Her dress is white. **Their wedding** was big. We had **our wedding** in a church.	**Mine** is blue. **Ours** was small. They had **theirs** in a garden.	When we use a possessive pronoun, we omit the noun. *mine* = my dress *ours* = our wedding *theirs* = their wedding
The groom's parents look happy.	**The bride's** do too.	After the possessive form of a noun, we can omit the noun. *The bride's* = the bride's parents

120 Lesson 4

Exercise 4 Variation

To provide practice with listening skills, have students close their books and listen to the audio. Repeat the audio as needed. Ask comprehension questions, such as: *What is she going to wear to her sister's wedding?* (her new blue dress) *Where is the wedding going to be?* (at a church) *Where are the newlyweds going for their honeymoon?* (They're going to stay at a friend's cottage.) Then have students open their books and complete Exercise 4.

Expansion

Exercise 4 Have students practice the conversation in pairs. Ask volunteers to role-play all or some of the conversation in front of the class.

Compare the three forms below.

Subject pronoun	Possessive Adjective	Possessive Pronoun
I	my	mine
you	your	yours
he	his	his
she	her	hers
it	its	—
we	our	ours
they	their	theirs

EXERCISE 5 Fill in the blanks with an appropriate possessive pronoun.

A: I heard your brother got married last month. How was the wedding? Was it anything like your wedding? I remember ___yours___ (example) very well.

B: It was very different from ___mine___ (1). ___His___ (2) was a very formal wedding in a church last month. ___Mine___ (3) was very informal, in a garden.

A: I prefer informal weddings. I don't like to get dressed up in a suit and tie. At ___mine___ (4), I just wore comfortable clothes.

B: Our honeymoon was a two-day trip. ___Theirs___ (5) was a two-week stay in a luxury hotel in Hawaii. Their honeymoon was expensive. ___Ours___ (6) was very economical. We drove to Chicago and stayed in a motel there.

A: I remember your wife made her own dress. You saved a lot of money.

B: My sister-in-law, Gina, spent a lot of money on her dress. ___It___ (7) cost over $1,000. My wife's was only about $100.

A: The cost of a wedding isn't the most important thing. The most important thing is the happiness that follows. My uncle's wedding cost over $30,000. ___It___ (8) was the most beautiful wedding you can imagine. But his marriage lasted only eight months.

Possessive Forms; Object Pronouns; Reflexive Pronouns; Questions 121

4.3 | Possessive Pronouns (*cont.*)

5. Point out that there is no corresponding possessive pronoun for *it/its*.

EXERCISE 5

CD 2, Track 3

1. Tell students that this exercise is a conversation about a wedding. Have students read the direction line. Go over the example in the book.
2. Have students complete Exercise 5 individually. Then check answers as a class.
3. If necessary, review grammar chart **4.3** on pages 120–121.

Exercise 5 Variation

To provide practice with listening skills, have students close their books and listen to the audio. Repeat the audio as needed. Ask comprehension questions, such as *Who got married last month?* (person B's brother) *Where was person B's wedding?* (in a garden) *Does person A like formal or informal weddings?* (informal weddings) Then have students open their books and complete Exercise 5.

Expansion

Exercise 5 Have students practice the conversation in pairs. Ask volunteers to role-play all or some of the conversation in front of the class.

EXERCISE 6

1. Have students read the direction line. Ask: *What do we write in the blanks?* (*I*, *I'm*, *me*, *my*, or *mine*)
2. Have students complete Exercise 6 individually. Check the answers as a class.
3. If necessary, review grammar charts **4.2** on page 119 and **4.3** on pages 120–121.

EXERCISE 7

1. Have students read the direction line. Ask: *What do we write in the blanks?* (*we*, *we're*, *us*, *our*, or *ours*)
2. Have students complete Exercise 7 in pairs. Circulate to observe pair work. Give help as needed.
3. If necessary, review grammar charts **4.2** on page 119 and **4.3** on pages 120–121.

EXERCISE 8

1. Have students read the direction line. Ask: *What do we write in the blanks?* (*you*, *you're*, *your*, or *yours*)
2. Have students complete Exercise 8 in pairs. Circulate to observe pair work. Give help as needed.
3. If necessary, review grammar charts **4.2** on page 119 and **4.3** on pages 120–121.

EXERCISE 9

1. Have students read the direction line. Ask: *What do we write in the blanks?* (*he*, *he's*, *his*, or *him*)
2. Have students complete Exercise 9 in small groups. Circulate to observe pair work. Give help as needed.
3. If necessary, review grammar charts **4.2** on page 119 and **4.3** on pages 120–121.

To save class time, have students do the exercise for homework.

EXERCISE 10

1. Have students read the direction line. Ask: *What do we write in the blanks?* (*she*, *she's*, *her*, or *hers*)
2. Have students complete Exercise 10 in small groups. Circulate to observe pair work. Give help as needed.
3. If necessary, review grammar charts **4.2** on page 119 and **4.3** on pages 120–121.

To save class time, have students do the exercise for homework.

EXERCISE 6 Fill in the blanks with *I*, *I'm*, *me*, *my*, or *mine*.

1. ___I'm___ a student.
2. ___I___ live in an apartment near school.
3. ___My___ apartment is on the first floor.
4. ___My___ parents often visit ___me___.
5. They don't have a computer. They use ___mine___.

EXERCISE 7 Fill in the blanks with *we*, *we're*, *us*, *our*, or *ours*.

1. ___Our___ classroom is large.
2. ___We___ study English here.
3. ___We're___ foreign students.
4. The teacher helps ___us___ learn English.
5. The teacher brings her book, and we bring ___ours___.

EXERCISE 8 Fill in the blanks with *you*, *you're*, *your*, or *yours*. Pretend you are talking directly to the teacher.

1. ___You're___ the teacher.
2. ___You___ come from the U.S.
3. My first language is Polish. ___Yours___ is English.
4. ___Your___ pronunciation is very good.
5. We see ___you___ every day.

EXERCISE 9 Fill in the blanks with *he*, *he's*, *his*, or *him*.

1. I have a brother. ___His___ name is Paul.
2. ___He's___ married.
3. ___He___ has four children.
4. My apartment is small. ___His___ is big.
5. I see ___him___ on the weekends.

EXERCISE 10 Fill in the blanks with *she*, *she's*, *her*, or *hers*.

1. I have a sister. ___Her___ name is Marilyn.
2. I visit ___Her___ twice a week.
3. ___She___ lives in a suburb.
4. ___She's___ a teacher. ___Her___ husband is a doctor.
5. My children go to private school. ___Hers___ go to public school.

EXERCISE 11 Fill in the blanks with *it, it's,* or *its.*

1. The school has a big library. ___It's___ comfortable and clean.
2. ___It___ has many books and magazines.
3. ___Its___ hours are from 8 a.m. to 8 p.m.
4. I use ___it___ every day.
5. ___It's___ on the first floor.

EXERCISE 12 Fill in the blanks with *they, they're, their,* or *theirs.*

1. My parents rent ___their___ apartment.
2. My apartment is small, but ___theirs___ is big.
3. ___They're___ very old now.
4. ___They___ live in a suburb.
5. I visit ___them___ on the weekends.

4.4 Questions with *Whose*

Whose + a noun asks a question about ownership.

Whose + Noun	Auxiliary Verb	Subject	Verb	Answer
Whose dress	did	the bride	borrow?	She borrowed her sister's dress.
Whose last name	will	the bride	use?	She'll use her husband's last name.
Whose flowers	are	those?		They're the bride's flowers.

Language Note:
You can drop the noun after *whose* if the meaning is clear.
Whose flowers are these? **Whose** are those?

EXERCISE 13 Write a question with *whose*. The answer is given.

EXAMPLE ___Whose flowers are these___? They're the bride's flowers.

1. ___Whose car is that___? That's my father's car.
2. ___Whose gifts are those___? Those are the newlyweds' gifts.
3. ___Whose necklace is she wearing___? She's wearing her sister's necklace.
4. ___Whose suit are you wearing___? I'm wearing my friend's suit.
5. ___Whose advice do you follow___? I follow my parents' advice.
6. ___Whose dress did the bride borrow___? The bride borrowed her sister's dress.

Possessive Forms; Object Pronouns; Reflexive Pronouns; Questions 123

Expansion

Exercise 13 Have students write five statements similar to the statements from Exercise 13 (e.g., *They're my keys. That's my friend's car. Those are my teacher's gifts.*). Then have students exchange papers with a partner to make questions for the statements (*Whose keys are these? Whose car is that? Whose gifts are those?*). Circulate to observe pair work. Give help as needed.

EXERCISE 11

1. Have students read the direction line. Ask: *What do we write in the blanks?* (*it, it's,* or *its*)
2. Have students complete Exercise 11 individually. Check the answers as a class.
3. If necessary, review grammar charts **4.2** on page 119 and **4.3** on pages 120–121.

EXERCISE 12

1. Have students read the direction line. Ask: *What do we write in the blanks?* (*they, they're, their, theirs,* or *them*)
2. Have students complete Exercise 12 individually. Check the answers as a class.
3. If necessary, review grammar charts **4.2** on page 119 and **4.3** on pages 120–121.

4.4 Questions with *Whose*

1. Have students cover up grammar chart **4.4** in their books. Pick up a student's book from his/her desk. Ask: *Whose book is this?* (e.g., Tina's book) Write it on the board. Then ask: *What was the question I asked?* Have a volunteer write it on the board.
2. Have students look at grammar chart **4.4.** Say: Whose + *noun asks about possession or ownership.*
3. Direct students to the Language Note. Say: *If the meaning is clear, you don't need to use the noun after* whose. Go over the example in the book.

EXERCISE 13

1. Have students read the direction line. Go over the example in the book.
2. Have students complete the exercise individually. Go over the answers with the class.
3. If necessary, review grammar chart **4.4** on page 123.

4.5 | Object Pronouns

1. Have students cover up grammar chart **4.5** in their books. Write the subject pronouns on the board. Activate prior knowledge. Say: *OK. Here are the subject pronouns. Can you write the object pronouns?* Have a volunteer write them on the board.
2. Have students look at grammar chart **4.5**. Say: *Compare our list with the grammar chart.* Go over any errors.
3. Review the examples in the chart. Ask: *What do subject pronouns take the place of?* (the subject of a sentence) *What do object pronouns take the place of?* (the object of a sentence) Say: *We can use an object pronoun to take the place of an object after the verb of a sentence.*
4. Explain that object pronouns can also take the place of an object after a preposition. Ask: *What prepositions do you know? (of, about, to, from, in,* etc.) Go over the examples in the book. Point out that we use *them* for plural people and plural things.
5. Then go back to the reading on pages 116–117. Ask students to circle the examples of verb + object pronoun and preposition + object pronoun.

EXERCISE 14

1. Have students read the direction line. Ask: *What do we write in the blanks?* (an object pronoun) Go over the example in the book.
2. Have students complete the exercise individually. Go over the answers with the class.
3. If necessary, review grammar chart **4.5** on page 124.

4.5 | Object Pronouns

We can use an object pronoun *(me, you, him, her, it, us,* or *them)* after the verb.

Object Noun	Object Pronoun	Explanation
Daniel loves **Sofia.** Sofia loves **Daniel.** You know **my parents.**	He loves **her** very much. She loves **him** very much. You met **them.**	We can use an object pronoun to substitute for an object noun.
Do you know **the guests?** The bride and groom sent **invitations.**	Yes, we know **them.** They sent **them** last month.	We use *them* for plural people and things.
I see **the bride.** The bride is with her **father.**	Everyone is looking ***at* her.** She will dance ***with* him.**	An object pronoun can follow a preposition (*at, with, of, about, to, from, in,* etc.).

Compare Subject and Object Pronouns

Subject	Object	Examples: Subject	Verb	Object
I	me	You	love	me.
you	you	I	love	you.
he	him	She	loves	him.
she	her	He	loves	her.
it	it	We	love	it.
we	us	They	love	us.
they	them	We	love	them.

EXERCISE 14 Fill in the blanks with an object pronoun in place of the underlined word.

EXAMPLE The groom doesn't walk down the aisle with the bride. Her father walks with ___*her*___.

1. The bride doesn't enter with the groom. He waits for ___*her*___, and she goes to ___*him*___.
2. The groom takes the ring. He puts ___*it*___ on the bride's hand.
3. The bride wears a veil. The groom lifts ___*it*___ to kiss ___*her*___.
4. The bride doesn't throw the bouquet to all the women. She throws ___*it*___ to the single women only.
5. People make toasts to the bride and groom. They wish ___*them*___ health and happiness.
6. The groom promises to love the bride, and the bride promises to love ___*him*___.

EXERCISE 15 Fill in the blanks with the correct subject pronoun, object pronoun, or possessive adjective. Answers may vary.

A: How was your cousin Lisa's wedding last Saturday?

B: *It* (example) was great.

A: How many guests were there?

B: Maybe about 200. I couldn't count *them* (1).

A: Wow! That's a lot. It sounds like an expensive wedding. How did they pay for *it* (2)?

B: Lisa and Ron worked when *they* (3) graduated from college and saved money for *their* (4) wedding. *Their* (5) parents helped *them* (6) a little, but they couldn't depend on *them* (7) too much. *Their* (8) parents aren't wealthy.

A: Did Lisa wear a traditional white dress?

B: Yes. In fact, *she* (9) wore *her* (10) mother's wedding dress. She looked beautiful in *it* (11).

A: Where did *they* (12) go on their honeymoon?

B: They went to Hawaii. I was surprised—they sent *me* (13) a postcard. They had a great time.

A: I hope *they* (14) will be happy. The wedding and honeymoon are important, but the marriage that follows is what really counts.

B: I agree with *you* (15). But I'm sure they'll be happy. *She* (16) loves *him* (17) and *he* (18) loves *her* (19) very much.

A: Did you take pictures?

B: Yes. Do you want to see *them* (20)? I took *them* (21) with my new digital camera.

A: I don't have time now. Can you show *me* (22) the pictures tomorrow?

B: Yes. I'll bring *them* (23) tomorrow to show *you* (24).

EXERCISE 15

CD 2, Track 4

1. Tell students that this exercise is a conversation about a wedding. Have students read the direction line. Do a brief review of subject pronouns, object pronouns, and possessive adjectives. Ask volunteers to write them on the board. Go over the example in the book.
2. Have students complete Exercise 15 individually. Direct students' attention to the picture of the postcard. Ask: *What is this?* (a postcard) *Where is it from?* (Hawaii)
3. If necessary, review grammar charts **4.2** on page 119 and **4.5** on page 124.

To save class time, have students do the exercise for homework.

Exercise 15 Variation

To provide practice with listening skills, have students close their books and listen to the audio. Repeat the audio as needed. Ask comprehension questions, such as: *When was Lisa's wedding?* (last Saturday) *Was her wedding big?* (yes) *Did her parents pay for the wedding?* (No. They helped a little.) *Whose dress did Lisa wear?* (her mother's) *Where did they go on their honeymoon?* (Hawaii) Then have students open their books and complete Exercise 15.

Expansion

Exercise 15 Have students work in pairs to practice the conversation or to create their own conversations about weddings they have attended in their own lives. Ask volunteers to role-play the conversations in front of the class.

New Wedding Trends (Reading)

1. Have students look at the photo on page 126. Ask: *Do you know of anyone who has gotten married on the beach or in any other interesting place?* Then have students look at the photo on page 127. Ask: *What are these people doing in this photo? Do you know of any unusual wedding customs from other cultures?*
2. Have students look at the title of the reading. Ask: *What is the reading about?* Have students use the title and photos to make predictions about the reading.
3. Preteach any vocabulary words your students may not know such as *unique, vow,* and *cherish.*

BEFORE YOU READ

1. Have students discuss the questions in pairs. Try to pair students of different cultures together.
2. Ask for a few volunteers to share their answers with the class.

To save class time, skip "Before You Read" or have students prepare answers for homework ahead of time.

Reading CD 2, Track 5

1. Have students first read the text silently. Tell them to pay special attention to direct and indirect objects after verbs. Then play the audio and have students read along silently.
2. Check students' comprehension. Ask questions such as: *Where are some places couples are having their weddings?* (beaches and mountain tops) *Why do couples send their guests "save-the-date" cards?* (so they can make plans to attend the wedding) *What are some traditions in African-American weddings?* (jumping over a broom; wearing traditional African clothing) *What do couples always do after a wedding?* (send thank-you cards to their guests)

To save class time, have students do the reading for homework ahead of time.

NEW WEDDING TRENDS[5]

Before You Read

1. American wedding customs are changing. Are wedding customs changing in your native culture?
2. In your native culture, what kind of vows do the bride and groom make to each other?

 Read the following article. Pay special attention to direct and indirect objects after verbs.

Wedding traditions are changing. More and more young couples are choosing to create a unique wedding experience for themselves and for their guests. In traditional weddings, a clergy **reads the bride and groom their vows.** "Do you, Mary Jones, take Roger Smith to be your husband, for better or for worse, for richer, for poorer, in sickness and in health, to love and to cherish, until death parts you?" The bride and groom simply **say, "I do"** in response to this question. But more and more couples today are writing their own vows and **saying them** in their own words. They face the guests while they **say** or **read their vows to each other.**

Churches and synagogues are still the most popular places for a wedding. But some couples are choosing to have a destination wedding. They get married on the beach, on a mountain top, or other unusual place. These weddings have fewer guests because of the expense of traveling. Often the bride and groom pay for the hotel rooms of their guests. They **tell their guests the date** at least three to four months in advance. Often they send **them "save-the-date" cards** so that their guests can make plans to attend the wedding.

Another new trend in weddings is to create a wedding based on the couple's ethnic background. For example, in an African-American wedding,

[5]A *trend* is a current style.

126 Lesson 4

Reading Variation

To practice listening skills, have students first listen to the audio alone. Ask a few comprehension questions. Repeat the audio if necessary. Then have them open their books and read along as they listen to the audio.

Reading Glossary

cherish: to love most dearly
unique: singular, one of a kind
vow: a solemn promise

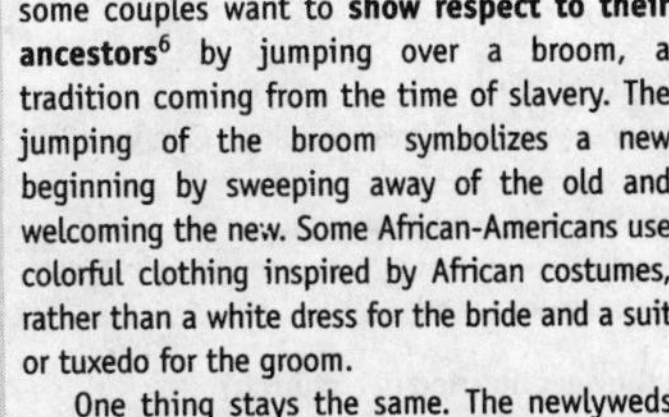

some couples want to **show respect to their ancestors**[6] by jumping over a broom, a tradition coming from the time of slavery. The jumping of the broom symbolizes a new beginning by sweeping away of the old and welcoming the new. Some African-Americans use colorful clothing inspired by African costumes, rather than a white dress for the bride and a suit or tuxedo for the groom.

One thing stays the same. The newlyweds **send the guests thank-you cards** by mail to thank them for attending the wedding and for the gifts they gave.

4.6 | Direct and Indirect Objects

Some verbs are followed by both a direct and an indirect object. The order of the objects depends on the verb.[7]

Examples	Explanation
Pattern A: Subj. / Verb / Indirect Obj. / Direct Obj. We gave the couple a wedding gift. They sent us a thank-you card. She read the groom her vows. They showed me their pictures. Pattern B: Subj. / Verb / Direct Obj. / *To* Indirect Obj. We gave a wedding gift to the couple. She read her vows to the groom.	With the following verbs, we follow Pattern A or Pattern B. bring, read, show give, sell, tell offer, send, write pay
He gave her a ring. He gave **it to her** on her birthday. Do you have the pictures? Can you show **them to me?**	When the direct object is a pronoun, we follow Pattern B.
Direct Obj. / *To* Indirect *Obj.* Please explain wedding customs to me. Please describe the wedding to us.	With the following verbs, we follow Pattern B. announce, mention, say describe, prove, suggest explain, report

[6] *Ancestors* are your grandparents, great-grandparents, great-great grandparents, etc.
[7] For a more detailed list of verbs and the order of direct and indirect objects, see Appendix I.

4.6 | Direct and Indirect Objects

1. Have students cover up grammar chart **4.6.** To present Pattern A, write the following sentence on the board:
   We gave the couple a wedding gift.
   Say: *Some verbs are followed by both direct and indirect objects. What are the direct and indirect objects in this sentence?* (d.o.—a wedding gift; i.o.—the couple) *Which comes first—the direct object or the indirect object?* (the indirect object)
   Then present Pattern B. Say: *We can also write the sentence like this: We gave a wedding gift to the couple.*
   Ask: *How is this sentence pattern different from the first one?* (the direct object comes before the indirect object; the indirect object has a *to* in front of it)
2. Then ask students to look at grammar chart **4.6.** Review the patterns and explanations for direct and indirect objects.
3. Explain that some verbs (*bring, give, offer,* etc.) can use either Pattern A or Pattern B. Direct students to the list of verbs in the grammar chart. Point out that when the direct object is a pronoun, Pattern B must be used (e.g., *He gave it to her.* NOT *He gave her it.*).
4. Then direct students to the second list of verbs. Say: *Put the direct object before the indirect object after these verbs (announce, describe, explain, etc.).* Point out that we can't use Pattern A with these verbs. For example, it's incorrect to say, "Please explain me wedding customs."
5. Now ask students to go back to the reading on pages 126 and 127 to find verbs with direct and indirect objects. Have students say if the order of the verb and objects are Pattern A or Pattern B (e.g., *A clergy reads the bride and groom their vows.—Pattern A*).

EXERCISE 16

CD 2, Track 6

1. Tell students that this exercise is a conversation about a wedding. Have students read the direction line. Go over the example in the book. Ask: *Can we write:* Give me it? (No. If the direct object is a pronoun, it always goes before the indirect object.)
2. Have students complete Exercise 16 individually. Go over the answers as a class.
3. If necessary, review grammar chart **4.6** on page 127.

4.7 | *Say* and *Tell*

1. Have students cover up grammar chart **4.6.** Activate prior knowledge. Ask: *Does anyone know the difference between the two verbs "say" and "tell"?* Write the two verbs on the board. Say: *They mean the same thing, but we use them differently.*
2. Create a matching exercise. Write the examples from the grammar chart on the board. On the other side of the board, write the explanations in a mixed-up order:
   a. She said her name.
   b. She told me her name.
   c. She said her name to me.
   d. They told the musicians to start the music.
   1. We say something to someone.
   2. We tell someone something.
   3. We tell someone to do something.
   4. We say something.
   Have students match the examples with the explanations.
3. Then ask students to look at grammar chart **4.7.** Say: *Now check your work.* Review the examples and explanations for *say* and *tell.*
4. Have students find an example of *say* and an example of *tell* in the reading on pages 126–127. Have students describe which pattern the sentences follow—*a, b, c,* or *d.*

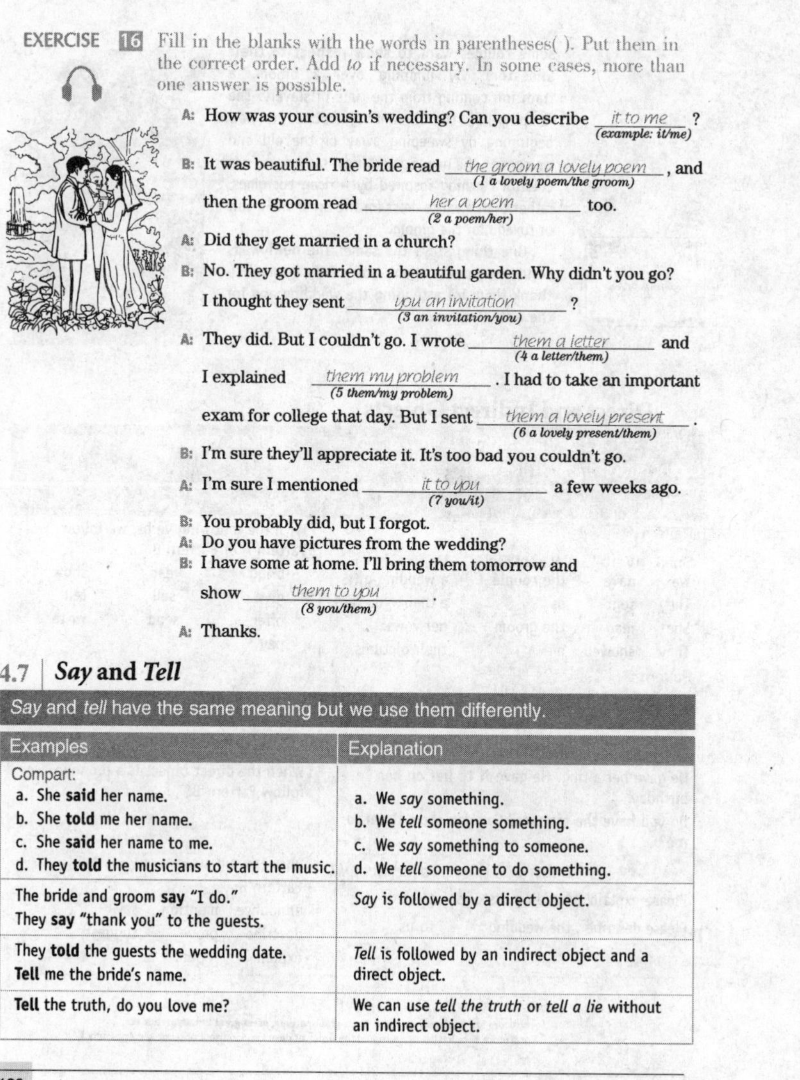

EXERCISE 16 Fill in the blanks with the words in parentheses( ). Put them in the correct order. Add *to* if necessary. In some cases, more than one answer is possible.

A: How was your cousin's wedding? Can you describe ___it to me___ (example: it/me)?

B: It was beautiful. The bride read ___the groom a lovely poem___ (1 a lovely poem/the groom), and then the groom read ___her a poem___ (2 a poem/her) too.

A: Did they get married in a church?

B: No. They got married in a beautiful garden. Why didn't you go? I thought they sent ___you an invitation___ (3 an invitation/you)?

A: They did. But I couldn't go. I wrote ___them a letter___ (4 a letter/them) and I explained ___them my problem___ (5 them/my problem). I had to take an important exam for college that day. But I sent ___them a lovely present___ (6 a lovely present/them).

B: I'm sure they'll appreciate it. It's too bad you couldn't go.

A: I'm sure I mentioned ___it to you___ (7 you/it) a few weeks ago.

B: You probably did, but I forgot.

A: Do you have pictures from the wedding?

B: I have some at home. I'll bring them tomorrow and show ___them to you___ (8 you/them).

A: Thanks.

4.7 | *Say* and *Tell*

Say and *tell* have the same meaning but we use them differently.

Examples	Explanation
Compart: a. She **said** her name. b. She **told** me her name. c. She **said** her name to me. d. They **told** the musicians to start the music.	a. We *say* something. b. We *tell* someone something. c. We *say* something to someone. d. We *tell* someone to do something.
The bride and groom **say** "I do." They **say** "thank you" to the guests.	*Say* is followed by a direct object.
They **told** the guests the wedding date. **Tell** me the bride's name.	*Tell* is followed by an indirect object and a direct object.
Tell the truth, do you love me?	We can use *tell the truth* or *tell a lie* without an indirect object.

128 Lesson 4

Exercise 16 Variation

To provide practice with listening skills, have students close their books and listen to the audio. Repeat the audio as needed. Ask comprehension questions, such as: *Who got married?* (person B's cousin) *What did the bride read to the groom?* (a poem) *Where did they get married?* (in a garden) Then have students open their books and complete Exercise 16.

Expansion

Exercise 16 Have students practice the conversation in pairs. Then ask volunteers to act out the conversation for the class.

EXERCISE 17 Fill in the blanks with the correct form of *say* or *tell*.

EXAMPLES The bride ___said___, "I love you."

They ___told___ me the date of the wedding.

1. You ___told___ me the groom's name, but I forgot it.
2. Can you ___tell___ me where the wedding is?
3. ___Tell___ the truth, do you love him?
4. The bride hates to ___say___ good-bye to her family.
5. During the ceremony, the bride and groom ___say___, "I do."
6. We ___told___ the band to play romantic music.
7. My neighbor wants to come to the wedding. I wasn't planning on inviting her, but I can't ___say___ no.
8. We ___told___ our daughter to economize on her wedding, but she ___said___ she wanted a fancy wedding.

ECONOMIZING ON A WEDDING

Before You Read

1. Why are weddings so expensive?
2. How can people economize on their weddings?

Read the following article. Pay special attention to the reflexive pronouns.

The average cost of a wedding in the U.S. today is $20,000 to $25,000 for about 200 guests. In days past, the bride's parents usually paid for the wedding. But as today's brides and grooms are older when they get married, they often pay for things **themselves.** There are many couples who put **themselves** in debt[8] to create a dream wedding.

(continued)

[8] When you are *in debt*, you owe money and have to pay it back.

Reading Variation

To practice listening skills, have students first listen to the audio alone. Ask a few comprehension questions. Repeat the audio if necessary. Then have them open their books and read along as they listen to the audio.

Reading Glossary

economize: to spend less than before
secondhand: owned or used by someone in the past

Culture Note

About 43 percent of couples spend more on their wedding than they had planned on spending. Many wedding debts now last longer than the actual marriages.

EXERCISE 17

1. Have students read the direction line. Go over the examples in the book.
2. Have students complete the exercise individually. Go over the answers with the class.
3. If necessary, review grammar chart **4.7** on page 128.

Economizing on a Wedding (Reading)

1. Have students look at the photo. Ask: *Who are these people? What do you think is happening in this photo?*
2. Have students look at the title of the reading. Ask: *What is the reading about?* Have students use the title and photo to make predictions about the reading.
3. Preteach any vocabulary words your students may not know such as *economize* and *secondhand.*

BEFORE YOU READ

1. Have students discuss the questions in pairs. Try to pair students of different cultures together.
2. Ask for a few volunteers to share their answers with the class.

To save class time, skip "Before You Read" or have students prepare answers for homework ahead of time.

Reading *CD 2, Track 7*

1. Have students first read the text silently. Tell them to pay special attention to the reflexive pronouns. Then play the audio and have students read along silently.
2. Check students' comprehension. Ask questions such as: *Why do couples often pay for their own weddings?* (They're older.) *Instead of spending $1,000 on a dress, what does the author suggest brides do?* (Buy a secondhand dress or make it themselves.) *What does one couple suggest for music?* (Hire a DJ for dancing instead of a live band.) *Is January a popular time to get married?* (no) *What's the best way to save money on a wedding?* (Don't invite a lot of people.)

To save class time, have students do the reading for homework ahead of time.

DID YOU KNOW?

Although American women and men are marrying at a later age now than they did during the 1950s, Americans historically have always married at relatively later ages. From the 1890s to 1940, the average age of marriage for American men and women were about the same as they are today.

Some recently married people give advice on how to economize on a wedding and still have a lovely, memorable event. Here are their tips:

- "I always pictured **myself** in a beautiful white dress. But when I went shopping and saw that most dresses are at least $1,000, I decided to look for a secondhand dress. I found something for $200, and it was lovely. When my sister got married, she made her dress **herself** and spent only $100 on fabric and lace. It isn't necessary to spend so much money on a dress. A bride is always beautiful."
- "We were going to use a professional printer for the invitations, but we decided to make the invitations **ourselves.** We designed them on the computer and added ribbons. The guests told us that they were beautiful and original."

- "I always wanted live music at my wedding. But when I saw the cost of musicians, I was shocked. My cousin plays piano well, so I asked her to play the piano for the wedding. And we used a DJ[9] for the dancing afterwards. We had to remind **ourselves** that the music wasn't the focus for the day, our marriage was."
- "Most couples want to get married in the summer. Ask **yourself** how important a summer wedding really is. You can cut costs by having a wedding at a less popular time. For example, a wedding in January is cheaper than a wedding in August."

Did You Know?

The average age of marriage is 27 for men and 25 for women.

According to some couples, it is not good to economize on some things.

- "Don't try to save money by sending invitations or thank-you cards through e-mail. Guests are offended. You should use postal mail."
- "We asked a friend to take pictures at our wedding but were very disappointed with the results. Our advice: Hire a professional photographer. You want to look at **yourselves** and guests for years to come."

The best way to economize is to cut the guest list and invite only your closest relatives and friends.

While most young couples want a perfect wedding, the most important thing is to have a good marriage.

[9]A *DJ* is a disk jockey, a person who plays recorded music from CDs.

130 Lesson 4

Culture Note

The United States has the highest marriage rates—and the highest divorce rates—of any other industrialized nation. Americans marry at a rate that is twice that of most Western European countries.

4.8 | Reflexive Pronouns

We use reflexive pronouns for the object when the subject and object are the same.
Compare:
The groom loves her.(object pronoun)
The bride loves herself.(reflexive pronoun)

Examples	Explanation
a. I pictured **myself** in a beautiful white dress. (D.O.) b. We tell **ourselves** that money makes us happy, but it's not true. (I.O.) c. They like to look at **themselves** in their wedding photos. (O.P.)	A reflexive pronoun can be a. a direct object (D.O.) b. an indirect object (I.O.) c. the object of a preposition (O.P.)
She made the dress **all by herself.** The bride and groom made the invitations **themselves.**	We often use a reflexive pronoun to mean alone, without help. We often add (*all*) *by* before the reflexive pronoun.
We enjoyed **ourselves** at the wedding. Help **yourself** to more cake. Make **yourself** at home.	We use reflexive pronouns in a few idiomatic expressions.

Forms

Subject	Verb	Reflexive Pronoun
I	see	myself.
You	see	yourself.
He	sees	himself.
She	sees	herself.
It	sees	itself.
We	see	ourselves.
You	see	yourselves.
They	see	themselves.

EXERCISE 18 Frank and Sylvia are like many American couples. They have problems balancing their relationship, children, careers, families, and other responsibilities. Read each one's story and fill in the blanks with a reflexive pronoun.

Sylvia's Story:

Now that I'm married, I don't have time for ___myself___ (example) anymore. We used to spend time with each other. Now that we have kids, we never have time for ___ourselves___ (1). We both work, but Frank doesn't help me with housework or with the kids. I have to do everything all by ___myself___ (2). My husband only thinks of ___himself___ (3). When he wants something, like a new digital camera or new software, he buys it.

Possessive Forms; Object Pronouns; Reflexive Pronouns; Questions 131

Exercise 18 Variation

To provide practice with listening skills, have students close their books and listen to the audio. Repeat the audio as needed. Ask comprehension questions, such as: *Does Frank help Sylvia with the housework?* (no) *Does Frank buy Sylvia lots of presents?* (no) *Does Frank like to go to the movies by himself?* (no) *Why doesn't Frank want to go to a counselor?* (because he doesn't like to tell people about their problems) Then have students open their books and complete Exercise 18.

4.8 | Reflexive Pronouns

1. Have students cover up grammar chart **4.8.** Then have students go back to the reading on pages 129 and 130. Say: *Find the reflexive pronouns in the reading. Circle them. Then find the subject of the sentence or phrase that contains the reflexive pronoun and underline it* (e.g., *They often pay for things themselves.*). Write students' examples on the board. Say: *When the object and the subject of the sentence are the same, we use a reflexive pronoun for the object.*
2. Write the following two sentences on the board:
   The groom loves her.
   The bride loves herself.
   Say: *Look at these two sentences. What is the difference between the two?* (In the first example, the object (*her*) is not the same person as the subject (*the groom*). In the second, the object (*the bride*) and the subject (*herself*) are the same.)
3. Review the forms of the reflexive pronouns. Write a list of the subject pronouns on the board. Ask volunteers to write the reflexive pronouns. Point out that *you* has both a singular reflexive pronoun (*yourself*) and a plural reflexive pronoun (*yourselves*).
4. Have students look at grammar chart **4.8.** Review the examples and explanations in the chart. Go over the reflexive pronoun as a direct object, as an indirect object, and as the object of a preposition.
5. Point out that the reflexive pronoun is often used to mean "alone" (without help). Often "(all) by" is added for emphasis. Direct students to the idiomatic expressions. Give students more examples. Have students make their own sentences using idiomatic expressions.

EXERCISE 18

CD 2, Track 8

1. Tell students that this exercise is about a husband and wife, Frank and Sylvia. Talk about married life. Have students read the direction line. Go over the example in the book.
2. Have students complete Exercise 18 individually. Go over the answers as a class.
3. If necessary, review grammar charts **4.8** on page 131.

EXERCISE 19

1. Have students read the direction line. Ask: *What do you like to do by yourself?* Go over the examples. Model the exercise for the class (e.g., *I like to go to the movies by myself.*).
2. Have students complete the exercise individually. Then have students compare sentences in pairs. Circulate to observe pair work.
3. If necessary, review grammar chart **4.8** on page 131.

To save class time, have students write their sentences for homework ahead of time.

He never buys me flowers or presents anymore. I tell _myself_ (4) that he still loves me, but sometimes I'm not so sure. Sometimes I think the problem is his fault, but sometimes I blame _myself_ (5).

Frank's Story:

Sylvia never has time for me anymore. We used to do things together. Now I have to do everything by _myself_ (6). If I want to go to a movie, she says that she's too busy or too tired or that the kids are sick. I rarely go to the movies, and if I do, I go by _myself_ (7). It seems that all I do is work and pay bills. Other married people seem to enjoy _themselves_ (8) more than we do. She says she wants me to help her with the housework, but she really prefers to do everything _herself_ (9) because she doesn't like the way I do things. She wants us to see a marriage counselor, but I don't like to tell other people about my problems. I like to solve my problems _myself_ (10).

What do you think Frank and Sylvia should do?

EXERCISE 19 ABOUT YOU Write two sentences telling about things you like to do by yourself. Write two sentences telling about things you don't like to do by yourself.

EXAMPLES *I like to shop by myself.*

I don't like to eat by myself.

Answers will vary.

______

______

132 Lesson 4

Expansion

Exercise 18 In small groups, have students discuss the question at the end of Exercise 18 (***What do you think Frank and Sylvia should do?***). Instruct groups to come up with three things Frank should do and three things Sylvia should do to improve their married life. Have groups share their answers. Make a class list and vote on the top three pieces of advice.

Exercise 18 Have students create similar monologues about being married or about living in large families. Encourage students to use reflexive pronouns whenever possible. Have volunteers perform their monologues in class.

EXERCISE 20 *Combination Exercise.* Fill in the blanks with the correct pronoun possessive form.

Frank and Sylvia used to do a lot of things together. They (example) went to movies, went out to restaurants, and took vacations together.

But now they (1) are always too busy for each other. They (2) have two children and spend most of their (3) time taking care of them (4).

Frank and Sylvia bought a house recently and spend their (5) free time taking care of it (6). It's an old house and needs a lot of work.

When Frank and Sylvia have problems, they (7) try to solve them (8) by themselves (9). But sometimes Sylvia goes to her (10) mother for advice. Frank never goes to his (11) mother. He doesn't want to bother her (12) with his (13) problems. Frank often complains that Sylvia cares more about the kids and the house than about him (14).

Sylvia wants to go to a marriage counselor, but Frank doesn't want to go with her (15). He always says to Sylvia, "We don't need a marriage counselor. We can solve our (16) problems by ourselves (17). You just need to pay more attention to me (18). If you want to see a counselor, you can go by yourself (19). I'm not going." Sylvia feels very frustrated. She thinks that the marriage isn't going to get better by itself (20).

QUESTIONS AND ANSWERS ABOUT AN AMERICAN WEDDING

Before You Read

1. Do you have any questions about American weddings?
2. How is a traditional American wedding different from a wedding in your native culture?

EXERCISE 20

1. Tell students that this exercise is about the married couple, Frank and Sylvia. Have students read the direction line. Go over the example. Model the exercise for the class.
2. Have students complete the exercise individually. Then have students compare their answers with a partner. Circulate to observe pair work.
3. If necessary, review grammar charts **4.2** on page 119, **4.5** on page 124, **4.6** on page 127, and **4.8** on page 131.

To save class time, have students do half of the exercise in class and complete the other half for homework. Or assign the entire exercise for homework.

Questions and Answers about an American Wedding (Reading)

1. Have students look at the photo on page 134. Ask: *What do you think the woman is doing?* (opening gifts; reading a card)
2. Have students look at the title of the reading. Ask: *What kind of questions do you have about American weddings?* Write students' questions on the board.
3. Preteach any vocabulary words your students may not know such as *cookware* and *appliances.*

BEFORE YOU READ

1. Have students discuss the questions in pairs. Try to pair students of different cultures together.
2. Ask for a few volunteers to share their answers with the class.

To save class time, skip "Before You Read" or have students prepare answers for homework ahead of time.

Reading 🎧 ***CD 2, Track 9***

1. Have students first read the text silently. Tell them to pay special attention to the questions. Then play the audio and have students read along silently.
2. Check students' comprehension. Ask questions such as: *What kind of gifts do brides get at a shower?* (towels, cookware, linens, and small appliances) *Who pays the hotel for the bridesmaids?* (the bride) *Is the groom's brother always the best man?* (No, it can be a friend or another relative.) *How much do friends usually spend on a wedding gift?* (about $100)

To save class time, have students do the reading for homework ahead of time.

Read the following questions and answers about American weddings. Pay special attention to questions.

Q: Who pays for the wedding?

A: In the past, the bride's parents paid for most of the wedding. Today only about 20 percent of weddings are the responsibility of the bride's parents. As men and women are getting married after starting careers and earning money, more and more weddings are becoming the responsibility of the bride and groom.

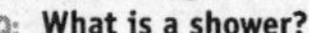

Q: What is a shower?

A: A shower is a party for the bride (and sometimes the groom) before the wedding. The purpose of the party is to give the couple gifts that will help them start their new home. Typical gifts are towels, cookware, linens[10], and small kitchen and household appliances.

Q: Who hosts the shower?

A: Usually the maid of honor hosts the shower. She invites friends and relatives of the bride and groom.

Q: When do they have the shower?

A: Usually the shower is two to six weeks before the wedding.

Q: How long does it take to plan a wedding?

A: Most couples plan their wedding for seven to twelve months.

Q: When do the couples send invitations?

A: They usually send the invitations about eight weeks before the wedding.

Q: When guests come in from out of town, **who pays for their hotel and transportation?**

A: The out-of-town guests pay for their own hotel. However, the groom pays for the hotel for his groomsmen and the bride pays for her bridesmaids. The guests usually pay for their own transportation.

Q: Whom does the groom choose as his best man?

A: Often the groom chooses his brother or best friend. However, he chooses the man he feels closest to. The groom chooses other close friends or male relatives as the groomsmen.

Q: When do the bride and groom open their gifts?

A: They open their gifts at home, not at the wedding.

Q: How do the guests know what the bride and groom want as gifts?

A: The bride and groom usually register for gifts at stores. They list the gift items they want and need for their new home, such as dishes, cookware, small appliances, and towels. When the guests go to buy a gift, they check the registry in the store. Of course, money is always a popular gift.

Q: How do I know how much money to give?

A: Most guests spend about $100 on a gift. People who are closer to the bride or groom often spend more. Casual friends usually spend less.

[10] *Linens* are sheets, pillowcases, and tablecloths.

Reading Variation

To practice listening skills, have students first listen to the audio alone. Ask a few comprehension questions. Repeat the audio if necessary. Then have them open their books and read along as they listen to the audio.

Reading Glossary

appliance: a device used for a specific function, usually electrical and used in the home
cookware: utensils that are used for cooking, such as pots and pans

Culture Note

Many couples hire a wedding consultant or wedding planner to help with planning and organizing their big event. Wedding planners typically charge anywhere from 10 percent to 15 percent of the total wedding budget for their services.

4.9 | Questions About the Subject or Complement

Questions about the complement include *do, does,* or *did.* Questions about hte subject do not include *do, does,* or *did.*

Examples	Explanation
Who wears a white dress? The bride **does.** **Who paid** for the wedding? The parents **did.** **How many people came** to the wedding? About 150 people **did.**	We usually answer a subject question with a subject and an auxiliary verb.
What happened after the wedding? The bride and groom **went** on a honeymoon.	*What happened* is a subject question. We usually answer with a different verb.
Who **has** the prettiest dress? Which woman **has** the prettiest dress? Which women **have** the prettiest dresses? How many people **want** to dance?	• After *who*, use the *-s* form for the simple present tense. • After *which* + noun, use either the base form or the *-s* form. • After *how many,* use the base form.

Compare these statements and related questions.

Wh- Word	*Do/Does/Did*	Subject	Verb	Complement
		The groom	paid for	the rings.
What	did	the bride	pay for?	
		Someone	paid for	the wedding.
		Who	paid for	the wedding?
		The groom	chooses	a best man.
Whom	does	he	choose?	
		The bride	chooses	her dress.
		Who	chooses	the rings?
		Out-of-town guests	stay	at a hotel.
Why	do	they	stay	at a hotel?
		Who	stays	at a hotel?
		Something	happened	next.
		What	happened	next?

Language Note:
In a question about the object, *whom* is very formal. Informally, many Americans say *who.*
Formal: *Whom* did your brother marry?
Informal: *Who* did your brother marry?

4.9 | Questions About the Subject or Complement

1. Have students go to the reading on page 134. Ask them to look at the questions in the reading. Say: *Underline the questions with* do *or* does (e.g., *When do they have the shower?*). *Are these questions about the subject or the complement?* (the complement—*two to four weeks before the wedding*) *Circle the questions with a verb in the* -s *form* (e.g., *Who pays for the wedding?*). *Are these questions asking about the subject or the complement?* (the subject—*the bride's parents/the bride and groom*)
2. Have students look at grammar chart **4.9** on page 135. Explain that when we use *do* or *does* in a question, we are asking about the complement of the sentence, not the subject. Say: *When we use the* -s *form in a question and not* do, does, *or* did, *we are asking a question about the subject.* Read the examples and the explanation.
3. Have students look back at the reading on page 134 to compare questions about the subject with questions about the complement.
4. Point out that although *What happened?* is a subject question, the answer usually has another verb (not *happen* or an auxiliary verb).
5. Review the forms to use after *who, which* + noun, and *how many.*
6. Have students label the questions in the comparison chart on page 135. Ask: *Which questions are about the complement and which questions are about the subject?*
7. Direct students to the Language Note. Explain that *whom* is very formal. Native speakers typically use *who.*

EXERCISE 21

1. Have students read the direction line. Go over the example in the book. Say: *These questions are all questions about the subject.*
2. Have students complete Exercise 21 individually. Go over the answers as a class.
3. If necessary, review grammar chart **4.9** on page 135.

EXERCISE 22

1. Have students read the direction line. Say: *First you'll write the questions. Then we'll answer the questions as a class.* Go over the examples in the book.
2. Have students write the questions individually. Then answer the questions as a class.
3. If necessary, review grammar chart **4.9** on page 135.

To save class time, have students write half or all of the questions for homework. Then have students ask the class questions if time allows.

EXERCISE 21 Read each statement. Then write a question about the words in parentheses( ). No answer is necessary.

EXAMPLE **Someone takes the bride to the groom. (who)**

Who takes the bride to the groom?

1. **Someone dances the first dance. (who)**
   Who dances the first dance?
2. **Someone holds the rings. (who)**
   Who holds the rings?
3. **Two people say, "I do." (how many people / "congratulations")**
   How many people say, "Congratulations?"
4. **The bridesmaids sometimes wear matching dresses.[11] (which woman / a white dress)**
   Which woman wears a white dress?
5. **The bride pays for her white dress. (who / the bridesmaids' dresses)**
   Who pays for the bridesmaids' dresses?

EXERCISE 22 ABOUT YOU Use the simple present tense of the verb in parentheses ( ) to ask a question about this class. Any student may volunteer an answer.

EXAMPLES **Who (ride) a bike to school?**

A: Who rides a bike to school?
B: I do.

How many students (have) the textbook?

A: How many students have the textbook?
B: We all do.

Answers will vary.

1. **Who (explain) the grammar?** *Who explains the grammar?*
2. **How many students (speak) Spanish?** *How many students speak Spanish?*
3. **What usually (happen) after class?** *What usually happens after class?*
4. **Who (need) help with this lesson?** *Who needs help with this lesson?*
5. **Who (have) a computer?** *Who has a computer?*
6. **Who (have) a digital camera?** *Who has a digital camera?*
7. **Who (live) alone?** *Who lives alone?*

[11] ***Matching dresses*** **are all the same color.**

136 Lesson 4

Expansion

Exercise 21 Have students create statements about wedding traditions in their native countries. Have students model their statements after the statements in Exercise 21 (e.g., *Someone carries coins for good luck. Who carries coins for good luck?*). Then have a partner ask questions about the subject.

EXERCISE 23 ABOUT YOU Use the simple past tense of the verb in parentheses ( ) to ask a question. Any student may volunteer an answer.

EXAMPLE Who (buy) a used textbook?
A: Who bought a used textbook?
B: I did.

Answers will vary.

1. Who (move) last year? *Who moved last year?*
2. Who (understand) the explanation? *Who understood the explanation?*
3. Who (take) a trip recently? *Who took a trip recently?*
4. Who (bring) a dictionary to class today? *Who brought a dictionary to class today?*
5. Who (pass) the last test? *Who passed the last test?*
6. Which students (come) late today? *Which students came late today?*
7. Which student (arrive) first today? *Which student arrived first today?*
8. How many students (do) today's homework? *How many students did today's homework?*
9. How many students (study) English in elementary school? *How many students studied English in elementary school?*
10. How many students (bring) a cell phone to class? *How many students brought a cell phone to class?*

EXERCISE 24 Read each statement. Then write a question about the words in parentheses ( ). Some of the questions are about the subject. Some are not. No answer is necessary.

EXAMPLES The bride wears a white dress. (what / the groom)
What does the groom wear?

The bride enters last. (who / first)
Who enters first?

The bride throws the bouquet. (when)
What does the groom wear?

Some women try to catch the bouquet. (which women)
Which women try to catch it?

The groom puts the ring on the bride's finger. (on which hand) OR (which hand . . . on)
On which hand does he put the ring? / Which hand does he put the ring on?

The band plays music. (what kind of music)
What kind of music does the band play?

Someone dances with the bride. (who)
Who dances with the bride?

EXERCISE 23

1. Have students read the direction line. Say: *You're going to write questions about the subject. Will your questions include* do, does *or* did? (no) Go over the example in the book. Say: *After you write the questions, we'll answer them as a class.*
2. Have students write the questions individually. Answer the questions as a class.
3. If necessary, review grammar chart **4.9** on page 135.

To save class time, do the exercise as a class.

EXERCISE 24

1. Have students read the direction line. Ask: *Are the questions about the subject?* (No. Some are about the complement.) Go over the examples in the book.
2. Have students write the questions individually. Then have students compare answers in pairs. Circulate to observe pair work. Give help as needed.
3. If necessary, review grammar chart **4.9** on page 135.

To save class time, have students do half of the exercise for homework and complete the other half in class. Or assign the entire exercise for homework.

EXERCISE 25

CD 2, Track 10

1. Tell students that the conversation in this exercise is between two women talking about their families. Direct students' attention to the photo. Then have students read the direction line. Go over the example in the book.
2. Have students complete Exercise 25 individually. Then have students compare answers in pairs. Circulate to observe pair work. Give help as needed.
3. If necessary, review grammar chart **4.9** on page 135.

To save class time, have students do half of the exercise for homework and complete the other half in class. Or assign the entire exercise for homework.

6. **Guests give presents. (what kind of presents)**
   What kind of presents do they give?
7. **Some people cry at the wedding. (who)**
   Who cries at the wedding?
8. **There's a dinner after the ceremony. (what / happen / after the dinner)**
   What happens after the dinner?

EXERCISE 25 In the conversation below, two women are talking about their families. Fill in the blanks to complete the questions. Some of the questions are about the subject. Some are about the object. Answers may vary.

A: **How do you have time to work, go to school, and take care of a family?**

B: **I don't have to do everything myself.**

A: **Who** *helps you* ? ***(example)***

B: **My husband helps me.**

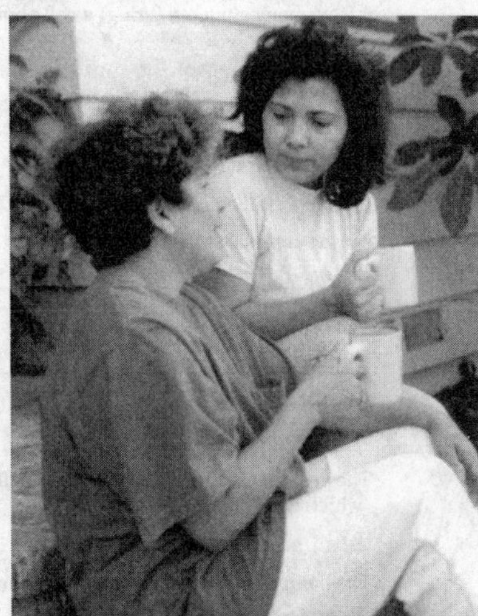

138 Lesson 4

Exercise 25 Variation

To provide practice with listening skills, have students close their books and listen to the audio. Repeat the audio as needed. Ask comprehension questions such as: ***Who helps at home while person B is at work or at school?*** (her husband) ***How many children does person B have?*** (five) ***Who is her babysitter?*** (the neighbor) Then have students open their books and complete Exercise 25.

A: I usually cook in my house. Who cooks in your house (1)?

B: Sometimes my husband cooks; sometimes I cook. We take turns.

A: I usually clean. Who cleans the house (2)?

B: I usually clean the house.

A: How many children do you have (3)?

B: I have five children.

A: How many children go to school (4)?

B: Three children go to school. The younger ones stay home.

A: Do you send them to public school or private school?

B: One of my sons goes to private school.

A: Which one (5)?

B: The oldest does. He's in high school now.

A: It's hard to take care of so many children. How do you find the time to go to class?

B: As I said, my husband helps me a lot. And sometimes I use a babysitter.

A: I'm looking for a sitter. Who(m) do you recommend (6)?

B: I recommend our neighbor, Susan. She's 16 years old, and she's very good with our children.

A: Maybe she's too busy to help me. How many families does she work for (7)?

B: I think she works for only one other family. I'll give you her phone number. If she's not busy, maybe she can work for you too.

A: Thanks. I can use some help.

EXERCISE 26 Fill in the blanks with *who, whom, who's,* or *whose.*

1. Who's your English teacher? Cindy Kane is my teacher.
2. Who do you live with? I live with my sister.
3. Who has the right answer? I have the right answer.
4. There's no name on this book. Whose is it?
5. Whose parents speak English? My parents do.

EXERCISE 26

1. Have students read the direction line. Say: *More than one answer may be right. You may use the question words more than once.*
2. Have students complete the exercise individually. Go over the answers as a class.
3. If necessary, review grammar charts **4.4** on page 123 and **4.9** on page 135.

Expansion

Exercise 25 Have students work in pairs to practice the conversation or write a conversation about their own family lives. Ask volunteers to role-play the conversation in front of the class.

Summary of Lesson 4

1. **Pronouns and Possessive Forms** Have students cover up the summary. Write the list of subject pronouns on the board. Write the headings of the other lists (*Object Pronoun, Possessive Adjective,* etc.). Ask students to fill in the rest of the chart. On the board, write the example sentences below the chart in the book without the pronouns:
   Robert and Lisa are my friends.
   ____ come from Canada.
   I like ____.
   Have students fill in the blanks. Do the same with the *wh-* question words. If necessary, have students review:
   4.2 Possessive Adjectives (p. 119)
   4.3 Possessive Pronouns (p. 120)
   4.5 Object Pronouns (p. 124)
   4.8 Reflexive Pronouns (p. 131)
   4.9 Questions About the Subject and Complement (p. 135).
2. **Possessive Form of Nouns** Rewrite the examples from the summary without the possessive form:
   the dress of the bride
   the house of the father
   Ask students to make the examples into possessive nouns. If necessary, have students review:
   4.1 Possessive Forms of Nouns (p. 117).
3. ***Say* and *Tell*** Rewrite the examples from the summary without *say* and *tell.* For example:
   He ____ his name.
   He ____ me his name.
   Ask students to fill in the blanks with *said* or *told.* If necessary, have students review:
   4.7 *Say* and *Tell* (p. 128).
4. **Questions About the Subject** Write the following statements on the board:
   Jamie has the rings. (who)
   Three bridesmaids have pink dresses. (how many)
   That bridesmaid has a red dress. (which)
   Those bridesmaids have pink flowers. (which)
   A man kissed the bride. (who)
   That man kissed the bride. (which)
   Ask students to make questions about the subject for each statement. If necessary, have students review:
   4.9 Questions About the Subject and the Complement (p. 135).

SUMMARY OF LESSON 4

1. Pronouns and Possessive Forms

Subject Pronoun	Object Pronoun	Possessive Adjective	Possessive Pronoun	Reflexive Pronoun
I	me	my	mine	myself
you	you	your	yours	yourself
he	him	his	his	himself
she	her	her	hers	herself
it	it	its	—	itself
we	us	our	ours	ourselves
you	you	your	yours	yourselves
they	them	their	theirs	themselves
who	whom	whose	whose	—

EXAMPLES
Robert and Lisa are my friends.
They come from Canada.
I like **them.**
Their wedding was beautiful.
My wedding was small.
Theirs was big.
They paid for the wedding **themselves.**

Who has a new car?
With **whom** do you live? (FORMAL)
Who do you live with? (INFORMAL)
Whose book is that?
This is my dictionary. **Whose** is that?

2. Possessive Form of Nouns

Singular Nouns
the **bride's** dress
my **father's** house
the **child's** toy
the **man's** hat
Charles' wife / **Charles's** wife

Plural Nouns
the **bridesmaids'** dresses
my **parents'** house
the **children's** toys
the **men's** hats

3. *Say* and *Tell*

He **said** his name.
He **told** me his name.
He **said** good-bye to his friends.
He **told** them to write often.

4. Questions About the Subject

Simple Present:
Who has the rings?
How many bridesmaids have a pink dress?
Which bridesmaid has a red dress?
Which bridesmaids have pink flowers?

Simple Past:
Who kissed the bride?
Which man kissed the bride?
What happened next?

140 Lesson 4

Summary Variation

Item 1 Break the class up into two teams. Create two identical charts on the board with only the subject pronouns filled in. See which team can fill in the chart the fastest.

EDITING ADVICE

1. Don't confuse *you're* (you are) and *your* (possessive form).

   ~~Your~~ *You're* late.

   ~~You're~~ *Your* class started ten minutes ago.

2. Don't confuse *he's* (he is) and *his* (possessive form).

   ~~His~~ *He's* married.

   ~~He's~~ *His* wife is a friend of mine.

3. Don't confuse *it's* (it is) and *its* (possessive form).

   This college is big. ~~Its~~ *It's* a state university.

   ~~It's~~ *Its* library has many books.

4. Don't confuse *his* (masculine possessor) and *her* (feminine possessor).

   My sister loves ~~his~~ *her* son.

   My brother loves ~~her~~ *his* daughter.

5. Don't confuse *my* and *mine*.

   I don't have ~~mine~~ *my* book today.

6. Don't confuse *they're* and *their*.

   ~~They're~~ *Their* last name is Williams.

7. Use the correct pronoun (subject or object).

   I have a daughter. I love ~~she~~ *her* very much.

8. For a compound subject, use "another person and I." Don't use *me* in the subject position.

   My father and ~~me~~ *I* like to go fishing.

   ~~Me and my father~~ *My father and I* like to go fishing.

Editing Advice

Have students close their books. Write the example sentences without editing marks or corrections on the board. For example:

1. *Your late. You're class started ten minutes ago.*
2. *His married.*

Ask students to correct each sentence and provide a rule or explanation for each correction. This activity can be done individually, in pairs, or as a class. After students have corrected each sentence, tell them to turn to pages 141–142. Say: *Now compare your work with the Editing Advice in the book.*

9. For a compound object, use "another person and me." Don't use *I* in the object position.

My parents gave my brother and ~~I~~ *me* a present.

10. Don't use *the* with a possessive form.

~~The my~~ *M*y wife's mother is very nice.

11. Don't use an apostrophe to make a plural form.

They invited many ~~guest's~~ *guests* to the wedding.

12. Don't use an auxiliary verb in a question about the subject.

Who ~~does~~ speak*s* Spanish?

13. Don't separate *whose* from the noun.

Whose is this book?

14. Don't confuse *whose* and *who's*.

~~Who's~~ *Whose* coat is that?

15. Use the correct word order for possession.

~~Mother my wife~~ *My wife's mother* helps us a lot.

16. Put the apostrophe after the *s* of a plural noun that ends in *s*.

My ~~parent's~~ *parents'* house is small.

17. The *s* in a possessive pronoun is not for a plural.

Theirs parents live in Canada.

18. Don't use a form of *be* with *what happened.*

What was happened to your new car?

19. Use correct word order with direct and indirect objects.

She explained ~~me the grammar~~ *the grammar to me*.

I gave ~~him it~~ *it to him*.

LESSON 4 TEST / REVIEW

PART 1 Find the mistakes with the underlined words, and correct them. Not every sentence has a mistake. If the sentence is correct, write *C*.

EXAMPLES The bride's the parents are very proud.

They are going to get married in their parents' house. C

1. Do you like the bridesmaid's dresses?
2. The groom puts the ring on the brides' left hand.
3. The bride throws his bouquet to the single women. her
4. The groom dances with her new wife. his
5. When will they open their friends gifts?
6. They're car has a sign that says "Just Married." Their
7. The groom's friend's often have a party for him before the wedding.
8. Your wedding was very beautiful. C
9. She married his best friend's brother. C
10. Her husband's mother's friend is wearing a beautiful dress. C
11. The womens' dresses are very elegant.
12. My sister's the wedding will be in March.
13. Your name is different from your husband's name. C
14. She visits hers parents once a week.
15. The groom graduated from college. His an accountant now. He's
16. Our friends invited my wife and me to their wedding. C
17. My wife and me went to a beautiful wedding. I
18. Who did get married in a church? got
19. Whose mother is that? I think it's mother the bride. the, of
20. How many people brought gifts to the wedding? C
21. Please describe me the painting. to me
22. Who throw the bouquet at an American wedding? The bride does. s
23. Theirs dresses are green. Mine is black.
24. The your wedding was lovely. Y
25. What was happened after the wedding?
26. Show me the wedding pictures. C

Possessive Forms; Object Pronouns; Reflexive Pronouns; Questions 143

Lesson 4 Test/Review

For additional practice, review, and assessment materials, see Assessment CD-ROM with *ExamView Pro*, *More Grammar Practice* Workbook 2, Interactive CD-ROM, and Web site http://elt.thomson.com/gic

PART 1

1. Part 1 may be used as an in-class test to assess student performance, in addition to the Assessment CD-ROM with *ExamView Pro*. Have students read the direction line. Collect for assessment.
2. If necessary, have students review: **Lesson 4.**

Lesson Review

To use Part 1 as a review, assign it as homework or use it as an in-class activity to be completed individually or in pairs. Check answers and review errors as a class. Reteach grammar points that students haven't mastered. Then student learning may be assessed using a test generated from the Assessment CD-ROM with *ExamView Pro*.

PART 2

1. Part 2 may also be used as an in-class test to assess student performance, in addition to the Assessment CD-ROM with *ExamView Pro*. Have students read the direction line. Instruct them to write the letter for the correct answer in the blank. Collect for assessment.
2. If necessary, have students review: **Lesson 4.**

PART 2 Choose the correct word to complete each sentence.

EXAMPLE **Do you like ___c___ neighbors?**

a. you b. you're c. your d. yours

1. Where do your parents live? ___b___ live in Colombia.
   a. My b. Mine c. Mine's d. Mines
2. ___a___ coat is that?
   a. Whose b. Who's c. Who d. Whom
3. ___a___ is usually white.
   a. The bride's dress b. The brides' dress
   c. Dress the bride d. The dress of bride
4. My sister's daughter is 18. ___b___ son is 16.
   a. His b. Her c. Hers d. Her's
5. What's ___c___?
   a. the name your son b. the name your son's
   c. your son's name d. your the son's name
6. Look at those dogs. Do you see ___c___?
   a. they b. its c. them d. it's
7. We have your phone number. Do you have ___c___?
   a. us b. our c. ours d. our's
8. What is ___b___?
   a. that building name b. the name of that building
   c. the name that building d. the name's that building
9. ___c___
   a. Whose is this sweater? b. Who's is this sweater?
   c. Whose sweater is this? d. Who's sweater is this?
10. ___d___ the correct answer?
    a. Who knew b. Whom knows c. Who does know d. Who knows
11. They have my address, but I don't have ___d___.
    a. their b. them c. they're d. theirs
12. We did it by ___d___.
    a. self b. oneself c. ourself d. ourselves

Lesson Review

To use Part 2 as a review, assign it as homework or use it as an in-class activity to be completed individually or in pairs. Check answers and review errors as a class. Reteach grammar points that students haven't mastered. Then student learning may be assessed using a test generated from the Assessment CD-ROM with *ExamView Pro*.

13. They can help ___d___.

a. theirself b. theirselves c. themself d. themselves

14. I know ___a___ very well.

a. myself b. mineself c. meself d. self

15. My teacher speaks Spanish. My ___c___ teacher doesn't.

a. husbands b. husbands' c. husband's d. the husband's

PART 3 Fill in the blanks with *said* or *told*.

1. She ___said___, "Excuse me."
2. She ___told___ them to study.
3. She ___told___ him the truth.
4. She ___said___ "hello" to her neighbor.
5. She ___told___ them the answers.
6. She ___told___ us about her trip.
7. She ___told___ an interesting story.
8. She ___told___ them her name.

PART 4 Complete the question. Some of these questions ask about the subject. Some do not. The answer is underlined.

EXAMPLES What ___does the bride wear___?

The bride wears a white dress and a veil.

Who ___usually cries at the wedding___?

The bride's mother usually cries at the wedding.

1. When ___does she throw the bouquet___?

She throws the bouquet at the end of the wedding party.

2. Which women ___try to catch the bouquet___?

The single women try to catch the bouquet.

3. On which hand ___does the groom put the ring___?

The groom puts the ring on the bride's left hand.

4. Whom ___does the groom kiss___?

The groom kisses the bride.

Possessive Forms; Object Pronouns; Reflexive Pronouns; Questions 145

PART 3

1. Part 3 may also be used as an in-class test to assess student performance, in addition to the Assessment CD-ROM with *ExamView Pro*. Have students read the direction line. Collect for assessment.
2. If necessary, have students review: **4.7** *Say* and *Tell* (p. 128).

PART 4

1. Part 4 may also be used as an in-class test to assess student performance, in addition to the Assessment CD-ROM with *ExamView Pro*. Have students read the direction line. Go over the examples. Remind students that some of the questions are about the complement and some are about the subject. Ask: *Which example has a question about the subject?* (the 2nd example) *How do you know?* (It doesn't contain *do*, *does*, or *did*.) Collect for assessment.
2. If necessary, have students review: **4.9** Questions About the Subject or Complement (p. 135).

Lesson Review

To use Parts 3 and 4 as a review, assign them as homework or use them as in-class activities to be completed individually or in pairs. Check answers and review errors as a class. Reteach grammar points that students haven't mastered. Then student learning may be assessed using a test generated from the Assessment CD-ROM with *ExamView Pro*.

PART 5

1. Part 5 may also be used as an in-class test to assess student performance, in addition to the Assessment CD-ROM with *ExamView Pro*. Have students read the direction line. Collect for assessment.
2. If necessary, have students review:
   4.8 Reflexive Pronouns (p. 131).

5. Whose *ring has a diamond*?
   The bride's ring has a diamond.
6. Whose *name does the bride use*?
   The bride uses her husband's last name.
7. Who *took pictures at your wedding*?
   A professional photographer took pictures at my wedding.
8. Whose *dress did you borrow*?
   I borrowed my sister's dress.
9. Whose *wedding was bigger*, yours or your sisters?
   My sister's wedding was bigger.
10. How many people *came to the wedding*?
    Over 250 people came to the wedding.
11. Who *cut the cake*?
    The bride and groom cut the cake.

PART 5 Fill in the blanks with a reflexive pronoun.

EXAMPLE She likes to talk about *herself*.

1. I made the cake all by *myself*.
2. The bride made her dress *herself*.
3. They prepared *themselves* financially before getting married.
4. We helped *ourselves* to another piece of cake.
5. The groom bought *himself* a new pair of shoes.
6. All of you should help *yourselves* to more cake and coffee.
7. Did you go to the wedding by *yourself* or did your wife go with you?

146 Lesson 4

Lesson Review

To use Part 5 as a review, assign it as homework or use it as an in-class activity to be completed individually or in pairs. Check answers and review errors as a class. Reteach grammar points that students haven't mastered. Then student learning may be assessed using a test generated from the Assessment CD-ROM with *ExamView Pro*.

EXPANSION ACTIVITIES

Classroom Activities

1. Form a small group. The group should have people from different cultures and countries, if possible. Talk about weddings and marriages in your native cultures and countries.
   a. Who chooses a husband for a woman?
   b. Who pays for the wedding?
   c. What happens at the wedding?
   d. What happens after the wedding?
   e. Do the guests bring gifts to the wedding? What kind of gifts do they give? Where do the bride and groom open the gifts?
   f. How many people attend a wedding?
   g. Where do people get married?
   h. Do people dance at a wedding?
   i. Who takes pictures?
   j. What color dress does the bride wear?
   k. At what age do people usually get married?
2. In a small group, interview one person who is married. Ask this person questions about his or her wedding.

   EXAMPLES Where did you get married?
   How many people did you invite?
   How many people came?
   Where did you go on your honeymoon?
3. According to an American tradition, the bride should wear:
   Something old,
   Something new,
   Something borrowed,
   Something blue.

   Do you have any traditions regarding weddings in your native culture?
4. Do you have a video of a wedding in your family? If so, can you bring it to class and tell the class about it? The teacher may have a video of an American wedding to show the class.

Expansion Activities

These expansion activities provide opportunities for students to interact with one another and further develop their speaking and writing skills. Encourage students to use grammar from this lesson whenever possible.

To save class time, assign parts of the activities as homework. Then use class time for interaction and communication. If students do not need additional speaking practice, some of the activities may be assigned as writing activities for homework, or skipped altogether.

CLASSROOM ACTIVITIES

1. After the groups discuss each question, have them report to the class. Write the nationalities and cultures represented in the class on the board. Write brief notes for each item under the country so that the class can compare.
2. If possible, put students from different countries and cultures together in groups.
3. If applicable, tell the students about your own wedding and if you followed these specific traditions. Put students from different nationalities in groups to discuss traditions. Have groups share interesting traditions with the class.
4. If students don't have videos, ask them to bring in photos to share with the rest of the class.

Classroom Activities Variation

Activity 1 Write nationalities represented in the class on the board. Have the class predict what each nationality would answer for each of the questions. Then ask volunteers from each nationality to say if each guess is correct or not.

CLASSROOM ACTIVITIES (*comt* .)

5. Have students write the advice individually. Then put students in groups to discuss the advice.

WRITE ABOUT IT

1. Direct students to the list of questions from Classroom Activity 1 (p. 147) for ideas to write about.
2. To help students prepare to write, have students get into pairs to talk about the problem they've had or are having.

TALK ABOUT IT

Have students discuss each point in pairs, in groups, or as a whole class.

INTERNET ACTIVITIES

1. Direct students to go to department store Web sites and not specialty stores that will only carry one type of gift. Brainstorm well-known department stores with the class and write them on the board.
2. Brainstorm key words to use while searching for information on planning a wedding (e.g., *wedding plans, plan a wedding*, and *wedding planning*).

5. Write some advice for newlyweds in each of the following categories. Discuss your sentences in a small group.

home	problem solving
children	mother-in-law
housework	money
careers	time together / time apart
family obligations	

Write About it

1. Write about a typical wedding in your native culture, or describe your own wedding.
2. Write about a problem you once had or have now. Tell what you did (or are doing) to help yourself solve this problem or how others helped you (or are helping you).

Talk About it

1. What kind of problems do most married people have today? Do you think American married couples have the same problems as couples in other countries?
2. Do you think married couples can solve their problems by themselves? At what point should they go to a marriage counselor?
3. Do you think married people should spend most of their time together, or should they spend time by themselves?
4. Do you think young people are realistic about marriage? How can they prepare themselves for the reality of marriage?
5. Some people go on TV in the U.S. and talk about themselves and their personal problems. What do you think about this?

Internet Activities

1. Do a search on *bridal registry* on the Internet. Make a list of the types of wedding gifts couples ask for.
2. Do a search on *weddings* on the Internet. Find out how Americans plan for a wedding.

Additional Activities at http://elt.thomson.com/gic

Write About it Variation

Have students exchange first drafts with a partner. Ask students to help their partners edit their drafts. Refer students to the Editing Advice on pages 141–142.

Internet Activities Variation

Activity 1 Tell students who don't have access to the Internet that they can also go to large department stores or specialty shops to look at typical gift registry information. Stores will often have premade lists that couples adapt for their own purposes.

Activity 2 Tell students who don't have access to the Internet that they can find information in libraries about planning a wedding.

Lesson | 5

LESSON

5

GRAMMAR
Singular and Plural
Count and Noncount Nouns
There + *Be*
Quantity Words

CONTEXT : Thanksgiving, Pilgrims, and American Indians
A Typical Thanksgiving
The Origin of Thanksgiving
Recipe for Turkey Stuffing
Taking the Land from the Native Americans
Navajo Code-Talkers

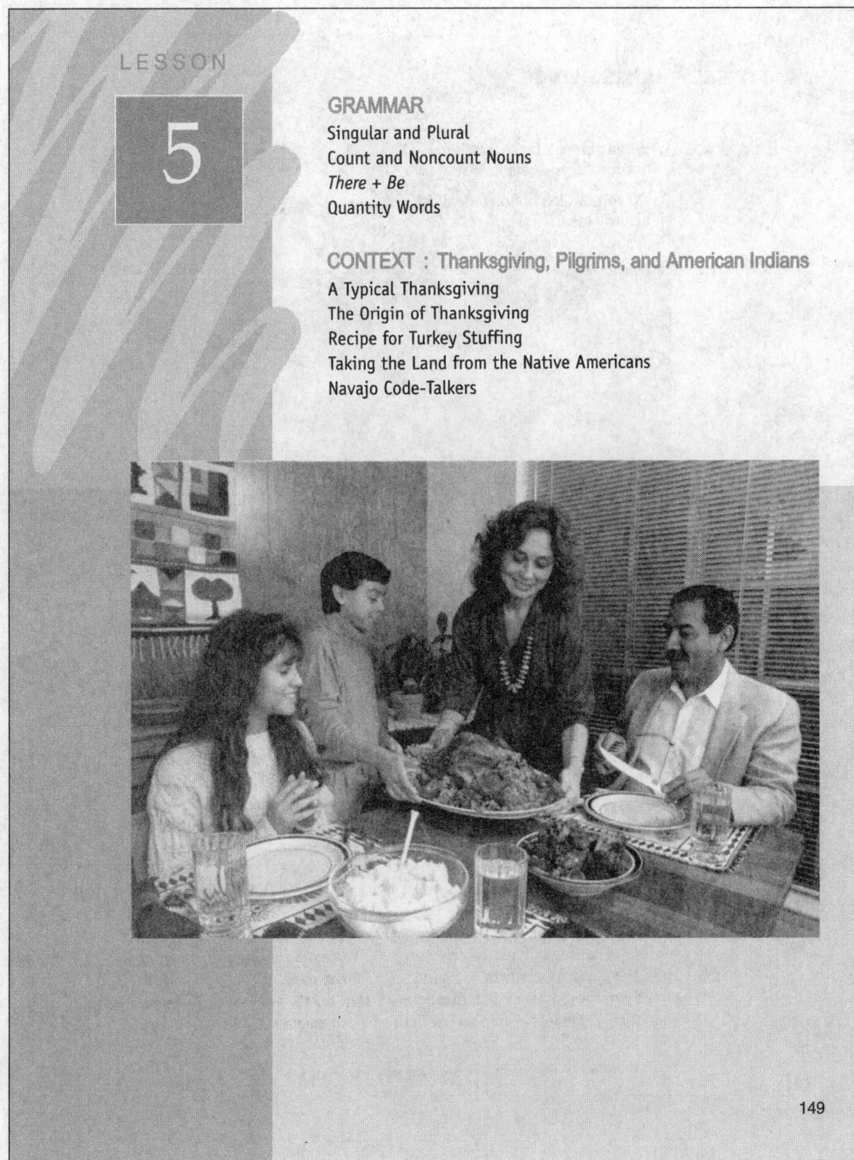

149

Lesson Overview

GRAMMAR

1. Briefly review what students learned in the last lesson. Ask: *What did we study in Lesson 4?* (possessive forms, object pronouns, reflexive pronouns, and questions)
2. Ask: *What will we study in this lesson?* (the singular and the plural, count and noncount nouns, *there* + *be*, and quantity words) *Can anyone give me an example of a count and a noncount noun?* (e.g., *apple, rice*) Have students give examples. Write the examples on the board. Then ask volunteers for sentences with *there + be* (e.g., *There is a mall in our town.*).

CONTEXT

1. Ask: *What will we learn about in this lesson?* (Thanksgiving, Pilgrims, and Native Americans) Activate students' prior knowledge. Ask: *What do you know about Thanksgiving? Who or what are Pilgrims? Does anyone know the names of any Native American tribes?*
2. Have students share their knowledge and personal experiences.

Photo

1. Direct students' attention to the photo. Ask: *What's happening in this picture?* (A family is celebrating Thanksgiving.)
2. Have students talk about some of their first American Thanksgiving experiences.

To save class time, have students do the Test/Review at the end of the lesson, or administer a lesson test generated from the Assessment CD-ROM with *ExamView® Pro.* Skip sections of the lesson that students have already mastered. You may also assign some sections for self-study for extra credit.

Expansion

Theme The topic for this lesson can be enhanced with the following ideas:

1. Sampling typical Thanksgiving dishes
2. Illustrations of the first Thanksgiving with Pilgrims and Native Americans
3. Books about Native American tribes
4. Native American artifacts and handicrafts

A Typical Thanksgiving (Reading)

1. Have students look at the photo of the parade. Ask: *Have you ever watched a Thanksgiving day parade in person or on TV? What kind of floats do you see in this parade?*
2. Have students look at the title of the reading. Ask: *What is the reading about?* Have students use the title, photo, and picture to make predictions about the reading.
3. Preteach any vocabulary words your students may not know, such as *snacks* and *diet*.

BEFORE YOU READ

1. Have students discuss the questions in pairs. Try to pair students of different cultures together.
2. Ask for a few volunteers to share their answers with the class.

To save class time, skip "Before You Read" or have students prepare answers for homework ahead of time.

Reading CD 2, Track 11

1. Have students first read the text silently. Tell them to pay special attention to singular and plural nouns. Then play the audio and have students read along silently.
2. Check students' comprehension. Ask questions such as: *When is Thanksgiving celebrated?* (the fourth Thursday of November) *When is the biggest travel day in the U.S.?* (the Sunday after Thanksgiving) *Does a typical Thanksgiving meal have a lot of calories?* (yes) *What are two activities people do on Thanksgiving?* (watch football and watch parades)

To save class time, have students do the reading for homework ahead of time.

A TYPICAL THANKSGIVING

Before You Read

1. When you celebrate a holiday, what kind of food do you prepare?
2. Do you think a holiday meal is a healthy meal?

Thanksgiving Day Parade

Read the following article. Pay special attention to singular and plural nouns.

Thanksgiving is a very special American holiday. We celebrate it on the fourth Thursday of November. **People** get together with family and **friends.** **Airports** are especially crowded as people travel to be with their **families** on this day. In fact, there are more **travelers** on the Sunday after Thanksgiving than any other day in the year.

On Thanksgiving, people eat a very big meal. While waiting for the **guests** to arrive, the host family usually puts out **snacks,** such as potato **chips** and **nuts.** The main part of the meal is **turkey.** Most people stuff the turkey with a mixture of **bread, onions, celery, nuts,** and **spices.** Some people add **fruit,** such as **apples** or **apricots** to the stuffing. Other parts of the meal include **sweet potatoes, mashed potatoes, gravy**[1], **corn bread,** and **cranberry sauce.** Then there is **dessert. Pumpkin pie** with whipped **cream** is a favorite dessert.

[1] *Gravy* is made from meat drippings, flour, water, and sometimes bacon fat.

150 Lesson 5

Reading Variation

To practice listening skills, have students first listen to the audio alone. Ask a few comprehension questions. Repeat the audio if necessary. Then have them open their books and read along as they listen to the audio.

Reading Glossary

diet: a weight loss program
snack: a small amount of food, usually eaten between meals

The typical Thanksgiving meal contains more than 3,000 **calories** and is 45 percent **fat.** Many people talk about going on a diet the day after Thanksgiving.

In addition to eating a big meal, many **people** relax and watch TV. It is a typical tradition to watch professional football on Thanksgiving day. The **men** are especially interested in football. Many **cities** also have a parade on Thanksgiving morning. New York City has a very big parade. **Millions** of people go to see the parade.

Thanksgiving is a relaxing and fun day for **families** and **friends.**

5.1 Noun Plurals

We use the plural to talk about more than one. Regular noun plurals add *-s* or *-es*. Some noun plurals are irregular.

Regular Noun Plurals

Word Ending	Example Noun	Plural Addition	Plural Form	Pronunciation
Vowel	bee banana	+ *s*	bees bananas	/z/
s, ss, sh, ch, x, z	church dish box watch class	+ *es*	churches dishes boxes watches classes	/əz/
Voiceless consonants	cat lip month	+ *s*	cats lips months	/s/
Voiced consonants	card pin	+ *s*	cards pins	/z/
Vowel + *y*	boy day	+ *s*	boys days	/z/
Consonant + *y*	lady story	~~*y*~~ + *ies*	ladies stories	/z/
Vowel + *o*	video radio	+ *s*	videos radios	/z/
Consonant + *o*	potato hero	+ *es*	potatoes heroes	/z/
Exceptions: photos, pianos, solos, altos, sopranos, autos, and avocados				
f or *fe*	leaf knife	~~*f*~~ + *ves*	leaves knives	/z/
Exceptions: beliefs, chiefs, roofs, cliffs, chefs, and sheriffs				

(*continued*)

Culture Note

Macy's Thanksgiving Day Parade is a famous annual event that began in 1924 when an enthusiastic group of Macy's employees decided to put on the first parade. Eighty years later, the parade is considered by Americans as the beginning of the holiday season. The only time the parade did not take place was for three years during World War II. During those years, Macy's donated the much needed rubber from the floats to the war effort. Now, in place of that small group of Macy's employees, more than four thousand volunteers help stage the magnificent display along two-and-a-half miles of Manhattan streets.

5.1 Noun Plurals

1. Copy the lists of nouns (singular and plural) from grammar chart **5.1** on the board. Keep nouns in the same groups and in the same order as in the chart in the book. For example:

   <u>*Singular*</u> <u>*Plural*</u>
   bee *bees*
   banana *bananas*

   church *churches*
   dish *dishes*
2. Have students cover up grammar chart **5.1** in their books. Say: *Study these spelling changes. Can you guess what the spelling rules for adding an -s are?* If students have difficulty, give them hints. Say: *Look at the endings of these five nouns:* church, dish, box, watch, and class. *What do you add to them to make them plural? (-es) So what's the rule?* (When the noun ends in *-ss*, *-sh*, *-ch*, or *-x*, add *-es*.) Continue with the same questions for the other groups of nouns.
3. Go over the pronunciation rules for plural nouns. Say: *There are three ways to pronounce the endings of plural nouns.* Across the board, write:
   (1)/s/ (2)/z/ (3)/əz/
   and pronounce each sound. Remind students that this is about pronunciation, not spelling or writing. Then say: *Listen to each word as I say it. Tell me which sound I'm making.* Say words from the grammar chart lists on page 151 in random order. Pronounce each word carefully. Have students guess where the word belongs and write it under the sound they tell you.
4. Have students look at grammar chart **5.1**. Say: *Compare our work with the book.* Review the rules in the grammar chart. Have students practice the pronunciation of the plural endings chorally or in pairs as needed.
5. Point out the exceptions. Nouns ending in a consonant + *-o* that do not add an *-e* are: *photos, pianos, solos, altos, sopranos, autos,* and *avocados.* Nouns that end in *-f* or *-fe* that don't change to *-ves* are: *beliefs, chiefs, roofs, cliffs, chefs,* and *sheriffs.*

5.1 | Noun Plurals (*cont.*)

6. Have students cover up the Irregular Noun Plurals section of the grammar chart **5.1** on page 152. Activate students' prior knowledge. Write the list of the singular nouns from the chart on the board. Ask volunteers to come up to the board and write the plural spellings.
7. Have students look at grammar chart **5.1.** Say: *Compare our nouns on the board with the plurals in the book. How many did we get right?* Review the information in the grammar chart. Explain to students that there are no rules for spelling changes with these nouns. English language learners must memorize the plural forms.
8. Demonstrate the pronunciation differences between *woman* and *women.* Say it several times and have students guess if you're saying the singular or plural. Then have students practice the pronunciation. Explain that sometimes you can use *persons* as the plural for *person* but that it's not common.

EXERCISE 1

1. Have students read the direction line. Go over the example in the book. Say: *Some of the nouns in this list are regular and some are irregular.*
2. Have students complete Exercise 1 individually. Then have them compare their answers in pairs. Tell students to practice the pronunciation of each plural. Circulate to observe pronunciation.
3. If necessary, review grammar chart **5.1** on pages 151–152.

Irregular Noun Plurals

Singular	Plural	Examples	Explanation
man woman mouse tooth foot goose	men women mice teeth feet geese	The **men** watched the football game. The **women** washed the dishes.	Vowel change
sheep fish deer	sheep fish deer	There are three **fish** in the bowl.	No change
child person	children people (or persons) Note: *People* is more commonly used than *persons.*	The **children** set the table. We invited a lot of **people** to dinner.	Different word form

EXERCISE 1 Write the plural form of each noun. Pronounce each plural form.

EXAMPLE hour *hours*

1. holiday *holidays*
2. turkey *turkeys*
3. cranberry *cranberries*
4. potato *potatoes*
5. child *children*
6. family *families*
7. spice *spices*
8. nut *nuts*
9. guest *guests*
10. man *men*
11. woman *women*
12. snack *snacks*
13. apple *apples*
14. peach *peaches*
15. tomato *tomatoes*
16. pie *pies*
17. knife *knives*
18. deer *deer*
19. watch *watches*
20. tax *taxes*
21. month *months*
22. goose *geese*
23. dish *dishes*
24. path *paths*

152 Lesson 5

Expansion

Exercise 1 Have a Spelling and Pronunciation Bee. Make a list of 40 or so nouns. Divide the class into Team A and Team B. Give one team member from Team A a noun, and tell them to spell the plural form on the board. Do the same with Team B. Then give a member from Team A a plural noun to pronounce. Do the same with Team B. To make the exercise more challenging, give extra points if the team can say (or act out) what the word means.

EXERCISE 2 Fill in the blanks with the plural form of the words in parentheses ( ).

A: Who prepares the Thanksgiving meal in your family?

B: The *women* (example: woman) in my family do most of the cooking. But the *men* (1 man) help a little too. My husband usually makes the *potatoes* (2 potato) and gravy. I always prepare the turkey. Even the *children* (3 child) help. Last year, my two *daughters* (4 daughter) made the cranberry sauce.

A: Do you use fresh *cranberries* (5 cranberry)?

B: Yes, we do. We boil them with sugar and add *apples* (6 apple) or orange *slices* (7 slice) and some *nuts* (8 nut).

A: How do you make the stuffing?

B: I use bread, garlic *cloves* (9 clove), *onions* (10 onion), butter, and *mushroom* (11 mushroom). I add *spices* (12 spice).

A: What do you make for dessert?

B: My neighbor always comes and brings several *pies* (13 pie).

A: Does she make them herself?

B: No, she doesn't make them. She buys them.

A: Thanksgiving is such a lovely holiday, isn't it?

B: I love it. The only thing I don't like is washing the *dishes* (14 dish) afterwards.

A: Why don't the *men* (15 man) wash the *dishes* (16 dish)?

B: They're too busy watching the football game. They always say that they'll wash them later, but the *women* (17 woman) are in a hurry to clean up. So we do it ourselves.

Singular and Plural; Count and Noncount Nouns; *There* + *Be*; Quantity Words 153

EXERCISE 2

CD 2, Track 12

1. Tell students that this exercise is about Thanksgiving dinner. Have students read the direction line. Go over the example in the book.
2. Have students complete Exercise 2 individually. Point out the picture of garlic.
3. If necessary, review grammar chart **5.1** on pages 151–152.

To save class time, have students do half of the exercise in class and complete the other half for homework. Or assign the entire exercise for homework.

Exercise 2 Variation

To provide practice with listening skills, have students close their books and listen to the audio. Repeat the audio as needed. Ask comprehension questions, such as: *Who prepares the Thanksgiving dinner?* (The women do. The men help a little.) *What are some of the ingredients of the stuffing?* (bread, garlic cloves, onions, butter, mushrooms, and spices) *Why don't the men wash the dishes?* (They're too busy watching football.) Then have students open their books and complete Exercise 2.

Expansion

Exercise 2 Have students practice the conversation in pairs or work together to create similar conversations about special dinners for other holidays or dinners from their native countries/cultures. Ask volunteers to role-play the conversation in front of the class.

5.2 | Using the Singular and Plural for Generalizations

1. Explain to students that a generalization says that something is true of all members of a group. Give an example. Say: *Students are noisy. That means that all students, everywhere are noisy. Is this true?* (no)
2. Have students look at grammar chart **5.2.** Review the information. Say: *To make a generalization about a singular noun, use* a *or* an. *To make a generalization about a plural noun, don't use any article.* Go over the example sentences. Ask: *What verb tense are these sentences in?* (simple present) Point out that we use the simple present when making generalizations.
3. Write the following words on the board:
   1. house
   2. cat
   3. shark
   Ask students to write two sentences for each item. Say: *Write a generalization for a plural and for a singular.* Have volunteers write their sentences on the board (e.g., *A house is better than an apartment. Houses are expensive.*).

EXERCISE 3

1. Say: *You're going to make generalizations on all these topics.* Go over the example in the book.
2. Have students complete Exercise 3 individually. Then have them compare their answers in pairs.
3. If necessary, review grammar chart **5.2** on page 154.

EXERCISE 4

1. Say: *You're going to make generalizations on all these professions.* Have students read the direction line. Go over the example. Ask a volunteer to model the example.
2. Have students complete Exercise 4 individually. Then have them compare their answers in pairs.
3. If necessary, review grammar chart **5.2** on page 154.

To save class time, have students do the exercise for homework.

5.2 | Using the Singular and Plural for Generalizations

We can use singular or plural to make a generalization. A generalization says something is true of all members of a group.

Examples	Explanation
a. **A football game** lasts about three hours. b. **Football games** last about three hours. a. **A sweet potato** is nutritious. b. **Sweet potatoes** are nutritious.	To make a generalization about the subject, use the indefinite article (*a* or *an*) with a singular subject (examples **a**) or no article with a plural subject (examples **b**).

EXERCISE 3 Make a generalization about the following nouns. Use the plural form. You may work with a partner.

EXAMPLE American teachers *are very informal.*

1. American children ______ Answers will vary.
2. American colleges ______
3. Buses in this city ______
4. Elderly Americans ______
5. American cities ______
6. American doctors ______
7. American women ______
8. American men ______
9. American holidays ______
10. Football games ______

EXERCISE 4 Make a generalization about these professions. Use the singular form. You may work with a partner.

EXAMPLE A taxi driver *has a dangerous job.*

1. A teacher ______ Answers will vary.
2. A doctor ______
3. A nurse ______
4. A garbage collector ______
5. A lawyer ______

154 Lesson 5

Expansion

Exercise 3 Have students get in groups to discuss their generalizations. Did anyone have the same generalizations? Ask students to report the group's opinions to the class.

6. A musician ______________________

7. A librarian ______________________

8. A movie star ______________________

9. An accountant ______________________

10. A newspaper reporter ______________________

5.3 | Special Cases of Singular and Plural

Examples	Explanation
a. The U.S. has over 290 **million** people. b. **Millions** of people go shopping the day after Thanksgiving.	a. Exact numbers use the singular form. b. Inexact numbers use the plural form.
One of my **neighbors** brought a pie to the Thanksgiving dinner. One of the **men** helped with the dishes.	We use the plural form in the following expressions: *one of* (*the, my, his, her*, etc.).
Every **guest** brought something. We washed all the **dishes.**	We use a singular noun and verb after *every*. We use a plural noun after *all*.
After dinner, the girl put on her **pajamas** and went to bed. We're wearing our best **clothes** today. 	Some words have no singular form: *pajamas, clothes, pants, slacks, (eye)glasses, scissors.*
Let's watch the **news.** It's on after dinner. Let's not discuss **politics** during dinner. It's not a good subject	Even though *news* and *politics* end in *-s*, they are singular.

Language Note:
Do not make adjectives plural.
He made three ***wonderful pies.***

EXERCISE 5 Find the mistakes with the underlined words, and correct them. Not every sentence has a mistake. If the sentence is correct, write *C*.

EXAMPLES Five man watched the football game. *(men)*

Ten guests came to dinner. C

1. The childrens helped serve the dinner.
2. One of her daughter came from New York on Thanksgiving.
3. Ten millions people passed through the airports that day.
4. Millions of people travel for Thanksgiving. C

Expansion

Exercise 4 Have students separate into groups to discuss their generalizations. Did anyone have the same generalizations? Ask students to report the group's opinions to the class.

5.3 | Special Cases of Singular and Plural

1. Have students cover up the explanations side of grammar chart **5.3** on page 155. Say: *Read the first two sentences. What is the difference between the use of* million *in sentence (a) and the use of* million *in sentence (b)?* (In sentence (a), *290 million* is an exact number and is in the singular; in sentence (b), *millions* is not an exact number and is in the plural form.) After students have made their guesses, ask them to look at the explanation.
2. Ask students to look at the use of *one of* in the next set of sentences. Say: *We use the plural when we say* one of the, one of my, one of his, etc. Have volunteers make sentences using *one of* (e.g., *One of my favorite books is* Pride and Prejudice.).
3. Direct students to the next two sentences. Ask: *Is the noun singular or plural after* every? (singular) *Is the noun singular or plural after* all? (plural)
4. Point out that some words have no singular form (*pajamas, clothes, pants*, etc.). Go over the examples.
5. Say: *Some nouns may look plural, but they're actually singular, such as* news, politics, *and* economics. Remind students that adjectives do not agree in number with nouns. Go over the example.

EXERCISE 5

1. Say: *You're going to correct the mistakes in each sentence.* Have students read the direction line. Ask: *Do all sentences have mistakes?* (no) Go over the examples in the book.
2. Have students complete Exercise 5 individually. Go over the answers as a class.
3. If necessary, review grammar chart **5.3** on page 155.

The Origin of Thanksgiving (Reading)

1. Have students look at the illustrations on pages 156 and 157. Say: *Look at the illustrations in the reading. Do you know who or what each of these drawings depict?* (Pilgrims, the Mayflower, a Native American, a deer, a squash)
2. Have students look at the title of the reading. Ask: *What is the reading about?* Have students use the title, pictures, and photo to make predictions about the reading.
3. Preteach any vocabulary words your students may not know, such as *health, survive,* and *fortune.*

BEFORE YOU READ

1. Have students discuss the questions in pairs. Try to pair students of different cultures together.
2. Ask for a few volunteers to share their answers with the class.

To save class time, skip Before You Read or have students prepare answers for homework ahead of time.

Reading *CD 2, Track 13*

1. Have students first read the text silently. Tell them to pay special attention to count and noncount nouns. Then play the audio and have students read along silently.
2. Check students' comprehension. Ask questions such as: *Who declared Thanksgiving an official holiday?* (President Lincoln) *Why did the Pilgrims come to America?* (They wanted to be able to practice their religion.) *Why were the Pilgrims in such bad condition after their first winter?* (They did not know how to survive in the new land.) *Who helped them learn survival skills?* (Squanto and American Indians)

To save class time, have students do the reading for homework ahead of time.

5. After the news is over, we can watch the football game.
6. His pants is new.
7. Five women prepared the dinner.
8. Every guests stayed to watch the game.
9. Thanksgiving is one of my favorite holiday.
10. Hundreds of people saw the parade.
11. My grandmother came for Thanksgiving. She's in her eighties.
12. Politics is not a good subject to discuss at the dinner table.
13. The child should go to bed. His pajamas are on the bed.
14. Do you like sweets potatoes?

THE ORIGIN OF THANKSGIVING

Before You Read

1. What do you know about the origin of American Thanksgiving?
2. Do you have a day of thanks in your native culture?

Read the following article. Pay special attention to count and noncount nouns.

On Thanksgiving, **Americans** come together to give thanks for all the good **things** in their **lives.** Thanksgiving officially began in 1863 when President Lincoln declared that Americans would have a day of thanks. What is the origin of this great day?

In 1620, a group of 120 **men, women,** and **children** left England for America on a ship called the Mayflower. They came to America in search of religious **freedom.** They started their new life in a deserted[2] Indian village in what is now the state of Massachusetts. But half of the Pilgrims did not survive their first cold, hard winter. In the spring, two American **Indians**[3] found the **people** from England in very bad condition. They didn't have enough **food,** and they were in bad **health.** Squanto, an English-speaking American Indian, stayed with them for several **months** and taught them how to

[2] *Deserted* means empty of people.
[3] The natives of America are called *American Indians, Indians,* or *Native Americans.*

156 Lesson 5

Reading Variation

To practice listening skills, have students first listen to the audio alone. Ask a few comprehension questions. Repeat the audio if necessary. Then have them open their books and read along as they listen to the audio.

Reading Glossary

fortune: chance; (good or bad) luck
health: the condition of a living thing's body and mind
survive: to continue to live or exist, especially for a long time or under hard conditions

survive in this new land. He brought them deer **meat** and animal **skins;** he showed them how to grow **corn** and other **vegetables;** he showed them how to use **plants** as **medicine;** he explained how to use **fish** for fertilizer[4]—he taught them many **skills** for survival in their new land.

By the time their second fall arrived, the Pilgrims had enough **food** to get through their second winter. They were in better **health.** They decided to have a Thanksgiving **feast**[5] to celebrate their good **fortune.**

They invited Squanto and neighboring Indian **families** of the Wampanoag tribe to come to their dinner. The Pilgrims were surprised when 90 Indians showed up. The Pilgrims did not have enough **food** for so many people. Fortunately, the Indian **chief** sent some of his people to bring food to the celebration. They brought five **deer, fish, beans, squash,** corn **bread, berries,** and many wild **turkeys.** The feast lasted for three **days.** There was a short time of **peace** and **friendship** between the Indians and the Pilgrims.

Now on Thanksgiving, we eat some of the traditional **foods** from this period in American history.

[4] *Fertilizer* is made of natural things. We put fertilizer in the earth to help plants grow.
[5] A *feast* is a large dinner.

Culture Note

Five years before Squanto (or Tisquantum) met and helped the Pilgrims in Plymouth, he had been kidnapped in what is now known as the Plymouth Bay, by an erstwhile English colonizer and shipped off to Spain to be sold as a slave. He was freed by some Catholic priests and eventually ended up in England where he learned the English language. Through his travels he came in contact with colonizers who eventually brought him back to his village, Patuxet, in Plymouth Bay.

5.4 | Noncount Nouns

1. Have students cover up grammar chart **5.4.** Write these five categories across the board:
   A. Nouns that have no distinct, separate parts. We look at the whole.
   B. Nouns that have parts that are too small or insignificant to count
   C. Nouns that are classes or categories of things. The members of the category are not the same.
   D. Nouns that are abstractions
   E. Subjects of study
2. Have students go back to the reading on pages 156–157. Say: *Find the noncount nouns in the reading. Which group do the nouns in the reading belong to? Write them in your notebooks under the correct group.* Have volunteers write the words on the board.
3. Then have students look at grammar chart **5.4.** Say: *Now let's look at the chart.* Go over any errors. Review all of the words in each category.
4. Remind students that noncount nouns do not have a plural. For example, we can't say *I breathed two airs yesterday.*

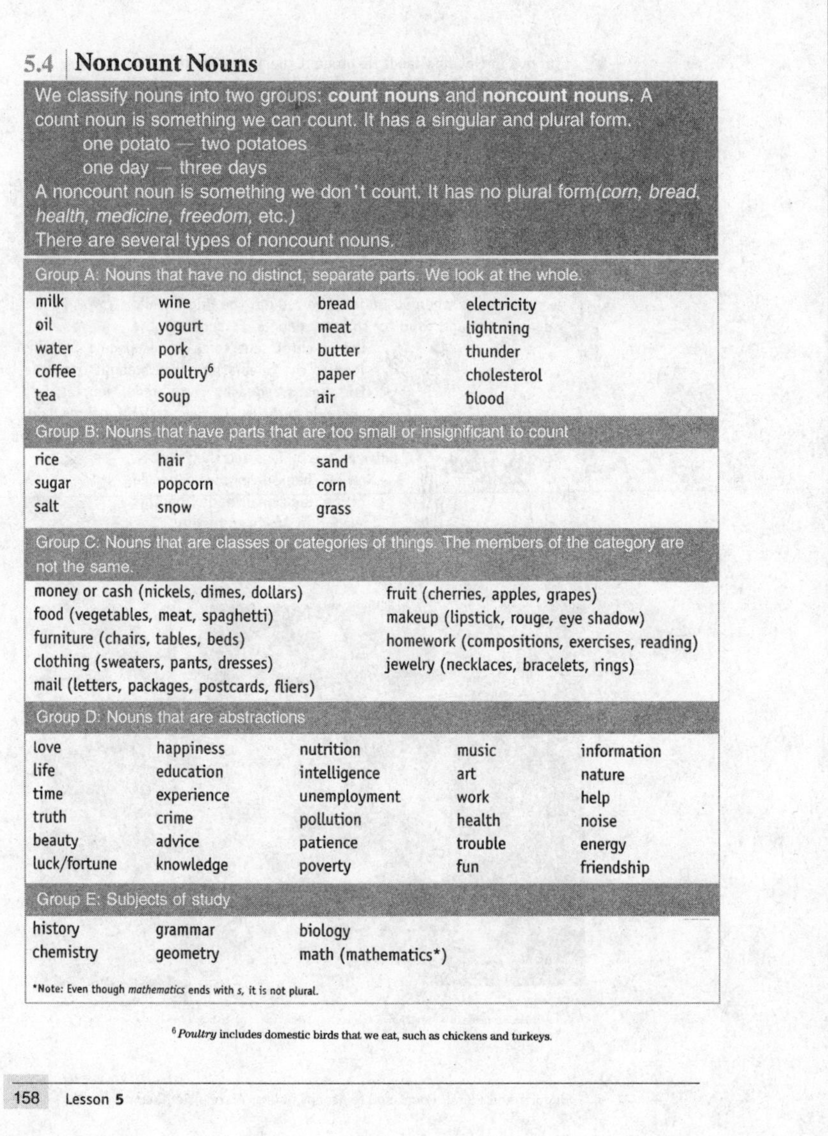

5.4 | Noncount Nouns

We classify nouns into two groups: **count nouns** and **noncount nouns.** A count noun is something we can count. It has a singular and plural form.
one potato — two potatoes
one day — three days
A noncount noun is something we don't count. It has no plural form*(corn, bread, health, medicine, freedom,* etc.*)*
There are several types of noncount nouns.

Group A: Nouns that have no distinct, separate parts. We look at the whole.			
milk	wine	bread	electricity
oil	yogurt	meat	lightning
water	pork	butter	thunder
coffee	poultry[6]	paper	cholesterol
tea	soup	air	blood

Group B: Nouns that have parts that are too small or insignificant to count		
rice	hair	sand
sugar	popcorn	corn
salt	snow	grass

Group C: Nouns that are classes or categories of things. The members of the category are not the same.	
money or cash (nickels, dimes, dollars)	fruit (cherries, apples, grapes)
food (vegetables, meat, spaghetti)	makeup (lipstick, rouge, eye shadow)
furniture (chairs, tables, beds)	homework (compositions, exercises, reading)
clothing (sweaters, pants, dresses)	jewelry (necklaces, bracelets, rings)
mail (letters, packages, postcards, fliers)	

Group D: Nouns that are abstractions				
love	happiness	nutrition	music	information
life	education	intelligence	art	nature
time	experience	unemployment	work	help
truth	crime	pollution	health	noise
beauty	advice	patience	trouble	energy
luck/fortune	knowledge	poverty	fun	friendship

Group E: Subjects of study		
history	grammar	biology
chemistry	geometry	math (mathematics*)

*Note: Even though *mathematics* ends with *s*, it is not plural.

[6] *Poultry* includes domestic birds that we eat, such as chickens and turkeys.

158 Lesson 5

Grammar Variation

Have students first look at chart **5.4.** Go over Groups A–E. Then have students go back to the reading on pages 156–157 to find and categorize noncount nouns.

EXERCISE 6 Fill in the blanks with a noncount noun from the box below.

advice	turkey	freedom ✓	friendship
health	food	corn	snow

EXAMPLE The Pilgrims wanted to find freedom in America.

1. They had poor health.
2. The Indians gave the Pilgrims a lot of advice about how to grow food.
3. Squanto taught them to plant corn.
4. The first winter was hard. It was cold and there was a lot of snow.
5. During the second winter, the Pilgrims had enough food.
6. In the beginning, there was friendship between the Pilgrims and the Indians.
7. Today people eat turkey on Thanksgiving.

5.5 | Count and Noncount Nouns[7]

Examples	Explanation
I eat a lot of **rice** and **beans.** rice = noncount noun beans = count noun	*Count* and *noncount* are grammatical terms, but they are not always logical. *Rice* is very small and is a noncount noun. *Beans* and *peas* are also very small, but they are count nouns.
a. We put some **fruit** in the cranberry sauce. b. Oranges and lemons are **fruits** that contain Vitamin C. a. We prepared a lot of **food** for Thanksgiving. b. Cranberries and sweet potatoes are typical **foods** for Thanksgiving.	a. Use *fruit* and *food* as noncount nouns when you mean fruit and food in general. b. Use *fruits* and *foods* as count nouns when you mean kinds of fruit or categories of food.
a. The Indians brought many **turkeys** to the feast. b. We eat **turkey** on Thanksgiving. a. He brought 3 **pies** to the Thanksgiving dinner. b. I ate some **pie** after dinner.	a. When referring to the whole thing (*turkey, pie*), these words are count nouns. b. When referring to a part, these words are noncount nouns.
a. Children like to eat **candy.** b. There are 3 **candies** on the table. 	a. When you talk about candy in general, *candy* is noncount. b. When you look at individual pieces of candy, you can use the plural form.
We have a lot of **information** about American history. The Indians gave the English people **advice** about how to plant food.	Some nouns that have a plural form in other languages are noncount in English. *Advice, information, knowledge, equipment, furniture,* and *homework* are always noncount nouns in English.

[7] For a list of nouns that can be both count or noncount, see Appendix G.

EXERCISE 6

1. Have students read the direction line. Go over the example in the book.
2. Have students complete Exercise 6 individually. Go over the answers as a class.
3. If necessary, review grammar chart **5.4** on page 158.

5.5 | Count and Noncount Nouns

1. Write on the board:
   rice
   beans
   fruit
   food
   candy
   Ask: *Are these count or noncount nouns?*
   Say: *Sometimes grammar rules are not logical.* Rice *is noncount, but* beans *are count. You have to learn the exceptions.* Fruit, food, *and* candy *are noncount nouns when they are used as a general term. For example:* The food at this hotel is good. *But if you mean kinds of food or kinds of fruit, they can be count nouns. For example:* Oranges and lemons are fruits that contain a lot of Vitamin C. Candy *is generally noncount, but if you are talking about pieces of candy, then you can use the plural form. For example:* There are three candies on the table.
2. Review the example sentences in the chart. Point out that some nouns that have a plural form in other languages are noncount in English, such as *information.* Go over the examples.

Expansion

Grammar Have students go back to the reading on pages 156 and 157. Say: *Make two lists of words from the reading: count and noncount.*

EXERCISE 7

1. Have students read the direction line. Ask: *If the noun is a count noun, what do we do?* (Write the plural form.) Go over the example.
2. Have students complete Exercise 7 individually. Then check the answers as a class.
3. If necessary, review grammar charts **5.4** on page 158 and **5.5** on page 159.

EXERCISE 7 Decide if the noun in parentheses ( ) is count or noncount. If it is a count noun, change it to the plural form, If it is a noncount noun, do not use the plural form.

EXAMPLE The *Pilgrims* (Pilgrim) wanted *freedom* (freedom).

American Indians have a lot of respect for *nature* (nature).

They love *flowers* (flower), *trees* (tree), *birds* (bird), and *fish* (fish).

Thanksgiving is a celebration of *peace* (peace) and *friendship* (friendship).

On Thanksgiving, Americans eat a lot of *food* (food) and sometimes gain weight.

Squanto gave the Pilgrims a lot of *advice* (advice) about planting *corn* (corn) and other *vegetables* (vegetable).

He had a lot of *knowledge* (knowledge) about the land.

The Pilgrims didn't have any *experience* (experience) with American food.

On the first Thanksgiving, Indians brought *meat* (meat), *beans* (bean), *bread* (bread), and *berries* (berry).

7. The Pilgrims celebrated because they had a lot of good *fortune* (fortune).

American Indians use *plants* (plant) for *medicine* (medicine).

My friends went to the Southwest last summer. They bought American Indian *jewelry* (jewelry), such as *rings* (ring) and *necklaces* (necklace).

Do you have a lot of *information* (information) about American *holidays* (holiday)?

160 Lesson 5

Expansion

Exercise 7 Have students work in pairs to write five sentences with count nouns and five sentences with noncount nouns. If possible, have students from the same culture or country work together. Say: *Write about a historical event that happened in your native country.* Ask a few volunteers to share their sentences with the class.

RECIPE FOR TURKEY STUFFING

Before You Read

1. Do you like to cook?
2. What is a favorite recipe of yours?

 Read the following recipe. Pay special attention to quantities.

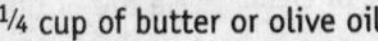

Turkey Stuffing

1/4 cup of butter or olive oil
2 cloves of garlic, minced[8]
1 cup of mushrooms
1 onion, chopped
3 stalks of celery, chopped
1/4 cup pieces of bacon
4 cups of dry bread, cut into cubes
1/4 teaspoon of salt
1/4 teaspoon of pepper
1/4 teaspoon of oregano
2 teaspoons of dry parsley
1 1/4 cup of hot chicken broth

Brown garlic in butter (or olive oil). Add mushrooms and sauté. Add the rest of the vegetables and cook until they begin to soften. Stir bacon bits into mixture, then lower heat to medium and add bread cubes and seasonings.

Continue cooking for approximately 5 more minutes, stirring continuously.

Add hot chicken broth and mix well. Cover and cook over low heat for at least 30 minutes, stirring frequently.

Use as turkey stuffing and bake with turkey OR place in a covered casserole dish and bake for 30 minutes in 350–375 degree oven.

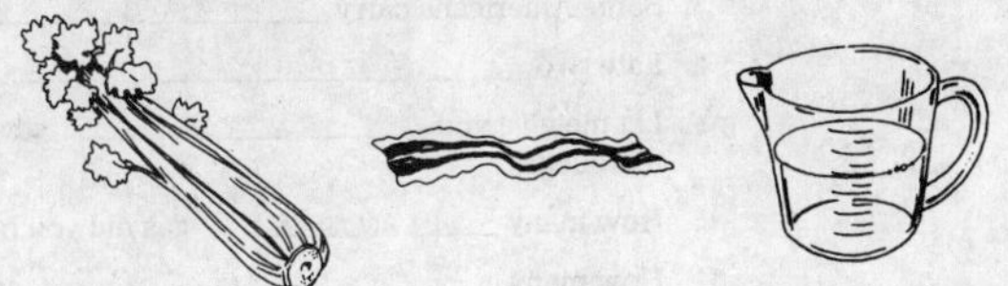

[8] *Minced* means cut into very small pieces.

Recipe for Turkey Stuffing (Reading)

1. Have students look at the title of the reading. Ask: *What is the reading about?* Have students use the title and pictures to make predictions about the reading.
2. Preteach any vocabulary words your students may not know, such as *brown, sauté,* and *casserole dish.*

BEFORE YOU READ

1. Have students discuss the questions in pairs. Try to pair students of different cultures together.
2. Ask for a few volunteers to share their answers with the class.

To save class time, skip "Before You Read" or have students prepare answers for homework ahead of time.

Reading *CD 2, Track 14*

1. Have students first read the text silently. Tell them to pay special attention to quantities. Then play the audio and have students read along silently.
2. Check students' comprehension. Ask questions such as: *When do you stir in bacon bits?* (after sautéing the mushrooms and vegetables) *How long do you cook it over low heat?* (30 minutes)

To save class time, have students do the reading for homework ahead of time.

Reading Variation

To practice listening skills, have students first listen to the audio alone. Ask a few comprehension questions. Repeat the audio if necessary. Then have them open their books and read along as they listen to the audio.

Reading Glossary

brown: to fry something until its color becomes brown
casserole dish: a deep dish for baking and serving mixed foods
sauté: to fry something quickly in a small amount of oil or butter

5.6 | Quantities with Count and Noncount Nouns

1. Have students cover up grammar chart **5.6.** Say: *We can use numbers with count nouns, but we can't use numbers with noncount nouns. We use units of measure such as a* bottle, a glass, a can, *etc. And we can count these units of measure.*
2. Write the following categories across the board in chart form: *container* *portion* *measurement* *shape or whole piece* *other*
   Then write a list of ten phrases on one side of the board: *a bag of flour, a pound of meat, a work of art, a slice of pizza, a carton of milk, a piece of meat, a quart of oil, a piece of information, a roll of film, an ear of corn.*
   Say: *Try to guess where these nouns and units of measure go.* Have volunteers fill in the chart on the board using the ten phrases.
3. Have students look at grammar chart **5.6.** Say: *Now compare your work with the chart.* Go over any errors. Review the example sentences in the chart and the units of measure.

EXERCISE 8

1. Have students read the direction line. Ask: *Are the nouns in these sentences count or noncount?* (noncount) Go over the example.
2. Have students complete the exercise individually. Check the answers as a class.
3. If necessary, review grammar chart **5.6** on page 162.

5.6 | Quantities with Count and Noncount Nouns

We can put a number before a count noun. We cannot put a number before a noncount noun. We use a unit measure, which we can count — two **cloves** of garlic.

By container	By portion	By measurement[9]	By shape or whole piece	Other
a bottle of water a carton of milk a jar of pickles a bag of flour a can of soda (pop) a cup of coffee a glass of water a bowl of soup	a slice (piece) of bread a piece of meat a piece of cake a strip of bacon a piece (sheet) of paper a slice of pizza a scoop of ice cream	an ounce of sugar a quart of oil a pound of meat a gallon of milk a pint of cream	a loaf of bread an ear of corn a piece of fruit a head of lettuce a candy bar a roll of film a tube of toothpaste a bar of soap a clove of garlic a stalk of celery	a piece of mail a piece of furniture a piece of advice a piece of information a work of art a homework assignment

EXERCISE 8 Fill in the blanks with a specific quantity or unit of measure. Answers may vary.

EXAMPLE I drink three *glasses of* water a day.

1. You should take a few *rolls of* film on your vacation.
2. I'm going to buy two *pieces of* meat to make dinner for the family.
3. *A gallon of* milk is heavy to carry.
4. She drinks two *cups of* coffee every morning.
5. Buy *a loaf of* bread for dinner.
6. He eats *three pieces of* fruit a day.
7. Some Americans carry *a bottle of* water with them.
8. I ate two *pieces of* cake.
9. Let me give you *a piece of* advice before you apply to colleges.
10. How many *gallons of* gas did you buy at the gas station?
11. How many *cloves of* garlic are you going to use in the recipe?
12. The recipe calls for 1/4 *cup of* butter or oil.
13. The recipe calls for 1/4 *teaspoon of* pepper.

[9] For a list of conversions from the American system of measurement to the metric system, see Appendix D.

162 Lesson 5

Expansion

Grammar Say: *Find all the quantities listed in the recipe from the reading on page 161.*

TAKING THE LAND FROM THE NATIVE AMERICANS

Before You Read

1. Who were the original inhabitants of your native country?
2. Are there any ethnic minorities in your native country? Do they have the respect of the majority population?

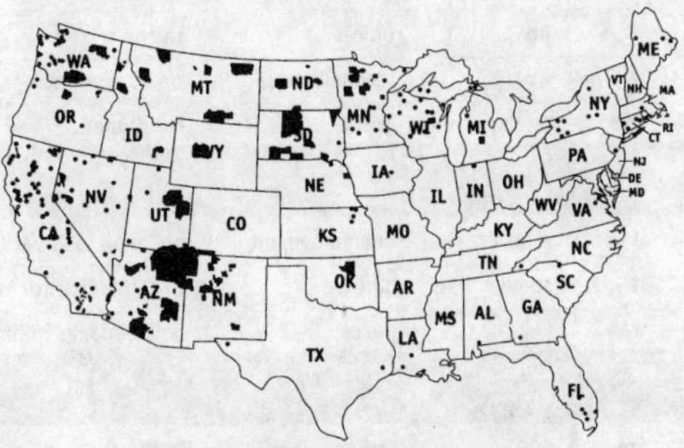

American Indian Reservations in the U.S.

 Read the following article. Pay special attention to *there* + a form of *be*.

Before the arrival of Europeans, **there were** between 10 and 16 million Native Americans in America. Today **there are** fewer than two million. What happened to these natives of America?

The friendship between the Indians and Europeans did not last for long. As more English people came to America, they did not need the help of the Indians, as the first group of Pilgrims did. The white people started to take the land away from the Indians. As Indians fought to keep their land, many of them were killed. Also, **there were** many deaths from diseases that Europeans brought to America. In 1830, President Andrew Jackson took the Indians' lands and sent them to live on reservations. Indian children had to learn English. Often they were punished for speaking their own language. As a result, **there are** very few Indians today who speak the language of their ancestors.[10]

Today **there are** about 500 tribes in the U.S., each with its own traditions. **There are** about 300 reservations, but only 22 percent of American Indians live on this land. **There is** a lot of unemployment and poverty on many reservations. As a result, many Indians move to big cities to find work. Many return to their reservations only for special celebrations such as Pow-Wows, when Indians wear their traditional clothing and dance to traditional music.

It is becoming harder and harder for Indians to keep their traditions and languages alive.

Did You Know?

Many place names in the U.S. are American Indian names. Chicago, for example, comes from an indian word meaning smelly onion.

[10] *Ancestors* are grandparents, great-grandparents, etc.

Singular and Plural; Count and Noncount Nouns; *There + Be*; Quantity Words 163

Reading Variation

To practice listening skills, have students first listen to the audio alone. Ask a few comprehension questions. Repeat the audio if necessary. Then have them open their books and read along as they listen to the audio.

Reading Glossary

punish: to discipline, make someone pay for doing something wrong

tribe: a group of people who usually speak the same language, live in the same area, often in villages, and have many relatives within the group

Taking the Land from the Native Americans (Reading)

1. Have students look at the map of the U.S. Explain that the darkened areas and dots show American Indian reservations. Ask: *Have you ever been on a reservation?*
2. Have students look at the title of the reading. Ask: *What is the reading about?* Have students use the title and the map to make predictions about the reading.
3. Preteach any vocabulary words your students may not know, such as *punish* and *tribe*.

BEFORE YOU READ

1. Have students discuss the questions in pairs. Try to pair students of different cultures together.
2. Ask for a few volunteers to share their answers with the class.

To save class time, skip "Before You Read" or have students prepare answers for homework ahead of time.

Reading *CD 2, Track 15*

1. Have students first read the text silently. Tell them to pay special attention to *there + be.* Then play the audio and have students read along silently.
2. Check students' comprehension. Ask questions such as: *What or who killed so many Indians?* (settlers, directly through war and indirectly by bringing disease) *Do most of the 2 million Native Americans now live on reservations?* (no, only 2 percent) *Why do many live off the reservations?* (There aren't many jobs, and there is a lot of poverty.)

To save class time, have students do the reading for homework ahead of time.

DID YOU KNOW?

It's been estimated that when the Europeans came to the Americas, approximately 1,000 languages were being spoken by Native Americans in North, Central, and South America. There are still about 700 languages spoken today—but by far fewer people. For example, about 200 languages are spoken in Canada and the U.S. by only 300,000 people. Many words, such as *moccasin, squash, chocolate, tobacco,* and *condor* in the English language today are borrowings from Indian languages.

5.7 | *There* + a Form of *Be*

1. Have students cover up grammar chart **5.7.** Write the following sentences on the board:
   There is a reservation in Wyoming.
   There is an onion in the recipe.
   There is a lot of unemployment on some reservations.
   There is some garlic in the recipe for stuffing.
   There are 500 Indian tribes in the U.S.
   There were many deaths from diseases when the Europeans arrived.
   Say: *Underline the subject in each sentence. Then say if the subject is a count or noncount noun. If it's a count noun, say if it's singular or plural.* Elicit the patterns for these sentences.
2. Have students look at grammar chart **5.7.** Review the example sentences in the chart. Point out the use of *there is/will be/was* with the singular subjects. Then point out the use of *a/an/one* with singular subjects.
3. Then have students look at the sentences with a noncount subject and with a plural subject. Ask: *What quantity words are they used with?* Have them compare and contrast the singular, plural, and noncount examples (*A lot of* and *some* are used with both count and noncount nouns. *Many* is used with plural count nouns.).
4. Finally, have students look at the negative forms. Have students explain when *not* is used and when *no* is used (With *not*, the verb is negative: *There wasn't a problem.* With *no*, the verb is affirmative: *There was no problem.* Also, we don't use *a/an/any* with *no*.).
   Ask: *When do you use* any? (With noncount nouns and a negative verb: *There isn't any milk.* With plural nouns and a negative verb: *There aren't any reservations.*) Go over all of the examples for negative forms.

5.7 | *There* + a Form of *Be*

We use *there* + a form of *be* to introduce a subject, either count or noncount, into the conversation. After the noun, we often give a time or place.

There	*Be*	*A / An / One*	Singular Subject	Complement
There	is	a	reservation	in Wyoming.
There	is	an	onion	in the recipe.
There	will be	a	football game	on TV tonight.
There	was	one	guest	for dinner.
There	*Be*	(Quantity Word)	Noncount Subject	Complement
There	is	a lot of	unemployment	on some reservations.
There	is	some	garlic	in the recipe for stuffing.
There	was		peace	between the Indians and the Pilgrims.
There	*Be*	(Quantity Word)	Plural Subject	Complement
There	are	500	Indian tribes	in the U.S.
There	were	many	deaths	from diseases after the Europeans arrived.
There	are	a lot of	calories	from diseases after the Europeans arrived.
There	are		reservations	in California.

Negative Forms

There	*Be + Not + A/An*	Singular Subject	Complement
There	wasn't a	problem	between the Pilgrims and Indians in 1620.
There	*Be + No*	Singular Subject	Complement
There	was no	problem	between the Pilgrims and Indians in 1620.
There	*Be + Not + (Any)*	Noncount	Complement
There	isn't any	milk	in the recipe.
There	*Be + No*	Noncount	Complement
There	is no	milk	in the recipe.
There	*Be + Not + (Any)*	Plural Subject	Complement
There	aren't any	reservations	in Illinois.
There	*Be + No*	Plural Subject	Complement
There	are no	reservations	in Illinois.

164 Lesson 5

Expansion

Grammar Have students go back to the reading on page 163 to look at constructions with *there.* Ask students what kind of subject each sentence has.

5.8 | Using *There*

We use *there* + a form of *be* to introduce a subject, either count or noncount, into the conversation.

Examples	Explanation
There's a reservation in Wyoming.	The contraction for *there is* = *there's*. We don't write a contraction for *there are*.
There is one onion and three celery stalks in the recipe. **There are** three celery stalks and one onion in the recipe. **There is** dessert and coffee after the dinner.	If two nouns follow *there*, use a singular verb (*is*) if the first noun is singular. Use a plural verb (*are*) if the first noun is plural.
Informal: **There's** a lot of reservations in California. Formal: **There are** a lot of reservations in California.	In conversation, you will sometimes hear *there's* with plural nouns.
There are over 500 tribes of Native Americans in the U.S. **They** each have their own traditions. There's a Navajo reservation in Arizona. **It's** very big. There's a Navajo woman in my chemistry class. **She** comes from Arizona.	After we introduce a noun with *there*, we can continue to speak of this noun with a pronoun (*they, it, she,* etc.)
Is there unemployment on some reservations? Yes, there is. **Are there** any reservations in California? Yes, there are. How many Navajo Indians **are there** in Arizona?	Observe the word order in questions with *there*.
Wrong: There's the Grand Canyon in Arizona. *Right:* The Grand Canyon is in Arizona.	*There* never introduces a specific or unique noun. Don't use a noun with the definite article (*the*) after *there*.

EXERCISE 9 Fill in the blanks with the correct form and tense.

EXAMPLE There ___*are*___ a lot of Indians in Oklahoma.

1. There ___*are*___ a lot of reservations in California.
2. There ___*were*___ more American Indians 200 years ago than there ___*are*___ today.
3. In the beginning, there ___*was*___ peace between the Indians and the Pilgrims.

Singular and Plural; Count and Noncount Nouns; *There* + *Be*; Quantity Words 165

5.8 | Using *There*

1. Have students cover up grammar chart **5.8.** Say: There + *a form of* be *(present, past, future) is used to introduce a subject into the conversation.*
2. Say: There's *is the contraction for* there is. *We do not make a contraction for* there are.
3. Write the following sentences on the board:
   There ___ one onion and three celery stalks in the recipe.
   There ___ three celery stalks and one onion in the recipe.
   There ___ dessert and coffee after the dinner.
   Say: *Fill in the blanks with* is *or* are.
4. Have students look at grammar chart **5.8.** Review the sentences with compound subjects. Go over any errors.
5. Point out that many native speakers will use the singular with a plural noun in informal speech (e.g., *There's a lot of reservations in California.*).
6. Say: There is *and* there are *are used to introduce a noun. Once it has been introduced, you use a pronoun.* Go over the examples in the chart.
7. Remind students to invert the *there is* and *there are* in questions to *is there* and *are there.* Go over the examples. Point out the short answers.
8. Explain to students that *there is* and *there are* are not used to introduce specific or unique nouns. Go over the example in the chart.

EXERCISE 9

1. Have students read the direction line. Say: *Not all sentences are in the present tense.* Go over the example in the book.
2. Have students complete the exercise individually. Check the answers as a class.
3. If necessary, review grammar charts **5.7** on page 164 and **5.8** on page 165.

Expansion

Grammar Have students work in pairs to write eight sentences about the classroom and school with *there* + a form of *be* (e.g., *There will be a new student in our class next week.*).

EXERCISE 10

1. Tell students that they are going to complete the sentences with a time or place. Have students read the direction line. Go over the example in the book.
2. Have students complete the exercise individually. Have students compare answers in pairs. Circulate to observe pair work. Give help as needed.
3. If necessary, review grammar charts **5.7** on page 164 and **5.8** on page 165.

To save class time, have students do the exercise as a class or for homework.

Navajo Code Talkers (Reading)

1. Have students look at the photo. Ask: *Who do you think this man is? What do you notice about his uniform?*
2. Have students look at the title of the reading. Ask: *What is the reading about?* Have students use the title and photo to make predictions about the reading.
3. Preteach any vocabulary words your students may not know, such as *code, skillful, battleship, submarine,* and *recognition.*

BEFORE YOU READ

1. Have students discuss the questions in pairs. Try to pair students of different cultures together.
2. Ask for a few volunteers to share their answers with the class.

To save class time, skip "Before You Read" or have students prepare answers for homework ahead of time.

4. Later, there ___were___ wars between the Indians and the white people who took their land.
5. ___Was___ ___there___ enough food to eat at the first Thanksgiving? Yes, there was.
6. How many people ___were___ ___there___ at the first Thanksgiving celebration?
7. Next week there ___will___ ___be___ a test on noncount nouns.
8. How many questions ___will___ ___there___ ___be___ on the test?

EXERCISE 10 Fill in the blanks with a time or place.

EXAMPLE There was a war *in my country from 1972 to 1975.*

1. There will be a test ___Answers will vary.___
2. There's a lot of snow ________________
3. There are a lot of people ________________
4. There are a lot of reservations ________________
5. There was a presidential election ________________

NAVAJO CODE TALKERS

Before You Read

1. Are some languages more complicated than others?
2. Why is a code important during wartime?

Expansion

Exercise 10 Ask: *What do you want to tell your partner about your native country? Write five sentences about your country with* there + *a form of* be. Have students exchange papers with their partners. Then have volunteers report interesting things they learned from their partners.

 Read the following article. Pay special attention to quantity words.

American Indian languages are very complicated. There are **many** different languages and each one has **several** dialects. **Some** languages, like Navajo, have **no** alphabet or symbols.

Philip Johnston was not an Indian but he grew up on the Navajo reservation and learned **a lot of** their language. Later, when Johnston served in World War I, he understood the importance of developing a code that the enemy could not understand. In World War II, the U.S. was at war with Japan. The Japanese were very skillful at breaking codes. In 1942, Johnston met with an American military general and explained his idea of using the Navajo language in code to send messages. Indians living on Navajo land in the Southwest U.S. could speak and understand the language. **Very few** non-Navajos could speak or understand it.

The general agreed to try this idea. The U.S. Marines recruited **200** native speakers of Navajo to create a code based on their language. There were **many** military words that did not exist in the Navajo language, so the Navajo recruits had to develop words for these things. For example, the commanding general was a "war chief"; a battleship was a "whale"; a submarine was an "iron fish."

In the first **two** days of code talking, more than 800 messages were sent without **any** errors.

During and after the war, the Navajo code talkers got **little** recognition for their great help in World War II. It wasn't until 1992 that the U.S. government honored the Navajo code talkers for their help in winning major battles of the war.

5.9 | Quantity Expressions—An Overview

We can use quantity expressions to talk about the quantity of count and noncount nouns.

There are about **two million** American Indians today.
There were about **400** code talkers during World War II.
Very few non-Navajos could speak the Navajo language.
Navajo code talkers got **little** recognition for their work.
The Pilgrims had **very little** food during the first winter.
The American Indians had **a lot of** knowledge about the land.
The Pilgrims didn't have **much** knowledge about the land.
Many Indians died from disease after the Europeans came.
Some Indians today live on reservations.
The Navajo language has **no** alphabet.
The Navajo language has **several** dialects.

Reading CD 2, Track 16

1. Have students first read the text silently. Tell them to pay special attention to quantity words. Then play the audio and have students read along silently.
2. Check students' comprehension. Ask questions such as: *Why was Navajo a great language for a code?* (There were not many people outside of the Navajo tribe who knew it. There was no writing system for the language.) *Who created the code based on the Navajo language?* (200 Navajo Indians recruited for the effort) *How many messages were passed in the first two days?* (more than 800)

To save class time, have students do the reading for homework ahead of time.

5.9 | Quantity Expressions—An Overview

1. Have students look at grammar chart **5.9.** Say: *We use quantity expressions to talk about the quantity of count and noncount nouns.* Go over each example sentence. Ask students if the subject is a count or noncount noun.
2. Then ask: *Which expressions do we use with count nouns? Which expressions do we use with noncount nouns.* Make two lists. Write students' responses on the board. Tell students they will learn more about these quantity expressions in the subsequent grammar charts.

Reading Variation

To practice listening skills, have students first listen to the audio alone. Ask a few comprehension questions. Repeat the audio if necessary. Then have them open their books and read along as they listen to the audio.

Reading Glossary

battleship: a large warship with long guns
code: a way of hiding the true meaning of communication from all except those people who have the keys to understand it
recognition: credit; praise for doing something well
skillful: able to do something well
submarine: a tube-shaped ship that can travel underwater

EXERCISE 11

1. Tell students that this exercise is based on the readings in this lesson. Have students read the direction line. Go over the example.
2. Have students complete the exercise individually. Check the answers as a class.
3. If necessary, review grammar chart **5.9** on page 167.

EXERCISE 11 Fill in the blanks to complete these statements. Answers may vary.

EXAMPLE There are 500 ___tribes___ of American Indians in the United States.

1. Two hundred native speakers of ___Navajo___ served as code talkers.
2. There is no word for ___battleship___ in Navajo.
3. The Navajo language has no ___alphabet___.
4. Before the arrival of the white people from Europe, there were at least ___10 million___ American Indians.
5. After the first cold winter in America, the Pilgrims didn't have much ___food___.
6. Many Pilgrims ___died___ during the first winter.
7. Some ___Indians___ helped the Pilgrims.
8. The Indians taught them many ___skills___ to help them survive.
9. The second year in America was much better. They had a lot of ___food___.
10. As more white people came to America, many ___Indians___ lost their land.
11. Many Indians can't find work on their reservations. There is a lot of ___unemployment___ on a reservation.

Native American at a Pow-Wow

Culture Note

The Pow-Wow is an event where Native Americans gather to celebrate their heritage with ceremonies and dancing. The dancing takes place in a round "arena." Pow-Wows have become so popular in the U.S. with spectators that many communities are hosting weeklong events with competitions, games, and vendors selling Native American crafts.

5.10 | *Some, Any, A, No*

	Examples	Explanation
Affirmative	There is **a** big reservation in the Southwest. There is **an** onion in the recipe.	Use *a* or *an* with singular count nouns.
Affirmative	I used **some** raisins in the recipe. I used **some** bread in the recipe.	Use *some* with both plural count nouns and noncount nouns.
Negative	I didn't eat **any** potatoes. I didn't eat **any** gravy.	Use *any* for negatives with both plural count nouns and noncount nouns.
Question	Did the code talkers make **any** mistakes? Did the enemy get **any** information?	Use *any* for questions with both plural count nouns and noncount nouns.
No* vs. *any	There isn't **any** sugar in the stuffing. There is **no** sugar in the stuffing. There aren't **any** potatoes in the soup. There are **no** potatoes in the soup.	Use *any* after a negative verb. Use *no* after an affirmative verb. *Wrong:* There *aren't no* potatoes in the soup.

Language Note:
1. Don't use the indefinite article after *no*.
   Wrong: I have no *an* answer to your question.
   Right: I have no answer to your question.
2. You will sometimes see *any* with a singular count noun.
   Which pen should I use for the test? You can use *any* pen.
   Any, in this case, means whichever you want. It doesn't matter which pen.

EXERCISE 12 ABOUT YOU Use *there* + *be* + the words given to tell about your hometown. If you use no, delete the article. You can add a statement to give more information.

EXAMPLES a mayor
There's a mayor in my hometown. He's a young man.

a subway
There's no subway in my hometown.

Answers will vary.

1. a university
2. a subway
3. an English language newspaper
4. an airport
5. a soccer team
6. a river
7. a jail
8. an art museum
9. an English language institute
10. a cemetery

Exercise 12 Variation

After students complete the exercise individually, have students ask and answer questions in pairs (e.g., *Is there a university? Is there a subway?*).

5.10 | *Some, Any, A, No*

1. Have students cover up grammar chart **5.10.** Create a fill-in exercise. On one side of the board, write the example sentences from the chart. On the other side of the board, write the explanations in random order, leaving out *some, any, a,* and *no.* For example:
   Use ____ for questions with both plural count and noncount nouns.
   Use ____ or ____ with singular count nouns.
   Say: *Study the sentences. Then fill in the explanations with* some, any, a, *or* no. Have volunteers fill in the blanks on the board.
3. Have students look at the grammar chart. Say: *Compare your work with the chart.* Go over any trouble spots.
4. Direct students to the Language Notes in the chart. Remind students that they can't use *no* and an article together. Point out that *any* used with a singular noun means *whichever.* Go over the examples.

EXERCISE 12

1. Tell students that this exercise is about their hometowns. Have students read the direction line. Ask: *When do we delete the article in front of the noun?* (if we use *no*) Go over the examples. Have volunteers model the examples. Remind students to write other sentences to give more information.
2. Have students complete the exercise individually. Then have them compare answers in pairs. Circulate to observe pair work. Give help as needed.
3. If necessary, review grammar chart **5.10** on page 169.

EXERCISE 13

1. Have students read the direction line. Go over the examples in the book.
2. Have students complete the exercise individually. Then have students check answers in pairs.
3. If necessary, review grammar chart **5.10** on page 169.

To save class time, have students do half of the exercise in class and complete the other half for homework. Or assign the entire exercise for homework.

EXERCISE 13 Fill in the blanks with *some, any, a, an,* or *no.*

EXAMPLES I have ___some___ money in my pocket.
Do you have ___any___ time to help me?
Do you have ___a___ new car?
I have ___no___ experience as a babysitter.

1. Do you have ___any___ questions about this exercise?
2. Do you have ___a___ dictionary with you?
3. Did you have ___any___ trouble with the homework?
4. If we have ___some___ extra time, we'll go over the homework.
5. The teacher can't help you now because he has ___no___ time.
6. The teacher can't help you now because he doesn't have ___any___ time.
7. I'm confused. I need ___an___ answer to my question.
8. I have ___some___ questions about the last lesson. Can you answer them for me?
9. I understand this lesson completely. I have ___no___ questions.
10. I understand this lesson completely. I don't have ___any___ questions.
11. I work hard all day and have ___no___ energy late at night.
12. I don't have ___a___ computer.

170 Lesson 5

Expansion

Exercise 13 Have students write five questions for their partners using *some, any, a, an,* or *no.* Then have students take turns asking and answering questions.

5.11 | A Lot Of, Much, Many

	Examples	Explanation
Affirmative	**A lot of** Indians served in the military. It takes **a lot of** time to develop a code.	Use *a lot of* with count and noncount nouns.
Affirmative	On Thanksgiving, we give thanks for the **many** good things in our lives. We eat **a lot of** food on Thanksgiving.	Use *many* with count nouns. Use *a lot of* with noncount nouns in affirmative statements. *Much* is rare in affirmative statements.
Negative	Today the Indians don't have **much** land. The Pilgrims didn't have **many** skills.	Use *much* with noncount nouns. Use *many* with count nouns.
Negative	Today the Indians don't have **a lot of** land. The Pilgrims didn't have **a lot of** skills.	Use *a lot of* with both count and noncount nouns.
Question	Did you eat **much** turkey? Did you eat **many** cookies?	Use *much* with noncount nouns. Use *many* with count nouns.
Question	Did you eat **a lot of** turkey? Did you eat **a lot of** cookies?	Use *a lot of* with both count and noncount nouns.
Question	**How much** experience did the code talkers have? **How many** code talkers were in the military?	Use *how much* with noncount nouns. Use *how many* with count nouns.

Language Note:
When the noun is omitted (in this case, water), use *a lot*, not *a lot of*.
Compare:
I usually drink **a lot of** water, but I didn't drink **a lot** today.

EXERCISE 14 Fill in the blanks with *much*, *many*, or *a lot (of)*. Avoid *much* in affirmative statements. In some cases, more than one answer is possible.

A: Did you prepare ___a lot of___ *(example)* food for Thanksgiving?

B: No, I didn't prepare ___much___ *(1)*.

A: You didn't? Why not?

B: This year I didn't invite ___many___ *(2)* people. I just invited my immediate family.

A: How ___many___ *(3)* people are there in your immediate family?

Singular and Plural; Count and Noncount Nouns; *There + Be*; Quantity Words 171

Exercise 14 Variation

To provide practice with listening skills, have students close their books and listen to the audio. Repeat the audio as needed. Ask comprehension questions, such as: *Is it difficult to prepare a turkey?* (no) *How long do you have to cook it for?* (many hours) *Did person B prepare all the food for the dinner?* (No. Her family helped out.) Then have students open their books and complete Exercise 14.

5.11 | *A Lot Of, Much, Many*

1. Have students cover up grammar chart **5.11**. Create a fill-in exercise. Write the sentences from the grammar chart on the board leaving out *a lot of*, *much*, and *many*. For example:
   ____ Indians served in the military.
   It takes ____ time to develop a code.
   Say: *Fill in the blanks with* a lot of, much, *and* many.
2. Tell students to look at grammar chart **5.11**. Say: *Compare your work with the chart.* Review the explanations. Go over any trouble spots.
3. Direct students' attention to the Language Note. Say: *In the case of* a lot of, *when you don't use the noun, then just use* a lot. Go over the example. Give another example:
   I didn't eat a lot of bread today.
   I don't like to eat a lot. It's not healthy.

EXERCISE 14

CD 2, Track 17

1. Have students read the direction line. Remind students that we don't use *much* in affirmative sentences. Go over the example.
2. Have students complete Exercise 14 individually. Go over the answers as a class.
3. If necessary, review grammar chart **5.11** on page 171.

5.12 | *A Lot Of* vs. *Too Much / Too Many*

1. Tell students to look at grammar chart **5.12.** Say: A lot of *is used to describe a large quantity. It is a neutral term. But* too much *and* too many *show that something is excessive. We use* too much *with noncount nouns and* too many *with count nouns.* Go over all the example sentences.
2. Direct students to the Language Note. Point out that sometimes you can use *a lot of* in place of *too much/too many.* However, this can only be done if there is a second statement pointing out that the quantity was excessive. Go over the example in the book. Give another example (e.g., *There were a lot of cars in the parking lot. We couldn't find any place to park.*).

B: Just seven. I bought a twelve-pound turkey. It was more than enough.

A: I don't know how to prepare a turkey. Is it ___a lot of___ (4) work to prepare a turkey?

B: Not really. But you have to cook it for ___many___ (5) hours.

A: Did you make ___many___ (6) other dishes, like sweet potatoes and cranberry sauce?

B: No. Each person in my family made something. That way I didn't have ___much___ (7) work. But we had ___a lot of___ (8) work cleaning up. There were ___many___ (9) dirty dishes. I hate washing dishes after a big dinner, so I'm planning to buy a dishwasher soon.

A: Does a dishwasher cost ___a lot of___ (10) money?

B: Yes, but I'd like to have one for that one day a year.

A: Maybe you should just use paper plates.

B: I know ___a lot of___ (11) people do that, but I want my dinner to look elegant. For me, paper plates are for picnics.

5.12 | *A Lot Of* vs. *Too Much / Too Many*

Examples	Explanation
a. **A lot of** Navajo Indians live in the Southwest. b. My friend left the reservation because there was **too much** unemployment and she couldn't find a job. a. **A lot of** people came to dinner. We all had a great time. b. **Too many** people came to dinner. There wasn't enough food for everyone.	Sentences (a) show a large quantity. No problem is presented. *A lot of* has a neutral tone. Sentences (b) show an excessive quantity. A problem is presented or implied. A sentence with *too much/too many* can have a complaining tone.
I feel sick. I ate **too much.**	We can put *too much* at the end of a verb phrase.

Language Note:
Sometimes you can use *a lot of* in place of *too much / too many.*

Too many people came to dinner. There wasn't enough food for everyone.
A lot of people came to dinner.There wasn't enough food for everyone.

172 Lesson 5

Expansion

Exercise 14 Have students practice the conversation in pairs. Ask volunteers to role-play all or part of the conversation in front of the class.

EXERCISE 15 Fill in the blanks with *a lot of*, *too much*, or *too many*. In some cases, more than one answer is possible.

EXAMPLE I love garlic. This recipe calls for ___a lot of___ garlic, so it's going to be delicious.

1. I can't eat this soup. It has ___too much___ salt.
2. A Thanksgiving dinner has about 3,000 calories. Most people eat ___too much___ and gain a few pounds.
3. The Navajo code talkers gave ___a lot of___ help during World War II.
4. The code talkers sent ___many___ messages successfully.
5. Before the Europeans arrived, there were ___a lot of___ Indians in America.
6. There are ___many___ American Indian languages.
7. You put ___too much___ pepper in the potatoes, and they taste terrible.
8. She's going to bake a cherry pie. She needs ___a lot of___ cherries.
9. I think I ate ___too many___ pieces of pumpkin pie. Now I feel sick.

EXERCISE 16 Use *a lot of*, *too many*, or *too many* to fill in the blanks in the story below. In some cases, more than one answer is possible.

My name is Coleen Finn. I'm a Ho-chunk Indian. My tribal land is in Wisconsin. But I live in Chicago because there is ___too much___ unemployment on my tribal land, and I can't find a good job there. There are ___a lot of___ (1) opportunities in Chicago, and I found a job as a secretary in the English Department at Truman College. I like my job very much. I have ___a lot of___ (2) responsibilities and I love the challenge.

Coleen Finn

I like Chicago, but I miss my land, where I still have ___a lot of___ (3) relatives and friends. I often go back to visit them whenever I get tired of life in Chicago. My friends and I have ___a lot of___ (4) fun together, talking, cooking our native food,

Singular and Plural; Count and Noncount Nouns; *There + Be*; Quantity Words 173

EXERCISE 15

1. Have students read the direction line. Go over the example in the book.
2. Have students complete the exercise individually. Then have students check answers in pairs.
3. If necessary, review grammar chart **5.12** on page 172.

EXERCISE 16

CD 2, Track 18

1. Have students read the direction line. Go over the example.
2. Have students complete Exercise 16 individually. Then have students compare answers in pairs. Circulate to observe pair work. Give help as needed.
3. If necessary, review grammar chart **5.12** on page 172.

To save class time, have students do the exercise as a class or for homework.

Expansion

Exercise 15 Have students write five sentences about school or work using *a lot of, too much,* and *too many.* Then have students compare sentences in pairs.

Exercise 16 Variation

To provide practice with listening skills, have students close their books and listen to the audio. Repeat the audio as needed. Ask comprehension questions, such as: *Who is Coleen Finn?* (a Ho-chunk Indian) *Does she live on a reservation?* (No. She lives in Chicago.) *Does she ever visit the reservation?* (yes) Then have students open their books and complete Exercise 16.

EXERCISE 17

1. Tell students that they're going to give information on things they do too much of. Have students read the direction line. Go over the example in the book. Model the example for the class.
2. Have students complete the exercise individually. Then have students checks answers in pairs.
3. If necessary, review grammar chart **5.12** on page 172.

To save class time, have students do the exercise for homework.

5.13 | *A Few, Several, A Little*

Have students look at grammar chart **5.13.** Say: A few, several, *and* a little *mean small quantities. We use* a few *and* several *with count nouns and* a little *with noncount nouns.* Go over the examples.

---

walking in nature, and attending Indian ceremonies, such as Pow-Wows. I need to get away from Chicago once in a while to feel closer to nature. Even though there are ___a lot of___ (5) nice things about Chicago, there are ___too many___ (6) cars and trucks in the big city and there is ___too much___ (7) pollution. A weekend with my tribe gives me time to relax and smell fresh air.

EXERCISE 17 ABOUT YOU Fill in the blanks after *too* with *much* or *many*. Then complete the statement.

EXAMPLE If I drink too ___much___ coffee, ___I won't be able to sleep tonight.___

Answers will vary.

1. If I try to memorize too ___many___ words, ______
2. If I make too ___many___ mistakes on my homework, ______
3. If I spend too ___much___ money on clothes, ______
4. If I drink too ___much___ coffee, ______
5. If I spend too ___much___ time with my friends, ______
6. If I stay up late too ___many___ times, ______

5.13 | *A Few, Several, A Little*

	Examples	Explanation
Count	The Navajo language has **several** dialects. She speaks **a few** languages. Put **a few** teaspoons of salt in the potato recipe.	Use *a few* or *several* with count nouns or with quantities that describe noncount nouns (*teaspoon, cup, bowl, piece,* etc.).
Noncount	He put **a little** salt in the potatoes. Please add **a little** milk to the coffee.	Use *a little* with noncount nouns.

EXERCISE 18 Fill in the blanks with *a few, several,* or *a little.* In some cases, more than one answer is possible.

EXAMPLE We have ___a little___ information about American Indians.

1. ___A few/Several___ Indians came to help the Pilgrims.
2. They taught the Pilgrims ___a few/several___ skills for planting.
3. They gave them ___a little___ help.
4. ___A few/Several___ Navajo Indians developed a code.
5. It took ___a little___ time to develop the code.
6. The Navajos had to create ___a few/several___ new words.
7. There were ___a few/several___ Japanese experts at code breaking.
8. You need ___a little___ butter for the recipe.
9. You need ___a little___ bread for the recipe.
10. You need ___a few/several___ cloves of garlic for the recipe.

5.14 A Few vs. Few; A Little vs. Little

A few and *a little* have a positive emphasis. *Few* and *little* (without a) have a negative emphasis.

Examples	Explanation
a. **A few** Indians helped the Pilgrims. b. **Few** non-Navajos could speak the Navajo language. c. **Very few** young American Indians speak the language of their ancestors.	a. *A few* means some or enough. b. and c. *Few* and *very few* mean not enough; almost none. We use *very* to emphasize the negative quantity.
a. There's **a little** food in the refrigerator. Let's make a sandwich. b. The Navajo code talkers got **little** recognition for their help in World War II. c. The Pilgrims had **very little** food the first winter.	a. *A little* means some or enough. b. and c. *Little* and *very little* mean not enough; almost none. We use *very* to emphasize the negative quantity.

Language Note:
Whether something is enough or not enough does not depend on the quantity. It depends on the perspective of the person. Is the glass half empty or half full?
☺ One person may say the glass is half full. She sees something positive about the quantity of water in the glass: The glass has *a little* water.
☹ Another person may say the glass is half empty. He sees something negative about the quantity of water in the glass. The glass has *(very) little* water.

EXERCISE 18

1. Have students read the direction line. Point out that more than one answer may be possible in some cases. Go over the example in the book.
2. Have students complete the exercise individually. Then have students check answers in pairs.
3. If necessary, review grammar chart **5.13** on page 174.

5.14 | *A Few* vs. *Few; A Little* vs. *Little*

1. Have students turn to the reading on page 167. Say: *Find the sentences that use* very few *and* little. *Do* very few *and* little *in these sentences mean* some *or* enough*? Or do they mean* not enough*?* (not enough)
2. Have students look at grammar chart **5.14.** Say: A few *and* a little *mean some or enough.* Few, very few, little, *and* very little *without the article mean* not enough. *Very* emphasizes the negative quantity.
3. Direct students to the Language Note. Explain the concept of half empty/half full. Go over the examples. Ask: *In the picture, who thinks the glass has a little water?* (the woman) *How do you know?* (She's smiling. She has a positive expression on her face.) *Who thinks the glass has (very) little water?* (the man) *How do you know?* (He is frowning. He has a negative expression on his face.)

Expansion

Grammar Take a survey. Ask students if they are a "glass is half empty" or a "glass is half full" kind of person.

EXERCISE 19

1. Have students read the direction line. Go over the examples. Point out that more than one answer may be possible in some cases. Ask a volunteer to explain the difference between the use of *a little* and *very little* in the examples.
2. Have students complete the exercise individually. Point out the picture of the gray whale. Go over the answers with the class.
3. If necessary, review grammar chart **5.14** on page 175.

To save class time, have students do half the exercise as a class and complete the other half for homework.

EXERCISE 19 Fill in the blanks with *a little, very little, a few,* or *very few*. In some cases, more than one answer is possible.

EXAMPLES He has *a little* extra money. He's going to buy a sandwich.

He has *very little* extra money. He can't buy anything.

1. I have *a little* food in my refrigerator. Let's make dinner at my house.
2. In some countries, people have *very little* food, and many people are starving.[11]
3. That worker has *very little* experience. He probably can't do that job.
4. That worker has *a little* experience. He can probably do that job.
5. I eat *a little* meat every day because I want protein in my diet.
6. I want to bake cookies, but I can't because I have *very little* sugar in the house.
7. When there is *very little* rain, plants can't grow.
8. Tomorrow there may be *a little* rain, so you should take an umbrella.
9. Twenty-five years ago, home computers were very rare. *Very few* people had a home computer.
10. Before I bought my computer, I talked to *a few* people about which computer to buy.
11. There are *a few* monkeys in the zoo. Let's go to see them.
12. There are *very few* gray whales in the world. These animals are an endangered species.[12]
13. If you want to study medicine, I can give you a list of *a few* good medical schools in the United States.
14. *Very few* high schools teach Latin. It is not a very popular language to study anymore.
15. I want to say *a few* words about my country. Please listen.
16. My father is a man of *very few* words. He rarely talks.
17. English is the main language of *a few* countries.
18. Women are still rare as political leaders. *Very few* countries have a woman president.

[11] *To starve* means to suffer or die from not having enough food.
[12] An *endangered species* is a type of living thing that is becoming more and more rare. The species is in danger of disappearing completely if it is not protected.

176 Lesson 5

Expansion

Exercise 19 Have students write eight sentences using *a little, very little, a few,* or *very few* about things they have in the house. Then have students compare sentences with a partner.

EXERCISE 20 ABOUT YOU Ask a question with "*Are there . . . ?*" and the words given about another student's hometown. The other student will answer with an expression of quantity. Practice count nouns.

EXAMPLE museums

A: Are there any museums in your hometown?
B: Yes. There are a lot of (a few, three) museums in my hometown.
OR
No. There aren't any museums in my hometown.

1. department stores *Are there any department stores in your hometown?*
2. churches *Are there any churches in your hometown?*
3. synagogues *Are there any synagogues in your hometown?*
4. skyscrapers *Are there any skyscrapers in your hometown?*
5. supermarkets *Are there any supermarkets in your hometown?*
6. open markets *Are there any open markets in your hometown?*
7. hospitals *Are there any hospitals in your hometown?*
8. universities *Are there any universities in your hometown?*
9. mosques *Are there any mosques in your hometown?*
10. bridges *Are there any bridges in your hometown?*

EXERCISE 21 ABOUT YOU Ask a question with "*Are there any . . . ?*" or "*Are there many . . . ?*" and the words given about another student's native country. The other student will answer with an expression of quantity. Practice count nouns.

EXAMPLE single mothers

A: Are there many single mothers in your country?
B: There are very few.

Answers will vary.

1. homeless people
2. working women
3. fast-food restaurants
4. factories
5. American businesses
6. nursing homes
7. rich people
8. good universities

EXERCISE 22 ABOUT YOU Ask a question with "*Is there . . . ?*" and the words given about another student's native country or hometown. The other student will answer with an expression of quantity. Practice noncount nouns.

EXAMPLE petroleum / in your native country

A: Is there much petroleum in your native country?
B: Yes. There's lot of petroleum in my native country.
OR
No. There isn't much petroleum in my native country.

In Your Native Country

1. petroleum *Is there much petroleum in your native country?*
2. industry *Is there much industry in your native country?*
3. agriculture *Is there much agriculture in your native country?*
4. tourism *Is there much tourism in your native country?*

In Your Hometown

5. traffic *Is there much traffic in your hometown?*
6. rain *Is there much rain in your hometown?*
7. pollution *Is there much pollution in your hometown?*
8. noise *Is there much noise in your hometown?*

Expansion

Exercises 20–22 Create two rings of students. Have half of the students stand in an outer ring around the classroom. Have the other half stand in an inner ring, facing the outer ring. Instruct students to ask and answer the questions from Exercises 20–22. Call out "turn" every minute or so. Students in the inner ring should move one space clockwise. Students now ask and answer questions with their new partners. Have students ask questions in random order. Make sure students look at each other when they're speaking.

EXERCISE 20

1. Tell students that they're going to interview each other about their hometowns. Have students read the direction line. Remind students that in this exercise they'll be practicing count nouns. Model the example in the book for the class with a volunteer. Quickly review the quantity expressions summarized in grammar chart **5.9** on page 167.
2. Have students complete the exercise in pairs. Circulate to observe pair work. Give help as needed.
3. If necessary, review grammar charts **5.10** on page 169, **5.11** on page 171, **5.12** on page 172, **5.13** on page 174, and **5.14** on page 175.

To save class time, have students write out the questions for homework ahead of time.

EXERCISE 21

1. Tell students that they're going to interview each other about their native countries. Have students read the direction line. Model the example in the book for the class with a volunteer.
2. Have students complete the exercise in pairs. Circulate to observe pair work. Give help as needed.
3. If necessary, review grammar charts **5.10** on page 169, **5.11** on page 171, **5.12** on page 172, **5.13** on page 174, and **5.14** on page 175.

To save class time, have students write out the questions for homework ahead of time.

EXERCISE 22

1. Tell students that they're going to interview each other about their hometowns or native countries. Have students read the direction line. Remind students that in this exercise they'll be practicing noncount nouns. Model the example in the book for the class with a volunteer.
2. Have students complete the exercise in pairs. Circulate to observe pair work. Give help as needed.
3. If necessary, review grammar charts **5.10** on page 169, **5.11** on page 171, **5.12** on page 172, **5.13** on page 174, and **5.14** on page 175.

To save class time, have students write out the questions for homework ahead of time.

EXERCISE 23

1. Tell students that they're going to interview each other. Have students read the direction line. Say: *This time we'll use* Do you have . . . ? *rather than* Is there/are there . . . ? Go over the examples in the book. Model the examples for the class with volunteers.
2. Have students complete the exercise in pairs. Circulate to observe pair work. Give help as needed.
3. If necessary, review grammar charts **5.10** on page 169, **5.11** on page 171, **5.12** on page 172, **5.13** on page 174, and **5.14** on page 175.

To save class time, have students write out the questions for homework ahead of time.

EXERCISE 24

1. Have students read the direction line. Say: *Make sure you write about different countries, not your own.* Go over the example in the book.
2. Have students complete the statements individually. Then have students compare answers in groups. Circulate to observe group work. If possible, have students from different native countries work together in groups. Give help as needed.
3. If necessary, review grammar charts **5.10** on page 169, **5.11** on page 171, **5.12** on page 172, **5.13** on page 174, and **5.14** on page 175.

To save class time, have students do the exercise for homework.

EXERCISE 23 ABOUT YOU Ask a student a question with "*Do you have . . .?*" and the words given. The other student will answer. Practice both count and noncount nouns.

EXAMPLES American friends

Answers will vary.

A: Do you have any American friends?
B: Yes. I have many (OR a lot of) American friends.
OR
No. I don't have many American friends.

free time

A: Do you have a lot of free time?
B: Yes. I have some free time.
OR
No. I have very little free time.

1. problems in the U.S.
2. American friends
3. relatives in New York
4. time to relax
5. brothers and sisters (siblings)
6. experience with small children
7. questions about American customs
8. trouble with English pronunciation
9. information about points of interest in this city
10. knowledge about computer programming

EXERCISE 24 Cross out the phrase that doesn't fit and fill in the blanks with an expression of quantity to make a **true** statement about another country you know about. Discuss your answers.

EXAMPLE ~~There's~~ / There isn't ___*much*___ unemployment in ___*Korea*___.

1. There's / There isn't ___Answers will vary.___ opportunity to make money in ______.
2. There are / There aren't ______ divorced people in ______.
3. There are / There aren't ______ foreigners in ______.
4. There's / There isn't ______ freedom in ______.
5. There are / There aren't ______ American cars in ______.

178 Lesson 5

Expansion

Exercise 23 Create two rings of students. Have half of the students stand in an outer ring around the classroom. Have the other half stand in an inner ring, facing the outer ring. Instruct students to ask and answer the questions from Exercise 23. Call out "turn" every minute or so. Students in the inner ring should move one space clockwise. Students now ask and answer questions with their new partners. Have students ask questions in random order. Make sure students look at each other when they're speaking.

6. There are / There aren't ________________ political problems in ________________.
7. There is / There isn't ________________ unemployment in ________________.
8. There is / There isn't ________________ crime in ________________.

SUMMARY OF LESSON 5

1. Study the words that are used before count and noncount nouns.

Singular Count	Plural Count	Noncount
a tomato	some tomatoes	some coffee
no tomato	no tomatoes	no coffee
	any tomatoes *(with questions and negatives)*	any coffee
	a lot of tomatoes	a lot of coffee
	many tomatoes	much coffee *(with questions and negatives)*
	a few tomatoes	a little coffee
	several tomatoes	
	How many tomatoes?	How much coffee?

2. Sentences with *There*
Count
There's an onion in the recipe.
There are two carrots in the recipe.
Noncount
There's some butter in the recipe.
How much salt **is there** in the recipe?

3. *Too Much / Too Many / A Lot Of*
   - *A lot of* + count or noncount noun (no problem is presented)
     She's a healthy woman. She gets **a lot of** exercise.
     She walks **a lot of** miles.
   - *Too much* + noncount noun (a problem is presented)
     She doesn't qualify for financial aid because her parents make **too much** money.
   - *Too many* + count noun (a problem is presented)
     There are **too many** students in the class. The teacher doesn't have time to help everyone.

Summary of Lesson 5

1. **Words Before Count/Noncount Nouns** Have students study the chart. Ask students to list the differences between the plural count and noncount columns (*many*—count / *much*—noncount; *a few*—count / *a little*—noncount; *several*—count; *how many*—count / *how much*—noncount).
   If necessary, have students review:
   5.10 *Some, Any, A, No* (p. 169)
   5.11 *A Lot Of, Much, Many* (p. 171)
   5.13 *A Few, Several, A Little* (p. 174).
2. **Sentences with *There*** Go over the sentences with count and noncount nouns. Remind students to use *there is* (singular) with noncount nouns.
   If necessary, have students review:
   5.7 *There* + a Form of *Be* (p. 164).
3. ***Too Much / Too Many / A Lot Of*** Go over the sentences. Remind students that *a lot of* means a large quantity. It can be used with both count and noncount nouns. It has a neutral emphasis. *Too much* (noncount nouns) and *too many* (count nouns) mean excessive.
   If necessary, have students review:
   5.12 *A Lot Of* vs. *Too Much / Too Many* (p. 172).

Expansion

Exercise 24 Discuss the groups' findings with the class. Ask students to talk about things they learned from group members about other countries.

Editing Advice

Have students close their books. Write the example sentences without editing marks or corrections on the board. For example:

1. *She has two childrens.*
2. *Every children need love.*

Ask students to correct each sentence and provide a rule or explanation for each correction. This activity can be done individually, in pairs, or as a class. After students have corrected each sentence, tell them to turn to pages 180–181. Say: *Now compare your work with the Editing Advice in the book.*

EDITING ADVICE

1. Some plural forms are irregular and don't take *-s*.

   She has two childrens.

2. Use a singular noun and verb after *every*.

   Every children need^s love.

3. Use the plural form of the noun after *one of*.

   One of my sister^s is a lawyer.

4. Don't use *a* or *an* before a plural noun.

   She bought a new socks. *(some)*

5. Don't put *a* or *an* before a noncount noun.

   I want to give you an advice. *some* **OR** *a piece of*

6. A noncount noun is always singular.

   I have many homeworks to do. *a lot of*

   She bought three ^pieces of^ furnitures.

7. Use *there* to introduce a noun.

   ^There are a^ Are lot of people in China.

8. Be careful with *there* and *they're*. They sound the same.

   They're are many problems in the world. *There*

9. Don't use a specific noun after *there*.

   There's the Golden Gate bridge ^is^ in San Francisco. *T*

10. Include *of* with a unit of measure.

    He bought three rolls ^of^ film.

11. Omit *of* after *a lot* when the noun is omitted.

    I have a lot of time, but my brother doesn't have a lot of.

12. Use *a little / a few* for a positive meaning. Use *little / few* for a negative meaning.

He can't help you because he has ~~a~~ (very) little time.

13. Don't use *too much* or *too many* if the quantity doesn't present a problem.

He's a lucky man. He has ~~too many~~ a lot of friends.

14. Don't use a double negative.

He doesn't have ~~no~~ any money. OR

He has no money.

LESSON 5 TEST/REVIEW

PART 1 Find the mistakes with the underlined words, and correct them. Not every sentence has a mistake. If the sentence is correct, write *C*.

EXAMPLES How ~~many milks~~ much milk did you drink?

How much time do you have? C

1. He doesn't have ~~no~~ a job.
2. One of my friend^s moved to Montana.
3. I can't go out tonight because I have too much work. C
4. Three ~~womens~~ women came into the room.
5. I had a lot of friends in my country, but in the U.S. I don't have ~~a lot of~~ many.
6. A lot of American^s own a computer.
7. A person can be happy if he has a few good friends. C
8. I have ~~much~~ a lot of information about my country.
9. Every ~~workers~~ worker in the U.S. pays taxes.
10. Are there any mistakes in this sentence? C
11. My mother gave me a lot of ~~advices~~ advice.
12. You need ~~a~~ luck to win the lottery.
13. ~~There's the~~ The White House is in Washington, D.C.
14. I can help you on Saturday because I'll have ~~too much~~ a lot of time.
15. ~~Are~~ There are a lot of students in the cafeteria, and I can't find a seat.

Lesson 5 Test/Review

For additional practice, review, and assessment materials, see Assessment CD-ROM with *ExamView Pro*, *More Grammar Practice* Workbook 2, Interactive CD-ROM, and Web site http://elt.thomson.com/gic

PART 1

1. Part 1 may be used as an in-class test to assess student performance, in addition to the Assessment CD-ROM with *ExamView Pro*. Have students read the direction line. Ask: *Do all sentences have a mistake?* (no) Collect for assessment.
2. If necessary, have students review: **Lesson 5.**

Lesson Review

To use Part 1 as a review, assign it as homework or use it as an in-class activity to be completed individually or in pairs. Check answers and review errors as a class. Reteach grammar points that students haven't mastered. Then student learning may be assessed using a test generated from the Assessment CD-ROM with *ExamView Pro*.

PART 2

1. Part 2 may also be used as an in-class test to assess student performance, in addition to the Assessment CD-ROM with *ExamView Pro*. Have students read the direction line. Collect for assessment.
2. If necessary, have students review: **Lesson 5.**

16. A few of my teacher speak English very fast.
17. Did you buy a new furniture for your apartment?
18. Some man are very polite.
19. I have many problems with my landlord.
20. Did you have much fun at the party? C
21. I have a new dishes in my kitchen.
22. Several students in this class speak French. C
23. I have a dog. I don't have any cat.
24. Many people like to travel. C
25. He doesn't need any help from you. C
26. I have a little time. I can help you. C
27. I have a little time. I can't help you.
28. He bought three pounds meat.
29. How much apples did you eat?
30. How many cup of coffees did you drink?
31. They're are four Mexican students in the class.
32. I want to give you an advice about your education.

PART 2 Fill in the blanks with the singular or plural form of the word in parentheses( ).

EXAMPLE The Pilgrims didn't have a lot of experience (experience) with American land.

1. The Indians had many wars (war) with white people (person) over their lands.
2. Some reservations (reservation) have a big problem with unemployment (unemployment) and poverty (poverty). There aren't enough jobs (job) for everyone.
3. My father gave me a lot of advice (advice). He told me that there are more jobs (job) in big cities (city) than on reservations.

182 Lesson 5

Lesson Review

To use Part 2 as a review, assign it as homework or use it as an in-class activity to be completed individually or in pairs. Check answers and review errors as a class. Reteach grammar points that students haven't mastered. Then student learning may be assessed using a test generated from the Assessment CD-ROM with *ExamView Pro*.

4. We like to visit the art museum. We like to see the *sculptures* (sculpture) and *paintings* (painting) by famous *artists* (artist).

We like all kinds of *art* (art).

5. My brother likes all kinds of *music* (music). He has a large collection of *CDs* (CD) and *tapes* (tape).

PART 3 Fill in the blanks with an appropriate measurement of quantity. In some cases, several answers are possible.

EXAMPLE I bought a *loaf* of bread.

1. I drank a *cup* of tea.
2. She drank a *glass* of milk.
3. I usually put a *teaspoon* of sugar in my coffee.
4. There's a *gallon* of milk in the refrigerator.
5. I'm going to buy a *piece* of furniture for my living room.
6. The teacher gave a long homework *assignment*.
7. My father gave me an important *piece* of advice.
8. I took three *rolls* of film on my vacation.
9. I need a *piece* of paper to write my composition.
10. We need to buy a *bar* of soap.

PART 3

1. Part 3 may also be used as an in-class test to assess student performance, in addition to the Assessment CD-ROM with *ExamView Pro*. Have students read the direction line. Go over the example. Ask: *What do we write in the blank?* (a measurement of quantity) Have students briefly review quantities on page 162. Collect for assessment.
2. If necessary, have students review:
   5.6 Quantities with Count and Noncount Nouns (p. 162).

Lesson Review

To use Part 3 as a review, assign it as homework or use it as an in-class activity to be completed individually or in pairs. Check answers and review errors as a class. Reteach grammar points that students haven't mastered. Then student learning may be assessed using a test generated from the Assessment CD-ROM with *ExamView Pro*.

PART 4

1. Part 4 may also be used as an in-class test to assess student performance, in addition to the Assessment CD-ROM with *ExamView Pro*. Have students read the direction line. Point out that this is a composition by an American Indian. Go over the example. Collect for assessment.
2. If necessary, have students review:
   5.10 *Some, Any, A, No* (p. 169)
   5.11 *A Lot Of, Much, Many* (p. 171)
   5.12 *A Lot Of* vs. *Too Much / Too Many* (p. 172)
   5.13 *A Few, Several, Little* (p. 174)
   5.14 *A Few* vs. *Few; A Little* vs. *Little* (p. 175).

PART 4 Read this composition by an American Indian. Circle the correct words to complete the composition.

My name is Joseph Falling Snow. I'm (*an*, *a*, *any*) Native American from a Sioux[13] reservation in South Dakota. I don't live in South Dakota anymore because I couldn't find (*a*, *any*, *no*) job. There's (*a little*, *a few*, *very little*, *very few*) work on my reservation. There's (*much*, *a lot of*, *many*) poverty. My uncle gave me (*a*, *an*, *some*, *any*) good advice. He told me to go to Minneapolis to find (*a*, *an*, *some*) job. Minneapolis is a big city, so there are (*much*, *many*, *any*) job opportunities there. It was easy for me to find a job as a carpenter. I had (*no*, *not*, *any*) trouble finding a job because I have (*a lot of*, *many*, *much*) experience.

My native language is Lakota, but I know (*any*, *a few*, *very few*) words in my language. Most of the people on my reservation speak English. (*A few*, *Any*, *A little*) older people still speak Lakota, but the language is dying out as the older people die.

(*A few*, *A little*, *Few*, *Little*) times a year, I go back to the reservation for a Pow-Wow. We wear our native costumes and dance our native dances. It gets very crowded at these times because (*much*, *any*, *a lot of*) people from our reservation and nearby reservations attend this celebration. We have (*much*, *many*, *a lot of*) fun.

[13] *Sioux* is pronounced /su/.

184 Lesson 5

Lesson Review

To use Part 4 as a review, assign it as homework or use it as an in-class activity to be completed individually or in pairs. Check answers and review errors as a class. Reteach grammar points that students haven't mastered. Then student learning may be assessed using a test generated from the Assessment CD-ROM with *ExamView Pro*.

EXPANSION ACTIVITIES

Classroom Activities

1. Work with a partner. Imagine that you have to spend a few weeks alone on a deserted island. You can take 15 things with you. What will you need to survive? Give reasons for each item.

   EXAMPLE I'll take a lot of water because I can't drink ocean water. It has salt in it.

2. Game: Where am I? Teacher: Write these words on separate index cards: *at the airport, downtown, at the library, at a supermarket, at a department store, on the highway, at the zoo, at church, at the beach, at home, on an elevator, on a bus, on an airplane, at the post office,* and *in the school cafeteria.* Students: One student picks an index card with a place name and says, "Where am I?" Other students have to guess where he / she is by asking questions.

   EXAMPLES Are you indoors or outdoors?
   Are there a lot of cars in this place?
   Is it noisy in this place?
   Are there a lot of people in this place?

3. Find a partner. Take something from your purse, pocket, book bag, or backpack. Say, "I have __________ with me." Then ask your partner if he or she has this. If you're not sure if the item is a count or noncount noun, ask the teacher.

   EXAMPLES I have a comb in my pocket. Do you have a comb in your pocket?
   I have some makeup in my purse. Do you have any makeup in your purse?
   I have some money from my country in my pocket. Do you have any money from your country?

Talk About it

Read the following quotes and discuss what they mean to you.

1. "Once I was in a big city and I saw a very large house. They told me it was a bank and that the white men place their money there to be taken care of, and that by and by they got it back with interest. We are Indians and we have no such bank. When we have plenty of money or blankets, we give them away to other chiefs and people, and by and by they return them with interest, and our hearts feel good. Our way of giving is our bank."

   —Chief Maquinna, Nootka tribe

Singular and Plural; Count and Noncount Nouns; *There + Be*; Quantity Words 185

Expansion Activities

These expansion activities provide opportunities for students to interact with one another and further develop their speaking and writing skills. Encourage students to use grammar from this lesson whenever possible.

To save class time, assign parts of the activities as homework. Then use class time for interaction and communication. If students do not need additional speaking practice, some of the activities may be assigned as writing activities for homework, or skipped altogether.

CLASSROOM ACTIVITIES

1. Have students complete the survival list with a partner. Remind students to use quantities such as *a lot of, a little, a bag of,* etc. Circulate to observe pair work.
2. Write the location phrases on cards. Model the activity for the class. Pick a card and have students ask you questions. Encourage them to use *there is / there are.*
3. Model the activity with a volunteer. Keep two lists on the board for count and noncount nouns. As students ask you questions, keep track of the words on the board.

TALK ABOUT IT

Have students discuss each quote in pairs, in groups, or as a whole class. Say: *When you discuss these quotes, say if you agree or disagree with what's being said, what you like or don't like about it, and if it's made you change the way you think about things.*

Classroom Activities Variation

Activity 1 After students have created their lists in pairs, make a list with the class on the board. Ask students if they had any different or interesting suggestions.

WRITE ABOUT IT

1. Before students begin to write, have volunteers talk about the groups in their native countries they plan to talk about. Write any helpful vocabulary on the board.
2. Brainstorm vocabulary for city and country living on the board with the class.

OUTSIDE ACTIVITY

Assign one of the movies to each student to ensure enough people watch all three movies.

INTERNET ACTIVITIES

1. Tell students to find tribes closest to them. Ask students to find out if any local tribes have museums or exhibits for tourists. Are any tribes going to host a Pow-Wow soon?
2. Have students write or print out a short summary about Pilgrims.

2. "Treat the Earth well. It was not given to you by your parents; it was loaned to you by your children."
3. "Today is a time of celebrating for you—a time of looking back to the first days of white people in America. But it is not a time of celebrating for me. It is with a heavy heart that I look back upon what happened to my people. When the Pilgrims arrived, we, the Wampanoags, welcomed them with open arms, little knowing that it was the beginning of the end. . . . Let us always remember, the Indian is and was just as human as the white people."
From a speech by a Wampanoag Indian given on Thanksgiving in 1970 in Massachusetts, at the 350th anniversary of the Pilgrim's arrival in America.

Write About it

1. Write about an ethnic minority in your native country or another country you know about. Where and how do they live? Use expressions of quantity.
2. Write a paragraph telling about the advantages or disadvantages of living in this city. You may write about pollution, job opportunities, weather, traffic, transportation, and crime. Use expressions of quantity.

Outside Activity

Rent one of the following movies and write a summary of the movie: *Smoke Signals*, *Windtalkers*, or *Dances with Wolves*.

Internet Activities

1. Search for American Indian Web sites. Find the names and locations of three tribes.
2. Search for more information about the Pilgrims. Why did they leave England? Where did they go before coming to America?

Additional Activities at http://elt.thomson.com/gic

Write About it Variation

Have students exchange first drafts with a partner. Ask students to help their partners edit their drafts. Refer students to the Editing Advice on pages 180–181.

Outside Activity Variation

Have students get into groups to talk about the movie they watched. Then have volunteers quickly summarize the movies for the class. Take a vote. Which movie was a favorite among the students who viewed it?

Internet Activities Variation

Remind students that if they don't have Internet access, they can use Internet facilities at a public library or they can use traditional research methods to find out information including looking at encyclopedias, magazines, books, journals, and newspapers.

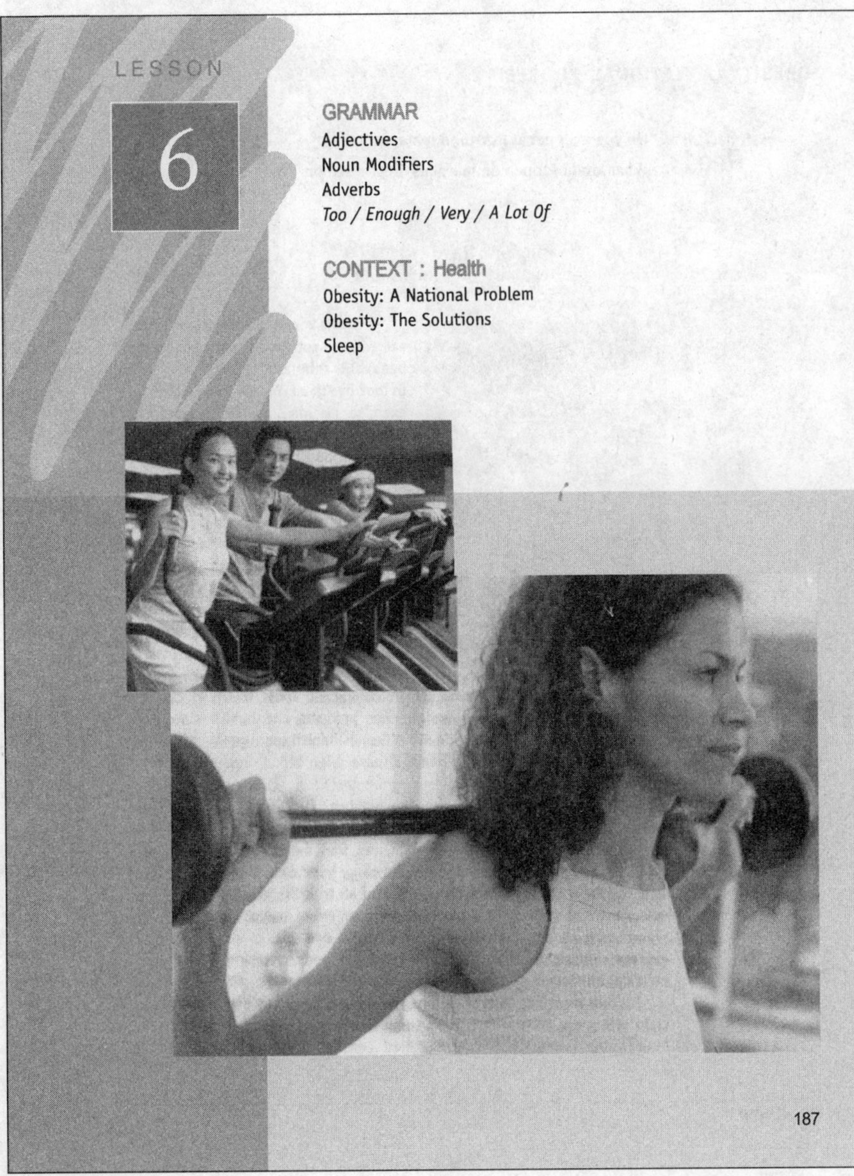

LESSON

6

GRAMMAR
Adjectives
Noun Modifiers
Adverbs
Too / Enough / Very / A Lot Of

CONTEXT : Health
Obesity: A National Problem
Obesity: The Solutions
Sleep

187

Lesson | 6

Lesson Overview

GRAMMAR

1. Briefly review what students learned in the last lesson. Ask: *What did we study in Lesson 5?* (the singular and the plural, count and noncount nouns, *there* + *be*, and quantity words)
2. Ask: *What are we going to study in this lesson?* (adjectives, noun modifiers, adverbs, *too, enough, very, a lot of*) *Can anyone give me an example of an adjective and an adverb?* (*pretty, slowly*) Have students give examples. Write the examples on the board. Then ask volunteers for noun modifiers (*health club*).

CONTEXT

1. Ask: *What will we learn about in this lesson?* (health, obesity, sleep) Activate students' prior knowledge. Ask: *What do you know about the problem of obesity in the U.S.?*
2. Have students share their knowledge and personal experiences.

Photo

1. Direct students' attention to the photos. Ask: *What's going on in these pictures?* (People are exercising in a gym. Some are doing cardio, and the woman in the large photo is lifting weights.)
2. Have students talk about how they exercise.

To save class time, have students do the Test/Review at the end of the lesson, or administer a lesson test generated from the Assessment CD-ROM with *ExamView® Pro.* Skip sections of the lesson that students have already mastered. You may also assign some sections for self-study for extra credit.

Expansion

Theme The topic for this lesson can be enhanced with the following ideas:

1. A flyer from a local gym
2. Nutritional information from fast-food restaurants

Obesity: A National Problem (Reading)

1. Have students look at the photos of the man eating a hamburger and of the junk food. Ask: *Do you eat a lot of unhealthy food, such as hamburgers, every day? How often do you eat junk food?*
2. Have students look at the title of the reading. Ask: *What is the reading about?* Have students use the title and the photos to make predictions about the reading.
3. Preteach any vocabulary words your students may not know, such as *average, cheap, tasty,* and *preventable.*

BEFORE YOU READ

1. Have students discuss the questions in pairs. Try to pair students of different cultures together.
2. Ask for a few volunteers to share their answers with the class.

To save class time, skip "Before You Read" or have students prepare answers for homework ahead of time.

Reading *CD 2, Track 19*

1. Have students first read the text silently. Tell them to pay special attention to adjectives and noun modifiers. Then play the audio and have students read along silently.
2. Check students' comprehension. Ask questions such as: *How many Americans are overweight?* (two-thirds) *Do Americans spend millions of dollars on weight-loss products and health clubs?* (No, they spend billions.) *What are some diseases related to obesity?* (heart disease, high blood pressure, diabetes, arthritis, and stroke) *What type of activity is today's lifestyle missing?* (physical activity)

To save class time, have students do the reading for homework ahead of time.

OBESITY: A NATIONAL PROBLEM

Before You Read

1. Do you ever eat at fast-food restaurants?
2. What kind of food commercials do you see on TV?

Read the following article.
Pay special attention to adjectives and noun modifiers.

Everyone knows that it's important to eat well and get **enough** exercise. We see **beautiful, thin** fashion models and want to look like them. We see commercials for **exercise** machines on TV showing **fit, thin, smiling** people exercising. **Health** clubs are full of people trying to get in shape. Sales of **diet** colas and low-calorie and low carbohydrate foods indicate that Americans want to be **thin.** However, two-thirds of **American** adults are **overweight,** and one in six American children is overweight. This is a **large** increase in the **last** 20 years, when 50 percent of adults and only five percent of children were **overweight.**

Fifty-eight percent of Americans are **concerned** about their weight. They spend billions of dollars on **weight-loss** products and **health** clubs. But weight is also becoming a **national** problem as **health** costs go up in response to diseases related to obesity: **heart** disease, **high blood** pressure, diabetes, arthritis, and stroke.

What is the reason for this **growing** problem? First, **today's** lifestyle does not include enough **physical** activity. When the U.S. was an **agricultural** society, farmers ate a **big, heavy** meal, but they burned off the calories by doing **hard physical** labor. **Modern** technology has removed **physical** activity from our **daily** lives. Seventy-five percent of all trips are less than a mile from home, but Americans drive. Only seventeen percent of **school** children walk to school even though most of them live within one mile of school. And the **average American** child spends 24 hours a week watching TV. In most **physical education** classes, kids are **active** for just three minutes.

Another reason for the **weight** problem is the **American** diet. The **average** child sees more than 10,000 **food** commercials a year. Most of these are for high-calorie foods, such as **sweetened** cereals, **sugary** soft drinks, **salty**

188 Lesson 6

Reading Variation

To practice listening skills, have students first listen to the audio alone. Ask a few comprehension questions. Repeat the audio if necessary. Then have them open their books and read along as they listen to the audio.

Reading Glossary

average: ordinary, common, neither very good nor very bad
cheap: costing very little, inexpensive
preventable: able to be prevented; avoidable (*syn.*)
tasty: flavorful

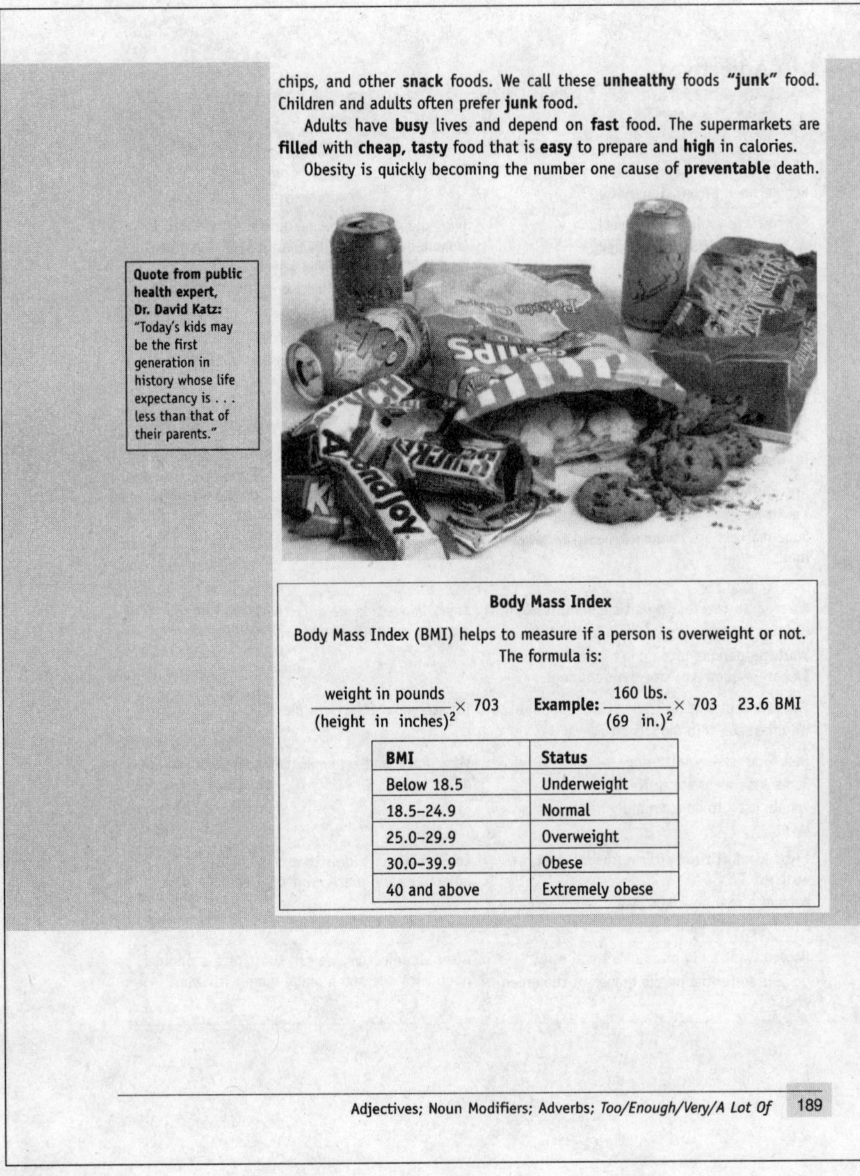

chips, and other **snack** foods. We call these **unhealthy** foods **"junk"** food. Children and adults often prefer **junk** food.

Adults have **busy** lives and depend on **fast** food. The supermarkets are **filled** with **cheap, tasty** food that is **easy** to prepare and **high** in calories.

Obesity is quickly becoming the number one cause of **preventable** death.

Quote from public health expert, Dr. David Katz: "Today's kids may be the first generation in history whose life expectancy is . . . less than that of their parents."

Body Mass Index

Body Mass Index (BMI) helps to measure if a person is overweight or not. The formula is:

$$\frac{\text{weight in pounds}}{(\text{height in inches})^2} \times 703 \qquad \textbf{Example: } \frac{160 \text{ lbs.}}{(69 \text{ in.})^2} \times 703 \quad 23.6 \text{ BMI}$$

BMI	Status
Below 18.5	Underweight
18.5–24.9	Normal
25.0–29.9	Overweight
30.0–39.9	Obese
40 and above	Extremely obese

Adjectives; Noun Modifiers; Adverbs; *Too/Enough/Very/A Lot Of* 189

Culture Note

Dr. David Katz is the founder and director of the Yale Prevention Research Center. He is also the director of Medical Studies in Public Health at Yale University. He has written a number of books and contributes to magazines and Web sites.

Expansion

Theme Have students use the equation to calculate their body mass index (BMI).

6.1 | Adjectives

1. Have students cover up grammar chart **6.1.** Activate prior knowledge. Say: *I'm going to read you a statement about adjectives, and you're going to tell me* true *or* false.
   1. *Adjectives go after nouns. (F)*
   2. *We can never put two adjectives before a noun. (F)*
   3. *An adjective can come after* it is. *(T)*
   4. *Words that end in* -ed *like* married, excited, *and* finished *are not adjectives. (F)*
   5. *Some words that end in* -ed *are adjectives, such as* married. *(T)*
   6. *You can make an adjective plural. (F)*
2. Then have students look at grammar chart **6.1.** Say: *Let's look at these examples and see if we were wrong or right.* Go over the examples and explanations.
3. Go over the *-ing* words that are adjectives.
4. Explain that the words *very, quite,* and *extremely* intensify the adjective. Review the conversational words that go in front of adjectives. Go over the meanings of each word (*kind of = a little; real = very; pretty = quite*).
5. Point out that after an adjective, we can substitute a singular noun with *one* and a plural noun with *ones.*

6.1 | Adjectives

An adjective describes a noun.

Examples	Explanation
We ate a **big** meal. People need **physical** activity.	An adjective can come before a noun.
Farmers ate a **big, heavy** meal. We see **beautiful, thin** models.	Two adjectives can come before a noun. Put a comma between the two adjectives if you can reverse the order of the adjectives or insert *and* between the adjectives without changing the meaning.
Fast food is **cheap.** Chips are **salty.** Burgers taste **delicious.** You look **healthy.**	An adjective can come after the verb *be* and after the sense-perception verbs: *look, seem, sound, smell, taste,* or *feel.*
It is **important** to eat well. It is **easy** to gain weight if you eat junk food.	An adjective can come after *it is.*
Are you **concerned** about your weight? I'm **tired** after work. Supermarkets are **filled** with easy-to-prepare foods.	Some *-ed* words are adjectives: *tired, worried, located, crowded, married, divorced, excited, disappointed, finished, frightened, filled,* or *concerned.*
We read an **interesting** article about weight. Obesity is a **growing** problem in the U.S. **Working** parents often don't have time to prepare a good meal for their children.	Some *-ing* words are adjectives: *interesting, growing, exciting, boring,* and *working.*
She is a **thin** model. We often see **thin** models on TV.	Do not make adjectives plural.
Fast food is **very** fattening. Some Americans are **quite** fat. People used to do **extremely** hard physical labor.	*Very, quite,* and *extremely* can come before adjectives.
I was **kind of** tired after work, so I just watched TV. We had a **real** delicious meal. I had a **pretty** hard day.	Conversational words that come before adjectives are: *pretty, sort of, kind of,* and *real.*
Do you want a big pizza or a small **one?** Do you prefer the purple grapes or the green **ones?**	After an adjective, we can substitute a singular noun with *one* and a plural noun with *ones.*

190 Lesson **6**

Expansion

Grammar Have students go to the reading on pages 150–151 in Lesson 5. Say: *Find as many adjectives as you can that correspond to each explanation in grammar chart **6.1**.*

EXERCISE 1 Fill in the blanks with an appropriate word. Answers may vary.

EXAMPLE Burgers and fries are _high_ in calories.

1. Fries are cooked in oil. They are very _unhealthy_.
2. I ate a terrible meal and I got _sick_.
3. Do you want a large cola or a small _one_?
4. She's very _concerned_ about her children's health because they prefer candy to fruit.
5. I didn't sleep at all last night. I'm very _tired_ today.
6. Have a piece of fresh apple pie. I just had a piece. It _tasted_ good.
7. Potato chips are very _salty_.
8. Ice cream is _high_ in calories.
9. Most Americans have _busy_ lives and don't make the time to eat well.
10. Obesity in the U.S. is a _growing_ problem. It is a much bigger problem today than it was 20 years ago.

EXERCISE 2 Circle the correct words in *italics* to complete this conversation.

A husband (H) and wife (W) are discussing weight.

H: We're gaining weight. We used to be *thin* / *thins*, but when we got *marry* / *married*, we started to gain weight.
(example) (1)

W: Let's go jogging after work. There's a *beautiful park* / *park beautiful* where we can go. It's *locate* / *located* just a few blocks away from our apartment.
(2) (3)

H: But after work I'm always too *tire* / *tired*. I just want to eat dinner and watch TV.
(4)

W: It's not good to eat a big meal so late at night. I know that's what most Americans do, but in other countries people eat a big meal during the day and *a small one* / *a small* at night.
(5)

H: What difference does it make?

Adjectives; Noun Modifiers; Adverbs; *Too/Enough/Very/A Lot Of* 191

EXERCISE 1

1. Say: *This exercise is based on the reading on pages 188–189.* Have students read the direction line. Go over the example.
2. Have students complete Exercise 1 individually. Go over the answers as a class.
3. If necessary, review grammar chart **6.1** on page 190.

EXERCISE 2

CD 2, Track 20

1. Have students read the direction line. Point out that this is a conversation between a husband and wife about weight. Ask: *What kind of words are in italics?* (adjectives) Go over the example.
2. Have students complete Exercise 2 individually. Then have students compare answers in pairs. Circulate to observe pair work. Give help as needed.
3. If necessary, review grammar chart **6.1** on page 190.

Exercise 2 Variation

To provide practice with listening skills, have students close their books and listen to the audio. Repeat the audio as needed. Ask comprehension questions, such as: *Was the couple in the conversation always overweight?* (No. They started putting on weight a few years ago.) *Can the husband eat a big meal in the middle of the day?* (No. He doesn't have time.) Then have students open their books and complete Exercise 2.

6.2 | Noun Modifiers

1. Have students look at grammar chart **6.2.** Say: *We can use a noun to describe another noun.* Point out that when two nouns come together, the second noun is more general. The first noun describes the second noun.
2. Say: *Gerunds are nouns that end with -ing. Sometimes a gerund describes a noun. It shows the purpose of a noun.* Go over the example sentences.
3. Explain that when two nouns come together, the first noun is always singular. Go over the examples in the chart.
4. Point out that sometimes possessive forms act as adjectives. Go over the examples in the chart.
5. Direct students' attention to the Pronunciation Note. Point out that when a noun modifies another noun, greater stress or emphasis is placed on the first noun. Have students practice pronouncing the examples in the chart chorally. Have them continue with other examples if necessary.

W: If we eat a big meal in the middle of the day, we have the rest of the day to burn off the calories.

H: I'm sure that's *an idea very good* / *a very good idea* (6) but I don't have time to eat a big meal in the middle of the day. My lunch break is *kind* / *kind of* (7) short.

W: We should cook more at home. We're always eating out in *expensive* / *expensives* (8) restaurants that have *fatty* / *fattied* (9) foods.

H: Maybe doctors will find a pill that will make us thin with no effort.

W: You know what they say, "No pain, no gain." It takes a lot of effort to lose weight.

6.2 | Noun Modifiers

Examples	Explanation
Do you have an **exercise machine?** A **farm worker** gets a lot of exercise. Some people eat at a **fast-food restaurant.** I joined a **health club.**	A noun can modify (describe) another noun. The second noun is more general than the first. An *exercise machine* is a machine. A *leg exercise* is an exercise.
I bought new **running** shoes. Do you ever use the **swimming** pool?	Sometimes a gerund describes a noun. It shows the purpose of the noun.
My **five-year-old** son prefers candy to fruit. **Potato** chips have a lot of grease. I can't read the small print on this box. I need my **eye**glasses.	The first noun is always singular. A five-**year**-old son is a son who is five **years** old. **Potato** chips are chips made from **potatoes.** **Eye**glasses are glasses for **eyes.**
Do you have your **driver's** license? I can't understand the **owner's** manual for my new DVD player. **Today's** lifestyle doesn't include much physical activity.	Sometimes a possessive form describes a noun.

Pronunciation Note:

When a noun describes a noun, the first noun usually receives the greater emphasis in speaking.

I wear my **running** shoes when I go to the **health** club and use the **exercise** machines.

192 Lesson 6

Expansion

Exercise 2 Have students practice the conversation in pairs. Ask volunteers to role-play all or part of the conversation in front of the class.

EXERCISE 3 Find the noun modifiers in the article on pages 188–189. Underline them.

EXERCISE 4 A mother (M) and son (S) are shopping at a big supermarket. Fill in the blanks by putting the nouns in parentheses ( ) in the correct order. Remember to use the singular form for the first noun.

S: What are we going to buy today? Just a few things?

M: No. We need a lot. Let's take a shopping cart (example: cart/shopping).

S: Can I sit in the child seat (1 child/seat)?

M: You're much too big. You're a six- year (2 year/years) -old boy.

S: Mom, buy me that cereal. It looks good. I saw it on a TV commercial (3 commercial/TV).

M: Let's read the ingredients on the cereal box (4 cereal/box) first. I want to see the sugar content (5 content/sugar) before we buy it. Let me put on my eyeglasses (6 glasses/eyes). Oh, dear. This cereal has 20 grams of sugar.

S: But I like sugar, Mom.

M: You know it causes tooth decay (7 teeth/decay). Remember what the dentist told you?

S: But I brush my teeth once a day.

M: I want you to use your toothbrush (8 teeth/brush) after every meal, not just once a day.

S: Mom, can we buy those potato chips (9 chips/potatoes)?

M: They have too much fat.

S: How about some soda?

M: You should drink more juice. How about some orange juice (10 juice/oranges)?

S: I don't like juice.

M: It seems you don't like anything that's good for you. Maybe we should shop at the health food (11 food/health) store next time.

S: Oh, Mom, you're no fun.

M: Let's get in the check-out line (12 line/check-out) and pay now.

Adjectives; Noun Modifiers; Adverbs; *Too/Enough/Very/A Lot Of* 193

EXERCISE 3

1. Have students read the direction line. Then have students go back to the reading on pages 188–189.
2. Have students complete Exercise 3 in pairs. Circulate to observe pair work.
3. If necessary, review grammar chart **6.2** on page 192.

EXERCISE 4

CD 2, Track 21

1. Have students read the direction line. Ask: *What are we going to write on the blanks?* (noun modifiers) Explain that this is a conversation between a mother and son while shopping at a supermarket. Point out the picture. Go over the example.
2. Have students complete Exercise 4 individually. Go over the answers as a class.
3. If necessary, review grammar chart **6.2** on page 192.

Exercise 4 Variation

To provide practice with listening skills, have students close their books and listen to the audio. Repeat the audio as needed. Ask comprehension questions, such as: *How old is the little boy?* (six years old) *What does the cereal have that the mother doesn't like?* (20 grams of sugar) *How often does his mother want her son to brush his teeth?* (after every meal) Then have students open their books and complete Exercise 4.

Expansion

Exercise 4 Have students practice the conversation in pairs. Ask volunteers to role-play all or part of the conversation in front of the class.

Obesity: The Solutions (Reading)

1. Have students look at the photo of the vending machines. Ask: *What are these machines called?* (vending machines) *What kind of food do you usually find in vending machines? Are there vending machines at this school? What about at your children's school? Do you ever eat food from a vending machine?* Have students look at the photo on page 195. Ask: *How often do you choose to eat fruits and vegetables instead of fattening processed foods?*
2. Have students look at the title of the reading. Ask: *What is the reading about?* Have students use the title and photos to make predictions.
3. Preteach any vocabulary words your students may not know, such as *recommendation* and *manufactured.*

BEFORE YOU READ

1. Have students discuss the questions in pairs. Try to pair students of different cultures.
2. Ask for a few volunteers to share their answers with the class.

To save class time, skip "Before You Read" or have students prepare answers for homework ahead of time.

Reading CD 2, Track 22

1. Have students first read the text silently. Tell them to pay special attention to adverbs. Then play the audio and have students read along silently.
2. Check students' comprehension. Ask questions such as: *What ways does the reading suggest we get active?* (ride a bike or walk places instead of driving) *Do nutritionists suggest we eat alone?* (No. They suggest we eat with our families.) *How many calories do teenagers consume from soft drinks?* (10 to 15 percent) *How do experts suggest we change our living arrangements to create healthier communities?* (build houses closer together, stores and activities should be within walking distance, build more sidewalks and bike paths)

To save class time, have students do the reading for homework ahead of time.

OBESITY: THE SOLUTIONS

Before You Read

1. Where and when do you eat your big meal of the day?
2. When you see commercials for food on TV, do you want to buy that food?

 Read the following article. Pay special attention to adverbs.

Millions of Americans are overweight. Health experts agree that the problem comes from a combination of things: the kind of food we eat, our lifestyle, and even technology. Experts have the following recommendations for living a healthier lifestyle.

1. Get active. Ride a bike or walk places instead of driving. Cars and other machines **greatly** reduce the need for physical activity. We can move from place to place **easily** and **quickly** and work **efficiently** without using much physical energy.
2. Eat a **well**-balanced meal, consisting of protein, grains, vegetables, and fruit. Unfortunately, many people often eat alone and **quickly.** Some even just eat snacks all day. Nutritionists recommend that families eat together like they used to. As they eat their big meal together **slowly,** they can discuss the events of their day and enjoy each other's company.
3. Take the soft drink and snack machines out of the schools and educate children **early** about nutrition and exercise. The typical teenager gets about 10 to 15 percent of his or her calories from soft drinks, which have no nutrition at all. Replace the food in the machines with water, juices, and healthy snacks such as raisins.

194 Lesson 6

Reading Variation

To practice listening skills, have students first listen to the audio alone. Ask a few comprehension questions. Repeat the audio if necessary. Then have them open their books and read along as they listen to the audio.

Reading Glossary

manufactured: something made for sale using machinery
recommendation: written or spoken praise about something or someone's good points

4. Be careful of the food messages you hear from advertisers that say, "Eat this. Buy that." Technology allows advertisers to send us messages **constantly** through commercials. Many of these foods are high in fat and calories. Choose natural foods, such as fruits and nuts, instead of manufactured foods.

In addition to what individuals can do, communities need to build their housing more **carefully.** In many communities in the U.S., it is hard to walk from place to place **easily** because there are no sidewalks. If we want people to get exercise in their communities, they need sidewalks and bike paths with stores and activities within walking distance.

Can you think of any other ways to solve the problem of obesity?

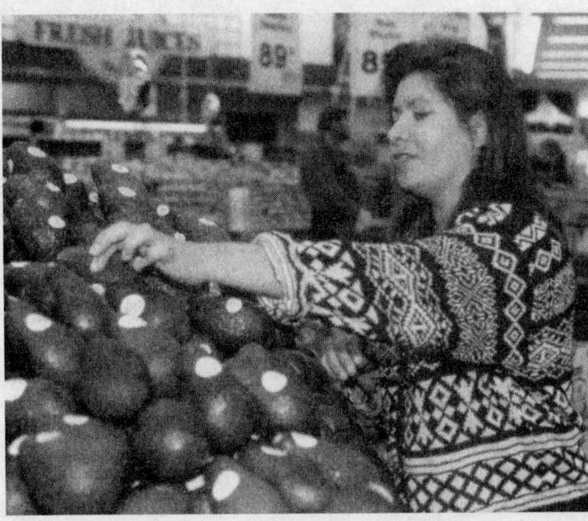

Culture Note

Many blame Americans' lack of activity on the way our living communities are developing—specifically the phenomenon known as *sprawl.* Sprawl is different from compact urban and town living. Typically, sprawl is characterized, among other things, by "excessive land consumption, lack of housing types and prices, repetitive one-story development, and the lack of public space and community centers." Sprawl is also car dependent. People who live in sprawl typically commute long distances to work, to shopping, and to other activities such as school. Much of a person's time is spent driving in vehicles instead of walking or carrying out other calorie-burning activities. Sprawl consumes more than 2 million acres of open space a year in the United States.

6.3 | Adverbs of Manner

1. Have students cover up grammar chart **6.3.** Tell students to go back to the reading on pages 194–195. Say: *Look at all the adverbs. What do you notice about them?* (They're formed from adjectives; all except for one end with an *-ly*; most adverbs come after the verb.) Write students' responses on the board.
2. Have students look at grammar chart **6.3.** Say: *We form most adverbs by putting* -ly *at the end of an adjective. An adverb usually follows the verb phrase.* Point out that *-ly* adverbs of manner can come before a verb but that this is more formal. Ask students if they noticed an adverb in this position in the reading (*greatly*).
3. Direct students to the next example. Say: Good *is the adjective;* well *is the adverb.*
4. Point out that adverbs describe verbs, and they also describe adjectives. When adverbs describe adjectives, they go before them. Go over the examples.
5. Explain that some adverbs have the same form as the adjective. These have to be memorized. Go over the examples. Point out that *hard* is an adjective and that it also is an adverb. *Hardly* is also an adverb, but it has a completely different meaning. Go over the examples. Repeat for *late* and *lately.*
6. Point out the list of adjectives that end in *-ly.* Because these adjectives don't have an adverb form, we must use them in an adverbial phrase—*in a friendly manner; in a lively way.*
7. Words like *very, so,* and *real* can come before an adverb. They intensify the meaning of the adverb. Review the examples.

6.3 | Adverbs of Manner

An adverb of manner tells *how* or *in what way* a person does something.

Examples	Explanation
Subject / Verb Phrase / Adverb He does his job **efficiently.** They ate lunch **quickly.** We walk together **slowly.**	We form most adverbs of manner by putting *-ly*[1] at the end of an adjective. An adverb usually follows the verb phrase.
Cars **greatly** reduce the need for physical activity. We **constantly** see ads on TV for food.	The *-ly* adverb of manner can come before the verb. This position is more formal.
Do you eat **well?**	The adverb for *good* is *well.*
You should eat a **well**-balanced meal. We live in a **carefully** planned community.	An adverb can come before an adjective.
ADJ: He is a **hard** worker. ADV: He works **hard.** ADJ: He wants a **fast** meal. ADV: Don't eat so **fast.** ADJ: He has an **early** class. ADV: We need to educate our children **early.** ADJ: I have a **late** class. ADV: I get home **late.**	Some adjectives and adverbs have the same form: *hard, fast, early,* and *late.*
She worked **hard** to prepare a good meal, but her son **hardly** ate anything.	*Hard* and *hardly* are both adverbs, but they have completely different meanings. *She worked **hard*** means she put a lot of effort into the work. *He **hardly** ate anything* means he ate almost nothing.
He came home **late** and missed dinner. **Lately,** he doesn't have time to eat a good meal.	*Late* and *lately* are both adverbs, but they have completely different meanings. *Late* means not on time. *Lately* means recently.
Compare: She is a **friendly** person. She behaves **in a friendly manner.** He is a **lively** person. He dances **in a lively way.**	Some adjectives end in *-ly*: *lovely, lonely, early, friendly, lively, ugly.* They have no adverb form. We use an adverbial phrase (*in a ___-ly way*) to describe the action.
He loses weight **very** *easily.* She cooks **extremely** *well.* He eats **so** *fast.* She exercises **real** *hard.* You eat **quite** *slowly.*	*Very, extremely, so, real,* and *quite* can come before an adverb.

[1] For the spelling of *-ly* adverbs, see Appendix C.

196 Lesson 6

Expansion

Grammar Have students write sentences with adverbs describing family members. Then have students talk about their family members in pairs.

EXERCISE 5 Fill in the blanks with an adverb from the box below (or choose your own adverb). Several answers may be possible.

cheaply	differently	constantly	poorly
briskly	regularly	quickly	well

EXAMPLE If you walk ___briskly___ every day, you can lose weight.

1. TV gives us messages ___constantly___, telling us to buy, buy, buy more food.
2. Do you eat ___quickly___ or slowly?
3. You should exercise ___regularly___ if you want to lose weight.
4. If you eat ___poorly___, you will not be healthy and strong.
5. If you eat ___well___, you will have no need to snack between meals.
6. In a fast-food restaurant, a family can eat ___cheaply___. In another kind of restaurant, they have to spend a lot of money.
7. Some immigrants eat ___differently___ when they come to the U.S. because they can't find food from their native countries.

EXERCISE 6 ABOUT YOU Write the adverb form of the word in parentheses ( ). Then check (✓) the activities that you do in this way. Make statements telling how you do these activities.

EXAMPLES ✓ shop ___carefully___ (careful)

I shop carefully. I always try to buy healthy food for my family.

___ dance ___well___ (good)

I don't dance well. I never learned.

Answers will vary.

1. ___ answer every question ___________ (honest)
2. ___ drive ___________ (fast)
3. ___ cook ___________ (good)
4. ___ talk ___________ (constant)
5. ___ work ___________ (hard)

EXERCISE 5

1. Have students read the direction line. Say: *You don't have to use the adverbs in the box. You can choose your own.* Go over the example in the book. Ask the class if they can think of another adverb that might work just as well in the example (*quickly, fast*).
2. Have students complete Exercise 5 individually. Go over the answers as a class.
3. If necessary, review grammar chart **6.3** on page 196.

EXERCISE 6

1. Have students read the direction line. Ask: *What are we going to do first?* (Write the adverb on the blank.) *Then what are we going to do?* (Check what's true for me.) Go over the examples in the book.
2. Have students complete Exercise 6 individually. Then have students compare responses in pairs. Ask: *Do you and your partner have a lot in common?* Circulate to observe pair work.
3. If necessary, review grammar chart **6.3** on page 196.

To save class time, have students do half of the exercise in class and complete the other half for homework. Or assign the entire exercise for homework.

Expansion

Exercise 6 Create two rings of students. Have half of the students stand in an outer ring around the classroom. Have the other half stand in an inner ring, facing the outer ring. Instruct students to make questions (and answer them) from the statements in Exercise 6 (e.g., *Do you answer every question honestly?*). Call out "turn" every minute or so. Students in the inner ring should move one space clockwise. Students now ask and answer questions with their new partners. Have students ask questions in random order. Make sure students look at each other when they're speaking.

6.4 | Adjective vs. Adverb

1. Have students cover up grammar chart **6.4.** Write the following sentences on the board:
   Jim is ***serious*** *about good health.*
   He takes his doctor's advice ***seriously.***
   Your composition looks ***good.***
   The teacher is looking at it ***carefully.***
   The children got ***hungry.***
   They ate lunch ***hungrily.***
   Her health is ***absolutely*** *perfect.*
   The refrigerator is ***completely*** *empty.*
   Say: *Study the use of adjectives and adverbs in these sentences. When do we use adjectives? When do we use adverbs?* Write student's ideas on the board.
2. Have students look at grammar chart **6.4.** Go through the examples and explanations.
3. Point out that when talking about health, we use *well* (e.g., *I don't feel well today.*). But in conversational, informal English, people often use *good* (e.g., *I don't feel good today.*). Point out the different usage for *usually* vs. *as usual.*

6. ___ study ___________ *(hard)*

7. ___ speak Spanish ___________ *(fluent)*

8. ___ type ___________ *(fast)*

9. ___ type ___________ *(accurate)*

10. ___ choose my food ___________ *(careful)*

6.4 | Adjective vs. Adverb

An adjective describes a noun. An adverb describes a verb (phrase).

Examples	Explanation
Jim is **serious** about good health. He takes his doctor's advice **seriously.**	*Serious* is an adjective. It describes Jim. *Seriously* is an adverb. It tells how he takes his doctor's advice.
a. Your composition looks **good.** b. The teacher is looking at it **carefully.** a. The soup tastes **delicious.** b. I tasted the soup **slowly** because it was hot.	a. Use an adjective, not an adverb, after the following verbs if you are describing the subject: *smell, sound, taste, look, seem, appear,* and *feel.* b. Use an adverb if you are telling *how* the action (the verb phrase) is done.
a. The children got **hungry.** b. They ate lunch **hungrily.**	Use an adjective, not an adverb, in expressions with *get: get hungry, get tired, get sick, get rich,* etc. a. *Hungry* describes the children. b. *Hungrily* describes how they ate lunch.
Her health is **absolutely** perfect. The refrigerator is **completely** empty. You should eat a **well**-balanced diet.	An adverb can come before an adjective in phrases such as these: completely right / extremely important pleasantly surprised / well known perfectly clear / absolutely wrong
He's sick. He doesn't feel **well** today.	For health, use *well.* In conversational English, people often use *good* for health. He's sick. He doesn't feel **good** today.
Compare: **As usual,** she cooked the dinner. Her husband **usually** cooks on Saturday.	Use the adjective, not the adverb, in the expression *as usual.*

198 Lesson 6

Expansion

Exercise 6 Have students write five more statements with the following phrases: *sing, spend money, play soccer, read, speak English.* Tell students to use their own adverbs. Then have students ask their partners about each activity (e.g., *Do you sing well?*).

EXERCISE 7 Fill in the blanks with the correct form of the adjective or adverb in parentheses( ).

Last week I was invited to a "potluck" dinner at my math teacher's house. This is my first month in the U.S., so I didn't know what that was. A ___good___ (example: good) friend of mine told me that this is a dinner where each person brings some food. I wanted to make a ___good___ (1 good) impression, so I prepared my ___favorite___ (2 favorite) dish from Mexico. I worked ___extremely___ (3 extreme) hard to make it look and taste ___good___ (4 good).

Most of the people at the dinner looked at my dish ___strangely___ (5 strange). They didn't know what it was. They thought ___foolishly___ (6 foolish) that Mexicans just eat tacos. They tasted my food ___carefully___ (7 careful), thinking that Mexicans make everything very hot and spicy. But I didn't. I know that some people don't like ___spicy___ (8 spicy) food, so I put the hot sauce on the side.

A student from India brought Indian food. I was ___surprised___ (9 surprised) to find out how hot Indian food is. The taste was very ___strange___ (10 strange) to me, but I ate it anyway.

The party was great. I went home very ___late___ (11 late). I had to get up early the next morning, so I ___hardly___ (12 hard) slept at all that night.

Adjectives; Noun Modifiers; Adverbs; *Too/Enough/Very/A Lot Of* 199

EXERCISE 7

CD 2, Track 23

1. Say: *This exercise is about a potluck dinner. A potluck dinner, is a group meal where everyone brings food and shares it with each other.* Use the picture to help students understand *potluck dinner.* Have students read the direction line. Go over the example.
2. Have students complete Exercise 7 individually. Go over the answers as a class.
3. If necessary, review grammar chart **6.4** on page 198.

Exercise 7 Variation

To provide practice with listening skills, have students close their books and listen to the audio. Repeat the audio as needed. Ask comprehension questions, such as: *Where was the potluck dinner?* (at the math teacher's house) *When did the student come to the U.S.?* (one month ago) *What kind of dish did the student bring?* (a Mexican dish) *What kind of food do most people not like?* (spicy food) Then have students open their books and complete Exercise 7.

Sleep (Reading)

1. Have students look at the title of the reading. Ask: *What is the reading about?* Have students use the title and the picture to make predictions about the reading.
2. Preteach any vocabulary words your students may not know, such as *complain* and *stimulated.*

BEFORE YOU READ

1. Have students discuss the questions in pairs. Try to pair students of different cultures together.
2. Ask for a few volunteers to share their answers with the class.

To save class time, skip "Before You Read" or have students prepare answers for homework ahead of time.

Reading *CD 2, Track 24*

1. Have students first read the text silently. Tell them to pay special attention to *too, enough, a lot of,* and *very.* Then play the audio and have students read along silently.
2. Check students' comprehension. Ask questions such as: *How many people get enough sleep?* (35 percent) *Who causes 100,000 auto accidents a year?* (sleepy drivers) *What are some things that are keeping Americans up at night?* (24-hour Internet and TV; malls, supermarkets, and laundromats that are open late) *Should you exercise late at night?* (no)

To save class time, have students do the reading for homework ahead of time.

DID YOU KNOW?

While Einsten may have said that he needed ten hours of sleep, other great men have said they needed very little, including Napoleon, Thomas Edison, and Winston Churchill.

SLEEP

Before You Read

1. How many hours do you sleep a night?
2. How many hours would you like to sleep a night?

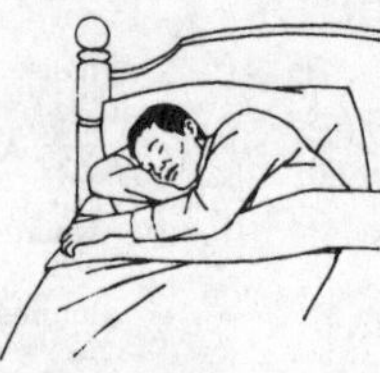

Read the following article. Pay special attention to *too, enough, a lot of,* and *very.*

Did You Know? Albert Einstein said he needed 10 hours of sleep a night to function well.

Most people need eight hours of sleep but don't get **enough.** Most Americans get less than seven hours a night. Only 35 percent get **enough sleep.** When people aren't rested **enough,** there are bad results. For example, if people drive when they're **too tired,** they can cause serious accidents on the road. According to the National Transportation Administration, sleepy drivers cause 100,000 accidents each year. There are many work-related accidents too. But that's not all. If you stay awake **too long,** your mind and nervous system begin to malfunction[2]. In the long term, if you don't get **enough sleep,** you will have less resistance to infection and disease.

Are we **too busy** to get enough sleep? Not always. Besides job and family responsibilities, Americans have **a lot of** other things that keep them out of bed. Twenty-four-hour-a-day Internet and TV keep us awake. Supermarkets, shopping malls, and laundromats are open late.

A lot of Americans report having trouble sleeping a few nights per week. About two-thirds complain to doctors about not getting **enough sleep.** Maybe they have **too much** stress in their lives or don't have good sleep habits. Sleep experts have some recommendations:

- Don't nap during the day.
- Don't get **too stimulated** before going to bed. Avoid activities such as watching TV or eating before bed.
- Go to bed at the same time every night.
- Avoid caffeine after lunchtime. If you drink **too much** coffee during the day, don't expect to get a good night's sleep.
- Exercise. Physical activity is **very** good for sleep. But if you exercise **too late** in the day, it will interfere with your sleep.

A good night's sleep is **very** important, so turn off the TV, shut down the computer, and sleep well.

[2] *To malfunction* means to function, or work, poorly.

200 Lesson **6**

Reading Variation

To practice listening skills, have students first listen to the audio alone. Ask a few comprehension questions. Repeat the audio if necessary. Then have them open their books and read along as they listen to the audio.

Reading Glossary

complain: to express dissatisfaction, such as with pain or something that is wrong
stimulated: to have increased energy or activity

6.5 | *Too* and *Enough*

Too indicates a problem. The problem is stated or implied. *Enough* means sufficient.

Examples	Explanation
adjective I'm **too tired** to drive. adverb She drove **too fast** and got a ticket.	Put *too* before adjectives and adverbs.
noncount noun a. Children eat **too much food** that is high in calories. count noun b. You spend **too many hours** watching TV. c. He doesn't sleep well because he worries **too much.**	a. Use *too much* before a noncount noun. b. Use *too many* before a count noun. c. *Too much* can come at the end of the verb phrase.
adjective Five hours of sleep is not **good enough.** adverb I walked **quickly enough** to raise my heart rate.	Put *enough* **after** adjectives and adverbs.
noun Some children don't get **enough exercise.** noun I don't have **enough time** to exercise.	Put *enough* **before** nouns.

Language Notes:

1. An infinitive phrase can follow a phrase with *too* and *enough.*
   He's **too young to *understand*** that candy isn't good for you.
   I don't have **enough money to *join*** a health club.
2. *Too good to be true* shows a positive surprised reaction.
   I just won a million dollars. It's **too good to be true.**

EXERCISE 8 Fill in the blanks to complete these statements. Answers may vary.

EXAMPLES Are Americans too ___busy___ to get a good night's sleep?
Some people don't get enough ___exercise___, so they're overweight.

1. It's hard to sleep if you exercise too ___late___ in the afternoon.
2. If you're too ___tired___ when you drive, you can fall asleep at the wheel.

Adjectives; Noun Modifiers; Adverbs; *Too/Enough/Very/A Lot Of* 201

Culture Note

Idiomatic Expressions with *Enough*

enough is enough: something is happening that is unpleasant and they want it to stop
I've had enough: had as much or more than wanted
leave well enough alone: if things are going tolerably well, leave them alone; your efforts to improve the situation may make things worse
sure enough: as expected
true enough: while something is accurate, it doesn't completely explain something

6.5 | *Too* and *Enough*

1. Have students cover up grammar chart **6.5** on page 201. Create a fill-in exercise. Write the following sentences from the grammar chart on the board:
   I'm too tired to drive.
   She drove too fast and got a ticket.
   Children eat too much food that is high in calories.
   You spend too many hours watching TV.
   He doesn't sleep well because he worries too much.
   Five hours of sleep is not good enough.
   I walked quickly enough to raise my heart rate.
   Some children don't get enough exercise.
   1. Use —— before a count noun.
   2. Put —— before nouns.
   3. Put —— after adjectives and adverbs.
   4. —— can come at the end of the verb phrase.
   5. Put —— before adjectives and adverbs.
   6. Use —— before a noncount noun.
   Say: *Study the sentences, then fill in the rules with* too, too much, too many, *or* enough. Have volunteers fill in the blanks on the board.
2. Then have students look at grammar chart **6.5.** Say: *Compare your work with the grammar chart.* Go over any trouble spots.
3. Direct students to the Language Notes. Point out that an infinitive phrase can follow *too* or *enough.* Review the idiomatic expression "too good to be true" and have volunteers make their own sentences using this expression (e.g., *It didn't rain once during my vacation. It was too good to be true.*).

EXERCISE 8

1. Tell students that this exercise is based on the reading on page 200. Have students read the direction line. Go over the examples in the book.
2. Have students complete Exercise 8 individually. Go over the answers as a class.
3. If necessary, review grammar chart **6.5** on page 201.

EXERCISE 9

1. Tell students that they are going to be finishing these sentences according to what's true for them. Have students read the direction line. Ask: *What's an infinitive?* (*to* + the base form of the verb) Go over the examples.
2. Have students complete Exercise 9 individually. Then have students compare answers in pairs. Circulate to observe pair work. Give help as needed.
3. If necessary, review grammar chart **6.5** on page 201.

To save class time, have students do the exercise as a class or do the exercise for homework.

EXERCISE 10

1. Have students read the direction line. Point out that this exercise is about a person complaining about the school cafeteria. Go over the example.
2. Have students complete Exercise 10 individually. Then check the answers as a class.
3. If necessary, review grammar chart **6.5** on page 201.

To save class time, have students do the exercise as a class or do the exercise for homework.

3. Some people spend too much ___time___ on the Internet. They should shut down the computer and go to bed.
4. If you drink too much ___coffee___, it can affect your sleep.
5. People drive everywhere. They don't ___walk___ enough.
6. When children eat too ___much___, they get fat.
7. Children shouldn't drink so much soda because it contains too many ___calories___.
8. Most Americans don't get enough ___sleep___.
9. Many people say, "I don't have enough ___time___ to do all the things I need to do."
10. It's never too ___late___ to change your bad habits.
11. His clothes don't fit him anymore because he got too ___big___.

EXERCISE 9 ABOUT YOU Complete each statement with an infinitive.

EXAMPLES I'm too young ___to retire.___

I'm not strong enough ___to move a piano.___

1. I'm not too old ___Answers will vary.___
2. I'm too young ______
3. I don't have enough money ______
4. I don't have enough time ______
5. I don't speak English well enough ______

EXERCISE 10 A person is complaining about the school cafeteria. Fill in the blanks with *too*, *too much*, or *too many*.

EXAMPLE It's ___too___ noisy, so I can't talk with my friends.

1. They serve ___too much___ junk food there.
2. The fries have ___too much___ grease.
3. The hamburgers have ___too many___ calories.
4. The food is ___too___ expensive.
5. The tables are ___too___ dirty.
6. There are ___too many___ people there, and sometimes there's no place to sit.

202 Lesson 6

Expansion

Exercise 9 Have students write three to five more unfinished statements with *too* and *enough*. Then have students complete their partners' sentences.

Exercise 10 Have students work in pairs to write complaints about their workplace, dormitory, condominium, etc.

6.6 | *Too* and *Very* and *A Lot Of*

Examples	Explanation
a. I'm **too** tired to drive. Would you drive for a while? b. I was **very** tired, but I stayed up late and studied for my test.	Don't confuse *very* and *too*. *Too* always indicates a problem in a specific situation. The problem can be stated or implied. *Very* is a neutral word.
a. The speed limit on the highway is 55, and you're driving 40. You're driving **too** slowly. b. The speed limit on this road is 15 miles per hour. You need to drive **very** slowly. a. My brother is 14 years old. He's **too** old to get into the movie theater at half price. b. My grandmother is 85. She's **very** old, but she's in great health.	In examples (a), *too* shows a problem in a specific situation. In examples (b), *very* does not show any problem.
a. You put **too much** salt in the soup, and I can't eat it. b. She puts **a lot of** sugar in her coffee. She likes it that way. a. I ate **too many** cookies, and now I feel sick. b. She baked **a lot of cookies** for the party. Everyone enjoyed them.	Don't confuse *a lot of* and *too much/too many*. a. *Too* always indicates a problem in a specific situation. b. *A lot of* is a neutral expression.

EXERCISE 11 Fill in the blanks with *too, too much, too many, a lot of,* or *very*.

A: Your dinner was ___very___ (example) delicious tonight.

B: I'm ___very___ (1) glad you liked it.

A: Everything was great. But the soup had ___too much___ (2) salt.

B: Oh. I thought you liked everything.

A: I did. Other than the salt, it was good. And I especially liked the potatoes.

B: I'm glad.

A: But you put a little ___too much___ (3) butter in the potatoes.

They were ___too___ (4) greasy.

B: Oh.

A: But don't worry. I ate them anyway.

6.6 | *Too* and *Very* and *A Lot Of*

1. Have students scan the reading on page 200 again. Ask them to pay special attention to the use of *too* and *very*. Ask: *Which indicates that there is a problem:* too *or* very?
2. Have students look at grammar chart **6.6.** Read through the examples and explanations. Point out that we often use an infinitive after *too.* We don't use an infinitive after *very.*
3. Tell students not to get confused with *a lot of* and *too much/too many. A lot of* is a neutral expression. *Too much/too many* indicates there is a problem. Go over the examples.

EXERCISE 11

CD 2, Track 25

1. Have students read the direction line. Go over the example.
2. Have students complete Exercise 11 individually. Go over the answers as a class.
3. If necessary, review grammar chart **6.6** on page 203.

Exercise 11 Variation

To provide practice with listening skills, have students close their books and listen to the audio. Repeat the audio as needed. Ask comprehension questions, such as: *How much salt did the soup have?* (too much) *Did person A eat the potatoes?* (yes) *Was the cake big enough?* (No. It was too small.) Then have students open their books and complete Exercise 11.

Summary of Lesson 6

1. **Adjectives and Adverbs** Have students cover up the Summary of Lesson 6 on page 204. Create the following exercise on the board:
   1. (quick) We ate____.
   We had a____lunch.
   2. (late) We had a____lunch.
   We ate____.
   3. (good) She is a____cook. She cooks____.
   4. (serious) She looks____.
   She is looking at the label ____.
   5. (usual) ____, he drank a cup of coffee.
   He____drinks coffee in the morning.
   Say: *Fill in the blanks with the correct form of adverb or adjective.* Then have students look at item 1 in the summary on page 204. Say: *Compare your work with the sentences.* If necessary, have students review:
   6.1 Adjectives (p. 190)
   6.3 Adverbs of Manner (p. 196)
   6.4 Adjective vs. Adverb (p. 198).
2. **Adjective Modifiers and Noun Modifiers** Have students cover up the Summary of Lesson 6 on page 204. Create the following exercise on the board: *two-week, old, exercise, short, new, running, driver's, valid*
   1. a____machine (adj.)
   an____machine (noun)
   2. ____shoes (adj.)
   shoes (noun)
   3. a vacation (adj.)
   a vacation (noun)
   4. a license (adj.)
   a____license (noun)
   Say: *Fill in the blanks with the correct form of adjective or noun modifier.* Then have students look at item 2 in the summary on page 204. Say: *Compare your work with the sentences.* If necessary, have students review:
   6.1 Adjectives (p. 190)
   6.2 Noun Modifiers (p. 192).

B: I'm afraid the steak was burned. I left it in the oven ___*too*___ (5) long.

A: Well, no one's perfect. I ate it anyway.

B: What about the cake I made? Did you like that?

A: Yes. It was ___*very*___ (6) good. The only problem was it was ___*too*___ (7) small. I was hoping to have another piece, but there was nothing left.

B: I thought you wanted to lose weight. You always say you're ___*too*___ (8) fat and need to go on a diet.

A: Fat? I'm not fat.

B: But you can't wear your old pants anymore.

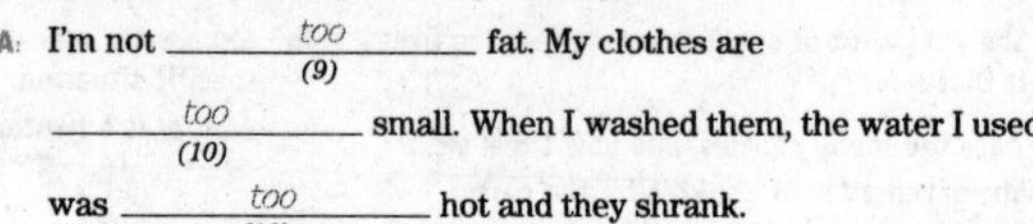

A: I'm not ___*too*___ (9) fat. My clothes are ___*too*___ (10) small. When I washed them, the water I used was ___*too*___ (11) hot and they shrank.

B: They didn't shrink. You gained weight.

SUMMARY OF LESSON 6

1. Adjectives and Adverbs

Adjectives	Adverbs
We had a **quick** lunch.	We ate **quickly.**
We had a **late** dinner.	We ate **late.**
She is a **good** cook.	She cooks **well.**
She looks **serious.**	She is looking at the label **seriously.**
As usual, he drank a cup of coffee.	He **usually** drinks coffee in the morning.

2. Adjective Modifiers and Noun Modifiers

Adjective Modifier	Noun Modifier
a **new** machine	an **exercise** machine
old shoes	**running** shoes
a **short** vacation	a **two-week** vacation
a **valid** license	a **driver's** license

204 Lesson 6

Expansion

Exercise 11 Have students practice the conversation in pairs. Ask volunteers to role-play all or part of the conversation in front of the class.

3. *Very / Too / Enough / Too Much / Too Many*
He's **very** healthy.
He's **too** young to retire.
I'm relaxed **enough** to drive.
I had **enough** sleep last night.
She doesn't eat ice cream because it has **too much** fat.
She doesn't eat ice cream because it has **too many** calories.
He loves coffee, but when he drinks **too much,** he can't sleep.

EDITING ADVICE

1. Adjectives are always singular.

   I had two importants meetings last week.

2. Certain adjectives end with *-ed*.

   d
   He was tire after his trip.

3. Put an adjective before the noun.

   very intelligent girl
   She is a ~~girl very intelligent~~.

4. Use *one(s)* after an adjective to take the place of a noun.

   one
   He has an old dictionary. She has a new.

5. Put a specific noun before a general noun.

   phone call
   She made a ~~call phone~~.

6. A noun modifier is always singular.

   She took a three-weeks vacation.

7. An adverb describes a verb. An adjective describes a noun.

   ly
   The teacher speaks English fluent.

   The teacher looks seriously.

8. Don't put the *-ly* adverb between the verb and the object.

   He opened (carefully) the envelope.

Summary of Lesson 6 (*cont.*)

3. *Very / Too / Enough / Too Much / Too Many* Have students cover up item 3 from the Summary of Lesson 6 on page 205. Create the following exercise on the board:

very, too, enough, too much, too many

1. *He's ____ healthy.*
2. *He's ____ young to retire.*
3. *I'm relaxed ____ to drive.*
4. *I had ____ sleep last night.*
5. *She doesn't eat ice cream because it has ____ fat.*
6. *She doesn't eat ice cream because it has ____ calories.*
7. *He loves coffee, but when he drinks ____, he can't sleep.*

Say: *Fill in the blanks with the correct word.* Then have students look at item 3 in the summary on page 205. Say: *Compare your work with the sentences.* If necessary, have students review:

6.5 *Too* and *Enough* (p. 201)
6.6 *Too* and *Very* and *A Lot Of* (p. 203).

Editing Advice

Have students close their books. Write the example sentences without editing marks or corrections on the board. For example:

1. *I had two importants meetings last week.*
2. *He was tire after his trip.*

Ask students to correct each sentence and provide a rule or explanation for each correction. This activity can be done individually, in pairs, or as a class. After students have corrected each sentence, tell them to turn to pages 205–206. Say: *Now compare your work with the Editing Advice in the book.*

Lesson 6 Test/Review

For additional practice, review, and assessment materials, see Assessment CD-ROM with *ExamView Pro*, *More Grammar Practice* Workbook 2, Interactive CD-ROM, and Web site http://elt.thomson.com/gic

PART 1

1. Part 1 may be used as an in-class test to assess student performance, in addition to the Assessment CD-ROM with *ExamView Pro*. Have students read the direction line. Ask: *Do all sentences have a mistake?* (no) Collect for assessment.
2. If necessary, have students review: **Lesson 6.**

9. Adverbs of manner that don't end in *-ly* follow the verb phrase.

   He late came home.

10. *Too* indicates a problem. If there is no problem, use *very*.

   Your father is too intelligent. (very)

11. *Too much / too many* is followed by a noun. *Too* is followed by an adjective or adverb.

   She's too much old to take care of herself.

12. Put *enough* after the adjective.

   He's enough old to get married. (old enough)

13. Don't use *very* before a verb.

   He very likes his job. (very much)

14. Don't confuse *hard* and *hardly*.

   I'm tired. I worked hardly all day.

15. Don't use *too much / too many* when there is no problem.

   I love juice. Every day I drink too much juice. (a lot of)

LESSON 6 TEST/REVIEW

PART 1 Find the mistakes with the underlined words, and correct them. Not every sentence has a mistake. If the sentence is correct, write *C*.

EXAMPLES When did you get your license driver's? (license)

He gets up early and walks the dog. C

1. Do you know where I can find the shoes department in this store?
2. She doesn't feel well today. C
3. The language English is very different from my language.
4. I'm very tire because I worked hard all week. (d)
5. Your answer seems wrongly.
6. My grandfather is too much old to work.
7. I don't like red apples. I like yellows ones.

206 Lesson 6

Lesson Review

To use Part 1 as a review, assign it as homework or use it as an in-class activity to be completed individually or in pairs. Check answers and review errors as a class. Reteach grammar points that students haven't mastered. Then student learning may be assessed using a test generated from the Assessment CD-ROM with *ExamView Pro*.

8. The singer's voice sounds sweet. C

9. I wrote carefully my name.

10. She bought a car very expensive.

11. I'm ~~too~~ very happy to meet you.

12. He stayed in the library late to finish his class project. C

13. She looked beautiful when she got ~~marry~~ married.

14. You speak English very fluently. C

15. He's not old enough to work. C

16. I like your new shoes very much. C

17. I made too much food for the party, and everyone had enough to eat. C

18. He hardly speaks a word of English. He just came to the U.S. C

19. She's going to take her driving test. She looks ~~nervously~~.

20. I'm completely surprised by the news of your marriage. C

21. I very like your new apartment.

22. If you spend too much time in front of the TV, you'll get fat. C

23. You have ~~too many~~ a lot of friends. You're a lucky person.

PART 2 Fill the blanks with the correct form, adjective or adverb, of the word in parentheses ( ).

EXAMPLES She has clear pronunciation. *(clear)*

She pronounces very clearly. *(clear)*

1. You need to find time to eat well *(good)*. Don't eat food that is bad *(bad)* for you.
2. Don't drive fast *(fast)*. It's important to arrive safely *(safe)*.
3. I can't understand you. Could you speak more slowly *(slow)*, please?
4. Some people learn languages easily *(easy)*.
5. Some people think that math is hard *(hard)*, but it's easy *(easy)* for me.

PART 2

1. Part 2 may also be used as an in-class test to assess student performance, in addition to the Assessment CD-ROM with *ExamView Pro*. Have students read the direction line. Collect for assessment.
2. If necessary, have students review:
   6.1 Adjectives (p. 190)
   6.3 Adverbs of Manner (p. 196)
   6.4 Adjective vs. Adverb (p. 198).

Lesson Review

To use Part 2 as a review, assign it as homework or use it as an in-class activity to be completed individually or in pairs. Check answers and review errors as a class. Reteach grammar points that students haven't mastered. Then student learning may be assessed using a test generated from the Assessment CD-ROM with *ExamView Pro*.

Expansion Activities

These expansion activities provide opportunities for students to interact with one another and further develop their speaking and writing skills. Encourage students to use grammar from this lesson whenever possible.

To save class time, assign parts of the activities as homework. Then use class time for interaction and communication. If students do not need additional speaking practice, some of the activities may be assigned as writing activities for homework, or skipped altogether.

CLASSROOM ACTIVITIES

1. Have students complete the food list individually. Then have students compare lists in groups (e.g., *I used to eat a lot of potato chips. Now I eat a lot of vegetables.*).

6. As ___usual___ (usual), we will have a test at the end of the lesson.
7. She spoke ___softly___ (soft), and I couldn't hear her ___well___ (good).
8. I need to learn English ___quickly___ (quick).
9. Do you exercise ___regularly___ (regular), or are you ___lazy___ (lazy)?
10. You seem ___tired___ (tired) today.
11. I'm very ___busy___ (busy).
12. She works very ___hard___ (hard), but she's ___happy___ (happy) with her job.
13. She is a ___lovely___ (lovely) woman. She's very ___friendly___ (friendly).
14. John sounds ___angry___ (angry), but he's not angry. He just talks ___loudly___ (loud).
15. You speak English ___extremely___ (extreme) well. You have ___perfect___ (perfect) pronunciation. Everything you say is ___absolutely___ (absolute) ___clear___ (clear).

EXPANSION ACTIVITIES

Classroom Activities

1. Make a list of things that you ate when you were younger that you don't eat now. Make a list of things that you eat now that you didn't eat when you were younger. Form a small group and compare your lists.

Things I ate before that I don't eat now:	Things I eat now that I didn't eat before:

208 Lesson 6

2. Make a list of your lifestyle changes in the past few years. Find a partner. Compare your list with your partner's list. Which of these activities affect your health?

Things I do (or don't do) now:	Things I did (or didn't do) before:
I watch TV more often.	*I hardly ever watched TV before.*
I shop once a week.	*I shopped almost every day when I lived in my country.*

3. Bad habits. Make a list of bad habits that you or someone in your family has.

EXAMPLES I don't get enough exercise.
My daughter talks on the phone too much.

4. Take something from your purse, pocket, or bag, but don't show it to anyone. Describe it. Another student will try to guess what it is.

5. Game: "In the manner of"

Teacher: Write these adverbs on separate pieces of paper or on index cards:

accurately	excitedly	gladly	quietly	smoothly
carefully	fearfully	indecisively	repeatedly	steadily
carelessly	fearlessly	neatly	simply	suddenly
comfortably	foolishly	promptly	slowly	surprisingly
efficiently				

Make sure the students know the meaning of each of these adverbs. Ask one student to leave the room. The other students pick one adverb. When the student returns to the room, he/she asks individuals to do something by giving imperatives. The others do this task in the manner of the adverb that was chosen. The student tries to guess the adverb.

EXAMPLES Edgar, write your name on the blackboard.
Sofia, take off one shoe.
Maria, open the door.
Elsa, walk around the room.
Nora, give me your book.

CLASSROOM ACTIVITIES (*cont.*)

2. Have students complete the lifestyle list individually. Then have students compare lists in pairs.
3. Have students write down all their bad habits. Then have students compare lists in pairs.
4. Put students in groups. Have students think of an object in their bag or pocket. Students may take it out and keep it hidden, or write the name of the object down on a piece of paper. Remind students that they're practicing adjectives (e.g., *Is it green? Is it long?*).
5. Review the meaning of each adverb before beginning the game. If necessary, review imperatives and/or have students write down a list of imperatives they might use for this game.

Classroom Activities Variation

Activity 3 Compare answers as a class. Make a *Top Ten Bad Habits* list on the board.

CLASSROOM ACTIVITIES (*cont*.)

6. After pairs have developed an evaluation form, discuss it as a class. Create a final form together on the board.

TALK ABOUT IT

Have students discuss each topic in pairs, in groups, or as a whole class.

1. Ask students to decide which students come from the most healthful cultures.
2. Ask students to discuss this idea and then decide "who they are" based on what they eat.
3. Survey the class. What's the average number of hours the students sleep?

WRITE ABOUT IT

1. Before students begin to write, brainstorm places to write about with the class. Write ideas on the board.
2. Remind students to use adjectives when describing their hometowns. If it's useful, consider brainstorming vocabulary for describing places (e.g., *busy streets, tree-lined avenues*, and *green parks*). Model the activity by giving a brief description of your hometown.
3. Say: *Before you start writing, make two lists—one of your native culture's food and one of American food. Then write adjectives that describe the food.*

INTERNER ACTIVITIES

1. Have volunteers talk about their diets and what they learned from the USDA.
2. If appropriate, survey the class to find out what percentage of the students is at the right weight for height.
3. Ask students to also find out what their height is in the English system.

In some schools, students evaluate teachers. Work with a partner and write an evaluation form for teachers at this school or for another profession you are familiar with.

EXAMPLES

	Strongly Agree	Agree	Disagree	Strongly Disagree
1. Begins class promptly. 2. Treats students with respect. 3. Explains assignments clearly.				

Talk About it

1. In a small group or with the entire class, discuss what kind of food you usually eat. Do you think people eat healthful food in your native culture?
2. Americans often say, "You are what you eat." What do you think this means?
3. Do you get enough sleep? How much is enough for you? Do you remember your dreams?

Write About it

1. Think of a place in this city (a museum, a government office, a park, a shopping center, the airport, etc.). Write a brief description of this place.
2. Write a paragraph about your hometown (or a specific place in your hometown). Use descriptions.
3. Write a short composition comparing food in your native culture to food in the U.S.

Internet Activities

1. Go to the Web site for the U.S. Department of Agriculture (USDA). Find an article about food and nutrition and bring it to class. How does your diet compare to the USDA's recommendations?
2. At a search engine, type in *height weight*. Find a copy of a height/weight chart. Print it. See if you are the right weight for your height.
3. Find a conversion chart from the metric system to the English system. See how much you weigh in pounds.

Additional Activities at http://elt.thomson.com/gic

210 Lesson 6

Classroom Activities Variation

Activity 6 Tell students that the final evaluation form will be used to evaluate your (the teacher's) class.

Expansion

Talk About it Have students share interesting dreams they have had. Then ask a few volunteers to "interpret" the meaning of their dreams.

Write About it Variation

Have students exchange first drafts with a partner. Ask students to help their partners edit their drafts. Refer students to the Editing Advice on pages 205–206.

Internet Activities Variation

Remind students that if they don't have Internet access, they can use Internet facilities at a public library or they can use traditional research methods to find information including looking at encyclopedias, magazines, books, journals, and newspapers.

LESSON

7

GRAMMAR
Time Words and Time Clauses
The Past Continuous Tense[1]

CONTEXT : Immigrants
Ellis Island
Albert Einstein—Immigrant from Germany
Gloria Estefan—Cuban Immigrant

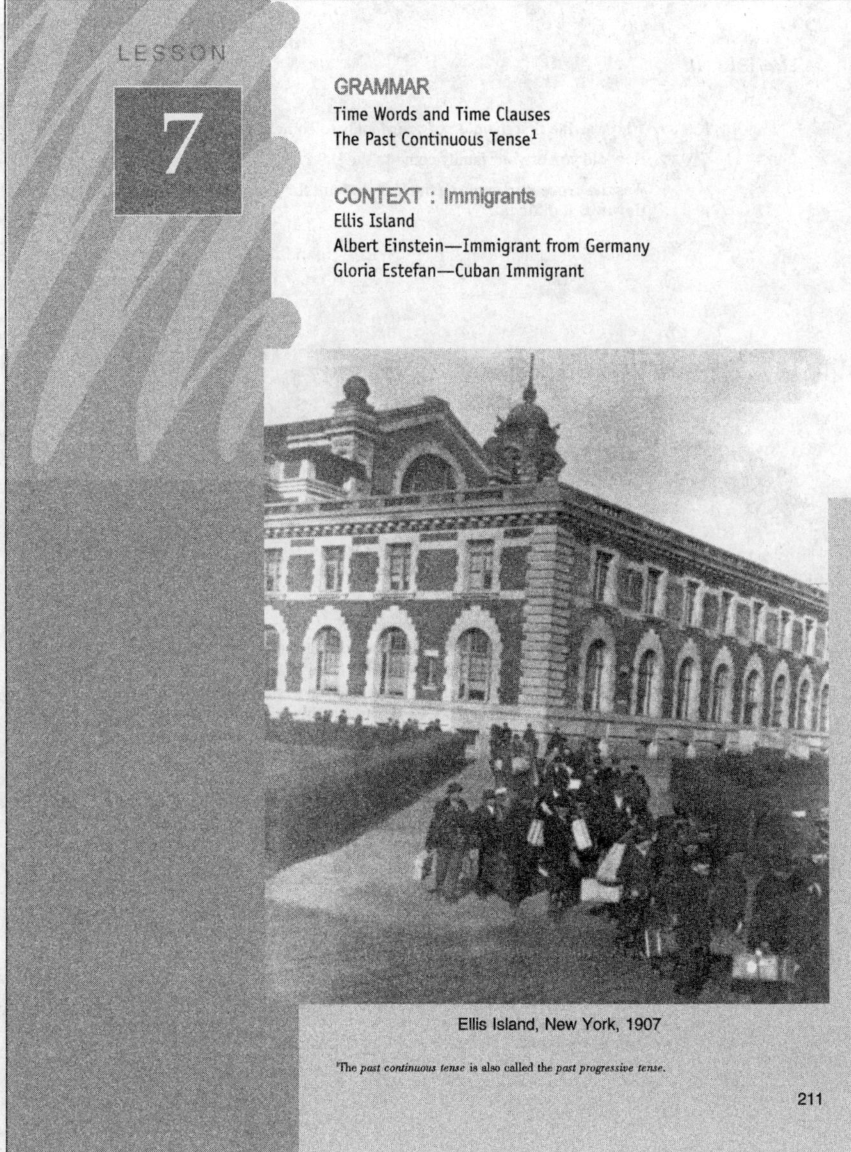

Ellis Island, New York, 1907

[1]The *past continuous tense* is also called the *past progressive tense*.

211

Lesson | 7

Lesson Overview

GRAMMAR

1. Briefly review what students learned in the last lesson. Ask: *What did we study in Lesson 6?* (adjectives, noun modifiers, adverbs, *too, enough, very, a lot of*)
2. Ask: *What are we going to study in this lesson?* (time words and time clauses; the past continuous tense) *What are some time words and time clauses?* (e.g., *when, until, before 2005*) Have students give examples. Write the examples on the board. Then ask volunteers for examples of the past continuous (e.g., *I was talking on the phone when my mother walked in.*).

CONTEXT

1. Ask: *What are we going to learn about in this lesson?* (immigrants, Ellis Island, Albert Einstein, Gloria Estefan) Activate students' prior knowledge. Ask: *Are you the first person in your family to leave your native country?*
2. Have students share their knowledge and personal experiences.

Photo

Direct students' attention to the photo. Ask: *What do you know about Ellis Island? What are the people doing?*

To save class time, have students do the Test/Review at the end of the lesson, or administer a lesson test generated from the Assessment CD-ROM with *ExamView® Pro.* Skip sections of the lesson that students have already mastered. You may also assign some sections for self-study for extra credit.

Expansion

Theme The topic for this lesson can be enhanced with the following ideas:

1. A book with pictures of Ellis Island
2. Statistics on immigration from the U.S. Census

Ellis Island (Reading)

1. Have students look at the photo. Say: *This is the Wall of Honor on Ellis Island. Whose names do you think are on it?*
2. Have students look at the title of the reading. Ask: *What is the reading about?* Have students use the title and photo to make predictions about the reading.
3. Preteach any vocabulary words your students may not know, such as *harbor, hope, registry, meet the requirements,* and *restore.*

BEFORE YOU READ

1. Have students discuss the questions in pairs. Try to pair students of different cultures together.
2. Ask for a few volunteers to share their answers with the class.

To save class time, skip "Before You Read" or have students prepare answers for homework ahead of time.

Reading CD 2, Track 26

1. Have students first read the text silently. Tell them to pay special attention to time words. Then play the audio and have students read along silently.
2. Check students' comprehension. Ask questions such as: *When was Ellis Island being used as an immigration processing station?* (from 1892–1924) *How many immigrants were processed at Ellis Island?* (12 million) *How many people had to return to their countries?* (250,000) *When was the restoration of Ellis Island completed?* (1990)

To save class time, have students do the reading for homework ahead of time.

DID YOU KNOW?

Many Americans like to study their genealogy—or family history. Ellis Island has become a center for genealogy. Millions of Americans try to trace their families' histories with the help of the immigration records from Ellis Island.

ELLIS ISLAND

Before You Read

1. Who was the first member of your family to come to the U.S.?
2. How did you or your family come to the U.S.?
3. Was the process of entering the U.S. difficult for your family? How was it difficult?

Read the following article. Pay special attention to time words.

Ellis Island today with Wall of Honor

Did You Know?

The largest number of immigrants in the U.S. between 1820 and 1996 came from Germany. The largest number of immigrants today come from Mexico, India, the Philippines, and China.

For many years, Ellis Island, an island in New York harbor, was the main door through which millions of immigrants entered the United States. **From** the time it opened **in** 1892 **until** the time it closed **in** 1924, the U.S. Bureau of Immigration used Ellis Island to receive and process new arrivals. **During** this time, 12 million foreigners passed through this door with the hope of becoming Americans. They came from Italy, Poland, Russia, Germany, China, and many other countries. Sometimes more than 10,000 people passed through the registry room in one 24-hour period. New arrivals often waited **for** many hours **while** inspectors checked to see if they met legal and medical standards. Most did not speak English, and they were tired, hungry, and confused. Two percent (250,000 people) did not meet the requirements to enter the U.S. and had to return to their countries.

After Congress passed an immigration law that limited the number and nationality of new immigrants, immigration slowed down and Ellis Island was closed as an immigration processing center. It remained abandoned **until** 1965, **when** President Lyndon Johnson decided to restore it as a monument. Restoration of Ellis Island was finished **by** 1990. Now visitors to this monument can see the building as it looked **from** 1918 **to** 1920. In addition, they can see the Wall of Honor with the names of many of those who passed through on their way to becoming American citizens.

212 Lesson 7

Reading Variation

To practice listening skills, have students first listen to the audio alone. Ask a few comprehension questions. Repeat the audio if necessary. Then have them open their books and read along as they listen to the audio.

Reading Glossary

harbor: a port
hope: desire that something will happen
meet the requirements: have or do what is necessary
registry: an office of official records
restore: to make something look like it did when it was new

7.1 | When, Until, While

Examples	Explanation
When immigration slowed down, Ellis Island was closed. **When** it reopened, visitors could see the history of immigration.	*When* means *at that time* or *starting at that time.*
Ellis Island was closed **until** 1990. Immigrants could not enter the U.S. **until** they passed an inspection.	*Until* means *before that time.*
While they waited, they were often tired, confused, and hungry. New arrivals waited **while** inspectors checked their documents. **While** they were crossing the ocean, they thought about their uncertain future.	*While* means *during that time.* We can sometimes use *when* in place of *while:* **When** they were crossing the ocean, they thought about their uncertain future.

EXERCISE 1 Fill in the blanks with *when, while,* or *until.* In some cases, more than one answer is possible.

EXAMPLE My grandfather came to the U.S. ___when___ he was 25 years old.

1. ___While/When___ he lived in Poland, he had a hard life.
2. ___When___ he left Poland, he didn't speak English at all.
3. ___While___ he was at Ellis Island, he had to wait for hours. He was nervous ___while___ he waited.
4. He was nervous ___until___ he got permission to enter the country. Then he felt more relaxed.
5. ___When___ he passed the inspection, he entered the country.

6. In Poland, he didn't study English. He didn't speak a word of English ___until___ he started to work in the U.S. Then he learned a little.
7. ___While___ he worked, he saved money to bring his wife and children to America.
8. My grandmother couldn't come to the U.S. ___until___ my grandfather had enough money to send for her and their children.
9. My grandfather lived in the U.S. ___when___ he died in 1968.

Grammar Variation

Have students cover up grammar chart **7.1**. Write the rules on the board with blanks:

a. ____ means during that time.
b. ____ means at that time or starting at that time.
c. ____ means before that time.

Have students go back to the reading on page 212. Say: *Look at the sentences with* when, until, *and* while. *Then fill in the blanks to complete the rules.*

7.1 | When, Until, While

1. Have students cover up grammar chart **7.1**. Create an exercise on the board:
   1. When immigration slowed down, Ellis Island was closed.
   2. Ellis Island was closed until 1990.
   3. While they waited, they were often tired, confused, and hungry.
   a. ____ means during that time.
   b. ____ means at that time or starting at that time.
   c. ____ means before that time.
   Say: *Study the sentences. Then fill in the blanks with* when, until, *and* while *to complete the rules.*
2. Then have students look at grammar chart **7.1**. Say: *Compare your answers with the chart.* Go over the examples and explanations.
3. Point out that we can sometimes also use *when* in place of *while.* Go over the example.

EXERCISE 1

1. Have students read the direction line. Go over the example. Remind students that sometimes more than one answer will be possible.
2. Have students complete Exercise 1 individually. Go over the answers as a class.
3. If necessary, review grammar chart **7.1** on page 213.

EXERCISE 2

1. Have students read the direction line. Say: *Make these sentences true for you.* Go over the example. Model the example for the class. Then have a volunteer model the example.
2. Have students complete Exercise 2 individually. Then have students compare answers in pairs. Circulate to observe pair work. Give help as needed.
3. If necessary, review grammar chart **7.1** on page 213.

EXERCISE 3

1. Have students read the direction line. Say: *Make these sentences true for you.* Go over the example. Have a volunteer model the example.
2. Have students complete Exercise 3 individually. Then have students compare answers in pairs. Circulate to observe pair work. Give help as needed.
3. If necessary, review grammar chart **7.1** on page 213.

To save class time, have students do the exercise as a class or for homework.

EXERCISE 4

1. Have students read the direction line. Say: *In this exercise, you're going to name things you've never done, seen,* or *had. Make sentences that are true for you.* Go over the example. Model the example for the class. Then have a volunteer model the example.
2. Have students complete Exercise 4 individually. Then have students compare answers in pairs. Circulate to observe pair work. Give help as needed.
3. If necessary, review grammar chart **7.1** on page 213.

To save class time, have students do half of the exercise in class and complete the other half in writing for homework. Or if students do not need speaking practice, the entire exercise may be skipped or done in writing.

EXERCISE 2 ABOUT YOU Add a main clause to complete each statement.

EXAMPLE Before I got to class today, *I finished all my homework.*

1. While I was in high school, ______ Answers will vary.
2. When I finished high school, ______
3. Until I came to this city / school, ______
4. When I arrived in the U.S., ______
5. Until I started this course, ______

EXERCISE 3 ABOUT YOU Finish the time expression to complete each statement.

EXAMPLE I stayed in my country until *a civil war broke out.*

1. I found my apartment / house while ______ Answers will vary.
2. I enrolled in this English class when ______
3. I didn't understand English until ______
4. I got married / found a job / bought a car / came to this country (*choose one*) when ______

EXERCISE 4 ABOUT YOU If you are from another country, name something *you never... until you came to the U.S.*

EXAMPLE Name something you never had.
I never had a car until I came to the U.S.

Answers will vary.

1. Name something you never did.
2. Name something or someone you never heard of.
3. Name something you never saw.
4. Name something you never thought about.
5. Name something you never had.
6. Name something you never ate.
7. Name something you never knew.

Expansion

Exercises 2 and 3 Have students write a paragraph about themselves using the sentences from the exercises and adding other information.

7.2 | *When* and *Whenever*

Examples	Explanation
When I went to New York last year, I visited Ellis Island.	*When* means *at that time* or *after that time.*
Whenever I go to New York, I go to the theaters there.	*Whenever* means *any time* or *every time.* With the general present, *when* and *whenever* have almost the same meaning.

EXERCISE 5 ABOUT YOU Add a main clause to complete each statement. Use the general present.

EXAMPLE Whenever I take a test, *I feel nervous.*

1. Whenever I feel sad or lonely, Answers will vary.
2. Whenever I get angry, ________
3. Whenever I need advice, ________
4. Whenever I receive a present, ________
5. Whenever I get a letter from my family, ________
6. Whenever I'm sick, ________
7. Whenever the weather is bad, ________
8. Whenever the teacher explains the grammar, ________

EXERCISE 6 ABOUT YOU Finish each sentence with a time clause.

EXAMPLES I feel nervous *before I take a test.*
I feel nervous *whenever I have to speak in class.*

1. I feel relaxed Answers will vary.
2. I get angry ________
3. I get bored ________
4. I can't concentrate ________
5. I'm happy ________
6. I'm in a bad mood ________
7. I sometimes daydream[2] ________
8. Time passes quickly for me ________

[2] *To daydream* means to dream while you are awake. Your mind does not stay in the present moment.

7.2 | *When* and *Whenever*

1. Have students look at grammar chart **7.2.** Say: *We use* when *with the past to refer to a specific time.* Whenever *is used to talk about any time or every time. In the present tense,* when *and* whenever *have similar meanings.*
2. Go over the example sentences. Then point out that you can substitute *when* for *whenever* in the second example.

EXERCISE 5

1. Have students read the direction line. Say: *Make sentences that are true for you.* Go over the example in the book. Model the example for the class.
2. Have students complete Exercise 5 individually. Have students compare answers in pairs. Circulate to observe pair work. Give help as needed. Have a few volunteers share answers with the class.
3. If necessary, review grammar chart **7.2** on page 215.

EXERCISE 6

1. Have students read the direction line. Ask: *What are some time words?* (*before, after, whenever, when*) Write the words on the board. Then say: *Make the statements true for you.* Go over the examples. Have volunteers model the examples.
2. Have students complete Exercise 6 individually. Then have students compare responses in pairs. Ask: *Do you and your partner have a lot in common?* Circulate to observe pair work. Give help as needed. Have a few volunteers share answers with the class.
3. If necessary, review grammar chart **7.2** on page 215.

To save class time, have students do half of the exercise in class and complete the other half for homework. Or assign the entire exercise for homework.

7.3 | Time Words

1. Have students cover up the examples in grammar chart **7.3.** Then have students work in pairs. Say: *Study the explanations for the use of time words. Then go to the reading on page 212 and try to find examples that match the explanations.* Tell students that not all the time words are used in the reading. Before having students look at the grammar chart, have volunteers explain the time words they found (*in, after, during, for, by, from . . . to, from . . . until, until*).
2. Have students look at grammar chart **7.3.** Go over the example sentences and explanations. Pay particular attention to the time words not used in the reading (*on; in,* as in after a period of time; *before;* and *ago*).

EXERCISE 7

1. Have students read the direction line. Ask: *What are some time words?* Have students give some examples. Then go over the example in the book.
2. Have students complete Exercise 7 individually. Go over the answers as a class.
3. If necessary, review grammar chart **7.3** on page 216.

7.3 | Time Words

Time Word	Examples	Explanation
on	We came to the U.S. **on** April 16, 2003. We came to the U.S. **on** Monday.	Use *on* with a specific date or day.
in	Ellis Island closed **in** 1924. My cousins came to the U.S. **in** August.	Use *in* with a specific year or month.
in vs. after	a. My brother will come to the U.S. **in** two months. b. My brother will come to the U.S. **after** he gets his visa.	a. Use *in* to mean after a period of time. b. Use *after* with an activity. *Wrong:* My brother will come to the U.S. *after* two months.
during	a. Many immigrants came to America **during** the war. b. Ellis Island was open from 1892 to 1924. **During** that time, 12 million immigrants came through there.	a. Use *during* with an event (*the war, the trip, the movie,* etc.). b. Use *during* with a period of time (*during that time, during the month of May, during the first week in August,* etc.).
for	**For** many years, Ellis Island was the main entrance for immigrants to America. My grandfather waited at Ellis Island **for** ten hours.	Use *for* with the quantity of years, months, weeks, days, etc. *Wrong:* They waited at Ellis Island *during* ten hours.
before vs. by	a. **Before 1990,** Ellis Island was closed. b. **By 1990,** restoration of Ellis Island was complete.	a. In the example to the left, if you use *before,* 1990 is not included. b. If you use *by,* 1990 is included.
before vs. ago	a. She got married **before** she came to the U.S. b. She got married three years **ago.**	Do not confuse *before* and *ago.* *Wrong:* She got married three years *before.*
from . . . to till until	Ellis Island was open **from** 1892 **to** 1924. You can visit Ellis Island **from** 9:30 *till* 5:00.	Use *from* with the starting time. Use *to, till,* or *until* with the ending time.

EXERCISE 7 Circle the correct time word to fill in the blanks.

EXAMPLE He lived with his parents (*during* / *until* / *by*) he was 19 years old.

1. (*When* / *During* / *Whenever*) he was a child, he lived with his grandparents.
2. (*During* / *For* / *While*) several years, he lived with his grandparents.
3. (*For* / *While* / *During*) his childhood, he lived with his grandparents.

216 Lesson 7

Expansion

Grammar Have students scan the reading on page 219 for time words. Say: *Don't read the text; just scan it for time words and circle them.* Then have students compare search results with a partner.

4. (*While* / *Until* / *When*) he got married, he lived with his grandparents. Then he found an apartment with his wife.

5. (*While* / *During* / *Whenever*) he was in elementary school, he lived with his grandparents.

6. (*Whenever* / *While* / *When*) he was ten years old, his grandparents gave him a bike.

7. She worked for her father (*during* / *while* / *whenever*) she was in college.

8. She worked for her father (*for* / *during* / *while*) her free time.

9. She worked for her father (*during* / *whenever* / *when*) she was single.

10. She worked for her father (*for* / *during* / *while*) three years.

11. She worked for her father full time (*while* / *when* / *during*) her summer vacation.

12. She worked for her father (*when* / *until* / *while*) she got married. Then she quit her job to take care of her husband and children.

13. She worked for her father 12 years (*before* / *ago* / *after*).

14. (*Until* / *Whenever* / *During*) her husband needs help in his business, she helps him out.

15. She can't help you now. She's busy. She'll help you (*by* / *after* / *in*) an hour.

16. Please finish this exercise (*by* / *in* / *until*) 8:30.

17. Please finish this exercise (*by* / *before* / *until*) you go home. The teacher wants it today.

18. Please finish this exercise (*in* / *after* / *by*) ten minutes.

19. He'll retire (*after* / *in* / *by*) two years.

20. He'll retire (*when* / *while* / *until*) he's sixty-five years old.

21. He'll work (*when* / *while* / *until*) he's sixty-five years old. Then he'll retire.

22. I'm not going to eat dinner (*when* / *while* / *until*) my wife gets home. Then we'll eat together.

23. The Ellis Island Museum is open everyday (*for* / *from* / *by*) 9:30 a.m. (*at* / *by* / *till*) 5:00 p.m.

24. The Ellis Island Museum is not open (*in* / *at* / *on*) December 25.

Time Words and Time Clauses; The Past Continuous Tense 217

Expansion

Exercise 7 Have students make four statements about their past and two statements about their future using time words. Have students exchange papers with a partner to compare. Ask volunteers to share their statements.

7.4 | The Past Continuous Tense—An Overview

1. Have students cover up grammar chart **7.4.** Ask: *How do you form the present continuous?* (*be* + verb-*ing*) *When do we use the present continuous?* (to show actions that are taking place at this moment) *Can you give an example?* (e.g., *We're studying grammar right now.*) Then ask: *How do you form the past continuous?* (*was/were* + verb-*ing*) *When do we use the past continuous?* (to show that something was in progress at a particular moment in time in the past) *Can you give an example*? (e.g., *In 1999, we were living in Colombia.*)
2. Have students look at grammar chart **7.4.** Go over the example sentences and explanations. Review how to form the negative and contractions.

Albert Einstein—Immigrant from Germany (Reading)

1. Have students look at the photo of Albert Einstein. Ask: *Do you recognize this man? Who is he?* (He's the genius who discovered the theory of relativity.)
2. Have students look at the title of the reading. Ask: *What is the reading about?* Have students use the title and photo to make predictions about the reading.
3. Preteach any vocabulary words your students may not know, such as *universe, memory, spare,* and *interrupt.*

BEFORE YOU READ

1. Have students discuss the questions in pairs. Try to pair students of different cultures together.
2. Ask for a few volunteers to share their answers with the class.

To save class time, skip "Before You Read" or have students prepare answers for homework ahead of time.

7.4 | The Past Continuous Tense—An Overview

We use the past continuous tense to show that something was in progress at a particular moment in time.

Examples	Explanation
In 1998, I **was living** in the U.S. In 1998, my parents **were living** in Ecuador.	To form the past continuous tense, we use *was* or *were* + verb-*ing*. I, he, she, it → *was* you, we, they → *were*
In 1998, I **wasn't living** in Ecuador. My parents **weren't living** with me.	To form the negative, put *not* after *was* or *were*. The contraction for *was not* is *wasn't*. The contraction for *were not* is *weren't*.

ALBERT EINSTEIN — IMMIGRANT FROM GERMANY

Before You Read

1. Can you name any famous immigrants to the U.S.?
2. Did anyone from your native culture become famous in the U.S.?

Pay special attention to the relationship of the past and the past continuous tenses.

Albert Einstein, 1879–1955

Did You Know?
After Einstein died, Princeton University kept his brain in a jar to study how the brain of a genius is different from an ordinary brain.

Of the many immigrants who came to the U.S., one will always be remembered throughout the world: Albert Einstein. Einstein changed our understanding of the universe. When people think of the word "genius," Einstein's name often comes to mind. However, in Einstein's early years, he was not successful in school or at finding a job.

Einstein was born in Germany in 1879 to Jewish parents. He loved math and physics, but he disliked the discipline of formal German schooling. Because of his poor memory for words, his teachers believed that he was a slow learner. Einstein left school before receiving his diploma and tried to pass the exam to enter the Swiss Polytechnic Institute, but he failed on his first attempt. On his second attempt, he passed. He graduated in 1900. He **was planning** to become a teacher of physics and math, but he could not find a job in those fields. Instead, he went to work in a patent[3] office as a third-class technical expert from 1902 to 1909. While he **was working** at this job, he **studied** and **wrote** in his spare time. In 1905, when he was only 26 years old, he published three papers that explained the basic structure of the universe. His theory of relativity explained the relationship of space and time. Einstein was finally respected for his brilliant discovery. He returned to Germany to accept a research position at the University of Berlin. However, in 1920, while he **was lecturing** at the university, anti-Jewish groups often **interrupted** his lectures, saying they were "un-German."

In 1920, Einstein visited the United States for the first time. During his visits, he talked not only about his scientific theories, but also about world peace. While he **was visiting** the U.S. again in 1933, the Nazis **came** to power in Germany. They took his property, burned his books, and removed him from his university job. The U.S. offered Einstein a home. In 1935, he became a permanent resident of the U.S., and in 1940, he became a citizen. He received many job offers from all over the world, but he decided to accept a position at Princeton University in New Jersey. He lived and worked there until he died in 1955.

Einstein's Life	
1879	Born in Germany
1902–1909	Worked in a Swiss patent office
1905	Published his theory of relativity
1919	Scientists recognized his theory to be correct
1933	Visited the U.S.
1940	Became a U.S. citizen
1955	Died

[3] A *patent* is a document that identifies the owner of a new invention. Only the person or company who has the patent can sell the invention.

Reading CD 2, Track 27

1. Have students first read the text silently. Tell them to pay special attention to the relationship of the past and the past continuous tenses. Then play the audio and have students read along silently.
2. Check students' comprehension. Ask questions such as: *Was Einstein successful at finding jobs when he was young?* (no) *Why did his teachers think he had learning problems?* (He had a poor memory for words.) *How old was Einstein when he wrote about the structure of the universe?* (26)

To save class time, have students do the reading for homework ahead of time.

DID YOU KNOW?

In 1955, Dr. Thomas Harvey removed Albert Einstein's brain during an autopsy and kept it in a jar for 43 years. Over the years, Harvey gave pieces of the brain to a few select researchers. Finally, after more than four decades he gave the brain to pathologists at Princeton University. Many people, including Einstein's family, said he should have never taken the brain. Others think he did a good job of protecting it for science.

Reading Variation

To practice listening skills, have students first listen to the audio alone. Ask a few comprehension questions. Repeat the audio if necessary. Then have students open their books and read along as they listen to the audio.

Reading Vocabulary

interrupt: to start talking or doing something in the middle of someone's conversation or activity
memory: the ability of the brain to remember
spare: extra; surplus; excess
universe: the stars, planets, other heavenly bodies, and space taken together

7.5 | The Past Continuous Tense—Forms

1. Have students look at grammar chart **7.5.** Review the affirmative and negative statements, questions, and short answers.
2. Write the following sentence on the board: *Steve and Mami Katz were living in the U.S.* Ask students to write affirmative and negative statements, questions, and short answers related to the statement.

BEFORE YOU READ

1. Have students read the direction line. Say: *Put the words in parentheses into the past continuous.* Go over the example in the book.
2. Have students complete Exercise 8 individually. Go over the answers as a class.
3. If necessary, review grammar chart **7.5** on page 220.

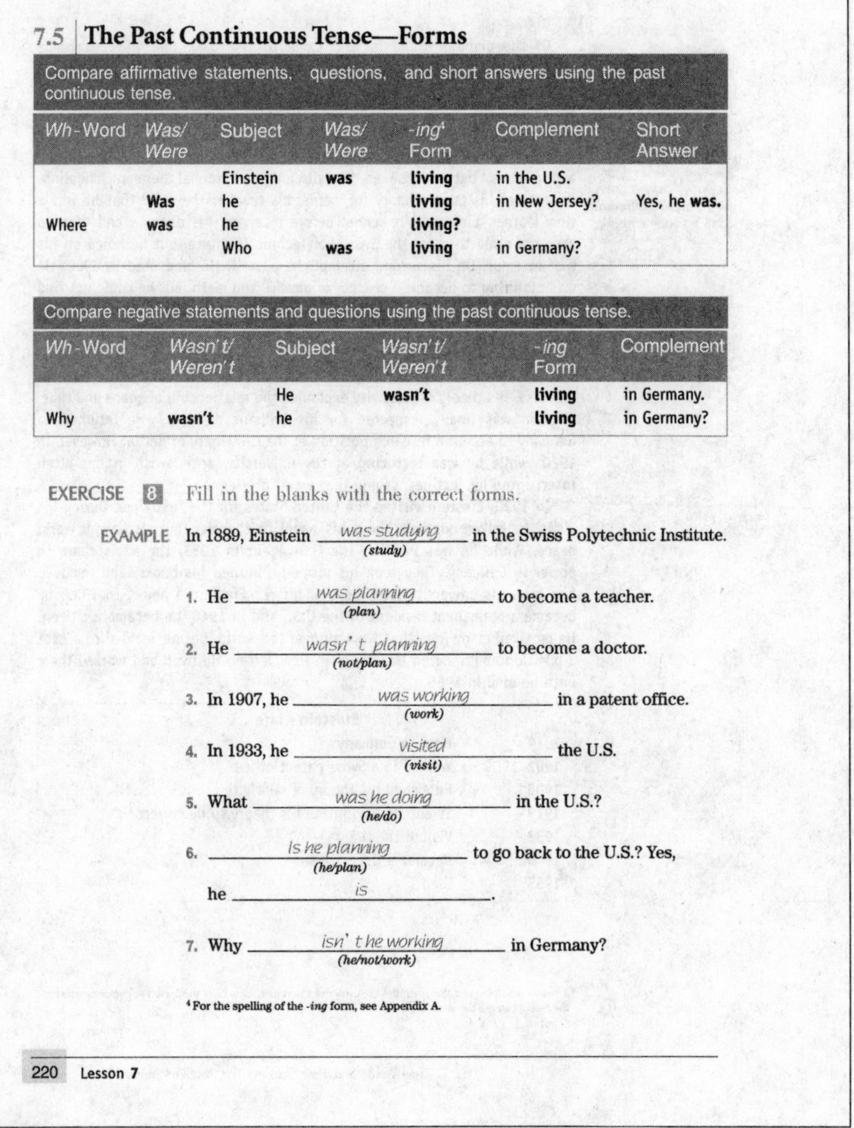

7.5 | The Past Continuous Tense—Forms

Compare affirmative statements, questions, and short answers using the past continuous tense.

Wh-Word	*Was/ Were*	Subject	*Was/ Were*	*-ing*[4] Form	Complement	Short Answer
		Einstein	**was**	**living**	in the U.S.	
	Was	he		**living**	in New Jersey?	Yes, he was.
Where	**was**	he		**living?**		
		Who	**was**	**living**	in Germany?	

Compare negative statements and questions using the past continuous tense.

Wh-Word	*Wasn't/ Weren't*	Subject	*Wasn't/ Weren't*	*-ing* Form	Complement
		He	**wasn't**	**living**	in Germany.
Why	**wasn't**	he		**living**	in Germany?

EXERCISE 8 Fill in the blanks with the correct forms.

EXAMPLE In 1889, Einstein ___*was studying*___ (study) in the Swiss Polytechnic Institute.

1. He ___*was planning*___ (plan) to become a teacher.
2. He ___*wasn't planning*___ (not/plan) to become a doctor.
3. In 1907, he ___*was working*___ (work) in a patent office.
4. In 1933, he ___*visited*___ (visit) the U.S.
5. What ___*was he doing*___ (he/do) in the U.S.?
6. ___*Is he planning*___ (he/plan) to go back to the U.S.? Yes, he ___*is*___.
7. Why ___*isn't he working*___ (he/not/work) in Germany?

[4] For the spelling of the *-ing* form, see Appendix A.

220 Lesson 7

Expansion

Grammar Have students write affirmative and negative statements, questions, and short answers about a historical figure or about a relative, such as a grandparent.

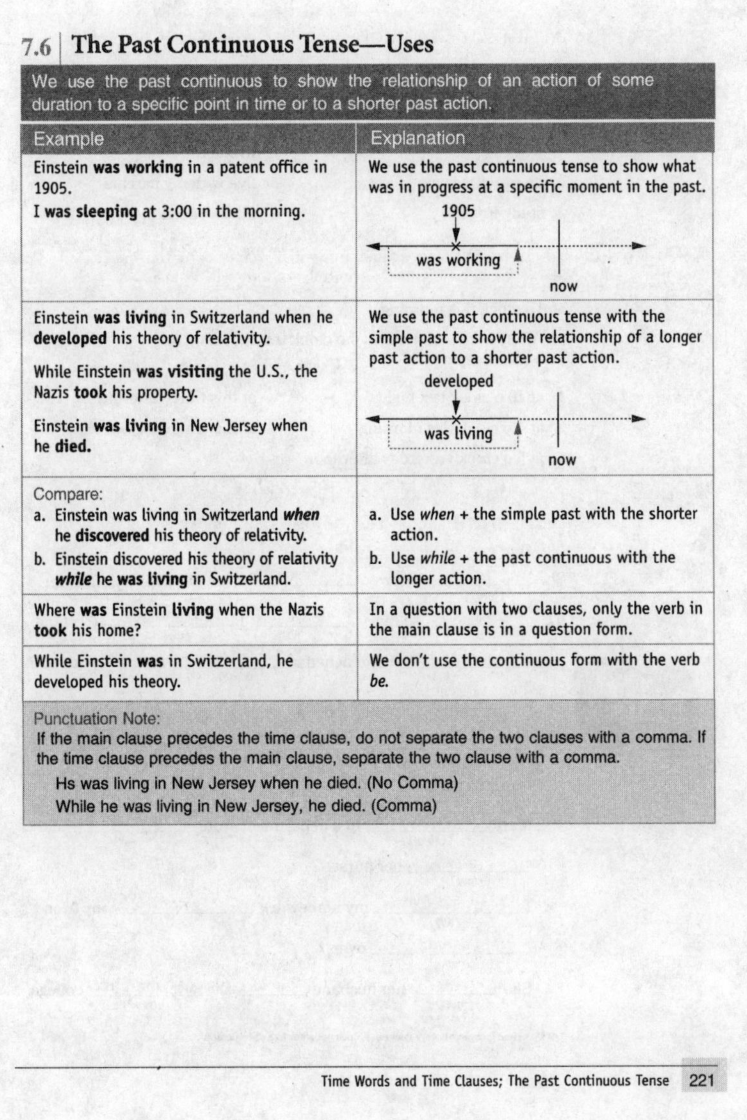

7.6 | The Past Continuous Tense—Uses

We use the past continuous to show the relationship of an action of some duration to a specific point in time or to a shorter past action.

Example	Explanation
Einstein **was working** in a patent office in 1905. I **was sleeping** at 3:00 in the morning.	We use the past continuous tense to show what was in progress at a specific moment in the past. 1905 / was working / now
Einstein **was living** in Switzerland when he **developed** his theory of relativity. While Einstein **was visiting** the U.S., the Nazis **took** his property. Einstein **was living** in New Jersey when he **died.**	We use the past continuous tense with the simple past to show the relationship of a longer past action to a shorter past action. developed / was living / now
Compare: a. Einstein was living in Switzerland ***when*** he **discovered** his theory of relativity. b. Einstein discovered his theory of relativity ***while*** he **was living** in Switzerland.	a. Use *when* + the simple past with the shorter action. b. Use *while* + the past continuous with the longer action.
Where **was** Einstein **living** when the Nazis **took** his home?	In a question with two clauses, only the verb in the main clause is in a question form.
While Einstein **was** in Switzerland, he developed his theory.	We don't use the continuous form with the verb *be*.

Punctuation Note:
If the main clause precedes the time clause, do not separate the two clauses with a comma. If the time clause precedes the main clause, separate the two clause with a comma.

Hs was living in New Jersey when he died. (No Comma)
While he was living in New Jersey, he died. (Comma)

Time Words and Time Clauses; The Past Continuous Tense 221

Expansion

Grammar Have students diagram on a timeline three to five of the past continuous sentences from the reading on page 219. Ask volunteers to show their timelines on the board.

7.6 | The Past Continuous Tense—Uses

1. On the board, draw a timeline similar to the timeline in grammar chart **7.6.** Explain the past continuous tense using the example from the book: *Einstein was working in a patent office in 1905.* As you write *was working,* explain that he may have been working before 1905 and after 1905. Mark *1905* on the timeline.
2. Then ask students to draw the timeline in their notebooks and to diagram the next sentence: *I was sleeping at 3:00 in the morning.* Ask a volunteer to create the timeline on the board.
3. Go over the next example using the timeline: *Einstein was living in Switzerland when he developed his theory of relativity.* Explain that the simple past describes an action that occurred once (e.g., *discovered, died, took*) while the continuous action was in progress. Then have students plot out the next two examples from the grammar chart on the timeline.
4. Point out that *when* is used with the clause that contains the simple past and *while* is used with the clause that contains the past continuous.
5. Say: *In questions with two clauses, only the verb in the main clause is in question form* (i.e., the verb precedes the subject). Review the example.
6. Point out that the continuous form is not used with *be* (wrong: *While Einstein was being in Switzerland, he developed . . .*).
7. Direct students to the Punctuation Note. Point out that if the time clause precedes the main clause, we need to separate the two clauses with a comma. Go over the examples.

EXERCISE 9

1. Have students read the direction line. Ask: *Were these things happening to you in January 2004?* Go over the example. Model the example for the class. Then have a volunteer model the example.
2. Have students complete Exercise 9 individually. Then have students ask and answer questions in pairs (e.g., *Were you going to school in January 2004? No, I wasn't.*). Circulate to observe pair work. Give help as needed.
3. If necessary, review grammar chart **7.6** on page 221.

EXERCISE 10

1. Have students read the direction line. Say: *You're going to ask your partner what he or she was doing at the times listed here.* Go over the example. Have a volunteer model the example with you.
2. Have students complete Exercise 10 in pairs. Circulate to observe pair work. Give help as needed.
3. If necessary, review grammar chart **7.6** on page 221.

EXERCISE 11

1. Say: *In this exercise, you have to decide when to use the simple past and when to use the past continuous. You also have to choose when to use* while *and* when. Ask: *Do we use* while *with the past continuous or with the simple past?* (past continuous) Have students read the direction line. Go over the examples.
2. Have students complete Exercise 11 individually. Point out the pictures of the teacher dropping the chalk, the fuse, and the woman who is ironing. Go over the answers as a class.
3. If necessary, review grammar chart **7.6** on page 221.

To save class time, have students do half of the exercise in class and complete the other half for homework. Or assign the entire exercise for homework.

EXERCISE 9 ABOUT YOU Tell if the following things were happening in January 2004.

EXAMPLE go to school
I was (not) going to school in January 2004.

Answers will vary.

1. work
2. go to school
3. study English
4. live in the U.S.
5. live with my parents
6. take a vacation

EXERCISE 10 ABOUT YOU Ask a question with "*What were you doing...?*" at these specific times. Another student will answer.

EXAMPLE at 6 o'clock this morning
A: What were you doing at 6 o'clock this morning?
B: I was sleeping.

Answers will vary.

1. at 10 o'clock last night
2. at 4 o'clock this morning
3. at 5 o'clock yesterday afternoon
4. at this time yesterday
5. at this time last year[5]

EXERCISE 11 Decide which of these two verbs has longer action. Fill in the correct tense (simple past or past continuous) of the verb in parentheses ( ) and *when* or *while*.

EXAMPLES She was taking (take) a shower when the telephone rang (ring).
It started (start) to rain while I was walking (walk) to school.

1. When the teacher was writing (write) on the blackboard, she dropped (drop) the chalk.
2. He fell (fall) and broke (break) his arm while he was climbing (climb) a tree.
3. Mary was shopping (shop) in a department store when she lost (lose) her purse.
4. I was doing (do) my homework when my friend came (come) over.
5. She met (meet) her husband while she was attending (attend) college.

[5] *At this time last year* is very general; it does not refer to a specific hour.

222 Lesson 7

Expansion

Exercises 9 and 10 Create two rings of students. Have half of the students stand in an outer ring around the classroom. Have the other half stand in an inner ring, facing the outer ring. Instruct students to ask each other questions from Exercises 9 and 10 (e.g., *Were you going to school in January 2004?*). Call out "turn" every minute or so. Students in the inner ring should move one space clockwise. Students now interview their new partners. Make sure students look at each other when they're asking and answering questions.

6. While I was driving (drive) to work, I ran (run) out of gas.[6]

7. When he arrived (arrive) at the airport, his friends were waiting (wait) for him.

8. They were eating (eat) dinner when someone knocked (knock) on the door.

9. While I was taking (take) a test, my pencil point broke (break).

10. The baby interrupted (interrupt) me when I was talking (talk) to a friend.

11. I broke (break) my tooth while I was eating (eat) a nut.

12. I met (meet) an old friend while I was walking (walk) in the park.

13. She was cooking (cook) dinner when the smoke alarm went (go) off.[7]

14. He was shoveling (shovel) snow when he lost (lose) his glove.

15. I blew (blow) a fuse when I was ironing (iron).

fuse

16. She was sleeping (sleep) when the baby started (start) to cry.

17. She broke (break) her favorite plate when she was washing (wash) the dishes.

[6] To *run out of* means to use up everything.
[7] When an alarm *goes off*, it starts to sound.

EXERCISE 12

CD 2, Track 28

1. Say: *There are three conversations in this exercise.* Have students read the direction line. Go over the example. Point out that Conversation 1 is between a wife and husband, Conversation 2 is between two students, and Conversation 3 is between a son and mother.
2. Have students complete Exercise 12 individually. Check answers as a class.
3. If necessary, review grammar chart **7.6** on page 221.

To save class time, have students do half of the exercise in class and complete the other half for homework. Or assign the entire exercise for homework.

EXERCISE 12 Fill in the blanks with the simple past or the past continuous form of the verb in parentheses ( ) in the following conversations.

Conversation 1, between a wife (W) and husband (H)

W: Look what I found today! Your favorite watch!

H: Where *did you find* (example: find) it?

W: In your top drawer. I *was putting* (1 put) away your socks when I *found* (2 find) it.

H: I wonder how it got there.

W: Probably while you *were putting* (3 put) something in that drawer, it *fell* (4 fall) off your wrist.

Conversation 2, between two students

A: When did you come to the U.S.?

B: Two months ago.

A: Really? But you speak English so well.

B: While I *was living* (1 live) in a refugee camp in Kenya, I studied English.

A: *Are you planning* (2 you/plan) to come to the U.S.?

B: Not really. I had no plans at all. I *was just waiting* (3 just/wait) in the refugee camp.

A: Are you from Kenya?

B: No. I'm from Sudan. But while I *was living* (4 live) in Sudan, a war *started* (5 start) there and I had to leave my country.

A: Are you here with your family?

B: No. I'm alone. When the war *started* (6 start), I *was living* (7 live) far away from my family. I escaped to Kenya, but I don't know where my family is today.

224 Lesson 7

Exercise 12 Variation

To provide practice with listening skills, have students close their books and listen to the audio. Repeat the audio as needed. Ask comprehension questions, such as: *In conversation 1, when did the man's wife find his watch?* (when she was putting away his socks) *In conversation 2, where did the student from the Sudan learn English?* (in a refugee camp in Kenya) *In conversation 3, when did the dad ask the mom to marry him?* (while they were eating in a beautiful restaurant) Then have students open their books and complete Exercise 12.

Conversation 3, between a son (S) and mother (M)

S: I *was looking* (1 look) through some old boxes when I *found* (2 find) this picture of you and Dad when you were young. By the way, how *did* you *meet* (3 meet) Dad?

M: One day I *was walking* (4 walk) in the park in my hometown when he *stopped* (5 stop) me to ask what time it was. We *started* (6 start) to talk, and then he *asked* (7 ask) me to go out with him.

S: Did you date for a long time?

M: We *dated* (8 date) for ten months. During that time, his family *was applying* (9 apply) for the green card lottery in the U.S. While we *were dating* (10 date), they *received* (11 receive) a letter that gave them permission to immigrate to the U.S.

S: What *happened* (12 happen)?

M: At first, I was worried that I'd never see your dad again. But he *wrote* (13 write) to me often and *called* (14 call) me whenever he could. About a year later, he *went* (15 go) back to our country to visit me. While we *were eating* (16 eat) in a beautiful restaurant, he *asked* (17 ask) me to marry him.

S: *Did you marry* (18 you/marry) him right away?

M: Yes, we got married a few weeks later and then he *returned* (19 return) to the U.S. But I couldn't go to the U.S. with him. I *had* (20 have) to wait for permission. Finally, I *got* (21 get) permission to come.

Expansion

Exercise 12 Have students practice the conversations in pairs. Ask volunteers to role-play all or part of the conversations in front of the class.

7.7 | Was/Were Going To

Have students look at grammar chart **7.7.** Say: Was / were going to + *base form means the same thing as* was / were planning to. Go over the examples and explanations.

EXERCISE 13

CD 2, Track 29

1. Have students read the direction line. Go over the example.
2. Have students complete Exercise 13 individually. Check answers as a class.
3. If necessary, review grammar chart **7.7** on page 226.

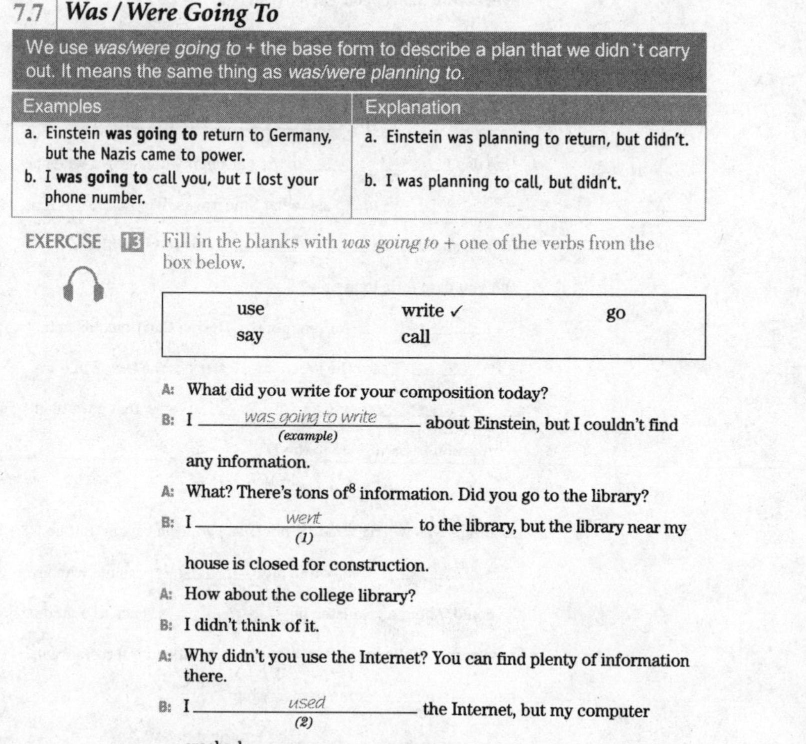

7.7 | *Was / Were Going To*

We use *was/were going to* + the base form to describe a plan that we didn't carry out. It means the same thing as *was/were planning to.*

Examples	Explanation
a. Einstein **was going to** return to Germany, but the Nazis came to power.	a. Einstein was planning to return, but didn't.
b. I **was going to** call you, but I lost your phone number.	b. I was planning to call, but didn't.

EXERCISE 13 Fill in the blanks with *was going to* + one of the verbs from the box below.

use	write ✓	go
say	call	

A: What did you write for your composition today?

B: I ___*was going to write*___ *(example)* about Einstein, but I couldn't find any information.

A: What? There's tons of[8] information. Did you go to the library?

B: I ___*went*___ *(1)* to the library, but the library near my house is closed for construction.

A: How about the college library?

B: I didn't think of it.

A: Why didn't you use the Internet? You can find plenty of information there.

B: I ___*used*___ *(2)* the Internet, but my computer crashed.

A: Why didn't you call me? I have Internet access at home. You're welcome to use my computer.

B: I ___*called*___ *(3)* you, but I lost your phone number.

A: I'm beginning to think you didn't really want to do your homework.

B: Maybe you're right. I'm kind of lazy.

A: I ___*said*___ *(4)* that, but I didn't want to hurt your feelings.

[8] *Tons of* means *a lot of.*

226 Lesson 7

Exercise 13 Variation

To provide practice with listening skills, have students close their books and listen to the audio. Repeat the audio as needed. Ask comprehension questions, such as: *Why didn't person B go to the local library?* (because it was closed for construction) *Was he going to use the Internet?* (Yes, but he couldn't because his computer crashed.) Then have students open their books and complete Exercise 13.

EXERCISE 14 Fill in the blanks to tell what prevented a plan from happening.

EXAMPLE He was going to return to his country, but *he couldn' t get permission.*

1. My cousin was going to come to the U.S., but Answers will vary.
2. He was going to work in the U.S. for only three months, but ______
3. We were going to return to our country, but ______
4. I was going to call my grandparents last night, but ______
5. We were going to rent an apartment in this city, but ______

GLORIA ESTEFAN—CUBAN IMMIGRANT

Before You Read

1. Is there anyone from your native culture who is famous in the U.S.?
2. Do you like Latin music?

Read the following article. Pay special attention to the verb tenses with *when* and *while*.

Immigrants who come to the U.S. bring their skills and talents. The U.S. benefits from these diverse abilities. One especially talented immigrant came from Cuba.

On September 1, 1957, Gloria Maria Fajardo was born in Havana, Cuba. **When** Fidel Castro **took** over in Cuba, Gloria was only two years old. Her father was taken as a political prisoner. Gloria and her mother moved to Miami to escape the Communist government.

Life as a child was not easy for Gloria. **When** Gloria's father **joined** the family in Miami a few years later, he **became** very sick. Gloria **took** care of him **while** her mother **worked**. She **practiced** singing and playing the guitar **while taking** care of her father.

In 1985, Gloria's mother asked her to sing some songs at a wedding. The bandleader at the wedding, Emilio Estefan, was very impressed by Gloria's singing and asked her to join his band, The Miami Sound Machine. (Emilio Estefan later became Gloria's husband.) The band played a combination of Cuban and American pop music. In 1989, Gloria started to perform solo and had several hit songs.

(continued)

Reading Variation

To practice listening skills, have students first listen to the audio alone. Ask a few comprehension questions. Repeat the audio if necessary. Then have them open their books and read along as they listen to the audio.

Reading Glossary

join: to get together with others
recover: to regain one's health
undergo: to suffer; bear

EXERCISE 14

1. Have students read the direction line. Say: *Complete the sentences with a logical phrase.* Go over the example. Model the example for the class (e.g., *He was going to return to his country, but he couldn't get permission.*).
2. Have students complete Exercise 14 individually. Then have students compare answers in pairs. Circulate to observe pair work. Give help as needed.
3. If necessary, review grammar chart **7.7** on page 226.

Gloria Estefan—Cuban Immigrant (Reading)

1. Have students look at the photo. Ask: *Who is Gloria Estefan?* (singer, songwriter, performer)
2. Have students look at the title of the reading. Ask: *What is the reading about?* Have students make predictions.
3. Preteach any vocabulary words your students may not know, such as *join, undergo,* and *recover.*

BEFORE YOU READ

1. Have students discuss the questions in pairs. Try to pair students of different cultures together.
2. Ask for a few volunteers to share their answers with the class.

To save class time, skip "Before You Read" or have students prepare answers for homework ahead of time.

Reading *CD 2, Track 30*

1. Have students first read the text silently. Tell them to pay special attention to the verb tenses with *when* and *while.* Then play the audio and have students read along silently.
2. Check students' comprehension. Ask questions such as: *When was Gloria Estefan born?* (1957) *While taking care of her father, what did Gloria do?* (practiced singing and playing the guitar) *Who heard her singing at the wedding?* (the leader of the Miami Sound Machine and her future husband, Emilio Estefan) *What happened one day while Gloria was traveling in her tour bus?* (The bus had an accident, and she broke her back.)

To save class time, have students do the reading for homework ahead of time.

7.8 | Simple Past vs. Past Continuous with *When*

1. Have students cover up grammar chart **7.8** on page 228. Write the following two sentences on the board:
   When the truck hit the tour bus, Gloria was hurt.
   When the truck hit the tour bus, Gloria and her husband were riding to a concert.
   Say: *Study the sentences. Which sentence shows what happened AFTER the tour bus was hit?* (*When the truck hit the tour bus, Gloria was hurt.*)
2. Then have students look at grammar chart **7.8.** Say: *In sentences with* when, *the simple past in the main clause shows what happened* ***after*** *an action. Identify the main clause of each sentence* (*Gloria was hurt; Gloria and her husband were riding to a concert.*). *In sentences with* when, *the past continuous in the main clause shows what was happening* ***at the same time*** *a shorter action occurred.* Go over the examples and explanations.

EXERCISE 15

1. Have students read the direction line. Go over the examples in the book.
2. Have students complete Exercise 15 individually. For items 5 and 6, point out pictures A and B. Go over the answers as a class.
3. If necessary, review grammar chart **7.8** on page 228.

Awards, fame, and fortune followed—until one day in 1990 when a tragedy happened. Gloria, her husband, and son **were riding** in her music tour bus **when** a truck **hit** the bus. Gloria's back was broken. She had to undergo painful surgery. Her career was on hold for a year. **When** she **recovered**, she **started** singing again.

Today, Gloria Estefan has a successful career and millions of fans among Americans and Latinos. Gloria's story is one of talent, a little luck, and a lot of hard work.

7.8 | Simple Past vs. Past Continuous with *When*

Both the simple past and the past continuous can be used in a sentence that has a *when* clause. However, the time sequence is completely different.

Examples	Explanation
a. ***When*** the truck hit the tour bus, Gloria **was** hurt. b. ***When*** the truck hit the tour bus, Gloria and her band **were riding** to a concert.	In sentences (a), the simple past in the main clause shows what happened ***after*** an action.
a. Einstein came to live in the U.S. **when** he lost his German citizenship. b. Einstein **was living** in the U.S. **when** he died.	In sentences (b), the past continuous in the main clause shows what was happening ***at the same time*** a shorter action occurred.

EXERCISE 15 Fill in the blanks with the simple past or the past continuous of the verb in parentheses ( ).

EXAMPLES When the movie was over, we *left* (leave) the theater.

We *were leaving* (leave) the theater when we met an old friend.

1. Gloria Estefan *was riding* (ride) in a bus when the accident happened.
2. Gloria Estefan *was going* (go) to the hospital when the accident happened.
3. Einstein *was living* (live) in the U.S. when he died.
4. A scientist *put* (put) Einstein's brain in a jar when he died.
5. When I got home, I *ate* (eat) dinner with my family. (picture A)
6. When I got home, my family *was eating* (eat) dinner. (picture B)

A

B

228 Lesson 7

Expansion

Grammar Have students go back to the reading on pages 227–228. Say: *Find the simple past and past continuous with* when. *Decide if* when *means* after *or* at the same time.

Culture Note

There are many Cuban Americans who have established themselves as leaders in many fields from entertainment to politics. One such important figure is Cuban-born Cristina Saralegui, famous talk-show host and magazine publisher. She is the granddaughter of communications magnate Francisco Saralegui. Cristina emigrated to the U.S. in 1960 at the age of 12. After college, she began working in her grandfather's magazines and eventually became the director of *Cosmopolitan en Español*. In 1989, *El Show de Cristina* aired for the first time and has been a hit ever since, earning many awards along the way. Cristina, following the footsteps of her late grandfather, now owns her own successful magazine named *Cristina!*

7. When I got to class, the teacher ___was giving___ (give) a test. Luckily I got there just in time.

8. When I got to class, the teacher ___gave___ (give) a test. I missed the first ten minutes of it.

9. When the phone rang, I ___was taking___ (take) a shower.

10. When the phone rang, my roommate ___answered___ (answer) it.

11. When she heard the news about the disaster, she ___started___ (start) to cry.

12. When she heard the news about the disaster, she ___was watching___ (watch) TV.

13. When the accident happened, I ___called___ (call) the police.

14. When the accident happened, I ___was driving___ (drive) to work. I called my boss to tell him I would be late.

7.9 Simple Past vs. Past Continuous

Examples	Explanation
Gloria took care of her father **while** her mother worked. **While** Einstein **worked** at a patent office, he studied and wrote.	We can connect two past actions that happened in the same time period with *while* and the simple past tense in both clauses.
While I **was reading** the story about Gloria Estefan, I **was underlining** the verbs. **While** we **were doing** the last exercise, the teacher **was helping** us.	We can connect two past actions that happened in the ***exact*** same time period with *while* and the past continuous tense in both clauses.
When the accident **happened**, Gloria had to stop performing.	Use *when* to mean *at a specific time*. Use the simple past tense.

EXERCISE 16 Fill in the blanks with *when* for an action at a specific time or *while* for an action that continues over time.

EXAMPLE She learned to play guitar ___while___ she took care of her father.

1. ___While___ her mother worked, Gloria stayed home with her sick father.

2. ___When___ Emilio Estefan met Gloria, he liked her very much.

7.9 Simple Past vs. Past Continuous

1. Have students cover up grammar chart **7.9** on page 229. Create a matching exercise. Write the following on the board:
   1. *Gloria took care of her father while her mother worked.*
   2. *While I was reading the story about Gloria Estefan, I was underlining the verbs.*
   3. *When the accident happened, Gloria had to stop performing.*
   a. *Two past actions happened at the exact same time.*
   b. *An action happened at a specific time.*
   c. *Two past actions happened in the same time period.*

   Say: *Match the sentence to the correct description.*
2. Then have students look at grammar chart **7.9.** Review the sentences and the explanations.

EXERCISE 16

1. Have students read the direction line. Say: *You have to decide whether to use* while *or* when. *Go over the example in the book.*
2. Have students complete Exercise 16 individually. Go over the answers as a class.
3. If necessary, review grammar chart **7.9** on page 229.

Expansion

Exercise 15 Have students write four sentences using the simple past and the past continuous with *when.* Say: *Write two sentences where* when *means* after. *Then write two more sentences where* when *means* at the same time.

7.10 | Using the *-ing* Form After Time Words

1. Have students look at grammar chart **7.10.** Say: *When the main clause and the time clause have the same subject, we can delete the subject of the time clause and use an -ing word.*
2. Go over the examples. Remind students that the clause with the time word is the time clause. Have students identify the main clauses and the time clauses in the example sentences.

EXERCISE 17

1. Have students read the direction line. Go over the example in the book. Say: *If you delete the subject in the first clause, you must use it in the following clause.*
2. Have students complete Exercise 17 individually. Go over the answers as a class.
3. If necessary, review grammar chart **7.10** on page 230.

3. Gloria was hurt very badly ___when___ a truck hit her bus.
4. ___When___ Gloria had an accident, she had to stop singing.
5. ___While___ she was recovering, she received a lot of mail from fans.
6. ___When___ she recovered, she went back to her singing career.

7.10 | Using the *-ing* Form After Time Words

When the main clause and the time clause have the same subject, we can delete the subject of the time clause and use a present participle (verb + *-ing*) after the time word.

Examples
Einstein left high school **before he finished** his studies.
Einstein left high school **before finishing** his studies.
After Einstein left high school, he studied mathematics and physics.
After leaving high school, Einstein studied mathematics and physics.
Gloria Estefan practiced the guitar **while she took** care of her father.
Gloria Estefan practiced the guitar **while taking** care of her father.

EXERCISE 17 Change these sentences. Use a present participle after the time word. Make any necessary changes.

EXAMPLE After ~~Einstein entered~~ *entering* the university, ~~he~~ *Einstein* developed his theory.

1. Einstein passed an exam before ~~he entered~~ *entering* the university.
2. He left high school before ~~he received~~ *receiving* his diploma.
3. After ~~Einstein developed~~ *developing* his theory of relativity, ~~he~~ *Einstein* became famous.
4. He became interested in physics after ~~he received~~ *receiving* books on science.
5. After ~~Einstein came~~ *coming* to the U.S., ~~he~~ *Einstein* got a job at Princeton.
6. Before ~~she came~~ *coming* to the U.S., Gloria lived in Cuba.
7. While ~~Gloria was~~ taking care of her father, ~~she~~ *Gloria* practiced the guitar.
8. Gloria was injured while ~~she was~~ riding in a music tour bus.
9. After ~~she recovered~~ *recovering* from her injuries, Gloria went back to making music.

230 Lesson 7

Expansion

Exercise 16 Have students work with a partner to write a paragraph about a famous immigrant or a person they know. Tell students to write about something that happened in his or her life. Instruct them to use the simple past and the past continuous tenses.

SUMMARY OF LESSON 7

1. Time Words

Time Word	Examples
When	**When** immigrants came to America, they passed through Ellis Island.
While	They waited **while** inspectors checked their health.
Until	Ellis Island remained closed **until** 1990.
Before	**Before** 1920, many immigrants came to America.
After	**After** 1920, Congress limited the number of immigrants.
From . . . to until	**From** 1892 **to** 1924, Ellis Island was an immigrant processing center.
till	The Ellis Island Museum is open **from** 9:30 **till** 5:00.
During	**During** this time, 12 million immigrants passed through Ellis Island.
For	New arrivals had to wait **for** hours.
In	**In** 1905, Einstein wrote about relativity. We will finish the test **in** an hour.
By	Restoration of Ellis Island was finished **by** 1990.
Ago	One hundred years **ago**, new arrivals passed through Ellis Island.
On	We came to the U.S. **on** Wednesday.

2. Uses of the past continuous tense:

A. To describe a past action that was in progress at a specific moment:
He **was sleeping** at 6 o'clock this morning.
Where **were** you **living** in December 2001?

B. With the past tense, to show the relationship of a longer past action to a shorter past action:
Gloria **was riding** in a bus when the accident **happened.**
Einstein **was living** in New Jersey when he **died.**
While Gloria **was taking** care of her father, she **practiced** the guitar.

C. To show past intentions:
I **was going to call** you, but I lost your phone number.
She **was going to cook** dinner, but she didn't have time.

Summary of Lesson 7

1. **Time Words** Have students cover up the Summary of Lesson 7 on page 231. Create a fill-in exercise using the chart on page 231. Reproduce the sentences without the time words on a handout or on the board. For example: ____ *immigrants came to America, they passed through Ellis Island.* Then have students compare their work with the sentences in the book. If necessary, have students review:
   7.3 Time Words (p. 216).
2. **Uses of the past continuous tense** Have students cover up the Summary of Lesson 7 on page 231. Create a matching exercise on the board:
   1. He was sleeping at 6 o'clock this morning.
   2. Gloria was riding in a bus when the accident happened.
   3. I was going to call you, but I lost your phone number.
   a. to show past intentions
   b. to describe a past action that was in progress at a specific moment
   c. to show the relationship of a longer past action to a shorter past action
   Say: *Match the sentence to the description.* Then have students compare their work with the sentences in the book. Go over all the example sentences. If necessary, have students review:
   7.4 The Past Continuous—An Overview (p. 218)
   7.6 The Past Continuous—Uses (p. 221)
   7.8 Simple Past vs. Past Continuous with *When* (p. 228)
   7.9 Simple Past vs. Past Continuous (p. 229).

Editing Advice

Have students close their books. Write the example sentences without editing marks or corrections on the board. For example:

1. *When entered the teacher, the students stood up.*
2. *While she spilled the milk, she started to cry.*

Ask students to correct each sentence and provide a rule or explanation for each correction. This activity can be done individually, in pairs, or as a class. After students have corrected each sentence, tell them to turn to page 232. Say: *Now compare your work with the Editing Advice in the book.*

Lesson 7 Test/Review

For additional practice, review, and assessment materials, see Assessment CD-ROM with *ExamView Pro*, *More Grammar Practice* Workbook 2, Interactive CD-ROM, and Web site http://elt.thomson.com/gic

PART 1

1. Part 1 may be used as an in-class test to assess student performance, in addition to the Assessment CD-ROM with *ExamView Pro*. Have students read the direction line. Ask: *Do all sentences have a mistake?* (no) Collect for assessment.
2. If necessary, have students review:
   7.1 *When, Until, While* (p. 213)
   7.3 Time Words (p. 216)
   7.6 The Past Continuous Tense—Uses (p. 221)
   7.7 *Was/Were Going To* (p. 226)
   7.8 Simple Past vs. Past Continuous with *When* (p. 228)
   7.9 Simple Past vs. Past Continuous (p. 229).

EDITING ADVICE

1. Put the subject before the verb in all clauses.
   When ~~entered the teacher~~ *the teacher entered*, the students stood up.
2. Use *when*, not *while*, if the action has no duration.
   ~~While~~ *When* she spilled the milk, she started to cry.
3. Don't confuse *during* and *for*.
   He watched TV ~~during~~ *for* three hours.
4. Don't confuse *until* and *when*.
   She will eat dinner ~~until~~ *when* her husband comes home.
5. Don't confuse *before* and *ago*.
   They came to the U.S. three years ~~before~~ *ago*.
6. After a time word, use an *-ing* form, not a base form.
   After ~~find~~ *finding* a job, he bought a car.

LESSON 7 TEST/REVIEW

PART 1 Find the mistakes with the underlined words, and correct them. Not every sentence has a mistake. If the sentence is correct, write *C*.

EXAMPLES She came to the U.S. two weeks before. *ago*
While I was walking in the park, I saw my friend. C

1. When he arrived, he ate dinner with his family. *C*
2. After leaving my country, I went to Thailand. *C*
3. When ~~arrived the teacher~~, *the teacher arrived* the students had a test.
4. I graduated ~~until~~ *when* I finished all my courses.
5. While she was washing the dishes, she dropped the glass. *C*
6. ~~While~~ *When* she dropped the glass, it broke.
7. He studied English until he became fluent. *C*
8. She served dinner when her guests arrived. *C*

232 Lesson 7

Lesson Review

To use Part 1 as a review, assign it as homework or use it as an in-class activity to be completed individually or in pairs. Check answers and review errors as a class. Reteach grammar points that students haven't mastered. Then student learning may be assessed using a test generated from the Assessment CD-ROM with *ExamView Pro*.

9. Einstein lived in the U.S. until he died. C

10. They went home ~~until~~ *when* the movie was over.

11. I'll be back in ten minutes. C

12. ~~During~~ *For* three weeks, he was on vacation.

13. Please return your library books by Friday. C

14. She found a job three weeks ~~before~~ *ago*.

15. He was sick for a week. C

16. I ate dinner an hour ago. C

17. Einstein was in the U.S. during the Second World War. C

18. I was going to call you, but I lost your phone number. C

PART 2 Fill in the blanks with the simple past or the past continuous form of the verb in parentheses ( ).

EXAMPLE He *was walking* (walk) to his car when he *lost* (lose) his glove.

1. What *were you doing* (you/do) at 4 p.m. yesterday afternoon? I tried to call you, but you weren't home.

2. She *was living* (live) in Paris when the war *started* (start).

3. I *found* (find) your necklace while I *was looking* (look) for my watch.

4. She *bought* (buy) a house three years ago.

5. He *met* (meet) his wife while he *was working* (work) in a restaurant.

6. When my grandfather *came* (come) to America, he *found* (find) a job in a factory.

7. When he *arrived* (arrive) at Ellis Island, his uncle *was waiting* (wait) for him.

PART 2

1. Part 2 may also be used as an in-class test to assess student performance, in addition to the Assessment CD-ROM with *ExamView Pro*. Have students read the direction line. Collect for assessment.
2. If necessary, have students review:
   7.6 The Past Continuous Tense—Uses (p. 221)
   7.8 Simple Past vs. Past Continuous with *When* (p. 228)
   7.9 Simple Past vs. Past Continuous (p. 229).

Lesson Review

To use Part 2 as a review, assign it as homework or use it as an in-class activity to be completed individually or in pairs. Check answers and review errors as a class. Reteach grammar points that students haven't mastered. Then student learning may be assessed using a test generated from the Assessment CD-ROM with *ExamView Pro*.

PART 3

1. Part 3 may also be used as an in-class test to assess student performance, in addition to the Assessment CD-ROM with *ExamView Pro*. Have students read the direction line. Point out that in some cases, more than one answer is possible. Collect for assessment.
2. If necessary, have students review:
   7.1 *When, Until, While* (p. 213)
   7.2 *When* and *Whenever* (p. 215)
   7.3 Time Words (p. 216)
   7.8 Simple Past vs. Past Continuous with *When* (p. 228)
   7.10 Using the *-ing* Form After Time Words (p. 230).

8. While she ___was using___ the computer,
(use)
it ___crashed___.
(crash)

9. He ___was cooking___ dinner when the fire
(cook)
___started___.
(start)

10. I ___was driving___ my car and ___listening___
(drive) (listen)
to the radio when I ___heard___ about the plane crash.
(hear)

PART 3 Fill in the blanks with an appropriate time word. Choose *when, whenever, while, until, before, after, by, ago, in, for, on, from, till, to,* or *during*. In some cases, more than one answer is possible.

EXAMPLE I will continue to work ___until___ I am 65 years old. Then I will retire.

1. ___When/Whenever___ it snows, there are a lot of traffic accidents.
2. I was walking to my friend's house ___when___ it started to rain. I was glad I had my umbrella with me.
3. ___While/When___ I was driving to school, I was listening to the radio.
4. ___After___ I finished my homework last night, I watched the news on TV.
5. I got my visa ___before___ coming to the U.S.
6. He must stay in his country ___until___ he gets permission to come to the U.S.
7. ___After___ he dropped his glasses, they broke.
8. We have to finish this lesson ___by/before___ 10 o'clock.
9. He found a job two months ___ago___.
10. He found a job three weeks ___after___ coming to the U.S.
11. He found a job ___in___ April.
12. It's 7:50. The movie will begin ___in___ ten minutes, at 8:00.
13. ___When___ the movie began, everyone became quiet.
14. ___While___ she was watching the sad movie, she started to cry.

234 Lesson 7

Lesson Review

To use Part 3 as a review, assign it as homework or use it as an in-class activity to be completed individually or in pairs. Check answers and review errors as a class. Reteach grammar points that students haven't mastered. Then student learning may be assessed using a test generated from the Assessment CD-ROM with *ExamView Pro*.

15. Einstein was 61 years old ___when___ he became a U.S. citizen.

16. Einstein lived in the U.S. ___for___ 22 years.

17. I had a doctor's appointment ___on___ Monday.

18. I work everyday ___from___ 9 a.m. ___to/till___ 5 p.m.

EXPANSION ACTIVITIES

Classroom Activities

1. Pick an important event in your life (*immigrating to a new country, moving to a new town, going to a new school, getting married,* etc.) and make a list of things you did before, during, and after the event. Discuss your answers with a small group.

Event: ______________________

Before	During	After

2. Form a small group. Turn to the person next to you and say a year or a specific time of the year. The person next to you tells what was happening in his or her life at that time.

EXAMPLES 1996
I was living with my parents.

January 2004
I was studying to be a nurse.

Talk About it

1. Read these quotes by Einstein. Discuss their meaning.
   - "Imagination is more important than knowledge."
   - "The only real valuable thing is intuition."
   - "A person starts to live when he can live outside himself."
   - "I never think of the future. It comes soon enough."
   - "Anyone who has never made a mistake has never tried anything new."

Expansion Activities

These expansion activities provide opportunities for students to interact with one another and further develop their speaking and writing skills. Encourage students to use grammar from this lesson whenever possible.

To save class time, assign parts of the activities as homework. Then use class time for interaction and communication. If students do not need additional speaking practice, some of the activities may be assigned as writing activities for homework or skipped altogether.

CLASSROOM ACTIVITIES

1. Have students complete the event chart individually. Then have students compare charts in pairs (e.g., *Before I came to the U.S., I was living with relatives in Belize.*).
2. Before the groups begin, model the activity with a few students. Have students go around the circle clockwise. After the person answers the question, he or she turns to the person on the left and says a year or specific time of the year.

TALK ABOUT IT

1. Put students in groups to discuss the quotes by Einstein. Tell students to try and rephrase the quotes.

Classroom Activities Variation

Activity 1 Have students ask and answer questions about an event that happened to them. Tell students to fill out the chart. Say: *Tell your partner the event you're going to talk about. For example:* I moved to the U.S. *Ask your partner questions about the event. For example:* What happened before you moved to the U.S.? Before I moved to the U.S., I was living with relatives in Belize.

TALK ABOUT IT (*cont.*)

2. Ask students if they know of any other famous geniuses. Write them on the board.
   Some famous geniuses:
   Charles Darwin (1809–1882): Naturalist
   Galileo Galilei (1564–1642): Physicist / Astronomer
   George Elliot (Mary Ann Evans) (1819–1880): Writer
   Leonardo DaVinci (1452–1519): Renaissance artist
   Marie Curie (1867–1934): Physicist
   Rembrandt (1606–1669): Artist
   Wolfgang Amadeus Mozart (1756–1791): Composer
3. Have students discuss their experiences with immigration in small groups. Tell students that they should talk about what happened or was happening before they came to the U.S., as well as what happened during and after the immigration process.

WRITE ABOUT IT

1. Suggest to students that they can also write about natural disasters that affected their country or region, such as earthquakes, tsunamis, floods, and volcanoes.
2. Ask volunteers to speak briefly about the famous person they've chosen to write about. Write ideas on the board.
3. Before they begin to write, put students in pairs to quickly tell each other the story of how they met their spouses or how their parents met.

OUTSIDE ACTIVITIES

1. Have students ask three to five people what they were doing when they heard about the September 11 terrorist attacks. Have students tell groups members what their friends and neighbors said.
2. Brainstorm important events with the class. Say: *Ask three to five people what they were doing when a specific event happened.* Have students discuss the results of their interviews in groups.

INTERNET ACTIVITIES

Remind students that if they don't have Internet access, they can use Internet facilities at a public library or they can use traditional research methods to find information, including looking at encyclopedias, magazines, books, journals, and newspapers.

- "Science is a wonderful thing if one does not have to earn one's living at it."
- "Peace cannot be kept by force. It can only be achieved by understanding."
- "Education is what remains after one has forgotten everything he learned in school."
- "Not everything that counts can be counted, and not everything that can be counted counts." (Sign hanging in Einstein's office at Princeton)

2. Einstein is often called a genius. Can you think of any other famous people who are geniuses?
3. In a small group or with the entire class, discuss your experience of immigration. Was the process difficult? How did you feel during the process?

Write About it

1. Write a paragraph about the changes that took place after a major historical event in your country or elsewhere in the world.

EXAMPLES After the Khmer Rouge took power in Cambodia . . .
After the coup failed in the former Soviet Union . . .
After the president of my country was assassinated . . .
After the fall of the Berlin Wall . . .

2. Write about the life of a famous person who interests you.
3. Write about how you met your spouse or how your father and mother met.

Outside Activities

1. Most people remember what they were doing when they heard shocking news. Do you remember what you were doing when you heard about the terrorist attacks in the U.S. on September 11, 2001? Ask another classmate or a friend or neighbor, "What were you doing when you heard about the attack on September 11?" Report this information to the class.
2. Is there another famous event that most people remember well? What was it? Ask people what they were doing when this event happened. Report your findings to the class.

Internet Activities

1. Look for the Ellis Island Web site. Find out what time the museum is open. See what names are on the wall of the museum. Is your family's name on the wall?
2. At a search engine, type in *famous immigrants*. Find information about an immigrant that you find interesting. Report this information to the class.

Additional Activities at http://elt.thomson.com/gic

Talk About it Variation

Item 1 Have students create presentations about famous geniuses or immigrants. Ask students to include pictures or illustrations. Have students discuss their presentations in groups. Display presentations around the classroom.

Write About it Variation

Item 1 Have students create timelines to accompany their paragraphs.

Have students exchange first drafts with a partner. Ask students to help their partners edit their drafts. Refer students to the Editing Advice on page 232.

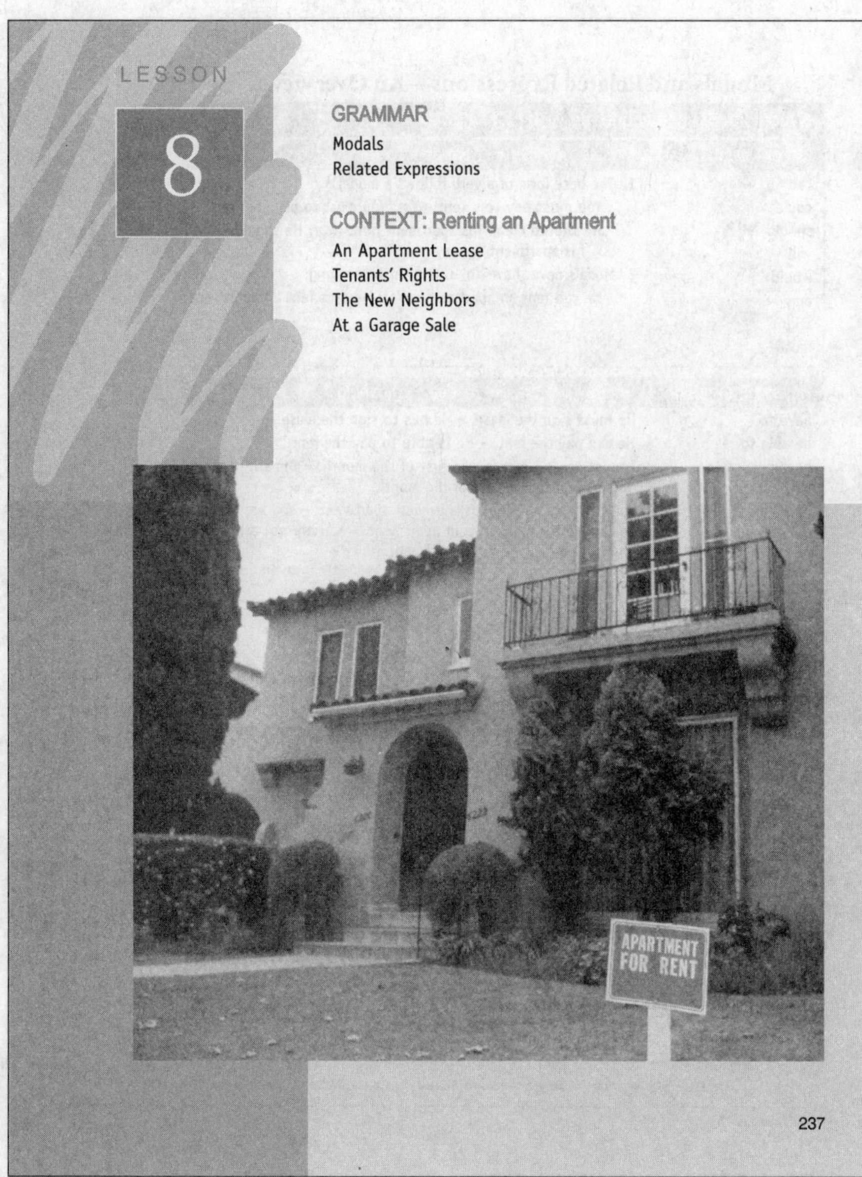

LESSON

8

GRAMMAR

Modals

Related Expressions

CONTEXT: Renting an Apartment

An Apartment Lease

Tenants' Rights

The New Neighbors

At a Garage Sale

237

Lesson | 8

Lesson Overview

GRAMMAR

1. Briefly review what students learned in the last lesson. Ask: *What did we study in Lesson 7?* (time words and time clauses; the past continuous)
2. Ask: *What are we going to study in this lesson?* (modals and related expressions) *Can anyone give me an example of a modal?* (e.g., *can, could, would*) Have students give examples. Write the examples on the board.

CONTEXT

1. Ask: *What are we going to learn about in this lesson?* (renting an apartment) Activate students' prior knowledge. Ask: *Do you rent an apartment?*
2. Have students share their knowledge and personal experiences.

To save class time, have students do the Test/Review at the end of the lesson, or administer a lesson test generated from the Assessment CD-ROM with *ExamView® Pro*. Skip sections of the lesson that students have already mastered. You may also assign some sections for self-study for extra credit.

Expansion

Theme The topic for this lesson can be enhanced with the following ideas:

1. Classified section of newspapers
2. Real estate magazines or circulars advertising apartments for rent
3. A copy of a lease

8.1 | Modals and Related Expressions—An Overview

1. Have students look at grammar chart **8.1** on page 238. Say: *Modals are followed by the base form of a verb. Modals never have an* -s, -ed, *or* -ing *ending.* Go over the list of modals and the example sentences.
2. Say: *There are some related expressions with verbs that act as modals and have the same meanings.* Go over the list of expressions and the examples.

An Apartment Lease (Reading)

1. Have students look at the lease on page 238. Ask: *Do you have a lease that looks something like this?*
2. Have students look at the title of the reading. Ask: *What is the reading about?* Have students make predictions about the reading.
3. Preteach any vocabulary words your students may not know, such as *damage, repair, wear and tear,* and *terms.* Point out the picture of the smoke detector on page 239.

BEFORE YOU READ

1. Have students discuss the questions in pairs.
2. Ask for a few volunteers to share their answers with the class.

To save class time, skip "Before You Read" or have students prepare answers for homework ahead of time.

8.1 | Modals and Related Expressions—An Overview

A modal adds meaning to the verb that follows it.

List of Modals	Modals are different from other verbs in several ways.
can could should will would may might must	1. The base form of a verb follows a modal.[1] You **must pay** your rent. (*Not:* You must to pay your rent.) He **should clean** his apartment now. (*Not:* He should cleaning his apartment now.) 2. Modals never have an *-s, -ed,* or *-ing* ending. He **can** rent an apartment. (*Not:* He cans rent an apartment.)

Related Expressions	Some verbs are like modals in meaning.
have to	He **must** sign the lease. = He **has to** sign the lease.
be able to	He **can** pay the rent. = He **is able to** pay the rent.
be supposed to	I **must** pay my rent by the first of the month. = **I'm supposed to** pay my rent by the first of the month.
be permitted to be allowed to	You **can't** change the locks in your apartment. = You **are not permitted to** change the locks in your apartment. = You **are not allowed to** change the locks in your apartment.

AN APARTMENT LEASE

Before You Read

1. Do you live in an apartment? Do you have a lease? Did you understand the lease when you signed it?
2. What kinds of things are not allowed in your apartment?

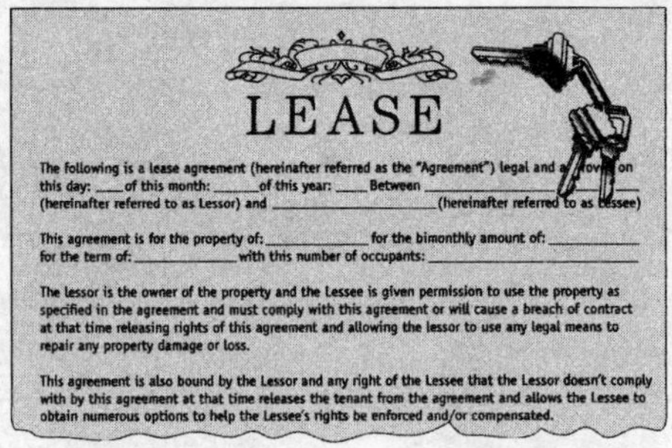

LEASE

The following is a lease agreement (hereinafter referred as the "Agreement") legal and a[illegible] on this day: ____of this month: ______of this year: ____ Between ____________________ (hereinafter referred to as Lessor) and ____________________(hereinafter referred to as Lessee)

This agreement is for the property of:____________ for the bimonthly amount of: __________ for the term of: ____________with this number of occupants: ________________

The lessor is the owner of the property and the Lessee is given permission to use the property as specified in the agreement and must comply with this agreement or will cause a breach of contract at that time releasing rights of this agreement and allowing the lessor to use any legal means to repair any property damage or loss.

This agreement is also bound by the Lessor and any right of the Lessee that the Lessor doesn't comply with by this agreement at that time releases the tenant from the agreement and allows the Lessee to obtain numerous options to help the Lessee's rights be enforced and/or compensated.

[1] Do not follow a modal with an infinitive. There is one exception: *ought to. Ought to* means *should.*

238 Lesson **8**

Read the following article. Pay special attention to modals and related expressions.

When people rent an apartment, they often **have to** sign a lease. A lease is an agreement between the owner (landlord[2]) and the renter (tenant). A lease states the period of time for the rental, the amount of the rent, and the rules the renter **must** follow. Some leases contain the following rules:

- Renters **must not** have a waterbed.
- Renters **must not** have a pet.
- Renters **must not** change the locks without the owner's permission.
- Renters **must** pay a security deposit.

Many owners ask the renters to pay a security deposit, in case there are damages. When the renters move out, the owners **are supposed to** return the deposit plus interest if the apartment is in good condition. If there is damage, the owners **can** use part or all of the money to repair the damage. However, they **may not** keep the renters' money for normal wear and tear (the normal use of the apartment).

Renters **do not have to** agree to all the terms of the lease. They can ask for changes before they sign. A pet owner, for example, can ask for permission to have a pet by offering to pay a higher security deposit.

There are laws that protect renters. For example, owners **must** provide heat during the winter months. In most cities, they **must** put a smoke detector in each apartment and in the halls. In addition, owners **can't** refuse to rent to a person because of sex, race, religion, nationality, or disability.

When the lease is up for renewal, owners can offer the renters a new lease or they can ask the renters to leave. The owners **are supposed to** notify the renters (usually at least 30 days in advance) if they want the renters to leave.

smoke detector

[2] A *landlord* is a man. A *landlady* is a woman.

Reading CD 3, Track 1

1. Have students first read the text silently. Tell them to pay special attention to modals and related expressions. Then play the audio and have students read along silently.
2. Check students' comprehension. Ask questions such as: *What do people have to sign when they rent an apartment?* (a lease) *What does the lease contain?* (rules for the landlord and the tenant) *What is a security deposit?* (It's money paid in advance to the landlord in case there is damage.)

To save class time, have students do the reading for homework ahead of time.

Reading Variation

To practice listening skills, have students first listen to the audio alone. Ask a few comprehension questions. Repeat the audio if necessary. Then have them open their books and read along as they listen to the audio.

Reading Glossary

damage: harm
repair: to fix something; make something work again
terms: items in a contract or agreement
wear and tear: use that causes damage

8.2 | Negatives with Modals

1. Have students cover up grammar chart **8.2.** Say: *Find all the negative modals in the reading (must not, may not, can't).* Ask: *How do you form the negative with modals?* (Put *not* after a modal.)
2. Have students look at grammar chart **8.2.** Say: *You can make a contraction with some modals.* Review the list of modals and their negative forms. Point out that the negative of *can* is *cannot. Can't* is the contraction. The negative of *will* is *will not.* The contraction is *won't.* And the negative of *may* is *may not,* and the negative of *might* is *might not.* There are no contractions for *may not* and *might not.*

EXERCISE 1

1. Have students read the direction line. Ask: *What do we write on the blanks?* (the negative of the underlined word) Go over the example.
2. Have students complete Exercise 1 individually. Go over the answers as a class.
3. If necessary, review grammar chart **8.2** on page 240.

8.2 | Negatives with Modals

Negatives and negative contractions	You form the negative of a modal by putting *not* after the modal. You can make a negative contraction with some, but not all, modals.
cannot → can't could not → couldn't should not → shouldn't will not → won't would not → wouldn't may not → (no contraction) might not → (no contraction) must not → mustn't	• The negative of *can* is *cannot* (one word) or *can't*. We **cannot** pay the rent. You **can't** have a dog in your apartment. • The negative contraction of *will not* is *won't*. We **will not** renew our lease. We **won't** stay here. • Don't make a contraction for *may not* or *might not*. You **may not** know legal terms. You **might not** understand the lease.

EXERCISE 1 Write the negative form of the underlined words. Use a contraction whenever possible.

EXAMPLE You must pay a security deposit. You *mustn't* have a waterbed.

1. I can have a cat in my apartment. I *can't* have a dog.
2. You should read the lease carefully. You *shouldn't* sign it without reading it.
3. The landlord must install a smoke detector. You *mustn't* remove it.
4. You may have visitors in your apartment. You *may not* make a lot of noise and disturb your neighbors.
5. If you damage something, the landlord can keep part of your deposit. He *can't* keep all of your deposit.
6. You might get back all of your security deposit. If you leave your apartment in bad condition, you *might not* get all of it back.

240 Lesson 8

Expansion

Grammar Do a drill. Have students close their books. Go quickly around the room saying modals and asking students to give you the negative form (e.g., Teacher: *would.* Student: *wouldn't*). This can also be done with the whole class answering as a chorus.

8.3 | Statements and Questions with Modals

Compare **affirmative** statements and questions with a modal.

Wh- Word	Modal	Subject	Modal	Verb (base form)	Complement	Short Answer
		He	**can**	have	a cat in his apartment.	
	Can	he		have	a waterbed?	No, he **can't.**
What	can	he		have	in his apartment?	
		Who	**can**	have	a dog?	

Compare **negative** statements and questions with a modal.

Wh- Word	Modal	Subject	Modal	Verb (base form)	Complement
		He	shouldn't	pay	his rent late.
Why	shouldn't	he		pay	his rent late?

EXERCISE 2 Read each statement. Fill in the blanks to complete the question.

EXAMPLE You should read the lease before you sign it. Why *should I* read the lease before I sign it?

Answers will vary.

1. You can't have a waterbed. Why *can't I have* a waterbed?
2. We must pay a security deposit. How much *must we pay* ?
3. Someone must install a smoke detector. Who *can install* a smoke detector?
4. The landlord can't refuse to rent to a person because of race, religion, or nationality. Why *can't the landlord refuse* to rent to a person for these reasons?
5. Tenants shouldn't make a lot of noise in their apartments. Why *shouldn't they make* a lot of noise?
6. I may have a cat in my apartment. *May I* have a dog in my apartment?
7. The landlord can have a key to my apartment. *Can the landlord* enter my apartment when I'm not home?

Modals; Related Expressions 241

8.3 | Statements and Questions with Modals

1. Have students cover up grammar chart **8.3.** Write the following statement on the board: *He can have a cat in his apartment.* Say: *Write a yes/no question, a negative short answer, an information question with* what, *and a question about the subject.* Then write the negative statement from the chart on the board: *He shouldn't pay his rent late.* Say: *Write a negative question for this statement.*
2. Have students look at grammar chart **8.3.** Say: *Now compare your work with the chart.* Go over any trouble spots with the class.

EXERCISE 2

1. Have students read the direction line. Go over the example.
2. Have students complete Exercise 2 individually. Go over the answers as a class.
3. If necessary, review grammar chart **8.3** on page 241.

Expansion

Exercise 2 Have students write three to five questions for their partners about their apartments (e.g., *Can you have pets?*). Have partners answer each other's questions.

8.4 | *Must, Have To, Have Got To*

1. Go over grammar chart **8.4.** Say: Must, have to, *and* have got to *all have the same meaning. However,* must *is very formal. Use* have to *or* have got to *in more informal settings.*
2. Go over the examples and explanations. Point out that *must, have to,* and *have got to* as imperatives all express the same sense of urgency.
3. Explain that *must* should not be used to express personal obligation. Point out that *must* doesn't have its own past form. The past of both *have to* and *must* is *had to.*
4. Direct students to the Language Notes. Explain that native speakers often pronounce *have to* as *hafta* and *got to* as *gotta.* Model the pronunciation for the class. Point out that we don't usually use *have got to* for questions or negatives.

EXERCISE 3

1. Have students read the direction line. Go over the example.
2. Have students complete Exercise 3 individually. Then go over the answers as a class.
3. If necessary, review grammar chart **8.4** on page 242.

8.4 | *Must, Have To, Have Got To*

Must has a very official tone. For nonofficial situations, we usually use *have to* or *have got to.*

Examples	Explanation
The landlord **must** give you a smoke detector. The tenant **must** pay the rent on the first of each month.	For formal obligations, use *must. Must* is often used in legal contracts, such as apartment leases.
The landlord **has to** give you a smoke detector. The landlord **has got to** give you a smoke detector.	In conversation or informal writing, we usually use *have to* or *have got to,* not *must.*
You **must** leave the building immediately. It's on fire! You **have to** leave the building immediately. It's on fire! You**'ve got to** leave the building immediately. It's on fire!	*Must, have to,* and *have got to* express a sense of urgency. All three sentences to the left have the same meaning. *Have got to* is usually contracted: I have got to = I've got to He has got to = He's got to
Our apartment is too small. We **have to** move. Our apartment is too small. We**'ve got to** move. The landlord **has to** give you a smoke detector.	Avoid using *must* for personal obligations. It sounds very official or urgent and is too strong for most situations. Use *have to* or *have got to.* (You can use *have to* in formal situations. But don't use *must* in informal situations.)
At the end of my lease last May, I **had to** move. I **had to** find a bigger apartment.	*Must* has no past form. The past of both *must* and *have to* is *had to. Have got to* has no past form.

Language Notes:
1. In fast, informal speech, *have to* is often pronounced "hafta." *Has to* is often pronounced "hasta." *Got to* is often pronounced "gotta." Listen to your teacher pronounce the sentences in the above box.
2. We don't usually use *have got to* for questions and negatives.

EXERCISE 3 Fill in the blanks with an appropriate verb. Answers may vary.

EXAMPLE The landlord must ___give___ you heat in cold weather.

1. You must ___sign___ the lease with a pen. A pencil is not acceptable.
2. The landlord must ___return___ your security deposit if you leave your apartment in good condition.

242 Lesson 8

3. The landlord must ___notify___ you if he wants you to leave at the end of your lease.

4. You must ___be___ quiet in your apartment at night. Neighbors want to sleep.

5. To get a driver's license, you must ___pass___ a driving test.

6. When you are driving, you must ___wear___ your seat belt.

7. When you see a red light, you must ___stop___

EXERCISE 4 ABOUT YOU Make a list of personal necessities you have.

EXAMPLE *I have to change the oil in my car every three months.*

1. Answers will vary.
2. ______
3. ______

EXERCISE 5 ABOUT YOU Make a list of things you had to do last weekend.

EXAMPLE *I had to do my laundry.*

1. Answers will vary.
2. ______
3. ______

EXERCISE 6 Finish these statements. Practice *have got to*. Answers will vary.

EXAMPLE When you live in the U.S., you've got to *learn English.*

1. When I don't know the meaning of a word, I've got to ______ Answers will vary.
2. English is so important in the U.S. We've got to ______
3. For this class, you've got to ______
4. If you rent an apartment, you've got to ______
5. If you want to drive a car, you've got to ______

Expansion

Exercise 4 Do a class survey. Find out what everyone's number one item is on the "have to do" list.

Exercise 6 Have students write three more sentence starters for their partners to finish using *have got to*.

EXERCISE 4

1. Ask: *What do you have to do on a regular basis? Car maintenance? House maintenance? Get your hair cut? Go grocery shopping?* Have students read the direction line. Go over the example. Model the example for the class.
2. Have students complete Exercise 4 individually. Then have students compare answers in pairs. Circulate to observe pair work. Give help as needed.
3. If necessary, review grammar chart **8.4** on page 242.

EXERCISE 5

1. Say: *In this exercise, you're going to write about the things you had to do last weekend. Write sentences that are true for you.* Have students read the direction line. Go over the example. Model the activity. Then have a volunteer give an example.
2. Have students complete Exercise 5 individually. Then have students compare answers in pairs. Circulate to observe pair work. Give help as needed.
3. If necessary, review grammar chart **8.4** on page 242.

EXERCISE 6

1. Have students read the direction line. Ask: *Which modal or expression are we going to use?* (*have got to*) Go over the example. Model the example.
2. Have students complete Exercise 6 individually. Then have students compare answers in pairs. Circulate to observe pair work. Give help as needed.
3. If necessary, review grammar chart **8.4** on page 242.

To save class time, have students do half of the exercise in class and complete the other half for homework. Or assign the entire exercise for homework.

8.5 | Obligation with *Must* or *Be Supposed To*

1. Have students look at grammar chart **8.5.** Say: *If you are not in a position of authority, avoid using* must. *Instead, use* be supposed to.
2. Explain that when you report on a law that was broken or a task that was not carried out, we use *be supposed to.*
3. Direct students to the Pronunciation Note. Explain that the *d* in *supposed to* is not pronounced. Model the pronunciation. Do a choral practice of the pronunciation with the class.

EXERCISE 7

1. Have students read the direction line. Ask: *When do we use* be supposed to*?* (when we're not in a position of authority) Go over the example.
2. Have students complete Exercise 7 in pairs. Go over the answers as a class.
3. If necessary, review grammar chart **8.5** on page 244.

8.5 | Obligation with *Must* or *Be Supposed To*

Examples	Explanation
Landlord to tenant: "You **must** pay your rent on the first of each month." Judge to landlord: "You have no proof of damage. You **must** return the security deposit to your tenant."	*Must* has an official, formal tone. A person in a position of authority (like a landlord or judge) can use *must*. Legal documents use *must*.
You're **supposed to** put your name on your mailbox. The landlord **is supposed to** give you a copy of the lease.	Avoid using *must* if you are not in a position of authority. Use *be supposed to*.
We're **not supposed to** have cats in my building, but my neighbor has one. The landlord **was supposed to** return my security deposit, but he didn't. I'm **supposed to** pay my rent on the first of the month, but sometimes I forget.	*Be supposed to*, not *must*, is used when reporting on a law or rule that was broken or a task that wasn't completed.

Pronunciation Note:
The ***d*** in *supposed to* is not pronounced.

EXERCISE 7 Make these sentences less formal by changing from *must* to *be supposed to.*

EXAMPLE **You must wear your seat belt.**
You're supposed to wear your seat belt.

1. **You must carry your driver's license with you when you drive.**
You're supposed to carry your driver's license with you when you drive.
2. **You must stop at a red light.**
You're supposed to stop at a red light.
3. **We must put money in the parking meter during business hours.**
We're supposed to put money in the parking meter during business hours.
4. **Your landlord must notify you if he wants you to leave.**
Your landlord is supposed to notify you if he wants you to leave.
5. **The landlord must give me a smoke detector.**
The landlord is supposed to give me a smoke detector.
6. **The teacher must give a final grade at the end of the semester.**
The teacher is supposed to give a final grade at the end of the semester.
7. **We must write five compositions in this course.**
We're supposed to write five compositions in this course.
8. **We must bring our books to class.**
We're supposed to bring our books to class.

EXERCISE 8 Finish these statements. Use *be supposed to* plus a verb. Answers may vary.

EXAMPLE I *'m supposed to pay my rent* on the first of the month.

1. Pets are not permitted in my apartment. I (not) *'m not supposed to have* a pet.
2. The landlord *is supposed to give* us heat in the winter months.
3. The tenants *are supposed to clean the apartment* before they move out.
4. The landlord *is supposed to install* a smoke detector in each apartment.
5. I *was supposed to pay* my rent last week, but I forgot.
6. My stove isn't working. My landlord *is supposed to fix* it.
7. We're going to move out next week. Our apartment is clean and in good condition. The landlord *is supposed to return* our security deposit.

EXERCISE 9 ABOUT YOU Write three sentences to tell what you are supposed to do for this course. You may work with a partner.

EXAMPLE *We're supposed to write three compositions this semester.*

1. Answers will vary.
2. ____
3. ____

Modals; Related Expressions 245

EXERCISE 8

1. Have students read the direction line. Say: *Remember. We also use* be supposed to *when we're reporting on a law or rule.* Go over the example in the book.
2. Have students complete Exercise 8 individually. Go over the answers as a class.
3. If necessary, review grammar chart **8.5** on page 245.

EXERCISE 9

1. Have students read the direction line. Go over the example. Then have a volunteer model the example.
2. Have students complete Exercise 9 individually. Then have students compare answers in pairs. Circulate to observe pair work. Give help as needed.
3. If necessary, review grammar chart **8.5** on page 244.

To save class time, have students do the exercise for homework.

Expansion

Exercise 8 Have students write statements about their apartments and lease agreements. Ask: *What are you and the landlord supposed to do?* Then have students compare information in pairs. Ask volunteers to describe their rental agreements in front of the class.

Exercise 9 Have students ask and answer questions in pairs about things they're supposed to do at home, at work, and at school this week (e.g., *What are you supposed to do at work this week? I'm supposed to organize the files in my office.*).

8.6 | *Can, May, Could,* and Alternate Expressions

1. Have students cover up grammar chart **8.6.** Create a matching exercise. Write the following on the board:
   1. I can clean the apartment by Friday. ______
   2. I can't understand the lease. ______
   3. I can't have a pet in my apartment. ______
   4. The landlord may not keep my deposit if my apartment is clean and in good condition. ______
   5. I couldn't speak English five years ago, but I can now. ______
   6. I could have a dog in my last apartment, but I can't have one in my present apartment. ______
   a. ability
   b. possibility
   c. permission
   Say: *Decide if each sentence is an example of ability, possibility, or permission. Write* a, b, *or* c.
2. Then have students look at grammar chart **8.6.** Go over the examples and explanations. Point out that *could* is the past of *can.*
3. Review all of the alternate expressions.
4. Direct students to the Language Notes. Go over the pronunciation of *can* and *can't.* Tell students that they must listen for the sound of the vowel and not the ending because the final *t* in *can't* is difficult to hear. Tell students that this is often confusing for native speakers as well. Point out that in short answers, *can* may sound like /kæn/. But tell students that in a short answer, they can easily distinguish between the two by listening for *yes* or *no.* Demonstrate the pronunciation with the sentences in the grammar chart.
5. Go over the meaning of the expression *can't afford.* Go around the room and ask students to tell you things they can't afford. Model the exercise (e.g., *I can't afford a Mercedes.*).

8.6 | *Can, May, Could,* and Alternate Expressions

Example with a Modal	Alternate Expression	Explanation
I **can** clean the apartment by Friday.	It **is possible** (for me) **to** clean the apartment by Friday.	Possibility
I **can't** understand the lease.	I **am not able to** understand the lease.	Ability
I **can't** have a pet in my apartment.	I **am not permitted to** have a pet. I **am not allowed to** have a pet.	Permission
The landlord **may not** keep my deposit if my apartment is clean and in good condition.	The landlord **is not permitted to** keep my deposit. The landlord **is not allowed to** keep my deposit.	Permission
I **couldn't** speak English five years ago, but I can now.	I **wasn't able to** speak English five years ago, but I can now.	Past Ability
I **could** have a dog in my last apartment, but I can't have one in my present apartment.	I **was permitted to** have a dog in my last apartment, but I can't have one in my present apartment.	Past Permission

Language Notes:
1. *Can* is not usually stressed in affirmative statements. Sometimes it is hard to hear the final *t*, so we must pay attention to the vowel sound to hear the difference between *can* and *can't*.
   Listen to your teacher pronounce these sentences:
   I can gó. /kIn/
   I cán't go. /kænt/
   In a short answer, we pronounce *can* as /kæn/.
   Can you help me later?
   Yes, I can. /kæn/
2. We use *can* in the following common expression:
   I *can't afford* a bigger apartment. I don't have enough money.

246 Lesson 8

Expansion

Grammar Prepare between 10 and 20 sentences with *can* and *can't.* Read the sentences and ask students to raise their hands if they hear *can* and to keep their hands down if they hear *can't.*

EXERCISE 10 Fill in the blanks with an appropriate permission word to talk about what is or isn't permitted at this school.

EXAMPLES We _aren't allowed to_ bring food into the classroom.

We _can_ leave the room without asking the teacher for permission.

1. We _Answers will vary._ eat in the classroom.
2. Students __________ talk during a test.
3. Students __________ use their dictionaries when they write compositions.
4. Students __________ write a test with a pencil.
5. Students __________ sit in any seat they want.
6. Students __________ use their textbooks during a test.

EXERCISE 11 Complete each statement. Answers may vary.

EXAMPLE The landlord may not _refuse to rent_ to a person because of his or her nationality.

1. The tenants may not _change_ the locks without the landlord's permission.
2. Each tenant in my building has a parking space. I may not _park_ in another tenant's space.
3. Students may not _talk_ during a test.
4. Teacher to students: "You don't need my permission to leave the room. You may _leave_ the room if you need to."
5. Some teachers do not allow cell phones in class. In Mr. Klein's class, you may not _use a cell phone_ during class.
6. My teacher says that after we finish a test, we may _leave_. We don't have to stay in class.

EXERCISE 10

1. Have students read the direction line. Explain that this exercise is about things that are permitted or not permitted at your school. Say: *There may be several ways to complete each statement correctly.* Go over the examples. Ask volunteers to give alternate expressions for the examples.
2. Have students complete Exercise 10 individually. Go over the answers as a class.
3. If necessary, review grammar chart **8.6** on page 246.

EXERCISE 11

1. Have students read the direction line. Go over the example. Remind students that answers will vary.
2. Have students complete Exercise 11 individually. Go over the answers as a class.
3. If necessary, review grammar chart **8.6** on page 246.

To save class time, have students do half of the exercise in class and complete the other half for homework.

Exercise 10 Variation

Have students complete the statements in as many correct ways as possible.

EXERCISE 12

1. Have students read the direction line. Say: *Write four statements or questions about the rules of the class, school, library, cafeteria,* etc. Go over the examples. Model an example for the class (e.g., *You can't use your books during a test.*).
2. Have students complete Exercise 12 in pairs. Circulate to observe pair work. Give help as needed.
3. If necessary, review grammar chart **8.6** on page 246.

EXERCISE 13

1. Have students read the direction line. Say: *Write three statements about what you could not do in your last school or class, and compare them with what you can do in this school or class.* Go over the example. Have a volunteer model an example for the class.
2. Have students complete Exercise 13 individually. Then have students compare statements in pairs. Circulate to observe pair work.
3. If necessary, review grammar chart **8.6** on page 246.

To save class time, have students do the exercise for homework.

EXERCISE 14

1. Have students read the direction line. Say: *Write three statements about what you could not do in your native country, and compare them with what you can do here in the U.S.* Go over the example. Have a volunteer model an example for the class.
2. Have students complete Exercise 14 individually. Then have students compare statements in pairs. Circulate to observe pair work.
3. If necessary, review grammar chart **8.6** on page 246.

To save class time, have students do the exercise for homework.

EXERCISE 12 ABOUT YOU Write statements to tell what is or is not permitted in this class, in the library, at this school, or during a test. If you have any questions about what is permitted, write a question for the teacher. You may work with a partner.

EXAMPLES *We aren't allowed to talk in the library.*

May we use our textbooks during a test?

Answers will vary.

EXERCISE 13 ABOUT YOU Write three sentences telling about what you couldn't do in another class or school that you attended.

EXAMPLE *In my high school, I couldn't call a teacher by his first name, but I can do it here.*

1. Answers will vary.
2.
3.

EXERCISE 14 ABOUT YOU If you come from another country, write three sentences telling about something that was prohibited there that you can do in the U.S.

EXAMPLE *I couldn't criticize the political leaders in my country, but I can do it now.*

1. Answers will vary.
2.
3.

248 Lesson 8

Expansion

Exercise 12 Have students talk about school rules in groups. What can't they do that they would like to do? (e.g., *We're not permitted to eat in class. They should change this rule. I work all day and don't have time to eat before class.*)

Exercise 14 Have students talk about what they could and couldn't do in their native countries. If possible, put students from different countries in groups together.

TENANTS' RIGHTS

Before You Read

1. What are some complaints you have about your apartment? Do you ever tell the landlord about your complaints?
2. Is your apartment warm enough in the winter and cool enough in the summer?

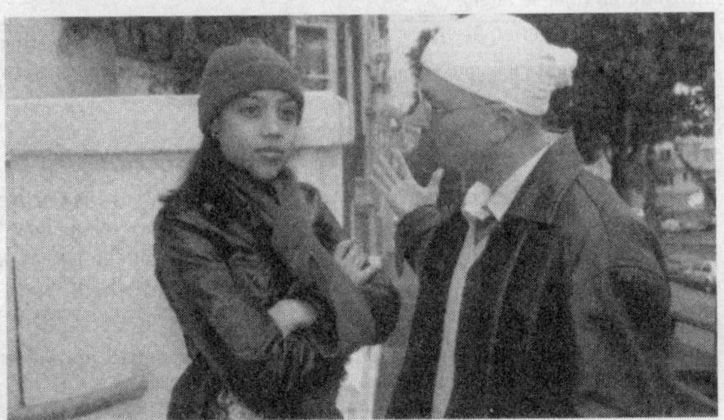

Read the following conversation. Pay special attention to *should* and *had beter.*

brochure

A: My apartment is always too cold in the winter. I've got to move.
B: You don't have to move. The landlord is supposed to give enough heat.
A: But he doesn't.
B: You **should** talk to him about this problem.
A: I did already. The first time I talked to him, he just told me I **should** put on a sweater. The second time I said, "You'd **better** give me heat, or I'm going to move."
B: You **shouldn't** get so angry. That's not the way to solve the problem. You know, there are laws about heat. You **should** get information from the city so you can know your rights.
A: How can I get information?
B: Tomorrow morning, you **should** call the mayor's office and ask for a brochure about tenants' rights. When you know what the law is exactly, you **should** show the brochure to your landlord.
A: And what if he doesn't want to do anything about it?
B: Then you **should** report the problem to the mayor's office.
A: I'm afraid to do that.
B: Don't be afraid. You have rights. Maybe you **should** talk to other tenants and see if you can do this together.

Modals; Related Expressions 249

Tenants' Rights (Reading)

1. Have students look at the photo. Ask: *What do you think is going on in this photo?* (e.g., *These people don't look happy. They look like they're talking about something serious.*)
2. Have students look at the title of the reading. Ask: *What is the reading about?* Have students use the title and photo to make predictions about the reading.
3. Preteach any vocabulary words your students may not know, such as *mayor.*

BEFORE YOU READ

1. Have students discuss the questions in pairs. Try to pair students of different cultures together.
2. Ask for a few volunteers to share their answers with the class.

To save class time, skip "Before You Read" or have students prepare answers for homework ahead of time.

Reading CD 3, Track 2

1. Have students first read the text silently. Tell them to pay special attention to *should* and *had better.* Then play the audio and have students read along silently.
2. Check students' comprehension. Ask questions such as: *Why is person A unhappy about the apartment?* (It's cold. There's not enough heat in the winter.) *Did person A talk to the landlord?* (Yes, twice.) *What does person B suggest?* (Call the mayor's office for information about tenants' rights.) *Does person A want to report the problem to the mayor's office?* (no)

To save class time, have students do the reading for homework ahead of time.

Reading Variation

To practice listening skills, have students first listen to the audio alone. Ask a few comprehension questions. Repeat the audio if necessary. Then have them open their books and read along as they listen to the audio.

Reading Glossary

mayor: the elected head of a city's government

Culture Note

If you're renting an apartment, you should always be aware of your rights as a tenant. States usually have laws on tenants' rights in the following areas: apartment sharing, heating season, eviction, security deposits, and pets.

8.7 | *Should; Had Better*

1. Have students cover up grammar chart **8.7.** Create a fill-in exercise. Write the following on the board:
   a. Use should *for advice.*
   b. Use must *for rules and laws.*
   c. Use had better *for warnings.*
   1. Your landlord ________ give you a smoke detector; it's the law.
   2. You ________ talk to the landlord about the problems.
   3. The landlord ________ give me heat, or I'm going to move.
   Say: *Study the three rules for* should, must, *and* had better. *Then fill in the blanks with the correct word.*
2. Go over the answers with the class (a. *must*; b. *should*; c. *had better*).
3. Then have students look at grammar chart **8.7.** Go over the examples and explanations.
4. Direct students to the Pronunciation Note. Explain that native speakers often don't say the *had* in *had better*. Demonstrate the pronunciation.

EXERCISE 15

1. Have students read the direction line. Go over the example in the book. Have a volunteer model #1.
2. Have students complete Exercise 15 individually. Then have students compare answers in pairs. Circulate to observe pair work. Give help as needed.
3. If necessary, review grammar chart **8.7** on page 250.

8.7 | *Should; Had Better*

Examples	Explanation
You **should** talk to the landlord about the problem. You **should** get information about tenants' rights. You **shouldn't** get so angry.	For advice, use *should*. *Should* = It's a good idea. *Shouldn't* = It's a bad idea.
Compare: Your landlord **must** give you a smoke detector. You **should** check the battery in the smoke detector occasionally.	Remember, *must* is very strong and is not for advice. It is for rules and laws. For advice, use *should*.
You **had better** give me heat, or I'm going to move. We'd **better not** make so much noise, or our neighbors will complain.	For a warning, use *had better (not)*. Something bad can happen if you don't follow this advice. The contraction for *had* (in *had better*) is *'d*. I'd you'd he'd she'd we'd they'd

Pronunciation Note:
Native speakers often don't pronounce the *had* or *'d* in *had better*. You will hear people say, "You better be careful; You better not make so much noise."

EXERCISE 15 Give advice using *should*. Answers may vary.

EXAMPLE **I'm going to move next week, and I hope to get my security deposit back.**
Advice: *You should clean the apartment completely.*

1. **I just rented an apartment, but the rent is too high for me alone.**
   Advice: *You should get a roommate.*
2. **My upstairs neighbors make a lot of noise.**
   Advice: *You should ask them to be quieter.*
3. **The battery in the smoke detector is old.**
   Advice: *You should replace the battery.*
4. **I want to paint the walls.**
   Advice: *You should ask the landlord for permission.*
5. **The rent was due last week, but I forgot to pay it.**
   Advice: *You should pay it now.*
6. **My landlady doesn't give us enough heat in the winter.**
   Advice: *You should talk to her about the problem.*

250 Lesson 8

7. I can't understand my lease.

Advice: *You should ask the landlord questions.*

8. I broke a window in my apartment.

Advice: *You should replace it.*

9. My landlord doesn't want to return my security deposit.

Advice: *You should write him a letter.*

10. The landlord is going to raise the rent by 40 percent.

Advice: *You should move.*

EXERCISE 16 Fill in the blanks with an appropriate verb (phrase) to complete this conversation. Answers may vary.

A: My mother is such a worrier.

B: What does she worry about?

A: Everything. Especially me.

B: For example?

A: Even if it's warm outside, she always says, "you'd better *take a sweater* (example) because it might get cold later," or "You'd better *bring an umbrella* (1) because it might rain." When I drive, she always tells me, "You'd better *slow down* (2), or you might get a ticket." If I stay out late with my friends, she tells me, "You'd better *come home early* (3), or you won't get enough sleep." If I read a lot, she says, "You'd better not *read so much* (4), or you'll ruin your eyesight."

B: Well, she's your mother. So naturally she worries about you.

A: But she worries about other things too.

B: Like what?

EXERCISE 16

CD 3, Track 3

1. Say: *In this conversation, a woman is talking about her mother who worries a lot.* Have students read the direction line. Go over the example.
2. Have students complete Exercise 16 individually. Then check answers as a class.
3. If necessary, review grammar chart **8.7** on page 251.

To save class time, have students do half of the exercise in class and complete the other half for homework.

Expansion

Exercise 15 Say to students: *Write down three to five problems you need advice for.* Have students exchange problems with a partner. Then have each partner write advice. Survey the class to find out if students were happy with the advice. Ask volunteers to read the problems and the advice.

Exercise 15 Have students write to an advice column seeking advice for a problem they have. Ask students not to put their names on the letters. If necessary, show students examples of advice columns such as *Dear Abby.* Collect the letters and read them out loud. Ask the class to give advice.

Exercise 16 Variation

To provide practice with listening skills, have students close their books and listen to the audio. Repeat the audio as needed. Ask comprehension questions, such as: *When person A drives fast, what does her mother say?* ("You'd better slow down, or you might get a ticket.") *What's going to happen if she reads too much?* (She'll ruin her eyes.) *Why does she have to take her shoes off when she enters the apartment?* (The neighbors might be bothered by the noise.) Then have students open their books and complete Exercise 16.

A: You'd better ___take off (5)___ your shoes when you enter the apartment, or the neighbors downstairs will hear us walking around.

We'd better ___be quiet (6)___, or the neighbors will complain about the noise in our apartment.

B: It sounds like she's a good neighbor.

A: That's not all. She unplugs the TV every night. She says, "I'd better ___unplug it (7)___, or the apartment will fill up with radiation."

And she doesn't want to use a cell phone. She says it has too much radiation. I think that's so silly.

B: I don't think that's silly. You'd better ___read (8)___ some articles about cell phones because they do produce radiation.

A: I don't even use my cell phone very much. But my mother always tells me, "You'd better ___bring it (9)___ in case I need to call you."

B: Do you live with your mother?

A: Yes, I do. I think I'd better ___move (10)___ to my own apartment, or she'll drive me crazy.

252 Lesson 8

Expansion

Exercise 16 Have students practice the dialogue in pairs. Then ask volunteers to role-play all or part of the dialogue in front of the class.

8.8 | Negatives of Modals

In negative statements, *must not, don't have to,* and *shouldn't* have very different meanings. *Must not, may not,* and *can't* have similar meanings.

Examples	Explanation
You **must not** change the locks without the landlord's permission. You **must not** take the landlord's smoke detector with you when you move.	Use *must not* for prohibition. These things are against the law or rule. *Must not* has an official tone.
I **can't** have a dog in my apartment. I **may not** have a waterbed in my apartment.	Use *cannot* or *may not* to show no permission. The meaning is about the same as *must not.* (*May not* is more formal than *cannot*).
The landlord **is not supposed to** keep your security deposit. You **are not supposed to** paint the walls without the landlord's permission. You **are not supposed to** park in another tenant's parking space.	*Be not supposed to* indicates that something is against the law or breaks the rules. *Be not supposed to* is more common than *must not.* Remember, *must not* has an official tone.
My landlord offered me a new lease. I **don't have to** move when my lease is up. The janitor takes out the garbage. I **don't have to** take it out.	*Not have to* indicates that something is not necessary, not required. A person can do something if he wants, but he has no obligation to do it.
If you turn on the air-conditioning, you **shouldn't** leave the windows open. You **shouldn't** make noise late at night.	*Shouldn't* is for advice, not for rules.
You'**d better not** play your music so loud, or your neighbors will complain to the landlord.	*Had better not* is used for a warning.
Compare: a. I **don't have to pay** my rent with cash. I can use a check. b. I **must not pay** my rent late. c. I **don't have to use** the elevator. I can use the stairs. d. There's a fire in the building. You **must not use** the elevator.	In affirmative statements, *must* and *have to* have very similar meanings. However, in negative statements, the meaning is very different. In the examples on the left: a. It is not necessary to use cash. b. It is against the rules to pay late. c. You have options: stairs or elevator. d. It is prohibited or dangerous to use the elevator.
Compare: a. You **must not change** the locks without permission from the landlord. b. You'**re not supposed to change** the locks without permission from the landlord. c. You **shouldn't leave** your door unlocked. A robber can enter your apartment.	a. *Must not* is for prohibition. b. *Be not supposed to* is also for prohibition, but it sounds less official or formal. c. *Should not* expresses that something is a bad idea. It does not express prohibition.

8.8 | Negatives of Modals

1. Have students cover up grammar chart **8.8.** Create a chart on the board with the following headers: *against the law/rules (formal), against the law/rules (informal), no permission, not necessary, not advisable,* and *warning.*
   Then write the following sentences from the chart on the board in random order:
   1. *My landlord offered me a new lease. I don't have to move when my lease is up.*
   2. *You'd better not play your music so loud, or your neighbors will complain to the landlord.*
   3. *You are not supposed to paint the walls without the landlord's permission.*
   4. *You must not change the locks without the landlord's permission.*
   5. *You shouldn't make noise late at night.*
   6. *I can't have a dog in my apartment.*

   Say: *Put the underlined modal or expression in the correct category.*
2. Then have students look at grammar chart **8.8.** Say: *Let's go through the examples and explanations and see if we were right.*
3. Direct students to the comparisons. Say: *Although* must *and* have to *have similar meanings in the affirmative, they mean completely different things in the negative.* Don't have to *means that it's not necessary, while* must not *means it's prohibited.* Read the examples.
4. Say: Must not *and* not supposed to *both mean that something is prohibited, although* must not *is more formal than* not supposed to. Should not *expresses that something is a bad idea. It does not express prohibition.*

EXERCISE 17

1. Have students read the direction line. Say: *When you say something that's addressed to every one in general, you use the pronoun* you. Go over the example in the book.
2. Have students complete Exercise 17 in pairs. Circulate to observe pair work. Give help as needed. Go over the answers as a class.
3. If necessary, review grammar chart **8.8** on page 253.

EXERCISE 18

1. Have students read the direction line. Say: *Make statements with* have to *and* don't have to *that are true for you.* Go over the examples in the book.
2. Have students complete Exercise 18 in pairs. Circulate to observe pair work. Give help as needed. Go over the answers as a class.
3. If necessary, review grammar chart **8.8** on page 253.

EXERCISE 17 Practice using *must not* for prohibition. Use *you* in the impersonal sense.

EXAMPLE **Name something you must not do.**
You must not steal.

Answers will vary.

1. **Name something you must not do on the bus.**
2. **Name something you mustn't do during a test.**
3. **Name something you mustn't do in the library.**
4. **Name something you must not do in the classroom.**
5. **Name something you mustn't do on an airplane.**

EXERCISE 18 ABOUT YOU Tell if you *have to* or *don't have to* do the following. For affirmative statements, you can also use *have got to.*

EXAMPLES **work on Saturdays**
I have to work on Saturdays. OR **I've got to work on Saturdays.**

wear a suit to work
I don't have to wear a suit to work.

Answers will vary.

1. **speak English every day**
2. **use a dictionary to read the newspaper**
3. **pay rent on the first of the month**
4. **type my homework**
5. **work on Saturdays**
6. **come to school every day**
7. **pay my rent in cash**
8. **use public transportation**
9. **talk to the teacher after class**
10. **cook every day**

254 Lesson 8

Expansion

Exercise 17 Survey the class. Find out what students answered for some of the items in Exercise 17.

Exercise 18 Create two rings of students. Have half of the students stand in an outer ring around the classroom. Have the other half stand in an inner ring, facing the outer ring. Instruct students to ask and answer questions based on the items from Exercise 18. Tell students to answer questions with a short answer (e.g., *Do you have to speak English every day? Yes, I have to/No, I don't have to.*). Call out "turn" every minute or so. Students in the inner ring should move one space clockwise. Students now interview their new partners. Make sure students look at each other when they're speaking.

EXERCISE 19 Ask a student who comes from another country these questions.

Answers will vary.

1. In your native country, does a citizen have to vote?
2. Do men have to serve in the military?
3. Do schoolchildren have to wear uniforms?
4. Do divorced fathers have to support their children?
5. Do people have to get permission to travel?
6. Do students have to pass an exam to get their high school or university diploma?
7. Do students have to pay for their own books?
8. Do citizens have to pay taxes?
9. Do people have to make an appointment to see a doctor?

EXERCISE 20 Fill in the blanks with *be not supposed to* (when there is a rule) or *don't have to* (when something is not necessary).

A: Would you like to see my new apartment?

B: Yes.

A: I'll take you there after class today. The teacher says we ___don't have to___ (example) go to the lab this afternoon. We can take the day off today.

(at the apartment)

B: Why do you carry your bicycle up to the third floor? Wouldn't it be better to leave it near the front door?

A: The landlord says we ___'re not supposed to___ (1) leave anything near the door. The rule is to leave the front lobby empty. Besides, I can take it up in the elevator. I ___don't have to___ (2) use the stairs, but I don't mind carrying it. My bicycle is light.

B: This is a great apartment. But it's so big. Isn't it expensive?

A: Yes, but I ___don't have to___ (3) pay the rent alone. I have a roommate.

B: I see you have lots of nice pictures on the walls. In my apartment, we ___'re not supposed to___ (4) make holes in the walls.

EXERCISE 19

1. Have students read the direction line. Say: *You're going to interview a classmate who is from the same country you're from.* Model #1 with a volunteer.
2. Have students complete Exercise 19 in pairs. Circulate to observe pair work. Give help as needed.
3. If necessary, review grammar chart **8.8** on page 253.

To save class time, have students do half of the exercise in class and complete the other half in writing for homework, answering the questions themselves. Or if students do not need speaking practice, the entire exercise may be skipped or done in writing.

EXERCISE 20

CD 3, Track 4

1. Say: *In this conversation, one student is showing another student his apartment.* Have students read the direction line. Go over the example in the book.
2. Have students complete Exercise 20 individually. Then have students compare answers in pairs. Circulate to observe pair work. Give help as needed.
3. If necessary, review grammar chart **8.8** on page 253.

To save class time, have students do half of the exercise in class and complete the other half for homework.

Exercise 19 Variation

Have students interview someone from a different country outside the class.

Expansion

Exercise 19 Discuss the questions as a class. Make a chart on the board. Write the countries represented in the class across the top. Write the number of the questions down the side. Poll the class, using a check for *yes* answers and an *X* for *no* answers.

Exercise 20 Variation

To provide practice with listening skills, have students close their books and listen to the audio. Repeat the audio as needed. Ask comprehension questions, such as: *Where does person A keep his bike?* (in his apartment) *Is the apartment expensive?* (yes) *Is he allowed to hang up pictures in his apartment?* (yes) Then have students open their books and complete Exercise 20.

EXERCISE 21

CD 3, Track 5

1. Say: *In this conversation, students are asking the teacher questions about an exam.* Have students read the direction line. Go over the example in the book. Say: *Remember, all the answers should be in the negative.*
2. Have students complete Exercise 21 individually. Then have students compare answers in pairs. Circulate to observe pair work. Give help as needed.
3. If necessary, review grammar chart **8.8** on page 253.

To save class time, have students do half of the exercise in class and complete the other half for homework. Or assign the entire exercise for homework.

A: You can't even put up pictures? If you use picture hooks, you *don't have to* (5) make big holes. Why don't you ask your landlord if you can do it? If you can, I can give you some picture hooks.

B: Thanks. In my apartment, the landlord has so many rules. For example, we *'re not supposed to* (6) hang our laundry out the window. We have to use the washing machine in the basement. And we *are not supposed to* (7) use electric heaters.

A: An electric heater can sometimes cause a fire. I'm sure the apartment has heaters for each room. And in the U.S. people don't usually hang clothes to dry out the window. People use driers.

B: There are so many different rules and customs here.

A: Don't worry. If you do something wrong, someone will tell you.

EXERCISE 21 Students (S) are asking the teacher (T) questions about the final exam. Fill in the blanks with the negative form of *have to, should, must, had better, can, may, be supposed to.* In some cases, more than one answer is possible.

S: Do I have to sit in a specific seat for the test?

T: No, you *don't have to* (example). You can choose any seat you want.

S: Is it OK if I talk to another student during a test?

T: No. Absolutely not. You *must not* (1) talk to another student during a test.

S: Is it OK if I use my book?

T: Sorry. You *can't* (2) use your book.

S: What if I don't understand something on the test? Can I ask another student?

T: You *had better not* (3) talk to another student, or I'll think you're getting an answer. Ask me if you have a question.

S: What happens if I am late for the test? Will you let me in?

256 Lesson 8

Exercise 21 Variation

To provide practice with listening skills, have students close their books and listen to the audio. Repeat the audio as needed. Ask comprehension questions, such as: *Do students have to sit in a specific seat for the exam?* (no) *Can they use their books during the exam?* (no) *Do they have to bring paper?* (no) Then have students open their books and complete Exercise 21.

T: Of course I'll let you in. But you ___shouldn't___ (4) come late. You'll need a lot of time for the test.

S: Do I have to bring my own paper for the final test?

T: If you want to, you can. But you ___don't have to___ (5) bring paper. I'll give you paper if you need it.

S: Must I use a pen?

T: You can use whatever you want. You ___don't have to___ (6) use a pen.

S: Do you have any advice on test-taking?

T: Yes. If you see an item that is difficult for you, go on to the next item. You ___shouldn't___ (7) spend too much time on a difficult item, or you won't finish the test.

S: Can I bring coffee into the classroom?

T: The school has a rule about eating or drinking in the classroom. You ___can't___ (8) bring food into the classroom.

S: If I finish the test early, must I stay in the room?

T: No, you ___don't have to___ (9) stay. You can leave.

Expansion

Exercise 21 Have students practice the conversation in pairs. Then ask volunteers to act out the conversation for the class.

The New Neighbors (Reading)

1. Have students look at the illustration. Ask: *What's going on in this picture?* (A neighbor is bringing cookies to someone who just moved in. The new neighbor is unpacking her things in the new apartment.)
2. Have students look at the title of the reading. Ask: *What is the reading about?* Have students use the title and picture to make predictions about the reading.
3. Preteach any vocabulary words your students may not know, such as *worry* and *whisper*. Point out the picture of the crib.

BEFORE YOU READ

1. Have students discuss the questions in pairs. Try to pair students of different cultures together.
2. Ask for a few volunteers to share their answers with the class.

To save class time, skip "Before You Read" or have students prepare answers for homework ahead of time.

Reading CD 3, Track 6

1. Have students first read the text silently. Tell them to pay special attention to *must.* Then play the audio and have students read along silently.
2. Check students' comprehension. Ask questions such as: *Where does Lisa live?* (downstairs) *Does the new neighbor have kids?* (Yes. She has a 10-month-old son.) *How does Lisa know that Paula has a baby?* (She saw a crib.) *What does Lisa's daughter spend a lot of time doing?* (talking on the phone)

To save class time, have students do the reading for homework ahead of time.

THE NEW NEIGHBORS

Before You Read

1. Are people friendly with their neighbors in your community?
2. Do you know any of your neighbors now?

Read the following conversation. Pay special attention to *must.*

Lisa (L) knocks on the door of her new upstairs neighbor, Paula (P).

L: Hi. You **must be** the new neighbor. I saw the moving truck out front this morning. Let me introduce myself. My name is Lisa. I live downstairs from you.
P: Nice to meet you, Lisa. My name is Paula. We just moved in.
L: I saw the movers carrying a crib upstairs. You **must have** a baby.
P: We do. We have a ten-month-old son. He's sleeping now. Do you have any kids?
L: Yes. I have a 16-year-old-daughter and an 18-year-old son.
P: It **must be** hard to raise teenagers.
L: Believe me, it is! I **must spend** half my time worrying about where they are and what they're doing. My daughter talks on the phone all day. She **must spend** half of her waking hours on the phone with her friends. They're always whispering to each other. They **must have** some big secrets.
P: I know what you mean. My brother has a teenage daughter.
L: Listen, I don't want to take up any more of your time. You **must be** very busy. I just wanted to bring you these cookies.
P: Thanks. That's very nice of you. They're still warm. They **must be** right out of the oven.
L: They are. Maybe we can talk some other time when you're all unpacked.

crib

Reading Variation

To practice listening skills, have students first listen to the audio alone. Ask a few comprehension questions. Repeat the audio if necessary. Then have them open their books and read along as they listen to the audio.

Reading Glossary

whisper: soft, quiet talking
worry: fear that something bad may happen; anxiety

Culture Note

Many towns and cities in the U.S. have newcomer clubs that provide new residents with the opportunity to meet people. They usually have events such as barbeques, potluck dinners, book clubs, and playgroups for kids. Many groups have general meetings as well as meetings for special interests and hobbies. Some newcomer clubs even have newsletters and Web sites.

8.9 | *Must* for Conclusions

In Section 8.4, we studied *must* to express necessity. *Must* has another use: we use it to show a logical conclusion or deduction based on information we have or observations we make. *Must,* in this case, is for the present only, not the future.

Examples	Explanation
a. The new neighbors have a crib. They **must have** a baby. b. Paula just moved in. She **must be** very busy. c. The teenage girls whisper all the time. They **must have** secrets.	a. You see the crib, so you conclude that they have a baby. b. You know how hard it is to move, so you conclude that she is busy. c. You see them whispering, so you conclude that they are telling secrets.
I didn't see Paula's husband. He **must not** be home.	For a negative deduction, use *must not*. Do not use a contraction.

EXERCISE 22 A week later, Paula goes to Lisa's apartment and notices certain things. Use *must* + base form to show Paula's conclusions about Lisa's life. Answers may vary.

EXAMPLE There is a bowl of food on the kitchen floor.
Lisa must have a pet.

1. There are pictures of Lisa and her two children all over the house. There is no picture of a man.
She must be divorced (or widowed).
2. There is a nursing certificate on the wall with Lisa's name on it.
She must be a nurse.
3. There are many different kinds of coffee on a kitchen shelf.
She must like coffee.
4. There are a lot of classical music CDs.
She must like classical music.
5. In Lisa's bedroom, there's a sewing machine.
She must know how to sew.
6. In the kitchen, there are a lot of cookbooks.
She must enjoy cooking.

8.9 | *Must* for Conclusions

1. Have students cover up grammar chart **8.9.** Ask students: *What does* must *mean?* (It's a formal way to say that something is necessary.) Have students go back to the reading on page 258. Say: *There is another use for* must. *Read through the text again. What does* must *mean in this reading?* Discuss students' ideas.
2. Have students look at grammar chart **8.9.** Read through the explanation at the top of the chart. Go over the example sentences and the explanations. Review the negative *must not.*

EXERCISE 22

1. Have students read the direction line. Say: *Read each statement about Lisa's apartment, and make a logical deduction about Lisa's life.* Go over the example.
2. Have students complete Exercise 22 individually. Go over the answers as a class.
3. If necessary, review grammar chart **8.9** on page 259.

Expansion

Grammar Have students work in pairs. Ask students to take three to five things out of their bags or pockets. Have students make logical conclusions about their partners' lives based on their personal items (e.g., a mystery novel—*You must like to read mysteries.*).

EXERCISE 23

CD 3, Track 7

1. Say: *In this conversation, Alma introduces herself to her new neighbor, Eva.* Have students read the direction line. Go over the example in the book.
2. Have students complete Exercise 23 individually. Then have students compare answers in pairs. Circulate to observe pair work. Give help as needed.
3. If necessary, review grammar chart **8.9** on page 259.

Family Calendar			
Week 1	Mom	Joey	Ann
Sunday	Church social dinner		
Monday	Carpool to school		Piano lesson
Tuesday	PTA Meeting	Art Class	
Wednesday	Take cat to Vet	Start Science project	Report Due
Thursday	Carpool to school		Library with Liz
Friday		Dentist	Dentist
Saturday		School play practice	

7. There's a piano in the living room.
   She must play the piano.
8. On the bookshelf, there are a lot of books about modern art.
   She must like modern art.
9. On the kitchen calendar, there's an activity filled in for almost every day of the week.
   She must be busy.
10. There are pictures of cats everywhere.
    She must love cats.

EXERCISE 23 Two neighbors, Alma (A) and Eva (E), meet in the hallway of their building. Fill in the blanks with an appropriate verb to show deduction.

A: Hi. My name's Alma. I live on the third floor. You must *be* (example) new in this building.

E: I am. We just moved in last week. My name's Eva.

A: I noticed your last name on the mailbox. It's Ković. That sounds like a Bosnian name. You must *be* (1) from Bosnia.

E: I am. How did you know?

A: I'm from Bosnia too. Did you come directly to the U.S. from Bosnia?

E: No. I stayed in Germany for three years.

A: Then you must *speak* (2) German.

E: I can speak it pretty well, but I can't write it well.

A: Are you going to school now?

E: Yes, I'm taking English classes at Washington College.

A: What level are you in?

E: I'm in Level 5.

A: Then you must *know* (3) my husband. He takes classes there too. He's in Level 5 too.

260 Lesson **8**

Expansion

Exercise 22 Have students try to make negative deductions about Lisa's life from each statement (e.g., ***Lisa must not have a husband.***).

Exercise 23 Variation

To provide practice with listening skills, have students close their books and listen to the audio. Repeat the audio as needed. Ask comprehension questions, such as: ***When did Eva move in?*** (last week) ***How did Alma guess that Eva was from Bosnia?*** (from her last name; Alma is from Bosnia, too.) ***Who is in Eva's class?*** (Alma's husband) Then have students open their books and complete Exercise 23.

E: There's only one guy with a Bosnian last name. That must *be* (4) your husband.

A: His name is Hasan.

B: Oh, yes, I know him. I didn't know he lived in the same building. I never see him here. He must not *be* (5) home very much.

A: He isn't. He has two jobs.

E: Do you take English classes?

A: Not anymore. I came here 15 years ago.

E: Then your English must *be* (6) perfect.

A: I don't know if it's perfect, but it's good enough.

8.10 | *Will* and *May / Might*

Examples	Explanation
My lease **will** expire on April 30. We **won't** sign another lease.	For certainty about the future, use *will*. The negative contraction for *will not* is *won't*.
a. My landlord **might** raise my rent at that time. a. I **may** move. b. I don't know what "tenant" means. Let's ask the teacher. She **might** know. b. The teacher **may** have information about tenants' rights.	*May* and *might* both have about the same meaning: possibility or uncertainty. a. about the future b. about the present
He **may not** renew our lease. He **might not** renew our lease.	We don't use a contraction for *may not* and *might not*.
Compare: a. **Maybe** I will move. b. I **might** move. a. **Maybe** he doesn't understand the lease. b. He **might** not understand the lease. a. **Maybe** the apartment is cold in winter. (*maybe* = adverb) b. The apartment **may** be cold in winter. (*may* + *be* = modal + verb)	*Maybe* is an adverb. It is one word. It usually comes at the beginning of the sentence and means *possibly* or *perhaps*. *May* and *might* are modals. They follow the subject and precede the verb. Sentences (a) and (b) have the same meaning. *Wrong:* I *maybe* will move. *Wrong:* He *maybe* doesn't understand. *Wrong:* The apartment *maybe* is cold.

Expansion

Exercise 23 Have students practice the conversation in pairs. Then have volunteers role-play all or part of the conversation in front of the class.

Exercise 23 Have students work in pairs to create a conversation between new neighbors. Tell students to make the conversation as true for them as possible. Then ask volunteers to role-play the conversations in front of the class.

8.10 | *Will* and *May/ Might*

1. Have students look at grammar chart **8.10.** Say: Will *and* may/ might *are used to express certainty, uncertainty, and possibility.* Review the example sentences and explanations for *will.* Point out that the contraction for *will not* is *won't.* Explain that *will* is used for certainty in the future. Go around the room and ask volunteers to make statements about their futures using *will* and *won't* (e.g., *I will register for English class next semester.*).
2. Say: May *and* might *both have the same meaning. They can express uncertainty or possibility about the future and about the present.* Review the example sentences and explanations. Point out that there are no contractions for *may not* and *might not.*
3. Say: Maybe *is an adverb. It means* possibly *or* perhaps. *It can mean the same thing as* may *and* might. *It usually comes at the beginning of the sentence.* Go over the example sentences.
4. Direct students to the wrong examples with *maybe.* Ask: *What's wrong with these sentences? Correct them (Maybe I'll move. Maybe he doesn't understand. Maybe the apartment is cold.).* Review word order with *may* and *might* (subject + *may / might* + verb).

EXERCISE 24

1. Have students read the direction line. Go over the example.
2. Have students complete Exercise 24 in pairs. Go over the answers as a class.
3. If necessary, review grammar chart **8.10** on page 261.

EXERCISE 25

1. Say: *Complete these sentences with information that is true for you.* Have students read the direction line. Go over the examples.
2. Have students complete Exercise 25 individually. Then have students compare answers in pairs. Circulate to observe pair work. Give help as needed.
3. If necessary, review grammar chart **8.10** on page 261.

To save class time, have students do half of the exercise in class and complete the other half for homework.

EXERCISE 26

CD 3, Track 8

1. Have students read the direction line. Go over the example in the book.
2. Have students complete Exercise 26 individually. Then have students compare answers in pairs. Circulate to observe pair work. Give help as needed.
3. If necessary, review grammar chart **8.10** on page 261.

To save class time, have students do half of the exercise in class and complete the other half for homework. Or assign the entire exercise for homework.

EXERCISE 24 The following sentences contain *maybe*. Take away *maybe* and use *may* or *might* + base form.

EXAMPLE **Maybe your neighbors will complain if your music is loud.**
Your neighbors might complain if your music is loud.

1. **Maybe my sister will come to live with me.**
   My sister may come to live with me. / My sister might come to live with me.
2. **Maybe she will find a job in this city.**
   She may find a job in this city. / She might find a job in this city.
3. **Maybe my landlord will raise my rent.**
   My landlord may raise my rent. / My landlord might raise my rent.
4. **Maybe I will get a dog.**
   I may get a dog. / I might get a dog.
5. **Maybe my landlord won't allow me to have a dog.** *My landlord may not allow me to have a dog. / My landlord might not allow me to have a dog.*
6. **Maybe I will move next year.**
   I may move next year. / I might move next year.
7. **Maybe I will buy a house soon.**
   I may buy a house soon. / I might buy a house soon.
8. **Maybe I won't stay in this city.**
   I may not stay in this city. / I might not stay in this city.
9. **Maybe I won't come to class tomorrow.**
   I may not come to class tomorrow. / I might not come to class tomorrow.
10. **Maybe the teacher will review modals if we need more help.**
   The teacher may review modals if we need more help. / The teacher might review modals if we need more help.

EXERCISE 25 ABOUT YOU Fill in the blanks with a possibility.

EXAMPLES **If I don't pay my rent on time,** *I might have to pay a late fee.*
If I make a lot of noise in my apartment, *the neighbors may complain.*

1. **When my lease is up,** Answers will vary.
2. **If I don't clean my apartment before I move out,** ______
3. **If I don't study for the next test,** ______
4. **If we don't register for classes early,** ______
5. **If I don't pass this course,** ______

EXERCISE 26 Fill in the blanks with possibilities. Answers may vary.

EXAMPLE **A: I'm going to move on Saturday. I might** *need* **help. Can you help me?**
B: I'm not sure. I may *go* **to the country with my family if the weather is nice. If I stay here, I'll help you.**

1. **A: My next door neighbor's name is Terry Karson. I see her name on the doorbell but I never see her.**
   B: Why do you say "her"? Your neighbor may *be a man*. **Terry is sometimes a man's name.**

262 Lesson 8

Expansion

Exercise 24 Have students discuss each statement with a partner. Ask: ***Which statements are a possibility for you? Change the information when necessary*** **(e.g.,** ***My brother might come to live with me.*****).**

Exercise 26 Variation

To provide practice with listening skills, have students close their books and listen to the audio. Repeat the audio as needed. Ask some comprehension questions, such as: *In conversation 1, who is Terry Karson?* (person A's next door neighbor) *Has person A ever seen Terry?* (no) *Is Terry a man or a woman?* (We don't know.) Then have students open their books and complete Exercise 26.

2. A: I need coins for the laundry room. Do you have any?

B: Let me look. I might ___have___ some. No, I don't have any. Look in the laundry room. There might ___be___ a dollar-bill changer there.

3. A: Do you know the landlord's address?

B: No, I don't. Ask the manager. She might ___know it___.

A: Where's the manager now?

B: I'm not sure. She might ___be___ in a tenant's apartment.

4. A: Do they allow cats in this building?

B: I'm not sure. I know they don't allow dogs, but they might ___allow___ cats.

5. A: We'd better close the windows before going out.

B: Why? It's a hot day today.

A: Look how gray the sky is. It might ___rain___.

6. A: Are you going to stay in this apartment for another year?

B: I'm not sure. I may ___leave___.

A: Why?

B: The landlord might ___raise___ the rent. If the rent goes up more than 25 percent, I'll move.

7. A: I have so much stuff in my closet. There's not enough room for my clothes.

B: There might ___be___ lockers in the basement where you can store your things.

A: Really? I didn't know that.

B: Let's look. I may ___have___ a key to the basement with me.

A: That would be great.

B: Hmm. I don't have one on me. Let's go to my apartment. My basement keys might ___be___ there.

Expansion

Exercise 26 Have students create short dialogues in pairs using *maybe, may,* and *might.* Then have volunteers role-play their dialogues in front of the class.

At a Garage Sale (Reading)

1. Have students look at the photo. Ask: *What's going on in the photo?* (People are at a garage sale looking through a variety of used items.)
2. Have students look at the title of the reading. Ask: *What is the reading about?* Have students use the title and photo to make predictions about the reading.
3. Preteach any vocabulary words your students may not know, such as *deposit.* Direct students to the illustration of the outlet on page 264 and to the footnotes on bargaining at the bottom of page 264.

BEFORE YOU READ

1. Have students discuss the questions in pairs. Try to pair students of different cultures together.
2. Ask for a few volunteers to share their answers with the class.

To save class time, skip "Before You Read" or have students prepare answers for homework ahead of time.

Reading CD 3, Track 9

1. Have students first read the text silently. Explain that this is a conversation between a seller and buyer at a garage sale. Tell students to pay special attention to modals and related expressions. Then play the audio and have students read along silently.
2. Check students' comprehension. Ask questions such as: *What item is the buyer interested in?* (a microwave) *How are they going to see if it's working well?* (They're going to plug it in and boil a cup of water.) *Why is the seller selling it?* (He's moving.) *How much is the seller asking for it?* ($40)

To save class time, have students do the reading for homework ahead of time.

AT A GARAGE SALE

Before You Read

1. People often have a garage sale or yard sale or an apartment sale before they move. At this kind of sale, people sell things that they don't want or need anymore. Did you ever buy anything at this kind of sale?
2. At a garage or yard sale, it is usually not necessary to pay the asking price. You may be able to bargain[3] with the seller. Can you bargain the price in other places?

This is a conversation at a garage sale between a seller (S) and a buyer (B). Read the conversation. Pay special attention to modals and related expressions.

outlet

S: I see you're looking at my microwave oven. **May** I answer any questions?
B: Yes. I'm interested in buying one. Does it work well?
S: It's only two years old, and it's in perfect working condition. **Would** you **like** to try it out?
B: Sure. **Could** you plug it in somewhere?
S: I have an outlet right here. **Why don't we** boil a cup of water so you can see how well it works.
A few minutes later . . .
B: It seems to work well. **Would** you tell me why you're selling it, then?
S: We're moving next week. Our new apartment already has one.
B: How much do you want for it?[4]
S: $40.

[3] When a buyer *bargains* with the seller, the buyer makes an offer lower than the asking price and hopes that he or she and the seller will agree on a lower price.
[4] We ask "How much is it?" when the price is fixed. We ask "How much do you want for it?" when the price is negotiable—you can bargain for it.

Reading Variation

To practice listening skills, have students first listen to the audio alone. Ask a few comprehension questions. Repeat the audio if necessary. Then have them open their books and read along as they listen to the audio.

Reading Glossary

deposit: a partial payment to hold goods or property until the buyer makes complete payment

B: **Will** you take $30?
S: **Can** you wait a minute? I'll ask my wife.

few minutes later . . .
S: My wife says she'll let you have it for $35.
B: OK. **May** I write you a check?
S: I'm sorry. I'**d rather** have cash.
B: **Would** you hold it for me for an hour? I can go to the ATM and get cash.
S: **Could** you leave me a small deposit? Ten dollars, maybe?
B: Yes, I can.
S: Fine. I'll hold it for you.

8.11 Using Modals and Questions for Politeness

Modals and questions are often used to make direct statements more polite.
Compare:
Plug it in. (very direct)
Would you plug it in? (more polite)

	Examples	Explanation
To ask permission	**May** / **Can** / **Could** } I write you a check?	*May* and *could* are considered more polite than *can* by some speakers of English.
To request that someone do something	**Can** / **Could** / **Will** / **Would** } you plug it in?	For a request, *could* and *would* are softer than *can* and *will.*
To express want or desire	**Would** you **like** to try out the microwave oven? Yes, I **would like** to see if it works. **I'd like** a cup of coffee.	*Would like* has the same meaning as *want. Would like* is softer than *want.* The contraction for *would* after a pronoun is **'d.**
To express preference	**Would** you **rather** pay with cash or by credit card? **I'd rather** pay by credit card (than with cash).	Use *or* in questions with *would rather.* Use *than* in statements.
To offer a suggestion	**Why don't you** go to the ATM to get cash? **Why don't we** boil a cup of water? **Compare:** Go to the ATM. Boil a cup of water.	We can make a suggestion more polite by using a negative question.

Modals; Related Expressions 265

Culture Note

Garage sales, also known as yard sales or tag sales, are usually held when the weather is good—in the spring or early fall in colder states. They are usually held on weekends. Unlike most transactions in the U.S., it's acceptable to bargain for a lower price at a garage sale.

8.11 | Using Modals and Questions for Politeness

1. Have students cover up grammar chart **8.11.** Create a matching exercise on the board:
   1. May I write you a check?
   2. Could you plug it in?
   3. I'd like a cup of coffee.
   4. I'd rather pay by credit card than with cash.
   5. Why don't we boil a cup of water?
   a. to express preference
   b. to ask permission
   c. to offer a suggestion
   d. to request that someone do something
   e. to express want or desire
   Say: *Match the use with the example.*
2. Have students look at grammar chart **8.11.** Say: *Compare your work with the chart.* Then review the modals for politeness. Explain that *can* for permission is not considered as polite as *may* or *could.* Point out that *could* and *would* for requests sound softer than *can* and *will.*
3. Review questions for politeness. Explain that *would you like* has the same meaning as *do you want.* However *would you like* is softer sounding and is considered more polite. Remind students that the contraction for *would* after pronouns is *'d.*
4. To ask for and express preferences, *would rather* is used. Go over the examples.
5. To make a suggestion more polite, English speakers often make a negative question using *why don't.* Go over the examples.

EXERCISE 27

1. Say: *In this exercise, you're going to practice* may, can, *and* could + I. Have students read the direction line. Go over the examples.
2. Have students complete Exercise 27 in pairs. Go over the answers as a class.
3. If necessary, review grammar chart **8.11** on page 265.

EXERCISE 28

1. Have students read the direction line. Say: *Now you're going to be asking someone to do something for you.* Go over the examples.
2. Have students complete Exercise 28 in pairs. Circulate to observe pair work. Go over the answers as a class.
3. If necessary, review grammar chart **8.11** on page 265.

EXERCISE 29

1. Say: *Now we're going to practice* would like. Have students read the direction line. Go over the example.
2. Have students complete Exercise 29 in pairs. Circulate to observe pair work. Go over the answers as a class.
3. If necessary, review grammar chart **8.11** on page 265.

EXERCISE 30

1. Say: *Now practice negative questions.* Have students read the direction line. Go over the examples.
2. Have students complete Exercise 30 in pairs. Circulate to observe pair work. Go over the answers as a class.
3. If necessary, review grammar chart **8.11** on page 265.

To save class time, have students do half of the exercise in class and complete the other half in writing for homework. Or if students do not need speaking practice, the entire exercise may be skipped or done in writing.

EXERCISE 27 Change each request to make it more polite. Practice *may, can,* and *could + I?*

EXAMPLES **I want to use your phone.**
May I use your phone?

I want to borrow a quarter.
Could I borrow a quarter?

Answers will vary.
1. **I want to help you.**
2. **I want to close the door.**
3. **I want to leave the room.**
4. **I want to write you a check.**

EXERCISE 28 Change these commands to make them more polite. Practice *can you, could you, will you,* and *would you?*

EXAMPLES **Call the doctor for me.**
Would you call the doctor for me?

Give me a cup of coffee.
Could you give me a cup of coffee, please?

Answers will vary.
1. **Repeat the sentence.**
2. **Give me your paper.**
3. **Spell your name.**
4. **Tell me your phone number.**

EXERCISE 29 Make these sentences more polite by using *would like.*

EXAMPLE **Do you want some help?**
Would you like some help?

1. **I want to ask you a question.** *I would like to ask you a question.*
2. **The teacher wants to speak with you.** *The teacher would like to speak with you.*
3. **Do you want to try out the oven?** *Would you like to try out the oven?*
4. **Yes. I want to see if it works.** *Yes. I would like to see if it works.*

EXERCISE 30 Make each suggestion more polite by putting it in the form of a negative question.

EXAMPLES **Plug it in.**
Why don't you plug it in?

Let's eat now.
Why don't we eat now?

1. **Take a sweater.** *Why don't you take a sweater?*
2. **Let's turn off the light.** *Why don't we turn off the light?*
3. **Turn left here.** *Why don't you turn left here?*
4. **Let's leave early.** *Why don't we leave early?*

266 Lesson 8

Expansion

Exercises 27–30 Play a game. Have the class sit in a circle. Toss a ball to one student and make a request or polite command such as *Could I borrow a dollar?* The student answers, tosses the ball to another student, and asks another question with a different modal or related expression. Tell students that they can't repeat a modal or expression that the last two or three students have used. Remind students that they can use negative questions. If necessary, write all of the modals and related expressions on the board before beginning the game.

EXERCISE 31 ABOUT YOU Make a statement of preference using *would rather.*

EXAMPLE own a house / a condominium
I'd rather own a condominium (than a house).

Answers will vary.

1. live in the U.S. / in another country
2. own a condominium / rent an apartment
3. have young neighbors / old neighbors
4. have wood floors / carpeted floors
5. live in the center of the city / in a suburb
6. drive to work / take public transportation
7. pay my rent by check / cash
8. have nosy neighbors / noisy neighbors

EXERCISE 32 ABOUT YOU Ask a question of preference with the words given. Another student will answer.

EXAMPLE eat Chinese food / Italian food
A: Would you rather eat Chinese food or Italian food?
B: I'd rather eat Italian food.

1. read fact / fiction
   Would you rather read fact or fiction?
2. watch funny movies / serious movies
   Would you rather watch funny movies or serious movies?
3. listen to classical music / popular music
   Would you rather listen to classical music or popular music?
4. visit Europe / Africa
   Would you rather visit Europe or Africa?
5. own a large luxury car / a small sports car
   Would you rather own a large luxury car or a small sports car?
6. watch a soccer game / take part in a soccer game
   Would you rather watch a soccer game or take part in a soccer game?
7. write a letter / receive a letter
   Would you rather write a letter or receive a letter?
8. cook / eat in a restaurant
   Would you rather cook or eat in a restaurant?

EXERCISE 31

1. Say: *In this exercise, you're going to talk about what you prefer.* Have students read the direction line. Go over the example. Have a volunteer model #1.
2. Have students complete Exercise 31 by asking and answering questions in pairs (e.g., *Would you rather live in the U.S. or in another country?*). Circulate to observe pair work. Give help as needed.
3. If necessary, review grammar chart **8.11** on page 265.

To save class time, have students do half of the exercise in class and complete the other half in writing for homework. Or if students do not need speaking practice, the entire exercise may be skipped or done in writing.

EXERCISE 32

1. Have students read the direction line. Say: *Now you're going to be asking someone what he or she prefers.* Go over the example. Model the example with a volunteer.
2. Have students complete Exercise 32 in pairs. Tell students to take turns asking and answering each question. Circulate to observe pair work. Give help as needed.
3. If necessary, review grammar chart **8.11** on page 265.

To save class time, have students do half of the exercise in class and complete the other half in writing for homework, answering the questions themselves. Or if students do not need speaking practice, the entire exercise may be skipped or done in writing.

Expansion

Exercise 31 Do a class survey. Find out how students answered each question. Write the results for the class on the board.

Exercise 32 Create two rings of students. Have half of the students stand in an outer ring around the classroom. Have the other half stand in an inner ring, facing the outer ring. Instruct students to ask and answer questions from Exercise 32. Call out "turn" every minute or so. Students in the inner ring should move one space clockwise. Students now ask and answer questions with their new partners. Make sure students look at each other when they're talking.

EXERCISE 33

CD 3, Track 10

1. Say: *We're going to make a conversation more polite.* Have students read the direction line. Explain that this is a conversation between a seller and a buyer at a garage sale. Go over the example in the book.
2. Have students complete Exercise 33 individually. Then have students compare answers in pairs. Circulate to observe pair work. Give help as needed.
3. If necessary, review grammar chart **8.11** on page 265.

To save class time, have students do half of the exercise in class and complete the other half for homework. Or assign the entire exercise for homework.

EXERCISE 33 This is a conversation between a seller (S) and a buyer (B) at a garage sale. Make this conversation more polite by using modals and other polite expressions in place of the underlined words. Answers may vary.

Answers will vary.

S: ~~What do you want?~~ *May I help you?* *(example)*

B: I'm interested in that lamp. Show it to me. Does it work? *(1)*

S: I'll go and get a light bulb. Wait a minute. *(2)*

A few minutes later . . .

B: Plug it in. *(3)*

S: You see? It works fine.

B: How much do you want for it?

S: This is one of a pair. I have another one just like it. They're $10 each. I prefer to sell them together. *(4)*

B: Give them both to me for $15. *(5)*

S: I'll have to ask my husband.

(*A few seconds later*)

My husband says he'll sell them to you for $17.

B: Fine. I'll take them. Will you take a check?

S: I prefer to have cash. *(6)*

B: I only have five dollars on me.

S: OK. I'll take a check. Show me some identification. *(7)*

B: Here's my driver's license.

S: That's fine. Write the check to James Kucinski.

B: Spell your name for me. *(8)*

S: K-U-C-I-N-S-K-I.

268 Lesson 8

Exercise 33 Variation

To provide practice with listening skills, have students close their books and listen to the audio. Repeat the audio as needed. Ask some comprehension questions such as: *What is the buyer interested in?* (a lamp) *How many lamps does the seller have?* (two) *Does the seller want to sell only one?* (No. The seller prefers to sell both together.) Then have students open their books and complete Exercise 33.

Expansion

Exercise 33 Have students practice the conversation in pairs. Then ask volunteers to role-play the conversation in front of the class.

SUMMARY OF LESSON 8

Modals		
Modal	Example	Explanation
can	I **can** stay in this apartment until March. I **can** carry my bicycle up to my apartment. You **can't** paint the walls without the landlord's permission. **Can** I borrow your pen? **Can** you turn off the light, please?	Permission Ability/Possibility Prohibition Asking permission Request
should	You **should** be friendly with your neighbors. You **shouldn't** leave the air-conditioner on. It wastes electricity.	A good idea A bad idea
may	**May** I borrow your pen? You **may** leave the room. You **may not** talk during a test. I **may** move next month. The landlord **may** have an extra key.	Asking permission Giving permission Prohibition Future possibility Present possibility
might	I **might** move next month. The landlord **might** have an extra key.	Future possibility Present possibility
must	The landlord **must** install smoke detectors. You **must not** change the locks. Mary has a cat box. She **must** have a cat.	Rule or law: Official tone Prohibition: Official tone Conclusion/Deduction
would	**Would** you help me move?	Request
would like	I **would like** to use your phone.	Want
would rather	I **would rather** live in Florida than in Maine.	Preference
could	In my country, I **couldn't** choose my own apartment. The government gave me one. In my country, I **could** attend college for free. **Could** you help me move? **Could** I borrow your car?	Past permission Past ability Request Asking permission

Summary of Lesson 8

Modals and Related Expressions Have students cover up the example column of the chart on pages 269–270. Have students work in pairs to write a sentence for each use of the modal or expression. Then ask volunteers to write their sentences on the board. Go over the chart and review trouble spots with the class. If necessary, have students review:

8.1 Modals and Related Expressions—An Overview (p. 238)
8.2 Negatives with Modals (p. 240)
8.3 Statements and Questions with Modals (p. 241)
8.4 *Must, Have To, Have Got To* (p. 242)
8.5 Obligation with *Must* or *Be Supposed To* (p. 244)
8.6 *Can, May, Could,* and Alternate Expressions (p. 246)
8.7 *Should; Had Better* (p. 250)
8.8 Negatives of Modals (p. 253)
8.9 *Must* for Conclusions (p. 259)
8.10 *Will* and *May / Might* (p. 261)
8.11 Using Modals and Questions for Politeness (p. 265).

Editing Advice

Have students close their books. Write the example sentences without editing marks or corrections on the board. For example:

1. I must to study.
I can helping you now.
2. He cans cook.

Ask students to correct each sentence and provide a rule or an explanation for each correction. This activity can be done individually, in pairs, or as a class. After students have corrected each sentence, tell them to turn to pages 270–271. Say: *Now compare your work with the Editing Advice in the book.*

Related Expressions		
Expression	**Example**	**Explanation**
have to	She **has to** leave. He **had to** leave work early today.	Necessity Past necessity
have got to	She **has got to** see a doctor. **I've got to** move.	Necessity
not have to	You **don't have to** pay your rent with cash. You can pay by check.	No necessity
had better	You **had better** pay your rent on time, or the landlord will ask you to leave. You**'d better** get permission before changing the locks.	Warning
be supposed to	**I am supposed to** pay my rent by the fifth of the month. **We're not supposed to** have a dog here.	Reporting a rule
be able to	The teacher **is able to** use modals correctly.	Ability
be permitted to be allowed to	**We're not permitted to** park here overnight. **We're not allowed to** park here overnight.	Permission

EDITING ADVICE

1. After a modal, we use the base form.
   I must ~~to~~ study.
   I can help~~ing~~ you now.
2. A modal has no ending.
   He can~~s~~ cook.
3. We don't put two modals together. We change the second modal to another form.
   She will ~~must~~ *have to* take the test.
4. Don't forget *to* after *be permitted, be allowed, be supposed,* and *be able.*
   We're not permitted *to* talk during a test.

270 Lesson 8

5. Don't forget *be* before ***permitted to, allowed to, supposed to,*** and ***able to.***

am
I ^ not supposed to pay my rent late.

6. Use the correct word order in a question.

should I
What ~~I should~~ do about my problem?

7. Don't use *can* for past. Use *could* + a base form.

couldn't go
I ~~can't went~~ to the party last week.

8. Don't forget *would* before *rather.*

'd
I ^ rather live in Canada than in the U.S.

9. Don't forget *had* before *better.*

'd
You ^ better take a sweater. It's going to get cold.

10. Don't forget *have* before *got to.*

've
It's late. I ^ got to go.

11. Don't use *maybe* before a verb.

may
It ~~maybe will~~ rain later.

Lesson 8 Test/Review

For additional practice, review, and assessment materials, see Assessment CD-ROM with *ExamView Pro*, *More Grammar Practice* Workbook 2, Interactive CD-ROM, and Web site http://elt.thomson.com/gic

PART 1

1. Part 1 may be used as an in-class test to assess student performance, in addition to the Assessment CD-ROM with *ExamView Pro*. Have students read the direction line. Ask: *Do all sentences have a mistake?* (no) Go over the examples. Collect for assessment.
2. If necessary, have students review: **Lesson 8.**

PART 2

1. Part 2 may also be used as an in-class test to assess student performance, in addition to the Assessment CD-ROM with *ExamView Pro*. Have students read the direction line. Explain that this is a conversation between two friends. Collect for assessment.
2. If necessary, have students review: **Lesson 8.**

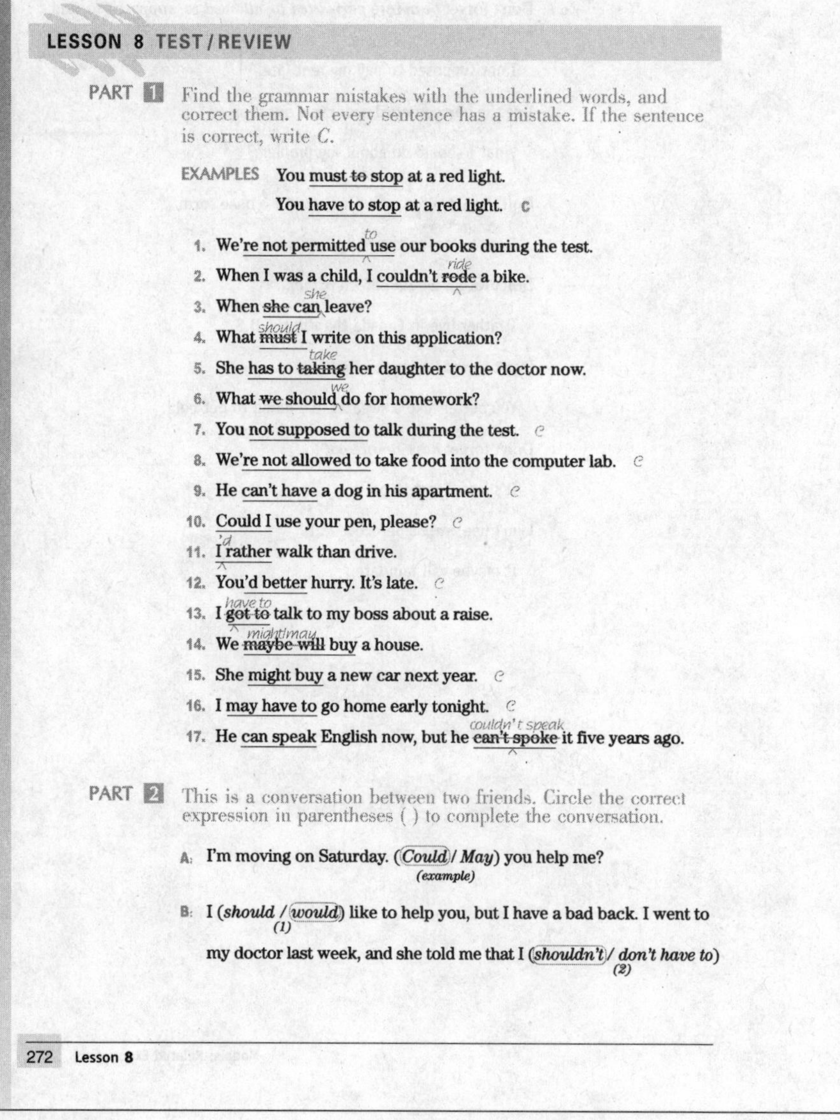

LESSON 8 TEST / REVIEW

PART 1 Find the grammar mistakes with the underlined words, and correct them. Not every sentence has a mistake. If the sentence is correct, write *C*.

EXAMPLES You must ~~to~~ stop at a red light.
You have to stop at a red light. C

1. We're not permitted use our books during the test.
2. When I was a child, I couldn't rode a bike.
3. When she can leave?
4. What must I write on this application?
5. She has to taking her daughter to the doctor now.
6. What we should do for homework?
7. You not supposed to talk during the test.
8. We're not allowed to take food into the computer lab.
9. He can't have a dog in his apartment.
10. Could I use your pen, please?
11. I rather walk than drive.
12. You'd better hurry. It's late.
13. I got to talk to my boss about a raise.
14. We maybe will buy a house.
15. She might buy a new car next year.
16. I may have to go home early tonight.
17. He can speak English now, but he can't spoke it five years ago.

PART 2 This is a conversation between two friends. Circle the correct expression in parentheses ( ) to complete the conversation.

A: I'm moving on Saturday. (*Could* / *May*) you help me? *(example)*

B: I (*should* / *would*) *(1)* like to help you, but I have a bad back. I went to my doctor last week, and she told me that I (*shouldn't* / *don't have to*) *(2)*

272 Lesson 8

Lesson Review

To use Part 1 as a review, assign it as homework or use it as an in-class activity to be completed individually or in pairs. Check answers and review errors as a class. Reteach grammar points that students haven't mastered. Then student learning may be assessed using a test generated from the Assessment CD-ROM with *ExamView Pro*.

lift anything heavy for a while. (Can / *Would*) I help you any other
(3)
way besides moving?

A: Yes. I don't have enough boxes. (*Should* / Would) you help me find some?
(4)

B: Sure. I (have to / *must*) go shopping this afternoon. I'll pick up some boxes while I'm at the supermarket.
(5)

A: Boxes can be heavy. You (*would* / had) better not lift them yourself.
(6)

B: Don't worry. I'll have someone put them in my car for me.

A: Thanks. I don't have a free minute. I (couldn't go / *can't went*) to class all last week. There's so much to do.
(7)

B: I know what you mean. You (*might* / must) be tired.
(8)

A: I am. I have another favor to ask. (Can / *Would*) I borrow your van on Saturday?
(9)

B: I (*should* / have to) work on Saturday. How about Sunday? I
(10)
(*must not* / don't have to) work on Sunday.
(11)

A: That's impossible. I ('ve got to / *should*) move out on Saturday. The new tenants are moving in Sunday morning.
(12)

B: Let me ask my brother. He has a van too. He (*must* / might) be able to let you use his van. He (has to / *should*) work Saturday too, but only for half a day.
(13) (14)

A: Thanks. I'd appreciate it if you could ask him.

B: Why are you moving? You have a great apartment.

A: We decided to move to the suburbs. It's quieter there. And I want to have a dog. I (*shouldn't* / 'm not supposed to) have a dog in my present apartment. But my new landlord says I (*might* / may) have a dog.
(15) (16)

B: I (*had* / would) rather have a cat. They're easier to take care of.
(17)

Lesson Review

To use Part 2 as a review, assign it as homework or use it as an in-class activity to be completed individually or in pairs. Check answers and review errors as a class. Reteach grammar points that students haven't mastered. Then student learning may be assessed using a test generated from the Assessment CD-ROM with *ExamView Pro*.

Expansion Activities

These expansion activities provide opportunities for students to interact with one another and further develop their speaking and writing skills. Encourage students to use grammar from this lesson whenever possible.

To save class time, assign parts of the activities as homework. Then use class time for interaction and communication. If students do not need additional speaking practice, some of the activities may be assigned as writing activities for homework or skipped altogether.

CLASSROOM ACTIVITIES

1. If the class is large, do this activity in groups. Ask volunteers to present one of the problems to the class or group or to create their own problems.

EXPANSION ACTIVITIES

Classroom Activities

1. A student will read one of the following problems out loud to the class, pretending that this is his or her problem. Other students will ask for more information and give advice about this problem.

EXAMPLE My mother–in–law comes to visit all the time. When she's here, she always criticizes everything we do. I told my wife that I don't want her here, but she says, "It's my mother, and I want her here." What should I do?

A: How long does she usually stay?
B: She might stay for about two weeks or longer.
C: How does she criticize you? What does she say?
B: She says I should help my wife more.
D: Well, I agree with her. You should help with house work.
B: My children aren't allowed to watch TV after 8 o'clock. But my mother–in–law lets them watch TV as long as they want.
E: You'd better have a talk with her and tell her your rules.

Problem 1. My mother is 80 years old, and she lives with us. It's very hard on my family to take care of her. We'd like to put her in a nursing home, where she can get better care. Mother refuses to go. What can we do?

Problem 2. I have a nice one-bedroom apartment with a beautiful view of a park and a lake. I live with my wife and one child. My friends from out of town often come to visit and want to stay at my apartment. In the last year, ten people came to visit us. I like to have visitors, but sometimes they stay for weeks. It's hard on my family with such a small apartment. What should I tell my friends when they want to visit?

Problem 3. My upstairs neighbors make noise all the time. I can't sleep at night. I asked them three times to be quieter, and each time they said they would. But the noise still continues. What should I do?

Write your own problem to present to the class. It can be real or imaginary. (Suggestions: a problem with a neighbor, your landlord, a teacher or class, a service you are dissatisfied with)

____
____
____

274 Lesson 8

2. Circle a game you like from the following list. Find a partner who also likes this game. Write a list of some of the rules of this game. Tell what you *can, cannot, should, have to,* and *must not* do.

chess	tennis	football	poker	other ______
checkers	baseball	soccer	volleyball	

EXAMPLE checkers

You have to move the pieces on a diagonal. You can only move in one direction until you get a king. Then you can move in two directions.

______

______

______

3. Many people get vanity license plates that tell something about their professions, hobbies, or families. Often words are abbreviated: M = am, U = you, 4 = for, 8 = the "ate" sound. Words are often missing vowels. If you see the following license plates, what conclusion can you make about the owner? You may work with a partner and get help from the teacher.

CALIFORNIA
EYE DOC
The Golden State

EXAMPLE EYE DOC *The owner must be an eye doctor.*

1. I TCH ENGLSH *The owner must be an English teacher.*
2. I LV CARS *The owner must love cars.*
3. I M GRANDMA *The owner must be a grandmother.*
4. MUSC LVR *The owner must love music.*
5. I LV DGS *The owner must love dogs.*
6. TENNIS GR8 *The owner must love tennis.*
7. I SK8 *The owner must be a skater.*
8. CRPNTR *The owner must be a carpenter.*
9. BSY MOM *The owner must be a busy mom.*
10. SHY GUY *The owner must be shy.*
11. DAD OF TWO *The owner must have two kids.*
12. RMNTIC GAL *The owner must be a romantic girl.*
13. NO TIME 4 U *The owner must be very busy.*
14. CITY GAL *The owner must be a girl who lives in the city.*
15. LDY DOC *The owner must be a woman doctor.*
16. LUV GLF *The owner must be a golf player.*
17. MXCAN GUY *The owner must be a Mexican man.*
18. I M GD COOK *The owner must be a good cook.*

CLASSROOM ACTIVITIES (*cont.*)

2. Have students mingle around the classroom asking questions to find a partner to work with (e.g., *Do you like to play poker? Do you know the rules?*). Have students write down the rules. If possible, have students join with another pair who wrote about the same game to compare rules.
3. Have students work with a partner to guess the meaning of the license plates.

Expansion

Classroom Activities For Activity 3, have students write three to five new vanity license plates. Ask students to have their partners guess what the meaning is and who the owner must be or must like.

CLASSROOM ACTIVITIES (*cont.*)

4. Put students from the same country in pairs. Have them present information about laws in their countries and how they compare to laws in the U.S. to the class.

TALK ABOUT IT

1. Put students in groups to discuss the procedures for getting a driver's license in this state. How do the requirements compare with getting a license in another state or country?
2. Ask students to tell their groups how they found the apartment they're living in now.

WRITE ABOUT IT

1. Tell students to make a list of the rules in their apartment buildings before they begin writing their paragraphs.
2. Tell students to make a list of the rules in this school before they begin writing their paragraphs.
3. Have students write a list of steps a student must take to register for classes at the school. Then ask them to write an e-mail to a friend interested in taking classes here.

OUTSIDE ACTIVITIES

1. Have students find tag sales that will be taking place in their neighborhoods over the weekend.
2. Ask students if they ever read advice columns in newspapers and magazines. Tell them to read two letters from a column, to circle the modals and expressions, and to say if they agree or disagree with the advice.
3. If possible, have students bring their leases to class. Ask students to explain the rules of their apartment buildings to a partner. Ask: *Are there any differences? Who has a better lease?*

INTERNET ACTIVITIES

Remind students that if they don't have Internet access, they can use Internet facilities at a public library, or they can use traditional research methods to find out information, including looking at encyclopedias, magazines, books, journals, and newspapers.

19. ALWAYS L8 *The owner must always be late.*
20. WE DANCE *The owner must be dancers.*

4. Work with a partner from your own country, if possible. Talk about some laws in your country that are different from laws in the United States. Present this information to the class.

EXAMPLE Citizens must vote in my country. In the U.S., they don't have to vote.

People are supposed to carry identification papers at all times. In the U.S., people don't have to carry identification papers.

In my country, citizens must not own a gun.

Talk About it

1. Compare getting a driver's license here with getting a driver's license in another country or state. Are the requirements the same?
2. How did you find your apartment?

Write About it

1. Write a short composition comparing rules in an apartment in this city with rules in an apartment in your hometown or native country.
2. Write about the differences between rules at this school and rules at another school you attended. Are students allowed to do things here that they can't do in another school?
3. Find out what a student has to do to register for the first time at this school. You may want to visit the registrar's office to interview a worker there. Write a short composition explaining to a new student the steps for admission and registration.

Outside Activitis

1. Look at the Sunday newspaper for notices about garage sales or apartment sales. What kind of items are going to be sold? If you have time, go to a sale. Report about your experience to the class.
2. Get a newspaper. Look for the advice column. Read the problems and the advice. Circle the modals. Do you agree with the advice?
3. Look at your lease. Can you understand what the rules are in your apartment?

Internet Activities

1. Try to find information online about tenants' rights in the city where you live. Circle the modals.
2. Find a phone directory online. Look up the names and addresses of moving companies in your city. Call a company to find out the price of a move.
3. Find apartments for rent online. Print a page. Discuss with your classmates the price of apartments and what is included.

Additional Activities at http://elt.thomson.com/gic

Write About it Variation

Item 3 Have students create a brochure for new students. Have them write down the procedure for registering, along with other rules, regulations, and tips that might be useful for new students. Display the brochures in the classroom.

Have students exchange first drafts with a partner. Ask students to help their partners edit their drafts. Refer students to the Editing Advice on pages 270–271.

LESSON

9

GRAMMAR

The Present Perfect

The Present Perfect Continuous[1]

CONTEXT: Searching the Web

Google

Genealogy

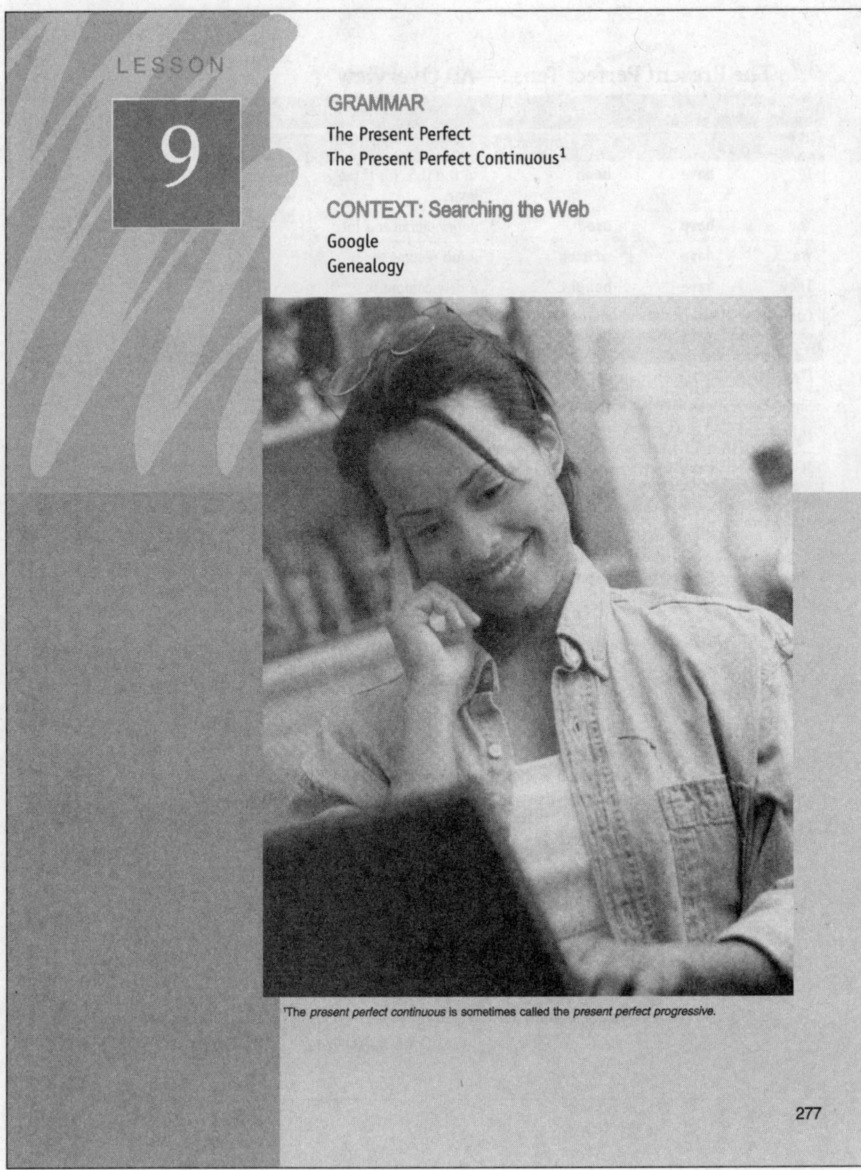

[1]The present perfect continuous is sometimes called the present perfect progressive.

277

Lesson | 9

Lesson Overview

GRAMMAR

1. Briefly review what students learned in the last lesson. Ask: *What did we study in Lesson 8?* (modals and related expressions)
2. Ask: *What are we going to study in this lesson?* (the present perfect and the present perfect continuous) *Can anyone give me an example of the present perfect?* (e.g., *I have seen* Star Wars *ten times.*) Have students give examples. Write the examples on the board. Then ask for examples of the present perfect continuous.

CONTEXT

1. Ask: *What will we learn about in this lesson?* (searching the Web) Activate students' prior knowledge. Ask: *Do you use the Internet a lot? What do you use it for?*
2. Have students share their knowledge and personal experiences.

To save class time, have students do the Test/Review at the end of the lesson, or administer a lesson test generated from the Assessment CD-ROM with *ExamView® Pro.* Skip sections of the lesson that students have already mastered. You may also assign some sections for self-study for extra credit.

Expansion

Theme The topic for this lesson can be enhanced with the following ideas:

1. A family tree
2. A scrapbook or family album of several generations

9.1 | The Present Perfect Tense—An Overview

1. Have students look at grammar chart **9.1** on page 278. Write on the board: have / has + *past participle.* Say: *We form the present perfect tense for* I, you, we, they, *and plural nouns with the auxiliary* have *plus the past participle. For* he, she, it, *and singular nouns, we use* has *plus the past participle.* Review the example sentences in the chart.
2. Say: *We can also use the present perfect with* there. *If a plural noun follows* there, *then we use* have. *If a singular noun follows* there, *then we use* has. Go over the examples.

Google (Reading)

1. Have students look at the photo. Ask: *Do you use Google? What is it?* (an Internet search engine) *Who do you think these two men are?* (the two founders of Google) For those who are not familiar with Google, point to the image of the Web page on page 279.
2. Have students look at the title of the reading. Ask: *What is the reading about?* Have students use the title and photo to make predictions about the reading.
3. Preteach any vocabulary words your students may not know, such as *expert, banner,* and *modestly.*

BEFORE YOU READ

1. Have students discuss the questions in pairs.
2. Ask for a few volunteers to share their answers with the class.

To save class time, skip "Before You Read" or have students prepare answers for homework ahead of time.

9.1 | The Present Perfect Tense—An Overview

We form the present perfect with *have* or *has* + the past participle.

Subject	*have*	Past Participle	Complement	Explanation
I	**have**	**been**	in the U.S. for three years.	Use *have* with *I, you, we, they,* and plural nouns.
You	**have**	**used**	your computer a lot.	
We	**have**	**written**	a job résumé.	
They	**have**	**bought**	a new computer.	
Computers	**have**	**changed**	the world.	
Subject	***has***	**Past Participle**	**Complement**	**Explanation**
My sister	**has**	**gotten**	her degree.	Use *has* with *he, she, it,* and singular nouns.
She	**has**	**found**	a job as a programmer.	
My father	**has**	**helped**	me.	
It	**has**	**rained**	a lot this month.	
There	***has/have***	***been***	**Complement**	**Explanation**
There	**has**	**been**	a problem with my computer.	After *there,* we use *has* or *have,* depending on the noun that follows. Use *has* with a singular noun. Use *have* with a plural noun.
There	**have**	**been**	many changes in the world.	

GOOGLE

Before You Read

1. Do you surf the Internet a lot? Why?
2. What search engine do you usually use?

Larry Page and Sergey Brin

278 Lesson 9

Grammar Variation

Write the following sentences on the board:
I have been in the U.S. for three years.
We have written a job résumé.
She has found a job as a programmer.
It has rained a lot this month.
There has been a problem with my computer all day.
Say: *Here are some sentences in the present perfect tense. Can you tell me the rules for forming this tense?* Have volunteers explain the rules for forming the present perfect.

 Read the following article. Pay special attention to the present perfect tense.

Since its start in 1998, Google **has become** one of the most popular search engines. It **has grown** from a research project in the dormitory room of two college students to a business that now employs approximately 1,000 people.

Google's founders, Larry Page and Sergey Brin, met in 1995 when they were in their 20s and graduate students in computer science at Stanford University in California. They realized that Internet search was a very important field and began working together to make searching easier. Both Page and Brin left their studies at Stanford to work on their project. Interestingly, they **have** never **returned** to finish their degrees.

Brin was born in Russia, but he **has lived** in the U.S. since he was five years old. His father was a mathematician in Russia. Page, whose parents were computer experts, **has been** interested in computers since he was six years old.

When Google started in 1998, it did 10,000 searches a day. Today it does 200 million searches a day in 90 languages. It indexes[2] three billion Web pages.

How is Google different from other search engines? **Have** you ever **noticed** how many ads and banners there are on other search engines? News, sports scores, stock prices, links for shopping, mortgage rates, and more fill other search engines. Brin and Page wanted a clean home page. They believed that people come to the Internet to search for specific information, not to be hit with a lot of unwanted data. The success of Google over its rivals[3] **has proved** that this is true.

Over the past few years, Google **has added** new features to its Web site: Google Images, where you can type in a word and get thousands of pictures; Google News, which takes you to today's news; Froogle, which takes you to a shopping site; and more. But one thing **hasn't changed:** the clean opening page that Google offers its users.

In 2003, *Fortune* magazine ranked Page and Brin among the top ten richest people under 30. So far these two men **haven't changed** their lifestyles very much. They continue to live modestly.

Did You Know?
The word "Google" started as a noun, the company's name. Today people use it as a verb: "I'm going to google the Civil War to get more information about it."

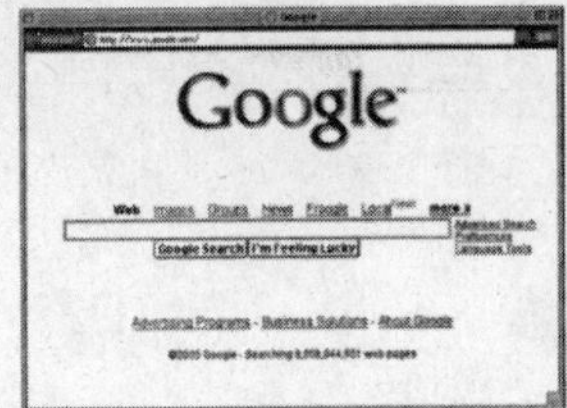

[2] *To index* means to sort, organize, and categorize information.
[3] *Rivals* are competitors.

Reading CD 3, Track 11

1. Have students first read the text silently. Tell them to pay special attention to the present perfect tense. Then play the audio and have students read along silently.
2. Check students' comprehension. Ask questions such as: *When did Page and Brin begin their business?* (when they were graduate students in California) *Where they both born in the U.S.?* (No. Brin was born in Russia.) *What's different about the look of Google compared to the look of other search sites.* (It's very clean. There are no advertisements.)

To save class time, have students do the reading for homework ahead of time.

DID YOU KNOW?

The name of the search engine Google was derived from the word *googol*, which is the number 1 followed by 100 zeroes. The word *googol* was coined by a nine-year-old boy—the nephew of an important American mathematician—Edward Kasner.

Reading Variation

To practice listening skills, have students first listen to the audio alone. Ask a few comprehension questions. Repeat the audio if necessary. Then have them open their books and read along as they listen to the audio.

Reading Glossary

banner: a graphic on a Web page that's often used as an advertisement
expert: a master at something; an authority
modest: describing a person who does not brag or boast

EXERCISE 1

1. Have students read the direction line. Go over the example.
2. Have students complete Exercise 1 individually. Go over the answers as a class.
3. If necessary, review grammar chart **9.1** on page 278.

9.2 | The Past Participle

1. Have students cover up grammar chart **9.2.** Write the following list of past forms and past participles on the board:

Past Form	*Past Participle*
walked	*walked*
talked	*talked*
studied	*studied*
cooked	*cooked*

Say: *These are regular verbs. What do you notice about the past form and the past participle?* (They're the same.)

2. Have students look at grammar chart **9.2.** Say: *Irregular verbs have irregular past participles. These participles have to be memorized. Some are the same as the past tense form, and some are completely different. Look at grammar chart 9.2 on page 280.*

EXERCISE 1 Underline the present perfect tense in each sentence. Then tell if the sentence is true or false.

EXAMPLE Google has become the number one search engine. T

1. Google has grown over the years. T
2. Sergey Brin has lived in the U.S. all his life. F
3. Larry Page and Sergey Brin have known each other since they were children. F
4. Larry Page has been interested in computers since he was a child. T
5. Brin and Page have returned to college to finish their degrees. F
6. Since they became rich, Brin and Page have changed their lifestyles. F
7. The word "Google" has become a verb. T

9.2 | The Past Participle

Forms			Explanation
Regular Verbs			The past participle of regular verbs ends in *-ed*. The past form and the past participle for regular verbs are the same.
Base Form	Past Form	Past Participle	
work	worked	**worked**	
improve	improved	**improved**	
Irregular Verbs			The past participle of irregular verbs is sometimes the same as the past form and sometimes different from it. For an alphabetical list of irregular past tenses and past participles, see Appendix M.
Base Form	Past Form	Past Participle	
have	had	**had** (*same as past*)	
write	wrote	**written** (*different from past*)	

9.3 | Irregular Past Participle Forms of Verbs[4]

Base Form	Past Form	Past Participle
become come run	became came ran	become come run
blow draw fly grow know throw	blew drew flew grew knew threw	blown drawn flown grown known thrown
swear tear wear	swore tore wore	sworn torn worn
break choose freeze speak steal	broke chose froze spoke stole	broken chosen frozen spoken stolen
begin drink ring sing sink swim	began drank rang sang sank swam	begun drunk rung sung sunk swum
arise bite drive ride rise write	arose bit drove rode rose wrote	arisen bitten driven ridden risen written
be eat fall forgive give mistake see shake take	was/were ate fell forgave gave mistook saw shook took	been eaten fallen forgiven given mistaken seen shaken taken
do forget get go lie prove show	did forgot got went lay proved showed	done forgotten gotten gone lain proven (or proved) shown (or showed)

[4] For an alphabetical listing of irregular past tenses and past participles, see Appendix M.

9.3 | Irregular Past Participle Forms of Verbs

1. Go over the list of verbs on the chart. Model the pronunciation of the past participles. Tell students that an alphabetical list can be found in Appendix M.
2. Have students try to find spelling patterns. Give them a hint. Say: *Sometimes the past participle is more closely related to the base form, and sometimes it resembles the past form. Sometimes a vowel is changed or a consonant added.* Review students' findings, and write them on the board.
3. There are eight categories in the irregular verbs chart:
   1. Past participle = base form
   2. Add *-n* to the base form (for *fly*, change *y* to *o* and add *w*)
   3. Remove final *-e*, add *-n* to the past form
   4. Add *-n* to the past form
   5. Change vowel from *a* in past form to *u*
   6. Add *-n* to base form, double consonant if last vowel sound is /d/ or /t/
   7. Add *-en* to base form
   8. Miscellaneous changes

Expansion

Grammar Have students go through the reading and circle the irregular past participles.

EXERCISE 2

1. Have students read the direction line. Go over the example.
2. Have students complete Exercise 2 individually. Go over the answers as a class.
3. If necessary, review grammar chart **9.3** on page 281.

9.4 | The Present Perfect—Contractions, Negatives

1. Have students cover up grammar chart **9.4**. Write the following sentences from the chart on the board:
   I've had a lot of experience with computers.
   He's been interested in computers since he was a child.
   I haven't studied programming.
   Brin hasn't finished his degree.
   Say: *Explain how to form the affirmative and negative contractions with the present perfect.* Have volunteers explain.
2. Go over the examples and explanations in the chart. Point out that most singular nouns can contract with *has*.
3. Direct students to the Language Note. Explain that an *'s* can mean *has* or *is*. Say: *The word following the contraction will tell you what the contraction means.* Go over the examples. Explain that in writing, we don't contract plural nouns with *have*. However, native speakers might do it in speech.

EXERCISE 2 Write the past participle of these verbs.

EXAMPLE eat *eaten*

1. go *gone*	16. come *come*
2. see *seen*	17. break *broken*
3. look *looked*	18. wear *worn*
4. study *studied*	19. choose *chosen*
5. bring *brought*	20. drive *driven*
6. take *taken*	21. write *written*
7. say *said*	22. put *put*
8. be *been*	23. begin *begun*
9. find *found*	24. want *wanted*
10. leave *left*	25. get *gotten*
11. live *lived*	26. fly *flown*
12. know *known*	27. sit *sat*
13. like *liked*	28. drink *drunk*
14. fall *fallen*	29. grow *grown*
15. feel *felt*	30. give *given*

9.4 | The Present Perfect—Contractions, Negatives

For an affirmative statement, we can make a contraction with the subject pronoun. For a negative statement, we can make a contraction using *have/has + n't*.

Examples	Explanation
I've had a lot of experience with computers. **We've** read the story about Google. **He's** been interested in computers since he was a child. **There's** been an increase in searching over the years.	We can make a contraction with subject pronouns and *have* or *has*. I have = I've He has = He's You have = You've She has = She's We have = We've It has = It's They have = They've There has = There's
Larry's lived in the U.S. all his life. **Sergey's** been in the U.S. since he was five years old.	Most singular nouns can contract with *has*.
I **haven't** studied programming. Brin **hasn't** finished his degree.	Negative contractions: *have not = haven't* *has not = hasn't*

Language Note:
The *'s* in *he's, she's, it's,* and *there's* can mean *has* or *is*. The word following the contraction will tell you what the contraction means.
He's working. = He *is* working.
He's worked. = He ***has*** worked.

Expansion

Exercise 2 Have students practice the pronunciation of each past participle in pairs. Circulate to observe pronunciation. Give help as needed.

EXERCISE 3 Fill in the blanks to form the present perfect. Make a contraction, if possible.

EXAMPLE You 've bought a new computer.

1. I 've learned a lot about computers.
2. We 've read the story about Google.
3. Larry has known Sergey since they were at Stanford University.
4. They (not) haven't known each other since they were children.
5. It 's been easy for me to learn about computers.
6. You 've used the Internet many times.
7. Larry and Sergey (not) haven't finished their degrees.

9.5 | Adding an Adverb

Subject	has/ have	Adverb	Past Participle	Complement	Explanation
Page and Brin	**have**	never	**finished**	their degrees.	You can put an adverb between the auxiliary verb (*have/has*) and the past participle.
They	**have**	already*	**made**	a lot of money.	
They	**have**	even	**become**	billionaires in their 30s.	
Larry Page	**has**	always	**been**	interested in computers.	
You	**have**	probably	**used**	a search engine.	

Language Note:
Already frequently comes at the end of the verb phrase.
They have made a lot of money **already.**

EXERCISE 4 Add the word in parentheses ( ) to the sentence.

EXAMPLE You have gotten an e-mail account. (probably)
You have probably gotten an e-mail account.

1. The teacher has given a test on this lesson. (not)
The teacher has not given a test on this lesson.
2. We have heard of Page and Brin. (never)
We have never heard of Page and Brin.

EXERCISE 3

1. Have students read the direction line. Go over the example. Remind students to use contractions whenever possible.
2. Have students complete Exercise 3 individually. Then go over the answers as a class.
3. If necessary, review grammar chart **9.4** on page 282.

9.5 | Adding an Adverb

1. Have students cover up grammar chart **9.5.** Then have students go back to the reading on page 279. Say: ***Find where adverbs have been used with the present perfect*** (*They have never returned . . .; Have you ever noticed . . .*). Then ask: ***Where do you put the adverb?*** (between *have/has* and the past participle)
2. Then have students look at grammar chart **9.5.** Go over the examples.
3. Direct students to the Language Note. Explain that *already* often comes at the end of the verb phrase.

EXERCISE 4

1. Have students read the direction line. Go over the example. Ask: ***What kind of word is in the parentheses?*** (an adverb)
2. Have students complete Exercise 4 individually. Then have students compare answers in pairs. Circulate to observe pair work. Give help as needed.
3. If necessary, review grammar chart **9.5** on page 283.

9.6 | The Present Perfect—Statements and Questions

1. Have students cover up grammar chart **9.6.** Write the following on the board:
   Larry has lived in the U.S. all his life.
   Say: *Write a yes/no question, a short answer, and then ask a question with* how long.
   Then write the following on the board:
   They haven't finished their degrees.
   Say: *Write a negative question based on this statement.*
2. Then have students look at grammar chart **9.6.** Say: *Compare your work with the chart.* Go over the examples and explanations.
3. Direct students to the Language Note. Point out that we can't make a contraction with a short affirmative answer. Go over the example.

EXERCISE 5

1. Say: *Ask a question about the statement.* Have students read the direction line. Go over the example. Have a volunteer do #1.
2. Have students complete Exercise 5 individually. Then have students compare answers in pairs. Circulate to observe pair work. Give help as needed.
3. If necessary, review grammar chart **9.6** on page 284.

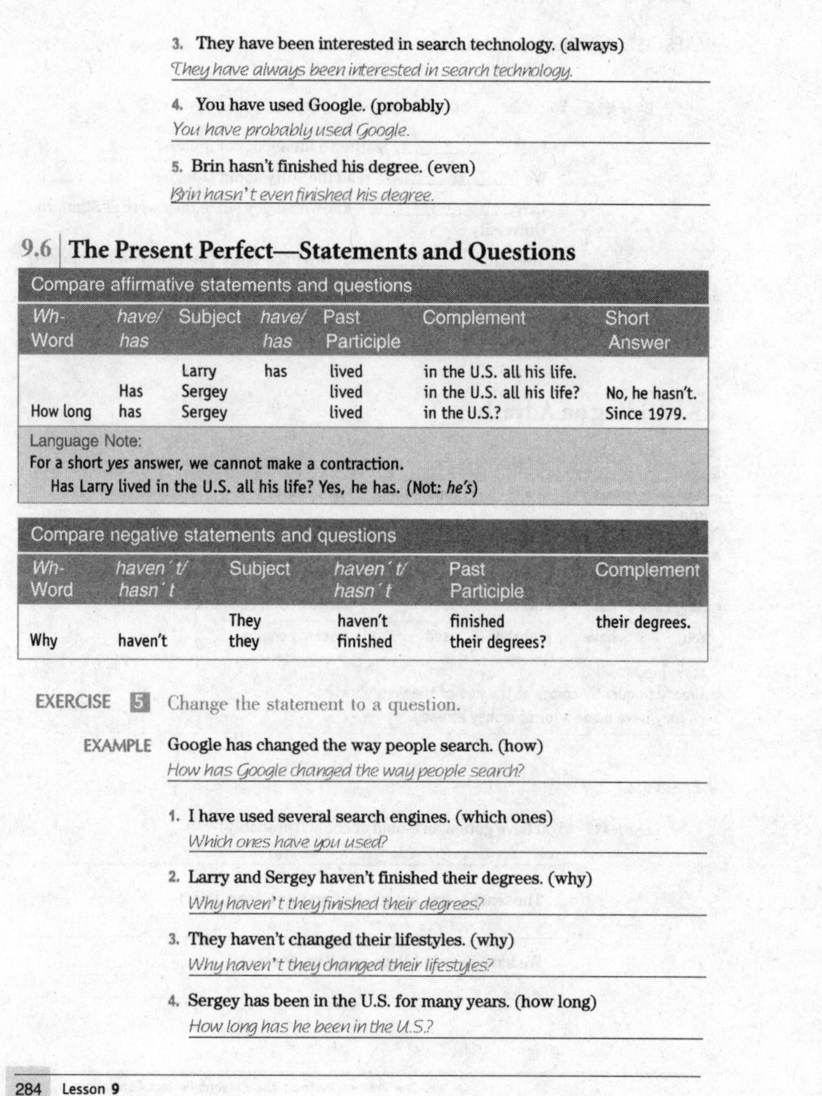

3. They have been interested in search technology. (always)
They have always been interested in search technology.

4. You have used Google. (probably)
You have probably used Google.

5. Brin hasn't finished his degree. (even)
Brin hasn't even finished his degree.

9.6 | The Present Perfect—Statements and Questions

Compare affirmative statements and questions

Wh- Word	*have/ has*	Subject	*have/ has*	Past Participle	Complement	Short Answer
		Larry	has	lived	in the U.S. all his life.	
	Has	Sergey		lived	in the U.S. all his life?	No, he hasn't.
How long	has	Sergey		lived	in the U.S.?	Since 1979.

Language Note:
For a short *yes* answer, we cannot make a contraction.
Has Larry lived in the U.S. all his life? Yes, he has. (Not: *he's*)

Compare negative statements and questions

Wh- Word	*haven't/ hasn't*	Subject	*haven't/ hasn't*	Past Participle	Complement
		They	haven't	finished	their degrees.
Why	haven't	they	finished	their degrees?	

EXERCISE 5 Change the statement to a question.

EXAMPLE Google has changed the way people search. (how)
How has Google changed the way people search?

1. I have used several search engines. (which ones)
Which ones have you used?
2. Larry and Sergey haven't finished their degrees. (why)
Why haven't they finished their degrees?
3. They haven't changed their lifestyles. (why)
Why haven't they changed their lifestyles?
4. Sergey has been in the U.S. for many years. (how long)
How long has he been in the U.S.?

284 Lesson 9

Expansion

Exercise 4 Have students write three to five sentences about their experiences with the Internet (e.g., *I have never used Google.*).

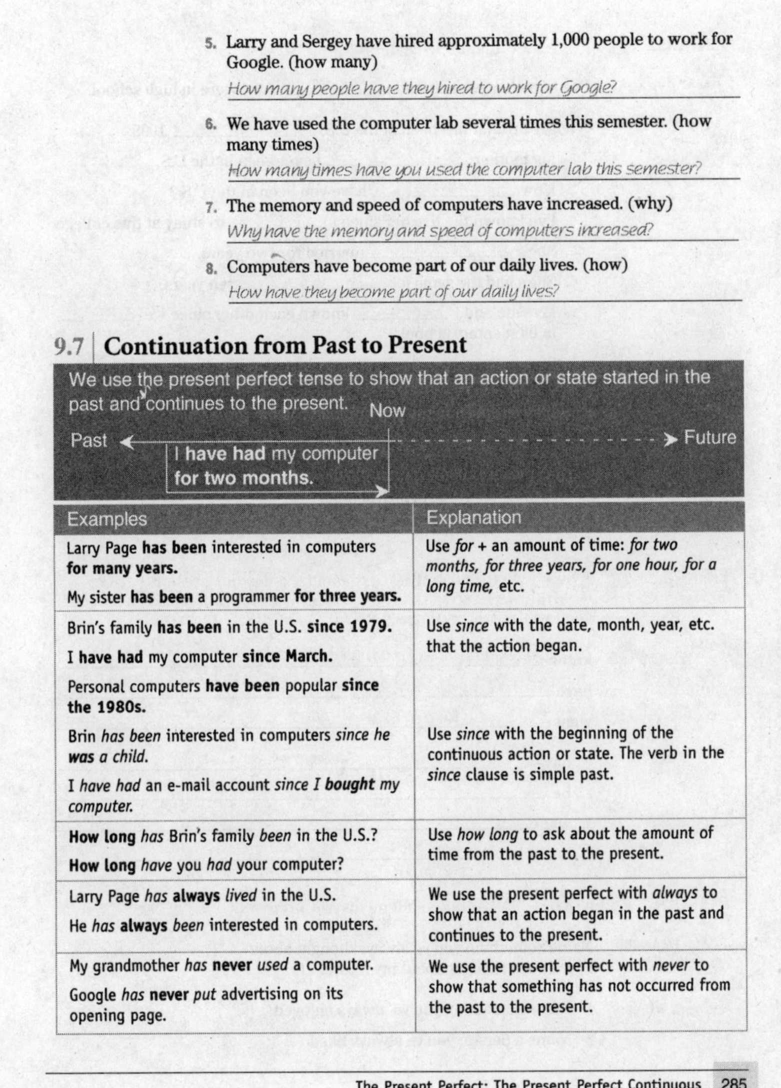

5. Larry and Sergey have hired approximately 1,000 people to work for Google. (how many)
   How many people have they hired to work for Google?

6. We have used the computer lab several times this semester. (how many times)
   How many times have you used the computer lab this semester?

7. The memory and speed of computers have increased. (why)
   Why have the memory and speed of computers increased?

8. Computers have become part of our daily lives. (how)
   How have they become part of our daily lives?

9.7 | Continuation from Past to Present

We use the present perfect tense to show that an action or state started in the past and continues to the present.

Now

Past ← **I have had** my computer **for two months.** → Future

Examples	Explanation
Larry Page **has been** interested in computers **for many years.** My sister **has been** a programmer **for three years.**	Use *for* + an amount of time: *for two months, for three years, for one hour, for a long time,* etc.
Brin's family **has been** in the U.S. **since 1979.** I **have had** my computer **since March.** Personal computers **have been** popular **since the 1980s.**	Use *since* with the date, month, year, etc. that the action began.
Brin *has been* interested in computers *since he was a child.* I *have had* an e-mail account *since I* **bought** my computer.	Use *since* with the beginning of the continuous action or state. The verb in the *since* clause is simple past.
How long *has* Brin's family *been* in the U.S.? **How long** *have* you *had* your computer?	Use *how long* to ask about the amount of time from the past to the present.
Larry Page *has* **always** *lived* in the U.S. He *has* **always** *been* interested in computers.	We use the present perfect with *always* to show that an action began in the past and continues to the present.
My grandmother *has* **never** *used* a computer. Google *has* **never** *put* advertising on its opening page.	We use the present perfect with *never* to show that something has not occurred from the past to the present.

9.7 | Continuation from Past to Present

1. Have students cover up grammar chart **9.7.** Write the following sentence from the reading on the board: *Since its start in 1998, Google has become one of the most popular search engines.*
   Ask: *When did Google start to become popular?* (in 1998) *Correct. In the past. Is Google still popular?* (yes) *So, today, in the present it is still popular.*
2. Have students look at grammar chart **9.7.** Say: *We use the present perfect tense to show that an action or a state started in the past and continues to the present.* Point out the timeline.
3. Go over the examples and explanations in the chart. Explain the use of the following with the present perfect:
   a. *for* + an amount of time
   b. *since* with dates
   c. *since* with a verb
   d. *how long*
   e. *always*
   f. *never*

Expansion

Grammar Have students write statements and questions about themselves and their families using *for, since, how long, always,* and *never.*

EXERCISE 6

1. Have students read the direction line. Go over the example.
2. Have students complete Exercise 6 individually. Then go over the answers with the class.
3. If necessary, review grammar chart **9.7** on page 285.

EXERCISE 7

1. Say: *In this exercise, you're going to write true statements about yourselves.* Have students read the direction line. Go over the examples. Model the examples for the class.
2. Have students complete Exercise 7 individually. Then have students compare answers in pairs. Circulate to observe pair work. Give help as needed.
3. If necessary, review grammar chart **9.7** on page 285.

To save class time, have students do the exercise for homework.

EXERCISE 8

1. Have students read the direction line. Go over the example in the book. Model the example for the class.
2. Have students complete Exercise 8 in pairs. Circulate to observe pair work. Give help as needed.
3. If necessary, review grammar chart **9.7** on page 285.

EXERCISE 6 Fill in the blanks with the missing words.

EXAMPLE I've known my best friend ___since___ we were in high school.

1. My brother has been in the U.S. ___since___ 1998.
2. My mother ___has___ never been in the U.S.
3. How ___long___ have you been in the U.S.?
4. I've known the teacher since I ___began___ to study at this college.
5. She's ___been___ married for two years.
6. She's had the same job ___for___ ten years.
7. My wife and I ___have___ known each other since we ___were___ in elementary school.
8. She ___'s___ been a student at this college ___since___ September.
9. I've had my car for three years. ___How___ long have you ___had___ your car?
10. I'm interested in art. I ___'ve___ ___been___ interested in art since I was in high school.
11. ___I've___ always wanted to have my own business.

EXERCISE 7 ABOUT YOU Write **true** statements using the present perfect with the words given and for, *since, always,* or *never.* Share your sentences with the class.

EXAMPLES know ___My parents have known each other for over 40 years.___

have ___I've had my car since 2002.___

want ___I've always wanted to learn English.___

1. have ___Answers will vary.___
2. be ______
3. want ______
4. know ______

EXERCISE 8 ABOUT YOU Make statements with *always.*

EXAMPLE Name something you've always thought about.
I've always thought about my future.

Answers will vary.
1. Name something you've always enjoyed.
2. Name a person you've always liked.

Expansion

Exercise 7 Ask volunteers to share what they wrote in Exercise 7.

3. Name something you've always wanted to do.
4. Name something you've always wanted to have.
5. Name something you've always been interested in.

EXERCISE 9 ABOUT YOU Make statements with *never.*

EXAMPLE Name a machine you've never used.
I've never used a fax machine.

Answers will vary.
1. Name a movie you've never seen.
2. Name a food you've never liked.
3. Name a subject you've never studied.
4. Name a city you've never visited.
5. Name a sport you've never played.
6. Name a food you've never tasted.

EXERCISE 10 ABOUT YOU Write four sentences telling about things you've always done (or been). Share your sentences with the class.

EXAMPLES *I' ve always cooked the meals in my family.*
I' ve always been lazy.

1. Answers will vary. ______
2. ______
3. ______
4. ______

EXERCISE 11 ABOUT YOU Write four sentences telling about things you've never done (or been) but would like to. Share your sentences with the class.

EXAMPLES *I've never studied photography, but I' d like to.*
I've never acted in a play, but I' d like to.

1. Answers will vary. ______
2. ______
3. ______
4. ______

EXERCISE 9

1. Have students read the direction line. Go over the example in the book. Model the example for the class.
2. Have students complete Exercise 9 in pairs. Circulate to observe pair work. Give help as needed.
3. If necessary, review grammar chart **9.7** on page 285.

EXERCISE 10

1. Have students read the direction line. Go over the examples. Ask a volunteer to model the exercise.
2. Have students complete Exercise 10 individually. Then have students compare answers in pairs. Circulate to observe pair work. Give help as needed.
3. If necessary, review grammar chart **9.7** on page 285.

To save class time, have students do half of the exercise in class and complete the other half for homework. Or assign the entire exercise for homework.

EXERCISE 11

1. Say: *Now talk about what you've never done or been.* Have students read the direction line. Go over the examples. Ask a volunteer to model the exercise.
2. Have students complete Exercise 11 individually. Then have students compare answers in pairs. Circulate to observe pair work. Give help as needed.
3. If necessary, review grammar chart **9.7** on page 285.

To save class time, have students do half of the exercise in class and complete the other half for homework. Or assign the entire exercise for homework.

Expansion

Exercises 8 and 9 Create two rings of students. Have half of the students stand in an outer ring around the classroom. Have the other half stand in an inner ring, facing the outer ring. Instruct students to ask and answer questions from Exercises 8 and 9 (e.g., *What have you always thought about? I've always thought about my future.*). Call out "turn" every minute or so. Students in the inner ring should move one space clockwise. Students now interview their new partners. Make sure students look at each other when they're talking.

Exercises 10 and 11 Ask volunteers to share some of their responses to Exercises 10 and 11.

9.8 | The Simple Present vs. the Present Perfect

1. Have students look at grammar chart **9.8.** Review the examples and explanations.
2. Ask students to circle words and expressions that accompany the present perfect (e.g., *since*, *always*, etc.).

EXERCISE 12

1. Have students read the direction line. Say: *You're going to ask me questions about my life and my job.* Go over the example.
2. Complete Exercise 12 as a class.
3. If necessary, review grammar chart **9.8** on page 288.

9.8 | The Simple Present vs. the Present Perfect

Examples	Explanation
a. Larry Page **is** in California. b. Larry Page **has been** in California since he was in his 20s.	Sentences (a) refer only to the present.
a. He **loves** computers. b. He **has** always **loved** computers.	Sentences (b) connect the past to the present.
a. Google **doesn't have** advertising on its homepage. b. Google **has** never **had** advertising on its homepage.	
a. **Do** you **work** at a computer company? Yes, I **do.** b. **Have** you always **worked** at a computer company? Yes, I **have.**	

EXERCISE 12 Read each statement about your teacher. Then ask the teacher a question beginning with the words given. Include *always* in your question. Your teacher will answer.

EXAMPLE You're a teacher. Have you *always been a teacher*?

No. I was an accountant before I became a teacher. I've only been a teacher for five years.

1. You teach English. Have you *always been an English teacher*?
2. You work at this college / school. Have you *always worked at this college/school*?
3. You think about grammar. Have you *always thought about grammar*?
4. English is easy for you. Has English *always been easy for you*?
5. Your last name is *Answers will vary.* Has your last name ________?
6. You're interested in languages. Have you *always been interested in languages*?
7. You live in this city. Have you *always lived in this city*?

288 Lesson 9

EXERCISE 13 Fill in the blanks with the missing words.

Two students meet by chance in the computer lab.

A: ___Have___ (example) you ___been___ in the U.S. for long?

B: No. I ___haven't___ (1).

A: How ___long___ (2) ___have___ (3) you been in the U.S

B: I ___'ve___ (4) ___been___ (5) here for about a year.

A: Where do you come from?

B: Burundi.

A: Burundi? I ___'ve___ (6) never ___heard___ (7) of it. Where is it?

B: It's a small country in Central Africa.

A: Do you have a map? Can you show me where it is?

B: Let's go on the Internet. We can do a search.

A: Did you learn to use a computer in your country?

B: No. When I came here, a volunteer at my church gave me her old computer. Before I didn't know anything about computers. I've ___learned___ (8) a lot about computers since I came here.

A: Oh, now I see Burundi. It's very small. It's near Congo.

B: Yes, it is.

A: Why did you come to the U.S.?

B: My country ___has had___ (9) political problems for many years. It wasn't safe to live there. My family left in 1995.

A: So you ___have___ (10) ___been___ (11) here since 1995?

B: No. First we lived in a refugee camp in Zambia.

A: I ___'ve___ (12) never ___heard___ (13) of Zambia either. Can we search for it on the Internet?

EXERCISE 13

CD 3, Track 12

1. Say: *In this conversation, two students are talking about their homes in Burundi and North Dakota.* Have students read the direction line. Go over the example.
2. Have students complete Exercise 13 individually. Go over the answers as a class.
3. If necessary, review grammar chart **9.8** on page 288.

To save class time, have students do half of the exercise in class and complete the other half for homework. Or assign the entire exercise for homework.

Exercise 13 Variation

To provide practice with listening skills, have students close their books and listen to the audio. Repeat the audio as needed. Ask comprehension questions, such as: *How long has student B been in the U.S.?* (about a year) *Where is student B from?* (Burundi) *Did student B use computers in Africa?* (no) Then have students open their books and complete Exercise 13.

Expansion

Exercise 13 Have students practice the conversation in pairs. Ask volunteers to role-play all or part of the conversation in front of the class.

Exercise 13 Have students work in pairs to create a similar conversation that is true for them. Then have volunteers role-play all or part of the conversation in front of the class.

9.9 | The Present Perfect vs. the Simple Past

1. Have students look at grammar chart **9.9.** Review the examples and explanations. Point out that the simple past shows a single action that happened in the past. The action did not continue. The present perfect describes an action that began in the past and continues into the present.
2. Explain that *when* is used with the simple present and *how long* is used with the present perfect.

B: Here it is.

A: You speak English very well. Is English the language of Burundi?

B: No. Kirundi is the official language. Also French. I 've (14) spoken (15) French since I was a small child. Where are you from?

A: I'm from North Dakota.

B: I 've (16) never heard (17) of North Dakota. Is it in the U.S.?

A: Of course. Let's search for an American map on the Internet. Here it is. Winter in North Dakota is very cold. It's cold here too.

B: I don't know how people live in a cold climate. I 've (18) never lived (19) in a cold climate before. I 've (20) always lived (21) near the Equator.

A: Don't worry. You'll be OK. You just need warm clothes for the winter.

B: I have class now. I've got to go.

A: I 've (22) learned (23) so much about your country in such a short time.

B: It's easy to learn things fast using a computer and a search engine.

9.9 | The Present Perfect vs. the Simple Past

Do not confuse the present perfect with the simple past.

Examples	Explanation
Compare: a. Sergey Brin **came** to the U.S. in 1979. b. Sergey Brin **has been** in the U.S. since 1979. a. Brin and Page **started** Google in 1998. b. Google **has been** popular since 1998.	Sentences (a) show a single action in the past. This action does not continue. Sentences (b) show the continuation of an action or state from the past to the present.
a. When **did** Brin **come** to the U.S.? b. How long **has** Brin **been** in the U.S.?	Question (a) with *when* uses the simple past tense. Question (b) with *how long* uses the present perfect tense.

290 Lesson 9

Expansion

Grammar Have students go back to the reading on page 279. Say: *Circle the verbs in the simple past.*

EXERCISE 14 Fill in the blanks with the simple past or the present perfect of the verb in parentheses ( ).

A: Do you like to surf the Internet?

B: Of course, I do. I *have had* (example: have) my Internet connection since 1999, and I love it. A couple of months ago, I *bought* (1 buy) a new computer with lots of memory and speed. And last month I *changed* (2 change) from a dial-up connection to a cable modem. Now I can surf much faster.

A: What kind of things do you search for?

B: Lots of things. I *'ve always wanted* (3 always/want) to learn about the stock market, and with the Web, I can start to learn. Last week I *made* (4 make) my first investment in the stock market.

A: Do you ever buy products online?

B: Sometimes I do. Last month, I *found* (5 find) a great Web site where I can download music for 99¢. So far I *'ve downloaded* (6 download) about a hundred songs, and I *'ve made* (7 make) several CDs. My old computer *does not have* (8 not/have) a CD burner, so I'm very happy with my new one.

A: *Did you sell* (9 you/sell) your old computer?

B: No. It was about eight years old. I just *left* (10 leave) it on top of the garbage dumpster. When I *passed* (11 pass) by a few hours later, it was gone. Someone *had taken* (12 take) it.

A: Was your new computer expensive?

B: Yes, but I *got* (13 get) a great deal online.

A: I *'ve had* (14 have) my computer for three years, and it seems so old by comparison to today's computers. But it's too expensive to buy a new one every year.

B: There's a joke about computers: "When is a computer old?"

A: I don't know. When?

B: As soon as you get it out of the box!

EXERCISE 14

CD 3, Track 13

1. Have students read the direction line. Go over the example.
2. Have students complete Exercise 14 individually. Go over the answers as a class.
3. If necessary, review grammar charts **9.8** on page 288 and **9.9** on page 290.

Exercise 14 Variation

To provide practice with listening skills, have students close their books and listen to the audio. Repeat the audio as needed. Ask comprehension questions, such as: *How long has person B had an Internet connection?* (since 1999) *Does person B buy things online?* (yes) *Did person B use to have a CD burner?* (No, but now person B does.) *What did person B do with his old computer?* (He left it on top of a dumpster.) Then have students open their books and complete Exercise 14.

Expansion

Exercise 14 Have students practice the conversation in pairs. Ask volunteers to role-play all or part of the conversation in front of the class.

9.10 | The Present Perfect Continuous—An Overview

Have students look at grammar chart **9.10.** Say: *We use the present perfect continuous to talk about an action that started in the past and continues to the present.* Review the examples.

Genealogy (Reading)

1. Have students look at the photo. Ask: *What do you think this represents?* (a family tree/the history of a family)
2. Have students look at the title of the reading. Ask: *What is the reading about? What is genealogy?* (the names and history of one's family) Have students use the title and photo to make predictions about the reading.
3. Preteach any vocabulary words your students may not know, such as *ancestors, amateur,* and *census.*

BEFORE YOU READ

1. Have students discuss the questions in pairs. Try to pair students of different cultures together.
2. Ask for a few volunteers to share their answers with the class.

To save class time, skip "Before You Read" or have students prepare answers for homework ahead of time.

DID YOU KNOW?

Researching family history is very popular in Britain as well. The BBC has an extensive Web page dedicated to helping people research their family histories. Many digital family histories are available on the BBC Web site for everyone to view.

9.10 | The Present Perfect Continuous—An Overview

We use the present perfect continuous to talk about an action that started in the past and continues to the present.

Affirmative	I **have been using** the Internet for two hours.
Negative	You **haven't been working** on your computer all day.
Question	**Have** you **been surfing** the Web for great deals?

GENEALOGY

Before You Read

1. Do you think it's important to know your family's history? Why or why not?
2. What would you like to know about your ancestors?

Read the following article. Pay special attention to the present perfect and the present perfect continuous tenses.

Did You Know? Family history is the second most popular hobby in the U.S. after gardening.

In the last 30 years, genealogy **has become** one of America's most popular hobbies. If you type *genealogy* in a search engine, you can find about 16 million hits. If you type *family history,* you will get about 10 million hits. The percentage of the U.S. population interested in family history **has been increasing** steadily. Forty-five percent of Americans in 1996 stated they were interested in genealogy. In 2000, that number rose to 60 percent according to a national survey. This increase probably has to do with the ease of searching on the Internet.

The number of genealogy Web sites **has been growing** accordingly as people ask themselves: Where does my family come from? How long **has** my family **been** in the U.S.? Why did they come here? How did they come here? What kind of people were my ancestors?

Reading Variation

To practice listening skills, have students first listen to the audio alone. Ask a few comprehension questions. Repeat the audio if necessary. Then have them open their books and read along as they listen to the audio.

Reading Glossary

amateur: a person who does activities, such as sports, for pleasure and without pay
ancestors: the persons from whom one is descended
census: a count by the government of the people in a country

Genealogy is a lifelong hobby for many. The average family historian **has been doing** genealogy for 14 years, according to a recent study. Most family historians are over 40. Cyndi Howells, from Washington State, quit her job in 1992 and **has been working** on her family history ever since. She **has created** a Web site to help others with their search. Her Web site has over 99,000 resources. Since its start in 1996, her Web site **has had** over 22 million visitors and more than 32 million page hits each month. Cyndi **has** also **been giving** lectures all over the country to genealogy groups. Cyndi's Web site **has won** an award three times for the best genealogy site on the Web.

While the Internet **has made** research easier for amateur genealogists, it is only the beginning for serious family historians. Researchers still need to go to courthouses and libraries to find public records, such as land deeds[5], obituaries[6], wedding notices, and tax records. Another good source of information is the U.S. Census. Early census records are not complete, but since the mid-1800s, the U.S. Census **has been keeping** detailed records of family members, their ages, occupations, and places of birth.

Are you interested in knowing more about your ancestors and their stories, their country or countries, and how you fit into the history of your family? Maybe genealogy is a good hobby for you.

9.11 | The Present Perfect Continuous—Forms

Subject	*have/has*	*been*	Present Participle	Complement
I	**have**	**been**	**using**	the Internet for two hours.
We	**have**	**been**	**reading**	about search engines.
You	**have**	**been**	**studying**	computers.
They	**have**	**been**	**living**	in California.
He	**has**	**been**	**writing**	since one o'clock.
She	**has**	**been**	**surfing**	the Internet all day.
It	**has**	**been**	**raining**	all day.

Language Notes:

1. To form the negative, put *not* between *have* or *has* and *been*.
   You **have *not* been** listening.
   She **hasn't been** working hard.
2. To form the question, reverse the subject and *have/has*.
   Has she been using her new computer?
   How long **have they** been living in the U.S.?

[5] A *land deed* is a document that shows who the owner of the land is.
[6] *Obituaries* are death notices posted in the newspaper.

The Present Perfect; The Present Perfect Continuous 293

Reading CD 3, Track 14

1. Have students first read the text silently. Tell them to pay special attention to the present perfect and the present perfect continuous tenses. Then play the audio and have students read along silently.
2. Check students' comprehension. Ask questions such as: *Is genealogy a popular hobby?* (yes) *Why is the popularity of genealogy increasing?* (probably because the Internet has made searching much easier) *How old are most family historians?* (over 40) *What did Cyndi Howells do so that she could work on her family history more?* (She quit her job.)

To save class time, have students do the reading for homework ahead of time.

9.11 | The Present Perfect Continuous—Forms

1. Have students cover up grammar chart **9.11.** Say: *Go back to the reading on pages 292 and 293. Find some examples of the present perfect continuous, and try to figure out the rule for forming it.* Then ask a volunteer to tell you how to form the present perfect continuous (*have/has* + *been* + present participle). Write it on the board. Ask students to say how they might form the negative (*have/has* + *not* + *been* + present participle). Then ask students to make questions from the reading (e.g., *Has Cyndi been giving lectures all over the country?*).
2. Have students look at grammar chart **9.11.** Review the examples and explanations.

9.12 | The Present Perfect Continuous—Statements and Questions

1. Have students cover up grammar chart **9.12.** Write the following on the board:
   Cyndi has been working on her family history.
   Say: *Write a yes/no question, a short answer, and an information question with* how long. Have volunteers write their statements and questions on the board. Then write this negative statement on the board:
   They haven't been using the public library.
   Say: *Write a negative question for this statement.* Have a volunteer write the negative question on the board.
2. Then have students look at grammar chart **9.12.** Say: *Compare your work with the chart.* Go over any trouble spots with the class.
3. Direct students to the short answers. Explain that only the auxiliary *have* or *has* is used with short answers. Also, words like *since* and *for* can be used alone with the date or time period (e.g., *Since 1992. For 12 years.*).

EXERCISE 15

1. Have students read the direction line. Go over the example in the book.
2. Have students complete Exercise 15 individually. Go over the answers as a class.
3. If necessary, review grammar chart **9.12** on page 294.

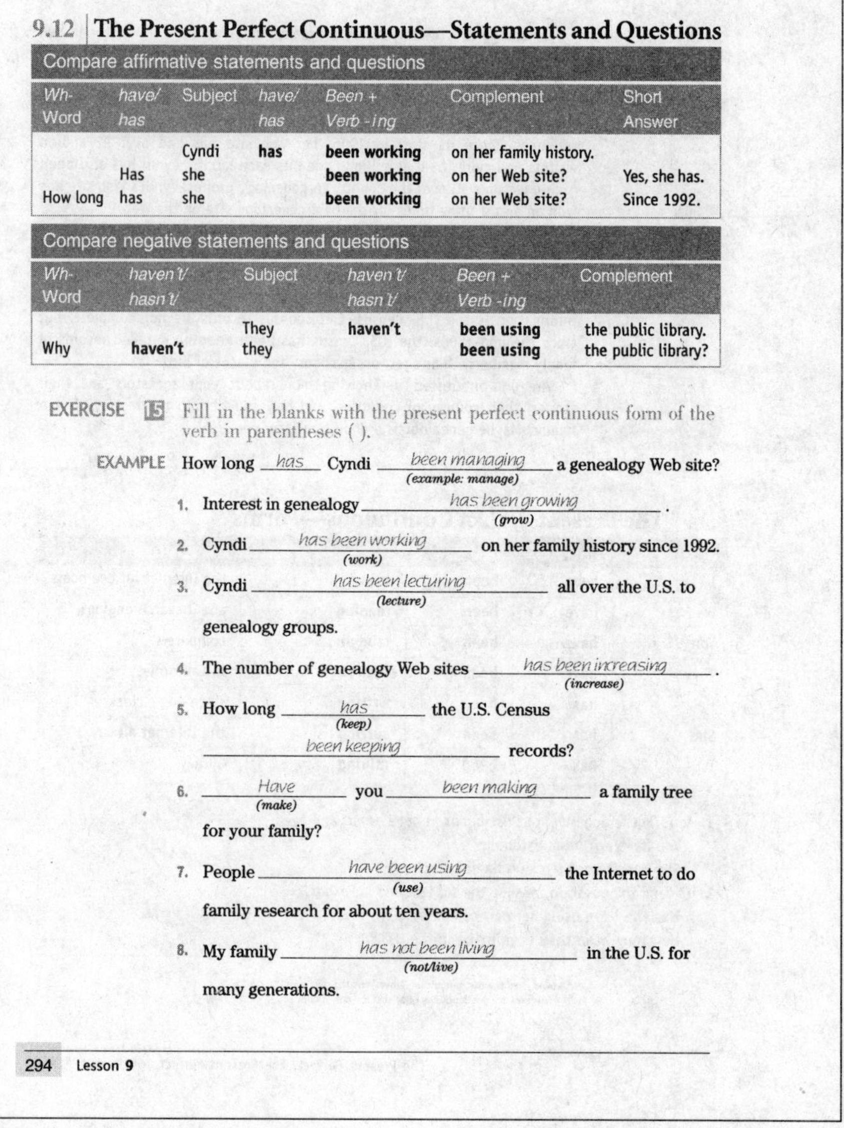

9.12 | The Present Perfect Continuous—Statements and Questions

Compare affirmative statements and questions

Wh- Word	have/ has	Subject	have/ has	Been + Verb -ing	Complement	Short Answer
		Cyndi	**has**	**been working**	on her family history.	
	Has	she		**been working**	on her Web site?	Yes, she has.
How long	has	she		**been working**	on her Web site?	Since 1992.

Compare negative statements and questions

Wh- Word	haven't/ hasn't	Subject	haven't/ hasn't	Been + Verb -ing	Complement
		They	**haven't**	**been using**	the public library.
Why	**haven't**	they		**been using**	the public library?

EXERCISE 15 Fill in the blanks with the present perfect continuous form of the verb in parentheses ( ).

EXAMPLE How long _has_ Cyndi _been managing_ (example: manage) a genealogy Web site?

1. Interest in genealogy _has been growing_ (grow).
2. Cyndi _has been working_ (work) on her family history since 1992.
3. Cyndi _has been lecturing_ (lecture) all over the U.S. to genealogy groups.
4. The number of genealogy Web sites _has been increasing_ (increase).
5. How long _has_ (keep) the U.S. Census _been keeping_ records?
6. _Have_ (make) you _been making_ a family tree for your family?
7. People _have been using_ (use) the Internet to do family research for about ten years.
8. My family _has not been living_ (not/live) in the U.S. for many generations.

294 Lesson 9

Expansion

Grammar Ask: *What have you been working on lately? Write five to ten sentences about a hobby or pastime you enjoy. Use the present perfect continuous tense to describe what you've been doing* (e.g., *I have been gardening since 1999. I have been working on creating a perennial garden in the back of the house. I have been planting bulbs every fall. I have been fertilizing the soil and watering the beds.*).

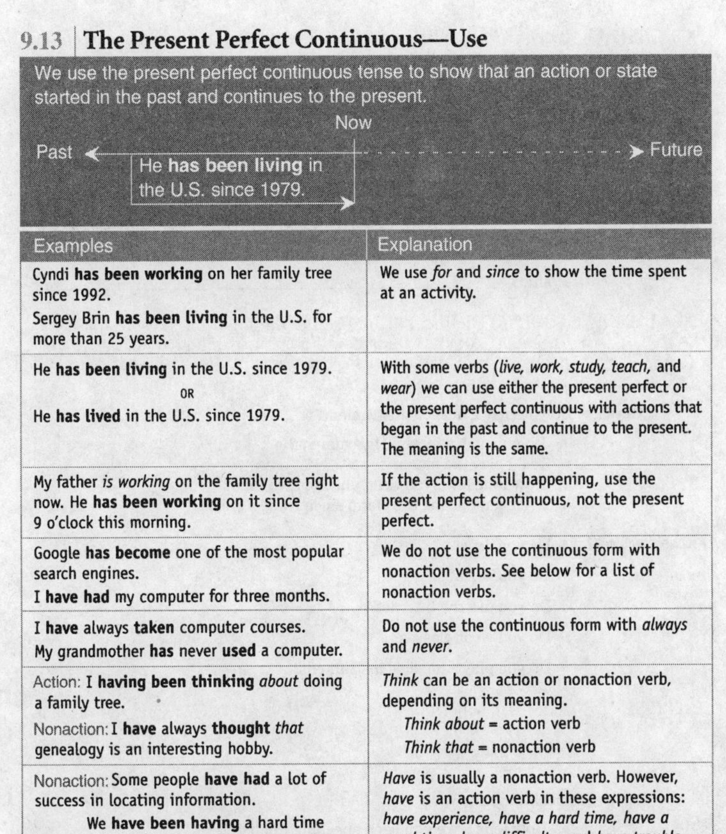

9.13 | The Present Perfect Continuous—Use

We use the present perfect continuous tense to show that an action or state started in the past and continues to the present.

Examples	Explanation
Cyndi **has been working** on her family tree since 1992. Sergey Brin **has been living** in the U.S. for more than 25 years.	We use *for* and *since* to show the time spent at an activity.
He **has been living** in the U.S. since 1979. OR He **has lived** in the U.S. since 1979.	With some verbs (*live, work, study, teach,* and *wear*) we can use either the present perfect or the present perfect continuous with actions that began in the past and continue to the present. The meaning is the same.
My father *is working* on the family tree right now. He **has been working** on it since 9 o'clock this morning.	If the action is still happening, use the present perfect continuous, not the present perfect.
Google **has become** one of the most popular search engines. I **have had** my computer for three months.	We do not use the continuous form with nonaction verbs. See below for a list of nonaction verbs.
I **have** always **taken** computer courses. My grandmother **has** never **used** a computer.	Do not use the continuous form with *always* and *never*.
Action: I **having been thinking** *about* doing a family tree. Nonaction: I **have** always **thought** *that* genealogy is an interesting hobby.	*Think* can be an action or nonaction verb, depending on its meaning. *Think about* = action verb *Think that* = nonaction verb
Nonaction: Some people **have had** a lot of success in locating information. We **have been having** a hard time locating information about our ancestors.	*Have* is usually a nonaction verb. However, *have* is an action verb in these expressions: *have experience, have a hard time, have a good time, have difficulty,* and *have trouble.*

Nonaction verbs:

like	know	see	cost
love	believe	smell	own
hate	think (that)	hear	have (for possession)
want	care (about)	taste	become
need	understand	feel	
prefer	remember	seem	

The Present Perfect; The Present Perfect Continuous 295

9.13 | The Present Perfect Continuous—Use

1. Have students cover up grammar chart **9.13.** Write the following sentence on the board along with the timeline: *He has been living in the U.S. since 1979.*
   Ask: *When did he start living in the U.S.?* (in 1979) *Correct. In the past. Is he still living here?* (yes) *So, today, he is still living in the U.S.*
2. Have students look at grammar chart **9.13.** Say: *We use the present perfect continuous tense to show that an action or state started in the past and continues to the present.* Point out the timeline.
3. Go over the examples and explanations in the chart. Explain the use of the following with the present perfect continuous:
   1. *for* + an amount of time
   2. *since* with dates
   3. some verbs (*live, work, study, teach, wear*) can be used for both
   4. if the action is still happening, use continuous
   5. don't use with *always* or *never*
   6. *think about* (action)
   7. expressions with *have*
4. Remind students that the present perfect continuous is used with action verbs. Point out the list of nonaction verbs in the chart.

EXERCISE 16

1. Say: *You're going to write true statements about your life.* Have students read the direction line. Go over the example. Say: *Remember, use* for *or* since *in your sentences.* Model the example for the class.
2. Have students complete Exercise 16 individually. Then have students compare answers in pairs. Circulate to observe pair work. Give help as needed.
3. If necessary, review grammar chart **9.13** on page 295.

EXERCISE 17

1. Say: *Now you're going to find out some information about your partner.* Have students read the direction line. Go over the example. Ask: *When do we ask a question with* how long? (when the answer to the first question is *yes*) Model the example with a volunteer.
2. Have students complete Exercise 17 in pairs. Circulate to observe pair work. Give help as needed.
3. If necessary, review grammar chart **9.13** on page 295.

To save class time, have students do half of the exercise in class and complete the other half in writing for homework, answering the questions themselves. Or if students do not need speaking practice, the entire exercise may be skipped or done in writing.

EXERCISE 18

1. Say: *Now you're going to ask me some questions.* Have students read the direction line. Go over the example.
2. Complete Exercise 18 as a class.
3. If necessary, review grammar chart **9.13** on page 295.

To save class time, have students write the questions for homework. Then have a few volunteers ask you the questions in class.

EXERCISE 16 ABOUT YOU Write true statements using the present perfect continuous with the words given and *for* or *since*. Share your sentences with the class.

EXAMPLE **work** *My brother has been working as a waiter for six years.*

1. **study English** ____ Answers will vary.
2. **work** ____
3. **live** ____
4. **use** ____
5. **study** ____

EXERCISE 17 ABOUT YOU Read aloud each of the following present tense questions. Another student will answer. If the answer is *yes*, add a present perfect continuous question with *"How long have you . . . ?"*

EXAMPLE **Do you play a musical instrument?**

A: **Do you play a musical instrument?**
B: **Yes. I play the piano.**
A: **How long have you been playing the piano?**
B: **I've been playing the piano since I was a child.**

Answers will vary.

1. **Do you drive?**
2. **Do you work?**
3. **Do you use the Internet?**
4. **Do you wear glasses?**
5. **Do you play a musical instrument?**

EXERCISE 18 Ask the teacher questions with *"How long . . . ?"* and the present perfect continuous form of the words given. The teacher will answer your questions.

EXAMPLE **speak English**

A: **How long have you been speaking English?**
B: **I've been speaking English all[7] my life.**

1. **teach English** *How long have you been teaching English?*
2. **work at this school** *How long have you been working at this school?*
3. **live in this city** *How long have you been living in this city?*
4. **use this book** *How long have you been using this book?*
5. **live at your present address** *How long have you been living at your present address?*

[7] We do not use the preposition *for* before *all*.

296 Lesson 9

Expansion

Exercise 17 Have students think of three to five more questions they would like to ask their partners. Then have students take turns asking and answering questions in pairs.

Exercise 18 If possible, bring in other teachers for students to interview in groups. Have students prepare extra questions ahead of time.

EXERCISE 19 Fill in the blanks in the following conversations. Answers may vary.

EXAMPLE A: Do you wear glasses?

B: Yes, I ___do___.

A: How long ___have___ you ___been wearing___ glasses?

B: I ___'ve been wearing___ glasses since I ___was___ in high school.

1. A: Are you working on your family history?

   B: Yes, I am.

   A: How long ___have___ you ___been working___ on your family history?

   B: I ___'ve been working___ on it for about ten years.

2. A: Is your sister surfing the Internet?

   B: Yes, she ___is___.

   A: How long ___has___ she ___been___ surfing the Internet?

   B: Since she woke up this morning!

3. A: Does your father live in the U.S.?

   B: Yes, he ___does___.

   A: How long ___has___ he been ___living___ in the U.S.?

   B: He ___'s been living___ in the U.S. since he ___was___ 25 years old.

4. A: Are you studying for the test now?

   B: Yes, I ___am___.

   A: How long ___have you been studying___ for the test?

   B: For ___Answers will vary.___.

5. A: Is your teacher teaching you the present perfect lesson?

   B: Yes, he ___is___.

   A: ___How___ long ___has he been teaching___ you this lesson?

   B: Since ___Answers will vary.___.

The Present Perfect; The Present Perfect Continuous 297

EXERCISE 19

CD 3, Track 15

1. Say: *In this exercise, you're going to listen to nine miniconversations.* Have students read the direction line. Go over the example.
2. Have students complete Exercise 19 individually. Go over the answers as a class.
3. If necessary, review grammar chart **9.13** on page 295.

To save class time, have students do half of the exercise in class and complete the other half for homework. Or assign the entire exercise for homework.

Exercise 19 Variation

To provide practice with listening skills, have students close their books and listen to the audio. Repeat the audio as needed. Ask comprehension questions, such as: *In conversation 1, what's person B doing?* (working on his/her family history) *How long has person B been working on it?* (for about ten years) Then have students open their books and complete Exercise 19.

6. A: Are they using the computers now?

B: Yes, they are.

A: How long have they been using them?

B: Since they started to write their compositions.

7. A: Are you using the Internet?

B: Yes, I am.

A: How long have you been using the Internet?

B: I've been using the Internet for two hours.

8. A: Do your grandparents live in the U.S.?

B: Yes, they do.

A: How long have they lived in the U.S.?

B: Since they were born.

9. A: Is she studying her family history?

B: Yes, she is.

A: How long has she been studying her family history?

B: Since she Answers will vary.

Expansion

Exercise 19 Have students practice the miniconversations in pairs. Ask volunteers to role-play the conversations in front of the class.

Photo

Direct students' attention to the photo on page 298. Say: *Describe what's probably going on in this picture* (A grandmother or great grandmother is talking to her grandchildren about their family's history.). Ask: *Do you have a lot of information about your family's history? Where do you get your information from? Do you have grandparents who tell you stories about your family?* Have students share personal experiences.

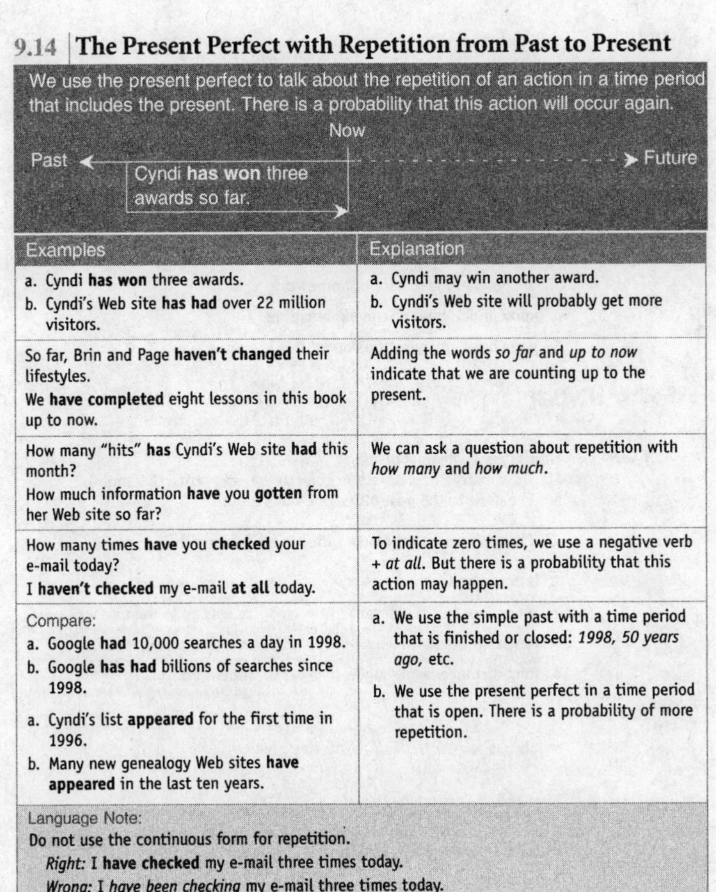

9.14 | The Present Perfect with Repetition from Past to Present

We use the present perfect to talk about the repetition of an action in a time period that includes the present. There is a probability that this action will occur again.

Examples	Explanation
a. Cyndi **has won** three awards. b. Cyndi's Web site **has had** over 22 million visitors.	a. Cyndi may win another award. b. Cyndi's Web site will probably get more visitors.
So far, Brin and Page **haven't changed** their lifestyles. We **have completed** eight lessons in this book up to now.	Adding the words *so far* and *up to now* indicate that we are counting up to the present.
How many "hits" **has** Cyndi's Web site **had** this month? How much information **have** you **gotten** from her Web site so far?	We can ask a question about repetition with *how many* and *how much*.
How many times **have** you **checked** your e-mail today? I **haven't checked** my e-mail **at all** today.	To indicate zero times, we use a negative verb + *at all*. But there is a probability that this action may happen.
Compare: a. Google **had** 10,000 searches a day in 1998. b. Google **has had** billions of searches since 1998. a. Cyndi's list **appeared** for the first time in 1996. b. Many new genealogy Web sites **have appeared** in the last ten years.	a. We use the simple past with a time period that is finished or closed: *1998, 50 years ago*, etc. b. We use the present perfect in a time period that is open. There is a probability of more repetition.

Language Note:
Do not use the continuous form for repetition.
Right: I **have checked** my e-mail three times today.
Wrong: I have been checking my e-mail three times today.

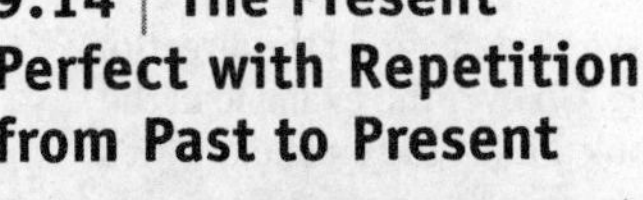

9.14 | The Present Perfect with Repetition from Past to Present

1. Have students cover up grammar chart **9.14.** Write the following sentence on the board along with the timeline: *Cyndi has won three awards so far.* Ask: *Do you think Cyndi might win more awards?* (Yes, the possibility that she'll win again is high.)
2. Have students look at grammar chart **9.14.** Say: *We use the present perfect to talk about the repetition of an action in a time period that includes the present. There is a probability that this action will occur again.* Point out the timeline.
3. Go over the examples and explanations in the chart. Point out that the expressions *so far* and *up to now* hint at the action continuing into the future. Questions about repetition are asked with *how many* and *how much*. The use of *at all* also indicates that an action may happen in the future (e.g., *I haven't checked my e-mail at all today (but I will check it at some point).*). Review the examples from the chart.
4. Explain to students that the simple past is used with closed time periods (e.g., *in 1998*). The present perfect is used with time periods that remain open (e.g., *since 1998*).
5. Direct students to the Language Note. Explain to students that we don't use the present perfect continuous for repetition. Go over the example sentences.

EXERCISE 20

1. Have students read the direction line. Go over the example in the book. Model the example with a volunteer, using *up to now*.
2. Have students complete Exercise 20 in pairs. Circulate to observe pair work. Give help as needed.
3. If necessary, review grammar chart **9.14** on page 299.

EXERCISE 21

1. Have students read the direction line. Go over the example in the book.
2. Have students complete Exercise 21 in pairs. Circulate to observe pair work. Give help as needed.
3. If necessary, review grammar chart **9.14** on page 299.

EXERCISE 22

1. Say: *You're going to write questions for your classmates or me* (the teacher). Have students read the direction line. Go over the examples in the book. Ask: *What words can we use for repetition?* (*so far* and *up to now*)
2. Have students write the questions individually. Then have students mingle in the classroom asking and answering questions. Give help as needed.
3. If necessary, review grammar chart **9.14** on page 299.

To save class time, have students write the questions for homework.

EXERCISE 20 ABOUT YOU Ask a *yes / no* question with *so far* or *up to now* and the words given. Another student will answer.

EXAMPLE **you / come to every class.**
A: Have you come to every class so far?
B: Yes, I have.
OR
B: No, I haven't. I've missed three classes.

Answers will vary.

1. **we / have any tests**
2. **this lesson / be difficult**
3. **the teacher / give a lot of homework**
4. **you / understand all the explanations**
5. **you / have any questions about this lesson**

EXERCISE 21 ABOUT YOU Ask a question with "*How many . . . ?*" and the words given. Talk about this month. Another student will answer.

EXAMPLE **times / go to the post office**
A: How many times have you gone to the post office this month?
B: I've gone to the post office once this month.
OR
I haven't gone to the post office at all this month.

1. **letters / write** *How many letters have you written this month?*
2. **times / eat in a restaurant** *How many times have you eaten in a restaurant this month?*
3. **times / get paid** *How many times have you gotten paid this month?*
4. **long-distance calls / make** *How many long-distance calls have you made this month?*
5. **books / buy** *How many books have you bought this month?*
6. **times / go to the movies** *How many times have you gone to the movies this month?*
7. **movies / rent** *How many movies have you rented this month?*
8. **times / cook** *How many times have you cooked this month?*

EXERCISE 22 ABOUT YOU Write four questions to ask another student or your teacher about repetition from the past to the present. Use *how much* or *how many*. The other person will answer.

EXAMPLES *How many cities have you lived in?*
How many English courses have you taken at this college?

1. Answers will vary.
2. ______
3. ______
4. ______

300 Lesson 9

Expansion

Exercises 20 and 21 Create two rings of students. Have half of the students stand in an outer ring around the classroom. Have the other half stand in an inner ring, facing the outer ring. Instruct students to ask and answer questions from Exercises 20 and 21. Tell students to answer questions with a short answer. Call out "turn" every minute or so. Students in the inner ring should move one space clockwise. Students now interview their new partners. Make sure students look at each other when they're talking.

9.15 | The Simple Past vs. the Present Perfect with Repetition

We use the present perfect with repetition in a present time period. There is probability of more repetition. We use the simple past with repetition in a past time period. There is no possibility of any more repetition during that period.

Examples	Explanation
How many hits **has** your Web site **had** today? It **has had** over 100 hits today. How many times **have** you **been** absent this semester? **I've been** absent twice so far.	To show that there is possibility for more repetition, use the present perfect. In the examples on the left, *today* and *this semester* are not finished. *So far* indicates that the number given may not be final.
Last month my Web site **had** 5,000 hits. How many times **were** you absent last semester?	To show that the number is final, use the simple past tense and a past time expression. *Yesterday, last week, last year, last semester,* etc. are finished. The number is final.
a. Brin and Page **have added** new features to Google over the years. b. Before she died, my grandmother **added** many details to our family tree.	a. Brin and Page are still alive. They can (and probably will) add new features to Google in the years to come. b. Grandmother is dead. The number of details she added is final.
Compare: a. I **have checked** my e-mail twice today. b. I **checked** my e-mail twice today. a. She **has gone** to the library to work on her family tree five times this month. b. She **went** to the library to work on her family tree five times this month.	With a present time expression (such as *today, this week, this month,* etc.), you may use either the present perfect or the simple past. In sentences (a), the number may not be final. In sentences (b), the number seems final.
Compare: a. In the U.S., I **have had** two jobs. b. In my native country, I **had** five jobs. a. In the U.S., I **have lived** in three apartments so far. b. In my native country, I **lived** in two apartments.	a. To talk about your experiences in this phase of your life, you can use the present perfect tense. b. To talk about a closed phase of your life, use the simple past tense. For example, if you do not plan to live in your native country again, use the simple past tense to talk about your experiences there.

EXERCISE 23 ABOUT YOU Fill in the blanks with the simple past or the present perfect to ask a question. A student from another country will answer.

EXAMPLES How many cars ___*have you owned*___ in the U.S.?
I've owned two cars in the U.S.

How many cars ___*did you own*___ in your country?
I owned only one car in my country.

The Present Perfect; The Present Perfect Continuous 301

9.15 | The Simple Past vs. the Present Perfect with Repetition

1. Have students look at grammar chart **9.15.** Say: *We can use both the simple past and the present perfect to express repetition. However, with the simple past, the repetition of the action happened in a time period in the past and won't be repeated again in the future.*
2. Go over the examples and explanations in the chart. Point out that the expressions *so far, today,* and *this semester* used with the present perfect indicate that the number may not be final. To show that the number is final, we use the simple past with a past time expression such as *yesterday, last week,* or *last semester.*
3. Explain to students that sometimes you can use either the simple past or the present perfect with a present time expression to mean the same thing. Go over the examples.

EXERCISE 23

1. Say: *In this exercise, you're going to complete the question and then respond with an answer that's true for you.* Have students read the direction line. Go over the examples.
2. Have students complete Exercise 23 in pairs. Circulate to observe pair work. Give help as needed.
3. If necessary, review grammar chart **9.15** on page 301.

Expansion

Grammar Have students go back to the reading on pages 292 and 293. Ask students to underline the verbs in the simple past, circle the verbs in the present perfect, and put a box around verbs in the present perfect continuous. Ask students to discuss the tense of each verb with a partner.

9.16 | The Present Perfect with Indefinite Past Time

1. Have students look at grammar chart **9.16.** Say: *We use the present perfect to refer to an action that occurred at an indefinite time in the past (that is, there was no specified time or date for the beginning of the action). Words that show indefinite time are:* ever, yet, *and* already.
Point out the example on the timeline in the grammar chart: *Have you ever used Google?* Say: *This question is not concerned with a specific time.*
2. Go over the examples and explanations in the chart. Point out that a question with *ever* asks about any time between the past and the present.
3. Say: Yet *and* already *refer to an indefinite time in the recent past.* Review the questions and short answers with *yet* and *already.*
4. Then say: *We can also use the present perfect with no reference to time at all.* Go over the examples.

1. How many apartments ___have you lived in___ in your country?
2. How many apartments ___have you lived in___ in the U.S.?
3. How many schools ___have you attended___ in your country?
4. How many schools ___have you attended___ in the U.S.?
5. How many jobs ___have you had___ in the U.S.?
6. How many jobs ___have you had___ in your country?

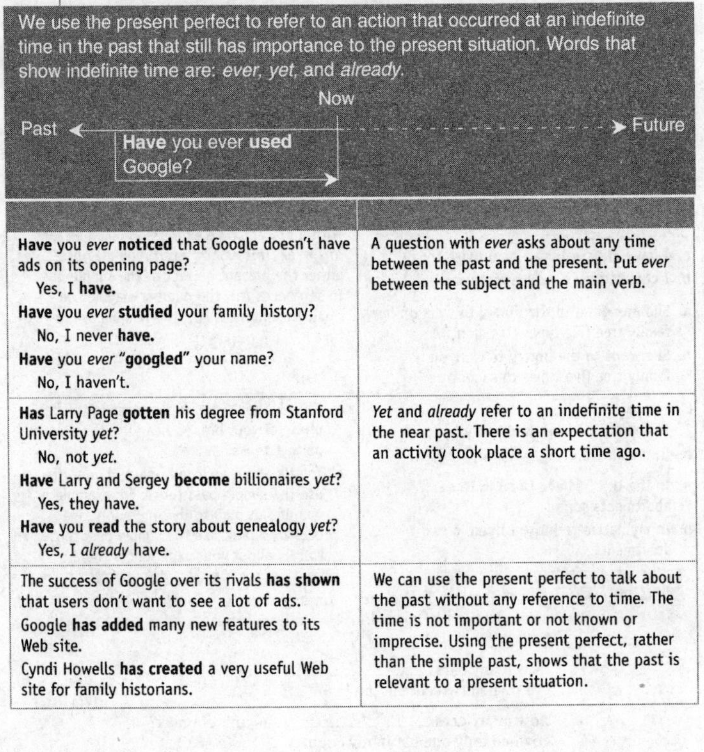

9.16 | The Present Perfect with Indefinite Past Time

We use the present perfect to refer to an action that occurred at an indefinite time in the past that still has importance to the present situation. Words that show indefinite time are: *ever, yet,* and *already.*

Have you *ever* **noticed** that Google doesn't have ads on its opening page? Yes, I **have.** **Have** you *ever* **studied** your family history? No, I never **have.** **Have** you *ever* **"googled"** your name? No, I haven't.	A question with *ever* asks about any time between the past and the present. Put *ever* between the subject and the main verb.
Has Larry Page **gotten** his degree from Stanford University *yet?* No, not *yet.* **Have** Larry and Sergey **become** billionaires *yet?* Yes, they have. **Have** you **read** the story about genealogy *yet?* Yes, I *already* have.	*Yet* and *already* refer to an indefinite time in the near past. There is an expectation that an activity took place a short time ago.
The success of Google over its rivals **has shown** that users don't want to see a lot of ads. Google **has added** many new features to its Web site. Cyndi Howells **has created** a very useful Web site for family historians.	We can use the present perfect to talk about the past without any reference to time. The time is not important or not known or imprecise. Using the present perfect, rather than the simple past, shows that the past is relevant to a present situation.

302 Lesson 9

Expansion

Exercise 23 Take a class survey. Find out how many apartments, schools, and jobs students have had in their native countries and in the U.S.

EXERCISE 24 ABOUT YOU Answer the following questions with: *Yes, I have; No, I haven't;* or *No, I never have.*

Answers will vary.

1. Have you ever "googled" your own name?
2. Have you ever researched your family history?
3. Have you ever made a family tree?
4. Have you ever used the Web to look for a person you haven't seen in a long time?
5. Have you ever added hardware to your computer?
6. Have you ever downloaded music from the Internet?
7. Have you ever used a search engine in your native language?
8. Have you ever sent photos by e-mail?
9. Have you ever received a photo by e-mail?
10. Have you ever bought anything from a Web site?
11. Have you ever built a computer?
12. Has your computer ever had a virus?

EXERCISE 25 ABOUT YOU Answer the questions with: *Yes, I have; Yes, I already have;* or *Not yet.*

Answers will vary.

1. Have you eaten lunch yet?
2. Have you finished lesson eight yet?
3. Have you done today's homework yet?
4. Have you paid this month's rent yet?
5. Have you learned the names of all the other students yet?
6. Have you visited the teacher's office yet?
7. Have you done Exercise 22 yet?
8. Have you learned the present perfect yet?
9. Have you learned all the past participles yet?

EXERCISE 24

1. Have students read the direction line. Say: *Give short answers to the following questions.* Ask: *Is there a difference between* No, I haven't *and* No, I never have*?* (no)
2. Have students ask and answer the questions in pairs. Circulate to observe pair work. Give help as needed.
3. If necessary, review grammar chart **9.16** on page 302.

EXERCISE 25

1. Have students read the direction line. Say: *Give short answers to the following questions.* Ask: *Is there a difference between* Yes, I have *and* Yes, I already have*?* (There's a slight difference. With *already*, there's an expectation that it just happened. *No, not yet* means that you expect to do the action soon.)
2. Have students ask and answer the questions in pairs. Circulate to observe pair work. Give help as needed.
3. If necessary, review grammar chart **9.16** on page 302.

To save class time, have students answer all or some of the questions in writing for homework.

Expansion

Exercises 24 and 25 Create two rings of students. Have half of the students stand in an outer ring around the classroom. Have the other half stand in an inner ring, facing the outer ring. Instruct students to ask and answer questions from Exercises 24 and 25. Call out "turn" every minute or so. Students in the inner ring should move one space clockwise. Students now ask and answer questions with their new partners. Make sure students look at each other when they're talking.

9.17 | Answering a Present Perfect Question

1. Have students cover up grammar chart **9.17.** Write the following sentence from the grammar chart on the board: *Have you ever used Google?* Go around the class and ask random students that question. Write their responses on the board.
2. Then have students look at grammar chart **9.17.** Say: *We can answer a present perfect question with the present perfect OR with the simple past.* If possible, point to several examples from students on the board. Say: *If the response does not have a specific time or number of times, use the present perfect. If the response has a specific time or number of times, use the simple past.* Go over the examples in the chart.

EXERCISE 26

1. Say: *Your partner is going to ask questions in the present perfect.* Have students read the direction line. Ask: *When do you use the simple past in the answer?* (when you give a specific time or number of times) Go over the examples in the book.
2. Have students ask and answer the questions in pairs. Circulate to observe pair work. Give help as needed.
3. If necessary, review grammar chart **9.17** on page 304.

9.17 | Answering a Present Perfect Question

We can answer a present perfect question with the simple past tense when a specific time is introduced in the answer. If a specific time is not known or necessary, we answer with the present perfect.

Examples	Explanation
Have you ever **used** Google? Answer A: Yes. I've **used** Google many times. Answer B: Yes. I **used** Google a few hours ago.	Answer A, with *many times,* shows repetition at an indefinite time. Answer B, with *a few hours ago,* shows a specific time in the past.
Have you ever **heard** of Larry Page? Answer A: No. I've **never** heard of him. Answer B: Yes. We **read** about him yesterday.	Answer A, with *never,* shows continuation from past to present. Answer B, with *yesterday,* shows a specific time in the past.
Have you **done** your homework yet? Answer A: Yes. I've **done** it already. Answer B: Yes. I **did** it this morning.	Answer A, with *already,* is indefinite. Answer B, with *this morning,* shows a specific time.
Have Brin and Page **become** rich? Answer A: Yes, they have. Answer B: Yes. They **became** rich before they were 30 years old.	Answer A is indefinite. Answer B, with *before they were 30 years old,* is definite.

EXERCISE 25 ABOUT YOU Ask a question with "*Have you ever . . . ?*" and the present perfect tense of the verb in parentheses ( ). Another student will answer. To answer with a specific time, use the past tense. To answer with a frequency response, use the present perfect tense. You may work with a partner.

EXAMPLES (go) to the zoo

A: Have you ever gone to the zoo?
B: Yes. I've gone there many times.

(go) to Disneyland

A: Have you ever gone to Disneyland?
B: Yes. I went there last summer.

1. (work) in a factory
   Have you ever worked in a factory?
2. (lose) a glove
   Have you ever lost a glove?
3. (run) out of gas[8]
   Have you ever run out of gas?
4. (fall) out of bed
   Have you ever fallen out of bed?

[8] *To run out of gas* means to use all the gas in your car while driving.

304 Lesson 9

5. (make) a mistake in English grammar *Have you ever made a mistake in English grammar?*
6. (tell) a lie
Have you ever told a lie?
7. (eat) raw[9] fish
Have you ever eaten raw fish?
8. (study) calculus
Have you ever studied calculus?
9. (meet) a famous person
Have you ever met a famous person?
10. (go) to an art museum
Have you ever gone to an art museum?
11. (stay) up all night
Have you ever stayed up all night?
12. (break) a window
Have you ever broken a window?
13. (get) locked out[10] of your house or car *Have you ever gotten locked out of your house or car?*
14. (see) a French movie
Have you ever seen a French movie?
15. (go) to Las Vegas
Have you ever gone to Las Vegas?
16. (travel) by ship
Have you ever traveled by ship?
17. (be) in love
Have you ever been in love?
18. (write) a poem
Have you ever written a poem?

EXERCISE 27 ABOUT YOU Write five questions with *ever* to ask your teacher. Your teacher will answer.

EXAMPLES *Have you ever gotten a ticket for speeding?*
Have you ever visited Poland?

1. Answers will vary.
2.
3.
4.
5.

EXERCISE 28 ABOUT YOU Ask a student from another country questions using the words given. The other student will answer.

EXAMPLE **your country / have a woman president**

A: Has your country ever had a woman president?
B: Yes, it has. We had a woman president from 1975 to 1979.

1. your country / have a civil war
Has your country ever had a civil war?
2. your country's leader / visit the U.S.
Has your country's leader ever visited the U.S.?
3. an American president / visit your country
Has an American president ever visited your country?
4. your country / have a woman president
Has your country ever had a woman president?
5. you / go back to visit your country
Have you ever gone back to visit your country?
6. there / be an earthquake in your hometown
Has there ever been an earthquake in your hometown?

[9] *Raw* means not cooked.
[10] *To get locked out* of your house means that you can't get in because you do not have keys with you to get inside.

EXERCISE 27

1. Say: *Now you get to ask me some questions.* Have students read the direction line. Go over the examples. Answer the questions.
2. Have students complete Exercise 27 in pairs. Circulate to observe pair work and to answer students' questions.
3. Have students ask you their questions and answer them.
4. If necessary, review grammar chart **9.17** on page 304.

EXERCISE 28

1. Say: *Ask your partner questions about his or her native country.* Have students read the direction line. Go over the example.
2. Have students complete Exercise 28 in pairs. Circulate to observe pair work. Give help as needed.
3. If necessary, review grammar chart **9.17** on page 304.

To save class time, have students do half of the exercise in class and complete the other half in writing for homework, answering the questions themselves. Or if students do not need speaking practice, the entire exercise may be skipped or done in writing.

Expansion

Exercise 26 Survey the class on some of the information from Exercise 26 (e.g., *Have you ever met a famous person?*). And ask students to expand on the topic (e.g., *Who did you meet? Where did you meet him or her?*).

Exercise 28 Have students from different countries discuss their answers to the questions from Exercise 28 in groups (e.g., ***Has your country ever had a civil war? Yes, my country has had many civil wars. My country is still going through a civil war.***).

EXERCISE 29

1. Say: *Now ask your partner questions about things he or she has done in the U.S.* Have students read the direction line. Go over the example.
2. Have students complete Exercise 29 in pairs. Circulate to observe pair work. Give help as needed.
3. If necessary, review grammar chart **9.17** on page 304.

EXERCISE 30

CD 3, Track 16

1. Say: *You're going to have to choose what tense to use. Answers may vary.* Have students read the direction line. Go over the examples in the book.
2. Have students complete Exercise 30 individually. Go over answers as a class.
3. If necessary, review grammar chart **9.17** on page 304.

To save class time, have students do half of the exercise in class and complete the other half for homework. Or assign the entire exercise for homework.

EXERCISE 25 ABOUT YOU Ask a student who has recently arrived in this country if he or she has done these things yet.

EXAMPLE buy a car

A: Have you bought a car yet?
B: Yes, I have. OR No, I haven't. OR I bought a car last month.

1. find a job
   Have you found a job yet?
2. make any American friends
   Have you made any American friends yet?
3. open a bank account
   Have you opened a bank account yet?
4. save any money
   Have you saved any money yet?
5. buy a car
   Have you bought a car yet?
6. write to your family
   Have you written to your family yet?
7. get a credit card
   Have you gotten a credit card yet?
8. buy a computer
   Have you bought a computer yet?
9. get a telephone
   Have you gotten a telephone yet?

EXERCISE 30 *Combination Exercise.* Fill in the blanks with the correct tense of the verb in parentheses ( ). Also fill in other missing words.

A: Your Spanish is a little different from my Spanish. Where are you from?

B: I'm from Guatemala.

A: How *long* (example) *have you been* (example: you/be) here?

B: I *'ve only been* (1 only/be) here for about six months. Where are you from?

A: Miami. My family comes from Cuba. They *left* (2 leave) Cuba in 1962, after the revolution. I *was* (3 be) born in the U.S. I'm starting to become interested in my family's history. I *'ve read* (4 read) several magazine articles about genealogy so far. It's fascinating. Are you interested in your family's history?

B: Of course I am. I *'ve been* (5 be) interested in it *for* (6) a long time. I *'ve been working* (7 work) on a family tree for many years.

A: When *did you start* (8 you/start)?

B: I *started* (9 start) when I *was* (10 be) 16 years old. Over the years, I *'ve found* (11 find) a lot of interesting

306 Lesson 9

Expansion

Exercise 29 Create two rings of students. Have half of the students stand in an outer ring around the classroom. Have the other half stand in an inner ring, facing the outer ring. Instruct students to ask and answer questions from Exercise 29 in random order. Call out "turn" every minute or so. Students in the inner ring should move one space clockwise. Students now ask and answer questions with their new partners. Make sure students look at each other when they're talking.

Exercise 30 Variation

To provide practice with listening skills, have students close their books and listen to the audio. Tell students: *You're going to hear a conversation between two students. They're talking about their family histories.* Repeat the audio as needed. Ask comprehension questions, such as: *Where are the two students from?* (Guatemala and Cuba) *Are they both interested in family history?* (yes) Then have students open their books and complete Exercise 30.

information about my family. Some of my ancestors were Mayans and some were from Spain and France. In fact, my great-great grandfather was a Spanish prince.

A: How _did you find_ (12 you/find) all that information?

B: I _'ve used_ (13 use) the Internet a lot. I _'ve also gone_ (14 also/go) to many libraries to get more information.

A: _Have you ever gone_ (15 ever/go) to Spain or France to look at records there?

B: Last summer I _went_ (16 go) to Spain, and I _found_ (17 find) a lot of information while I was there.

A: How many ancestors _have you found_ (18 you/find) so far?

B: So _far_ (19) I _'ve found_ (20 find) about 50, but I'm still looking.

A: How can I get started?

B: There's a great Web site called "Cyndi's list." I'll give you the Web address, and you can get started there.

The Present Perfect; The Present Perfect Continuous 307

Expansion

Exercise 30 Have students practice the conversation in pairs. Ask volunteers to role-play all or part of the conversation in front of the class.

Exercise 30 Have students work in pairs to create their own conversations about their family histories. Have volunteers role-play all or part of their conversations in front of the class.

Summary of Lesson 9

1. Compare the present perfect and the simple past. Have students cover up the summary on page 308. Create a matching exercise on the board.

a. The action of the sentence began in the past and includes the present.
b. The action of the sentence is completely past.
c. Repetition from past to present
d. Repetition in a past time period
e. The action took place at an indefinite time between the past and the present.
f. The action took place at a definite time in the past.

1. We have had four tests so far.
2. She used the Internet three times yesterday.
3. I've done the homework already.
4. Did you visit the art museum last month?
5. My father came to the U.S. in 1992.
6. My father has had his job in the U.S. for many years.

Say: *First match the sentences with the description. Then identify each sentence as simple past or present perfect.* Have students look at the chart on page 308. Say: *Compare your work with the chart.* Review all the examples. Go over any trouble spots with the class. If necessary, have students review:

9.1 The Present Perfect Tense—An Overview (p. 278)
9.7 Continuation from Past to Present (p. 285)
9.9 The Present Perfect vs. the Simple Past (p. 290)
9.14 The Present Perfect with Repetition from Past to Present (p. 299)
9.15 The Simple Past vs. the Present Perfect with Repetition (p. 301)
9.16 The Present Perfect with Indefinite Past Time (p. 302).

SUMMARY OF LESSON 9

1. Compare the present perfect and the simple past.

Present Perfect	Simple Past
A. The action of the sentence began in the past and includes the present:	A. The action of the sentence is completely past:
past ← now → future	past ← now → future
My father **has been** in the U.S. since 1992.	My father **came** to the U.S. in 1992.
My father **has had** his job in the U.S. for many years.	My father **was** in Canada for two years before he came to the U.S.
How long **have** you **been** interested in genealogy?	When **did** you **start** your family tree?
I've always **wanted** to learn more about my family's history.	When I was a child, I always **wanted** to spend time with my grandparents.

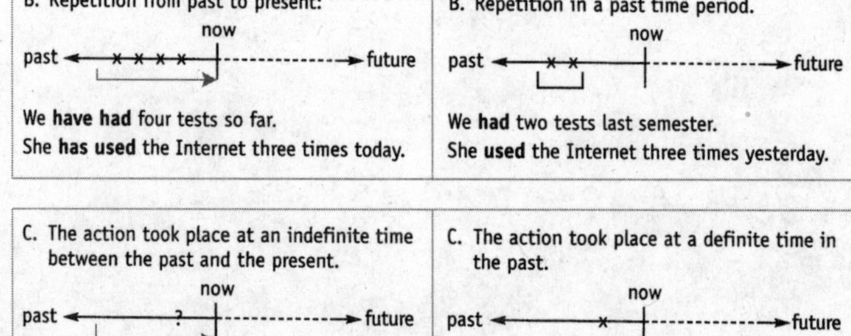

Present Perfect	Simple Past
B. Repetition from past to present:	B. Repetition in a past time period.
past ← × × × × now → future	past ← × × now → future
We **have had** four tests so far. She **has used** the Internet three times today.	We **had** two tests last semester. She **used** the Internet three times yesterday.

Present Perfect	Simple Past
C. The action took place at an indefinite time between the past and the present.	C. The action took place at a definite time in the past.
past ← ? now → future	past ← × now → future
Have you ever **made** a family tree? **I've done** the homework already. **Have** you **visited** the art museum yet?	**Did** you **make** a family tree last month? I **did** the homework last night. **Did** you **visit** the art museum last month?

308 Lesson 9

2. Compare the present perfect and the present perfect continuous.

Present Perfect	Present Perfect Continuous
A. A continuous action (nonaction verbs) I **have had** my car for five years.	A. A continuous action (action verbs) **I've been driving** a car for 20 years.
B. A repeated action Cyndi's Web site **has won** several awards.	B. A nonstop action The U.S. census **has been keeping** records since the 1880s.
C. Question with *how many* How many times **have** you **gone** to New York?	C. Question with *how long* How long **has** he **been living** in New York?
D. An action that is at an indefinite time, completely in the past. Cyndi **has created** a Web site.	D. An action that started in the past and is still happening. Cyndi **has been working** on her family history since 1992.

EDITING ADVICE

1. Don't confuse the *-ing* form and the past participle.

   She has been ~~taken~~ *taking* a test for two hours.

   She has ~~giving~~ *given* him a present.

2. Use the present perfect, not the simple present, to describe an action or state that started in the past and continues to the present.

   He has ^ *had* a car for two years.

   How long ~~do~~ *have* you work^*ed* in a factory?

3. Use *for*, not *since*, with the amount of time.

   I've been studying English ~~since~~ *for* three months.

4. Use the simple past, not the present perfect, with a specific past time.

   He ~~has come~~ *came* to the U.S. five months ago.

   When ~~have~~ *did* you come to the U.S.?

5. Use the simple past, not the present perfect, in a *since* clause.

   He has learned a lot of English since he ~~has come~~ *came* to the U.S.

The Present Perfect; The Present Perfect Continuous 309

Summary of Lesson 9 (*cont.*)

2. Compare the present perfect and the present perfect continuous. Have students cover up the summary on page 309. Create a matching exercise. On the board, write:

1. *continuous action (nonaction verbs)*
2. *continuous action (action verbs)*
3. *repeated action*
4. *nonstop action*
5. *question with* how many
6. *question with* how long
7. *action that is at an indefinite time, completely in the past*
8. *action that started in the past and is still happening*

Then write the example sentences from the chart for each use. Say: *First match the sentences with the use. Then identify each sentence as present perfect or present perfect continuous.* Have students look at the chart on page 309. Say: *Compare your work with the chart.* Review all the examples. Go over any trouble spots with the class. If necessary, have students review:

9.1 The Present Perfect Tense—An Overview (p. 278)
9.10 The Present Perfect Continuous—An Overview (p. 292)
9.13 The Present Perfect Continuous—Use (p. 295)
9.14 The Present Perfect with Repetition from Past to Present (p. 299)
9.16 The Present Perfect with Indefinite Past Time (p. 302).

Editing Advice

Have students close their books. Write the example sentences without editing marks or corrections on the board. For example:

She has been taken a test for two hours.
She has giving him a present.

Ask students to correct each sentence and provide a rule or an explanation for each correction. This activity can be done individually, in pairs, or as a class. After students have corrected each sentence, tell them to turn to pages 309–310. Say: *Now compare your work with the Editing Advice in the book.*

Lesson 9 Test/Review

For additional practice, review, and assessment materials, see Assessment CD-ROM with *ExamView Pro*, *More Grammar Practice* Workbook 2, Interactive CD-ROM, and Web site http://elt.thomson.com/gic

PART 1

1. Part 1 may be used as an in-class test to assess student performance, in addition to the Assessment CD-ROM with *ExamView Pro*. Have students read the direction line. Ask: *Do all sentences have a mistake?* (no) Go over the examples. Collect for assessment.
2. If necessary, have students review: **Lesson 9.**

6. Use correct word order. Put the adverb between the auxiliary and the main verb.

   He has ~~seen never~~ *never seen* a French movie.

   Have you ~~gone ever~~ *ever gone* to France?

7. Use correct word order in questions.

   How long ~~you have~~ *have you* been a teacher?

8. Use *yet* for negative statements; use *already* for affirmative statements.

   I haven't eaten dinner ~~already~~ *yet*.

9. Don't forget the verb *have* in the present perfect (continuous).

   I ^*have* been living in New York for two years.

10. Don't forget the *-ed* of the past participle.

    He's listen^*ed* to that CD many times.

11. Use the present perfect, not the continuous form, with *always, never, yet, already, ever,* and *how many*.

    How many times have you ~~been going~~ *gone* to Paris?

    I've never ~~been visiting~~ *visited* Paris.

12. Don't use *time* after *how long*.

    How long ~~time~~ have you had your job?

LESSON 9 TEST/REVIEW

PART 1 Find the mistakes with the underlined words, and correct them. Not every sentence has a mistake. If the sentence is correct, write *C*.

EXAMPLES I <u>have</u> *had* my car for six years.

We've <u>always wanted</u> to learn English. C

1. Since I'<u>ve come</u> *came* to the U.S., I've been studying English.
2. Have you ever <u>eating</u> *eaten* Chinese food?
3. How long <u>you've</u> *have you* been in the U.S.?

Lesson Review

To use Part 1 as a review, assign it as homework or use it as an in-class activity to be completed individually or in pairs. Check answers and review errors as a class. Reteach grammar points that students haven't mastered. Then student learning may be assessed using a test generated from the Assessment CD-ROM with *ExamView Pro*.

4. Have you ~~gone ever~~ ever gone to Canada?

5. I've ~~know~~ known my best friend since I was a child.

6. She's a teacher. She's been a teacher ~~since~~ for ten years.

7. I've never gone to Mexico.

8. How long time has your father been working as an engineer?

9. Has he ever gone to Paris? Yes, he went to Paris last year. C

10. He works in a restaurant. He's been working there since 1995.

11. Have you ever ~~study~~ studied biology?

12. Have they finished the test yet? C

13. She's done the homework ~~yet~~ already.

PART 2 Fill in the blanks with the simple past, the present perfect, or the present perfect continuous form of the verb in parentheses ( ). In some cases, more than one answer is possible.

Conversation 1

A: Have (example: study) you ever studied computer programming?

B: Yes. I studied (1 study) it in college. And I worked (2 work) as a programmer for five years. But my job is boring.

A: Have you ever thought (3 think) about changing jobs?

B: Yes. Since I was (4 be) a child, I've always wanted (5 always/want) to be an actor. When I was in college, I was (6 be) in a few plays, but since I graduated (7 graduate), I haven't had (8 not/have) time to act.

Conversation 2

A: How long have you been (1 you/be) in the U.S.?

B: For about two years.

A: Has your life changed (2 change) a lot since you came (3 come) to the U.S.?

The Present Perfect; The Present Perfect Continuous 311

PART 2

1. Part 2 may also be used as an in-class test to assess student performance, in addition to the Assessment CD-ROM with *ExamView Pro*. Have students read the direction line. Collect for assessment.
2. If necessary, have students review: **Lesson 9.**

Lesson Review

To use Part 2 as a review, assign it as homework or use it as an in-class activity to be completed individually or in pairs. Check answers and review errors as a class. Reteach grammar points that students haven't mastered. Then student learning may be assessed using a test generated from the Assessment CD-ROM with *ExamView Pro*.

PART 3

1. Part 3 may also be used as an in-class test to assess student performance, in addition to the Assessment CD-ROM with *ExamView Pro*. Have students read the direction line. Collect for assessment.
2. If necessary, have students review: **Lesson 9.**

B: Oh, yes. Before I ___came___ (4 come) here, I ___lived___ (5 live) with my family. Since I came here, I ___'ve lived___ (6 live) alone.

A: ___Have you always lived___ (7 always/live) in the same apartment in this city?

B: No. I ___'ve moved___ (8 move) three times so far. And I plan to move again at the end of the year.

A: Do you plan to have a roommate?

B: Yes, but I ___haven't found___ (9 not/find) one yet.

PART 3 Fill in the blanks with the simple present, the simple past, the present perfect, or the present perfect continuous form of the verb in parentheses ( ). In some cases, more than one answer is possible.

Paragraph 1

I ___use___ (1 use) the Internet every day. I ___have used___ (2 use) it for three years. I ___started___ (3 start) to use it when I ___became___ (4 become) interested in genealogy. I ___have been working___ (5 work) on my family tree for three years. Last month, I ___found___ (6 find) information about my father's ancestors. My grandfather ___lives___ (7 live) with us now and likes to tell us about his past. He ___was___ (8 be) born in Italy, but he ___came___ (9 come) here when he was very young, so he ___has lived___ (10 live) here most of his life. He doesn't remember much about Italy. I ___haven't found___ (11 not/find) any information about my mother's ancestors yet.

312 Lesson 9

Lesson Review

To use Part 3 as a review, assign it as homework or use it as an in-class activity to be completed individually and/or in pairs. Have students practice the conversations in pairs. Check answers and review errors as a class. Reteach grammar points that students haven't mastered. Then student learning may be assessed using a test generated from the Assessment CD-ROM with *ExamView Pro*.

Paragraph 2

I ___came___ (1 come) to the U.S. when a war ___broke___ (2 break) out in my country. I ___'ve lived___ (3 live) in the U.S. for five years. At first, everything ___was___ (4 be) very hard for me. I ___didn't know___ (5 not/know) any English when I ___arrived___ (6 arrive). But I ___'ve studied___ (7 study) English for the past five years, and now I ___speak___ (8 speak) it pretty well. I ___haven't started___ (9 not/start) my college education yet, but I plan to next semester.

EXPANSION ACTIVITIES

Classroom Activities

1. Form a group of between 4 and 6 students. Find out who in your group has done each of these things. Write that person's name in the blank.

a. ________ has made a family tree.
b. ________ has found a good job.
c. ________ has been on a ship.
d. ________ has never eaten Mexican food.
e. ________ hasn't done today's homework yet.
f. ________ has never seen a French movie.
g. ________ has taken a trip to Canada.
h. ________ has acted in a play.
i. ________ has gone swimming in the Pacific Ocean.
j. ________ has flown in a helicopter.
k. ________ has served in the military.
l. ________ has worked in a hotel.
m. ________ has never studied chemistry.
n. ________ has taken the TOEFL test.
o. ________ has just gotten a "green card."

Expansion Activities

These expansion activities provide opportunities for students to interact with one another and further develop their speaking and writing skills. Encourage students to use grammar from this lesson whenever possible.

To save class time, assign parts of the activities as homework. Then use class time for interaction and communication. If students do not need additional speaking practice, some of the activities may be assigned as writing activities for homework, or skipped altogether.

CLASSROOM ACTIVITIES

1. Rather than having students check off the things they've done first, encourage students to read through the list together as a group.

CLASSROOM ACTIVITIES (*cont.*)

2. Model the activity. Make a presentation of your family tree on the board or on handouts for your students.

WRITE ABOUT IT

1. Tell students to choose a topic to write about and make a list of the things that have changed in their lives before they begin writing their paragraph.
2. Have students make a list of the achievements of the person they're going to write about.

OUTSIDE ACTIVITITY

Have students prepare for the interview with the American by brainstorming a list of questions (e.g., *Do you know which ancestors first came to the U.S.? When did they come?*).

INTERNET ACTIVITIES

Remind students that if they don't have Internet access, they can use Internet facilities at a public library or they can use traditional research methods to find out information including looking at encyclopedias, magazines, books, journals, and newspapers.

2. Draw your family tree for the past three generations, if you can. Why do you think so many people are interested in genealogy? What is valuable about finding your family's history?

Write About it

1. Write a composition about one of the following:

   How your life has changed (*choose one*):

   a. since you came to the U.S.
   b. since you got married
   c. since you had a baby
   d. since you started college
   e. since you graduated from high school

2. Write about an interesting member of your family. What has he or she done that you think is interesting?

Outside Activities

Interview an American who has relatives who have been in the U.S. for several generations. Does this person know the stories of his or her ancestors and their native countries? What is something interesting you discovered from this interview?

Internet Activities

1. On the Internet, find Cyndi Howell's genealogy Web site. Find out about people who have the same last name as yours.
2. Type the word *genealogy* at a search engine. How many Web sites did you find?
3. Go to a search engine and type in *Larry Page, Sergey Brin.* Find an interesting fact about one of them that you didn't know. Bring it to class.

Additional Activities at http://elt.thomson.com/gic

314 Lesson 9

Classroom Activities Variation

Activity 2 Have students create visual presentations of their family tree. Encourage students to be creative. Display the family trees around the room. Ask volunteers to talk about their families.

Write About it Variation

Item 2 Have students create a presentation of their family member to show the class. Ask students to include photos if possible. Display the presentations around the room.

Have students exchange first drafts with a partner. Ask students to help their partners edit their drafts. Refer students to the Editing Advice on pages 309–310.

Internet Activities Variation

Activity 1 If students don't have access to the Internet, suggest that they find one of Cyndi Howell's books, *Cyndi's List* or *Netting Your Ancestors*, in the library. Have them look through the book and find one or two places they think might help them locate some of their ancestors.

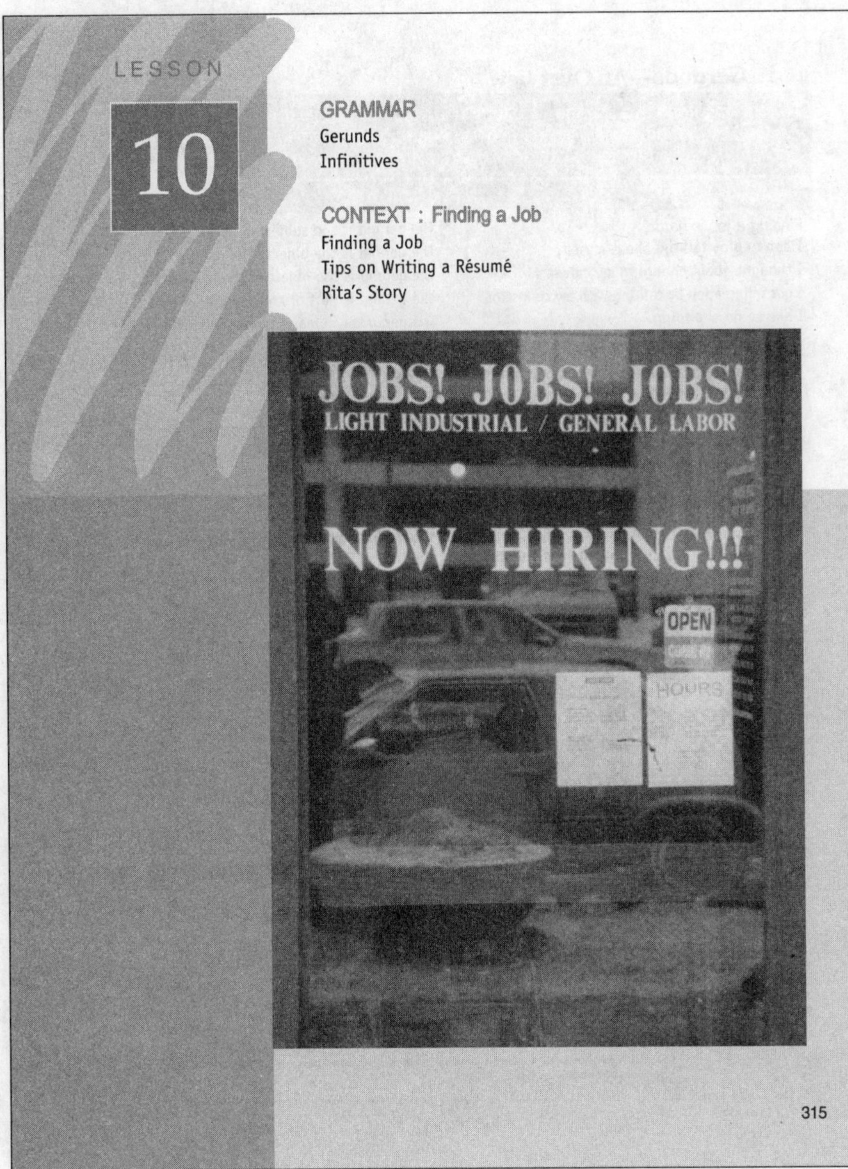

Lesson 10

Lesson Overview

GRAMMAR

1. Briefly review what students learned in the last lesson. Ask: *What did we study in Lesson 9?* (the present perfect and present perfect continuous)
2. Ask: *What are we going to study in this lesson?* (gerunds and infinitives) *Can anyone give me an example of a gerund?* (e.g., *I like **walking**.*) Have students give examples. Write the examples on the board. Then ask for examples of infinitives (e.g., *I like **to walk**.*).

CONTEXT

1. Ask: *What will we learn about in this lesson?* (finding a job) Activate students' prior knowledge. Ask: *Do you have a job? How did you find it? Did you need to write a résumé?*
2. Have students share their knowledge and personal experiences.

To save class time, have students do the Test/Review at the end of the lesson, or administer a lesson test generated from the Assessment CD-ROM with *ExamView® Pro*. Skip sections of the lesson that students have already mastered. You may also assign some sections for self-study for extra credit.

Expansion

Theme The topic for this lesson can be enhanced with the following ideas:

1. The classified section of a newspaper
2. Samples of résumés and cover letters

10.1 | Gerunds—An Overview

1. Have students cover up grammar chart **10.1** on page 316. Create a matching exercise. Write the following on the board:
   1. Finding a job is hard.
   2. I don't enjoy talking about myself.
   3. I thought about changing my career.
   4. I got information by talking with my counselor.
   a. subject
   b. object
   c. object of the preposition
   d. part of an adverbial phrase
   Ask: *What role does the gerund play in each of the sentences?*
   Review the example sentences in the chart.
2. Then have students look at grammar chart **10.1.** Say: *Now compare your answers with the chart.* Go over the examples. Point out that gerunds are often in many expressions with *go.*
3. Explain that we put *not* in front of a gerund to make it negative. Go over the examples.

Finding a Job (Reading)

1. Have students look at the photo. Ask: *What do you think is going on in the photo?* (These people may be ending a job interview.)
2. Have students look at the title of the reading. Ask: *What is the reading about?* Have students use the title and photo to make predictions about the reading.
3. Preteach any vocabulary words your students may not know, such as *résumé* and *in charge.*

BEFORE YOU READ

1. Have students discuss the questions in pairs.
2. Ask for a few volunteers to share their answers with the class.

To save class time, skip "Before You Read" or have students prepare answers for homework ahead of time.

10.1 | Gerunds—An Overview

To form a gerund, we use the *–ing* form of a verb *(finding, learning, eating, running)*. A *gerund phrase* is a gerund + a noun phrase *(finding a job, learning English)*. A gerund (phrase) can appear in several positions in a sentence.

Examples	Explanation
Finding a job is hard. I don't enjoy **talking** about myself. I thought about **changing** my career. I got information **by talking** with my counselor. I like to **go shopping.**	• The gerund is the subject. • The gerund is the object. • The gerund is the object of the preposition. • The gerund is part of an adverbial phrase. • The gerund is in many expressions with *go.*
Not having a job is frustrating. You can impress the boss by **not being** late.	We can put *not* in front of a gerund to make it negative.

FINDING A JOB

Before You Read

1. Have you ever had a job interview in this city?
2. What is your profession or job? What profession or job do you plan to have in the future?

 Read the following article. Pay special attention to gerunds.

Finding a job in the United States takes specific skills. The following advice will help you find a job.

- Write a good résumé. Describe your accomplishments.[1] Avoid **including** unnecessary information. Your résumé should be one page, if possible.

[1] *Accomplishments* are the unusual good things you have done, such as awards you have won or projects you have successfully managed.

316 Lesson **10**

Did You Know?

According to the Bureau of Labor Statistics, the fastest growing field is for medical assistants. The growth for this career between 2002 and 2012 is expected to be 59 percent.

- Find out about available jobs. One way is by **looking** in the newspaper or on the Internet. Another way is by **networking. Networking** means **exchanging** information with anyone you know—family, friends, neighbors, classmates, former coworkers, professional groups—who might know of a job. These people might also be able to give you insider information about a company, such as who is in charge and what it is like to work at their company. According to an article in the *Wall Street Journal*, 94 percent of people who succeed in **finding** a job say that **networking** was a big help.
- Practice the interview. The more prepared you are, the more relaxed you will feel. If you are worried about **saying** or **doing** the wrong thing, practice will help.
- Learn something about the company. You can find information by **going** to the company's Web site. **Getting** information takes time, but it pays off.

You can get help in these skills—**writing** a résumé, **networking**, **preparing** for an interview, **researching** a company—by **seeing** a career counselor. Most high schools and colleges have one who can help you get started.

Finding a job is one of the most difficult jobs. Some people send out hundreds of résumés and go on dozens of interviews before **finding** a job. And it isn't something you do just once or twice in your lifetime. For most Americans, **changing** jobs many times in a lifetime is not uncommon.

Tips for Getting a Job

Preparation:

1. Learn about the organization and have a specific job or jobs in mind.
2. Review your résumé.
3. Practice an interview with a friend or relative.
4. Arrive at least 15 minutes before the scheduled time of your interview.

Personal appearance:

1. Be well groomed[2] and dress appropriately.
2. Do not chew gum.

The interview:

1. Relax and answer each question concisely.
2. Use good manners. Shake hands and smile when you meet someone.
3. Be enthusiastic. Tell the interviewer why you are a good candidate for the job.
4. Ask questions about the position and the organization.
5. Thank the interviewer when you leave and in writing as a follow-up.

Information to bring to an interview:

1. Social Security card.
2. Government-issued identification (driver's license).
3. Résumé or application. Include information about your education, training, and previous employment.
4. References. Employers typically require three references. Get permission before using anyone as a reference. Make sure that each will give you a good reference. Avoid using relatives as references.

[2] When you are *well groomed*, your appearance is neat and clean.

Gerunds; Infinitives 317

Reading Variation

To practice listening skills, have students first listen to the audio alone. Ask a few comprehension questions. Repeat the audio if necessary. Then have them open their books and read along as they listen to the audio.

Reading Glossary

in charge: to be in control or command
résumé: a short statement of one's work history and education used to get a new job

Reading *CD 3, Track 17*

1. Have students first read the text silently. Tell them to pay special attention to gerunds. Then play the audio and have students read along silently.
2. Check students' comprehension. Ask questions such as: *How long should your résumé be?* (one page) *What does* networking *mean?* (exchanging information with anyone you know) *If you're prepared for an interview, how will you feel?* (relaxed) *Do Americans change jobs frequently?* (yes)

To save class time, have students do the reading for homework ahead of time.

DID YOU KNOW ?

According to the Bureau of Labor Statistics, the ten fastest growing occupations are:

1. medical assistants
2. network systems and data communications analysts
3. physician assistants
4. social and human service assistants
5. home health aids
6. medical records and health information technicians
7. physical therapist aids
8. computer software engineers, applications
9. computer software engineers, systems software
10. physical therapist assistants

10.2 | Gerund as Subject

Have students look at grammar chart **10.2.** Go over the examples and explanations. Explain that gerunds can be used as the subject of a sentence. When used as a subject, they take a singular verb. Put *not* in front of a gerund to make it negative.

EXERCISE 1

1. Have students read the direction line. Say: *Make a logical sentence using the gerund as the subject.* Remind students that answers will vary. Go over the example.
2. Have students complete Exercise 1 individually. Go over the answers as a class.
3. If necessary, review grammar chart **10.2** on page 318.

EXERCISE 2

1. Have students read the direction line. Go over the example. Have a volunteer model the example.
2. Have students complete Exercise 2 individually. Then have students compare answers in pairs. Circulate to observe pair work. Give help as needed.
3. If necessary, review grammar chart **10.2** on page 318.

To save class time, have students complete the statements for homework.

10.2 | Gerund as Subject

Examples	Explanation
Gerund Phrase **Finding a good job** takes time. **Writing a résumé** isn't easy.	We can use a gerund or gerund phrase as the subject of the sentence.
Exchanging ideas with friends **is** helpful. **Visiting** company Web sites **takes** time.	A gerund subject takes a singular verb.
Not preparing for an interview could have a bad result.	We can put *not* in front of a gerund to make it negative.

EXERCISE 1 The following things are important before a job interview. Make a sentence with each one, using a gerund phrase as the subject.

EXAMPLE get a good night's sleep
Getting a good night's sleep will help you feel rested and alert for an interview.

1. take a bath or shower
   Answers will vary.
2. select serious-looking clothes
3. prepare a résumé
4. check your résumé carefully
5. get information about the company
6. prepare answers to possible questions

EXERCISE 2 Complete each statement with a gerund (phrase) as the subject.

EXAMPLE *Learning a foreign language* takes a long time.

1. Answers will vary. is one of the most difficult jobs.
2. ______ is one of the best ways to find a job.
3. ______ is not permitted in this classroom.
4. ______ is difficult for a foreign student.
5. ______ takes a long time.
6. ______ is not polite.

318 Lesson 10

Expansion

Exercise 1 Have students work in pairs to make a flyer giving advice to students going on a job interview. Display the flyers around the class.

7. ______________________ makes me feel good.

8. ______________________ makes me nervous.

9. ______________________ scares me.

10. ______________________ is against the law.

EXERCISE 3 ABOUT YOU In preparing for an interview, it is good to think about the following questions. Answer these questions. Use a gerund in some of your answers, but do NOT try to use a gerund in every answer. It won't work. Give a lot of thought to your answers and compare them with your classmates' answers.

EXAMPLES What are your strengths?

Working with others; learning quickly; thinking fast in difficult situations.

What are your strong and weak subjects in school?

I'm strong in math. I'm weak in history.

1. What are your strengths?

   Answers will vary.

2. What are some of your weaknesses?

3. List your accomplishments and achievements. (They can be achievements in jobs, sports, school, etc.)

4. What are your interests?

5. What are your short-term goals?

6. What are your long-term goals?

7. What are things you like? Think about personalities, tasks, environments, types of work, and structure.

8. What are some things you dislike? Think about personalities, tasks, environments, types of work, and structure.

9. Why should we hire you?

Gerunds; Infinitives 319

EXERCISE 3

1. Say: *The questions in this next exercise will help you prepare for an interview.* Have students read the direction line. Say: *Remember, you don't have to try to use a gerund in every answer.* Go over the examples.
2. Have students complete Exercise 2 individually. Then have students compare answers in pairs. Circulate to observe pair work. Give help as needed.
3. If necessary, review grammar chart **10.2** on page 318.

To save class time, have students answer the questions for homework.

Expansion

Exercise 2 Do a class survey. How did students complete each statement?

Exercise 3 Have students carry out mock interviews. Tell students to find a new partner. One student plays the interviewer while the other is the job applicant. Students may also perform the interview in front of a group of students.

EXERCISE 4

1. Have students read the direction line. Go over the examples.
2. Have students complete Exercise 4 in groups. Circulate to observe group work. Give help as needed.
3. If necessary, review grammar chart **10.2** on page 318.

To save class time, have students do half of the exercise in class and complete the other half for homework.

10.3 | Gerund After Verb

1. Have students cover up grammar chart **10.3.** Have students go back to the reading on pages 316–317. Say: *In the reading, there is one verb that is immediately followed by a gerund; circle it (avoid).*
2. Have students look at grammar chart **10.3.** Explain that some verbs can be followed by a gerund. Review the list with the class. Go over the examples.
3. Say: Go + *gerund is used in many expressions.* Review the list of gerunds with *go.* Go over the example sentences.
4. Review the expressions *mind, put off,* and *can't help.*

EXERCISE 4 Write a list of personal behaviors during an interview that would hurt your chances of getting a job. You may work with a partner or in a small group.

EXAMPLES *Chewing gum during the interview looks bad.*

Not looking directly at the interviewer can hurt your chances.

1. Answers will vary.
2. ______
3. ______
4. ______
5. ______

10.3 | Gerund After Verb

Some verbs are commonly followed by a gerund (phrase). The gerund (phrase) is the object of the verb.

Examples	Explanation
Have you considered **going** to a job counselor? Do you appreciate **getting** advice? You can discuss **improving** your skills. You should practice **answering** interview questions.	The verbs below can be followed by a gerund: admit, discuss, mind, put off appreciate, dislike, miss, quit avoid, enjoy, permit, recommend can't help, finish, postpone, risk consider, keep, practice, suggest
I have many hobbies. I like to **go fishing** in the summer. I **go skiing** in the winter. I like indoor sports too. I **go bowling** once a month.	*Go* + gerund is used in many idiomatic expressions. go boating, go jogging go bowling, go sailing go camping, go shopping go dancing, go sightseeing go fishing, go skating go hiking, go skiing go hunting, go swimming
a. I don't **mind** *wearing* a suit to work. b. Don't **put off** *writing* your résumé. Do it now. c. I have an interview tomorrow morning. I **can't help** *feeling* nervous.	a. *I mind* means that something bothers me. *I don't mind* means that something is OK with me; it doesn't bother me. b. *Put off* means postpone. c. *Can't help* means to have no control over something.

320 Lesson 10

Expansion

Exercise 4 Have groups report to the class about behaviors that might hurt your chances of getting a job.

EXERCISE 5 ABOUT YOU Fill in the blanks with an appropriate gerund (or noun) to complete these statements. Share your answers with the class.

EXAMPLE I don't mind *shopping for food*, but I do[3] mind *cooking it*.

1. I usually enjoy ___Answers will vary.___ during the summer.
2. I don't enjoy ______
3. I don't mind ______ but I do mind ______
4. I appreciate ______ from my friends.
5. I need to practice ______ if I want to improve.
6. I often put off ______
7. I need to keep ______ if I want to be successful.
8. I should avoid ______ if I want to improve my health.
9. I miss ______ from my hometown.

EXERCISE 6 ABOUT YOU Make a list of suggestions and recommendations for a tourist who is about to visit your hometown. Read your list to a partner, a small group, or the entire class.

EXAMPLES *I recommend taking warm clothes for the winter.*

You should avoid drinking tap water.

1. I recommend:
   Answers will vary.
2. You should avoid:

EXERCISE 7 ABOUT YOU Tell if you like or don't like the following activities. Explain why.

Answers will vary.

EXAMPLES go shopping
I like to go shopping for clothes because I like to try new styles.

go bowling
I don't like to go bowling because I don't think it's an interesting sport.

1. go fishing	3. go jogging	5. go hunting
2. go camping	4. go swimming	6. go shopping

[3] *Do* makes the verb more emphatic. In this sentence, it shows contrast with *don't mind*.

Gerunds; Infinitives 321

EXERCISE 5

1. Have students read the direction line. Go over the example. Say: *If you can't think of a gerund, you can also use just a noun.* Have a volunteer model the example.
2. Have students complete Exercise 5 individually. Then have students compare answers in pairs. Circulate to observe pair work. Give help as needed.
3. If necessary, review grammar chart **10.3** on page 320.

EXERCISE 6

1. Ask: *What advice do you have for tourists visiting your native country?* Have students read the direction line. Go over the examples.
2. Have students complete Exercise 6 individually. Then have students compare answers in pairs. Circulate to observe pair work. Give help as needed.
3. If necessary, review grammar chart **10.3** on page 320.

To save class time, have students do the exercise for homework.

EXERCISE 7

1. Have students read the direction line. Go over the examples. Say: *You have to give a reason why you do or don't like something. Use* because.
2. Have students complete Exercise 7 in pairs. Circulate to observe pair work. Give help as needed.
3. If necessary, review grammar chart **10.3** on page 320.

To save class time, have students do half of the exercise in class and complete the other half in writing for homework. Or assign the entire exercise for homework.

Expansion

Exercise 6 Have students make brochures about their hometowns. Tell them to include their recommendations from Exercise 6.

Exercise 7 Create two rings of students. Have half of the students stand in an outer ring around the classroom. Have the other half stand in an inner ring, facing the outer ring. Instruct students to ask and answer questions from Exercise 7 in random order (e.g., *Do you like to go shopping? I like to go shopping for clothes because I like to try new styles.*). Call out "turn" every minute or so. Students in the inner ring should move one space clockwise. Students now interview their new partners. Make sure students look at each other when they're talking.

10.4 | Gerund After Preposition

1. Have students cover up grammar chart **10.4.** Have students go back to the reading on pages 316–317. Say: *Try to find gerunds that follow prepositions. Underline the preposition and the gerund* (e.g., *succeed in finding, worried about saying or doing*, etc.).
2. Then have students look at grammar chart **10.4.** Say: *A gerund can follow a preposition. It's important to choose the correct preposition after a verb or an adjective.*
3. Review the verb + preposition combinations. Go over the common combinations. Check that students understand the meanings of the expressions.
4. Review the adjective + preposition combinations. Go over the common combinations. Check that students understand the meanings of the expressions.

10.4 | Gerund After Preposition[4]

A gerund can follow a preposition. It is important to choose the correct preposition after a verb or adjective.

Preposition combinations		Common combinations	Examples
Verb + Preposition	verb + *about*	care about complain about dream about forget about talk about think about worry about	I **care about doing** well on an interview. My sister **dreams about becoming** a doctor.
	verb + *to*	adjust to look forward to object to	I am **looking forward to getting** a job and **saving** money.
	verb + *on*	depend on insist on plan on	I **plan on going** to a career counselor.
	verb + *in*	believe in succeed in	My father **succeeded in finding** a good job.
Adjective + Preposition	adjective + *of*	afraid of capable of guilty of proud of tired of	I'm **afraid of losing** my job.
	adjective + *about*	concerned about excited about upset about worried about sad about	He is **upset about not getting** the job.
	adjective + *for*	responsible for famous for grateful to . . . for	Who is **responsible for hiring** in this company?
	adjective + *at*	good at successful at	I'm not very **good at writing** a résumé.
	adjective + *to*	accustomed to used to	I'm not **accustomed to talking** about my strengths.
	adjective + *in*	interested in successful in	Are you **interested in getting** a better job?

[4] For a list of verbs and adjectives followed by a *preposition*, see Appendix H.

322 Lesson **10**

Expansion

Grammar Have students write four sentences with prepositions and gerunds. Say: *Write two sentences with an adjective followed by a preposition and gerund, and two sentences with a verb followed by a preposition and gerund.*

Language Notes:

1. *Plan, afraid,* and *proud* can be followed by an infinitive too.
   I plan **on seeing** a counselor./I plan **to see** a counselor.
   I'm afraid **of losing** my job./I'm afraid **to lose** my job.
   He's proud **of being** a college graduate./He's proud **to be** a college graduate.
2. Notice that in some expressions, *to* is a preposition followed by a gerund, not part of an infinitive.
   Compare:
   I need **to write** a résumé. (infinitive)
   I'm not accustomed **to writing** a résumé. (*to* + gerund)

EXERCISE 8 ABOUT YOU Complete the questions with a gerund (phrase). Then ask another student these questions.

EXAMPLE Are you lazy about *doing your homework?*

1. Do you ever worry about ______ Answers will vary.
2. Do you plan on ______
3. Do you ever think about ______
4. When you get tired of ______, what do you do?
5. Are you interested in ______

EXERCISE 9 ABOUT YOU Fill in the blanks with a preposition and a gerund (phrase) to make a **true** statement.

EXAMPLE I plan *on going back to Haiti soon.*

1. I'm afraid ______ Answers will vary.
2. I'm not afraid ______
3. I'm interested ______
4. I'm not interested ______
5. I want to succeed ______
6. I'm not very good ______
7. I'm accustomed ______
8. I'm not accustomed ______
9. I plan ______
10. I don't care ______

10.4 | Gerund After Preposition (*cont.*)

5. Direct students to the Language Notes. Review the verbs that can also be followed by an infinitive. Tell students that the sentences have the same meaning. Point out that *to* does not always indicate an infinitive. Sometimes *to* is a preposition preceding a gerund. Compare the sentences.
6. Remind students to look at Appendix H for a list of verbs and adjectives followed by a preposition.

EXERCISE 8

1. Say: *You're going to ask your partner some questions.* Have students read the direction line. Go over the example. Have two volunteers model the example.
2. First have students complete the questions. Then have students take turns asking and answering the questions in pairs. Circulate to observe pair work. Give help as needed.
3. If necessary, review grammar chart **10.4** on pages 322–323.

EXERCISE 9

1. Say: *Complete these statements and make them true for you.* Have students read the direction line. Go over the example. Have a volunteer model the example.
2. Have students complete Exercise 9 individually. Then have students compare answers in pairs. Circulate to observe pair work. Give help as needed.
3. If necessary, review grammar chart **10.4** on pages 322–323.

To save class time, have students do half of the exercise in class and complete the other half for homework.

Expansion

Exercise 8 Have students discuss their statements as a class. Do many students have the same interests or fears?

EXERCISE 10

1. Ask: *How have things changed for you since coming to live in the U.S.? Do you have the same dreams and worries? Or have things changed a lot for you?* Have students read the direction line. Go over the examples in the book.
2. Have students complete Exercise 10 individually. Then have students compare answers in pairs. Circulate to observe pair work. Give help as needed.
3. If necessary, review grammar chart **10.4** on pages 322–323.

To save class time, have students do the exercise for homework.

EXERCISE 10 ABOUT YOU Fill in the blanks to complete each statement. Compare your experiences in the U.S. with your experiences in your native country. You may share your answers with a small group or with the entire class.

EXAMPLES In the U.S., I'm afraid of *walking alone at night.*

In my native country, I was afraid of *not being able to give my children a good future.*

1. In the U.S., I'm interested in Answers will vary.
   In my native country, I was interested in ______
2. In the U.S., I worry about ______
   In my native country, I worried about ______
3. In the U.S., I dream about ______
   In my native country, I dreamed about ______
4. In the U.S., I look forward to ______
   In my native country, I looked forward to ______
5. In the U.S., people often complain about ______
   In my native country, people often complain about ______
6. In the U.S., families often talk about ______
   In my native country, families often talk about ______
7. American students are accustomed to ______
   Students in my native country, are accustomed to ______

324 Lesson 10

Expansion

Exercise 10 Do a class survey. How many students feel they have changed a lot? Ask volunteers to explain.

10.5 | Gerund in Adverbial Phrase

Examples	Explanation
You should practice interview questions **before going** on an interview. I found my job **by looking** in the newspaper. She took the test **without studying.**	We can use a gerund in an adverbial phrase that begins with a preposition: *before, by, after, without,* etc.

EXERCISE 11 Fill in the blanks to complete the sentences.

EXAMPLE The best way to improve your vocabulary is by *reading.*

1. One way to find a job is by *Answers will vary.*
2. It is very difficult to find a job without ______
3. The best way to improve your pronunciation is by ______
4. The best way to quit a bad habit is by ______
5. One way to find an apartment is by ______
6. I can't speak English without ______
7. It's impossible to get a driver's license without ______
8. You should read the instructions of a test before ______

EXERCISE 12 Fill in the blanks in the conversation below with the gerund form. Where you see two blanks, use a preposition before the gerund. Answers may vary.

A: I need to find a job. I've had ten interviews, but so far no job.

B: Have you thought *about* *going* (example) to a job counselor?

A: No. Where can I find one?

B: Our school office has a counseling department. I suggest *making* (1) an appointment with a counselor.

A: What can a job counselor do for me?

B: Do you know anything about interviewing skills?

Gerunds; Infinitives 325

Exercise 12 Variation

To provide practice with listening skills, have students close their books and listen to the audio. Repeat the audio as needed. Say: *You're going to hear two friends talking about searching for jobs in the U.S.* Ask comprehension questions, such as: *Who does his friend suggest he talk to about finding a job?* (a job counselor) *What is the job counselor going to help him with?* (preparing for job interviews) *What does he dislike doing?* (talking about himself) Then have students open their books and complete Exercise 12.

10.5 | Gerund in Adverbial Phrase

1. Have students look at grammar chart **10.5.** Say: *We can use a gerund in an adverbial phrase that begins with a preposition:* before, by, after, without, *etc.* Review the example sentences.
2. Ask: *How can you tell the difference between a gerund in an adverbial phrase and a gerund after a preposition?* (The preposition in an adverbial phrase is not preceded by a verb or an adjective.)
3. Have students go back to the reading on pages 316–317. Ask students to find all of the gerunds and adverbial phrases. Have them compare that construction with the gerunds after a preposition.

EXERCISE 11

1. Have students read the direction line. Go over the example. Ask: *What kind of words are we going to put on the blanks?* (gerunds)
2. Have students complete Exercise 11 individually. Then go over the answers as a class.
3. If necessary, review grammar chart **10.5** on page 325.

EXERCISE 12

CD 3, Track 18

1. Have students read the direction line. Go over the example in the book. Ask: *What are we going to write on the blanks?* (gerunds) *What are we going to write if there are two blanks?* (a preposition and a gerund)
2. Have students complete Exercise 12 individually. Go over the answers as a class.
3. If necessary, review grammar chart **10.5** on page 325.

To save class time, have students do half of the exercise in class and complete the other half for homework. Or assign the entire exercise for homework.

A: No.

B: Well, with the job counselor, you can talk *about* (2) *leaving* (3) a good impression during an interview. You can practice *answering* (4) questions that the interviewer might ask you.

A: Really? How does the counselor know what questions the interviewer will ask me?

B: Many interviewers ask the same general questions. For example, the interviewer might ask you, "Do you enjoy *working* (5) with computers?" Or she might ask you, "Do you mind *working* (6) overtime and on weekends?" Or "Are you good *at* (7) *working* (8) with other people?"

A: I dislike *talking* (9) about myself.

B: That's what you have to do in the U.S.

A: What else can the counselor help me with?

B: If your skills are low, you can talk about *improving* (10) your skills. If you don't know much about computers, for example, she can recommend *taking* (11) more classes.

A: It feels like I'm never going to find a job. I'm tired *of* (12) *looking* (13) and not finding anything.

B: If you keep *looking* (14), you will succeed *in* (15) *finding* (16) a job. I'm sure. But it takes time and patience.

Expansion

Exercise 12 Have students practice the conversation in pairs. Ask volunteers to role-play all or part of the conversation in front of the class.

10.6 | Infinitives—An Overview

To form an infinitive,we use *to* + the base form of a verb (*to find, to help, to run, to be*).

Examples	Explanation
I want **to find** a job.	An infinitive is used after certain verbs.
I want you **to help** me.	An object can be added before an infinitive.
I'm happy **to help** you.	An infinitive can follow certain adjectives.
It's important **to write** a good résumé.	An infinitive follows certain expressions with *it*.
He went to a counselor **to get** advice.	An infinitive is used to show purpose.

TIPS[5] ON WRITENG A RÉSUMÉ

Before You Read

1. Have you ever written a résumé? What is the hardest part about writing a résumé?
2. Do people in your native country have to write a résumé?

Read the following article. Pay special attention to infinitives.

It's important **to write** a good, clear résumé. A résumé should be limited to one page. It is only necessary **to describe** your most relevant work.[6] Employers are busy people. Don't expect them **to read** long résumés.

You need **to present** your abilities in your résumé. Employers expect you **to use** action verbs **to describe** your experience. Don't begin your sentences with "I". Use past tense verbs like: *managed, designed, created,* and *developed*. It is not enough **to say** you improved something. Be specific. How did you improve it?

Before making copies of your résumé, it is important **to check** the grammar and spelling. Employers want **to see** if you have good communications skills. Ask a friend or teacher **to read** and **give** an opinion about your résumé.

It isn't necessary **to include** references. If the employer wants you **to provide** references, he or she will ask you **to do** so during or after the interview.

Don't include personal information such as marital status, age, race, family information, or hobbies.

Be honest in your résumé. Employers can check your information. No one wants **to hire** a liar.

[5] A *tip* is a small piece of advice.
[6] *Relevant work* is work that is related to this particular job opening.

Reading Variation

To practice listening skills, have students first listen to the audio alone. Ask a few comprehension questions. Repeat the audio if necessary. Then have them open their books and read along as they listen to the audio.

Reading Glossary

hire: to pay for the services of; employ
liar: a person who doesn't tell the truth
relevant: loosely connected; appropriate

10.6 | Infinitives—An Overview

1. Have students cover up grammar chart **10.6.** Create a matching exercise on the board:
   1. I want to find a job.
   2. I want you to help me.
   3. I'm happy to help you.
   4. It's important to write a good résumé.
   5. He went to a counselor to get good advice.
   a. An infinitive follows certain expressions with it.
   b. An object can be added before an infinitive.
   c. An infinitive is used after certain verbs.
   d. An infinitive is used to show purpose.
   e. An infinitive can follow certain adjectives.
   Say: *Match the explanation to the sentence.*
2. Then have students look at grammar chart **10.6.** Say: *Compare your work with the chart.* Go over any trouble spots with the class.

Tips on Writing a Résumé (Reading)

1. Have students look briefly at the resume on page 328. Ask: *Do you have a résumé? Does it look like this résumé? How is it different? What are résumés like in your native country?*
2. Have students look at the title of the reading. Ask: *What is the reading about?* Have students use the title and the résumé to make predictions about the reading.
3. Preteach any vocabulary words your students may not know, such as *relevant, hire,* and *liar.*

BEFORE YOU READ

1. Have students discuss the questions in pairs.
2. Ask for a few volunteers to share their answers with the class.

To save class time, skip "Before You Read" or have students prepare answers for homework ahead of time.

Reading CD 3, Track 19

1. Have students first read the text silently. Tell them to pay special attention to infinitives. Then play the audio and have students read along silently.
2. Check students' comprehension. Ask questions such as: *Do employers want to see every job you've ever had on a résumé?* (Not necessarily. They want to see only relevant work.) *What kind of verbs should you use in a résumé?* (action verbs) *What should you check your résumé for?* (errors) *Should you put personal information about yourself or your family in the résumé?* (no)

To save class time, have students do the reading for homework ahead of time.

TINA WHITE
1234 Anderson Avenue
West City, MA 01766
tina.white@met.com
617-123-1234 (home)
617-987-9876 (cellular)

EXPERIENCE

COMPUTER SALES MANAGER
Acme Computer Services, Inc., Concord, MA
March 2003–Present

- Manage computer services department, overseeing 20 sales representatives throughout New England.
- Exceeded annual sales goal by 20 percent in 2004.
- Created online customer database, enabling representatives and company to track and retain customers and improve service.
- Developed new training program and materials for all company sales representatives.

OFFICE MANAGER
West Marketing Services, West City, MA
June 1999–March 2003

- Implemented new system for improving accounting records and reports.
- Managed, trained, and oversaw five customer service representatives.
- Grew sales contracts for support services by 200 percent in first two years.

EDUCATION AND TRAINING
Northeastern Community College, Salem, MA
Associates Degree Major: Accounting
Institute of Management, Boston, MA
Certificate of Completion. Course: Sales Management

COMPUTER SKILLS
Proficient in use of MS Windows, PowerPoint, Excel, Access, Outlook, MAC OS, and several accounting and database systems

Culture Note

The American résumé is different from the European CV or *curriculum vitae*. The résumé is a brief marketing tool that summarizes a person's professional career and educational background. It's usually a one- or two-page document. The CV is a formal package that describes in detail a person's professional and educational background. It is often printed on high quality paper and bound. Supporting documents (such as publications) are often included in the package. The résumé does not contain any personal information (e.g., marital status) about the applicant, whereas the CV will often include personal information and a photo of the applicant.

10.7 | Infinitive as Subject

An infinitive can be the subject of a sentence. We begin the sentence with *it* and delay the infinitive.

Examples	Explanation
It is important **to write** a good résumé. It isn't necessary **to include** all your experience. It takes time **to find** a job.	We can use an infinitive after these adjectives: dangerous, good, necessary, difficult, great, possible, easy, hard, sad, expensive, important, wrong, fun, impossible
It is necessary **for the manager** to choose the best candidate for the job. It isn't easy **for me** to talk about myself. It was hard **for her** to leave her last job.	Include *for* + noun or object pronoun to make a statement that is true of a specific person.
Compare Infinitive and Gerund Subjects: It's important **to arrive** on time. **Arriving** on time is important.	There is no difference in meaning between an infinitive subject and a gerund subject.

EXERCISE 13 Fill in the blanks with an appropriate infinitive to give information about résumés and interviews. Answers may vary.

EXAMPLE It is necessary ___to have___ a Social Security card.

1. It isn't necessary ___to write___ *all* your previous experience. Choose only the most relevant experience.
2. It's important ___to check___ your spelling and grammar before sending a résumé.
3. It is a good idea ___to practice___ interview questions before going on an interview.
4. It is important ___to look___ your best when you go on an interview, so choose your clothes carefully.
5. It isn't necessary ___to include___ references on a résumé. You can simply write, "References available upon request."
6. It's important ___to describe___ your past work experience in detail, using words like *managed, designed, supervised,* and *built.*

Gerunds; Infinitives 329

10.7 | Infinitive as Subject

1. Have students look at grammar chart **10.7.** Say: *Like gerunds, infinitives can also be used as the subject of a sentence.* Go over the example sentences.
2. Review the list of adjectives you can use before the infinitive as a subject.
3. Say: *To make a statement that is true for a particular person, use* for + *noun/object pronoun.* Go over the example sentences.
4. Point out that there is no difference in meaning between an infinitive and a gerund when used as a subject.

EXERCISE 13

1. Have students read the direction line. Go over the example in the book.
2. Have students complete Exercise 13 individually. Then have students compare answers in pairs. Circulate to observe pair work. Give help as needed.
3. If necessary, review grammar chart **10.7** on page 329.

Expansion

Grammar Have students go back to the reading on page 327. Say: *Underline the* it *expressions and all the infinitives used as subjects.*

EXERCISE 14

1. Have students read the direction line. Go over the examples in the book. Ask a volunteer to identify the object in one of the example sentences.
2. Have students complete Exercise 14 individually. Then have students compare answers in pairs. Circulate to observe pair work. Give help as needed.
3. If necessary, review grammar chart **10.7** on page 329.

To save class time, have students do half of the exercise in class and complete the other half for homework.

EXERCISE 15

1. Say: *In this exercise, you're going to say what's important for you to do or have.* Go over the example in the book. Ask a volunteer to model the example.
2. Have students complete Exercise 15 in pairs. Circulate to observe pair work. Give help as needed.
3. If necessary, review grammar chart **10.7** on page 329.

To save class time, have students do half of the exercise in class and complete the other half in writing for homework. Or if students do not need speaking practice, the entire exercise may be skipped or done in writing.

EXERCISE 16

1. Have students read the direction line. Go over the example in the book. Ask a volunteer to model the example.
2. Have students complete Exercise 16 individually. Then have students compare answers in pairs. Circulate to observe pair work. Give help as needed.
3. If necessary, review grammar chart **10.7** on page 329.

To save class time, have students do the exercise for homework.

EXERCISE 14 Complete each statement with an infinitive phrase. You can add an object, if you like.

EXAMPLES **It's easy** *to shop in an American supermarket.*

It's necessary *for me to pay my rent by the fifth of the month.*

1. **It's important** ______ Answers will vary.
2. **It's impossible** ______
3. **It's possible** ______
4. **It's necessary** ______
5. **It's dangerous** ______
6. **It isn't good** ______
7. **It's expensive** ______
8. **It's hard** ______

EXERCISE 15 ABOUT YOU Tell if it's important or not important for you to do the following.

EXAMPLE **own a house**
It's (not) important for me to own a house.

Answers will vary.

1. **get a college degree**
2. **find an interesting job**
3. **have a car**
4. **speak English well**
5. **read and write English well**
6. **study American history**
7. **become an American citizen**
8. **own a computer**
9. **have a cell phone**
10. **make a lot of money**

EXERCISE 16 Write a sentence with each pair of words below. You may read your sentences to the class.

EXAMPLE **hard / the teacher**
It's hard for the teacher to pronounce the names of some students.

1. **important / us (the students)**
   ______ Answers will vary.
2. **difficult / Americans**
   ______

330 **Lesson 10**

Expansion

Exercise 14 Have students discuss their statements in groups. Ask: ***What statements does everyone agree with? What statements does everyone disagree with?***

Exercise 15 Do a class survey. What's important to the majority of the students? What's not important?

3. easy / the teacher

4. necessary / children

5. difficult / a woman

6. difficult / a man

EXERCISE 17 Write a list of things that a foreign student or immigrant should know about life in the U.S. Use gerunds or infinitives as subjects. You may work with a partner.

EXAMPLES *It is possible for some students to get financial aid.*

Learning English is going to take longer than you expected.

1. Answers will vary.
2.
3.
4.
5.
6.

10.8 Infinitive After Adjective

Some adjectives can be followed by an infinitive.

Examples	Explanation
I would be happy **to help** you with your résumé. Are you prepared **to make** copies of your résumé?	Adjectives often followed by an infinitive are: afraid happy prepared ready glad lucky proud sad

Gerunds; Infinitives 331

EXERCISE 17

1. Have students read the direction line. Go over the examples in the book. Say: *In this exercise, try to use both infinitives and gerunds.* Ask: *Is there a gerund in one of the example sentences?* (Yes, *learning*.)
2. Have students complete Exercise 17 individually. Then have students compare answers in pairs. Circulate to observe pair work. Give help as needed.
3. If necessary, review grammar chart **10.7** on page 329.

To save class time, have students do half of the exercise in class and complete the other half for homework. Or assign the entire exercise for homework.

10.8 Infinitive After Adjective

Have students look at grammar chart **10.8.** Say: *Some adjectives can be followed by an infinitive.* Go over the example sentences and the list of adjectives. Remind students that these infinitives are not subjects with *it* expressions.

Expansion

Exercise 16 Ask volunteers to share their answers with the class.

Exercise 17 Variation

Have students work in pairs to create a pamphlet for new students. Ask students to use infinitives and gerunds as subjects. Display pamphlets around the room.

EXERCISE 18

CD 3, Track 20

1. Say: *In this conversation, two women are talking about an upcoming job interview.* Have students read the direction line. Go over the example.
2. Have students complete Exercise 18 individually. Go over the answers as a class.
3. If necessary, review grammar chart **10.8** on page 331.

EXERCISE 19

1. Say: *Make statements that are true for you.* Go over the example. Have a volunteer model the example.
2. Have students complete Exercise 19 individually. Then have students compare answers in pairs. Circulate to observe pair work. Give help as needed.
3. If necessary, review grammar chart **10.8** on page 331.

To save class time, have students do half of the exercise in class and complete the other half for homework.

EXERCISE 18 Complete this conversation with appropriate infinitives. Answers may vary.

EXAMPLE A: I have my first interview tomorrow. I'm afraid *to go* (example) alone. Would you go with me?

B: I'd be happy *to go* (1) with you and wait in the car. But nobody can go with you on an interview. You have to do it alone. It sounds like you're not ready *to have* (2) a job interview. You should see a job counselor and get some practice before you have an interview. I was lucky *to have* (3) a great job counselor. She prepared me well.

A: I don't have time to make an appointment with a job counselor before tomorrow. Maybe you can help me.

B: I'd be happy *to help* (4) you. Do you have some time this afternoon? We can go over some basic questions.

A: Thanks. I'm glad *to have* (5) you as my friend.

B: That's what friends are for.

EXERCISE 19 ABOUT YOU Fill in the blanks.

EXAMPLE I'm lucky *to be in the U.S.*

1. I was lucky ________ Answers will vary.
2. I'm proud ________
3. I'm sometimes afraid ________ alone.
4. I'm not afraid ________
5. In the U.S., I'm afraid ________
6. Are we ready ________
7. I'm not prepared ________

332 Lesson 10

Exercise 18 Variation

To provide practice with listening skills, have students close their books and listen to the audio. Repeat the audio as needed. Say: *In this conversation, two women are talking about an upcoming job interview.* Ask comprehension questions, such as: *Is person A nervous about the job interview?* (yes) *Is person B going to go into the interview with her?* (No. She said that she'll wait in the car.) *Is person A going to see a job counselor?* (No. She doesn't have time.) Then have students open their books and complete Exercise 18.

Expansion

Exercise 18 Have students practice the conversation in pairs. Ask volunteers to role-play the conversation in front of the class.

Exercise 19 Have volunteers share some of their answers with the class.

10.9 | Infinitive After Verb

Some verbs are commonly followed by an infinitive (phrase).	
Examples	**Explanation**
I need **to find** a new job. I decided **to quit** my old job. I prefer **to work** outdoors. I want **to make** more money.	We can use an infinitive after the following verbs: agree, decide, like, promise ask, expect, love, refuse attempt, forget, need, remember begin, hope, plan, start continue, learn, prefer, try want

Pronunciation Note:
The *to* in infinitives is often pronounced "ta" or, after a *d* sound, "da." *Want to* is often pronounced "wanna." Listen to your teacher pronounce the sentences in the above box.

EXERCISE 20 ABOUT YOU Ask a question with the words given in the present tense. Another student will answer.

EXAMPLE like / work with computers
A: Do you like to work with computers?
B: Yes, I do. OR No, I don't.

1. plan / look for a job
Do you plan to look for a job?
2. expect / make a lot of money at your next job
Do you expect to make a lot of money at your next job?
3. like / work with computers
Do you like to work with computers?
4. prefer / work the second shift
Do you prefer to work the second shift?
5. need / see a job counselor
Do you need to see a job counselor?
6. hope / become rich some day
Do you hope to become rich some day?
7. like / work with people
Do you like to work with people?
8. try / keep up with changes in technology
Do you try to keep up with changes in technology?
9. want / learn another language
Do you want to learn another language?
10. continue / speak your native language at home
Do you continue to speak your native language at home?

Gerunds; Infinitives 333

10.9 | Infinitive After Verb

1. Have students cover up grammar chart **10.9.** Then have students go back to the reading on pages 327–328. Ask: *What verbs are followed by an infinitive? Make a list.*
2. Have students look at grammar chart **10.9.** Ask: *Are the verbs from the reading on the list in the chart?* Go over the examples.
3. Direct students to the Pronunciation Note. Model the pronunciation of the *to* (*ta*) in infinitives. Model the pronunciation of *want to* (*wanna*). Have students listen as you pronounce all the sentences in the chart.

EXERCISE 20

1. Have students read the direction line. Go over the example in the book. Say: *Give a short answer to the questions.*
2. Have students complete Exercise 20 in pairs. Circulate to observe pair work. Give help as needed.
3. If necessary, review grammar chart **10.9** on page 333.

Expansion

Exercise 20 Create two rings of students. Have half of the students stand in an outer ring around the classroom. Have the other half stand in an inner ring, facing the outer ring. Instruct students to ask and answer questions from Exercise 20. Tell students to answer questions with a short answer. Call out "turn" every minute or so. Students in the inner ring should move one space clockwise. Students now interview their new partners. Make sure students look at each other when they're talking.

Culture Note

Job interviews are stressful, which is why it's best to be prepared and to practice, practice, practice. There are many books with lists of possible questions an interviewer might ask and with helpful hints on how to best answer the questions. Here are some typical interview questions:
What are your strengths and weaknesses?
Why did you go into this field?
What is success and how do you measure it?
Tell me about a situation at your last job that you feel you handled well.
Tell me about a situation at your last job that you feel you handled badly.
Why do you want to work here?
Why should we hire you?

EXERCISE 21

1. Have students read the direction line. Go over the examples in the book. Ask: *What tenses are these sentences in?* (The first is in the simple present. The second is in the present continuous.) *You can write these sentences in any tense.*
2. Have students complete Exercise 21 individually. Then have students compare sentences in pairs. Circulate to observe pair work.
3. If necessary, review grammar chart **10.9** on page 333.

To save class time, have students do half of the exercise in class and complete the other half for homework. Or assign the entire exercise for homework.

EXERCISE 22

1. Have students read the direction line. Model #1 for the students (e.g., *I like to stay home on the weekends because I'm never home during the week. I'm always at work.*). Point out the illustration of a chessboard.
2. Have students complete Exercise 22 individually. Have students discuss their answers in groups or as a class.
3. If necessary, review grammar chart **10.9** on page 333.

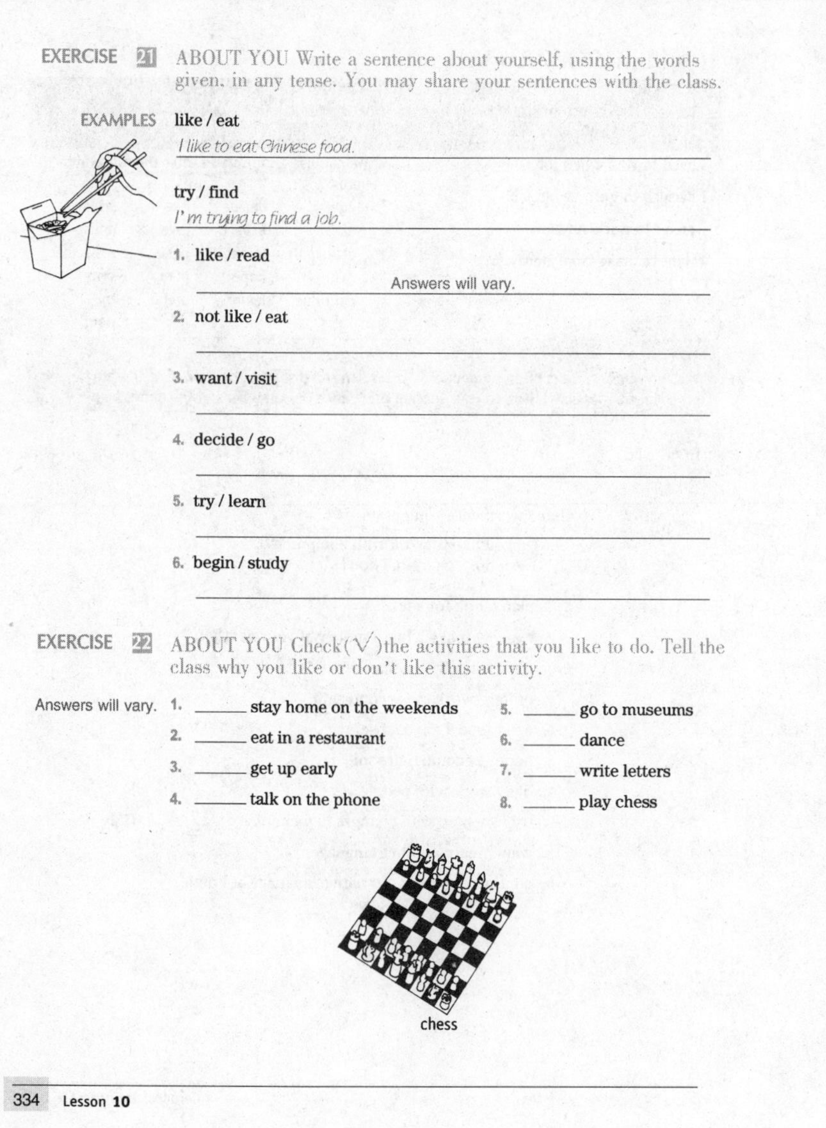

EXERCISE 21 ABOUT YOU Write a sentence about yourself, using the words given, in any tense. You may share your sentences with the class.

EXAMPLES like / eat
I like to eat Chinese food.

try / find
I'm trying to find a job.

1. like / read
 Answers will vary.
2. not like / eat
3. want / visit
4. decide / go
5. try / learn
6. begin / study

EXERCISE 22 ABOUT YOU Check (✓) the activities that you like to do. Tell the class why you like or don't like this activity.

Answers will vary.

1. ______ stay home on the weekends
2. ______ eat in a restaurant
3. ______ get up early
4. ______ talk on the phone
5. ______ go to museums
6. ______ dance
7. ______ write letters
8. ______ play chess

chess

334 Lesson 10

Expansion

Exercise 22 Have students ask and answer questions in pairs (e.g., *Do you like to stay home on weekends? Yes, I do. / No, I don't.*).

10.10 Gerund or Infinitive After Verb

Some verbs can be followed by either a gerund or an infinitive with almost no difference in meaning.

Examples	Explanation
I started **looking** for a job a month ago. I started **to look** for a job a month ago.	The verbs below can be followed by either a gerund or an infinitive with almost no difference in meaning:
He continued **working** until he was 65 years old. He continued **to work** until he was 65 years old.	attempt, deserve, prefer, begin, hate, start, can't stand[7], like, try, continue, love

Language Notes:

1. The meaning of *try* + infinitive is a little different from the meaning of *try* + gerund.
   Try + infinitive means to make an effort.
   I'll **try to improve** my résumé.
   You should **try to relax** during the interview.
2. *Try* + gerund means to use a different technique when one technique doesn't produce the result you want.
   I wanted to reach you yesterday, but I couldn't. I **tried calling** your home phone, but I got your answering machine. I **tried calling** your cell phone, but it was turned off. I **tried e-mailing** you, but you didn't check your e-mail.

EXERCISE 23 ABOUT YOU Complete each statement using either a gerund (phrase) or an infinitive (phrase). Practice both ways.

EXAMPLES I started *to learn English four years ago.* (learn)

I started *studying French when I was in high school.* (study)

1. I started Answers will vary. (come) to this school in ______
2. I began ______ (study) English ______
3. I like ______ (watch) on TV.
4. I like ______ (live)
5. I hate ______ (wear)
6. I love ______ (eat)

[7] *Can't stand* means hate or can't tolerate. I *can't stand* waiting in a long line.

Gerunds; Infinitives 335

10.10 Gerund or Infinitive After Verb

1. Have students look at grammar chart **10.10.** Say: *Some verbs can take an infinitive or a gerund without changing meaning.* Review the list of verbs and go over the example sentences.
2. Direct students to the Language Notes. Say: Try *has different meanings when used with an infinitive or with a gerund. With an infinitive,* try *means to make an effort. With a gerund, it means to use a different technique when what you're presently doing isn't working.* Go over the examples in the chart.

EXERCISE 23

1. Have students read the direction line. Go over the examples. Say: *Complete some sentences with a gerund and others, with an infinitive.*
2. Have students complete Exercise 23 individually. Go over the answers as a class.
3. If necessary, review grammar chart **10.10** on page 335.

Expansion

Exercise 23 Have students ask and answer questions in pairs (e.g., *When did you start coming to this school? In September 2004.*).

10.11 | Object Before Infinitive

1. Have students look at grammar chart **10.10.** Say: *We can use an object after the verb and before the infinitive.* Go over the example sentences. Review object pronouns if necessary.
2. Say: *We often use objects after the verbs on the list.* Go over the verbs.
3. Point out that the verb *help* can be followed by an object + base form or an object + infinitive. Go over the example sentences.

EXERCISE 24

CD 3, Track 21

1. Say: *In this conversation, two friends are talking about their jobs.* Have students read the direction line. Go over the examples.
2. Have students complete Exercise 24 individually. Go over the answers as a class.
3. If necessary, review grammar chart **10.11** on page 336.

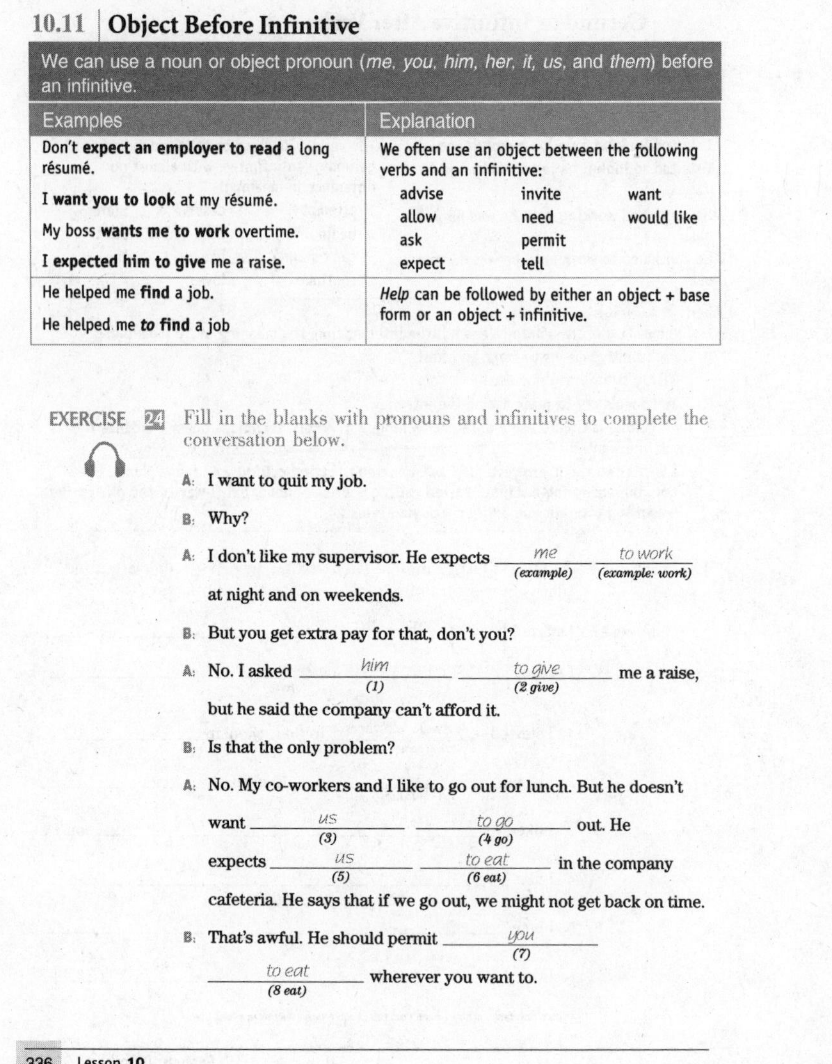

10.11 | Object Before Infinitive

We can use a noun or object pronoun (*me, you, him, her, it, us,* and *them*) before an infinitive.

Examples	Explanation
Don't **expect an employer to read** a long résumé. I **want you to look** at my résumé. My boss **wants me to work** overtime. I **expected him to give** me a raise.	We often use an object between the following verbs and an infinitive: advise, invite, want, allow, need, would like, ask, permit, expect, tell
He helped me **find** a job. He helped me ***to* find** a job	*Help* can be followed by either an object + base form or an object + infinitive.

EXERCISE 24 Fill in the blanks with pronouns and infinitives to complete the conversation below.

A: I want to quit my job.

B: Why?

A: I don't like my supervisor. He expects *me* (example) *to work* (example: work) at night and on weekends.

B: But you get extra pay for that, don't you?

A: No. I asked *him* (1) *to give* (2 give) me a raise, but he said the company can't afford it.

B: Is that the only problem?

A: No. My co-workers and I like to go out for lunch. But he doesn't want *us* (3) *to go* (4 go) out. He expects *us* (5) *to eat* (6 eat) in the company cafeteria. He says that if we go out, we might not get back on time.

B: That's awful. He should permit *you* (7) *to eat* (8 eat) wherever you want to.

336 Lesson 10

Exercise 24 Variation

To provide practice with listening skills, have students close their books and listen to the audio. Repeat the audio as needed. Ask comprehension questions such as: *Why doesn't person A like his supervisor?* (He expects him to work late and on weekends. He also doesn't like him to eat out for lunch.) *What does person A say about his manager?* (She never says anything nice—even when he does a good job.) *What does person A ask person B?* (He asks him if there are any openings at his company.) Then have students open their books and complete Exercise 24.

A: That's what I think. I also have a problem with my manager. She never gives anyone a compliment. When I do a good job, I expect

her (9) *to say* (10 say) something nice. But she only says something when we make a mistake.

B: It's important to get positive feedback too.

A: Do you know of any jobs in your company? I'd like *you* (11) *to ask* (12 ask) your boss if he needs anyone.

B: I don't think there are any job openings in my company. My boss has two sons in their twenties. He wants *them* (13) *to work* (14 work) for him on Saturdays. But they're so lazy. The boss allows *them* (15) *to come* (16 come) late and *to leave* (17 leave) early. He would never permit *us* (18) *to do* (19 do) that. We have to be on time exactly, or he'll take away some of our pay.

A: Maybe I should just stay at my job. I guess no job is perfect.

EXERCISE 25 Tell if the teacher wants or doesn't want the students to do the following.

EXAMPLES do the homework
The teacher wants us to do the homework.

use the textbook during a test
The teacher doesn't want us to use the textbook during a test.

talk to another student during a test
The teacher doesn't want us to talk to another student during a test.
study before a test
The teacher wants us to study before a test.
copy another student's homework in class
The teacher doesn't want us to copy another student's homework in class.
learn English
The teacher wants us to learn English.
speak our native languages
The teacher doesn't want us to speak our native language.
improve our pronunciation
The teacher wants us to improve our pronunciation.

EXERCISE 25

1. Have students read the direction line. Go over the examples.
2. Have students complete Exercise 25 individually. Have students compare answers in pairs. Circulate to observe pair work.
3. If necessary, review grammar chart **10.10** on page 336.

To save class time, have students do half of the exercise in class and complete the other half in writing for homework. Or if students do not need speaking practice, the entire exercise may be skipped or done in writing.

Expansion

Exercise 19 Have students practice the conversation in pairs. Ask volunteers to role-play the conversation in front of the class.

Exercise 19 Have students work in pairs to create a similar conversation, making it true for them. Ask volunteers to role-play the conversation in front of the class.

EXERCISE 26

1. Have students read the direction line. Go over the examples.
2. Have students complete Exercise 26 in pairs. Circulate to observe pair work.
3. If necessary, review grammar chart **10.11** on page 336.

To save class time, have students do half of the exercise in class and complete the other half in writing for homework. Or if students do not need speaking practice, the entire exercise may be skipped or done in writing.

EXERCISE 27

1. Have students read the direction line. Go over the examples. Have a volunteer model the activity.
2. Have students complete Exercise 27 individually. Then have students compare answers in pairs. Circulate to observe pair work.
3. If necessary, review grammar chart **10.11** on page 336.

To save class time, have students do the exercise for homework.

10.12 | Infinitive to Show Purpose

Have students look at grammar chart **10.12.** Say: *We use the infinitive to show purpose.* Go over the example sentences. Explain that you can also say *in order to* to show purpose. Go over the example sentences.

EXERCISE 28

1. Have students read the direction line. Go over the example. Have a volunteer do #1.
2. Have students complete Exercise 28 individually. Then have students compare answers in pairs. Circulate to observe pair work.
3. If necessary, review grammar chart **10.12** on page 338.

EXERCISE 26 ABOUT YOU Tell if you expect or don't expect the teacher to do the following.

EXAMPLES **give homework**
I expect him / her to give homework.
give me private lessons
I don't expect him / her to give me private lessons.

Answers will vary.

1. **correct the homework**
2. **give tests**
3. **speak my native language**
4. **help me after class**
5. **come to class on time**
6. **pass all the students**
7. **know a lot about my native country**
8. **answer my questions in class**
9. **teach us American history**
10. **pronounce my name correctly**

EXERCISE 27 ABOUT YOU Write sentences to tell what one member of your family wants (or doesn't want) from another member of your family.

EXAMPLES *My father doesn't want my brother to watch so much TV.*
My brother wants me to help him with his math homework.

1. ______ Answers will vary. ______
2. ______
3. ______
4. ______

10.11 | Infinitive to Show Purpose

We use the infinitive to show purpose.

Examples	Explanation
You can use the Internet **to find** job information. I need a car **to get** to work. I'm saving my money **to buy** a car.	*To* is the short form of *in order to.*
You can use the Internet **in order to find** job information. I need a car **in order to get** to work. I'm saving my money **in order to buy** a car.	The long form is *in order to.*

EXERCISE 28 Fill in the blanks with an infinitive to show purpose. Answers will vary.

EXAMPLE **I bought the Sunday newspaper** *to look for a job*.

1. **I called the company** *to make* **an appointment.**
2. **She wants to work overtime** *to earn more money*.

Expansion

Exercises 25 and 26 Have a class discussion about what students expect or don't expect you (the teacher) to do and what they think you want or don't want them to do.

3. You should use the Internet *to look for* jobs.
4. You can use a résumé writing service *to write* your résumé.
5. My interview is in a far suburb. I need a car *to get to* the interview.
6. Use express mail *to send it* faster.
7. In the U.S., you need experience *to get* a job, and you need a job *to get* experience.
8. I need two phone lines. I need one *to talk* on the phone with my friends and relatives. I need the other one *to make* business calls.
9. I'm sending a letter that has a lot of papers in it. I need extra stamps *to mail* this letter.
10. You should go to the college admissions office *to request* a copy of your transcripts.
11. After an interview, you can call the employer *to say* that you're very interested in the position.

AN APARTMENT LEASE

Before You Read

1. What are some differences in the American workplace and the workplace in other countries?
2. In your native culture, is it a sign of respect or disrespect to look at someone directly?

Read the following story. Pay special attention to *used to*, *be used to*, and *get used to*.

I've been in the U.S. for two years. I **used to** study British English in India, so I had a hard time **getting used to** the American pronunciation. But little by little, I started to **get used to** it. Now I understand Americans well, and they understand me.

I **used to be** an elementary school teacher in India. But for the past two years in the U.S., I've been working in a hotel cleaning rooms. I have to work the second shift. **I'm not used to working** nights. I don't like it because I don't see my children very much. When I get home from work, they're asleep.

(Continued)

Culture Note

Over the years, workplace attire has become more and more casual. However, some fields, such as law or finance, still maintain a more formal, conservative dress code. In corporate New York, for example, employees are expected to wear dark, conservative suits. Some companies may relax the code one day of the week, such as Fridays, and allow employees to wear very casual attire. Often, these days are known as casual Fridays or dress down days.

Reading Variation

To practice listening skills, have students first listen to the audio alone. Ask a few comprehension questions. Repeat the audio if necessary. Then have them open their books and read along as they listen to the audio.

Rita's Story (Reading)

1. Have students look at the illustrations on page 340. Ask: *What's going on in these pictures?* (In the first picture, a woman is wearing traditional Indian clothing. She's sitting in a comfortable chair. It looks like she's about to read a book. She looks happy. In the second picture, the same woman is vacuuming. It looks like she has a name tag on her shirt. This might mean that she works in the cleaning business.)
2. Have students look at the title of the reading. Ask: *What is the reading about?* Have students use the title and pictures to make predictions about the reading.
3. Preteach any vocabulary words your students may not know, such as *shift* and *impolite*.

BEFORE YOU READ

1. Have students discuss the questions in pairs.
2. Ask for a few volunteers to share their answers with the class.

To save class time, skip "Before You Read" or have students prepare answers for homework ahead of time.

Reading *CD 3, Track 22*

1. Have students first read the text silently. Tell them to pay special attention to *used to*, *be used to*, and *get used to*. Then play the audio and have students read along silently.
2. Check students' comprehension. Ask questions such as: *Did Rita learn English before she came to the U.S.?* (Yes. But she studied British English.) *What did she use to do in India?* (She was an elementary school teacher.) *What is she doing now?* (She cleans rooms in a hotel.) *Who prepares dinner at her house?* (her husband) *Does Rita like wearing a uniform?* (No. In India, she liked to wear traditional clothes.)

To save class time, have students do the reading for homework ahead of time.

My husband is home in the evening and cooks for them. In India, I **used to do** all the cooking, but now he has to help with household duties. He didn't like it at first, but now he's **used to it.**

When I started looking for a job, I had to **get used to** a lot of new things. For example, I had to learn to talk about my abilities in an interview. In India, it is considered impolite to say how wonderful you are. But my job counselor told me that I had to **get used to** it because that's what Americans do. Another thing **I'm not used to** is wearing American clothes. In India, I **used to wear** traditional Indian clothes to work. But now I wear a uniform to work. I don't like to dress like this. I prefer traditional Indian clothes, but my job requires a uniform. There's one thing I **can't get used to:** everyone here calls each other by their first names. It's our native custom to use a term of respect with people we don't know.

It has been hard to **get used to** so many new things, but little by little, I'm doing it.

340 Lesson 10

Reading Glossary

impolite: showing bad manners; rude

shift: a segment of work time

10.13 | *Used To* vs. *Be Used To*

Used to + base form is different from *be used to* + gerund.

Examples	Explanation
Rita **used to be** an elementary school teacher. Now she cleans hotel rooms. She **used to wear** traditional Indian clothes. Now she wears a uniform to work. She **used to cook** dinner for her family in India. Now her husband cooks dinner.	*Used to* + base form tells about a past habit or custom. This activity has been discontinued.
Her husband **didn't use to cook** in India.	The negative is *didn't use to* + base form. (Remove the *d* at the end.)
I'm used to working in the day, not at night. Women in India **are used to wearing** traditional clothes.	*Be used to* + gerund or noun means *be accustomed to*. Something is a person's custom and is therefore not difficult to do.
People who studied British English **aren't used to the American pronunciation.**	The negative is *be* + *not* + *used to* + gerund or noun. (Do not remove the *d* of **used to.**)
If you emigrate to the U.S., you have to **get used to many new things.** Children from another country usually **get used to living** in the U.S. easily. But it takes their parents a long time to **get used to a new life.**	*Get used to* + gerund or noun means *become accustomed to.*
I **can't get used to** the cold winters here. She **can't get used to** calling people by their first names.	For the negative, we usually say *can't get used to.*

EXERCISE 29 ABOUT YOU Write four sentences comparing your former behaviors to your behaviors or customs now.

EXAMPLES *I used to live with my family. Now I live with a roommate.*

I used to worry a lot. Now I take it easy most of the time.

1. Answers will vary.
2. ______
3. ______
4. ______

Gerunds; Infinitives 341

10.13 | *Used To* vs. *Be Used To*

1. Have students cover up grammar chart **10.13.** Write the following on the board:
   1. Rita used to be an elementary school teacher.
   2. I'm used to working in the day, not at night.
   3. If you emigrate to the U.S., you have to get used to many new things.
   Ask: *Which sentence means* to be accustomed to (sentence 2), *which means* to become accustomed to (sentence 3), *and which sentence means that something was a past habit or custom* (sentence 1)*?*
2. Have students look at grammar chart **10.13.** Say: Used to + *the base form means that an activity was a habit or custom in the past.* Be used to + *a gerund or a noun means that you're comfortable with that thing or activity.* Get used to + *a gerund or a noun means* become accustomed to something.
3. Review how to form the negative of each expression.

EXERCISE 29

1. Have students read the direction line. Ask: *Are we going to use* used to + *gerund or noun, or are we going to use* used to + *the base form? (used to* + base form) Go over the examples in the book. Model the exercise for the class.
2. Have students complete Exercise 29 individually. Then have students compare statements in pairs. Circulate to observe pair work. Have a few volunteers share some of their statements with the class.
3. If necessary, review grammar chart **10.13** on page 341.

Expansion

Grammar Have students go back to the reading on pages 339 and 340. Ask students to make three lists: *past habit*; *custom or familiarity*; and *become accustomed to*. Say: *Write the sentences with* used to *from the reading under each category.*

EXERCISE 30

1. Ask: *How did you use to do things in your native country?* Have students read the direction line. Go over the example in the book. Have a volunteer model the exercise.
2. Have students complete Exercise 30 individually. Then have students compare sentences in pairs. Circulate to observe pair work. Give help as needed.
3. If necessary, review grammar chart **10.13** on page 341.

EXERCISE 31

1. Have students read the direction line. Go over the example in the book. Explain that this is about a student who wrote about things that are new for her in an American classroom. Ask: *In the example, is the person comfortable or not comfortable taking multiple-choice tests?* (not comfortable) Say: *Now you say what you're used to—essay tests or multiple-choice tests.* Have a volunteer say what she or he is used to.
2. Have students complete the exercise individually. Then have students tell their partners what they're used to. Circulate to observe pair work. Give help as needed.
3. If necessary, review grammar chart **10.13** on page 341.

To save class time, have students do the exercise for homework.

EXERCISE 30 ABOUT YOU Write sentences comparing the way you used to live in your country or in another city and the way you live now. Read your sentences to the class.

EXAMPLE *I used to go everywhere by bus. Now I have a car.*

1. Answers will vary.
2. __________
3. __________
4. __________

EXERCISE 31 A student wrote about things that are new for her in an American classroom. Fill in the blanks with a gerund. Then tell if *you* are used to these things or not.

EXAMPLE I'm not used to *taking* multiple-choice tests. In my native country, we have essay tests.

1. I'm not used to *sitting* at small desks. In my native country, we sit at large tables.
2. I'm not used to *calling* the teacher by his / her first name. In my country, we say "Professor."
3. I'm not used to *writing* in a textbook. In my native country, we don't write in the books because we borrow them from the school.
4. I'm not used to *wearing* jeans to class. In my native country, students wear a uniform.
5. I'm not used to *working* and studying at the same time. Students in my native country don't work. Their parents support them.

342 Lesson 10

Expansion

Exercise 30 Ask volunteers to share some of their statements with the class.

6. I'm not used to ___paying___ a lot of money to attend college. In my native country, college is free.

7. I'm not used to ___sitting___ when a teacher asks me a question. In my native country, students stand to answer a question.

EXERCISE 32 ABOUT YOU Name four things that you had to get used to in the U.S. or in a new town or school. (These things were strange for you when you arrived.)

EXAMPLES I had to get used to ___living in a small apartment.___

I had to get used to ___American pronunciation.___

1. I had to get used to ___Answers will vary.___
2. I had to get used to ______
3. I had to get used to ______
4. I had to get used to ______

EXERCISE 33 ABOUT YOU Answer each question with a complete sentence. Practice *be used to* + gerund or noun.

EXAMPLE What are you used to drinking in the morning?
I'm used to drinking coffee in the morning.

Answers will vary.

1. What kind of work are you used to?
2. What kind of relationship are you used to having with co-workers?
3. What kind of food are you used to (eating)?
4. What kind of weather are you used to?
5. What time are you used to getting up?
6. What kinds of clothes are you used to wearing to work or class?
7. What kinds of things are you used to doing every day?
8. What kinds of classroom behaviors are you used to?
9. What kinds of things are you used to doing alone?

EXERCISE 32

1. Say: *In this exercise, you're going to write about what you've had to become accustomed to—or what you've had to get comfortable with—in the U.S., or in a new town or school.* Have students read the direction line. Go over the examples. Model the exercise for the class.
2. Have students complete Exercise 32 individually. Then have students compare sentences with a partner. Circulate to observe pair work. Give help as needed.
3. If necessary, review grammar chart **10.13** on page 341.

EXERCISE 33

1. Ask: *What are you used to doing?* Have students read the direction line. Go over the example. Model the activity for the class.
2. Have students complete Exercise 33 by asking and answering questions in pairs (e.g., *What kind of work are you used to? I'm used to restaurant work. I've worked in a lot of restaurants.*). Circulate to observe pair work. Give help as needed.
3. If necessary, review grammar chart **10.13** on page 341.

To save class time, have students do half of the exercise in class and complete the other half in writing for homework, answering the questions themselves. Or if students do not need speaking practice, the entire exercise may be skipped or done in writing.

Expansion

Exercise 31 Do a class survey. Find out what students are used to.

Exercise 32 Have students discuss in groups what they had to get used to when they moved to the U.S. Then have groups report the results of their discussions to the class. Was there something everyone had in common?

EXERCISE 34

CD 3, Track 23

1. Say: *In this conversation, two friends are talking about what they're used to and not used to.* Have students read the direction line. Have a volunteer do the first item.
2. Have students complete Exercise 34 individually. Go over the answers as a class.
3. If necessary, review grammar chart **10.13** on page 341.

To save class time, have students do half of the exercise in class and complete the other half for homework. Or assign the entire exercise for homework.

EXERCISE 34 Circle the correct words to complete this conversation.

A: How's your new job?

B: I don't like it at all. I have to work the night shift. I can't get used to *(sleep / sleeping)* (1) during the day.

A: I know. That's hard. I used to *(work / working)* (2) the night shift, and I hated it. That's why I quit.

B: But the night shift pays more money.

A: I know it does, but I was never home for my children. Now my kids speak more English than Spanish. They used to *(speaking / speak)* (3) Spanish well, but now they mix Spanish and English. They play with their American friends all day or watch TV.

B: My kids are the same way. But *(I'm / I)* (4) used to it. It doesn't bother me.

A: I can't *(get / be)* (5) used to it. My parents came to live with us, and they don't speak much English. So they can't communicate with their grandchildren anymore.

B: My parents used to *(living / live)* (6) with us too. But they went back to Mexico. They didn't like the winters here. They couldn't get *(use / used)* (7) to the cold weather.

A: Do you think Americans are *(used to / use to)* (8) cold weather?

B: I'm not sure. My coworker was born in the U.S., but she says she hates winter. She *(is used to / used to)* (9) live in Texas, but now she lives here in Minnesota.

A: Why did she move here if she hates the cold weather?

B: The company where she used to *(work / working)* (10) closed down and she had to find another job. Her cousin helped her find a job here.

A: Before I came to the U.S., I thought everything here would be perfect. I didn't *(use / used)* (11) to *(think / thinking)* (12) about the problems. But I guess life in every country has its problems.

344 Lesson 10

Exercise 34 Variation

To provide practice with listening skills, have students close their books and listen to the audio. Tell students: *In this conversation, two friends are talking about what they're used to and not used to.* Repeat the audio as needed. Ask comprehension questions, such as: *What does person B do during the day?* (sleep) *What does person B do during the night?* (work) *Does person B like working the night shift?* (no) Then have students open their books and complete Exercise 34.

SUMMARY OF LESSON 10

Gerunds	
Examples	**Explanation**
Working all day is hard.	As the subject of the sentence
I don't enjoy **working** as a taxi driver.	After certain verbs
I **go shopping** after work.	In many idiomatic expressions with *go*
I'm worried about **finding** a job.	After prepositions
She found a job by **looking** in the newspaper.	In adverbial phrases

Infinitives	
Examples	**Explanation**
I need **to find** a new job.	After certain verbs
My boss wants me **to work** overtime.	After an object
I'm ready **to quit.**	After certain adjectives
It's important **to have** some free time. It's impossible for me **to work** 80 hours a week.	After certain impersonal expressions beginning with *it*.
I work (in order) **to support** my family.	To show purpose

Gerund or Infinitive—No Difference in Meaning	
Gerund	**Infinitive**
I like **working** with computers. I began **working** three months ago.	I like **to work** with computers. I began **to work** three months ago.
Writing a good résumé is important.	It's important **to write** a good résumé.

Gerund or Infinitive—Difference in Meaning	
Infinitive (Past Habit)	**Gerund (Custom)**
Rita **used to be** a teacher in India. Now she works in a hotel.	She **isn't used to working** the night shift. It's hard for her.
Rita **used to wear** traditional Indian clothes to work. Now she wears a uniform.	Rita studied British English. She had to **get used to hearing** the American pronunciation.

Gerunds; Infinitives 345

Summary of Lesson 10

1. **Gerunds** Have students cover up the summary on page 345. Create a matching exercise on the board. On one side, write the example sentences. On the other side, write the explanations in random order. Ask students to match the sentences with the explanations. If necessary, have students review:
   10.1 Gerunds—An Overview (p. 316)
   10.2 Gerund as Subject (p. 318)
   10.3 Gerund After Verb (p. 320)
   10.4 Gerund After Preposition (pp. 322–323)
   10.5 Gerund in Adverbial Phrase (p. 325).
2. **Infinitives** Have students cover up the summary on page 345. Create a matching exercise on the board. On one side, write the example sentences. On the other side, write the explanations in random order. Ask students to match the sentences with the explanations.
   Say: *Now look at the summary on page 345. Compare your work with the chart on infinitives.* Go over any trouble spots. If necessary, have students review:
   10.6 Infinitives—An Overview (p. 327)
   10.7 Infinitive as Subject (p. 329)
   10.8 Infinitive After Adjective (p. 331)
   10.9 Infinitive After Verb (p. 333)
   10.10 Gerund or Infinitive After Verb (p. 335)
   10.11 Object Before Infinitive (p. 336)
   10.12 Infinitive to Show Purpose (p. 338).
3. **Gerund or Infinitive—No Difference in Meaning** Have students look at the summary on page 345. Remind students that some verbs can take an infinitive and a gerund with no change in meaning. Ask students to try to list some of the verbs that take both. Go over the example sentences. If necessary, have students review:
   10.10 Gerund or Infinitive After Verb (p. 335).
4. **Gerund or Infinitive—Difference in Meaning** Have students look at the summary on page 345. Review *used to* + base form; *be used to* + gerund or noun; and *get used to* + gerund or noun. If necessary, have students review:
   10.13 *Used To* vs. *Be Used To* (p. 341).

Editing Advice

Have students close their books. Write the example sentences without editing marks or corrections on the board. For example:

1. He read the whole book without use a dictionary.
2. She insisted in driving me home.

Ask students to correct each sentence and provide a rule or an explanation for each correction. This activity can be done individually, in pairs, or as a class. After students have corrected each sentence, tell them to turn to pages 346–347. Say: *Now compare your work with the Editing Advice in the book.*

EDITING ADVICE

1. Use a gerund after a preposition.

   He read the whole book without ~~use~~ *using* a dictionary.

2. Use the correct preposition.

   She insisted ~~in~~ *on* driving me home.

3. Use a gerund after certain verbs.

   I enjoy ~~to~~ walk*ing* in the park.

   He went ~~to~~ shop*ping* after work.

4. Use an infinitive after certain verbs.

   I decided *to* buy a new car.

5. Use a gerund, not a base form, as a subject.

   ~~Find~~ *Finding* a good job is important.

6. Don't forget to include *it* for a delayed infinitive subject.

   ~~Is~~ *It is* important to find a good job.

7. Don't use the past form after *to*.

   I decided to ~~bought~~ *buy* a new car.

8. After *want, expect, need, advise,* and *ask,* use an object pronoun, not a subject pronoun, before the infinitive. Don't use *that* as a connector.

   He wants ~~that I~~ *me to* drive.

   The teacher expects ~~we~~ *us to* do the homework.

9. Use *for,* not *to,* when introducing an object after impersonal expressions beginning with *it.* Use the object pronoun after *for.*

   It's important ~~to~~ *for* me to find a job.

   It's necessary for ~~he~~ *him* to be on time.

10. Use *to* + base form, not *for*, to show purpose.

I called the company ~~for~~ *to* make an appointment.

11. Don't put *be* before *used to* for the habitual past.

~~I'm~~ I used to live in Germany. Now I live in the U.S.

12. Don't use the *-ing* form after *used to* for the habitual past.

We used to ~~having~~ *have* a dog, but he died.

13. Don't forget the *d* in *used to*.

I use*d* to live with my parents. Now I live alone.

LESSON 10 TEST/REVIEW

PART 1 Find the mistakes with the underlined words, and correct them. Not every sentence has a mistake. If the sentence is correct, write *C*.

EXAMPLES He wrote the composition without ~~cheek~~ *checking* his spelling.

Do you like to play tennis? C

1. Using the Internet is fun. *C*
2. I recommend ~~to see~~ *seeing* a job counselor.
3. Do you enjoy learning a new language? *C*
4. ~~Save~~ *Saving* your money is important for your future.
5. It's important ~~to~~ *for* me to know English well.
6. It's impossible for ~~she~~ *her* to work 60 hours a week.
7. Do you go ~~fish~~ *fishing* with your brother every week?
8. Do you want the teacher to review modals? *C*
9. He got rich by working hard and investing his money. *C*
10. The teacher tried to explained the present perfect, but we didn't understand it.
11. ~~Is~~ *It is* necessary to come to class on time.
12. Do you want to watch TV? *C*
13. She use*d* to take the bus every day. Now she has a car and drives everywhere.
14. It's necessary for me *to* have a good education.

Gerunds; Infinitives 347

Lesson 10 Test/Review

For additional practice, review, and assessment materials, see Assessment CD-ROM with *ExamView Pro*, *More Grammar Practice* Workbook 2, Interactive CD-ROM, and Web site http://elt.thomson.com/gic

PART 1

1. Part 1 may be used as an in-class test to assess student performance, in addition to the Assessment CD-ROM with *ExamView Pro*. Have students read the direction line. Ask: *Do all sentences have a mistake?* (no) Go over the examples. Collect for assessment.
2. If necessary, have students review: **Lesson 10.**

Lesson Review

To use Part 1 as a review, assign it as homework or use it as an in-class activity to be completed individually or in pairs. Check answers and review errors as a class. Reteach grammar points that students haven't mastered. Then student learning may be assessed using a test generated from the Assessment CD-ROM with *ExamView Pro*.

PART 2

1. Part 2 may also be used as an in-class test to assess student performance, in addition to the Assessment CD-ROM with *ExamView Pro*. Have students read the direction line. Explain that this is a conversation between Molly and her friend about Molly's work situation. Collect for assessment.
2. If necessary, have students review: **Lesson 10.**

15. She came to the U.S. ~~for~~ find a better job. *to*
16. He's interested in becoming a nurse. *C*
17. We're thinking ~~to spend~~ our vacation in Acapulco. *about spending*
18. We've always lived in a big city. We're used to living in a big city. *C*
19. I'm used to live with my family. Now I live alone.
20. She's from England. She can't get used to ~~drive~~ on the right side of the road. *driving*
21. My mother wants ~~that~~ I call her every day. *me to*
22. Are you worried about ~~lose~~ your job? *losing*

PART 2 Fill in the blanks in the conversation below. Use a gerund or an infinitive. In some cases, either the gerund or the infinitive is possible. Answers may vary.

A: Hi, Molly. I haven't seen you in ages. What's going on in your life?

B: I've made many changes. First, I quit *working* (example) in a factory. I disliked *doing* (1) the same thing every day. And I wasn't used to *being* (2) on my feet all day. My boss often wanted me *to work* (3) overtime on Saturdays. I need *to be* (4) with my children on Saturdays. Sometimes they want me *to take* (5) them to the zoo or to the museum. And I need *to help* (6) them with their homework too.

A: So what do you plan on *doing* (7)?

B: I've started *going* (8) to college *to take* (9) some general courses.

A: What career are you planning?

B: I'm not sure. I'm interested in *working* (10) with children. Maybe I'll become a teacher's aide. I've also thought about *working* (11) in a day care center. I care about *helping* (12) people.

348 Lesson 10

Lesson Review

To use Part 2 as a review, assign it as homework or use it as an in-class activity to be completed individually and/or in pairs. Have students practice the conversation in pairs. Check answers and review errors as a class. Reteach grammar points that students haven't mastered. Then student learning may be assessed using a test generated from the Assessment CD-ROM with *ExamView Pro*.

A: Yes, it's wonderful *helping* (13) other people, especially children. It's important *to have* (14) a job that you like. So you're starting a whole new career.

B: It's not new, really. Before I came to the U.S., I used *to be* (15) a kindergarten teacher in my country. But my English wasn't so good when I came here, so I found a job in a factory. I look forward to *returning* (16) to my former profession or doing something similar.

A: How did you learn English so fast?

B: By *talking* (17) with people at work, by *watching* (18) TV, and by *reading* (19) the newspaper. It hasn't been easy for me *to learn* (20) American English. I studied British English in my country, but here I have to get used to *hearing* (21) things like "gonna" and "wanna." At first I didn't understand Americans, but now I'm used to their pronunciation. I've had to make a lot of changes.

A: You should be proud of *making* (22) so many changes in your life so quickly.

B: I am.

A: Let's get together some time and talk some more.

B: I'd love to. I love to dance. Maybe we can go *dancing* (23) together sometime.

A: That would be great. And I love *shopping* (24). Maybe we can go shopping together sometime.

Expansion Activities

These expansion activities provide opportunities for students to interact with one another and further develop their speaking and writing skills. Encourage students to use grammar from this lesson whenever possible.

To save class time, assign parts of the activities as homework. Then use class time for interaction and communication. If students do not need additional speaking practice, some of the activities may be assigned as writing activities for homework or skipped altogether.

CLASSROOM ACTIVITIES

1. Have students complete the chart individually. Then have students discuss their answers in groups or with the whole class.
2. Tell students they can answer *yes*, *no*, or *I don't know* to each statement. Remind students that if they haven't worked in the U.S., they can ask an American or someone who has job experience in the U.S. to fill out the chart.

EXPANSION ACTIVITIES

Classroom Activities

1. If you have a job, write a list of five things you enjoy and don't enjoy about your job. If you don't have a job, you can write about what you enjoy and don't enjoy about this school or class. Share your answers with the class.

I enjoy:	I don't enjoy:
I enjoy talking to people.	*I don't enjoy working at 6 a.m.*

2. Compare the work environment in the U.S. to the work environment in another country. Discuss your answers in a small group or with the entire class. (If you have no experience with American jobs, ask an American to fill in his / her opinions about the U.S.)

	The U.S.	Another Country
1. Coworkers are friendly with each other at the job.		
2. Coworkers get together after work to socialize.		
3. Arriving on time for the job is very important.		
4. The boss is friendly with the employees.		
5. The employees are very serious about their jobs.		
6. The employees use the telephone for personal use.		
7. Everyone wears formal clothes.		
8. Employees get long lunch breaks.		
9. Employees get long vacations.		
10. Employees call the company if they are sick and can't work on a particular day.		
11. Employees are paid in cash.		
12. Employees often take work home.		

350 Lesson 10

3. Find a partner. Pretend that one of you is the manager of a company and the other one is looking for a job in that company. First decide what kind of company it is. Then write the manager's questions and the applicant's answers. Perform your interview in front of the class.

Talk About it

1. Talk about your experiences in looking for a job in the U.S.
2. Talk about the environment where you work.
3. Talk about some professions that interest you.
4. Talk about some professions that you think are terrible.

Write About it

1. Write your résumé and a cover letter.
2. Write about a job you wouldn't want to have. Tell why.
3. Write about a profession you would like to have. Tell why.
4. Write about your current job or a job you had in the past. Tell what you like(d) or don't (didn't) like about this job.

Internet Activities

1. Type *career* in a search engine. See how many "hits" come up.
2. Find some career counseling Web sites. Find a sample résumé in your field or close to your field. Print it out and bring it to class.
3. From one of the Web sites you found, get information on one or more of the following topics:
   - how to write a cover letter
   - how to find a career counselor
   - how to plan for your interview
   - how to network
   - what questions to ask an interviewer
4. See if your local newspaper has a Web site. If it does, find the Help Wanted section of this newspaper. Bring job listings that interest you to class.

Additional Activities at http://elt.thomson.com/gic

Write About it Variation

Item 3 Have students create a presentation on the profession they're most interested in. Ask them to include as many facts about the profession as possible (e.g., current needs for those professionals, salary ranges, the level and kind of education needed, etc.).

Have students exchange first drafts with a partner. Ask students to help their partners edit their drafts. Refer students to the Editing Advice on pages 346–347.

CLASSROOM ACTIVITIES (*cont.*)

3. Quickly brainstorm with students the types of questions that they may be asked during an interview. Ask volunteers to share experiences from interviews they may have had.

TALK ABOUT IT

Have students discuss each topic in pairs, in groups, or as a class.

1. Ask students to talk about where they looked (ads in newspapers, on the Internet, window signs, etc.), how long they looked before they got an interview, and if they had to fill out an application.

2. Ask students to discuss the physical facility (the plant, the building, the store, etc.) and the social environment.

3. Have students talk about the advantages and disadvantages of the professions they're interested in.

4. Ask students to talk about the professions they are least interested in and to be specific about the reasons. Do they have experience in this profession, or do they know anyone who is in the profession?

WRITE ABOUT IT

1. Ask students to bring in a résumé and cover letter(s) that they might already have. Provide samples of good résumés and cover letters. Have students bring in advertisements for jobs they are interested in applying for.

2. and 3. Have students make a list of things that are important to them (e.g., spending time with family, owning a house, travel) and what they are looking for in a job (e.g., interesting work, high salary). Say: *Writing your thoughts down will help you think about the kind of job or profession that's best suited for your needs and goals.*

4. Ask students to talk about at least three things they liked and three things they didn't like about the job.

INTERNET ACTIVITIES

Remind students that if they don't have Internet access, they can use Internet facilities at a public library or they can use traditional research methods to find out information, including looking at encyclopedias, magazines, books, journals, and newspapers.

LESSON

11

GRAMMAR
Adjective Clauses

CONTEXT: Making Connections—Old Friends and New
Finding Old Friends
Internet Matchmaking

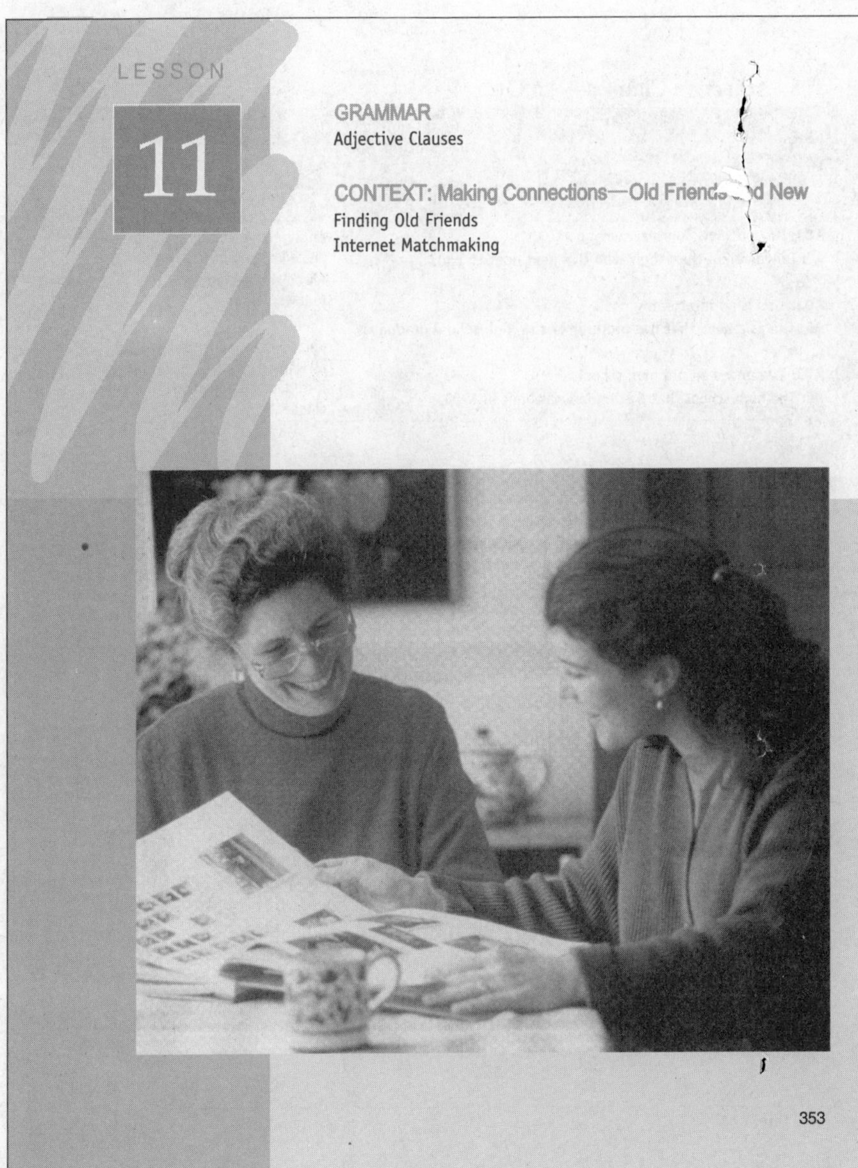

353

Lesson 11

Lesson Overview

GRAMMAR

1. Briefly review what students learned in the last lesson. Ask: *What did we study in Lesson 10?* (gerunds and infinitives)
2. Ask: *What are we going to study in this lesson?* (adjective clauses) *Can anyone give me an example of an adjective clause?* (e.g., *This is the book that I bought yesterday.*) Have students give examples. Write the examples on the board.

CONTEXT

1. Ask: *What will we learn about in this lesson?* (finding old friends and making new friends) Activate students' prior knowledge. Ask: *Have you ever gotten in contact with an old friend you haven't seen in a long time? How do you make new friends? Have you ever used an online dating agency?*
2. Have students share their knowledge and personal experiences.

To save class time, have students do the Test/Review at the end of the lesson, or administer a lesson test generated from the Assessment CD-ROM with *ExamView® Pro.* Skip sections of the lesson that students have already mastered. You may also assign some sections for self-study for extra credit.

Expansion

Theme The topic for this lesson can be enhanced with the following ideas:

1. A high school yearbook
2. Pages printed from dating Web sites and online people-finding services

11.1 | Adjective Clauses—An Overview

1. Have students cover up grammar chart **11.1** on page 354. Write the following on the board:
Do you know your new neighbors?
Do you know the people who live next door to you?
Ask: *Which sentence has the adjective clause?* (the second sentence) *What is* new? (It's an adjective.) *Does the adjective come before or after the noun?* (before) *Where does the adjective clause come?* (after)
2. Then have students look at grammar chart **11.1.** Review the example sentences in the chart. Say: *Relative pronouns introduce an adjective clause. What are the relative pronouns that introduce these adjective clauses?* (*who* and *that*)

Finding Old Friends (Reading)

1. Have students look at the photo. Ask: *What is a high school yearbook?* (a book for high school students that records important events) *Do you have one?*
2. Have students look at the title of the reading. Ask: *What is the reading about?* Have students use the title and photo to make predictions about the reading.
3. Preteach any vocabulary words your students may not know, such as *lose touch, emerge,* and *reunion.*

BEFORE YOU READ

1. Have students discuss the questions in pairs.
2. Ask for a few volunteers to share their answers with the class.

To save class time, skip "Before You Read" or have students prepare answers for homework ahead of time.

11.1 | Adjective Clauses—An Overview

An adjective is a word that describes a noun. An adjective clause is a group of words (with a subject and a verb) that describes a noun. Compare adjectives (ADJ.) and **adjective clauses** (AC) below.

Examples	Explanation
ADJ: Do you know your **new** neighbors? **AC:** Do you know the people **who live next door to you?**	An adjective (ADJ) precedes a noun. An adjective clause (AC) follows a noun.
ADJ: This is an **interesting** book. **AC:** This is a book **that has pictures of the high school graduates.**	
ADJ: I attended an **old** high school. **AC:** The high school **that I attended** was built in 1920.	Relative pronouns, such as *who* and *that,* introduce an adjective clause.

FINDING OLD FRIENDS

Before You Read

1. Do you keep in touch with old friends from elementary school or high school?
2. Have you ever thought about contacting someone you haven't seen in years?

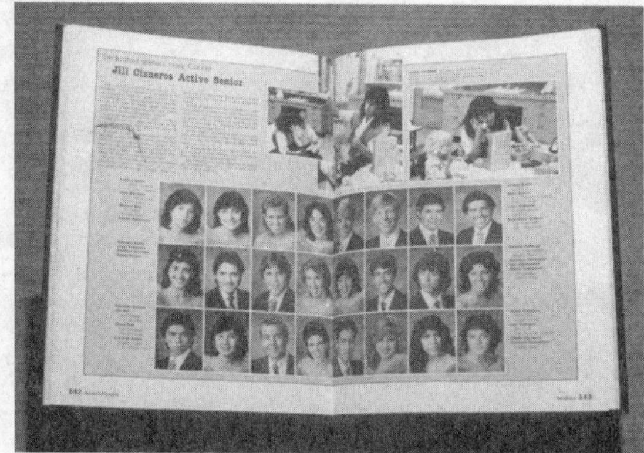

High School Yearbook

354 Lesson **11**

Culture Note

Americans are a mobile group of people. The 2000 census found that almost half of all Americans had moved since 1995. Although many Americans move a number of times in their lifetimes, some people are more mobile than others. Hispanics tend to move more than whites. Mobility varies from state to state. Nevada has a very transient population. More than 60 percent of its population resided in a different place in 2000 than in 1995. In 2000, 60 percent of the population was living in their hometowns. The states with the most "homebodies" are Louisiana, Pennsylvania, and Michigan.

Read the following article. Pay special attention to adjective clauses.

Americans move numerous times during their lives. As a result, they often lose touch with old friends. Usually, during their twenties and thirties, people are too busy building their careers and starting their families to think much about the past. But as people get older, they often start to wonder about the best friend **they had in high school,** the soldier **with whom they served in the military,** the person **who lived next door** when they were growing up, or their high school sweetheart. Many people want to connect with the past.

Before the Internet, finding a lost love or an old friend required searching through old phone books in libraries in different cities, a detective, and a lot of luck. It was especially hard to find married women **who changed their names.**

Now with the Internet, old friends can sometimes find each other in seconds. Several Web sites have emerged to meet people's growing desire to make connections with former classmates. There are Web sites **that list the students in high schools and colleges in the U.S.** People **who went to high school in the U.S.** can list themselves according to the school **they attended** and the year **they graduated.** A man might go to these Web sites looking for the guys **he played football with** or a long-lost friend—and find the name of a first love **whom he hasn't seen in years.**

One Web site, Classmates.com, claims that more than 30 million Americans have listed themselves on their site. Married women **who have changed their names** list themselves by their maiden names so that others can recognize them easily.

Another way **that people make connections with old classmates** is through reunions. Some high school graduating classes meet every ten years. They usually have dinner, remember the time **when they were young,** and exchange information about what they are doing today. They sometimes bring their high school yearbooks, **which have pictures of the graduates** and other school memories.

Some classes have their reunions in the schools **where they first met.** Others have their reunions in a nice restaurant. There are Web sites **that specialize in helping people find their former classmates and plan reunions.**

In America's highly mobile society, it takes some effort to connect with old friends. Looking back at fond memories, renewing old friendships, making new friends, and even starting a new romance with an old love can be the reward for a little work on the Internet.

Reading *CD 3, Track 24*

1. Have students first read the text silently. Tell them to pay special attention to adjective clauses. Then play the audio and have students read along silently.
2. Check students' comprehension. Ask questions such as: *Why do Americans often lose touch with old friends?* (Americans move a lot during their lives.) *When do Americans typically get interested in their old friends?* (when they're older, after building families and careers) *How did people find old friends before the Internet?* (They went to libraries and looked in phonebooks from other towns, and they hired detectives.) *Do Americans still have class reunions?* (yes)

To save class time, have students do the reading for homework ahead of time.

Reading Variation

To practice listening skills, have students first listen to the audio alone. Ask a few comprehension questions. Repeat the audio if necessary. Then have them open their books and read along as they listen to the audio.

Reading Glossary

emerge: to appear
lose touch: no longer have communication with
reunion: a time when people who have something in common (college, family) get together again

EXERCISE 1

1. Say: *This exercise is based on the reading.* Have students read the direction line. Go over the example.
2. Have students complete Exercise 1 individually. Go over the answers as a class.
3. If necessary, review grammar chart **11.1** on page 354.

EXERCISE 2

1. Say: *In this exercise, you're going to go back to Exercise 1.* Have students read the direction line. Go over the example. Have a volunteer model the example.
2. Have students complete Exercise 2 individually. Then have students compare answers in pairs. Circulate to observe pair work. Give help as needed.
3. If necessary, review grammar chart **11.1** on page 354.

To save class time, have students complete the exercise for homework.

11.2 | Relative Pronoun as Subject

1. Have students look at grammar chart **11.2.** Say: Who, that, *and* which *can be the subject of the adjective clause.* Who *and* that *are used for people.* That *and* which *are used for things.* Go over the examples and explanations. Ask: *How do you know if the relative pronoun is the subject?* Point out the first example sentence and say: *If the relative pronoun can be replaced by a subject and made into a complete sentence, then the relative pronoun is acting as the subject of the clause.* Point out the second example sentence. Show students how to replace the relative pronoun with the subject to make a sentence.
2. Direct students to the Language Notes. Point out that *which* is not used as often as *that.* Explain that the verb in the adjective clause has to agree with the subject. Say: *If the subject is plural, the verb is plural. If the subject is singular, the verb is singular.*

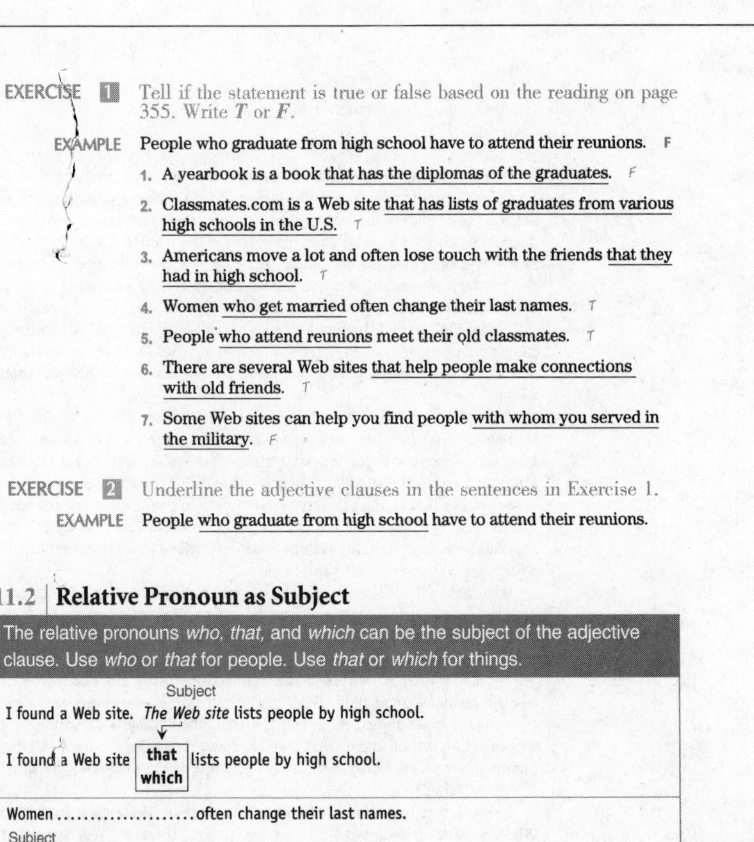

EXERCISE 1 Tell if the statement is true or false based on the reading on page 355. Write *T* or *F*.

EXAMPLE People who graduate from high school have to attend their reunions. F

1. A yearbook is a book that has the diplomas of the graduates. F
2. Classmates.com is a Web site that has lists of graduates from various high schools in the U.S. T
3. Americans move a lot and often lose touch with the friends that they had in high school. T
4. Women who get married often change their last names. T
5. People who attend reunions meet their old classmates. T
6. There are several Web sites that help people make connections with old friends. T
7. Some Web sites can help you find people with whom you served in the military. F

EXERCISE 2 Underline the adjective clauses in the sentences in Exercise 1.

EXAMPLE People who graduate from high school have to attend their reunions.

11.2 | Relative Pronoun as Subject

The relative pronouns *who, that,* and *which* can be the subject of the adjective clause. Use *who* or *that* for people. Use *that* or *which* for things.

Subject
I found a Web site. *The Web site* lists people by high school.

I found a Web site **that / which** lists people by high school.

Women ....often change their last names.
Subject
Women get married.

Women **who / that** get married often change their last names.

Language Notes:
1. *Which* is less common than *that*.
2. A present tense verb in the adjective clause must agree in number with its subject.
   A woman who **gets** married usually changes her name.
   Women who **get** married usually change their names.

356 Lesson 11

EXERCISE 3 Fill in the blanks with *who* or *that* + the correct form of the verb in parentheses ( ).

EXAMPLE A yearbook has photos *that show* (show) the activities of the high school.

1. He has a yearbook *that has* (have) pictures of all his classmates.
2. People *who go* (go) to a reunion exchange information about their lives.
3. Classmates.com is a Web site *that helps* (help) people make connections with old friends.
4. There are Web sites *that specialize* (specialize) in helping people plan a reunion.
5. People *who plan* (plan) a reunion have to contact former classmates.

EXERCISE 4 Fill in the blanks with *who* or *that* + the correct form of the verb in parentheses ( ). Then complete the statement. Answers will vary.

EXAMPLE People *who work* (work) hard *are often successful.*

1. People *Answers will vary.* (exercise) regularly ______
2. A person ______ (use) a cell phone while driving ______
3. Students ______ (be) absent a lot ______
4. Schools ______ (not/have) computers ______
5. A computer ______ (be) more than five years old ______
6. People ______ (have) digital cameras ______
7. Colleges ______ (have) evening classes ______
8. A college ______ (have) a day-care center ______
9. Students ______ (have) a full-time job ______

Adjective Clauses 357

EXERCISE 3

1. Have students read the direction line. Go over the example. Ask: *Can we use* that *for people?* (yes)
2. Have students complete Exercise 3 individually. Go over the answers as a class.
3. If necessary, review grammar chart **11.2** on page 356.

EXERCISE 4

1. Have students read the direction line. Go over the example. Model the exercise for the class (e.g., *People who work hard are often too tired to have fun.*).
2. Have students complete Exercise 4 individually. Have students compare answers in pairs. Circulate to observe pair work. Give help as needed.
3. If necessary, review grammar chart **11.2** on page 356.

To save class time, have students do half of the exercise in class and complete the other half for homework.

Expansion

Exercise 3 Have students decide whether each sentence in Exercise 3 is similar to the first example or to the second example in grammar chart **11.2** on page 356.

Exercise 4 Do a class survey. Find out what students wrote for selected items.

EXERCISE 5

1. Have students read the direction line. Go over the example. Model the example for the class.
2. Have students complete Exercise 5 individually. Then have students compare answers in pairs. Circulate to observe group work. Give help as needed.
3. If necessary, review grammar chart **11.2** on page 356.

To save class time, have students do the exercise for homework.

11.3 | Relative Pronoun as Object

1. Have students look at grammar chart **11.3.** Say: Who, whom, that, *and* which *can be the object of the adjective clause.* Go over the examples and explanations.
2. Direct students to the Language Notes. Point out that the relative pronoun is often not said when it is the object of the adjective clause. Explain that *whom* is considered more formal than *who. Who* is more common than *whom.*

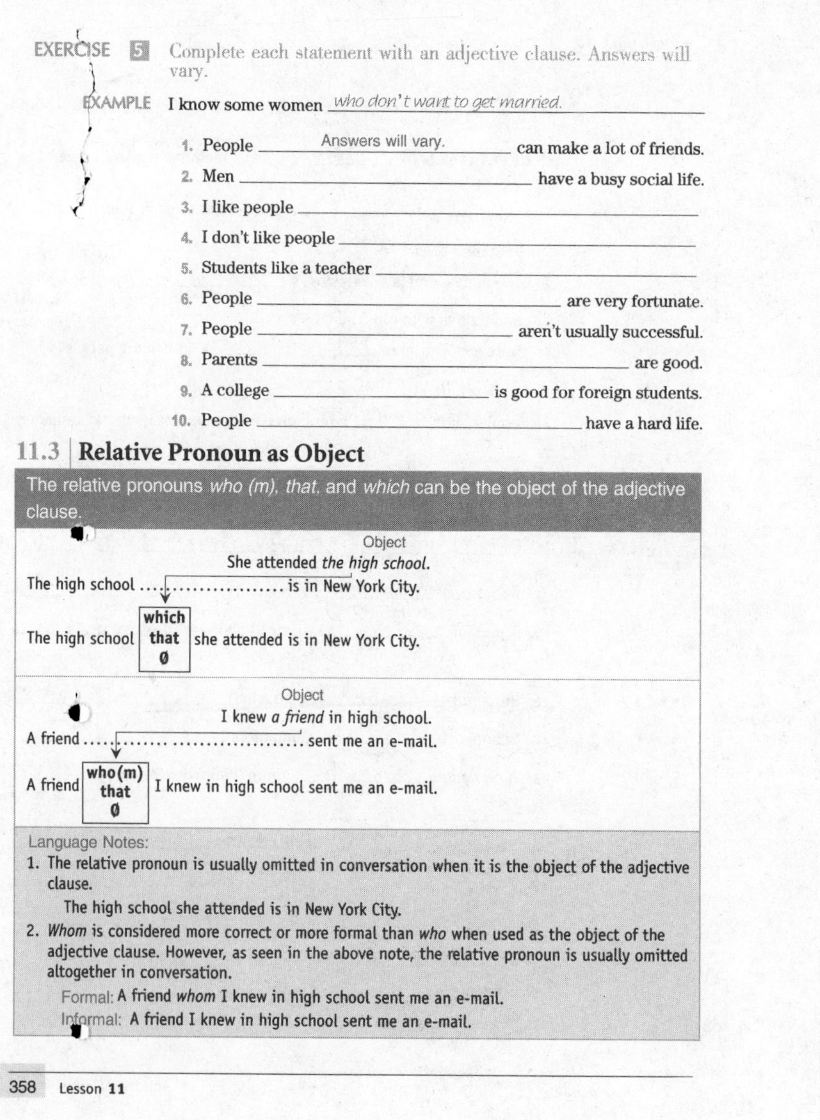

EXERCISE 5 Complete each statement with an adjective clause. Answers will vary.

EXAMPLE I know some women *who don't want to get married.*

1. People ___Answers will vary.___ can make a lot of friends.
2. Men ______ have a busy social life.
3. I like people ______
4. I don't like people ______
5. Students like a teacher ______
6. People ______ are very fortunate.
7. People ______ aren't usually successful.
8. Parents ______ are good.
9. A college ______ is good for foreign students.
10. People ______ have a hard life.

11.3 | Relative Pronoun as Object

The relative pronouns *who (m), that,* and *which* can be the object of the adjective clause.

Object
She attended *the high school.*
The high school .... is in New York City.

The high school [which / that / Ø] she attended is in New York City.

Object
I knew *a friend* in high school.
A friend .... sent me an e-mail.

A friend [who(m) / that / Ø] I knew in high school sent me an e-mail.

Language Notes:
1. The relative pronoun is usually omitted in conversation when it is the object of the adjective clause.
   The high school she attended is in New York City.
2. *Whom* is considered more correct or more formal than *who* when used as the object of the adjective clause. However, as seen in the above note, the relative pronoun is usually omitted altogether in conversation.
   Formal: A friend *whom* I knew in high school sent me an e-mail.
   Informal: A friend I knew in high school sent me an e-mail.

358 Lesson 11

Expansion

Exercise 5 Have volunteers share some of their statements with the class. How many students agree?

EXERCISE 6 In each sentence below, underline the adjective clause.

EXAMPLE I've lost touch with some of the friends I had in high school.

1. The high school I attended is in another city.
2. The teachers I had in high school are all old now.
3. We didn't have to buy the textbooks we used in high school.
4. She married a man she met at her high school reunion.
5. The friends I've made in this country don't know much about my country.

EXERCISE 7 A mother (M) is talking to her teenage daughter (D). Fill in the blanks to complete the conversation. Answers may vary.

M: I'd like to contact an old friend I ___had___ (example) in high school. I wish I could find her. I'll never forget the good times ___we had___ (1) in high school. When we graduated, we said we'd always stay in touch. But then we went to different colleges.

D: Didn't you keep in touch by e-mail?

M: When I was in college, e-mail didn't exist. At first we wrote letters. But little by little we wrote less and less until, eventually, we stopped writing.

D: Do you still have the letters she ___wrote___ (2)?

M: Yes, I do. They're in a box in the basement.

D: Why don't you write to the address on the letters?

M: That doesn't make sense. The address she ___wrote___ (3) on the letters was of the college town where she lived. I don't know what happened to her after she left college.

D: Have you tried calling her parents?

M: The phone number ___they had___ (4) is now disconnected. Maybe her parents have died.

D: Have you looked on Classmates.com?

M: What's that?

EXERCISE 6

1. Have students read the direction line. Go over the example. Say: *Remember, in these sentences the relative pronoun has been left out.*
2. Have students complete Exercise 6 individually. Go over the answers as a class.
3. If necessary, review grammar chart **11.3** on page 358.

EXERCISE 7

CD 3, Track 25

1. Say: *In this conversation, a mother and daughter are talking about how to contact old friends.* Have students read the direction line. Go over the example. Remind students that answers may vary.
2. Have students complete Exercise 7 individually. Go over the answers as a class.
3. If necessary, review grammar chart **11.3** on page 358.

To save class time, have students do the exercise for homework.

Expansion

Exercise 6 Have students insert the relative pronoun into the sentence.

Exercise 7 Variation

To provide practice with listening skills, have students close their books and listen to the audio. Repeat the audio as needed. Say: *In this conversation, a mother and daughter are talking about how to contact old friends.* Ask comprehension questions, such as: *Who wants to contact an old friend?* (the mother) *Why didn't they keep in touch by e-mail?* (E-mail didn't exist when they were younger.) *Are everyone's names on the* Classmates.com *Web site?* (No. Only the people who add their names.) Then have students open their books and complete Exercise 7.

EXERCISE 8

CD 3, Track 26

1. Say: *In this conversation, two people are talking about making new friends.* Have students read the direction line. Go over the example. Remind students that answers may vary. Point out the photo of the person meditating on page 361.
2. Have students complete Exercise 8 individually. Go over the answers as a class.
3. If necessary, review grammar chart **11.3** on page 358.

To save class time, have students do half of the exercise in class and complete the other half for homework.

D: It's a Web site that ___has___ (5) lists of people. The list is categorized by the high school you ___graduated from___ (6) and the dates you ___went___ (7) there.

M: Is everyone in my high school class on the list?

D: Unfortunately, no. Only the people ___who___ (8) add their names are on the list.

M: But my friend probably got married. I don't know the name of the man ___who she___ (9) married.

D: That's not a problem. You can search for her by her maiden name.

M: Will this Web site give me her address and phone number?

D: No. But for a fee, you can send her an e-mail through the Web site. Then if she wants to contact you, she can give you her personal information.

M: She'll probably think I'm crazy for contacting her almost 25 years later.

D: I'm sure she'll be happy to receive communication from a good friend ___she___ (10) hasn't seen in years. When I graduate from high school, I'm never going to lose contact with the friends ___I've___ (11) made. We'll always stay in touch.

M: That's what you think. But as time passes and your lives become more complicated, you may lose touch.

D: But today we have e-mail.

M: Well, e-mail is a help. Even so, the direction you ___choose___ (12) in life is different from the direction your friends choose.

EXERCISE 8 Fill in the blanks with appropriate words to complete the conversation. Answers may vary.

A: I'm lonely. I have a lot of friends in my native country, but I don't have enough friends here. The friends ___I have there___ (example) send me e-mail all the time, but that's not enough. I need to make new friends here.

B: Haven't you met any people here?

A: Of course. But the people ___I've___ (1) here don't have my interests.

B: What are you interested in?

360 Lesson **11**

Expansion

Exercise 7 Have students practice the conversation in pairs. Ask volunteers to role-play all or part of the conversation in front of the class.

Exercise 8 Variation

To provide practice with listening skills, have students close their books and listen to the audio. Repeat the audio as needed. Say: *In this conversation, two people are talking about making new friends.* Ask comprehension questions, such as: *Why is person A lonely?* (Person A doesn't have enough friends in the States.) *What are person A's interests?* (reading, meditating, going for quiet walks) *What are Americans interested in?* (parties, TV, sports, movies, going to restaurants) Then have students open their books and complete Exercise 8.

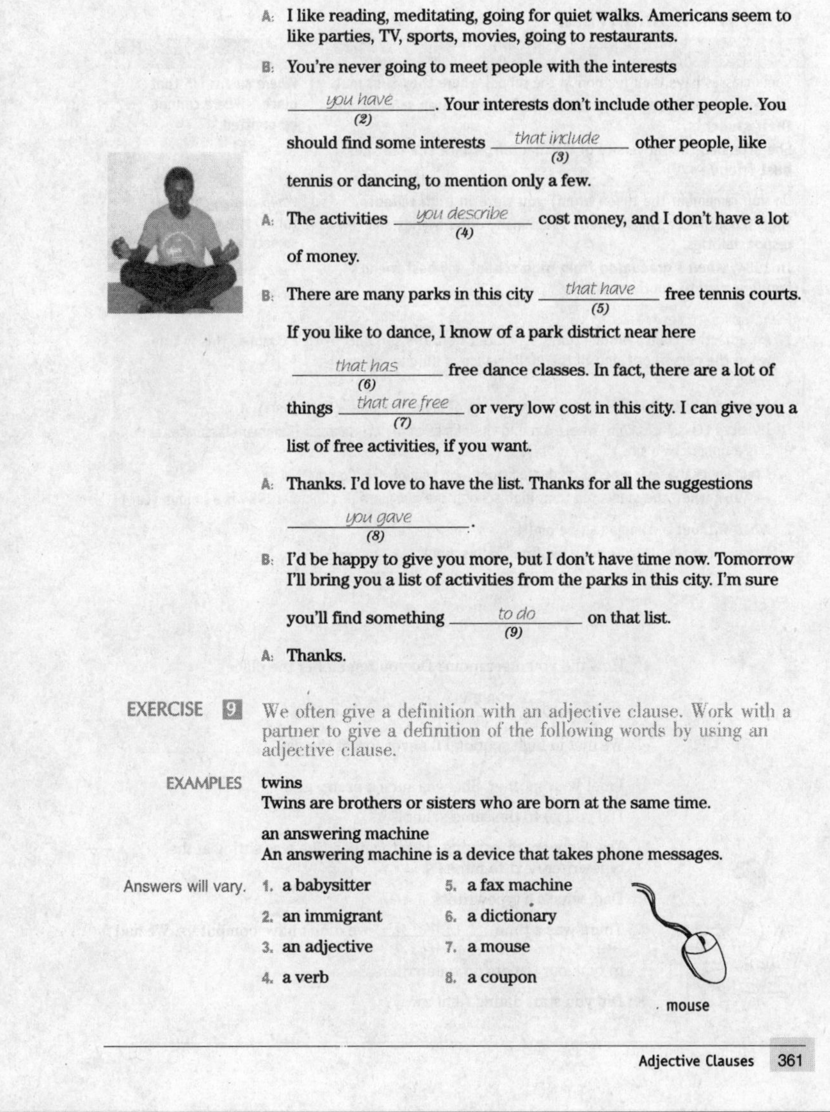

A: I like reading, meditating, going for quiet walks. Americans seem to like parties, TV, sports, movies, going to restaurants.

B: You're never going to meet people with the interests _you have_ (2). Your interests don't include other people. You should find some interests _that include_ (3) other people, like tennis or dancing, to mention only a few.

A: The activities _you describe_ (4) cost money, and I don't have a lot of money.

B: There are many parks in this city _that have_ (5) free tennis courts. If you like to dance, I know of a park district near here _that has_ (6) free dance classes. In fact, there are a lot of things _that are free_ (7) or very low cost in this city. I can give you a list of free activities, if you want.

A: Thanks. I'd love to have the list. Thanks for all the suggestions _you gave_ (8).

B: I'd be happy to give you more, but I don't have time now. Tomorrow I'll bring you a list of activities from the parks in this city. I'm sure you'll find something _to do_ (9) on that list.

A: Thanks.

EXERCISE 9 We often give a definition with an adjective clause. Work with a partner to give a definition of the following words by using an adjective clause.

EXAMPLES twins
Twins are brothers or sisters who are born at the same time.
an answering machine
An answering machine is a device that takes phone messages.

Answers will vary.

1. a babysitter
2. an immigrant
3. an adjective
4. a verb
5. a fax machine
6. a dictionary
7. a mouse
8. a coupon

mouse

EXERCISE 9

1. Have students read the direction line. Go over the examples. Have a volunteer complete #1. Point out the illustration of a mouse.
2. Have students complete Exercise 9 in pairs. Go over the answers as a class.
3. If necessary, review grammar chart **11.3** on page 358.

To save class time, have students do half of the exercise in class and complete the other half in writing for homework. Or if students do not need speaking practice, the entire exercise may be skipped or done in writing.

Expansion

Exercise 8 Have students practice the conversation in pairs. Ask volunteers to role-play all or part of the conversation in front of the class.

Exercise 8 Have students work in pairs to create a similar conversation, making it true for them. Ask volunteers to perform their conversations in front of the class.

Exercise 9 On a small piece of paper, have students write down one word they'd like to have a classmate define. Put the words in a hat, and ask each student to draw a paper and try to define the word on the spot.

11.4 | *Where* and *When*

1. Have students cover up grammar chart **11.4.** Have students go back to the reading on page 355. Say: *Look for the sentences in bold that have* where *and* when. *What do you think* where *and* when *mean in these sentences?* (*in that place* and *at that time*) Write students' answers on the board.
2. Then have students look at grammar chart **11.4** on page 362. Say: Where *means* in that place. Go over the example sentences. Explain that *where* can't be omitted.
3. Say: When *means* at that time. Point out that *when* can often be omitted. Go over the example sentences.
4. Direct students to the Punctuation Notes. Go over the examples and explanations.

EXERCISE 10

CD 3, Track 27

1. Say: *In this conversation, a father is talking to his son about how he met his wife.* Have students read the direction line. Go over the example. Point out the picture of the man using a typewriter.
2. Have students complete Exercise 10 individually. Go over the answers as a class.
3. If necessary, review grammar chart **11.4** on page 362.

11.4 | *Where* and *When*

Examples	Explanation
Some classes have their reunion in the school **where they first met.** There are Web sites **where you can find lists of high schools and their students.** She attended the University of Washington, **where she met her best friend.**	*Where* means "in that place." *Where* cannot be omitted.
Do you remember the time **(when) you were in high school?** High school was a time **(when)** I had many good friends and few responsibilities. In 1984, **when I graduated from high school,** my best friend's family moved to another state.	*When* means "at that time." *When* can sometimes be omitted.

Punctuation Notes:

1. An adjective clause is sometimes separated from the sentence with a comma. This is true when the person or thing in the main clause is unique.

Compare:

I visited a Web site **where** I found the names of my classmates. (No Comma)
I visited Classmates.com, **where** I found the names of my classmates. (Comma: Classmates.com is a unique Web site.)
I remember the year **when** I graduated from high school. (No Comma)
In 1984, **when** she graduated from high school, she got married. (Comma: 1984 is a unique year.)

2. *When* without a comma can be omitted.
I remember the year I graduated from high school.

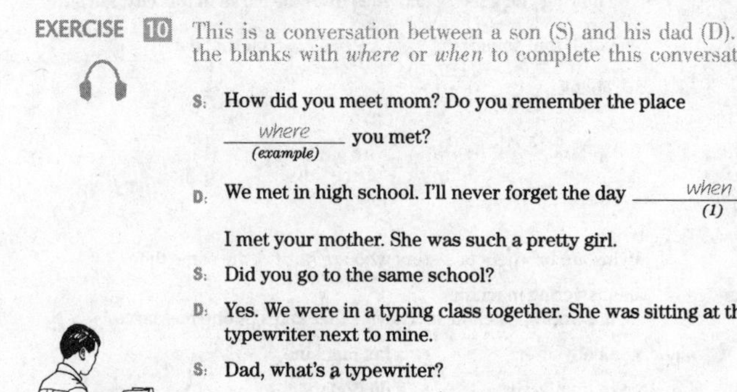

EXERCISE 10 This is a conversation between a son (S) and his dad (D). Fill in the blanks with *where* or *when* to complete this conversation.

S: How did you meet mom? Do you remember the place ___*where*___ (example) you met?

D: We met in high school. I'll never forget the day ___*when*___ (1) I met your mother. She was such a pretty girl.

S: Did you go to the same school?

D: Yes. We were in a typing class together. She was sitting at the typewriter next to mine.

S: Dad, what's a typewriter?

D: There was a time ___*when*___ (2) we didn't have computers. We had to type our papers on typewriters.

S: Did you start dating right away?

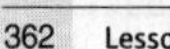

362 Lesson 11

Exercise 10 Variation

To provide practice with listening skills, have students close their books and listen to the audio. Repeat the audio as needed. Say: *In this conversation, a father is talking to his son about how he met his wife.* Ask comprehension questions, such as: *Where did he meet his wife?* (in typing class) *Why doesn't his son know what a typewriter is?* (They're not used anymore.) *Where did they use to meet?* (in a soda shop) Then have students open their books and complete Exercise 10.

D: No. We were friends. There was a time when (3) people were friends before they started dating. There was a soda shop near school where (4) we used to meet.

S: What's a soda shop, Dad?

D: It's a store where (5) you could buy milk shakes, sodas, and hamburgers. We used to sit there after school drinking one soda with two straws.

S: That doesn't seem too romantic to me.

D: But it was.

S: So did you get married as soon as you graduated from high school?

D: No. I graduated from high school at a time when (6) there was a war going on in this country. Mom went to college and I went into the army. We wrote letters during that time. When I got out of the army, I started college. So we got married about seven years after we met.

11.5 | Formal vs. Informal

Examples	Explanation
Informal: I lost touch with the friends I used to go to high school **with.** Formal: I lost touch with the friends **with whom** I used to go to high school.	Informally, most native speakers put the preposition at the end of the adjective clause. The relative pronoun is usually omitted.
Informal: I saved the yearbook my friends wrote **in.** Formal: I saved the yearbook **in which** my friends wrote.	In very formal English, the preposition comes before the relative pronoun, and only *whom* and *which* may be used. *That* is not used directly after a preposition.

EXERCISE 11 Change the sentences to formal English.

EXAMPLE What is the name of the high school you graduated from?
What is the name of the high school from which you graduated?

1. He found his friend that he served in the military with.
He found his friend whom he served with in the military.
2. I can't find the friend I was looking for.
I can't find the friend for whom I was looking.
3. The high school she graduated from was torn down.
The high school from which she graduated was torn down.

11.5 | Formal vs. Informal

Have students look at grammar chart **11.5.** Say: *Most native speakers put a preposition at the end of an adjective clause. In very formal speech, the preposition comes before the relative pronoun. If you use this formal style, only* whom *and* which *are used.* Go over the example sentences.

EXERCISE 11

1. Say: *You're going to make these sentences formal by using prepositions before* whom *and* which. Have students read the direction line. Go over the example.
2. Have students complete the exercise individually. Go over the answers as a class.
3. If necessary, review grammar chart **11.5** on page 363.

Expansion

Exercise 10 Have students practice the conversation in pairs. Then ask volunteers to role-play the conversation in front of the class.

Exercise 10 Have students work in pairs to write a similar conversation about meeting a boyfriend, girlfriend, husband, or wife. Ask volunteers to role-play the conversation in front of the class.

Internet Matchmaking (Reading)

1. Have students look at the photo. Ask: *What's going on in this photo?* (A woman is looking at photos of people on her computer screen.)
2. Have students look at the title of the reading. Ask: *What is the reading about?* Have students use the title and photo to make predictions about the reading.
3. Preteach any vocabulary words your students may not know, such as *values* and *widow*.

BEFORE YOU READ

1. Have students discuss the questions in pairs.
2. Ask for a few volunteers to share their answers with the class.

To save class time, skip "Before You Read" or have students prepare answers for homework ahead of time.

Reading CD 3, Track 28

1. Have students first read the text silently. Tell them to pay special attention to adjective clauses beginning with *whose*. Then play the audio and have students read along silently.
2. Check students' comprehension. Ask questions such as: *Why do some people fill out lengthy questionnaires on online dating sites?* (so they can be matched with someone with the same interests and values) *Why was Don Trenton looking for a wife?* (His first wife died, and he wanted to provide a stable family for his son.) *Why are there more women than men in the older age group looking to meet someone?* (Women typically have higher life expectancies than men.)

To save class time, have students do the reading for homework ahead of time.

DID YOU KNOW?

In 2003, seventy-one percent of men 65 and older were married, while only forty-one percent of women over the age of 65 were married.

4. Do you remember the teacher I was talking about?
Do you remember the teacher about whom I was talking?

5. In high school, the activities I was interested in were baseball and band.
In high school, the activities in which I was interested were baseball and band.

INTERNET MATCHMAKING

Before You Read

1. Where do you meet new people?
2. Do you know anyone who has tried an online dating service?

Read the following article. Pay special attention to adjective clauses beginning with *whose*.

Is it possible to find love on the Internet? About 40 million people a month visit an online dating service in hopes of finding true love. Some of these dating sites let you easily search the pictures and biographical descriptions of people who list themselves there. You can search by age and location. Other Web sites make you fill out lengthy questionnaires so that they can match you with people **whose interests** and **values** are similar to yours. Most of these sites charge a fee for this service.

Meg Olson, a 40-year-old woman from Michigan who wanted to get married, was simply not meeting men. She used an online dating site and met Don Trenton, 42, **whose wife** had recently died. After e-mailing, they started to talk on the phone and realized how many things they had in common. They met, started dating, and a year later, they were married. Don, **whose son** was six years old at the time, wanted to create a stable family for his son.

There are sites for all kinds of interests and connections. Some sites specialize in a specific religion or ethnic group. There are sites for senior citizens. Sadie Kaplan is a 75-year-old widow who wants to meet men **whose age** and **interests** are similar to her own. However, it's harder for women in this age group to meet men because women live longer than men. Because the life expectancy for women is much higher than it is for men (79 for women, 73 for men), many of the women in her age group are widows.

As people live busier and busier lives, they sometimes don't have the time to go out and meet new people. Dating Web sites provide a fast, easy way for people to find romance.

Did You Know?
Fifty-three percent of women 75 years old and older live alone. Twenty-one percent of men over 75 live alone.

364 Lesson **11**

Reading Variation

To practice listening skills, have students first listen to the audio alone. Ask a few comprehension questions. Repeat the audio if necessary. Then have them open their books and read along as they listen to the audio.

Reading Glossary

values: ideals; standards of a society
widow: a woman whose husband has died

11.6 | *Whose* + Noun

Whose is the possessive form of *who*. It substitutes for *his, her, its, their*, or the possessive form of the noun.

He met a woman.

Her values are similar to his own.

He met a woman **whose** values are similar to his own.

Don wanted to create a family.

Don's son was six years old.

Don, **whose** son was six years old, wanted to create a family.

Language Note:
Use *who* to substitute for a person. Use *whose* for possession or relationship.

Compare:

She married a man **who** has a child.

She married a man **whose interests** are similar to hers.

Punctuation Note:
An adjective clause is sometimes separated from the sentence with a comma. This is true when the person or thing in the main clause is unique.

Compare:

Some dating Web sites match you with someone **whose values** are similar to your own.

Sally met Harry, **whose values** were similar to her own. (Harry is unique.)

EXERCISE 12 This is a conversation between two friends. Fill in the blanks. Answers may vary.

A: I know you're trying to meet a man. I have a cousin whose *wife* (example) died last year. He's your age. He's ready to start dating.

B: Tell me more about him.

A: He likes sports and the outdoors.

B: You know I don't like sports. I prefer to stay home and read or watch movies. I want to meet someone whose *interests* (1) are the same as mine.

A: I'm sure you can become interested in football and fishing.

B: I'm not so sure about that. What kind of work does he do?

A: He's a traveling salesman. He's almost never home.

B: I prefer to meet a man whose *work* (2) doesn't take him away from home all the time. What else can you tell me about him?

Adjective Clauses 365

11.6 | *Whose* + Noun

1. Have students look at grammar chart **11.6.** Say: Whose *is the possessive form of* who. *It substitutes for possessive pronouns or the possessive form of the noun.* Review the example sentences.
2. Direct students to the Language Note. Say: Who *is used for a person.* Whose *is used for possession or relationship.* Go over the example sentences. Review the Punctuation Note.

EXERCISE 12

CD 3, Track 29

1. Say: *In this conversation, two friends are talking about dating.* Have students read the direction line. Go over the example in the book.
2. Have students complete Exercise 12 individually. Go over answers as a class.
3. If necessary, review grammar chart **11.6** on page 365.

Exercise 12 Variation

To provide practice with listening skills, have students close their books and listen to the audio. Repeat the audio as needed. Say: *You're going to hear two friends talking about dating.* Ask comprehension questions, such as: *What is person A's cousin interested in?* (sports and the outdoors) *Is person B interested in the same things?* (no) *Does person B want to raise a family? Why or why not?* (No. Her children are older. She doesn't want a new husband with young kids.) Then have students open their books and complete Exercise 12.

EXERCISE 13

1. Say: *Complete these statements so that they are true for you.* Have students read the direction line. Go over the example. Model the example for the students.
2. Have students complete the exercise individually. Then have students compare answers in pairs. Circulate to observe pair work. Give help as needed.
3. If necessary, review grammar chart **11.6** on page 365.

To save class time, have students do half of the exercise in class and complete the other half for homework.

EXERCISE 14

1. Say: *First you're going to complete these statements made by women. Then you're going to complete the statements made by men.* Have students read the direction line. Go over the example.
2. Have students complete the exercise individually. Then have students compare answers in pairs. Circulate to observe pair work. Give help as needed.
3. If necessary, review grammar chart **11.6** on page 365.

To save class time, have students do half of the exercise in class and complete the other half for homework.

A: He has a three-year-old son and a five-year-old daughter.

B: I don't want to marry a man whose *children* (3) are small. My kids are grown up, and I don't want to start raising kids again.

A: It's okay. His mother lives with him now, and she helps take care of the kids.

B: I don't want to date a man whose *mother* (4) lives with him.

A: But she's a nice woman. She's my aunt.

B: I'm sure she is, but I'm 45 and don't want to live with someone's mother.

A: You know my intentions are good.

B: I have a lot of friends whose *intentions* (5) are good, but then I meet the man and find we have nothing in common. I think it's better if I meet a man on my own.

EXERCISE 13 ABOUT YOU Fill in the blanks.

EXAMPLE I would like to own a car that *has enough room for my large family.*

1. My mother is a woman who ______ Answers will vary.
2. My city is a place where ______
3. My childhood was a time when ______
4. My favorite kind of book is one that ______
5. A great teacher is a person who ______
6. I have a friend whose ______
7. I have a computer that ______
8. I like to shop at a time when ______
9. I don't like people who ______

EXERCISE 14 *Combination Exercise. Part A:* Some women were asked what kind or man they'd like to marry. Fill in the blanks with a response, using the words in parentheses ( ).

EXAMPLE I'd like to marry a man *whose values are the same as mine.*
(His values are the same as mine.)

1. I'd like to marry a man *who I can trust.*
(I can trust him.)
2. I don't want a husband *who doesn't put his family first.*
(He doesn't put his family first.)

366 Lesson 11

Expansion

Exercise 12 Have students practice the conversation in pairs. Ask volunteers to role-play all or part of the conversation in front of the class.

3. I want to marry a man *who makes a good living.*
(He makes a good living.)

4. I'd like to marry a man *whose mother lives far away.*
(His mother lives far away.)

5. I'd like to marry a man *who's older than I am.*
(He's older than I am.)

6. I'd like to marry a man *who wants to have children.*
(He wants to have children.)

7. (Women: Add your own sentence telling what kind of man you'd like to marry, or what kind of man you married.)
Answers will vary.

Part B: Some men were asked what kind of woman they'd like to marry. Fill in the blanks with a response, using the words in parentheses ( ).

EXAMPLE I'd like to marry a woman *who knows how to cook.*
(She knows how to cook.)

1. I'd like to marry a woman *who has a sense of humor.*
(She has a sense of humor.)

2. I'd like to marry a woman *whose wisdom I can admire.*
(I can admire her wisdom.)

3. I'd like to marry a woman *whose manners are good.*
(Her manners are good.)

4. I'd like to marry a woman *whose family is supportive.*
(Her family is supportive.)

5. I'd like to marry a woman *who I've known for a long time.*
(I have known her for a long time.)

6. I'd like to marry a woman *who wants to have a lot of kids.*
(She wants to have a lot of kids.)

7. (Men: Add your own sentence telling what kind of woman you'd like to marry, or what kind of woman you married.)
Answers will vary.

EXERCISE 15 *Combination Exercise.* Fill in the blanks with appropriate words to complete the conversation. Answers may vary.

A: I'm getting married in two months.

B: Congratulations. Are you marrying the woman *you met* *(example)* at Mark's party last year?

Adjective Clauses 367

EXERCISE 15

CD 3, Track 30

1. Say: *In this conversation, a man is talking to his friend about his upcoming wedding.* Have students read the direction line. Go over the example.
2. Have students complete Exercise 15 individually. Go over the answers as a class.
3. If necessary, review grammar chart **11.6** on page 365.

To save class time, have students do half of the exercise in class and complete the other half for homework. Or assign the entire exercise for homework.

Expansion

Exercise 14 Have students discuss the statements from Parts A and B in groups. If possible, have students break into groups of all women and all men. Ask the women to say if they agree with the statements in Part A, and ask the men to say if they agree with the statements in Part B. Then get together as a class to discuss all the statements.

Exercise 15 Variation

To provide practice with listening skills, have students close their books and listen to the audio. Repeat the audio as needed. Say: *In this conversation, a man is talking to his friend about his upcoming wedding.* Ask comprehension questions, such as: *Does person B know the woman person A is going to marry?* (no) *Where did person A meet his fiancée?* (online) *Why are they going to live in the U.S.?* (He's got a good job here.) Then have students open their books and complete Exercise 15.

EXERCISE 16

1. Have students read the direction line. Go over the example in the book. Say: *After you finish completing the statements, say if you agree or disagree with them.*
2. Have students complete Exercise 16 individually. Then have students compare answers in pairs. Circulate to observe pair work. Give help as needed.
3. If necessary, review grammar chart **11.6** on page 365.

To save class time, have students do half of the exercise in class and complete the other half for homework. Or assign the entire exercise for homework.

A: Oh, no. I broke up with that woman a long time ago. I'm going to marry a woman *I met* (1) online about ten months ago.

B: What's your fiancée's name? Do I know her?

A: Sarah Liston.

B: I know someone whose *name* (2) is Liston. I wonder if they're from the same family.

A: I doubt it. Sarah comes from Canada.

B: Where are you going to live after you get married? Here or in Canada?

A: We're going to live here. Sarah's just finishing college and doesn't have a job yet. This is the place *where* (3) I have a good job, so we decided to live here.

B: Where are you going to get married?

A: At my parents' friend's house. They have a very big house and garden. The wedding's going to be in the garden.

B: My wife and I made plans to get married outside too, but we had to change our plans because it rained that day.

A: That's OK. The woman *who I marry* (4) is more important than the place *where* (5) we get married. And the life *we have* (6) together is more important than the wedding day.

B: You're right about that!

EXERCISE 16 *Combination Exercise.* Use the words in parentheses ( ) to form an adjective clause. Then read the sentences and tell if you agree or disagree. Give your reasons.

EXAMPLE A good friend is a person *I can trust* (I can trust her.).

1. A good friend is a person *(who) I see* (I see him.) almost every day.
2. A good friend is a person *who would lend me money* (She would lend me money.).
3. A good friend is a person *who knows everything about me* (He knows everything about me.).
4. A person *who has different political opinions* (He has different political opinions.) cannot be my friend.

368 Lesson 11

Expansion

Exercise 15 Have students practice the conversation in pairs. Ask volunteers to role-play the conversation in front of the class.

5. A person who doesn' t speak my native language cannot be my good friend.
(She doesn't speak my native language.)

6. A person whose religious beliefs are different from mine cannot be my good friend.
(His religious beliefs are different from mine.)

7. A person who lives far away cannot be a good friend.
(She lives far away.)

8. I would discuss the problems (that) I have with a good friend.
(I have problems.)

9. This school is a place (where) I can make many new friends easily.
(I can make many new friends easily at this school.)

10. Childhood is the only time in one's life when it is easy to make friends.
(It is easy to make friends at this time.)

SUMMARY OF LESSON 11

Adjective Clauses

1. Pronoun as Subject
   She likes men **who have self-confidence.**
   The man **that arrived late** took a seat in the back.
2. Pronoun as Object
   I'd like to meet the man **(who / m) (that) she married.**
   The book **(which) (that) I'm reading** is very exciting.
3. Pronoun as Object of Preposition
   FORMAL: The person **about whom** I'm talking is my cousin.
   INFORMAL: The person **(who)** I'm talking **about** is my cousin.
   FORMAL: The club **of which** I am a member meets at the community center.
   INFORMAL: The club **(that)** I am a member **of** meets at the community center.
4. *Whose* + Noun
   I have a friend **whose brother lives in Japan.**
   The students **whose last names begin with A or B** can register on Friday afternoon.
5. *Where*
   He moved to New Jersey, **where** he found a job.
   The apartment building **where** he lives has a lot of immigrant families.

Summary of Lesson 11

Adjective Clauses Have students cover up the summary on pages 369–370. Create a fill-in exercise on the board:

who, whom, that, which, whose, where, when

1. *I have a friend ________ brother lives in Japan.*
2. *She came to the U.S. at a time ________ she was young enough to learn English easily.*
3. *The book ________ I'm reading is very exciting.*
4. *The person about ________ I'm talking is my cousin.*
5. *The club ________ I am a member of meets at the community center.*
6. *The man ________ arrived late took a seat in the back.*

Say: *Fill in the blanks with the appropriate word. Answers may vary.* Then have students name the sentences where the relative pronoun is a subject, an object, or an object of a preposition. Finally, have students point out the one formal sentence.

If necessary, have students review:

11.1 Adjective Clauses—An Overview (p. 354)
11.2 Relative Pronoun as Subject (p. 356)
11.3 Relative Pronoun as Object (p. 358)
11.4 *Where* and *When* (p. 362)
11.5 Formal vs. Informal (p. 363)
11.6 *Whose* + Noun (p. 365).

Expansion

Exercise 16 Have students discuss the statements in groups. Then take a class vote on each statement: who agrees and who disagrees?

Editing Advice

Have students close their books. Write the example sentences without editing marks or corrections on the board. For example:

1. *I know a woman what has ten cats.*
2. *I know a man has been married four times.*

Ask students to correct each sentence and provide a rule or an explanation for each correction. This activity can be done individually, in pairs, or as a class. After students have corrected each sentence, tell them to turn to pages 370–371. Say: *Now compare your work with the Editing Advice in the book.*

6. *When*
   She came to the U.S. at a time **when** she was young enough to learn English easily.
   She came to the U.S. in 1995, **when** there was a war going on in her country.

EDITING ADVICE

1. Use *who, that,* or *which* to introduce an adjective clause. Don't use *what.*

   I know a woman ~~what~~ *who* has ten cats.

2. If the relative pronoun is the subject, don't omit it.

   I know a man ^*who* has been married four times.

3. Use *whose* to substitute for a possessive form.

   I live next door to a couple ~~their~~ *whose* children make a lot of noise.

4. If the relative pronoun is used as the object, don't put an object after the verb of the adjective clause.

   I had to pay for the library book that I lost ~~it~~.

5. Don't use *which* for people.

   The man ~~which~~ *who* bought my car paid me by check.

6. Use subject-verb agreement in all clauses.

   I have a friend who live^*s* in Madrid.

   People who talks too much bother me.

7. Don't use an adjective clause when a simple adjective is enough.

   I don't like long movies.
   ~~I don't like movies that are long.~~

8. An adjective clause is a dependent clause. It is never a sentence.

   I sold my car to a man~~.~~ ~~Who~~ *who* lives on the next block.

9. Put a noun before an adjective clause.

   A student w
   Who needs help should ask the teacher.

10. Put the adjective clause immediately after the noun it describes.

The car is beautiful that you bought.

11. Use *where*, not *that*, to mean "in a place."

where
The store that I buy my textbooks is having a sale this week.

12. Use *whom* and *which*, not *that*, if the preposition precedes the relative pronoun.

which
She would never want to go back to the country from that she came.

13. Use correct word order in an adjective clause (subject before verb).

my father caught
The fish that caught my father was very big.

14. Don't confuse *whose* (possessive form) and *who's (who is)*.

who's
A woman whose in my math class is helping me study for the test.

LESSON 11 TEST/REVIEW

PART 1 Find the mistakes with the underlined words, and correct them. Not every sentence has a mistake. If the sentence is correct, write *C*.

EXAMPLES Do you know the man ~~whose~~ who's standing in the back of the theater?

Could you please return the book I lent you last week? C

1. The wallet which found ~~my friend~~ my friend has no identification.
2. The coat is too small that I bought last week.
3. I don't know the people who lives next door to me.
4. I have to return the books that I borrowed from the library. C
5. I don't like neighbors ~~what~~ who make a lot of noise.
6. I don't like the earrings that I bought ~~them~~.
7. I have a friend who lives in Houston.
8. ~~Who~~ Anyone who speaks English well doesn't have to take this course.
9. I can't understand a word you are saying. C
10. I prefer to have an English teacher ~~which~~ who speaks my language.
11. Everyone whose last name begins with *A* should stand up. C

Lesson 11 Test/Review

For additional practice, review, and assessment materials, see Assessment CD-ROM with *ExamView Pro*, *More Grammar Practice* Workbook 2, Interactive CD-ROM, and Web site http://elt.thomson.com/gic

PART 1

1. Part 1 may be used as an in-class test to assess student performance, in addition to the Assessment CD-ROM with *ExamView Pro*. Have students read the direction line. Ask: *Do all sentences have a mistake?* (no) Go over the examples. Collect for assessment.
2. If necessary, have students review: **Lesson 11.**

Lesson Review

To use Part 1 as a review, assign it as homework or use it as an in-class activity to be completed individually or in pairs. Check answers and review errors as a class. Reteach grammar points that students haven't mastered. Then student learning may be assessed using a test generated from the Assessment CD-ROM with *ExamView Pro*.

PART 2

1. Part 2 may also be used as an in-class test to assess student performance, in addition to the Assessment CD-ROM with *ExamView Pro*. Have students read the direction line. Collect for assessment.
2. If necessary, have students review: **Lesson 11.**

12. The store ~~that~~ *where* I buy my groceries is open 24 hours a day.
13. I don't understand a thing you are talking about. *C*
14. The woman with whom he came to the party was not his wife. *C*
15. I don't know anyone, ~~W~~ho *w* has a record player any more.
16. We rented an apartment that doesn't have a refrigerator. *C*
17. A couple ~~who's~~ *whose* children are small has a lot of responsibilities.
18. I have a friend ~~her~~ *whose* brother just graduated from medical school.

PART 2 Fill in the blanks to complete the adjecive clause. Answers may vary.

EXAMPLE You lost a glove. Is this yours?
No. The glove *that I lost* is brown.

1. A: My neighbor's children make a lot of noise.
   B: That's too bad. I don't like to have neighbors *whose children make a lot of noise.*
2. A: I have a new cat. Do you want to see him?
   B: What happened to the other cat *you had*
   A: She died last month.
3. A: Do you speak French?
   B: Yes, I do. Why?
   A: The teacher is looking for a student *who speaks French* to help her translate a letter.
4. A: Did you meet your boyfriend on an Internet dating site?
   B: No. I didn't like any of the men *I met* on the Internet.
5. A: Does your last name begin with *A*?
   B: Yes, it does. Why?
   A: Registration is by alphabetical order. Students *whose last names begin with A* can register after two o'clock today.
6. A: Did you go to your last high school reunion?
   B: No. I was out of town on the day *the reunion was held*.
   A: Do you usually go to your reunions?
   B: Yes. I love to keep in touch with the people *I went to high school with*
7. A: Are you planning to marry Charles?
   B: No. He lives with his mother. I want to marry a man *whose mother* lives far away.

372 Lesson 11

Lesson Review

To use Part 2 as a review, assign it as homework or use it as an in-class activity to be completed individually or in pairs. Check answers and review errors as a class. Then have students practice the miniconversations. Reteach grammar points that students haven't mastered. Then student learning may be assessed using a test generated from the Assessment CD-ROM with *ExamView Pro*.

EXPANSION ACTIVITIES

Classroom Activities

1. Tell if you agree or disagree with the statements below. Discuss your answers.

	I agree.	I disagree.
a. People who have different religions can have a good marriage.		
b. People who come from different countries or have different languages can have a good marriage.		
c. Women who marry younger men can be happy.		
d. It's possible to fall in love with someone you've just met.		
e. Young people who want to get married should get the approval of their parents.		
f. A man shouldn't marry a divorced woman who has children.		
g. Couples who have children shouldn't get divorced.		
h. Older women whose husbands have died should try to get married again.		
i. A man should always marry a woman who is shorter than he is.		
j. Couples who live with a mother-in-law usually have problems.		
k. A woman shouldn't marry a man who has a lower level of education.		

2. Write a short definition or description of an object or a person. Read your definition to a small group. The others will try to guess what it is. Continue to add to your definition until someone guesses it.

EXAMPLE It's an animal that lives in the water.
Is it a fish?
No, it isn't. It's an animal that needs to come up for air.
Is it a dolphin?
Yes, it is.

3. Write a word from your native language that has no English translation. It might be the name of a food or a traditional costume. Define the word. Read your definition to a small group or to a partner.

EXAMPLE A *sari* is a typical Indian dress for women. It is made of a cloth that a woman wraps around her. She wraps one end around her waist. She puts the other end over her shoulder.

4. Bring to class something typical from your country. Demonstrate how to use it.

EXAMPLE a samovar
This is a pot that we use in Russia to make tea.

Expansion Activities

These expansion activities provide opportunities for students to interact with one another and further develop their speaking and writing skills. Encourage students to use grammar from this lesson whenever possible.

To save class time, assign parts of the activities as homework. Then use class time for interaction and communication. If students do not need additional speaking practice, some of the activities may be assigned as writing activities for homework, or skipped altogether.

CLASSROOM ACTIVITIES

1. First have students complete the chart individually. Then have students discuss their answers in groups or with the whole class.
2. To help students, write the names of objects and people on small cards and have students pick a card from a hat.
3. If possible, have students from different countries and cultures work together in groups.
4. If possible, bring in objects from other countries or cultures in case students forget theirs.

Classroom Activities Variation

Activity 4 Put strange objects that students might not recognize on the table. Have students take guesses at what they are and demonstrate their use.

CLASSROOM ACTIVITIES (*cont.*)

5. If you provide a list of words and definitions for students to choose from, it may be more interesting to choose words that sound similar to words students already know, such as the example in the book.

TALK ABOUT IT

Have students discuss each topic in pairs, in groups, or as a class.

WRITE ABOUT IT

1. Before they begin their compositions, have students make a list of all the qualities that describe the friend they're going to write about.
2. Have students first make a chart to list the dating customs in the U.S. and in their native countries.

INTERNET ACTIVITIES

Remind students that if they don't have Internet access, they can use Internet facilities at a public library, or they can use traditional research methods to find out information, including looking at encyclopedias, magazines, books, journals, and newspapers.

5. Dictionary game. Form a small group. One student in the group will look for a hard word in the dictionary. (Choose a noun. Find a word that you think no one will know.) Other students will write definitions of the word. Students can think of funny definitions or serious ones. The student with the dictionary will write the real definition. Students put all the definitions in a box. The student with the dictionary will read the definitions. The others have to guess which is the real definition.

EXAMPLE parapet
Sample definition: A parapet is a small pet that has wings, like a parakeet.
Real definition: A parapet is a low wall that runs along the edge of a roof or balcony.

(The teacher can provide a list of words and definitions beforehand, writing them on small pieces of paper. A student can choose one of the papers that the teacher has prepared.)

Talk About it

1. Do you think the Internet is a good way to meet a romantic partner? Why or why not?
2. How do people in your native culture find a spouse?
3. Talk about the kind of person who makes a good husband, wife, father, mother, or friend.
4. If you are married, tell where or how you met your spouse.
5. Are you surprised that there are Internet sites for seniors who are single and looking for a partner?
6. In your native culture, do people usually keep in touch with the friends they made in school?
7. Are there class reunions in your native country?

Write About it

1. Write a short composition describing your best friend from your school days.
2. Write a short composition describing the difference between dating customs in the U.S. and in your native culture.

Internet Activities

1. Visit an online dating service. Bring in a profile of a person that you think is interesting.
2. Visit an online dating service for senior citizens. Bring in a profile of a person that you think is interesting.
3. Visit a Web site that lists classmates. If you graduated from high school in the U.S., see if your high school is listed.
4. Visit a Web site that plans reunions. Find out some of the steps that are necessary in planning a reunion.

Additional Activities at http://elt.thomson.com/gic

374 Lesson 11

Expansion

Write About it Have students exchange first drafts with a partner. Ask students to help their partners edit their drafts. Refer students to the Editing Advice on pages 370–371.

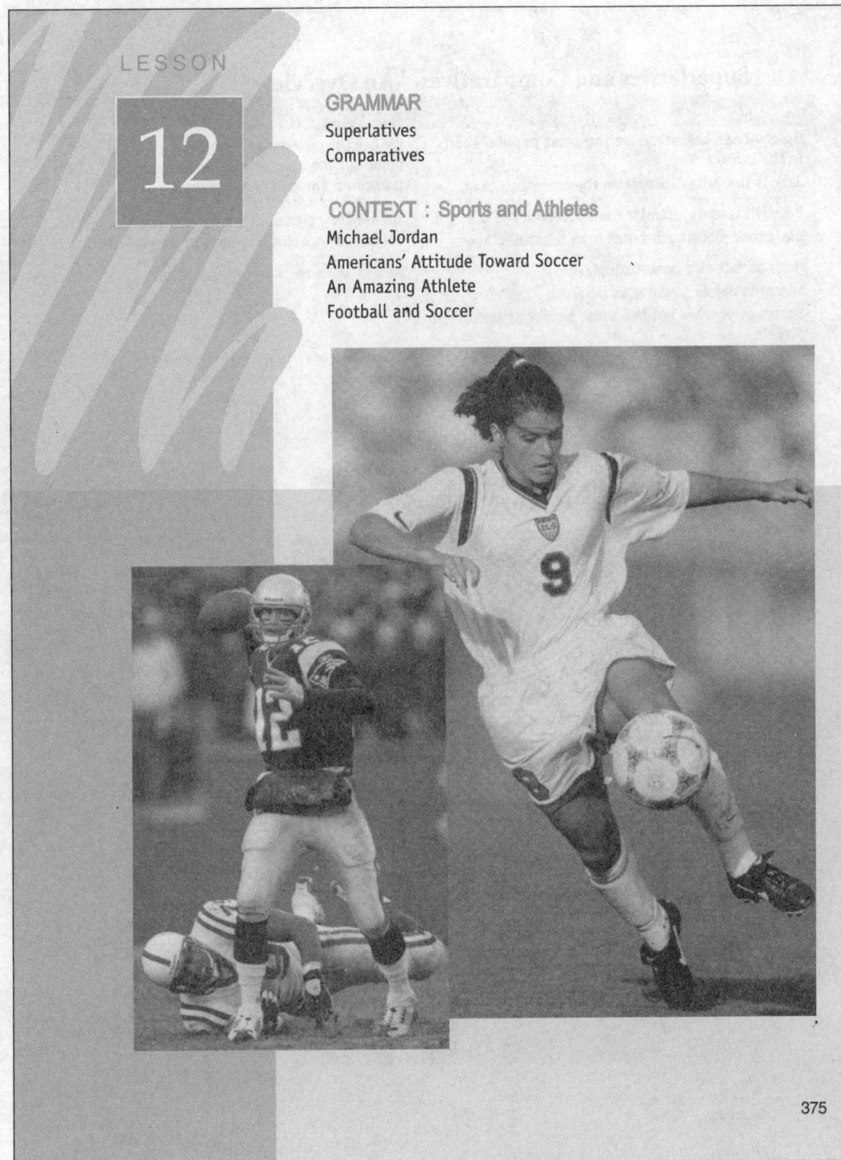

LESSON

12

GRAMMAR
Superlatives
Comparatives

CONTEXT : Sports and Athletes
Michael Jordan
Americans' Attitude Toward Soccer
An Amazing Athlete
Football and Soccer

375

Lesson 12

Lesson Overview

GRAMMAR

1. Briefly review what students learned in the last lesson. Ask: *What did we study in Lesson 11?* (adjective clauses)
2. Ask: *What are we going to study in this lesson?* (superlatives and comparatives) *Can anyone give me an example of a superlative?* (e.g., *the best book, the tallest mountain*) Have students give examples. Write the examples on the board. Then have students give examples of comparatives (e.g., *This winter was colder than winter last year.*).

CONTEXT

1. Ask: *What are we going to learn about in this lesson?* (sports and athletes) Activate students' prior knowledge. Ask: *Do you play any sports? What are your favorite sports? Who are your favorite athletes?*
2. Have students share their knowledge and personal experiences.

To save class time, have students do the Test/Review at the end of the lesson, or administer a lesson test generated from the Assessment CD-ROM with *ExamView® Pro.* Skip sections of the lesson that students have already mastered. You may also assign some sections for self-study for extra credit.

Expansion

Theme The topic for this lesson can be enhanced with the following ideas:

1. Books and pictures of sports and famous athletes
2. Video clips of famous sports moments

12.1 | Superlatives and Comparatives—An Overview

1. Have students cover up grammar chart **12.1** on page 376. Write the following on the board:
   1. Baseball is more popular than soccer in the U.S.
   2. He is as tall as a basketball player.
   3. Jack is the tallest player on the team.
   Ask: *Which sentence shows equality?* (2) *Which sentence is comparing two things?* (1) *Which sentence points out the number one item out of a group of three or more?* (3)
2. Then have students look at grammar chart **12.1.** Review the example sentences and explanations in the chart.

Michael Jordan (Reading)

1. Have students look at the photos on pages 376 and 377. Ask: *Who is Michael Jordan?* (a star basketball player who is now retired) *Have you ever seen him play? What award is he receiving?* (the Jackie Robinson Foundation Robie Award for Humanitarianism)
2. Have students look at the title of the reading. Ask: *What is the reading about?* Have students use the title and photos to make predictions about the reading.
3. Preteach any vocabulary words your students may not know, such as *record* and *comeback.*

BEFORE YOU READ

1. Have students discuss the questions in pairs.
2. Ask for a few volunteers to share their answers with the class.

To save class time, skip "Before You Read" or have students prepare answers for homework ahead of time.

12.1 | Superlatives and Comparatives—An Overview

Examples	Explanation
Baseball and basketball are **the most popular** sports in the U.S. Jack is **the tallest player** on the basketball team.	We use the superlative form to point out the number one item or items in a group of three or more.
Baseball is **more popular than** soccer in the U.S. Basketball players are **taller than** baseball players.	We use the comparative form to compare two items or groups of items.
He is **as tall as** a basketball player. Soccer is not **as popular as** baseball. Soccer players are not **the same height as** basketball players.	We can show equality or inequality.

MICHAEL JORDAN

Before You Read
1. Do you like sports? Which are your favorites?
2. Who are your favorite athletes?

376 Lesson 12

 Read the following article. Pay special attention to superlative forms.

Michael Jordan is probably **the best known** basketball player in the world. His career started in the early 1980s, when he played college basketball with the University of North Carolina. Although he was not **the tallest** or **the strongest** player, he won the attention of his coach for being an excellent athlete. Probably his **most important** achievement[1] at that time was scoring the winning basket in the 1983–1984 college championship game.

Jordan left college early to join the Chicago Bulls, a professional basketball team. He led the Bulls to **the best** record in professional basketball history. He was voted **the most valuable** player five times. Jordan holds several records: **the highest** scoring average (31.7 points per game) and **the most** points in a playoff game (63). Many people think that Michael Jordan was **the most spectacular** basketball player of all time. A statue of Jordan in Chicago has these words, "**The best** there ever was. **The best** there ever will be." Jordan retired from the Chicago Bulls in 1999 at the age of 35.

Jordan came out of retirement in 2001 to play a few more seasons with another team, the Washington Wizards. When he announced his comeback, he said he would donate his $1 million salary the first year to the families of the victims of the September 11, 2001 terrorist attacks. He retired from basketball for good in 2003, at the age of 40. L.A. Laker superstar Magic Johnson said it well when he said, "There's Michael, then there's all the rest of us."

Jordan's popularity with his fans brought him to the attention of advertisers. Jordan is paid a lot of money to have his name appear on sports products and to appear in TV commercials. *Forbes Magazine* in 2004 ranked him the fourth **highest** paid athlete and the seventh **highest** paid celebrity.

In his retirement, Jordan works with charities. He created The Jordan Institute for Families, an organization that tries to help solve the problems facing poor families. He is hoping to help families accomplish their dreams.

Did You Know?

When Michael Jordan tried out for the basketball team in high school, he didn't make it on the first try.

[1] An *achievement* is something you attain through practice or hard work.

Superlatives; Comparatives 377

Reading CD 4, Track 1

1. Have students first read the text silently. Tell them to pay special attention to superlative forms. Then play the audio and have students read along silently.
2. Check students' comprehension. Ask questions such as: *Why did Michael Jordan attract a lot of attention from his basketball coach in college?* (He was an excellent athlete.) *Did he graduate from college?* (No. He left early to pursue a professional basketball career.) *When did Jordan retire from the Chicago Bulls?* (in 1999 at age 35) *After he retired from the Bulls, did he ever play again?* (Yes. He played for a while with the Washington Wizards.)

To save class time, have students do the reading for homework ahead of time.

DID YOU KNOW?

As a young athlete, Michael Jordan liked a number of sports—his favorite was baseball. He became interested in basketball to beat his brother at small pick-up games. As a sophomore in high school, Michael Jordan was not chosen for the varsity team. He had to play on the junior varsity team until finally, as a junior, he became a varsity player.

Reading Variation

To practice listening skills, have students first listen to the audio alone. Ask a few comprehension questions. Repeat the audio if necessary. Then have them open their books and read along as they listen to the audio.

Reading Glossary

comeback: a return to the top level of success
record: the best time, distance, etc., in an athletic event

12.2 | The Superlative Form

1. Have students cover up grammar chart **12.2** on page 378. Write the following on the board:
   Jordan was not the tallest player on the team.
   Jordan was probably the most spectacular player of all time.
   Jordan is one of the richest athletes in the world.
   Jordan is one of the best athletes who has ever lived.
   Who is the best athlete in the world?
   Briefly explain each sentence. Say: *For short adjectives, we add* -est. *For longer adjectives, we add* most *to the adjective.* *We often use the expression* one of the *with superlatives.* *We often use an adjective clause with* ever *with the superlative.* *Some adjectives are irregular—and so their superlative forms will be irregular.*
2. Then have students look at grammar chart **12.2.** Review the example sentences and explanations in the chart.
3. Direct students to the Language Note. Point out the use of *the* before superlatives. Explain that *the* is not used if there is a possessive form. Go over the examples.

EXERCISE 1

1. Say: *This exercise is based on the reading.* Have students read the direction line. Go over the example.
2. Have students complete Exercise 1 individually. Go over the answers as a class.
3. If necessary, review grammar chart **12.2** on page 378.

12.2 | The Superlative Form

We use the superlative form to point out the number one item of a group of three or more. The superlative has two forms, depending on the number of syllables in the adjective or adverb.

Examples	Explanation
Jordan was not **the tallest** player on his team. Jordan was not **the strongest** player on his team.	Use: *the* + [short adjective/adverb] + *-est* We often put a prepositional phrase after a superlative phrase: *in the world, on his team, in the U.S., of all time.*
Jordan was probably **the most spectacular** player of all time. He was **the most valuable** player on this team.	Use: *the most* + [long adjective/adverb]
Jordan is **one of the richest athletes** in the world. Jordan was **one of the oldest players** on his team.	We often say "one of the" before a superlative form. The noun that follows is plural.
Jordan is one of the best athletes **who has ever lived.** His last game with the Bulls was one of the most exciting games **I have ever seen.**	An adjective clause with *ever* and the present perfect tense often completes a superlative statement.
Who is **the best** athlete in the world?	Some superlatives are irregular. See 12.3 for more information.

Language Notes:
Use **the** before a superlative form. Omit **the** if there is a possessive form before the superlative form.
Jordan was **the team's most valuable** player. (*Not:* Jordan was the *team's* the most valuable player.)
My oldest brother loves basketball, (*Not: My the oldest* brother loves basketball.)

EXERCISE 1 Tell if the statement is true (*T*) or false (*F*). Underline the superlative forms. Not every sentence has a superlative form.

EXAMPLE Michael Jordan is one of the best basketball players in the world. T

1. Magic Johnson said, "Jordan is the best there ever was, the best there ever will be." F
2. Jordan was voted the most valuable player more than one time. T
3. Jordan is one of the richest athletes in the world. T
4. Jordan scored the most points in a playoff game. T
5. Jordan retired for good at the age of 35. F
6. One year, Jordan donated his $1 million dollar salary to the families of the victims of September 11. T

378 Lesson 12

Expansion

Grammar Have students write three sentences about a famous athlete from their native countries. Say: *Use the sentences in the reading and grammar chart **12.2** as a model.*

12.3 | Comparative and Superlative Forms of Adjectives and Adverbs

Explanation	Simple	Comparative	Superlative
One-syllable adjectives and adverbs*	tall fast	taller faster	the tallest the fastest
Two-syllable adjectives that end in *-y*	easy happy	easier happier	the easiest the happiest
Other two-syllable adjectives	frequent active	more frequent more active	the most frequent the most active
Some two-syllable adjectives have two forms.	simple	simpler more simple	the simplest the most simple
Other two-syllable adjectives that have two forms are *handsome, quiet, gentle, narrow, clever, friendly, angry, polite, stupid*.	common	commoner more common	the commonest the most common
Adjectives with three or more syllables	important difficult	more important more difficult	the most important the most difficult
-ly adverbs	quickly brightly	more quickly more brightly	the most quickly the most brightly
Irregular adjectives and adverbs	good/well bad/badly far little a lot	better worse farther less more	the best the worst the farthest the least the most

Spelling Rules for Short Adjectives and Adverbs

Rule	Simple	Comparative	Superlative
Add *-er* and *-est* to short adjectives and adverbs.	tall fast	taller faster	tallest fastest
For adjectives that end in *y*, change *y* to *i* and add *-er* and *-est*.	easy happy	easier happier	easiest happiest
For adjectives that end in *e*, add *-r* and *-st*.	nice late	nicer later	nicest latest
For words ending in consonant-vowel-consonant, double the final consonant, then add *-er* and *-est*.**	big sad	bigger sadder	biggest saddest

Language Notes:

* Exceptions:	bored tired	more bored more tired	the most bored the most tired

** Exception: Do not double final *w*: new–newer–newest

Superlatives; Comparatives 379

12.3 | Comparative and Superlative Forms of Adjectives and Adverbs

1. Have students cover up grammar chart **12.3.** Write the following adjectives on the board:
tall, fast
easy, happy
frequent, active
important, difficult
Ask: *What do you notice about each pair of adjectives?* If students have difficulty, give them a hint. Say: *Look at the syllables.*
2. Then have students look at grammar chart **12.3.** Say: *Let's look at how we form the comparative and superlative forms. For short adjectives, we usually add* -er *for the comparative form. For the superlative, we add* -est. *For longer adjectives, we add* more *before the adjective to form the comparative and* most *before the adjective to form the superlative. There are exceptions.* Tired *and* bored, *which are one syllable adjectives, use* more *and* most *for the comparative and superlative forms.* Go over the examples and explanations for each kind of adjective. Explain that some two-syllable adjectives have two forms.
3. Point out that *-ly* adverbs use *more* and *most.* The last category of adjectives and adverbs are irregular; their forms have to be memorized. Explain that except for *good/well* and *bad/badly*, the adjective and adverb are the same.
4. Direct students to the bottom chart to review the rules for spelling short adjectives and adverbs. Have students cover up the *rule* column of the chart. Say: *Study these adjectives and adverbs with their superlative and comparative forms. Can you guess the rules?*
5. Have volunteers write the rules on the board. Then have students look at the complete grammar chart. Say: *Now compare your work with the chart.* Go over the examples and rules.
6. Direct students to the Language Notes. Explain that you don't double a final *w*.

EXERCISE 2

1. Have students read the direction line. Go over the examples.
2. Have students complete Exercise 2 individually. Then have students compare answers in pairs. Circulate to observe pair work. Give help as needed.
3. If necessary, review grammar chart **12.3** on page 379.

EXERCISE 3

1. Have students read the direction line. Explain that this exercise is about Michael Jordan. Go over the example.
2. Have students complete Exercise 3 individually. Then have students compare answers in pairs. Circulate to observe pair work. Give help as needed.
3. If necessary, review grammar chart **12.3** on page 379.

To save class time, have students do half of the exercise in class and complete the other half for homework.

EXERCISE 2 Give the comparative and superlative forms of each word.

EXAMPLES	fat	*fatter*	*the fattest*
	important	*more important*	*the most important*
1.	interesting	*more interesting*	*the most interesting*
2.	young	*younger*	*the youngest*
3.	beautiful	*more beautiful*	*the most beautiful*
4.	good	*better*	*the best*
5.	common	*commoner/more common*	*the commonest/ the most common*
6.	thin	*thinner*	*the thinnest*
7.	carefully	*more carefully*	*the most carefully*
8.	pretty	*prettier*	*the prettiest*
9.	bad	*worse*	*the worst*
10.	famous	*more famous*	*the most famous*
11.	lucky	*luckier*	*the luckiest*
12.	simple	*simpler/more simple*	*the simplest/ the most simple*
13.	high	*higher*	*the highest*
14.	delicious	*more delicious*	*the most delicious*
15.	far	*farther*	*the farthest*
16.	foolishly	*more foolishly*	*the most foolishly*

EXERCISE 3 Many people have said that Jordan is or was the superlative in these categories. Write the superlative form in each blank.

EXAMPLE He was *the most elegant* athlete. (elegant)

1. He was *the most popular* athlete. (popular)
2. He was *the greatest* athlete. (great)
3. He was *the most powerful* athlete. (powerful)
4. He was *the most graceful* athlete. (graceful)
5. He is *the best*-known American basketball player in the world. (good)

380 Lesson 12

Expansion

Exercise 2 Put together a list of 40 or so adjectives. Divide the class into two teams. Give each team a word to change into the comparative and superlative. One member from each team writes the comparative and superlative on the board. The members of the team have to take turns going up to the board. The team that gets the most number of adjectives correct wins.

6. He was the most valuable player.
(valuable)

7. He is one of the richest people in the world.
(rich)

8. He is one of the best -dressed people in the world.
(good)

EXERCISE 4 Write the superlative form of the word in paretheses ( ).

1. Michael Schumacher is one of the fastest race car drivers in the world.
(fast)

2. Training for the Olympics is one of the most difficult things for an athlete.
(difficult)

3. Soccer is the most popular sport in the world.
(popular)

4. Sumo wrestlers are the fattest athletes.
(fat)

5. Michael Jordan was the most valuable player on the Chicago Bulls.
(valuable)

6. Swimming and gymnastics are the most watched events during the Summer Olympics.
(watched)

EXERCISE 4

1. Have students read the direction line. Have a volunteer do #1. Point out the photo of Michael Schumacher and the illustration of the sumo wrestler on page 381 and the photo of Yao Ming on page 382.
2. Have students complete Exercise 4 individually. Have students compare answers in pairs. Circulate to observe pair work. Give help as needed.
3. If necessary, review grammar chart **12.3** on page 379.

To save class time, have students do the exercise for homework.

Expansion

Exercise 3 Have students write similar sentences about other athletes they know (e.g., *Pelé was the greatest soccer player in the history of the sport.*).

EXERCISE 5

1. Ask: *What's your opinion on these topics?* Have students read the direction line. Go over the examples. Have volunteers model the examples.
2. Have students complete Exercise 5 individually. Then have students compare answers in pairs. Circulate to observe group work. Give help as needed.
3. If necessary, review grammar chart **12.3** on page 379.

To save class time, have students do half of the exercise in class and complete the other half for homework. Or assign the entire exercise for homework.

7. Yao Ming is one of *the tallest* (tall) basketball players in the world.

8. *The most common* (common) name for soccer in the world is "football."

9. Running a marathon was one of *the hardest* (hard) things I've ever done.

10. In your opinion, what is *the most interesting* (interesting) sport?

EXERCISE 5 ABOUT YOU Write a superlative sentence giving your opinion about each of the following items. You may find a partner and compare your answers to your partner's answers.

EXAMPLES big problem in the world today

I think the biggest problem in the world today is hunger.

big problem in the U.S. today

I think crime is one of the biggest problems in the U.S. today.

1. good way to make friends
   Answers will vary.
2. quick way to learn a language
3. good thing about life in the U.S.
4. bad thing about life in the U.S.
5. terrible tragedy in the world
6. big problem in (*choose a country*)

382 Lesson **12**

Expansion

Exercise 5 Have volunteers share some of their statements with the class. How many students agree?

EXERCISE 6 ABOUT YOU Write superlative sentences about your experience with the words given. Use the present perfect form after the superlative.

EXAMPLE big / city / visit

London is the biggest city I have ever visited.

1. tall / building / visit

   Answers will vary.
2. beautiful / actress / see
3. difficult / subject / study
4. far / distant / travel
5. bad / food / eat
6. good / vacation / have
7. good / athlete / see
8. hard / job / have
9. interesting / sporting event / see

EXERCISE 7 ABOUT YOU Fill in the blanks.

EXAMPLE *Swimming across a lake alone at night* was one of the most dangerous things I've ever done.

1. Answers will vary. is one of the most foolish things I've ever done.
2. ______ is one of the hardest decisions I've ever made.
3. ______ is one of the most dangerous things I've ever done.

Superlatives; Comparatives 383

EXERCISE 6

1. Say: *In this exercise, you're going to use the present perfect with* ever. Have students read the direction line. Go over the example. Model the example for the class.
2. Have students complete Exercise 6 individually. Go over the answers as a class.
3. If necessary, review grammar chart **12.3** on page 379.

To save class time, have students do half of the exercise in class and complete the other half for homework.

EXERCISE 7

1. Ask: *What kind of difficult situations have you been in?* Have students read the direction line. Go over the example. Model the example for the class.
2. Have students complete Exercise 7 individually. Have students compare answers in pairs. Circulate to observe pair work.
3. If necessary, review grammar chart **12.3** on page 379.

To save class time, have students do the exercise for homework.

Expansion

Exercise 6 Take a class survey for selected items in the exercise. Write the responses on the board.

Exercise 7 Variation

Have students write the answers to the three questions on a small piece of paper without signing their names. Fold up the papers and put them all in a box. Read the papers randomly and have students guess who the answers refer to.

12.4 | Superlatives and Word Order

1. Have students cover up grammar chart **12.4.** Write the following on the board:
Who is the best basketball player?
Interest in soccer is growing the most quickly in the U.S.
Ask: *Where's the superlative adjective in the first sentence—before or after the noun?* (before) *Where's the superlative adverb in the second sentence?* (after the verb)
2. Then have students look at grammar chart **12.4** on page 384. Go over the examples and explanations. Remind students that *the best, the worst, the most,* and *the least* can be either adjectives or adverbs. Say: *If they're adjectives, they go before the noun. If they're adverbs, they go after the verb.*
3. Explain that if an adjective and noun are connected to another noun by the verb *be,* there are two possible ways to write the sentence. Go over the examples.

EXERCISE 8

1. Say: *You're going to talk about your family members: Who drives the best? Who's the best athlete?* Have students read the direction line. Go over the example. Say: *Remember to check if the phrase is an adjective and noun, or a verb and an adverb. Then you have to turn it into a superlative.* Have a volunteer model the example.
2. Have students complete Exercise 8 in pairs. Go over the answers as a class. Ask for volunteers to share their answers.
3. If necessary, review grammar chart **12.4** on page 384.

12.4 | Superlatives and Word Order

Examples	Explanation
Who is **the best basketball player?** (Superlative Adjective: best; Noun Phrase: basketball player) Who is **the most popular player?** (Superlative Adjective: most popular; Noun: player)	A superlative adjective comes **before** a noun or noun phrase.
Football is **the most popular sport** in the U.S. OR **The most popular sport** in the U.S. is football.	When the verb *be* connects a noun to a superlative adjective + noun, there are two possible word orders.
Interest in soccer **is growing the most quickly** in the U.S. (Verb: is growing; Superlative Adverb: the most quickly) Michael Jordan **shot baskets the most gracefully.** (Verb Phrase: shot baskets; Superlative Adverb: the most gracefully)	We put superlative adverbs **after** the verb (phrase).
Michael Jordan **played the best** with the Bulls. (Verb: played; Superlative: the best) Fans **loved Michael Jordan the most.** (Verb Phrase: loved Michael Jordan; Superlative: the most)	We put *the most, the least, the best,* and *the worst* **after** a verb (phrase).
Who scored **the most points?** (Superlative: the most; Noun: points) The Bulls had **the best record.** (Superlative: the best; Noun: record)	We put *the most, the least, the best,* and *the worst* **before** a noun.

EXERCISE 8 ABOUT YOU Name the person who is the superlative in your family in each of the following categories.

EXAMPLE works hard
My mother works the hardest in my family.

Answers will vary.

1. drives well
2. lives far from me
3. speaks English confidently
4. spends a lot of money
5. is well dressed
6. watches a lot of TV
7. worries a lot
8. lives well
9. works hard
10. is athletic
11. is a big sports fan
12. is learning English quickly

384 Lesson 12

Expansion

Exercise 8 Have students practice asking and answering questions about family members with a partner (e.g., *Who drives the best in your family? My brother does.*).

AMERICANS' ATTITUDE TOWARD SOCCER

Before You Read

1. Are you interested in soccer?
2. What's your favorite team?

 Read the following article. Pay special attention to comparisons.

Soccer is by far the most popular sport in the world. Almost every country has a professional league. In many countries, top international soccer players are **as** well-known **as** rock stars or actors. However, in 1994 when the World Cup soccer competition was held in the U.S., there was not a lot of interest in soccer among Americans. Many people said that soccer was boring.

Recently, Americans' attitude toward soccer has been changing. In 1999, when the Women's World Cup was played in the U.S., there was **more** interest than ever before. Little by little, soccer is becoming **more popular** in the U.S. The number of children playing soccer is growing. In fact, soccer is growing **faster** than any other sport. For elementary school children, soccer is now the number two sport after basketball. **More** kids play soccer than baseball. Many coaches believe that soccer is **easier** to play than baseball or basketball, and that there aren't **as many** injuries **as** with sports such as hockey or football.

Interest in professional soccer in the U.S. is still much **lower** than in other countries. The number of Americans who watch professional basketball, football, or hockey is still much **higher** than the number who watch Major League Soccer. However, **the more** parents show interest in their children's soccer teams, **the more** they will become interested in professional soccer.

Superlatives; Comparatives 385

Americans' Attitude Toward Soccer (Reading)

1. Have students look at the photo on page 385. Ask: *Is this a familiar scene in your native country?*
2. Have students look at the title of the reading. Ask: *What is the reading about?* Have students use the title and photo to make predictions about the reading.
3. Preteach any vocabulary words your students may not know, such as *league* and *injury.*

BEFORE YOU READ

1. Have students discuss the questions in pairs.
2. Ask for a few volunteers to share their answers with the class.

To save class time, skip "Before You Read" or have students prepare answers for homework ahead of time.

Reading *CD 4, Track 2*

1. Have students first read the text silently. Tell them to pay special attention to comparisons. Then play the audio and have students read along silently.
2. Check students' comprehension. Ask questions such as: *What did Americans use to say about soccer?* (It was boring.) *What big game was played in the U.S. in 1999?* (the Women's World Cup) *In elementary school, soccer is second to which sport?* (basketball) *Do more kids play baseball than soccer?* (no)

To save class time, have students do the reading for homework ahead of time.

Reading Variation

To practice listening skills, have students first listen to the audio alone. Ask a few comprehension questions. Repeat the audio if necessary. Then have them open their books and read along as they listen to the audio.

Reading Glossary

injury: a wound; damage
league: a group of sports teams that compete against each other

Culture Note

Two major American sports started out as imports, cricket and rugby, and then morphed into the very American sports we see today—baseball and American football. Soccer, in many an American's mind, never took on an American personality, and was forever doomed as an immigrant's game. These feelings cemented during the World Wars when Americans sought refuge in isolationism. Attitudes are changing, especially as the world becomes smaller thanks to innovations in communication technology. As American teams get better and more competitive, the public's interest in the sport heightens.

12.5 | Comparatives

1. Have students look at grammar chart **12.5** on page 386. Say: *For short adjectives and adverbs, the comparative form ends in* -er. *Use* more *before longer adjectives and before adverbs that end in* -ly. Go over the examples.
2. Explain that the comparative is used to compare two items. Point out that *than* is used before the second item of comparison.
3. Say: *If there is no comparison with a second item, omit* than. Write the example from the chart on the board.
4. Say: Much *and* little *can be used in front of a comparative.* Go over the examples in the chart.
5. Explain that there are two ways to make comparisons when pronouns are used after *than*: a formal way and an informal way. Say: *In the formal way, you use an auxiliary verb after the pronoun. In the informal way, you use an object pronoun and no verb.* Go over the examples.

EXERCISE 9

1. Have students read the direction line. Go over the example.
2. Have students complete Exercise 9 individually. Go over the answers as a class.
3. If necessary, review grammar chart **12.5** on page 386.

12.5 | Comparatives

We use the comparative form to compare two items. The comparative has two forms, depending on the number of syllables in the adjective or adverb.

Examples	Explanation
Soccer players are **shorter than** basketball players. Interest in baseball is **higher than** interest in soccer in the U.S.	Use: short adjective/short adverb + *-er* + *than*
Basketball is **more popular than** soccer in the U.S. Interest in soccer is growing **more quickly than** interest in hockey.	Use: *more* + longer adjective + *than* *more* + *-ly* adverb + *than*
My brother plays soccer **better than** I do.	Some comparative forms are irregular. See 12.3 for more information.
Basketball is popular in the U.S., but football is **more popular.** Michael Jordan is tall, but other basketball players are **taller.**	Omit *than* if the second item of comparison is not included.
Interest in soccer is ***much* lower** in the U.S. than in other countries. I like soccer ***a little* better** than I like baseball.	*Much* or *a little* can come before a comparative form.
You are taller than **I am.** (FORMAL) You are taller than **me.** (INFORMAL) I can play soccer better than **he can.** (FORMAL) I can play soccer better than **him.** (INFORMAL)	When a pronoun follows *than,* the correct form is the subject pronoun (*he, she, I,* etc.). Usually an auxiliary verb follows (*is, do, did, can,* etc.). Informally, many Americans use the object pronoun (*him, her, me,* etc.) after *than.* An auxiliary verb does not follow.
The more they practice, **the better** they play. **The older** you are, **the harder** it is to learn a new sport.	We can use two comparisons in one sentence to show cause and result.

EXERCISE 9 Circle the correct word to complete each statement.

EXAMPLE In the U.S., soccer is *more* / *less* popular than basketball.

1. Football players have *more* / *fewer* injuries than soccer players.
2. In the U.S., soccer is growing *faster* / *slower* than any other sport.
3. In 1999, there was *more* / *less* interest in soccer than in 1994.

386 Lesson 12

4. Professional soccer is *more* / (*less*) popular in the U.S. than in other countries.

5. In the U.S., soccer players are *more* / (*less*) famous than movie stars.

EXERCISE 10 Fill in the blanks with the comparative form of the word in parentheses ( ).

EXAMPLE In the U.S., basketball is *more popular than* (popular) soccer.

1. Tall people are often *better* (good) basketball players *than* short people.
2. Do you think volleyball is *more fun than* (fun) tennis?
3. Which do you think is *more difficult* (difficult), skiing or surfing?
4. A soccer ball is *larger than* (large) a tennis ball.
5. Children learn sports *more easily than* (easily) adults.
6. People who exercise a lot are in *better* (good) shape *than* people who don't.
7. Do you think soccer is *more interesting than* (interesting) football?
8. Do you think soccer is *more exciting* (exciting) than baseball?

EXERCISE 11 ABOUT YOU Compare the people of your native country (or a place you know wall) to Americans (in general). Give your own opinion.

EXAMPLE tall
Americans are taller than Koreans.

Answers will vary.

1. polite	4. tall	7. wealthy
2. friendly	5. thin	8. educated
3. formal	6. serious	9. happy

Superlatives; Comparatives 387

Expansion

Exercise 10 Have students get into groups to discuss their comparisons. If possible, have students from different cultures and nationalities work together.

EXERCISE 10

1. Have students read the direction line. Go over the example.
2. Have students complete the exercise individually. Go over the answers as a class.
3. If necessary, review grammar chart **12.5** on page 386.

To save class time, have students do half of the exercise in class and complete the other half for homework.

EXERCISE 11

1. Say: *Now you're going to make comparisons between people from your native country and people from the U.S.* Have students read the direction line. Go over the example. Have a volunteer model the example.
2. Have students complete the exercise in pairs. Circulate to observe pair work. Give help as needed.
3. If necessary, review grammar chart **12.5** on page 386.

To save class time, have students do half of the exercise in class and complete the other half in writing for homework. Or if students do not need speaking practice, the entire exercise may be skipped or done in writing.

EXERCISE 12

1. Say: *Now compare the U.S. and your native country.* Have students read the direction line. Go over the examples. Remind students to explain their responses.
2. Have students complete the exercise in pairs. Circulate to observe pair work. Give help as needed.
3. If necessary, review grammar chart **12.5** on page 386.

To save class time, have students do half of the exercise in class and complete the other half in writing for homework. Or if students do not need speaking practice, the entire exercise may be skipped or done in writing.

12.6 | Comparatives and Word Order

1. Have students cover up grammar chart **12.6.** Make a matching exercise on the board. Write the following sentences:
   1. Basketball is more popular than soccer in the U.S.
   2. Jordan played basketball more gracefully than any other player.
   3. There is less interest in hockey than there is in basketball.
   4. My sister likes soccer more than I do.
   a. Put more, less, better, *and* worse *after a verb.*
   b. Put comparative adverbs after the verb.
   c. Put the comparative adjective after the verb be *or other linking verbs:* seem, feel, look, sound, *etc.*
   d. Put more, less, fewer, better, *and* worse *before a noun.*
   Say: *Now match the examples with the explanations.* Have volunteers do the matching on the board.
2. Have students look at grammar chart **12.6.** Say: *Now compare your work with the grammar chart.* Go over the examples and explanations.

EXERCISE 13

1. Have students read the direction line. Go over the examples.
2. Have students complete Exercise 13 individually. Go over the answers as a class.
3. If necessary, review grammar chart **12.6** on page 388.

EXERCISE 12 ABOUT YOU Compare the U.S. and your native country (or a place you know well). Explain your response.

EXAMPLES cars
Cars are cheaper in the U.S. Most people in my native country can't afford a car.

education
Education is better in my native country. Everyone must finish high school.

Answers will vary.

1. rent	4. education	7. gasoline
2. housing	5. medical care	8. the government
3. cars	6. food	9. clothes (or fashions)

12.6 | Comparatives and Word Order

Examples	Explanation
Basketball **is more popular** than soccer in the U.S. (Be / Comparative Adjective) Football **looks more dangerous** than soccer. (Linking Verb / Comparative Adjective)	Put the comparative adjective after the verb be or other linking verbs: *seem, feel, look, sound,* etc.
Jordan **played basketball more gracefully** than any other player. (Verb Phrase / Comparative Adverb) Soccer **is growing faster** than any other sport. (Verb / Comparative Adverb)	Put the comparative adverb **after** the verb (phrase).
There is **less interest** in hockey than there is in basketball. (Comparative Noun) Soccer players have **fewer injuries** than football players. (Comparative Noun)	We can put *more, less, fewer, better,* and *worse* **before** a noun.
My sister **likes soccer more** than I do. (Verb Phrase / Comparative) I **play soccer worse** than my sister does. (Verb Phrase / Comparative)	You can put *more, less, better,* and *worse* **after** a verb (phrase).

EXERCISE 13 Find the mistakes with word order and correct them. Not every sentence has a mistake. If the sentence is correct, write *C*.

EXAMPLES A football team has players more than a baseball team.
A golf ball is smaller than a tennis ball. C

1. A basketball player is taller than a gymnast. C
2. A baseball game has action less than a soccer game.

388 Lesson 12

Expansion

Exercise 12 Have students get into groups to discuss their comparisons. If possible, have students from different cultures and nationalities work together.

3. Football players use padding more than soccer players.
4. Michael Jordan more beautifully played basketball than other players.
5. I more like baseball than basketball.
6. Team A won more games than Team B. C
7. Team A better played than Team B.

EXERCISE 14 ABOUT YOU Use a comparative adverb to compare the people of your native country (or a place you know well) to Americans (in general). Give your own opinion.

EXAMPLE drive well
Mexicans drive better than Americans.

Answers will vary.

1. dress stylishly	4. live long	7. have freedom
2. work hard	5. worry a little	8. have a good life
3. spend a lot	6. live comfortably	9. exercise a lot

EXERCISE 15 ABOUT YOU Compare this school to another school you attended. Use *better, worse, more, less,* or *fewer* before the noun.

EXAMPLE classroom / space
This classroom has more space than a classroom in my native country.

Answers will vary.

1. class / students	4. library / books
2. school / courses	5. school / facilities[2]
3. teachers / experience	6. school / teachers

EXERCISE 16 *Combination Exercise.* Fill in the blanks with the comparative or superlative form of the word in parentheses ( ). Include *than* or *the* when necessary.

EXAMPLES In the U.S., baseball is _more popular than_ (popular) soccer.

Baseball is one of _the most popular_ (popular) sports in the U.S.

1. A tennis ball is _softer than_ (soft) a baseball.
2. An athlete who wins the gold medal is _the best_ (good) athlete in his or her sport.
3. Who is _the tallest_ (tall) player on the Chicago Bulls today?
4. I am _more interested_ (interested) in baseball _than_ in basketball.
5. In my opinion, soccer is _the most exciting_ (exciting) sport.
6. Weightlifters are _more muscular_ (muscular) than golfers.

[2] *Facilities* are things we use, such as a swimming pool, cafeteria, library, exercise room, or student union.

Superlatives; Comparatives 389

Expansion

Exercise 14 Have students get into groups to discuss their comparisons. If possible, have students from different cultures and nationalities work together.

EXERCISE 14

1. Say: *Now you're going to make comparisons about how Americans do things compared to people from your native country. You're going to use adverbs.* Have students read the direction line. Go over the example. Have a volunteer model the example.
2. Have students complete the exercise in pairs. Circulate to observe pair work. Give help as needed.
3. If necessary, review grammar chart **12.6** on page 388.

EXERCISE 15

1. Say: *Now you're going to make comparisons between different schools.* Have students read the direction line. Go over the example. Have a volunteer model the example.
2. Have students complete the exercise in pairs. Circulate to observe pair work. Give help as needed.
3. If necessary, review grammar chart **12.6** on page 388.

To save class time, have students do half of the exercise in class and complete the other half in writing for homework. Or if students do not need speaking practice, the entire exercise may be skipped or done in writing.

EXERCISE 16

1. Have students read the direction line. Go over the examples.
2. Have students complete the exercise individually. Go over the answers as a class.
3. If necessary, review grammar chart **12.6** on page 388.

To save class time, have students do half of the exercise in class and complete the other half for homework. Or assign the entire exercise for homework.

An Amazing Athlete (Reading)

1. Have students look at the photo. Ask: *What's going on in this photo?* (A man is climbing a mountain.)
2. Have students look at the title of the reading. Ask: *What is the reading about?* Have students use the title and photo to make predictions about the reading.
3. Preteach any vocabulary words your students may not know, such as *tough*, *excel*, and *tolerate*.

BEFORE YOU READ

1. Have students discuss the questions in pairs.
2. Ask for a few volunteers to share their answers with the class.

To save class time, skip "Before You Read" or have students prepare answers for homework ahead of time.

Reading CD 4, Track 3

1. Have students first read the text silently. Tell them to pay special attention to comparisons. Then play the audio and have students read along silently.
2. Check students' comprehension. Ask questions such as: *Was Erik always blind?* (No. He lost his sight in his early teens.) *What sport did he discover didn't require the athlete to see?* (first wrestling, then rock climbing) *Is he very different from sighted mountain climbers?* (No. He is skilled and strong.) *When during the climb up Mount Everest did he have an advantage over his teammates?* (when visibility was zero because of the weather)

To save class time, have students do the reading for homework ahead of time.

DID YOU KNOW ?

Interesting Everest Facts

Oldest person to climb Mount Everest—Yuchuiro Miura (70) Japan (2003)

Youngest person to climb Mount Everest—Temba Tseri (15) Nepal (2001)

Fastest ascent—Pemba Dorje Sherpa (8 hours 10 minutes) Nepal (2004)

Fittest climber—Goran Kropp (Rode a bicycle from his home in Sweden to Everest, climbed the mountain without oxygen, and then rode his bike all the way home to Sweden.) Sweden (1996)

7. Golf is a *slower* (slow) sport *than* soccer.
8. A basketball team has *fewer* (few) players *than* a baseball team.
9. Even though January is *the coldest* (cold) month of the year, football players play during this month.
10. My friend and I both jog. I run *farther* (far) than my friend.
11. Who's a *better* (good) soccer player—you or your brother?

AN AMAZING ATHLETE

Before You Read

1. Can people with disabilities do well in sports?
2. Why do people want to climb the tallest mountain in the world?

 Read the following article. Pay special attention to comparisons.

Erik Weihenmayer is **as tough as** any mountain climber. In 2001 he made his way to the top of the highest mountain in the world—Mount Everest—at the age of 33. But Erik is **different from** other mountain climbers in one important way—he is completely blind. He is the first sightless person to reach the top of the tallest mountain.

Erik was an athletic child who lost his vision in his early teens. At first he refused to use a cane or learn Braille, insisting he could do **as well as** any teenager. But he finally came to accept his disability and to excel within it. He couldn't play **the same** sports **as** he used to. He would never be able to play basketball or catch a football again. But then he discovered wrestling, a

Did You Know?

The oldest person to climb Mount Everest was 70 years old.

390 Lesson 12

Reading Variation

To practice listening skills, have students first listen to the audio alone. Ask a few comprehension questions. Repeat the audio if necessary. Then have them open their books and read along as they listen to the audio.

Reading Glossary

excel: to do very well
tolerate: to endure; to suffer
tough: strong

sport where sight was not **as** important **as** feel and touch. Then, at 16, he discovered rock climbing, which **was like** wrestling in some ways; a wrestler and a rock climber get information through touch. Rock climbing led to mountain climbing, the greatest challenge of his life.

Teammates climbing with Erik say that he isn't **different from** a sighted mountaineer. He has **as much** training **as** the others. He is **as** strong **as** the rest. The major difference is he is not **as** thin **as** most climbers. But his strong upper body, flexibility, mental toughness, and ability to tolerate physical pain make him a perfect climber. The only accommodation for Erik's blindness is to place bells on the jackets of his teammates so that he can follow them easily.

Climbing Mount Everest was a challenge for every climber on Erik's team. The reaction to the mountain air for Erik was **the same as** it was for his teammates: lack of oxygen causes the heart to beat slower than usual and the brain does not function **as clearly as** normal. In some ways, Erik had an advantage over his teammates: as they got near the top, the vision of all climbers was restricted. So at a certain altitude, all his teammates **were like** Erik—nearly blind.

To climb Mount Everest is an achievement for any athlete. Erik Weihenmayer showed that his disability wasn't **as important as** his ability.

Did You Know?

Almost 90 percent of Everest climbers fail to reach the top. At least 180 have died while trying.

12.7 | *As . . . As*

Examples	Explanation
Erik is **as strong as** his teammates. At high altitudes, the brain doesn't function **as clearly as** normal. Erik can climb mountains **as well as** sighted climbers.	We can show that two things are equal or unequal in some way by using: *as* + adjective/adverb + *as*.
Erik is not **as thin as** most climbers. Skiing is not **as difficult as** mountain climbing.	When we make a comparison of unequal items, we put the lesser item first.
Baseball is popular in the U.S. Soccer is not **as popular.**	Omit the second *as* if the second item of comparison is omitted.

Usage Notes:

1. A very common expression is as soon as possible. Some people say A.S.A.P for short.
   I'd like to see you as soon as possible.
   I'd like to see you *A.S.A.P.*
2. These are some common expressions using as. . . as.
   as poor as a church mouse
   as old as the hills
   as quiet as a mouse
   as stubborn as a mule
   as sick as a dog
   as proud as a peacock
   as gentle as a lamb
   as happy as a lark

mule

peacock

DID YOU KNOW ?

The worst year for deaths occurred in 1996, when 15 people lost their lives. The worst day was May 10, 1996, when eight died near the summit. That climb was detailed in the book *Into Thin Air* written by journalist and climber Jon Krakauer.

12.7 | *As . . . As*

1. Have students look at grammar chart **12.7.** Say: *We can show two things are equal or unequal by using:* as + *adjective or adverb* + as. Go over the example sentences.
2. Say: *The lesser item goes first.* Go over the example sentences.
3. Explain that you can omit the second *as* if the second item is omitted. Go over the example.
4. Direct students to the Usage Notes. Go over the explanations and examples. Point out that *A.S.A.P.* is either pronounced as initials ("A-S-A-P") or one word ("asap").

EXERCISE 17

1. Have students read the direction line. Go over the example.
2. Have students complete the exercise individually. Go over the answers as a class.
3. If necessary, review grammar chart **12.7** on page 391.

EXERCISE 18

1. Say: *In this exercise, you can compare yourself to other people or you can compare two other people.* Have students read the direction line. Go over the examples. Have volunteers model the examples.
2. Have students complete the exercise in pairs. Circulate to observe pair work. Give help as needed.
3. If necessary, review grammar chart **12.7** on page 391.

To save class time, have students do half of the exercise in class and complete the other half in writing for homework. Or if students do not need speaking practice, the entire exercise may be skipped or done in writing.

EXERCISE 19

1. Say: *Now compare yourself to me.* Have students read the direction line. Go over the example. Have a volunteer model the example.
2. Have students complete the exercise individually. Then have students compare answers in pairs. Circulate to observe pair work. Give help as needed.
3. If necessary, review grammar chart **12.7** on page 391.

To save class time, have students do half of the exercise in class and complete the other half in writing for homework. Or if students do not need speaking practice, the entire exercise may be skipped or done in writing.

EXERCISE 17 Write true(*T*) or false(*F*).

EXAMPLE In wrestling, the sense of sight is as important as the sense of touch. F

1. Rock climbing is not as dangerous as mountain climbing. T
2. At high altitudes, you can't think as clearly as you can at lower altitudes. T
3. Erik was not as strong as his teammates. F
4. When Erik became blind, he wanted to do as well as any other teenager. T
5. Erik could not go as far as his teammates. F
6. Erik was as prepared for the climb as his teammates. T

EXERCISE 18 ABOUT YOU Compare yourself to another person. (Or compare two people you know.) Use the following adjectives and *as. . . as*. You may add a comparative statement if there is inequality.

EXAMPLES thin
I'm not as thin as my sister. (She's thinner than I am.)

old
My mother is not as old as my father. (My father is older than my mother.)

Answers will vary.

1. old	4. patient	7. religious	10. talkative
2. educated	5. lazy	8. friendly	11. athletic
3. intelligent	6. tall	9. strong	12. interested in sports

EXERCISE 19 ABOUT YOU Use the underlined word to compare yourself to the teacher.

EXAMPLE speak Spanish well
The teacher doesn't speak Spanish as well as I do. (I speak Spanish better.)

Answers will vary.

1. arrive at class promptly
2. work hard in class
3. understand American customs well
4. speak quietly
5. speak English fluently
6. understand a foreigner's problems well
7. write neatly
8. speak fast

392 Lesson 12

Expansion

Exercise 18 Have students compare themselves to each other. Have students take turns with their partners asking and answering questions (e.g., *Are you as old as I am? No, I'm not. I'm only 17.*).

Exercise 19 Have volunteers share their answers with the class.

12.8 | *As Many/Much . . . As*

Examples	Explanation
Soccer players don't have **as many injuries as** football players. Erik had **as much training as** his teammates.	We can show that two things are equal or not equal in quantity by using *as many* + count noun + *as* or *as much* + noncount noun + *as.*
I don't play soccer **as much as** I used to. She doesn't like sports **as much as** her husband does.	We can use *as much as* after a verb phrase.

EXERCISE 20 ABOUT YOU *Part A:* Fill in the blanks.

EXAMPLE I drive about *30* (number) miles a week.

1. I'm Answers will vary. (feet/inches) tall.
2. The highest level of education that I completed is ______ ______ (*high school, bachelor's degree, master's degree, doctorate*)
3. I work ______ (number) hours a week.
4. I study ______ (number) hours a day.
5. I exercise ______ (number) days a week.
6. I'm taking ______ (number) courses now.
7. I have ______ (number) siblings.[3]
8. I live ______ (number) miles from this school.

Part B: Find a partner and compare your answers to your partner's answers. Write statements with the words given and (*not*) *as. . . as* or (*not*) *as much / many as.*

EXAMPLE drive *I don't drive as much as Lisa.*

1. tall Answers will vary.
2. have education ______
3. work ______
4. study ______

[3] *Siblings* are a person's brothers and sisters.

Superlatives; Comparatives 393

12.8 | *As Many/Much . . . As*

1. Have students look at grammar chart **12.8.** Say: *We can show two things are equal or not equal in quantity by using:* as many + *count noun +* as *or* as much + *noncount noun +* as. Go over the example sentences.
2. Say: *We can use* as much as *after a verb phrase.* Go over the examples.

EXERCISE 20

1. Say: *First complete the statements to make them true for you. Then compare your information with a partner.* Have students read the direction line. Go over the examples in Parts A and B. Have two volunteers model the exercise.
2. Have students complete the statements individually. Then have students compare answers in pairs. Circulate to observe pair work. Give help as needed.
3. If necessary, review grammar chart **12.8** on page 393.

Expansion

Exercise 20 Have volunteers share some of their answers with the class.

EXERCISE 21

1. Have students read the direction line. Go over the example in the book.
2. Have students complete Exercise 21 in pairs. Circulate to observe pair work. Give help as needed.
3. If necessary, review grammar chart **12.8** on page 393.

EXERCISE 22

1. Say: *Now compare schools.* Have students read the direction line. Go over the example in the book.
2. Have students complete Exercise 22 in pairs. Circulate to observe pair work. Give help as needed.
3. If necessary, review grammar chart **12.8** on page 393.

To save class time, have students do half of the exercise in class and complete the other half in writing for homework. Or if students do not need speaking practice, the entire exercise may be skipped or done in writing.

EXERCISE 23

1. Have students read the direction line. Explain that students will be comparing their city with another city they know. Go over the example in the book.
2. Have students complete Exercise 23 individually. Then have students compare answers in pairs. Circulate to observe pair work. Give help as needed.
3. If necessary, review grammar chart **12.8** on page 393.

To save class time, have students do half of the exercise in class and complete the other half for homework. Or assign the entire exercise for homework.

5. **exercise frequently** ______
6. **take courses** ______
7. **have siblings** ______
8. **live far from school** ______

EXERCISE 21 Compare men and women (in general). Give your own opinion. Use *as many as* or *as much as*.

Answers will vary.

EXAMPLE **show emotion**
Men don't show as much emotion as women. (Women show more emotion than men.)

1. **earn**
2. **spend money**
3. **talk**
4. **gossip**
5. **use bad words**
6. **have responsibilities**
7. **have freedom**
8. **have free time**

EXERCISE 22 ABOUT YOU Compare this school and another school you attended. Use *as many as*.

EXAMPLE **classrooms**
This school doesn't have as many classrooms as King College. (King College has more classrooms.)

Answers will vary.

1. **teachers**
2. **classrooms**
3. **floors (or stories)**
4. **English courses**
5. **exams**
6. **students**

EXERCISE 23 Make a comparison between this city and another city you know well using the categories below.

EXAMPLE **public transportation** *The buses are cleaner in Boston than in this city.*
OR *The buses in this city are not as crowded as the buses in Boston.*

1. **traffic** Answers will vary.
2. **people** ______
3. **gardens and parks** ______
4. **public transportation** ______
5. **museums** ______
6. **universities** ______
7. **houses** ______
8. **buildings** ______
9. **stores or shopping** ______

394 Lesson 12

Expansion

Exercise 21 Have students discuss their answers in groups. Ask students to give details in their answers (e.g., *I agree. I think men still don't share as much emotion as women. I also think that's changing. Now men show more emotion than their fathers.*).

Exercise 23 Have a class discussion about cities. Find out which cities students wrote about. Write them on the board. Ask students to share their opinions.

12.9 | *The Same . . . As*

Examples	Explanation
Pattern A: Erik had **the same ability as** his teammates. A soccer ball isn't **the same shape as** a football.	We can show that two things are equal or not equal in some way by using *the same* + noun + *as*.
Pattern B: Erik and his teammates had **the same ability.** A soccer ball and a football aren't **the same shape.**	Omit *as* in Pattern B.
Language Note: We can make statements of equality with many nouns, such as *size, shape, color, value, religion,* or *nationality.*	

EXERCISE 24 Make statements with *the same. . . as* using the words given.

EXAMPLES a golf ball / a tennis ball (size)
A golf ball isn't the same size as a tennis ball.

1. a soccer ball / a volleyball (shape)
A soccer ball is the same shape as a volleyball.
2. a soccer player / a basketball player (height)
A soccer player isn't the same height as a basketball player.
3. an amateur athlete / a professional athlete (ability)
An amateur athlete doesn't have the same ability as a professional athlete.
4. a soccer player / a football player (weight)
A soccer player isn't the same weight as a football player.
5. team A's uniforms / team B's uniforms (color)
Team A's uniforms aren't the same color as team B's uniforms.

EXERCISE 25 ABOUT YOU Talk about two relatives or friends of yours. Compare them using the words given.

EXAMPLE age
My mother and my father aren't the same age.
OR
My mother isn't the same age as my father. (My father is older than my mother.)

Answers will vary.

1. age
2. height
3. weight
4. nationality
5. religion
6. (have) level of education

EXERCISE 26 ABOUT YOU Work with a partner. Make a true affirmative or negative statement with the words given.

EXAMPLES the same nationality
I'm not the same nationality as Alex. I'm Colombian, and he's Russian.
the same color shoes
Martina's shoes are the same color as my shoes. They're brown.

Superlatives; Comparatives 395

12.9 | The Same . . . As

1. Have students look at grammar chart **12.9.** Say: *We can show two things are equal or not equal by using:* the same + *noun* + as. Go over the example sentences.
2. Say: *There are two ways to write the comparison with* same as. Point out Pattern A and Pattern B. Go over the examples.
3. Direct students to the Language Note. Say: *You can use many nouns with* the same . . . as: the same size as, the same color as, the same religion as, *etc.*

EXERCISE 24

1. Have students read the direction line. Go over the examples.
2. Have students complete the statements individually. Go over the answers as a class.
3. If necessary, review grammar chart **12.9** on page 395.

EXERCISE 25

1. Say: *Now compare two relatives or two friends of yours.* Have students read the direction line. Go over the example. Have two volunteers model the example.
2. Have students complete the statements individually. Then have students compare answers in pairs. Circulate to observe pair work. Give help as needed.
3. If necessary, review grammar chart **12.9** on page 395.

To save class time, have students do half of the exercise in class and complete the other half in writing for homework. Or if students do not need speaking practice, the entire exercise may be skipped or done in writing.

EXERCISE 26

1. Have students read the direction line. Go over the examples. Have two volunteers model the examples.
2. Have students complete the exercise in pairs. Circulate to observe pair work. Give help as needed.
3. If necessary, review grammar chart **12.9** on page 395.

12.10 | Equality with Nouns or Adjectives

1. Have students cover up grammar chart **12.10.** Say: *To show equality with nouns, use* the same . . . as. *To show equality with adjectives or adverbs, use* as . . . as. *For example:* Michael is not the same height as John. Michael is shorter. Michael isn't as tall as John. Write the examples on the board.
2. Go through the list of nouns and adjectives and the example sentences.

EXERCISE 27

1. Have students read the direction line. Go over the example.
2. Have students complete the statements individually. Go over the answers as a class.
3. If necessary, review grammar chart **12.10** on page 396.

Answers will vary.
1. the same hair color
2. the same eye color
3. (speak) the same language
4. (like) the same sports
5. (have) the same level of English
6. the same nationality

12.10 | Equality with Nouns or Adjectives

For equality or inequality with nouns, use *the same . . . as.* For inequality with adjectives and adverbs, use the comparative form.

Noun	Adjective	Examples
height	tall, short	A soccer player is not **the same height as** a basketball player. A soccer player is **shorter.**
age	old, young	He's not **the same age as** his wife. His wife is **older.**
weight	fat, thin	Wrestler A is not **the same weight as** wrester B. Wrestler B is **fatter.** 
length	long, short	This shelf is not **the same length as** that shelf. This shelf is **shorter.**
price	expensive, cheap	This car is not **the same price as** that car. This car is **cheaper.**
size	big, small	These shoes are not **the same size as** those shoes. These shoes are **smaller.** 

EXERCISE 27 Change the following to use the comparative form. Answers may vary.

EXAMPLE Lesson 11 is not the same length as Lesson 12.
Lesson 11 is *shorter*.

1. I am not the same height as my brother.
   My brother is Answers will vary.
2. You are not the same age as your husband.
   You are ______________.
3. I am not the same height as a basketball player.
   A basketball player is ______________.
4. My left foot isn't the same size as my right foot.
   My right foot is ______________.
5. My brother is not the same weight as I am.
   My brother is ______________.

396 Lesson 12

Expansion

Grammar Have students write sentences showing equality with adjectives for each example in the grammar chart (e.g., *A soccer player is not as tall as a basketball player.*).

Exercise 27 Have students write sentences showing equality with adjectives for each item in the exercise (e.g., *Lesson 11 is not as long as Lesson 12.*).

FOOTBALL AND SOCCER

Before You Read
1. Which do you like better, football or soccer?
2. How are soccer players different from football players?

Read the following article. Pay special attention to similarities and differences.

tackle

It may seem strange that Americans give the name "football" to a game played mostly by throwing and carrying a ball with one's hands. But Americans give the name football to a sport that is very **different from** soccer.

Many of the rules in soccer and American football are the **same**. In both games, there are 11 players on each side, and a team scores its points by getting the ball past the goal of the other team. The playing fields for both teams are also very much **alike**.

When the action begins, the two games look very **different**. In addition to using their feet, soccer players are allowed to hit the ball with their heads. In football, the only person allowed to touch the ball with his feet is a special player known as the kicker. Also, in football, tackling the player who has the ball is not only allowed but encouraged, whereas tackling any player in soccer will get the tackler thrown out of the game.

(continued)

Reading Variation

To practice listening skills, have students first listen to the audio alone. Ask a few comprehension questions. Repeat the audio if necessary. Then have them open their books and read along as they listen to the audio.

Reading Glossary

block: to stand in the way
tackle: the act of knocking a player carrying the ball to the ground

Football and Soccer (Reading)

1. Have students look at the photos. Say: *Describe what's going on in these photos.*
2. Have students look at the title of the reading. Ask: *What is the reading about?* Have students use the title and photos to make predictions about the reading.
3. Preteach any vocabulary words your students may not know, such as *tackle* and *block*. For *tackle*, point out the illustration on page 397.

BEFORE YOU READ

1. Have students discuss the questions in pairs.
2. Ask for a few volunteers to share their answers with the class.

To save class time, skip "Before You Read" or have students prepare answers for homework ahead of time.

Reading *CD 4, Track 4*

1. Have students first read the text silently. Tell them to pay special attention to similarities and differences. Then play the audio and have students read along silently.
2. Check students' comprehension. Ask questions such as: *Do American football and soccer have anything in common?* (Yes. For example, many of the rules are the same. Both have 11 players. You score by getting the ball past the goal. And the playing fields are similar.) *Can all American football players kick the ball?* (no, only the kickers) *Do soccer players tackle?* (no) *Do football players wear shorts?* (no)

To save class time, have students do the reading for homework ahead of time.

12.11 Similarity with *Like* and *Alike*

1. Have students cover up grammar chart **12.11.** Write the four sentences from the grammar chart on the board. Label them *Pattern A* and *Pattern B.* Say: *Find the patterns in the two groups of sentences.* Elicit the two patterns from students, and write them on the board.
2. Have students look at grammar chart **12.11** on page 398. Say: *Now check your work.* Point out the illustration of a football player, a soccer player, and a rugby player.
3. Review the patterns. Then direct students to the Language Note. Point out that sense perception verbs are often used with *like* and *alike.* Review the list of verbs.

Football players and soccer players don't **dress alike** or even **look alike** in many ways. Since blocking and tackling are a big part of American football, the players are often very large and muscular and wear heavy padding and helmets. Soccer players, on the other hand, are usually thinner and wear shorts and polo shirts. This gives them more freedom of movement to show off the fancy footwork that makes soccer such a popular game around the world.

While both games are very **different,** both have a large number of fans that enjoy the exciting action.

12.11 | Similarity with *Like* and *Alike*

We can show that two things are similar (or not) with *like* and *alike.*

Examples	Explanation
Pattern A: A soccer player **looks like** a rugby player. A soccer player doesn't **dress like** a football player.	Pattern A: Noun 1 + verb + *like* + Noun 2
Pattern B: A soccer player and a rugby player **look alike.** A soccer player and a football player don't **dress alike.**	Pattern B: Noun 1 + Noun 2 + verb + *alike*

Language Note:
We often use the sense perception verbs (*look, sound, smell, taste, feel,* and *seem*) with *like* and *alike*. We can also use other verbs with *like*: *act like, sing like, dress like,* etc.

398 Lesson **12**

EXERCISE 28 Make a statement with the words given.

EXAMPLE taste / Pepsi / Coke
Pepsi tastes like Coke (to me).
OR
Pepsi and Coke taste alike (to me).

Answers will vary.

1. taste / diet cola / regular cola
2. taste / 2% milk / whole milk
3. look / an American classroom / a classroom in another country
4. sound / Asian music / American music
5. feel / polyester / silk
6. smell / cologne / perfume
7. look / salt / sugar
8. taste / salt / sugar
9. act / American teachers / teachers in other countries
10. dress / American teenagers / teenagers in other countries

EXERCISE 29 Fill in the blanks. In some cases, more than one answer is possible.

EXAMPLE Players on the same team dress ___alike___.

1. Twins ___look___ alike.
2. Americans and people from England don't sound ___alike___. They have different accents.
3. My daughter is only 15 years old, but she ___acts like___ an adult. She's very responsible and hard-working.
4. My son is only 16 years old, but he ___looks like___ an adult. He's tall and has a beard.
5. Teenagers often wear the same clothing as their friends. They like to ___dress alike___.
6. Soccer players don't look ___like___ football players at all.
7. Do you think I'll ever ___sound like___ an American, or will I always have an accent?

EXERCISE 28

1. Have students read the direction line. Go over the example. Say: *You can use Pattern A or Pattern B.*
2. Have students complete the exercise in pairs. Go over the answers as a class.
3. If necessary, review grammar chart **12.11** on page 398.

EXERCISE 29

1. Have students read the direction line. Go over the example. Say: *Sometimes you may need to provide the verb, sometimes just* like *or* alike, *and sometimes you'll need to provide both.*
2. Have students complete the exercise individually. Go over the answers as a class.
3. If necessary, review grammar chart **12.11** on page 398.

To save class time, have students do half of the exercise in class and complete the other half for homework. Or assign the entire exercise for homework.

Expansion

Exercise 28 Ask students to rewrite each sentence using the pattern they didn't use the first time they completed the exercise.

12.12 | *Be Like*

1. Have students look at grammar chart **12.12.** Say: *We can show that two things are similar or not similar in internal characteristics with* be like *and* be alike. Tell students to look down at the bottom of the chart. Say: *Compare these two sentences. One describes physical characteristics, and the other describes internal characteristics.* Go over the examples.
2. Have students look at the top of the grammar chart. Say: *There are two patterns for* be like *and* be alike*: Pattern A and Pattern B.* Write the patterns on the board. Say: *Use* be like *when the two nouns being compared are separated, and use* be alike *when the two nouns being compared are together.*

8. Children in private schools usually wear a uniform. They ___dress___ alike.
9. My children learned English very quickly. Now they sound ___like___ Americans. They have no accent at all.
10. Dogs don't ___look like___ cats at all. Dogs are very friendly. Cats are more distant.

12.12 | *Be Like*

We can show that two things are similar (or not) in internal characteristics with *be like* and *be alike.*

Explanation	Examples
Pattern A: For Erik, mountain climbing **is like** wrestling in some ways. Touch is more important than sight. Erik **was like** his teammates in many ways—strong, well trained, mentally tough, and able to tolerate pain.	Pattern A: Noun 1 + *be* + *like* + Noun 2
Pattern B: For Erik, wrestling and mountain climbing **are alike** in some ways. Erik and his teammates **were alike** in many ways.	Pattern B: Noun 1 + Noun 2 + *be* + *alike*
Compare: a. Erik **looks like** an athlete. He's tall and strong.	Use *look like* to describe physical appearance.
b. Erik **is like** his teammates. He has a lot of experience and training.	Use *be like* to describe an internal characteristic.

EXERCISE 30 ABOUT YOU Work with a student from another country. Ask a question with the words given. Use *be like*. The other student will answer.

EXAMPLE families in the U.S. / families in your native country

Answers will vary.

A: Are families in the U.S. like families in your native country?

B: No, they aren't. Families in my native country are very big. Family members live close to each other.

1. an English class in the U.S. / an English class in your native country
Is an English class in the U.S. like an English class in your native country?
2. your house (or apartment) in the U.S. / your house (or apartment) in your native country
Is your house in the U.S. like your house in your native country?
3. the weather in this city / the weather in your hometown
Is the weather in this city like the weather in your hometown?
4. food in your country / American food
Is the food in your country like American food?
5. women's clothes in your native country / women's clothes in the U.S.
Are women' s clothes in your native country like women' s clothes in the U.S.?
6. a college in your native country / a college in the U.S.
Is a college in your native country like a college in the U.S.?
7. American teachers / teachers in your native country
Are American teachers like teachers in your native country?
8. American athletes / athletes in your native country
Are American athletes like athletes in your native country?

12.13 | Same or Different

We show that two things are the same (or not) by using *the same as*. We show that two things are different by using *different from*.

Explanation	Examples
Pattern A: Football is not **the same as** soccer. Football is **different from** soccer.	Pattern A: Noun 1 is *the same as* Noun 2. Noun 1 is *different from* Noun 2.
Pattern B: Football and soccer are not **the same.** Football and soccer are **different.**	Pattern B: Noun 1 and Noun 2 are *the same.* Noun 1 and Noun 2 are *different.*

Language Note:
You will hear some Americans say *different than*.

EXERCISE 30

1. Have students read the direction line. Go over the example. Say: *Remember, only use* be like.
2. Have students complete the exercise in pairs. Circulate to observe pair work. Give help as needed.
3. If necessary, review grammar chart **12.12** on page 400.

12.13 | Same or Different

1. Have students look at grammar chart **12.13.** Say: *We can show that two things are the same or are not the same by using* the same as. *We can show that things are different by using* different from.
2. Say: *There are two patterns for* the same as *and* different from: *Pattern A and Pattern B.* Write the patterns on the board. Say: *Use* the same as *and* different from *when the two nouns being compared are separated, and use* the same *and* different *when the two nouns being compared are together.* Go over the example sentences.
3. Direct students to the Language Note. Say: *Some Americans say* different than *and not* different from.

Expansion

Exercise 30 Now have students rewrite the questions from Exercise 30 using *be alike.*

EXERCISE 31

1. Have students read the direction line. Go over the examples. Say: *You can use Pattern A or Pattern B.*
2. Have students complete the exercise in pairs. Go over the answers as a class.
3. If necessary, review grammar chart **12.13** on page 401.

EXERCISE 32

CD 4, Track 5

1. Say: *In this conversation, one friend talks about his twin brother with another friend.* Have students read the direction line. Go over the example. Say: *You may need to use* like/alike; be like/be alike; the same ... as; *or* the same as/different from.
2. Have students complete the exercise individually. Go over the answers as a class.
3. If necessary, review grammar charts **12.9** on page 395, **12.10** on page 396, **12.11** on page 398, **12.12** on page 400, and **12.13** on page 401.

EXERCISE 31 Tell if the two items are the same or different.

EXAMPLES boxing, wrestling
Boxing and wrestling are different.

fall, autumn
Fall is the same as autumn.

1. Michael Jordan, Michael Schumacher *Michael Jordan and Michael Schumacher are different.*
2. baseball in Cuba, baseball in the U.S. *Baseball in Cuba is the same as baseball in the U.S.*
3. the Chicago Bulls, the Chicago Bears *The Chicago Bulls and the Chicago Bears are different.*
4. a kilometer, 1,000 meters *A kilometer is the same as 1,000 meters.*
5. L.A., Los Angeles *L.A. is the same as Los Angeles.*
6. a mile, a kilometer *A mile and a kilometer are different.*
7. football, rugby *Football and rugby are different.*
8. football rules, soccer rules *Football rules and soccer rules are different.*

EXERCISE 32 *Combination Exercise.* Fill in the blanks in the following conversation.

A: I heard that you have a twin brother.

B: Yes, I do.

A: Do you and your brother look *alike* (example)?

B: No. He *doesn't* (1) look *like* (2) me at all.

A: But you're twins.

B: We're fraternal twins. That's different *from* (3) identical twins who have the *same* (4) genetic code. We're just brothers who were born at *the same* (5) time. We're not even the same *height* (6). I'm much taller than he is.

A: But you're *the same* (7) in many ways, aren't you?

B: No. We're completely *different* (8). I'm athletic and I'm on the high school football team, but David hates sports. He's a much *better* (9) student than I am. He's much more *like* (10) our mother, who loves to read and learn new things, and I*'m like* (11) our father, who's athletic and loves to build things.

A: What about your character?

B: I'm outgoing and he's very shy. Also we don't dress *alike* (12) at all.

402 Lesson 12

Expansion

Exercise 31 Ask students to rewrite each sentence using a different pattern than the one they used the first time they completed the exercise.

Exercise 32 Variation

To provide practice with listening skills, have students close their books and listen to the audio. Repeat the audio as needed. Say: *In this conversation, one friend talks about his twin brother with another friend.* Ask comprehension questions, such as: *Do the twin brothers look alike?* (No. They're fraternal twins.) *Is person B shorter or taller than his brother?* (taller) *Does person B's brother like sports?* (no) *Do they dress alike?* (no) Then have students open their books and complete Exercise 32.

He likes to wear neat, conservative clothes, but I prefer torn jeans and T-shirts.

A: From your description, it seems (13) like you're not even from the same family.

B: We have one thing in common. We were both interested in the same (14) girl at school. We both asked her out, but she didn't want to go out with either one of us!

EXERCISE 33 *Combination Exercise*. This is a conversation between two women. Fill in the blanks with an appropriate word to complete the comparisons.

A: In the winter months, my husband doesn't pay as much (example) attention to me as (1) he does to his football games.

B: Many women have the same problem as (2) you do. These women are called football "widows" because they lose their husbands during football season.

A: I feel like (3) a widow. My husband is in front of the TV all day on the weekends. In addition to the football games, there are pre-game shows. These shows last as (4) long as the game itself.

B: I know what you mean. He's no different from (5) my husband. During football season, my husband is more (6) interested in watching TV than (7) he is in me. He looks like (8) a robot sitting in front of the TV. When I complain, he tells me to sit down and join him.

A: It sounds like (9) all men act alike (10) during football season.

B: To tell the truth, I don't like football at all.

A: I don't either. I think soccer is much more (11) interesting than football.

Superlatives; Comparatives 403

Expansion

Exercise 32 Have students practice the conversation in pairs. Then ask volunteers to role-play all or part of the conversation in front of the class.

Exercise 32 Have students write a similar conversation about one of the students and a brother or sister. Then ask volunteers to role-play all or part of the conversation in front of the class.

Exercise 33 Variation

To provide practice with listening skills, have students close their books and listen to the audio. Repeat the audio as needed. Say: *In this conversation, two women are talking about their husbands' interest in football.* Ask comprehension questions, such as: *What is the name given to women whose husbands watch too much football?* (football widows) *When person B complains, what does her husband say?* (to come sit down and join him) *Do the two women like football?* (No. They like soccer better.) *What is their favorite sport?* (shopping) Then have students open their books and complete Exercise 33.

EXERCISE 33

CD 4, Track 6

1. Say: *In this conversation, two women are talking about their husbands' interest in football.* Have students read the direction line. Go over the example.
2. Have students complete the exercise individually. Go over the answers as a class.
3. If necessary, review **Lesson 12.**

To save class time, have students do half of the exercise in class and complete the other half for homework. Or assign the entire exercise for homework.

Summary of Lesson 12

1. **Simple, Comparative, and Superlative Forms** Have students cover up the Summary of Lesson 12. Create a fill-in exercise on the board:
   (tall)
   1. Jacob is ______ .
   2. Mark is ______ Jacob.
   3. Bart is ______ member of the basketball team.
   (popular)
   4. Golf is ______ in the U.S.
   5. Baseball is ______ golf.
   6. Soccer is ______ game in the world.
   Say: *Fill in the blanks with the appropriate form of the adjective.*
   If necessary, have students review:
   12.2 The Superlative Form (p. 378)
   12.3 Comparative and Superlative Forms of Adjectives and Adverbs (p. 379)
   12.5 Comparatives (p. 386).
2. **Other Kinds of Comparisons** Create an exercise on the board:
   1. She looks (as young/as young as) her daughter.
   2. She speaks English (as fluently/as fluently as) her husband.
   3. She is (the same age/the same age as) her husband.
   4. She and her husband are (the same age/the same age as).
   5. She works (as many hours/as many hours as) her husband.
   6. She doesn't have (as much time/as much time as) her husband.
   7. She works (as much/as much as) her husband.
   Say: *Circle the correct answer.*
   If necessary, have students review:
   12.7 *As . . . As* (p. 391)
   12.8 *As Many/Much . . . As* (p. 393).

B: Soccer is very different ___from___ (12) football. I think the action is ___more___ (13) exciting. And it's more fun to watch the foot work of the soccer players. Football players look ___like___ (14) big monsters with their helmets and padded shoulders. They don't look handsome at all.

A: Soccer is not ___as___ (15) popular in the U.S. ___as___ (16) it is in other countries. I wonder why.

B: What's your favorite team?

A: I like the Chicago Fire.

B: In my opinion they're not ___as___ (17) good as the Los Angeles Galaxy. But to tell the truth, I'm not very interested in sports at all. When our husbands start watching football next season, let's do our favorite sport: shopping. We can spend ___as much___ (18) time shopping as they spend in front of the TV.

A: I was just thinking the same thing! You and I think ___alike___ (19). Instead of being football widows, they can be shopping "widowers."

SUMMARY OF LESSON 12

1. Simple, Comparative, and Superlative Forms

   SHORT WORDS
   Jacob is **tall.**
   Mark is **taller than** Jacob.
   Bart is **the tallest** member of the basketball team.

   LONG WORDS
   Golf is **popular** in the U.S.
   Baseball is **more popular than** golf.
   Soccer is **the most popular** game in the world.

2. Other Kinds of Comparisons
   She looks **as young as** her daughter.
   She speaks English **as fluently as** her husband.
   She is **the same age as** her husband.
   She and her husband are **the same age.**
   She works **as many hours as** her husband.
   She doesn't have **as much time as** her husband.
   She works **as much as** her husband.

Expansion

Exercise 33 Have students practice the conversation in pairs. Ask volunteers to role-play all or part of the conversation in front of the class.

3. Comparisons with *Like*
She's **like** her mother. (She and her mother **are alike.**) They're both athletic.
She **looks like** her sister. (She and her sister **look alike.**) They're identical twins.
Coke **tastes like** Pepsi. (They taste **alike.**)
Western music doesn't **sound like** Asian music. (They don't **sound alike.**)

4. Comparisons with *Same* and *Different*
Football is **different from** soccer.
My uniform is **the same as** my teammates' uniforms.

EDITING ADVICE

1. Don't use a comparison word when there is no comparison.

New York is a bigger city.

2. Don't use *more* and *-er* together.

He is ~~more~~ older than his teacher.

3. Use *than* before the second item of comparison.

He is younger ~~that~~ *than* his wife.

4. Use *the* before a superlative form.

The Nile is ^*the* longest river in the world.

5. Use a plural noun in the phrase "one of the [superlative] [nouns]."

Chicago is one of the biggest ~~city~~ *cities* in the U.S.

6. Use the correct word order.

She ~~more speaks~~ *speaks more* than her husband.
I have ~~time more~~ *more time* than you.

7. Use *be like* for similar character. Use *look like* for a physical similarity.

He is look^*s* like his brother. They both have blue eyes and dark hair.
He is ~~look~~ like his sister. They are both talented musicians.

Summary of Lesson 12 (*cont.*)

3. Comparisons with *Like* Create an exercise on the board. Say: *Rewrite the sentence with* like *or* alike.
1. *She's like her mother.*
_______________.
2. *She and her sister look alike.*
_______________.
3. *Coke tastes like Pepsi.*
_______________.
4. *Western music and Asian music don't sound alike.*
_______________.

If necessary, have students review:
12.11 Similarity with *Like* and *Alike* (p. 398)
12.12 *Be Like* (p. 400).

4. Comparisons with *Same* and *Different* Create an exercise on the board. Say: *Complete the sentences with the appropriate forms of* same *and* different.
1. *Football is _______ soccer.*
2. *My uniform is _______ my teammates' uniforms.*

If necessary, have students review:
12.13 Same or Different (p. 401).

Editing Advice

Have students close their books. Write the example sentences without editing marks or corrections on the board. For example:

1. *New York is a bigger city.*
2. *He is more older than his teacher.*

Ask students to correct each sentence and provide a rule or an explanation for each correction. This activity can be done individually, in pairs, or as a class. After students have corrected each sentence, tell them to turn to pages 405–406. Say: *Now compare your work with the Editing Advice in the book.*

Lesson 12 Test/Review

For additional practice, review, and assessment materials, see Assessment CD-ROM with *ExamView Pro*, *More Grammar Practice* Workbook 2, Interactive CD-ROM, and Web site http://elt.thomson.com/gic

PART 1

1. Part 1 may be used as an in-class test to assess student performance, in addition to the Assessment CD-ROM with *ExamView Pro*. Have students read the direction line. Ask: *Do all sentences have a mistake?* (no) Go over the examples. Collect for assessment.
2. If necessary, have students review: **Lesson 12.**

8. Don't use *the* and a possessive form together.

   ~~My the~~ youngest son likes soccer.

9. Use the correct negative for *be like, look like, sound like, feel like,* etc.

   don't
   I'm ~~not~~ look like my father.

   does
   He is not act like a professional athlete.

LESSON 12 TEST/REVIEW

PART 1 Find the mistakes with the underlined words, and correct them. Not every sentence has a mistake. If the sentence is correct, write *C*.

EXAMPLES She is look^s like her sister. They both have curly hair.

A house in the suburbs is much more expensive than a house in the city. C

1. I am ~~the same~~ *as* tall as my brother.
2. New York City is the ~~larger~~ *largest* city in the U.S.
3. That man is smarter ~~that~~ *than* his wife.
4. The youngest student in the class has ~~more~~ better grades than you.
5. A big city has ^*more* crime ~~more~~ than a small town.
6. I have three sons. My oldest son is married. *C*
7. I visited many American cities, and I think that San Francisco is the ~~more~~ *most* beautiful city in the U.S.
8. New York is one of the largest ~~city~~ *cities* in the world.
9. My uncle is the most intelligent person in my family. *C*
10. She ^*types* faster ~~types~~ than I do.
11. Texas is one of the biggest state^*s* in the U.S.
12. He ^*drives* more carefully ~~drives~~ than his wife.
13. Paul is one of the youngest students in this class. *C*
14. She is richer than her best friend, but her friend is happier ~~than~~.
15. My ~~the~~ best grade this semester was A–.
16. She ~~isn't~~ *doesn't* look like her sister at all. She's short and her sister is tall.

406 Lesson 12

Lesson Review

To use Part 1 as a review, assign it as homework or use it as an in-class activity to be completed individually or in pairs. Check answers and review errors as a class. Reteach grammar points that students haven't mastered. Then student learning may be assessed using a test generated from the Assessment CD-ROM with *ExamView Pro*.

PART **2** Fill in the blanks.

EXAMPLE Pepsi is ___the same___ color ___as___ Coke.

1. She's 35 years old. Her husband is 35 years old. She and her husband are ___the same___ age.
2. She earns $30,000 a year. Her husband earns $35,000. She doesn't earn as ___much as___ her husband.
3. The little girl ___looks___ like her mother. They both have brown eyes and curly black hair.
4. My name is Sophia Weiss. My teacher's name is Judy Weiss. We have ___the same___ last name.
5. Chinese food is different ___from___ American food.
6. A dime isn't the same ___as___ a nickel. A dime is smaller.
7. She is as tall as her husband. They are the same ___height___.
8. I drank Pepsi and Coke, and I don't know which is which. They have the same flavor. To me, Pepsi ___is___ like Coke.
9. She ___is___ like her husband in many ways. They're both intelligent and hard-working. They both like sports.
10. **A:** Are you like your mother?
    B: Oh, no. We're not ___alike___ at all! We're completely different.
11. Please finish this test ___as soon as___ possible!
12. *Borrow* and *lend* don't have ___the same___ meaning. *Borrow* means take. *Lend* means give.
13. My two sisters look ___alike___. In fact, some people think they're twins.

PART 2

1. Part 2 may also be used as an in-class test to assess student performance, in addition to the Assessment CD-ROM with *ExamView Pro*. Have students read the direction line. Collect for assessment.
2. If necessary, have students review:
   12.7 *As . . . As* (p. 391)
   12.11 Similarity with *Like* and *Alike* (p. 398)
   12.12 *Be Like* (p. 400)
   12.13 Same or Different (p. 401).

Lesson Review

To use Part 2 as a review, assign it as homework or use it as an in-class activity to be completed individually or in pairs. Check answers and review errors as a class. Reteach grammar points that students haven't mastered. Then student learning may be assessed using a test generated from the Assessment CD-ROM with *ExamView Pro*.

Expansion Activities

These expansion activities provide opportunities for students to interact with one another and further develop their speaking and writing skills. Encourage students to use grammar from this lesson whenever possible.

To save class time, assign parts of the activities as homework. Then use class time for interaction and communication. If students do not need additional speaking practice, some of the activities may be assigned as writing activities for homework, or skipped altogether.

CLASSROOM ACTIVITIES

1. Try to have students work with a partner they don't know very well. To encourage students to use all of the grammar learned in this lesson, direct students to the summary on pages 404–405.
2. Have groups report the results of their discussions to the class.
3. Have each pair report to the class. Compile students' comparisons on the board.

EXPANSION ACTIVITIES

Classroom Activities

1. **Work with a partner. Find some differences between the two of you. Then write five sentences that compare you and your partner. Share your answers in a small group or with the whole class.**

   EXAMPLES I'm taller than Alex.
   Alex is taking more classes than I am.

2. **Form a small group (about 3–5 people) with students from different native countries, if possible. Make comparisons about your native countries. Include a superlative statement. (If all the students in your class are from the same native country, compare cities in your native country.)**

   EXAMPLES Cuba is closer to the U.S. than Peru is.
   China has the largest population.
   Cuba doesn't have as many resources as China.

3. **Work with a partner. Choose one of the categories below, and compare two examples from this category. Use any type of comparative method. Write four sentences. Share your answers with the class.**

   a. **countries** e. **cities** i. **sports**
   b. **cars** f. **animals** j. **athletes**
   c. **restaurants** g. **types of transportation**
   d. **teachers** h. **schools**

   EXAMPLE animals
   A dog is different from a cat in many ways.
   A dog can't jump as high as a cat.
   A dog is a better pet than a cat, in my opinion.
   A cat is not as friendly as a dog.
   ____
   ____
   ____
   ____

4. Compare the U.S. to another country you know. Tell if the statement is true in the U.S. or in the other country. Form a small group and explain your answers to the others in the group.

	Country ______	The U.S.
People have more free time.		
People have more political freedom.		
Families are smaller.		
Children are more polite.		
Teenagers have more freedom.		
People are friendlier.		
The government is more stable.		
Health care is better.		
There is more crime.		
There are more poor people.		
People are generally happier.		
People are more open about their problems.		
Friendship is more important.		
Women have more freedom.		
Schools are better.		
Job opportunities are better.		
Athletes make more money.		
Children have more fun.		
People dress more stylishly.		
Families are closer.		
People are healthier.		

5. Game—Test your knowledge of world facts.
Form a small group. Answer the questions below with other group members. When you're finished, check your answers. (Answers are at the bottom of the next page.) Which group in the class has the most correct answers?

1. Which athlete said, "I'm the greatest"?
   Michael Jordan Pelé (Muhammad Ali) Serena Williams
2. Where is the tallest building in the world?
   New York City Chicago Tokyo (Taipei)

CLASSROOM ACTIVITIES (*cont.*)

4. First have students complete the chart individually. Then have students get into groups to discuss their answers.
5. Give groups a time limit to complete the world facts quiz.

3. What country has the largest population?
   the U.S. India (China) Russia

4. Which country has the largest area?
   the U.S. China Canada (Russia)

5. What is the tallest mountain in the world?
   Mount McKinley (Mount Everest)
   Mount Kanchenjunga Mount Lhotse

6. Which state in the U.S. has the smallest population?
   Alaska (Wyoming) Rhode Island Vermont

7. What is the longest river in the world?
   the Mississippi the Missouri (the Nile) the Amazon

8. What is the biggest animal?
   the elephant the rhinoceros the giraffe (the whale)

9. What is the world's largest island?
   (Greenland) New Guinea Borneo Madagascar

10. What country has the most time zones?
    China (Russia) the U.S. Canada

11. What is the world's largest lake?
    Lake Superior Lake Victoria
    (the Caspian Sea) the Aral Sea

12. Which planet is the closest to the Earth?
    Mercury Venus (Mars) Saturn

13. Where is the world's busiest airport?
    (Chicago) New York Los Angeles London

14. Which is the most popular magazine in the U.S.?
    Time *Sports Illustrated* (*TV Guide*) *People Weekly*

15. What language has the largest number of speakers?
    English (Chinese) Spanish Russian

16. Which country has the most neighboring countries?
    (China) Russia Saudi Arabia Brazil

The answers are: 1. Ali 2. Taipei 3. China 4. Russia 5. Mount Everest 6. Wyoming 7. the Nile 8. the whale 9. Greenland 10. Russia 11. the Caspian Sea 12. Mars 13. Chicago 14. *TV Guide* 15. Chinese 16. China (It has 16 neighboring countries.)

Classroom Activities Variation

Activity 5 For a more challenging quiz, have students close their books. Read the questions—but not the multiple-choice answers. Have groups write their answers on a piece of paper. Then, have groups exchange papers with other groups to be corrected. Go over the answers as a class. Which group got the highest number of correct answers?

6. Look at the list of jobs below. Use the superlative form to name a job that matches each description. You may discuss your answers in a small group or with the entire class.

EXAMPLE interesting
In my opinion, a psychologist has the most interesting job.

coach	referee
psychologist	letter carrier
computer programmer	athlete
high school teacher	actress
factory worker	photojournalist
doctor	firefighter
police officer	politician
engineer	nurse

(*you may add other professions*)

a. interesting ____________________
b. dangerous ____________________
c. easy ____________________
d. tiring ____________________
e. dirty ____________________
f. boring ____________________
g. exciting ____________________
h. important ____________________
i. challenging ____________________
j. difficult ____________________

Write About it

Write a short composition comparing one of the sets of items below:

- two stores where you shop for groceries
- watching a movie at home and at a movie theater
- two friends of yours
- you and your parents
- football and soccer (or any two sports)
- clothing styles in the U.S. and your native country
- life in the U.S. (in general) and life in your native country
- your life in the U.S. and your life in your native country
- the American political system and the political system in your native country
- schools (including teachers, students, classes, etc.) in the U.S. and schools in your native country
- American families and families in your native country

CLASSROOM ACTIVITIES (*cont.*)

6. First have students complete the statements individually. Then have students get into groups to discuss their answers.

WRITE ABOUT IT

Before they begin their compositions, have students make a list of all the qualities that are the same or different for the set of items they've decided to write about.

Expansion

Write About it Have students exchange first drafts with a partner. Ask students to help their partners edit their drafts. Refer students to the Editing Advice on pages 405–406.

TALK BOUT IT

Have students discuss each topic in pairs, in groups, or as a whole class.

OUTSIDE ACTIVITY

Have students prepare the questions in class before carrying out the interview (e.g., *What is the most prestigious job in the U.S.?*).

INTERNET ACTIVITIES

Remind students that if they don't have Internet access, they can use Internet facilities at a public library, or they can use traditional research methods to find out information including looking at encyclopedias, magazines, books, journals, and newspapers.

Talk About it

1. Do athletes in other countries make a lot of money?
2. Do children in most countries participate in sports? Which sports?

Outside Activity

Interview someone who was born in the U.S. Get his or her opinion about the superlative of each of the following items. Share your findings with the class.

- prestigious job in the U.S.
- beautiful city in the U.S.
- popular TV program
- terrible tragedy in American history
- big problem in the U.S.
- handsome or beautiful actor
- good athlete
- good sports team

Internet Activities

1. Find an article about Michael Jordan on the Internet. Print the article and circle some interesting facts.
2. Find an article about an athlete that you admire. Print the article and circle some interesting facts.
3. Find an article about Enrique Oliu. Summarize the article. What makes Oliu so special?
4. Visit the Olympics Web site or a Web site with sports statistics and information. Find out which country has won the most medals in a particular sport. Which sport is the newest to be an Olympic event? Which athlete has the most Olympic medals?

Additional Activities at www.http://elt.thomson.com/gic

412 Lesson 12

Outside Activity Variation

Have students practice the interview in class with another student before doing the interview with someone who was born in the U.S. Later students can compare answers. How many of them were the same? Different?

Culture Note

Enrique Oliu is a sportscaster who has been blind since birth. For a number of years, he has been providing color commentary for Spanish-speaking radio for the Tampa Bay Devil Rays—a minor league baseball team. How does he do it? He has an amazing memory. His wife, Debbie Oliu, reads him articles about the games and the players, and he also memorizes information about the players, including their game statistics. During the game, his wife sits behind him and describes what's going on.

LESSON

13

GRAMMAR
Passive Voice and Active Voice

CONTEXT : The Law
Jury Duty
Unusual Lawsuits

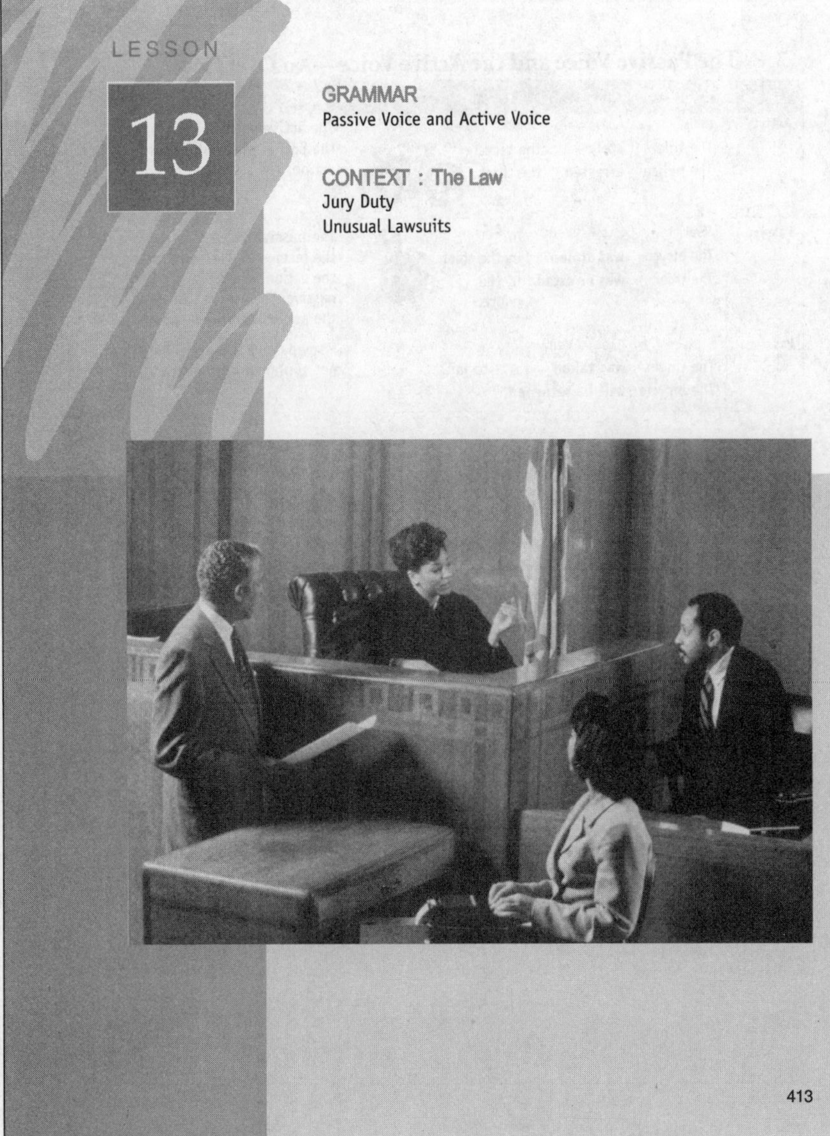

413

Lesson 13

Lesson Overview

GRAMMAR

1. Briefly review what students learned in the last lesson. Ask: *What did we study in Lesson 12?* (superlatives and comparatives)
2. Ask: *What are we going to study in this lesson?* (passive voice and active voice) *Can you give an example of the passive voice and the active voice?* (e.g., *Someone stole the bicycle; the bicycle was stolen.*) Have students give examples. Write the examples on the board.

CONTEXT

1. Ask: *What are we going to learn about in this lesson?* (jury duty, the law, lawsuits) Activate students' prior knowledge. Ask: *Does the system of law in your native country include a jury of peers?*
2. Have students share their knowledge and personal experiences.

To save class time, have students do the Test/Review at the end of the lesson, or administer a lesson test generated from the Assessment CD-ROM with *ExamView® Pro*. Skip sections of the lesson that students have already mastered. You may also assign some sections for self-study for extra credit.

Expansion

Theme The topic for this lesson can be enhanced with the following ideas:

1. A juror's notice and a pamphlet for prospective jurors
2. A video of *The People's Court* or *Judge Hatchett*

13.1 | The Passive Voice and the Active Voice—An Overview

1. Have students cover up grammar chart **13.1** on page 414. Create a matching exercise. Write the following on the board:
   1. The thief was arrested by the police.
   2. The bicycle will be returned.
   3. The police arrested the thief.
   a. The active voice focuses on the person who performs the action.
   b. The passive voice focuses on the receiver of the action.
   c. Many passive sentences do not contain a by *phrase.*
   Say: *Match the sentences with the explanations.*
2. Then have students look at grammar chart **13.1.** Say: *Compare your work with the chart.* Review the example sentences and explanations in the chart.

Jury Duty (Reading)

1. Have students look at the photo on page 414. Ask: *What is going on in this photo?* (a lawyer is talking to a jury) *Do you know anyone who has served on a jury?*
2. Have students look at the title of the reading. Ask: *What is the reading about?* Have students use the title and photo to make predictions about the reading.
3. Preteach any vocabulary words your students may not know, such as *protect, charge, consider,* and *open-minded.*

BEFORE YOU READ

1. Have students discuss the questions in pairs.
2. Ask for a few volunteers to share their answers with the class.

To save class time, skip "Before You Read" or have students prepare answers for homework ahead of time.

13.1 | The Passive Voice and the Active Voice—An Overview

	Examples			Explanation
Active	Subject	Active Verb	Object	The **active voice** focuses on the person who performs the action. The subject is active.
	The thief	**stole**	the bicycle.	
	The police	**arrested**	the thief.	
Passive	Subject	Passive Verb	By Phrase	The **passive voice** focuses on the receiver or the result of the action. The subject is passive. The person who does the action is in the *by* phrase.
	The bicycle	**was stolen**	by the thief.	
	The thief	**was arrested**	by the police.	
Passive	Subject	Passive Verb		Many passive sentences do not contain a *by* phrase.
	The thief	**was taken**	to jail.	
	The bicycle	**will be returned.**		

JURY DUTY

Before You Read

1. Have you ever been to court?
2. Have you ever seen a courtroom in a movie or TV show?

Read the following article. Pay special attention to the passive voice.

All Americans **are protected** by the Constitution. No one person can decide if a person is guilty of a crime. Every citizen has the right to a trial by jury. When a person **is charged** with a crime, he **is considered** innocent until the jury decides he is guilty.

Most American citizens **are chosen** for jury duty at some time in their lives. How **are** jurors **chosen?** The court gets the names of citizens from lists of taxpayers, licensed drivers, and voters. Many people **are called** to the courthouse for the selection of a jury. From this large number, 12 people **are chosen.** The lawyers and the judge ask each person questions to see if the person is going to be fair. If the person has made any judgment about the case before hearing the facts presented in the trial, he **is** not **selected.** If the juror doesn't understand enough English, he **is not selected.** The court needs jurors who can understand the facts and be open-minded. When the final jury selection **is made,** the jurors must raise their right hands and promise to be fair in deciding the case.

Sometimes a trial goes on for several days or more. Jurors **are** not **permitted** to talk with family members and friends about the case. In some cases, jurors **are** not **permitted** to go home until the case is over. They stay in a hotel and **are** not **permitted** to watch TV or read newspapers that give information about the case.

After the jurors hear the case, they have to make a decision. They go to a separate room and talk about what they heard and saw in the courtroom. When they are finished discussing the case, they take a vote.

Jurors **are paid** for their work. They receive a small amount of money per day. Employers must give a worker permission to be on a jury. Being on a jury **is considered** a very serious job.

13.2 | The Passive Voice

Examples	Explanation
Be / Past Participle The jurors **are** **chosen** from lists. My sister **was** **selected** to be on a jury. The jurors **will be** **paid** for jury duty.	The passive voice uses a form of *be* (any tense) + the past participle.
Compare Active (A) and Passive (P): (A) Ms. Smith *paid* her employees at the end of the week. (P) Ms. Smith *was paid* for being a juror.	The verb in active voice (A) shows that the subject (Ms. Smith) performed the action of the verb. The verb in passive voice (P) shows that the subject (Ms. Smith) did not perform the action of the verb.
I was helped **by the lawyer.** My sister was helped **by him** too.	When a performer is included after a passive verb, use *by* + noun or object pronoun.

Passive Voice and Active Voice 415

Reading Variation

To practice listening skills, have students first listen to the audio alone. Ask a few comprehension questions. Repeat the audio if necessary. Then have them open their books and read along as they listen to the audio.

Reading Glossary

charge: a statement of blame against
consider: to regard, think, believe
open-minded: willing to listen to or consider the opinions and ideas of others
protect: to defend against harm or loss

Reading *CD 4, Track 7*

1. Have students first read the text silently. Tell them to pay special attention to the passive voice. Then play the audio and have students read along silently.
2. Check students' comprehension. Ask questions such as: *Who decides if a person is innocent or guilty?* (a jury) *Where does the court get names of prospective jury members?* (from lists of taxpayers, licensed drivers, and voters) *How many people are chosen to be a jury?* (12) *Can the jurors talk with friends and family about the case?* (no) *Are jurors paid for their work?* (Yes. They are paid a small amount.)

To save class time, have students do the reading for homework ahead of time.

13.2 | The Passive Voice

1. Have students look at grammar chart **13.2** on page 415. Go over the examples and explanations. Explain how to form the passive (a form of *be* + the past participle). Ask: *How do you form the past participle for regular verbs?* (It's the same as the past form: *talk/talked*; *walk/walked.*)
2. Explain that in the active voice, the performer is the subject. The verb is the action the subject performs. Go over the example. Say: *In the passive, the action is performed on the subject. When a performer is included, use* by + *noun or object pronoun.* Go over examples.

EXERCISE 1

1. Have students read the direction line. Go over the examples.
2. Have students complete Exercise 1 individually. Go over the answers as a class.
3. If necessary, review grammar chart **13.2** on page 415.

13.3 | Passive Voice—Form and Use

1. Have students cover up grammar chart **13.3** on page 416. Create a matching exercise. Write the following on the board:
   1. They have taken a vote.
   2. They took a vote.
   3. They will take a vote.
   4. They must take a vote.
   5. They take a vote.
   a. Simple Present
   b. Simple Past
   c. Future
   d. Present Perfect
   e. Modal
   Say: *Match the verb tense with the example sentence. Then write a passive sentence from the active sentence.*
2. Then have students look at grammar chart **13.3.** Say: *Compare your work with the chart.* Review the example sentences and explanations in the chart. Go over any trouble spots with the class.
3. Direct students to the Language Notes. Point out that an adverb can be placed between the auxiliary verb (*be, have, will,* or a modal) and the past participle. Tell students that there is no need to repeat the verb *be* when two verbs are connected by *and.* Go over the example.

EXERCISE 1 Read the following sentences. Decide if the underlined verb is active (*A*) or passive (*P*).

EXAMPLES I received a letter from the court. A

I was told to go to court on May 10. P

1. The jury voted at the end of the trial. *A*
2. The jurors received $20 a day. *A*
3. Some jurors were told to go home. *P*
4. Not every juror will be needed. *P*
5. Twelve people were selected for the jury. *P*
6. The judge told the jurors about their responsibilities. *A*
7. My sister has been selected for jury duty three times. *P*
8. You will be paid for jury duty. *P*
9. A juror must be at least 18 years old and an American citizen. *A*
10. The judge and the lawyers ask a lot of questions. *A*

13.3 | Passive Voice—Form and Use

Form: The passive voice can be used with different tenses and with modals. The tense of the sentence is shown by the verb *be.* Use the past participle with every tense.

Tense	Active	Passive (*Be* + Past Participle)
Simple Present	They **take** a vote.	A vote **is taken.**
Simple Past	They **took** a vote.	A vote **was taken.**
Future	They **will take** a vote. They **are going to take** a vote.	A vote **will be taken.** A vote **is going to be taken.**
Present Perfect	They **have taken** a vote.	A vote **has been taken.**
Modal	They **must take** a vote.	A vote **must be taken.**

Language Notes:

1. An adverb can be placed between the auxiliary verb and the main verb.
   The jurors **are *always* paid.**
   Noncitizens **are *never* selected** for jury duty.
2. If two verbs in the passive voice are connected with *and,* do not repeat *be.*
   The jurors **are taken** to a room and **shown** a film about the court system.

416 Lesson 13

Use: The passive voice is used more frequently without a performer than with a performer.

Examples	Explanation
English **is spoken** in the U.S. Independence Day **is celebrated** in July.	The passive voice is used when the action is done by people in general.
The jurors **are given** a lunch break. The jurors **will be paid** at the end of the day. Jurors **are** not **permitted** to talk with family members about the case.	The passive voice is used when the actual person who performs the action is of little or no importance.
a. The criminal **was arrested.** b. The students **will be given** a test on the passive voice.	The passive voice is used when it is obvious who performed the action. In (a), it is obvious that the police arrested the criminal. In (b), it is obvious that the teacher will give a test.
Active: The lawyers **presented** the case yesterday. Passive: The case **was presented** in two hours. Active: The judge and the lawyers **choose** jurors. Passive: People who don't understand English **are not chosen.**	The passive voice is used to shift the emphasis from the performer to the receiver of the action.

EXERCISE 2 Change to the passive voice. (Do not include a *by* phrase.)

	ACTIVE	PASSIVE
EXAMPLE	They chose him.	*He was chosen.*
1.	They will choose him.	*He will be chosen.*
2.	They always choose him.	*He is always chosen.*
3.	They can't choose him.	*He can't be chosen.*
4.	They have never chosen us.	*We have never been chosen.*
5.	They didn't choose her.	*She hasn't been chosen.*
6.	They shouldn't choose her.	*She shouldn't be chosen.*

13.3 | Passive Voice—Form and Use (*cont.*)

4. Have students look at the section of the grammar chart on page 417. Say: *The passive voice is used more frequently without a performer than with a performer.* Go over each example and explanation.
5. Direct students to the first example. Ask: *How would these sentences be written if there were performers?* (e.g., *People speak English in the U.S.; People celebrate Independence Day in July.*) Ask: *Is people important? What is important in these sentences?* (The language that is spoken in the U.S., and not that people speak the language, is important. When Independence Day is celebrated, not who celebrates it, is important.) Review the remaining examples in this way.

EXERCISE 2

1. Have students read the direction line. Go over the example.
2. Have students complete Exercise 2 individually. Go over the answers with the class.
3. If necessary, review grammar chart **13.3** on pages 416–417.

Expansion

Grammar Have students go back to the reading on page 415. Ask students to try changing some sentences into the active voice. Discuss the performer in each sentence (e.g., *The Constitution protects all Americans* would be a good sentence if the reading were about the U.S. Constitution and not about the jury system.).

EXERCISE 3

1. Have students read the direction line. Go over the example. Remind students that the verbs in this exercise should be in the present tense.
2. Have students complete Exercise 3 individually. Then have students compare answers in pairs. Circulate to observe pair work. Give help as needed.
3. If necessary, review grammar chart **13.3** on pages 416–417.

To save class time, have students do half of the exercise in class and complete the other half for homework.

EXERCISE 4

1. Have students read the direction line. Go over the example. Remind students that the verbs in this exercise should be in the past tense.
2. Have students complete Exercise 4 individually. Have students compare answers in pairs. Circulate to observe pair work. Give help as needed.
3. If necessary, review grammar chart **13.3** on pages 416–417.

To save class time, have students do half of the exercise in class and complete the other half for homework.

EXERCISE 3 Fill in the blanks with the passive voice of the verb in parentheses ( ). Use the present tense.

EXAMPLE Jurors *are chosen* (choose) from lists.

1. Only people over 18 years old *are selected* (select) for jury duty.
2. Questionnaires *are sent* (send) to American citizens.
3. The questionnaire *is filled* (fill) out and *returned* (return).
4. Many people *are called* (call) to the courthouse.
5. Not everyone *is chosen* (choose).
6. The jurors *are asked* (ask) a lot of questions.
7. Jurors *are not permitted* (not/permit) to discuss the case with outsiders.
8. Jurors *are given* (give) a paycheck at the end of the day for their work.

EXERCISE 4 Fill in the blanks with the passive voice of the verb in parentheses ( ). Use the past tense.

EXAMPLE I *was sent* (send) a letter.

1. I *was told* (tell) to go to the courthouse on Fifth Street.
2. My name *was called* (call).
3. I *was given* (give) a form to fill out.
4. A video about jury duty *was shown* (show) on a large TV.
5. The jurors *were taken* (take) to the third floor of the building.
6. I *was asked* (ask) a lot of questions by the lawyers.
7. I *wasn't chosen* (not/choose).
8. I *was sent* (send) home before noon.

EXERCISE 5 Fill in the blanks with the passive voice of the verb in parentheses ( ). Use the present perfect tense.

EXAMPLE The jurors *have been given* (give) a lot of information.

1. Many articles *have been written* (write) about the courts.
2. Many movies *have been made* (make) about the courts.
3. Many people *have been chosen* (choose) for jury duty.
4. Your name *has been selected* (select) for jury duty.
5. The jurors *have been paid* (pay) for their work.
6. The check *has been left* (leave) at the door.
7. The money *has been put* (put) in an envelope.

EXERCISE 6 The people called to jury duty are getting instructions about what to expect. Fill in the blanks with the passive voice of the verb in parentheses ( ). Use the future tense.

EXAMPLE You *will be taken* (take) to a courtroom.

1. You *will be told* (tell) to stand up when the judge enters the room.
2. Each of you *will be asked* (ask) a lot of questions.
3. The lawyers *will be introduced* (introduce).
4. Information about the case *will be given* (give) to you.
5. You *will not be allowed* (not/allow) to eat in the courtroom.

Passive Voice and Active Voice 419

EXERCISE 5

1. Have students read the direction line. Go over the example. Remind students that the verbs in this exercise should be in the present perfect tense.
2. Have students complete Exercise 5 individually. Then have students compare answers in pairs. Circulate to observe pair work. Give help as needed.
3. If necessary, review grammar chart **13.3** on pages 416–417.

To save class time, have students do the exercise for homework.

EXERCISE 6

1. Have students read the direction line. Explain that this exercise is about instructions for jury duty. Go over the example. Remind students that the verbs in this exercise should be in the future tense.
2. Have students complete Exercise 6 individually. Have students compare answers in pairs. Circulate to observe pair work. Give help as needed.
3. If necessary, review grammar chart **13.3** on pages 416–417.

To save class time, have students do the exercise for homework.

Expansion

Exercise 6 Have students practice in pairs speaking to the jury like a judge. Ask volunteers to perform in front of the class. Arrange twelve students into a mock jury.

EXERCISE 7

1. Have students read the direction line. Go over the example. Remind students to use the same tense of the underlined verb.
2. Have students complete Exercise 7 individually. Then have students compare answers in pairs. Circulate to observe pair work. Give help as needed.
3. If necessary, review grammar chart **13.3** on pages 416–417.

To save class time, have students do half of the exercise in class and complete the other half for homework. Or assign the entire exercise for homework.

6. Twelve of you *will be selected* (select).

7. If you do not speak and understand English well, you *will not be picked* (not/pick).

8. Besides the 12 jurors, two alternates[1] *will be chosen* (choose).

9. The rest of you *will be sent* (send) home.

10. All of you *will be paid* (pay).

EXERCISE 7 Fill in the blanks with the passive voice of the underlined verbs. Use the same tense.

EXAMPLE The jury took a vote. The vote *was taken* after three hours.

1. The lawyers asked a lot of questions. The questions *asked* to find facts.

2. The court will pay us. We *will be paid* $20 a day.

3. They told us to wait. We *were told* to wait on the second floor.

4. They gave us instructions. We *were given* information about the law.

5. People pay for the services of a lawyer. Lawyers *are paid* a lot of money for their services.

6. You should use a pen to fill out the form. A pen *should be used* for all legal documents.

7. They showed us a film about the court system. We *were shown* the film before we went to the courtroom.

[1] An *alternate* takes the place of a juror who cannot serve for some reason (such as illness).

13.4 | Negatives and Questions with Passive Voice

Compare affirmative statements to negative statements and questions with the passive voice.	
Simple Past	**Present Perfect**
The jurors **were paid.**	I **have been chosen** for jury duty several times.
They **weren't paid** a lot.	I **haven't been chosen** this year.
Were they **paid** in cash?	**Have** you ever **been chosen?**
No, they **weren't.**	No, I **haven't.**
How much **were** they **paid?**	How many times **have** you **been chosen?**
Why **weren't** they **paid** in cash?	Why **haven't** you **been chosen?**

Language Note:
Never use *do*, *does*, or *did* with the passive voice.
Wrong: The juror ***didn't*** paid.

EXERCISE 8 Change to the negative form of the underlined words.

EXAMPLE I was selected for jury duty last year. I *was't selected* this year.

1. The jurors are paid. They *are not paid* a lot of money.
2. Twelve people were chosen. People who don't speak English well *weren't chosen*.
3. Jurors are allowed to talk with other jurors about the case. They *aren't allowed* to talk to friends and family about the case.
4. We were told to keep an open mind. We *weren't told* how to vote.
5. We have been given instructions. We *haven't been given* our checks yet.

EXERCISE 9 Change the statements to questions using the words in parentheses ( ).

EXAMPLE The jurors are paid. (how much)
How much are the jurors paid?

1. Some people aren't selected. (why)
Why aren't some jurors selected?
2. The jurors are given a lunch break. (when)
When are the jurors given a lunch break?

Passive Voice and Active Voice 421

Expansion

Exercise 9 Ask students to write answers for the questions in Exercise 9. Some of the answers can be found in the reading; others can be made up.

13.4 | Negatives and Questions with Passive Voice

1. Have students look at grammar chart **13.4** on page 421. Go over each sentence in the simple past and the present perfect.
2. Direct students to the Language Note. Remind students that the verb *be* is used in the passive—so you can't use *do, does,* or *did* with the passive.

EXERCISE 8

1. Have students read the direction line. Go over the example.
2. Have students complete Exercise 8 individually. Go over the answers as a class.
3. If necessary, review grammar chart **13.4** on page 421.

EXERCISE 9

1. Have students read the direction line. Go over the example.
2. Have students complete Exercise 9 individually. Go over the answers as a class.
3. If necessary, review grammar chart **13.4** on page 421.

To save class time, have students do half of the exercise in class and complete the other half for homework. Or assign the entire exercise for homework.

Unusual Lawsuits (Reading)

1. Have students look at the photos on pages 422 and 423. Ask: *What's happening in these pictures?* (A woman is sipping hot coffee and eating toast. A man is talking on his cell phone while driving.)
2. Have students look at the title of the reading. Ask: *What is the reading about?* Have students use the title and photos to make predictions about the reading.
3. Preteach any vocabulary words your students may not know, such as *lawsuit.*

BEFORE YOU READ

1. Have students discuss the questions in pairs.
2. Ask for a few volunteers to share their answers with the class.

To save class time, skip "Before You Read" or have students prepare answers for homework ahead of time.

3. I wasn't chosen for the jury. (why)
Why weren't you chosen for the jury?
4. You were given information about the case. (what kind of information)
What kind of information were you given about the case?
5. A film will be shown. (when)
When will a film be shown?
6. Several jurors have been sent home. (why)
Why have several jurors been sent home?
7. The jurors should be paid more money. (why)
Why should jurors be paid more money?
8. We were told to go to the courtroom. (when)
When were we told to go to the courtroom?
9. The jury has been instructed by the judge. (why)
Why has the jury been instructed by the judge?

UNUSUAL LAWSUITS

Before You Read

1. Are drivers permitted to use cell phones in the area where you live?
2. Have you read about any unusual court cases in the newspaper or heard about any on TV?

Read the following article. Pay special attention to the active and passive voice.

When a person is **injured** or **harmed,** it is the court's job to determine who is at fault. Most of these cases never **make** the news. But a few of them **appear** in the newspapers and on the evening news because they are so unusual.

In 1992, a fast-food restaurant **was sued** by a 79-year-old woman in New Mexico who **spilled** hot coffee on herself while driving. She **suffered** third-degree burns on her body. At first the woman **asked** for $11,000 to cover her medical expenses. When the restaurant **refused,** the case **went** to court and the woman **was awarded** nearly $3 million dollars.

In 2002, a group of teenagers **sued** several fast-food chains for serving food that **made** them fat. The case **was thrown** out of court. According to Congressman Ric Keller, Americans **have to** "get away from this new culture where people always try to play the victim and blame others for their problems." Mr. Keller, who is overweight and **eats** at fast-food chains once every two weeks, **said** that suing "the food industry is not going to make a single individual any skinnier. It **will** only **make** the trial attorneys' bank accounts fatter."

In June 2004 an Indiana woman **sued** a cell phone company for causing an auto accident in which she was involved. The court **decided** that the manufacturer of a cell phone cannot **be held** responsible for an auto accident involving a driver using its product. In March 2000, a teenage girl in Virginia was **struck** and **killed** by a driver conducting business on a cell phone. The girl's family **sued** the driver's employer for $30 million for wrongful death. They said that it was the company's fault because employees **are expected** to conduct business while driving. The family **lost** its case.

We **are protected** by the law. But as individuals we **need to take** personal responsibility and not blame others for our mistakes. The court system **is designed** to protect us; it **is** up to us to make sure that trials remain serious.

Did You Know?

In the United States about 148 million people used cell phones in 2003, compared with approximately 4.3 million in 1990.

Source: The Cellular Telecommunications & Internet Association

Reading *CD 4, Track 8*

1. Have students first read the text silently. Tell them to pay special attention to the active and the passive voice. Then play the audio and have students read along silently.
2. Check students' comprehension. Ask questions such as: *What happened to the 79-year-old woman in New Mexico?* (She spilled hot coffee on herself while she was driving. She suffered serious burns.) *How much did she win in the lawsuit?* (Eventually, she won $3 million dollars.) *Did the teenagers win their lawsuit against a fast-food chain?* (No. The lawsuit was thrown out of court.) *Who was killed by a driver talking on a cell phone?* (a teenage girl)

To save class time, have students do the reading for homework ahead of time.

DID YOU KNOW ?

Many states are now creating laws regulating the use of cell phones while driving. Many states are now mandating the use of hands-free devices based on studies that indicate that the driver is most distracted while dialing or locating the phone. However, the National Safety Counsel has new evidence that suggests it is the phone conversation that distracts the driver the most.

Reading Variation

To practice listening skills, have students first listen to the audio alone. Ask a few comprehension questions. Repeat the audio if necessary. Then have them open their books and read along as they listen to the audio.

Reading Glossary

lawsuit: a legal action bringing a problem or claim to a court of law

13.5 | Choosing Active Voice or Passive Voice

1. Have students look at grammar chart **13.5** on page 424. Say: *When the sentence has a specific performer, we can use an active or a passive construction. In English, we usually use active constructions when there is a choice. When we do use a passive construction, the performer is mentioned in a* by *phrase.* Go over the examples.
2. Say: *When there is no specific performer, we use a passive construction.* Go over the examples.
3. Say: *The passive voice is often used after* it *when talking about findings, discoveries, or general beliefs.* Go over the examples.
4. Say: *With some verbs, you can't use the passive. These verbs do not take an object.* Go over the examples.
5. Demonstrate the difference in pronouns in active and passive constructions. Go over the examples.
6. Direct students to the Language Note. Say: Have *and* want *are generally not used in passive constructions.* Go over the examples.

13.5 | Choosing Active Voice or Passive Voice

Examples	Explanation
(A) A driver using a cell phone **caused** the accident. (P) The accident **was caused** by a driver using a cell phone. (A) A driver **struck** and **killed** a teenager. (P) A teenager **was struck** and **killed** by a driver.	When the sentence has a specific performer, we can use either the active (A) or passive (P) voice. The active voice puts more emphasis on the person who performs the action. The passive voice puts more emphasis on the action or the result. The performer is mentioned in a *by* phrase (*by the driver, by a woman, by the court*). The active voice is more common than the passive voice when there is a specific performer.
(P) The obesity case **was thrown** out of court. (P) The manufacturer of a cell phone **cannot be held** responsible for a car accident. (P) Some employees **are expected** to conduct business while driving.	When there is no specific performer or the performer is obvious, the passive voice is usually used.
(P) It **was found** that six percent of accidents are the result of driver distraction. (P) It **is believed** that cell phone use distracts drivers.	Often the passive voice is used after *it* when talking about findings, discoveries, or general beliefs.
(A) The woman **went** to court. (A) The accident **happened** in Virginia. (A) Unusual court cases **appear** in the newspaper. (A) The teenager **died.**	Some verbs have no object. We cannot make these verbs passive. Some verbs with no object are: happen go fall become live sleep come look die seem work recover be remain arrive stay appear seem run sound grow depend wake up leave (a place)
(A) **She** sued **them.** (P) **They** were sued by **her.** (A) **He** helps **us.** (P) **We** are helped by **him.**	Notice the difference in pronouns in an active sentence and a passive sentence. After *by,* the object pronoun is used.

Language Note:
Even though ***have*** and ***want*** are followed by an object, these verbs are not usually used in the passive voice.
He **has** a cell phone. (*Not:* A cell phone is had by him.)
She **wants** a new car. (*Not:* A new car is wanted by her.)

424 Lesson 13

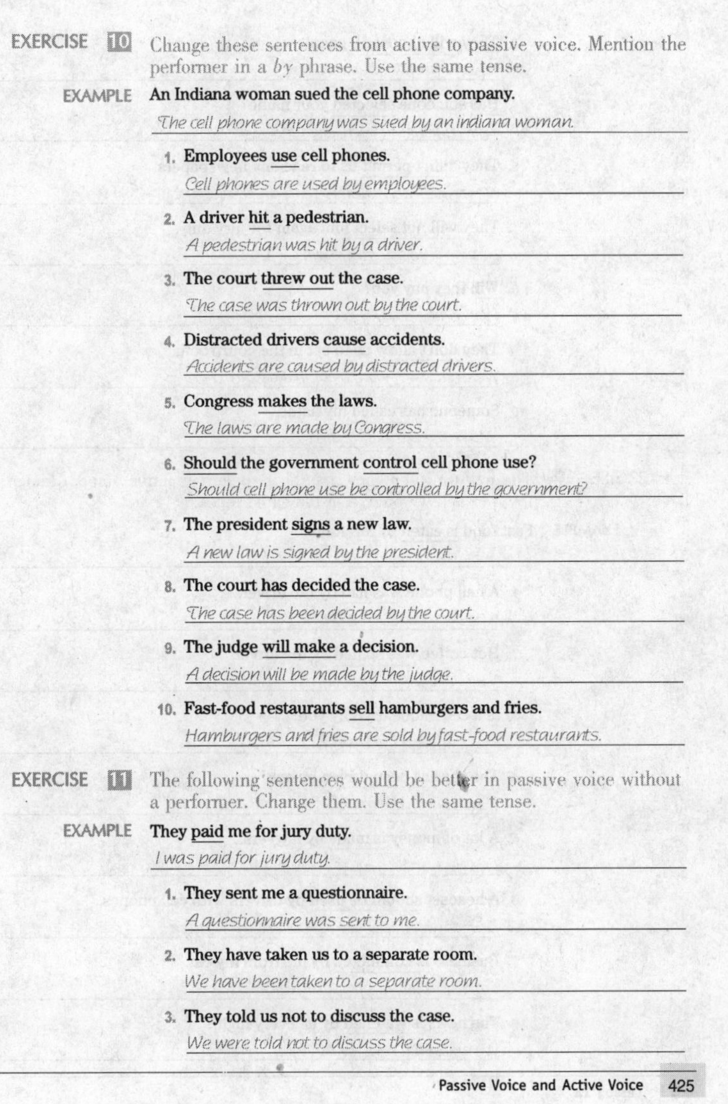

EXERCISE 10 Change these sentences from active to passive voice. Mention the performer in a *by* phrase. Use the same tense.

EXAMPLE **An Indiana woman sued the cell phone company.**
The cell phone company was sued by an indiana woman.

1. **Employees use cell phones.**
Cell phones are used by employees.
2. **A driver hit a pedestrian.**
A pedestrian was hit by a driver.
3. **The court threw out the case.**
The case was thrown out by the court.
4. **Distracted drivers cause accidents.**
Accidents are caused by distracted drivers.
5. **Congress makes the laws.**
The laws are made by Congress.
6. **Should the government control cell phone use?**
Should cell phone use be controlled by the government?
7. **The president signs a new law.**
A new law is signed by the president.
8. **The court has decided the case.**
The case has been decided by the court.
9. **The judge will make a decision.**
A decision will be made by the judge.
10. **Fast-food restaurants sell hamburgers and fries.**
Hamburgers and fries are sold by fast-food restaurants.

EXERCISE 11 The following sentences would be better in passive voice without a performer. Change them. Use the same tense.

EXAMPLE **They paid me for jury duty.**
I was paid for jury duty.

1. **They sent me a questionnaire.**
A questionnaire was sent to me.
2. **They have taken us to a separate room.**
We have been taken to a separate room.
3. **They told us not to discuss the case.**
We were told not to discuss the case.

Passive Voice and Active Voice 425

EXERCISE 10

1. Have students read the direction line. Go over the example.
2. Have students complete the exercise individually. Go over the answers as a class.
3. If necessary, review grammar chart **13.5** on page 424.

EXERCISE 11

1. Have students read the direction line. Go over the example.
2. Have students complete the exercise individually. Then have students compare answers in pairs. Circulate to observe pair work. Give help as needed.
3. If necessary, review grammar chart **13.5** on page 424.

To save class time, have students do half of the exercise in class and complete the other half for homework.

Expansion

Exercise 10 Have students write five sentences in the active voice. Ask students to use all the tenses including modals. Then have students exchange sentences with a partner. Have the partner change the active sentence into a passive sentence.

EXERCISE 12

1. Have students read the direction line. Go over the example. Remind students to use the same tense as the underlined verb.
2. Have students complete the exercise individually. Then have students compare answers in pairs. Circulate to observe pair work. Give help as needed.
3. If necessary, review grammar chart **13.5** on page 424.

To save class time, have students do the exercise for homework.

4. They will choose 12 people.
   Twelve people will be chosen.
5. Has someone selected your name?
   Has your name been selected?
6. They didn't permit us to read any newspapers.
   We weren't permitted to read any newspapers.
7. They will not select him again for jury duty.
   He won't be selected again for jury duty.
8. Will they pay you?
   Will you be paid?
9. They don't allow us to eat in the courtroom.
   We aren't allowed to eat in the courtroom.
10. Someone has called my name.
    My name has been called.

EXERCISE 12 The following sentences would be better in active voice. Change them to active voice. Use the same tense.

EXAMPLE Fast food is eaten by Mr. Keller.
Mr. Keller eats fast food.

1. A cell phone was had by the driver.
   The driver had a cell phone.
2. Hot coffee was spilled by the driver.
   The driver spilled hot coffee.
3. Is a cell phone used by you?
   Do you use a cell phone?
4. The car has been driven by me.
   I have driven the car.
5. A lot of money is made by lawyers.
   Lawyers make a lot of money.
6. A headset should be used by drivers with cell phones.
   Drivers with cell phones should use a headset.
7. Business is conducted by me from my car.
   I conduct business from my car.
8. The news is watched by us every night.
   We watch the news every night.

426 Lesson 13

9. Fast food is eaten by a lot of teenagers.

Teenagers eat a lot of fast food.

10. The accident will be reported by them.

They'll report the accident.

EXERCISE 13 Fill in the blanks with the active or passive voice of the verb in parentheses ( ). Use the tense or modal given.

In about 40 countries, laws *have been passed* (example: present perfect: pass) that prohibit drivers from using cell phones. In the U.S., the law *depends* (1 present: depend) on the place where you *live* (2 present: live). In New York, for example, the use of hand-held cell phones while driving *is prohibited* (3 present: prohibit), but the use of hands-free units *is permitted* (4 present: permit). A driver who *doesn't obey* (5 present: not/obey) this law can be fined $100 for a first offense, $200 for a second, and $500 after that. Other states *have started* (6 present perfect: start) to become tougher on drivers who use cell phones.

However, even when drivers *use* (7 present: use) hands-free cell phones, they still *cause* (8 present: cause) accidents. Drivers *must take* (9 must/take) their hands off the wheel to make or end a call. The problem *can be reduced* (10 can/reduce) if drivers *use* (11 present: use) voice-activated cell phones.

But the problem of driver distraction is not only a result of cell phones. According to one study conducted, it was found that six percent of accidents *are caused* (12 present: cause) by drivers who are not paying attention. But the distractions were not just from cell phones. This study *determined* (13 past: determine) that drivers *are distracted* (14 present: distract) by many things: eating, putting on makeup,

EXERCISE 13

CD 4, Track 9

1. Say: *This exercise is about the use of cell phones while driving.* Have students read the direction line. Go over the example.
2. Have students complete the exercise individually. Go over the answers as a class.
3. If necessary, review grammar chart **13.5** on page 424.

To save class time, have students do half of the exercise in class and complete the other half for homework. Or assign the entire exercise for homework.

Exercise 13 Variation

To provide practice with listening skills, have students close their books and listen to the audio. Repeat the audio as needed. Say: *This listening selection is about the use of cell phones while driving.* Ask comprehension questions, such as: *Are all laws about cell phone use while driving the same in every state in the U.S.?* (No. The laws vary from state to state.) *Is the cell phone the only distraction in the car?* (No. Eating, putting on makeup, reading, reaching for things, and changing stations on the radio are all distractions that have caused accidents.) Then have students open their books and complete Exercise 13.

EXERCISE 14

CD 4, Track 10

1. Say: *In this conversation, two friends are talking about jury duty.* Have students read the direction line. Go over the example.
2. Have students complete the exercise individually. Have students compare answers in pairs. Circulate to observe pair work.
3. If necessary, review grammar chart **13.5** on page 424.

To save class time, have students do half of the exercise in class and complete the other half for homework. Or assign the entire exercise for homework.

reading, reaching for things, changing stations on the radio—as well as by cell phone use. It is clear that all drivers ___*need*___ (15 present: *need*) to give driving their full attention.

EXERCISE 14 Fill in the blanks with the passive or active voice of the verb in parentheses ( ). using the past tense.

A: Why weren't you at work last week? Were you sick?

B: No. I ___*was chosen*___ (example: choose) to be on a jury.

A: How was it?

B: It was very interesting. A man ___*was arrested*___ (1 arrest) for fighting with a police officer.

A: Oh. How was the jury selection process?

B: The jury selection was interesting too. But it took half a day to choose 12 people.

A: Why?

B: The judge and lawyers ___*interviewed*___ (2 interview) more than 50 people.

A: Why so many people?

B: Well, several people ___*didn't understand*___ (3 not/understand) the judge's questions. They ___*didn't speak*___ (4 not/speak) English very well. And a woman ___*told*___ (5 tell) the judge that she was very sick. The judge ___*gave*___ (6 give) her permission to leave. I don't know why the other people ___*weren't chosen*___ (7 not/choose).

A: What kind of questions ___*were you asked*___ (8 you/ask) by the judge and lawyers?

B: First the lawyers ___*wanted*___ (9 want) to see if we could be fair. Some jurors ___*said*___ (10 say) that they had a bad experience with a police officer. Those jurors ___*were not selected*___ (11 not/select).

A: Why not?

Exercise 14 Variation

To provide practice with listening skills, have students close their books and listen to the audio. Repeat the audio as needed. Say: *In this conversation, two friends are talking about jury duty.* Ask comprehension questions, such as: *How long did it take to choose the jury?* (half a day) *How many people were interviewed?* (more than 50) *Why were some people rejected?* (They couldn't speak English very well. Others had bad experiences with police officers.) Then have students open their books and complete Exercise 14.

B: Because the judge probably thought they couldn't be fair in this case.

A: How long did the trial last?

B: Only two days.

A: Did you talk (12 you/talk) about the case with your family when you went (13 go) home the first night?

B: Oh, no. We were told (14 tell) not to talk to anyone about the case. When it was over, I told (15 tell) my wife and kids about it.

A: How long did it take the jurors to make a decision?

B: About two hours. One of the jurors didn't agree (16 not/agree) with the other 11 jurors. We talked (17 talk) about the evidence until she changed her mind.

A: Did your boss pay (18 your boss/pay) you for the days you missed work?

B: Of course. He had to pay me. That's the law.

A: Now that you've done it once, you won't have to do it again. Right?

B: That's not true. This was the second time I was chosen (19 choose).

SUMMARY OF LESSON 13

1. Active and Passive Voice

Active	Passive
He **drove** the car.	The car **was driven** by him.
He **didn't drive** the car.	The car **wasn't driven** by him.
He **will drive** the car.	The car **will be driven** by him.
He **has driven** the car.	The car **has been driven** by him.
He often **drives** the car.	The car **is** often **driven** by him.
He **should drive** the car.	The car **should be driven** by him.
Did he **drive** the car?	**Was** the car **driven** by him?
When **did** he **drive** the car?	When **was** the car **driven** by him?

Expansion

Exercise 14 Have students practice the conversation in pairs. Ask volunteers to role-play all or part of the conversation in front of the class.

Summary of Lesson 13

1. **Active and Passive Voice** Have students cover up the Summary of Lesson 13. Create an exercise on the board:
   1. *He drove the car.*
   2. *The car wasn't driven by him.*
   3. *The car will be driven by him.*
   4. *He has driven the car.*
   5. *The car is often driven by him.*
   6. *He should drive the car.*
   7. *Did he drive the car?*
   8. *When was the car driven by him?*

   Say: *If the sentence is active, make it passive. If it's passive, make it active.* If necessary, have students review:

   13.3 Passive Voice—Form and Use (p. 416).

Summary of Lesson 13 (*cont.*)

2. The Active Voice Say: *The active voice is preferred in English. With verbs that don't take an object, only the active voice can be used.* Go over the examples. If necessary, have students review:

13.5 Choosing Active Voice or Passive Voice (p. 424).

3. The Passive Voice Create a matching exercise on the board:

1. My cell phone was made in Japan.
2. The criminal was taken to jail.
3. Cell phones are used all over the world.
4. The court paid me. I was paid at the end of the day.
5. It was discovered that many accidents are the result of driver distraction.
6. A fast-food company was sued by a woman in New Mexico.
a. Use the passive when the emphasis shifts from the performer to the receiver.
b. Use the passive voice when the performer is not known or is not important.
c. Use the passive when the performer is obvious.
d. Use the passive with it *when talking about findings, discoveries, and beliefs.*
e. Use the passive when the performer is everybody or people in general.
f. Use the passive when we want to emphasize the receiver more than the performer.

Say: *Match the example with the explanation. Read through all of the choices before making a decision.* If necessary, have students review:

13.5 Choosing Active Voice or Passive Voice (p. 424).

2. The Active Voice

Examples	Explanation
I **bought** a new cell phone. He **eats** fast food. We **will drive** the car.	In most cases, the active voice is used when there is a choice between active and passive.
The accident **happened** last month. She **went** to court.	When there is no object, the active voice must be used. There is no choice.

3. The Passive Voice

Examples	Explanation
I **was chosen** for jury duty. My cell phone **was made** in Japan.	Use the passive voice when the performer is not known or is not important.
The criminal **was taken** to jail. Some employees **are expected** to conduct business while driving.	Use the passive voice when the performer is obvious.
Cell phones **are used** all over the world. Jury duty **is considered** a responsibility of every citizen.	Use the passive voice when the performer is everybody or people in general.
The court paid me. I **was paid** at the end of the day. The coffee was very hot. The coffee **was bought** at a fast-food restaurant.	Use the passive voice when the emphasis is shifted from the performer to the receiver of the action.
It **was discovered** that many accidents are the result of driver distraction. It **is believed** that a person can get a fair trial in the U.S.	Use the passive voice with *it*, when talking about findings, discoveries, or beliefs.
Accidents **are caused** by distracted drivers. A fast-food company **was sued** by a woman in New Mexico.	Use the passive voice when we want to emphasize the receiver of the action more than the performer. (In this case, the performer is included in a *by* phrase.)

430 Lesson 13

EDITING ADVICE

1. Never use *do, does,* or *did* with the passive voice.

   The money ~~didn't find~~ wasn't found.

   Where ~~did~~ were the jurors taken?

2. Don't use the passive voice with *happen, die, sleep, work, live, fall,* or *seem.*

   My grandfather ~~was~~ died four years ago.

3. Don't confuse the *-ing* form with the past participle.

   The criminal was ~~taking~~ taken to jail.

4. Don't forget the *-ed* ending for a regular past participle.

   My cousin was select^ed to be on a jury.

5. Don't forget to use *be* with a passive sentence.

   The books ^were found on the floor by the janitor.

6. Use the correct word order with adverbs.

   I was told (never) about the problem.

LESSON 13 TEST/REVIEW

PART 1 Find the mistakes with the underlined words, and correct them. Not every sentence has a mistake. If the sentence is correct, write *C.*

EXAMPLES The same mistake has ^been made many times.

We were told not to say anything. C

1. Children should ^be taught good behavior.
2. Parents should teach children good behavior. C
3. I ~~never~~ was ^never given any information about the test.
4. I have ~~been~~ had my car for three years.

Editing Advice

Have students close their books. Write the example sentences without editing marks or corrections on the board. For example:

1. The money didn't find.
2. Where did the jurors taken?

Ask students to correct each sentence and provide a rule or an explanation for each correction. This activity can be done individually, in pairs, or as a class. After students have corrected each sentence, tell them to turn to page 431. Say: *Now compare your work with the Editing Advice in the book.*

Lesson 13 Test/Review

For additional practice, review, and assessment materials, see Assessment CD-ROM with *ExamView Pro, More Grammar Practice* Workbook 2, Interactive CD-ROM, and Web site http://elt.thomson.com/gic

PART 1

1. Part 1 may be used as an in-class test to assess student performance, in addition to the Assessment CD-ROM with *ExamView Pro.* Have students read the direction line. Ask: *Do all sentences have a mistake?* (no) Go over the examples. Collect for assessment.
2. If necessary, have students review: **Lesson 13.**

Lesson Review

To use Part 1 as a review, assign it as homework or use it as an in-class activity to be completed individually or in pairs. Check answers and review errors as a class. Reteach grammar points that students haven't mastered. Then student learning may be assessed using a test generated from the Assessment CD-ROM with *ExamView Pro.*

PART 2

1. Part 2 may also be used as an in-class test to assess student performance, in addition to the Assessment CD-ROM with *ExamView Pro*. Have students read the direction line. Collect for assessment.
2. If necessary, have students review:
   13.3 Passive Voice—Form and Use (p. 416).

PART 3

1. Part 3 may also be used as an in-class test to assess student performance, in addition to the Assessment CD-ROM with *ExamView Pro*. Have students read the direction line. Collect for assessment.
2. If necessary, have students review:
   13.3 Passive Voice—Form and Use (p. 416)
   13.4 Negatives and Questions with Passive Voice (p. 421).

5. **The driver was given a ticket for driving without a seatbelt.** *C*
6. **Where did your gloves find?** *you find*
7. **They were find in the back seat of a taxi.** *found*
8. **Something was happened to my bicycle.**
9. **This carpet has been cleaned many times.** *C*
10. **The answers don't written in my book.** *aren't*

PART 2 Change sentences from active to passive voice. Do not mention the performer. (The performer is in parentheses.) Use the same tense as the underlined verb.

EXAMPLE **(Someone) took my dictionary.**
My dictionary was taken.

1. **(People) speak English in the U.S.**
   English is spoken in the U.S.
2. **(You) can use a dictionary during the test.**
   A dictionary can be used during the test.
3. **(The police) took the criminal to jail.**
   The criminal was taken to jail.
4. **(People) have seen the president on TV many times.**
   The president has been seen on TV many times.
5. **(Someone) will take you to the courtroom.**
   You will be taken to the courtroom.
6. **(Someone) has broken the mirror into small pieces.**
   The mirror has been broken into small pieces.
7. **(People) expect you to learn English in the U.S.**
   You are expected to learn English in the U.S.
8. **(They) don't allow cameras in the courtroom.**
   Cameras aren't allowed in the courtroom.

PART 3 Change the sentences from passive to active voice. Use the same tense.

EXAMPLE **You were told by me to bring your books.**
I told you to bring your books.

1. **You have been told by the teacher to write a composition.**
   The teacher has told you to write a composition.

432 Lesson 13

Lesson Review

To use Parts 2 and 3 as a review, assign them as homework or use them as in-class activities to be completed individually or in pairs. Check answers and review errors as a class. Reteach grammar points that students haven't mastered. Then student learning may be assessed using a test generated from the Assessment CD-ROM with *ExamView Pro*.

2. Your phone bill must be paid.
You must pay your phone bill.

3. You are not allowed by the teacher to use your books during a test.
The teacher does not allow you to use your books during a test.

4. The tests will be returned by the teacher.
The teacher will return the tests.

5. When are wedding gifts opened by the bride and groom?
When do the bride and groom open wedding gifts?

6. Your missing car was not found by the police.
The police did not find your missing car.

PART 4 Fill in the blanks with the passive or active form of the verb in parentheses ( ). Use an appropriate tense.

EXAMPLES The tests *will be returned* (will/return) tomorrow.

The teacher *will return* (will/return) the tests.

1. My neighbor had a heart attack and *was taken* (take) to the hospital in an ambulance yesterday.
2. I *will visit* (will/visit) my neighbor in the hospital tomorrow.
3. I *saw* (see) the movie *Star Wars* five times.
4. This movie *was seen* (see) by millions of people.
5. I *have* (have) a lot of friends.
6. I *have been helped* (help) many times by my friends.
7. Ten people *died* (die) in the fire last night.
8. Five people *were rescued* (rescue) by the fire department in yesterday's fire.
9. Her husband *comes* (come) home from work at six o'clock every day.

PART 4

1. Part 4 may also be used as an in-class test to assess student performance, in addition to the Assessment CD-ROM with *ExamView Pro*. Have students read the direction line. Collect for assessment.
2. If necessary, have students review: **13.5** Choosing Active Voice or Passive Voice (p. 424).

Lesson Review

To use Part 4 as a review, assign it as homework or use it as an in-class activity to be completed individually or in pairs. Check answers and review errors as a class. Reteach grammar points that students haven't mastered. Then student learning may be assessed using a test generated from the Assessment CD-ROM with *ExamView Pro*.

Expansion Activities

These expansion activities provide opportunities for students to interact with one another and further develop their speaking and writing skills. Encourage students to use grammar from this lesson whenever possible.

To save class time, assign parts of the activities as homework. Then use class time for interaction and communication. If students do not need additional speaking practice, some of the activities may be assigned as writing activities for homework or skipped altogether.

CLASSROOM ACTIVITIES

1. Have students fill out the chart on the judicial system in their native countries. Then have students get together in groups to talk about one or more countries.
2. Have students fill out the chart on the celebration of holidays in their native countries. Then have students get together in groups to talk about one or more countries.
3. Divide the class into two groups to make presentations on cell phone use in cars. Ask students to display their main points on the board, on posters, on a handout, or in some other form of presentation.

---

10. He ___was driven___ home by his coworker last night.
    (drive)

11. The answer to your question ___isn't known___ by anyone.
    (not/know)

12. Even the teacher ___didn't know___ the answer to your question.
    (not/know)

EXPANSION ACTIVITIES

Classroom Activities

1. Form a small group and talk about the legal system in another country. Use the chart below to get ideas.

   Country: ______________

	Yes	No
People are treated fairly in court.		
Citizens are selected to be on a jury.		
People are represented by lawyers in court.		
Lawyers make a lot of money.		
Famous trials are shown on TV.		
Punishment is severe for certain crimes.		
The death penalty is used in some cases.		
The laws are fair.		

2. Form a small group and tell about how a holiday is celebrated in your native culture. Use the chart below to get ideas.

	Yes	No
Gifts are given.		
The house is cleaned.		
Special clothing is worn.		
The house is decorated with special symbols of the holiday.		
Special food is prepared.		
Stores and businesses are closed.		
Special programs are shown on TV.		
Candles are used.		

3. Form two groups. One group should make a presentation telling why cell phone use should be permitted in cars. One group should make a presentation telling why cell phone use should *not* be permitted in cars.

Talk About it

1. Would you like to be on a jury? Why or why not?
2. In a small group, discuss your impressions of the American legal system from what you've seen on TV, from what you've read, or from your own experience.
3. Do you think drivers who use cell phones while driving cause accidents?
4. What laws should be changed in the U.S.? What laws should be added?
5. Do you think fast-food restaurants are responsible for obesity in the U.S.?

Write About it

1. Write about an experience you have had with the court system in the U.S. or your native country.
2. Write about a famous court case that you know of. Do you agree with the decision of the jury?
3. Write about the advantages of owning a cell phone.

Outside Activities

1. Watch a court movie, such as *The Firm, Witness to the Prosecution, Inherit the Wind, A Time to Kill, To Kill a Mockingbird, Presumed Innocent, Twelve Angry Men, A Civil Action*, or *The Client*. Write about your impressions of the American court system after watching one of these movies.
2. Watch a court TV show, such as *People's Court* or *Judge Judy*. What do you think of the judges' decisions on these shows?
3. Ask an American if he or she has ever been selected for a jury. Ask him or her to tell you about this experience.

Internet Activities

1. At a search engine, type in *Insurance Information Institute* and *cell phones*. Find some statistics about drivers who use cell phones. Bring the information to class. Is there anything that surprises you?
2. Look for information about one of these famous American trials:
   a. the O.J. Simpson trial
   b. the Leopold and Loeb trial
   c. the Sacco and Vanzetti trial
   d. the Amistad trials
   e. the Scopes trial
   f. the Rosenberg trial
   g. the Bruno Hauptmann trial

(continued)

Expansion

Write About it Have students exchange first drafts with a partner. Ask students to help their partners edit their drafts. Refer students to the Editing Advice on page 431.

TALK ABOUT IT

Have students discuss each topic in pairs, in groups, or as a whole class.

WRITE ABOUT IT

1. Before they begin writing, have students make an outline of the events that happened, if relevant.
2. Instruct students to write a quick summary of the famous case. Then have students express their opinions in a few lines.
3. Have students list both the advantages and disadvantages of owning a cell phone.

INTERNET ACTIVITIES

1. Make sure not all students watch the same movie.
2. Have students write a quick summary of at least one case they saw on a court TV show. Then ask students what their impression was of the show and if they agreed or disagreed with the judge's decision.
3. Have students prepare questions for the interview beforehand in class.

INTERNET ACTIVITIES

1. Before students search the Internet, have them brainstorm the types of statistics they might find, as well as additional key words they may use to help narrow their searches, such as *statistics* or *deaths*.
2. After searching the Internet, have students report on their findings.
   a. The O.J. Simpson Trial—O.J. Simpson, a famous American and former football player, was accused of killing his wife, Nicole Brown, and her friend Ron Goldman. After a controversial nine-month trail, Simpson was found not-guilty. Many feel that regardless of the outcome of the trial, he was guilty. He was found responsible for her death in the civil trial.
   b. The Leopold and Loeb trial—Two intelligent and educated sons of wealthy families, in an attempt to commit the perfect crime, kidnapped and murdered a young boy. They pleaded guilty and were sentenced to life in prison. Loeb died in prison, and Leopold was released after 34 years.

CLASSROOM ACTIVITIES (*cont.*)

c. The Sacco and Vanzetti trial—Sacco and Vanzetti were aliens, atheists, anarchists, and conscientious objectors of the war (WWI). They were accused of the murder of a guard at a shoe company in Massachusetts. They both had guns and lied about their activities. Supporters felt they were victims of communist hysteria. They were convicted in 1921 and later executed. The trial lasted two months. Their appeals were denied.
d. The Amistad trials—In 1839, a slave ship sailing from Cuba was taken over in a mutiny led by African slave Cinque. They were eventually captured by the American navy and put on trial in Connecticut. The case was eventually taken to the Supreme Court, where the Court ordered the slaves to be freed immediately. The trials lasted for approximately one year.
e. The Scopes trial—John Scopes was a biology teacher who taught evolution in his Tennessee classroom, even though it had been just made illegal in Tennessee and in other states. Townspeople who wanted to generate some publicity for their depopulated town decided to test the law in court. At the end of the long two-month trial in 1925, Scopes was found guilty and was fined. It was the hope of the defense to take the trial to the Supreme Court. It was thrown out of the appeals court.
f. The Rosenberg trial—Husband and wife, Julius and Ethel Rosenberg, were tried and executed for selling secrets about U.S. efforts to build atomic weapons to the Soviets. The prosecution was built on very poor evidence. People all around the world, including the Pope, begged for leniency. They were executed in 1953.
g. The Bruno Hauptmann trial—Bruno Hauptmann was convicted and executed in 1936 for the kidnapping and murder of Charles Lindbergh's (famous aviator) baby. The trial took place in 1935 and lasted one month.

Answer these questions about one of the trials:

- What was the defendant accused of?
- When did the trial take place?
- How long did the trial last?
- Was the defendant found guilty?

Additional Activities at http://elt.thomson.com/gic

Internet Activities Variation

Remind students that if they don't have Internet access, they can use Internet facilities at a public library, or they can use traditional research methods to find out information, including looking at encyclopedias, magazines, books, journals, and newspapers.

LESSON

14

GRAMMAR
Articles
Other / Another
Indefinite Pronouns

CONTEXT : Money
Kids and Money
Changing the American Dollar
The High Cost of a College Education

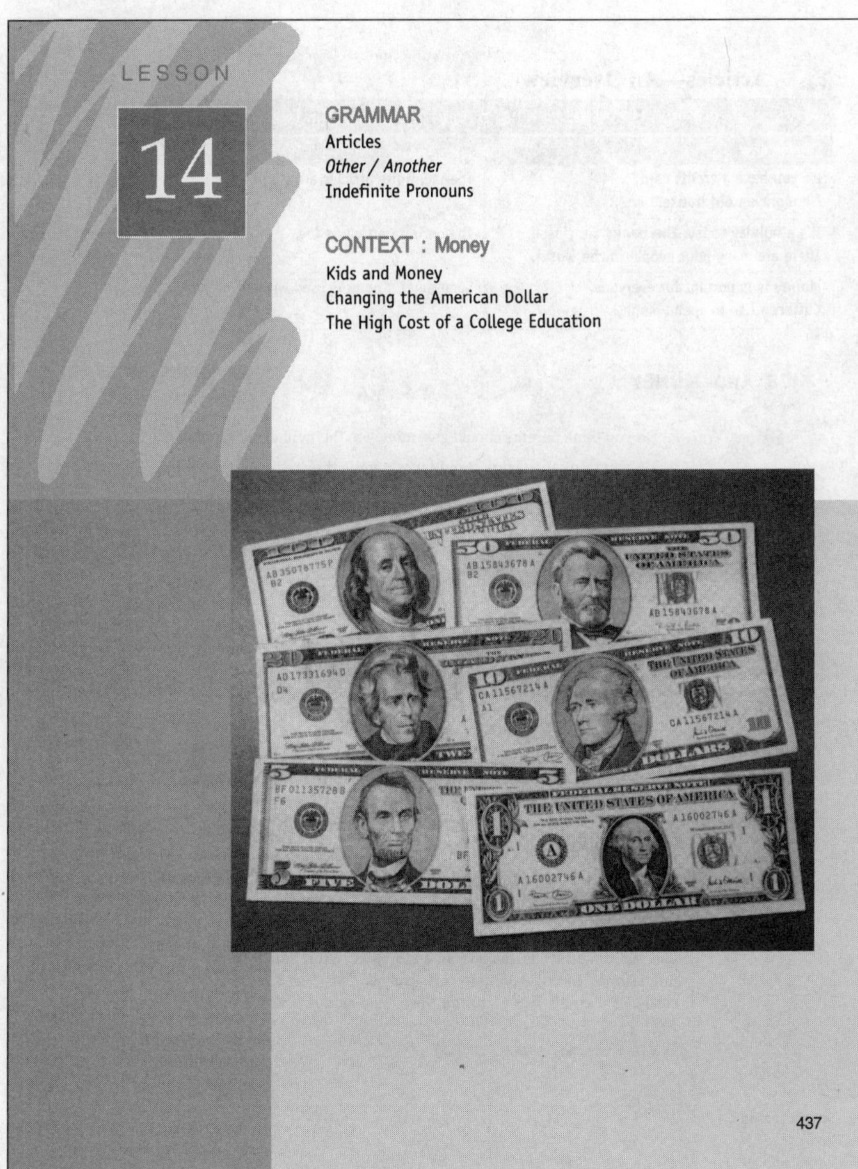

437

Lesson 14

Lesson Overview

GRAMMAR

1. Briefly review what students learned in the last lesson. Ask: *What did we study in Lesson 13?* (passive voice and active voice)
2. Ask: *What are we going to study in this lesson?* (articles; *other/another*, indefinite pronouns) *What are some articles?* (e.g., *a, the*) Have students give examples. Write the examples on the board. Then ask for examples of sentences using indefinite pronouns (e.g., *I don't have a car. But I'm going to need **one** next year when I move to the suburbs.*).

CONTEXT

1. Ask: *What are we going to learn about in this lesson?* (kids and money; changing the American dollar; the high cost of a college education) Activate students' prior knowledge. Ask: *How old were you when you started earning money? Did you save it or did you spend it?*
2. Have students share their knowledge and personal experiences.

To save class time, have students do the Test/Review at the end of the lesson, or administer a lesson test generated from the Assessment CD-ROM with *ExamView® Pro*. Skip sections of the lesson that students have already mastered. You may also assign some sections for self-study for extra credit.

Expansion

Theme The topic for this lesson can be enhanced with the following ideas:

1. Catalogs from state and private colleges and universities with tuition and housing costs
2. American money: new and old
3. Coins and bills from other countries

14.1 | Articles—An Overview

Have students look at grammar chart **14.1** on page 438. Say: *The indefinite articles are* a/an, *and the definite article is* the. Point out that nouns are sometimes used without an article. Go over the examples.

Kids and Money (Reading)

1. Have students look at the photo on page 438. Ask: *What is going on in this photo?* (two kids are shopping)
2. Have students look at the title of the reading. Ask: *What is the reading about?* Have students use the title and photo to make predictions about the reading.
3. Preteach any vocabulary words your students may not know, such as *gratitude, generosity, guilt, allowance,* and *chores.*

BEFORE YOU READ

1. Have students discuss the questions in pairs.
2. Ask for a few volunteers to share their answers with the class.

To save class time, skip "Before You Read" or have students prepare answers for homework ahead of time.

Reading CD 4, Track 11

1. Have students first read the text silently. Tell them to pay special attention to nouns and the articles that precede them. Then play the audio and have students read along silently.
2. Check students' comprehension. Ask questions such as: *In 2001, how much did kids on average spend a week?* ($104) *Why are some parents buying their children things?* (because they feel guilty for not spending a lot of time with them) *What do some children receive an allowance for?* (Some children have regular chores they do in exchange for an allowance.) *When should parents start talking to their children about money?* (when they start saying *I want. . . .*)

To save class time, have students do the reading for homework ahead of time.

14.1 | Articles—An Overview

Articles precede nouns and tell whether a noun is definite or indefinite.

Examples	Explanation
Do you have **a credit card?** I bought **an old house.**	The indefinite articles are *a* and *an*.
It's a holiday today. **The banks** are closed. There are many poor people in **the world.**	The definite article is *the.*
Money is important for everyone. **Children** like to spend money.	Sometimes a noun is used without an article.

KIDS AND MONEY

Before You Read

1. Do you think parents should give money to their children? At what age?
2. Do you think teenagers should work while they're in high school?

Read the following article. Pay special attention to nouns and the articles that precede them. (Some nouns have no article.)

Kids in the U.S. like to spend **money.** In 2001, kids between the ages of 12 and 19 spent an average of $104 a week. Much of today's **advertising** is directed at kids. When you go into **a store,** you often hear **toddlers**[1] who are just learning to talk saying to their parents, "Buy me **a toy.** Buy me **some candy.**" Some kids feel **gratitude** when they receive **a dollar** or **a toy** from

[1] A *toddler* is a child between the ages of one and three.

Reading Variation

To practice listening skills, have students first listen to the audio alone. Ask a few comprehension questions. Repeat the audio if necessary. Then have them open their books and read along as they listen to the audio.

Reading Glossary

allowance: money for everyday expenses
chores: routine tasks or jobs
generosity: readiness to give; giving
gratitude: thankfulness
guilt: feeling of having done something wrong or shameful; remorse

a **grandparent.** But some kids feel a sense of entitlement[2]. Even during **the** hard economic **times** of the early 1990s, sales of **soft drinks, designer blue jeans, fast food, sneakers, gum,** and **dolls** remained high. One factor in parents' **generosity** is **guilt.** As **parents** become busier in their **jobs,** they often feel guilty about not spending **time** with their **kids.** Often they deal with their **guilt** by giving their kids **money** and **gifts.**

To help children understand **the value** of **money, parents** often give their **children an allowance. The child's spending** is limited to **the money** he or she receives each week. How much should parents give **a child** as **an allowance?** Some parents give **the child a dollar** for each year of his or her age. **A five-year-old** would get five dollars. **A fifteen-year-old** would get fifteen dollars. Some parents pay their kids extra for **chores,** such as taking out **the garbage** or shoveling **snow.** Other parents believe kids should do chores as part of their family responsibilities.

When is **the right time** to start talking to **kids** about **money?** According to Nathan Dungan, **a financial expert,** the right time is as soon as **kids** can say, "I want." By **the time** they start **school,** they must know there are **limits.**

Did You Know?

In a study of young people aged 12 to 17, 58 percent said they wouldn't bother to pick up off the sidewalk anything less than a dollar.

14.2 The Indefinite Article—Classifying or Identifying the Subject

Examples	Explanation
A doll is **a toy.** A toddler is **a small child.** An allowance is **a weekly payment** to children. A penny is **a one-cent coin.** "Big" is **an adjective.** "Inflation" is **an economic term.**	After the verb *be,* we use the indefinite articles *a* or *an* + singular count noun to define or classify the subject of the sentence. We are telling who or what the subject is. Singular subject + *is* + *a(n)* + (adjective) + noun
Jeans are **popular clothes.** Teenagers are **young adults.** Chores are **everyday jobs.**	When we classify or define a plural subject, we don't use an article. Plural subject + *are* + (adjective) + noun

Language Note:
We can also use *be* in the past tense to give a definition.
The Depression **was** a difficult time in American history.
Abraham Lincoln **was** an American president.

[2] A sense of *entitlement* is a feeling that you have the right to receive something.

DID YOU KNOW?

When young children (6–8 years of age) in the U.S. lose a tooth, they put it under their pillow at night. The next day, money "magically" appears in its place compliments of the Tooth Fairy. Parents are now complaining that children expect more than the traditional quarter these days because of what they hear friends at school are getting. Tooth Fairy inflation has caused parents to fork over more money or to be creative. Many parents now give their children special gold dollar coins available at the post office or online at the U.S. mint.

14.2 The Indefinite Article—Classifying or Identifying the Subject

1. Have students look at grammar chart **14.2** on page 439. Say: *To tell who or what the subject is, we use* a *or* an *with a singular count noun after* be. Go over the examples.
2. Explain that when we classify a plural subject, we don't use an article. Go over examples.
3. Direct students to the Language Note. Say: *We can also classify things in the past.* Go over the examples.

EXERCISE 1

1. Have students read the direction line. Go over the example.
2. Have students complete Exercise 1 individually. Go over the answers as a class.
3. If necessary, review grammar chart **14.2** on page 439.

EXERCISE 2

1. Have students read the direction line. Go over the example.
2. Have students complete Exercise 2 individually. Go over the answers as a class.
3. If necessary, review grammar chart **14.2** on page 439.

To save class time, have students do half of the exercise in class and complete the other half for homework.

14.3 The Indefinite Article—Introducing a Noun

1. Have students look at grammar chart **14.3** on page 440. Say: A *and* an *introduce a singular noun.* Go over the examples.
2. Say: Some *or* any *introduce a plural noun or a noncount noun.* Any *is used only in negatives and questions.* Some *and* any *do not have to be used.* Go over the examples.

EXERCISE 1 Define the following words. Answers may vary.

EXAMPLE A toddler *is a small child.*

1. A teenager *Answers will vary.*
2. A quarter
3. A dime
4. A credit card
5. A wallet
6. Gold
7. Silver and gold

EXERCISE 1 Tell who these people are or were by classifying them. These people were mentioned in previous lessons in this book. Answers will vary.

EXAMPLE Martin Luther King, Jr. *was an African-American leader.*

1. Albert Einstein *was a scientist.*
2. Michael Jordan *is a basketball player.*
3. Erik Weihenmayer *is a blind mountain climber.*
4. Oprah Winfrey *is a TV celebrity.*
5. George Dawson *was an African-American author.*
6. Navajos *are American Indians.*
7. George Washington and Abraham Lincoln *were U.S. presidents.*

14.3 The Indefinite Article—Introducing a Noun

Examples	Explanation
She has **a son.** Her son has **a job.** Her son has **a checking account.**	Use *a* or *an* to introduce a singular noun.
He has **(some)** toys. He doesn't have **(any)** video games. Does he have **(any)** CDs?	Use *some* and *any* to introduce a plural noun. Use *any* for negatives and questions. *Some* and *any* can be omitted.
He has **(some)** money. He doesn't have **(any)** cash. Does he have **(any)** time?	Use *some* and *any* to introduce a noncount noun. Use *any* for negatives and questions. *Some* and *any* can be omitted.

Expansion

Exercise 2 Have students write five sentences telling who some important or famous people from their native countries or cultures are. Then have students exchange papers with a partner from a different country.

EXERCISE 3 Fill in the blanks with the correct word: *a, an, some,* or *any.*

EXAMPLE There are ___some___ symbols on the back of a credit card.

1. Do you have ___an___ account with the bank?
2. Do you have ___any___ money in your savings account?
3. I have ___a___ twenty-dollar bill in my pocket.
4. I have ___some___ quarters in my pocket.
5. I have ___some___ money with me.
6. Do you have ___any___ credit cards?
7. I don't have ___any___ change.
8. Buy me ___a___ toy.
9. Buy me ___some___ candy.
10. I need ___a___ dollar.
11. Many teenagers want to have ___a___ job.
12. Does your little brother get ___an___ allowance?

EXERCISE 4 A mother (M) and a son (S) are talking. Fill in the blanks with *a, an, some,* or *any.*

S: I want to get ___a___ *(example)* job.

M: But you're only 16 years old.

S: I'm old enough to work. I need to make ___some___ (1) money.

M: But we give you ___an___ (2) allowance each week. Isn't that enough money for you?

S: You only give me $15 a week. That's not even enough to buy ___a___ (3) CD or take ___a___ (4) girl to ___a___ (5) movie.

M: If you work, what are you going to do about school? You won't have ___any___ (6) time to study. Do you know how hard it is to work and do well in school?

S: Of course, I do. You know I'm ___a___ (7) good student. I'm sure I won't have ___any___ (8) problems working part time.

EXERCISE 3

1. Have students read the direction line. Go over the example.
2. Have students complete Exercise 3 individually. Go over the answers with the class.
3. If necessary, review grammar chart **14.3** on pages 440.

EXERCISE 4

CD 4, Track 12

1. Say: *In this conversation, a mother and her son are talking about getting a job.* Have students read the direction line. Go over the example.
2. Have students complete the exercise individually. Then have students compare answers in pairs. Circulate to observe pair work. Give help as needed.
3. If necessary, review grammar chart **14.3** on page 440.

To save class time, have students do half of the exercise in class and complete the other half for homework. Or assign the entire exercise for homework.

Exercise 4 Variation

To provide practice with listening skills, have students close their books and listen to the audio. Repeat the audio as needed. Say: *In this conversation, a mother and her son are talking about getting a job.* Ask comprehension questions, such as: *Why does he want to get a job?* (to make money) *What is his mother worried about?* (that he won't have enough time for school work) *What does he want to buy with his money?* (clothes, a car) Then have students open their books and complete Exercise 4.

M: Well, I'm worried about your grades falling. Maybe we should raise your allowance. That way you won't have to work.

S: I want to have my own money. I want to buy ___some___ (9) new clothes. And I'm going to save money to buy ___a___ (10) car someday.

M: Why do you want a car? You have ___a___ (11) bike.

S: Bikes are great for exercise, but if my job is far away, I'll need a car for transportation.

M: So, you need ___a___ (12) job to buy ___a___ (13) car, and you need ___a___ (14) car to get work.

S: Yes. You know, a lot of my friends work, and they're good students.

M: Well, let me think about it.

S: Mom, I'm not ___a___ (15) baby anymore. I need ___a___ (16) job.

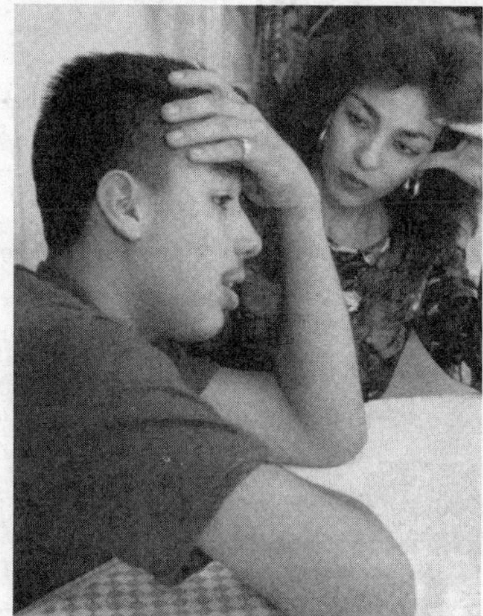

Expansion

Exercise 4 Have students practice the conversation in pairs. Ask volunteers to role-play all or part of the conversation in front of the class.

14.4 | The Definite Article

We use *the* to talk about a specific person or thing or a unique person or thing.	
Examples	**Explanation**
The book talks about kids and money. **The author** wants to teach kids to be responsible with money. 	The sentences to the left refer to a specific object or person that is present. There is no other book or author present, so the listener knows which noun is referred to.
Many kids in **the world** are poor. **The first** chapter talks about small children. **The back** of the book has information about the author. When is **the right** time to talk to kids about money?	Sometimes there is only one of something. There is only one world, only one first chapter, only one back of a book. We use *the* with the following words: *first, second, next, last, only, same,* and *right.*
Where's **the** teacher? I have a question about **the** homework.	When students in the same class talk about **the** teacher, **the** textbook, **the** homework, **the** chalkboard, they are talking about a specific one that they share.
Did you read **the article about money?** Children often spend **the money they get from their grandparents.**	The sentences to the left refer to a specific noun that is defined in the phrase or clause after the noun: *the article* ***about money;*** *the money* ***they get from their grandparents.***
I'm going to **the** store after work. Do you need anything? **The** bank is closed. I'll go tomorrow. You should make an appointment with **the** doctor.	We often use *the* with certain familiar places and people when we refer to the one that we usually use: the bank, the beach, the bus the zoo, the post office, the train the park, the doctor, the movies the store
a. I saw **a child** in the supermarket with her mother. b. **The child** kept saying, "Buy me this, buy me that." a. She used **a credit card.** b. She put **the credit card** back in her purse.	a. A noun is first introduced as an indefinite noun (with *a* or *an*). b. When referring to the same noun again, the definite article *the* is used.
My grandparents gave me lots of presents. **Kim's kids** have lots of toys.	Don't use the definite article with a possessive form. *Wrong:* My the grandparents *Wrong:* Kim's the kids

14.4 | The Definite Article

1. Have students cover up grammar chart **14.4** on page 443. Create a matching exercise on the board:
   1. *Did you read* ***the article about money****?*
   2. *Many kids in* ***the world*** *are poor.*
   3. *I'm going to* ***the store*** *after work. Do you want anything?*
   4. ***The author*** *wants to teach kids to be responsible with money.*
   5. *Where's* ***the teacher****? I have a question about* ***the homework****.*

   a. *Refers to a specific object or person present*
   b. *When there is only one of something*
   c. *When we refer to something (such as a classroom text) that we share with others*
   d. *When we refer to a specific noun that is defined in the phrase after the noun*
   e. *When we refer to the thing or the one that we usually use*

   Say: *Match the example with the explanation.*
2. Then have students look at grammar chart **14.4** on page 443. Say: *Compare your work with the chart.* Go over the examples and the explanations.
3. Explain that when a noun is first introduced, it has an indefinite article. When you refer to it again, you use the definite article *the.* Go over the examples.
4. Explain that you don't use the definite article with possessive forms. Go over the examples.

EXERCISE 5

CD 4, Track 13

1. Say: *There are three short conversations in this exercise.* Have students read the direction line. Go over the example. Point out the photo of the ATM and the illustration of the dollar-bill changer.
2. Have students complete the exercise individually. Go over the answers as a class.
3. If necessary, review grammar chart **14.4** on pages 443.

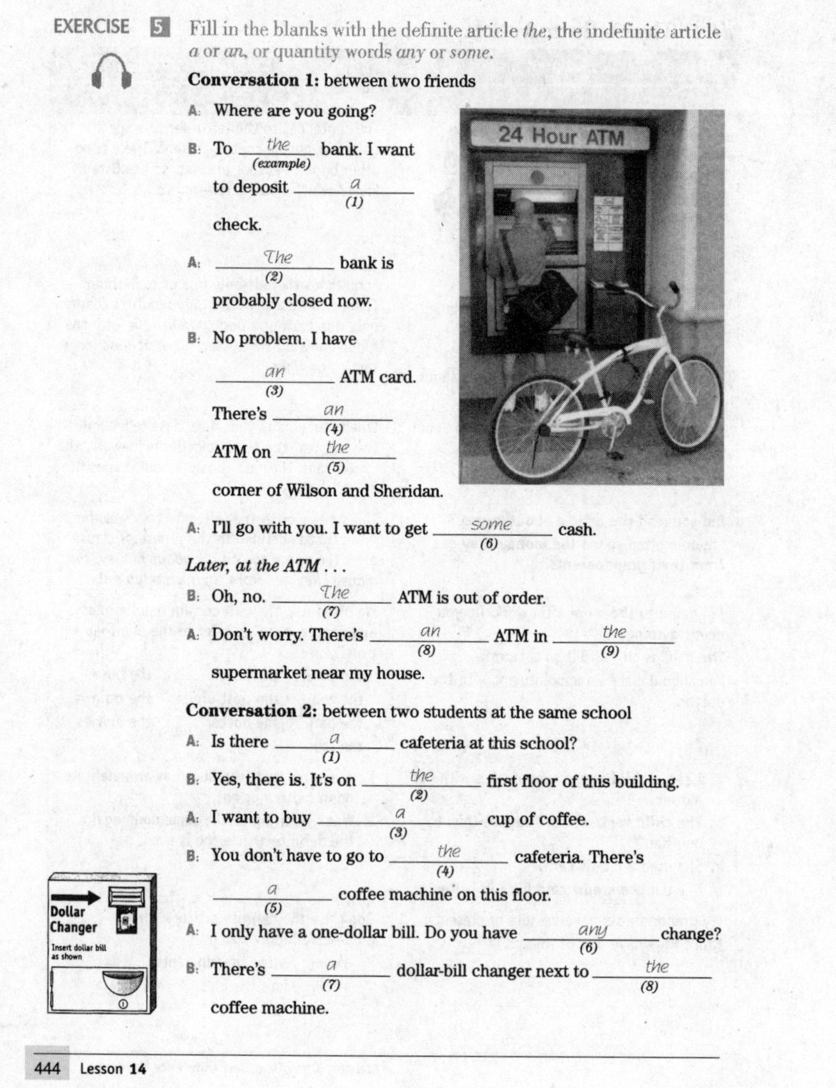

EXERCISE 5 Fill in the blanks with the definite article *the*, the indefinite article *a* or *an*, or quantity words *any* or *some*.

Conversation 1: between two friends

A: Where are you going?

B: To ___the___ bank. I want to deposit ___a___ check.
(example) (1)

A: ___The___ bank is probably closed now.
(2)

B: No problem. I have ___an___ ATM card. There's ___an___ ATM on ___the___ corner of Wilson and Sheridan.
(3) (4) (5)

A: I'll go with you. I want to get ___some___ cash.
(6)

Later, at the ATM . . .

B: Oh, no. ___The___ ATM is out of order.
(7)

A: Don't worry. There's ___an___ ATM in ___the___ supermarket near my house.
(8) (9)

Conversation 2: between two students at the same school

A: Is there ___a___ cafeteria at this school?
(1)

B: Yes, there is. It's on ___the___ first floor of this building.
(2)

A: I want to buy ___a___ cup of coffee.
(3)

B: You don't have to go to ___the___ cafeteria. There's ___a___ coffee machine on this floor.
(4) (5)

A: I only have a one-dollar bill. Do you have ___any___ change?
(6)

B: There's ___a___ dollar-bill changer next to ___the___ coffee machine.
(7) (8)

444 Lesson 14

Exercise 5 Variation

To provide practice with listening skills, have students close their books and listen to the audio. Repeat the audio as needed. Say: *You'll hear three short conversations.* Ask comprehension questions, such as: *What do they want to do in conversation 1?* (get cash from a bank or an ATM) *What does the student want to do in conversation 2?* (get coffee) *What's happening in conversation 3?* (The teacher is late.) Then have students open their books and complete Exercise 5.

Conversation 3: between two students (A and B) in the same class

A: Where's ___the___ (1) teacher? It's already 7:00.

B: Maybe she's absent today.

A: I'll go to ___the___ (2) English office and ask if anyone knows where she is.

B: That's ___a___ (3) good idea.

A few minutes later . . .

A: I talked to ___the___ (4) secretary in ___the___ (5) English office. She said that ___the___ (6) teacher just called. She's going to be about 15 minutes late. She had ___a___ (7) problem with her car.

14.5 | Making Generalizations

When we make a generalization, we say that something is true of ALL members of a group.

Examples	Explanation
a. **Children** like to copy their friends. b. **A child** likes to copy his or her friends. a. **Video games** are expensive. b. **A video game** is expensive.	There are two ways to make a generalization about a countable subject: a. Use *a* or *an* + singular noun OR b. Use no article + plural noun.
Money doesn't buy happiness. **Love** is more important than money. **Honesty** is a good quality.	To make a generalization about a noncount subject, don't use an article.
a. Children like **toys.** a. People like to use **credit cards.** b. Everyone needs **money.** b. No one has enough **time.**	Don't use an article to make a generalization about the object of the sentence. a. Use the plural form for count nouns. b. Noncount nouns are always singular.

Language Note:
Do not use *some* or *any* with generalizations.
Compare:
I need **some money** to buy a new bike.
Everyone needs **money.**

14.5 | Making Generalizations

1. Have students look at grammar chart **14.5** on page 445. Say: *When we make a generalization, we say that something is true of all members of a group.* Explain that to make a generalization with a singular count noun, we use *a* or *an.* To make a generalization about a plural noun, we don't use an article. Go over the examples.
2. Say: *For noncount nouns, don't use an article.* Go over the examples.
3. Explain that when you're making a generalization about the object of a sentence, you use a plural noun and no article with count nouns. With objects that are noncount nouns, don't use an article. Go over the examples.
4. Direct students to the Language Note. Point out that you don't use *some* or *any* with generalizations.

Expansion

Exercise 5 Have students practice the conversations in pairs. Ask volunteers to perform all or part of the conversations in front of the class.

EXERCISE 6

1. Say: *In this exercise, you're going to talk about the specific things on this page, or you're going to make generalizations with singular, plural, and noncount nouns.* Have students read the direction line. Go over the examples. Remind students that to make generalizations with singular nouns, we use *a* or *an*.
2. Have students complete Exercise 6 individually. Go over the answers with the class.
3. If necessary, review grammar chart **14.5** on page 445.

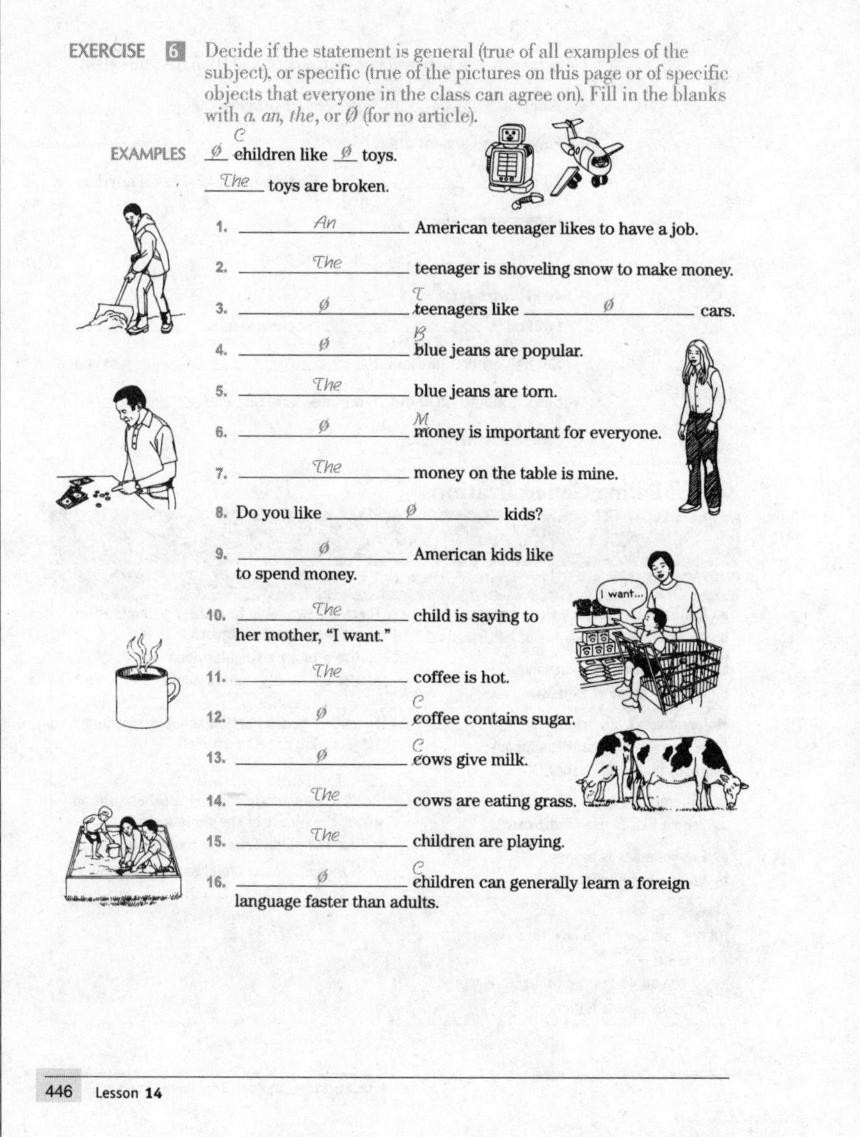

EXERCISE 6 Decide if the statement is general (true of all examples of the subject), or specific (true of the pictures on this page or of specific objects that everyone in the class can agree on). Fill in the blanks with *a, an, the*, or Ø (for no article).

EXAMPLES Ø children like Ø toys.
The toys are broken.

1. An American teenager likes to have a job.
2. The teenager is shoveling snow to make money.
3. Ø teenagers like Ø cars.
4. Ø blue jeans are popular.
5. The blue jeans are torn.
6. Ø money is important for everyone.
7. The money on the table is mine.
8. Do you like Ø kids?
9. Ø American kids like to spend money.
10. The child is saying to her mother, "I want."
11. The coffee is hot.
12. Ø coffee contains sugar.
13. Ø cows give milk.
14. The cows are eating grass.
15. The children are playing.
16. Ø children can generally learn a foreign language faster than adults.

446 Lesson 14

Expansion

Exercise 6 Have students work in pairs to write four sentences about specific things in the room and four sentences with generalizations.

EXERCISE 7 ABOUT YOU Tell if you like the following or not. For count nouns (C), use the plural form. For noncount nouns (NC), use the singular form.

EXAMPLES coffee (NC) I like coffee. apple (C) I don't like apples.

Answers will vary.

1. tea (NC)	4. potato chip (C)	7. cookie (C)
2. corn (NC)	5. milk (NC)	8 pizza (NC)
3. peach (C)	6. orange (C)	9. potato (C)

EXERCISE 8 Fill in the blanks with *the, a, an, some, any,* or Ø (for no article.) In some cases, more than one answer is possible.

A: Where are you going?

B: I'm going to *the* (example) post office. I need to buy *some* (1) stamps.

A: I'll go with you. I want to mail *a* (2) package to my parents.

B: What's in *the* (3) package?

A: *some/Ø* (4) shirts for my father, *a* (5) coat for my sister, and *some/Ø* (6) money for my mother.

B: You should never send *Ø* (7) money by mail.

A: I know. My mother never received *the* (8) money that I sent in my last letter. But what can I do? I don't have *a* (9) checking account.

B: You can buy *a* (10) money order at *the* (11) bank.

A: How much does it cost?

B: Well, if you have *an* (12) account in *the* (13) bank, it's usually free. If not, you'll probably have to pay a fee.

A: What about *the* (14) currency exchange on Wright Street? Do they sell *Ø* (15) money orders?

B: Yes.

A: Why don't we go there? We can save *some* (16) time. It's on *the* (17) same street as *the* (18) post office.

EXERCISE 7

1. Say: *You're going to talk about what you like and what you don't like.* Have students read the direction line. Go over the examples.
2. Have students complete Exercise 7 in pairs. Circulate to observe pair work. Give help as needed.
3. If necessary, review grammar chart **14.5** on page 445.

To save class time, have students do half of the exercise in class and complete the other half in writing for homework. Or if students do not need speaking practice, the entire exercise may be skipped or done in writing.

EXERCISE 8

CD 4, Track 14

1. Say: *In this conversation, you'll hear two friends talk about sending money through the mail.* Have students read the direction line. Go over the example. Remind students that some nouns won't need an article.
2. Have students complete the exercise individually. Then have students compare answers in pairs. Circulate to observe pair work. Give help as needed.
3. If necessary, review grammar chart **14.5** on page 445.

To save class time, have students do half of the exercise in class and complete the other half for homework.

Exercise 8 Variation

To provide practice with listening skills, have students close their books and listen to the audio. Repeat the audio as needed. Say: *In this conversation, you'll hear two friends talk about sending money through the mail.* Ask comprehension questions, such as: *What is person A going to send at the post office?* (a package to her family) *What's in the package?* (shirts, a coat, and money) *Why does she need to get a money order?* (It's not safe to send cash in the mail.) Then have students open their books and complete Exercise 8.

Expansion

Exercise 8 Have students practice the conversation in pairs. Ask volunteers to role-play all or part of the conversation in front of the class.

EXERCISE 9

CD 4, Track 15

1. Say: ***In this conversation, you'll hear two friends talk about money.*** Have students read the direction line. Go over the example. Remind students that some nouns won't need an article.
2. Have students complete the exercise individually. Then have students compare answers in pairs. Circulate to observe pair work. Give help as needed.
3. If necessary, review grammar chart **14.5** on page 445.

To save class time, have students do half of the exercise in class and complete the other half for homework. Or assign the entire exercise for homework.

EXERCISE 9 Two women are talking. Fill in the blanks with *the, a, an, some, any,* or Ø (for no article). Answers may vary.

A: I bought my daughter ___*a*___ *(example)* new doll for her birthday. She's been asking me to buy it for her for two months. But she played with ___*the*___ (1) doll for about three days and then lost interest.

B: That's how ___*Ø*___ (2) kids are. They don't understand ___*the*___ (3) value of money.

A: You're right. They think that ___*Ø*___ (4) money grows on ___*Ø*___ (5) trees.

B: I suppose it's our fault. We have to set ___*a*___ (6) good example. We buy a lot of things we don't really need. We use ___*Ø*___ (7) credit cards instead of ___*Ø*___ (8) cash and worry about paying the bill later.

A: I suppose you're right. Last month we bought ___*a*___ (9) new flat screen TV. We were at the store looking for a DVD player when we saw it. It's so much nicer than our old TV, so we decided to get it and put our ___*Ø*___ (10) old TV in ___*the*___ (11) basement. I suppose we didn't really need it.

B: Last weekend my husband bought ___*a*___ (12) new CD player. And he bought ___*some*___ (13) new CDs. I asked him what was wrong with our old CD player, and he said that it only played two CDs at a time. ___*The*___ (14) new CD player has room for 10 CDs.

Exercise 9 Variation

To provide practice with listening skills, have students close their books and listen to the audio. Repeat the audio as needed. Say: *In this conversation, you'll hear two friends talk about money.* Ask comprehension questions, such as: *Who has to set a good example for kids?* (the parents) *What do they use instead of cash?* (credit cards) *What did they put in the basement?* (their old TV) Then have students open their books and complete Exercise 9.

A: Well, when we complain about our kids, we should realize that they are imitating us.

B: We need to make some (15) changes in our own behavior. I'm going to start a (16) budget tonight. I'm going to start saving ∅ (17) money each month.

A: Me too.

14.6 | General or Specific with Quantity Words

If we put *of the* after a quantity word (*all, most, some,* etc.), we are making something specific. Without *of the*, the sentence is general.

Examples	Explanation
General: **All** children like toys. **Most** American homes have a television. **Many** teenagers have jobs. **Some** people are very rich. **Very few** people are billionaires.	We use *all, most, many, some, (a) few,* and *(a) little* before general nouns.
Specific: a. **All (of) the students** in this class have a textbook. b. **Most of the students** in my art class have talent. c. **Many of the topics** in this book are about life in America. d. **Some of the people** in my building come from Haiti. e. **Very few of the students** in this class are American citizens. f. **Very little of the time** spent in this class is for reading. g. **None of the classrooms** at this school has a telephone.	We use *all of the, most of the, many of the, some of the, (a) few of the, (a) little of the,* and *none of the* before specific nouns. After *all, of* is often omitted. **All the students** in this class have a textbook. After *none of the* + plural noun, a singular verb is correct. However, you will often hear a plural verb used. None of the classrooms ***have*** a telephone.

Language Note:
Remember the difference between *a few* and *(very) few, a little* and *(very) little*. When we omit *a*, the emphasis is on the negative. We are saying the quantity is not enough. (See Lesson 5, Section 5.14 for more information.)
Few people wanted to have a party. The party was canceled.
A few people came to the meeting. We discussed our plans.

14.6 | General or Specific with Quantity Words

1. Have students look at grammar chart **14.6** on page 449. Say: *When we put* of the *after a quantity word, we are making something specific.* Go over the examples. Explain that these sentences make generalizations.
2. Then have students read the sentences with *of the*. Explain that after *all*, the word *of* can be omitted. *None* is singular and should be followed by a singular verb. But point out that many native speakers use a plural verb after *none*. Go over the example.
3. Direct students to the Language Note. Point out that by omitting *a* before *few* and *little*, you make the emphasis negative. Go over the examples.

Expansion

Exercise 9 Have students practice the conversation in pairs. Ask volunteers to role-play all or part of the conversation in front of the class.

Exercise 9 Have students work in pairs to create a similar conversation with their own information. Ask volunteers to perform all or part of the conversation in front of the class.

Grammar Have students change the general sentences in the grammar chart to specific sentences by adding *of the* and some additional information (e.g., *All of the children at the party liked the toys.*).

EXERCISE 10

1. Say: *In this exercise, you're going to make general statements about Americans.* Have students read the direction line. Go over the example.
2. Have students complete the exercise individually. Then have students compare answers in pairs. Circulate to observe pair work. Give help as needed.
3. If necessary, review grammar chart **14.6** on page 449.

EXERCISE 11

1. Have students read the direction line. Say: *Now you're going to be completing specific statements.* Go over the examples. Say: *Remember that* none *is singular and so the verb has to be singular.*
2. Have students complete the exercise individually. Then have students compare answers in pairs. Circulate to observe pair work. Give help as needed.
3. If necessary, review grammar chart **14.6** on page 449.

To save class time, have students do half of the exercise in class and complete the other half for homework. Or assign the entire exercise for homework.

EXERCISE 10 Fill in the blanks with *all, most, some,* or *(very) few* to make a general statement about Americans. Discuss your answers.

EXAMPLE *Most* Americans have a car.

1. Answers will vary. Americans have educational opportunities.
2. ________ Americans have a TV.
3. ________ American families have more than eight children.
4. ________ Americans know where my native country is.
5. ________ Americans shake hands when they meet.
6. ________ Americans use credit cards.
7. ________ Americans are natives of America.
8. ________ American citizens can vote.
9. ________ Americans speak my native language.
10. ________ Americans are unfriendly to me.

EXERCISE 11 ABOUT YOU Fill in the blanks with a quantity word to make a **true** statement about specific nouns. If you use *none,* change the verb to the singular form.

EXAMPLES *All of the* students in this class want to learn English.

None of the students in this class come*s* from Australia.

1. Answers will vary. students in this class speak Spanish.
2. ________ students brought their books to class today.
3. ________ students are absent today.
4. ________ students want to learn English.
5. ________ students have jobs.
6. ________ students are married.
7. ________ students are going to return to their native countries.
8. ________ lessons in this book end with a review.
9. ________ pages in this book have pictures.
10. ________ tests in this class are hard.

Expansion

Exercise 10 Have students discuss their answers in groups. Who agrees? Who disagrees? Have groups report to the class.

Exercise 11 Do a class survey. Did most of the class have the same answers? Write the results on the board.

CHANGING THE AMERICAN DOLLAR

Before You Read

1. Does American money look different from money in another country (size, color, etc.)?
2. Compare a one-dollar bill to a twenty-dollar bill. Do you see differences in design?

Read the following article. Pay special attention to *other* and *another*.

Did You Know?
Before 1928, the U.S. dollar was much bigger than the dollars we use today. The size of the dollar was reduced to save money on paper.

The appearance of the American dollar did not change for a long time—from 1928 to 1996. But with advances in technology in recent years, it has become easier for counterfeiters[3] to copy dollar bills, making frequent changes necessary.

Look at the two twenty-dollar bills above. (Or see if you and your classmates have old and new bills.) You can see that on one twenty-dollar bill, the picture of Andrew Jackson is in an oval. On **the other** one, the picture is not in an oval. One bill has no background. **The other** bill has an eagle on the left and the words "Twenty USA" on the right. **Another** important change is in the color. The old bills are green. The new ones have some color. In the lower right corner of the old bill, the number "20" is in green. On the new bill, the "20" changes from gold to green, depending on how the light hits it. There are **other** changes too. If you have an old and a new bill, try to find **the other** differences.

The latest change to the U.S. bills began in 2003. The government decided to change the appearance of the twenty-dollar bill first, then the fifty- and one hundred-dollar bills. It has not been decided if the five- and ten-dollar bills will be changed. **The other** two bills ($1 and $2) will not be changed. Counterfeiters are not interested in small amounts of money. As new bills come into use, the old ones are "retired."

Some aspects of the bills remain the same: size, paper, the pictures on the front and back, and the motto "In God We Trust." In order to stay ahead of counterfeiters, the U.S. Treasury plans to redesign new bills every seven to ten years.

(continued)

[3] A *counterfeiter* is a person who makes copies of bills illegally.

Reading Variation

To practice listening skills, have students first listen to the audio alone. Ask a few comprehension questions. Repeat the audio if necessary. Then have them open their books and read along as they listen to the audio.

Changing the American Dollar (Reading)

1. Have students look at the pictures of the bills on page 451. Say: *Study the two twenty-dollar bills. Do you see any differences?*
2. Have students look at the title of the reading. Ask: *What is the reading about?* Have students use the title and pictures to make predictions about the reading.
3. Preteach any vocabulary words your students may not know such as *counterfeiters.* Direct students to the footnote at the bottom of page 451.

BEFORE YOU READ

1. Have students discuss the questions in pairs.
2. Ask for a few volunteers to share their answers with the class.

To save class time, skip "Before You Read" or have students prepare answers for homework ahead of time.

Reading *CD 4, Track 16*

1. Have students first read the text silently. Tell them to pay attention to *other* and *another.* Then play the audio and have students read along silently.
2. Check students' comprehension. Ask questions such as: *Why is the government now changing the look of U.S. money?* (Technology has made it easier to counterfeit money.) *Has the color of the twenty-dollar bill changed?* (Yes. It used to be all green, but now some more colors have been added.) *Will five- and ten-dollar bills be changed?* (No decision has been made.) *How often will the bills be changed?* (every seven to ten years)

To save class time, have students do the reading for homework ahead of time.

DID YOU KNOW?

There have been many dollar coins minted in the U.S. The first was minted in 1794, and the most recent is the Sacagawea golden dollar. Sacagawea was a Shoshone Indian who became part of the Lewis and Clark Expedition of the West. She acted as an interpreter and a guide. The dollar coin has never enjoyed wide acceptance in the U.S. Many experts feel this is because the paper dollar bill has never been withdrawn and because there has been little effort to advertise the coins.

14.7 | *Another* and *Other*

1. Have students look at grammar chart **14.7** on page 452. Say: The other *with a singular and plural noun is definite.* Other *with a plural noun and* another *with a singular noun are indefinite.* The other + *singular noun indicates that there is only one remaining.* The other + *plural noun indicates all the remaining ones.* Go over the examples.
2. Say: Another *is indefinite.* Another + *singular noun indicates that it is one of several.* Other + *plural noun indicates that they are some of several.* Go over the examples.

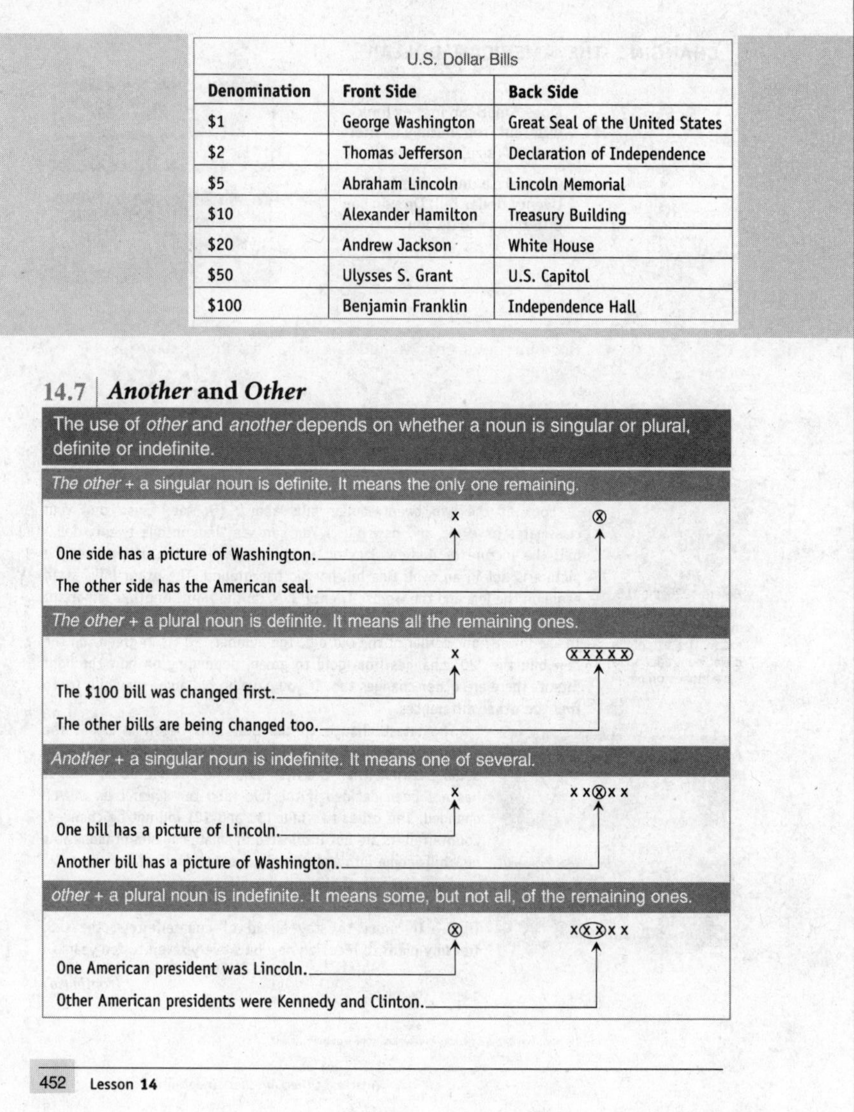

U.S. Dollar Bills

Denomination	Front Side	Back Side
$1	George Washington	Great Seal of the United States
$2	Thomas Jefferson	Declaration of Independence
$5	Abraham Lincoln	Lincoln Memorial
$10	Alexander Hamilton	Treasury Building
$20	Andrew Jackson	White House
$50	Ulysses S. Grant	U.S. Capitol
$100	Benjamin Franklin	Independence Hall

14.7 | *Another* and *Other*

The use of *other* and *another* depends on whether a noun is singular or plural, definite or indefinite.

The other + a singular noun is definite. It means the only one remaining.

One side has a picture of Washington.
The other side has the American seal.

The other + a plural noun is definite. It means all the remaining ones.

The $100 bill was changed first.
The other bills are being changed too.

Another + a singular noun is indefinite. It means one of several.

One bill has a picture of Lincoln.
Another bill has a picture of Washington.

other + a plural noun is indefinite. It means some, but not all, of the remaining ones.

One American president was Lincoln.
Other American presidents were Kennedy and Clinton.

452 Lesson 14

Expansion

Grammar Ask students to go back to the reading on page 451. Say: *See if you can find examples in the reading to match the explanations in the grammar box (On* ***the other one****, the picture is not in an oval.* ***Another*** *important* ***change*** *is in the color. There are* ***other changes****, too. If you have an old bill and a new bill, try to find* ***the other differences****.).*

14.8 | More About *Another* and *Other*

Examples	Explanation
One change is the color. Another **one** is the frame around the face. The two-dollar bill is not common. The other **ones** are common.	We can use pronouns, *one* or *ones*, in place of the noun.
The two-dollar bill is not common. The **others** are common.	When the plural noun or pronoun (*ones*) is omitted, change *other* to *others*.
I have two bank accounts. One is for savings. **My other** account is for checking.	*The* is omitted when we use a possessive form. *Wrong:* My *the* other account is for checking.
I'm busy now. Can you come **another** time? Can you come **any other** time? Can you come **some other** time?	After *some* or *any*, *another* is changed to *other.* *Wrong:* Can you come *any* another time?
This dollar bill is old. You can't put it in the vending machine. You have to use **another** one.	*Another* is sometimes used to mean a different one.

EXERCISE 12 Fill in the blanks with *the other, another, the others, others,* or *other.*

EXAMPLE One side of the one-dollar bill has a picture of George Washington. ___*The other*___ side has a picture of the American seal.

1. Some bills were changed in 2003. ___*Other*___ bills were changed in 2004. Not all bills were changed.
2. Franklin, on the $100 bill, and Hamilton, on the $10 bill, were not American presidents. All ___*the other*___ bills have pictures of American presidents.
3. Franklin was an important person in American history. ___*The other*___ important people were Thomas Jefferson and John Hancock.
4. One bill has a picture of Lincoln. ___*Another*___ one has a picture of George Washington.
5. George Washington was an American president. ___*Other*___ presidents were Lincoln, Roosevelt, and Truman.
6. There were two presidents named Roosevelt. One was Theodore Roosevelt. ___*The other*___ was Franklin Roosevelt.

Articles; *Other/Another;* Indefinite Pronouns 453

14.8 | More About *Another* and *Other*

1. Have students cover up grammar chart **14.8** on page 453. Create a matching exercise:
   1. We can use one *or* ones *in place of the noun.*
   2. When the plural noun or pronoun (ones) is omitted, change other *to* others.
   3. The *is omitted when we use a possessive form.*
   4. After some *or* any, another *is changed to* other.
   5. Another *is sometimes used to mean a different one.*
   a. This dollar bill is old. You have to use another one.
   b. I have two bank accounts. One is for savings. My other account is for checking.
   c. Can you come any other time?
   d. One change is the color. Another one is the frame around the face.
   e. My two-dollar bill is not common. The others are common.
   Say: *Match the example to the explanation.*
2. Then have students look at grammar chart **14.8** on page 453. Say: *Check your work with the chart.* Review all the examples and explanations.

EXERCISE 12

1. Have students read the direction line. Go over the example.
2. Have students complete the exercise individually. Then go over the answers as a class.
3. If necessary, review grammar charts **14.7** on page 452 and **14.8** on page 453.

EXERCISE 13

CD 4, Track 17

1. Say: *In this conversation, a grandfather and his grandson are talking about buying sneakers.* Have students read the direction line. Go over the example.
2. Have students complete the exercise individually. Go over the answers as a class.
3. If necessary, review grammar charts **14.7** on page 452 and **14.8** on page 453.

To save class time, have students do half of the exercise in class and complete the other half for homework. Or assign the entire exercise for homework.

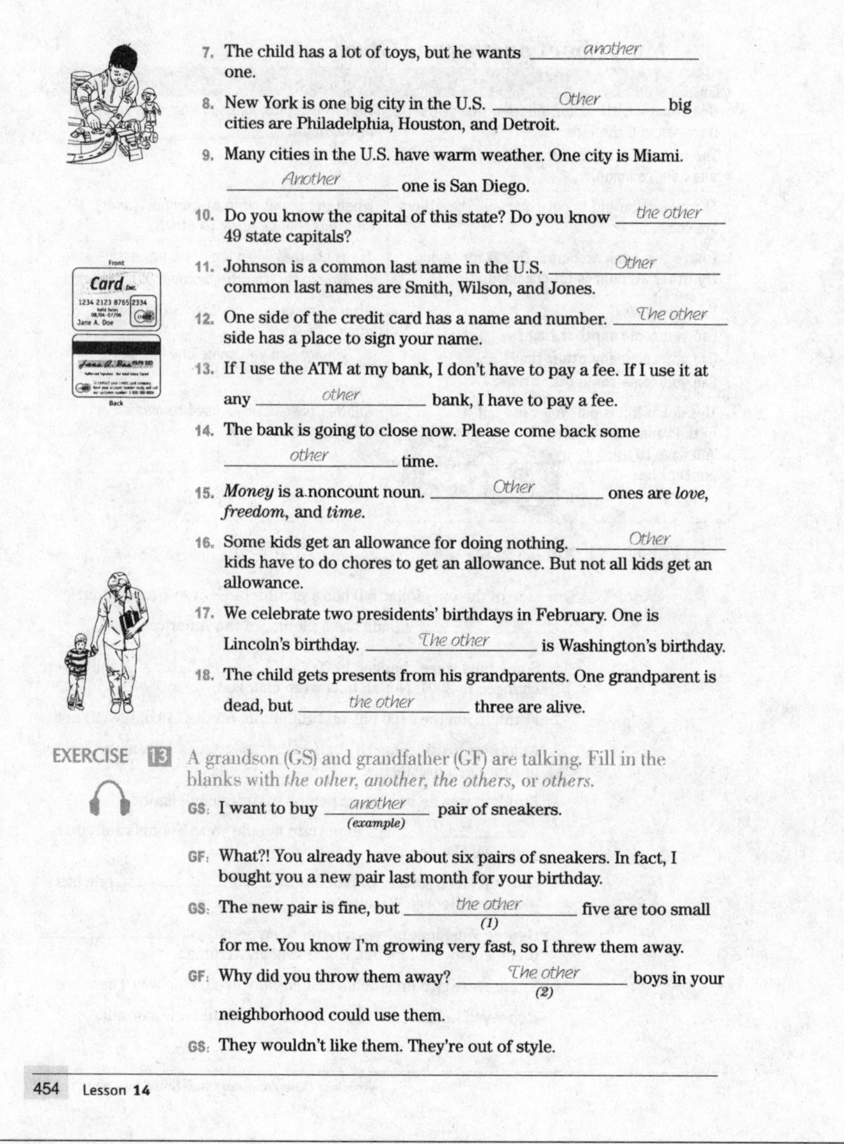

7. The child has a lot of toys, but he wants ___another___ one.
8. New York is one big city in the U.S. ___Other___ big cities are Philadelphia, Houston, and Detroit.
9. Many cities in the U.S. have warm weather. One city is Miami. ___Another___ one is San Diego.
10. Do you know the capital of this state? Do you know ___the other___ 49 state capitals?
11. Johnson is a common last name in the U.S. ___Other___ common last names are Smith, Wilson, and Jones.
12. One side of the credit card has a name and number. ___The other___ side has a place to sign your name.
13. If I use the ATM at my bank, I don't have to pay a fee. If I use it at any ___other___ bank, I have to pay a fee.
14. The bank is going to close now. Please come back some ___other___ time.
15. *Money* is a noncount noun. ___Other___ ones are *love, freedom,* and *time.*
16. Some kids get an allowance for doing nothing. ___Other___ kids have to do chores to get an allowance. But not all kids get an allowance.
17. We celebrate two presidents' birthdays in February. One is Lincoln's birthday. ___The other___ is Washington's birthday.
18. The child gets presents from his grandparents. One grandparent is dead, but ___the other___ three are alive.

EXERCISE 13 A grandson (GS) and grandfather (GF) are talking. Fill in the blanks with *the other, another, the others,* or *others.*

GS: I want to buy ___another___ *(example)* pair of sneakers.

GF: What?! You already have about six pairs of sneakers. In fact, I bought you a new pair last month for your birthday.

GS: The new pair is fine, but ___the other___ (1) five are too small for me. You know I'm growing very fast, so I threw them away.

GF: Why did you throw them away? ___The other___ (2) boys in your neighborhood could use them.

GS: They wouldn't like them. They're out of style.

454 Lesson 14

Exercise 13 Variation

To provide practice with listening skills, have students close their books and listen to the audio. Repeat the audio as needed. Say: *In this conversation, a grandfather and his grandson are talking about buying sneakers.* Ask comprehension questions, such as: *How many pairs of sneakers does the boy have?* (six) *How many pairs of sneakers don't fit him anymore?* (five) *What's wrong with the other pair?* (They're not in style anymore.) *What does the grandfather think he should do with the shoes that don't fit?* (He thinks the boy should give them to other boys in the neighborhood.) Then have students open their books and complete Exercise 13.

GF: You kids are so wasteful today. What's wrong with the sneakers I bought you last month? If they fit you, why do you need ___another___ (3) pair?

GS: Everybody in my class at school has red sneakers with the laces tied backward. The sneakers you gave me are not in style any more.

GF: Do you always have to have what all ___the other___ (4) kids in school have? Can't you think for yourself?

GS: Didn't you ask your parents for stuff when you were in junior high?

GF: My parents were poor, and my two brothers and I worked to help them. When we couldn't wear our clothes anymore because we outgrew them, we gave them to ___other___ (5) families nearby. And our neighbors gave us the things that their children outgrew. One neighbor had two sons. One son was a year older than me. ___The other___ (6) one was two years younger. So we were constantly passing clothes back and forth.

GS: What about style? When clothes went out of style, didn't you throw them out?

GF: No. We never threw things out. Styles were not as important to us then. We didn't waste our parents' money thinking of styles. In fact, my oldest brother worked in a factory and gave all his salary to our parents. My ___other___ (7) brother and I helped our father in his business. My dad didn't give us a salary or an allowance. It was our duty to help him.

GS: You don't understand how important it is to look like all ___the other___ (8) kids.

GF: I guess I don't. I'm old fashioned. Every generation has ___another___ (9) way of looking at things.

Expansion

Exercise 13 Have students practice the conversation in pairs. Then ask volunteers to role-play all or part of the conversation in front of the class.

The High Cost of a College Education (Reading)

1. Have students look at the photo on page 456. Ask: *What's going on in this photo?* (A father and son are having a serious conversation about something.)
2. Have students look at the title of the reading. Ask: *What is the reading about?* Have students use the title and photo to make predictions about the reading.
3. Preteach any vocabulary words your students may not know such as *potential* and *diploma*.

BEFORE YOU READ

1. Have students discuss the questions in pairs.
2. Ask for a few volunteers to share their answers with the class.

To save class time, skip "Before You Read" or have students prepare answers for homework ahead of time.

Reading *CD 4, Track 18*

1. Have students first read the text silently. Tell them to pay attention to *one, some, any, it,* and *them.* Then play the audio and have students read along silently.
2. Check students' comprehension. Ask questions such as: *Why is the father concerned?* (His son is telling him that he doesn't want to go to college.) *Why does the father want his son to go to college?* (He'll earn a better living with a college degree. He'll earn more money in his lifetime.) *How will he pay for college?* (The father has been saving money since his son was born.) *What else will the son need to do in order to pay for college?* (He'll need to get a scholarship and apply for grants and loans.)

To save class time, have students do the reading for homework ahead of time.

DID YOU KNOW?

The federal government provides about 70 percent of all financial aid for postsecondary education. In 2005, federal aid will be more than 60 billion dollars.

THE HIGH COST OF A COLLEGE EDUCATION

Before You Read

1. Have you received any financial aid to take this course?
2. Do you know how much it costs to get a college degree in the U.S.?

Read the following conversation between a son (S) and a dad (D). Pay attention to *one, some, any* (indefinite pronouns) and *it* and *them* (definite pronouns).

S: I decided not to go to college, Dad.
D: What? Do you know how important a college education is?
S: College is expensive. Besides, if I don't go to college now, I can start making money immediately. As soon as I earn **some,** I'd like to buy a car. Besides, my friends aren't going to college.
D: I'm not concerned about **them.** I'm interested in you and your future. I was just reading an article in a magazine about how much more money a college graduate earns than a high school graduate. Here's the article. Look at **it.** It says, "According to U.S. Census Bureau statistics, people with a bachelor's degree earn over 60 percent more than those with only a high school diploma. Over a lifetime, the gap in earning potential between a high school diploma and a B.A. (or higher) is more than $1,000,000."
S: Wow. I never realized that I could earn much more with a college degree than without **one.** Look. But the article also says, "In the 2003-2004 school year, the average tuition at a four-year private college was $27,000, and at a four-year public college, it was $10,000." How can you afford to send me to college?

Did You Know?

In 2002, about 60 percent of undergraduates received some form of financial aid: grants, loans, and scholarships.

Reading Variation

To practice listening skills, have students first listen to the audio alone. Ask a few comprehension questions. Repeat the audio if necessary. Then have them open their books and read along as they listen to the audio.

Reading Glossary

diploma: an academic certificate; an official paper stating that someone has passed a course of study
potential: capacity to be or do something

D: I didn't just start to think about your college education today. I started to think about **it** when you were born. We saved money each month to buy a house, and we bought **one**. And we saved **some** each month for your college tuition.

S: That's great, Dad.

D: I also want you to apply for financial aid. There are grants, loans, and scholarships you should also look into. Your grades are good. I think you should apply for a scholarship.

S: I'll need to get an application.

D: I already thought of that. I brought **one** home today. Let's fill **it** out together.

S: Dad, if a college degree is so important to you, why didn't you get **one?**

D: When I was your age, we didn't live in the U.S. We were very poor and had to help our parents. You have a lot of opportunities for grants and scholarships, but we didn't have **any** when I was young.

S: Thanks for thinking about this from the day I was born.

Grants and Scholarships

Grants and scholarships provide aid that does not have to be repaid. However, some require that recipients maintain good grades or take certain courses.

Loans

Loans are another type of financial aid and are available to both students and parents. Like a car loan or a mortgage for a house, an education loan must eventually be repaid. Often, payments do not begin until the student finishes school. The interest rate on education loans is commonly lower than for other types of loans.

Source: http://www.ed.gov/pubs

Amount You Would Need to Save to Have $10,000 Available When Your Child Begins College

(Assuming a 5 percent interest rate.)

			Amount Available When Child Begins College		
If you start saving when your child is	Number of years of saving	Approximate monthly savings	Principal	Interest earned	Total savings
Newborn	18	$29	$6,197	$3,803	$10,000
Age 4	14	41	6,935	3,065	10,000
Age 8	10	64	7,736	2,264	10,000
Age 12	6	119	8,601	1,399	10,000
Age 16	2	397	9,531	469	10,000

Source of chart: http://www.ed.gov/pubs/Prepare/pt4.html

14.9 | Definite and Indefinite Pronouns

1. Have students cover up grammar chart **14.9** on page 458. Create an exercise on the board:
   1. I've always thought about your education. I started to think about ________ when you were born.
   2. I received two college applications. I have to fill ________ out.
   3. A college degree is important. It's hard to make a lot of money without ________.
   4. The father knew it was important to save money. He saved ________ every month.
   5. You received five brochures for colleges. Did you read ________?
   Say: *Complete the sentences with* some, any, one, it, *or* them.
2. Then have students look at grammar chart **14.9** on page 458. Say: *Check your work with the chart.* Review all the examples and explanations.
3. Direct students to the Language Note. Say: *We often use* any *and* some *before* more. Go over the examples.

EXERCISE 14

CD 4, Track 19

1. Have students read the direction line. Then have students look at the photo on page 459. Ask: *What's going on in this photo?* (The mother looks like she's showing her daughter something. They look serious.) Go over the example.
2. Have students complete the exercise individually. Go over the answers as a class.
3. If necessary, review grammar chart **14.9** on page 458.

14.9 | Definite and Indefinite Pronouns

Examples	Explanation
I've always thought about <u>your education</u>. I started to think about **it** when you were born. I received <u>two college applications</u>. I have to fill **them** out. The father wants <u>his son</u> to go to college. The father is going to help **him.**	We use definite pronouns *him, her, them,* and *it* to refer to definite count nouns.
<u>A college degree</u> is important. It's hard to make a lot of money without **one.** I don't have <u>a scholarship</u>. I hope I can get **one.**	We use the indefinite pronoun *one* to refer to an indefinite singular count noun.
a. The father knew it was important to save <u>money</u>. He saved **some** every month. b. You received <u>five brochures</u> for colleges. Did you read **any?** c. You have a lot of <u>opportunities</u> today. When I was your age, we didn't have **any.**	We use *some* (for affirmative statements) and *any* (for negative statements and questions) to refer to an indefinite noncount noun (a) or an indefinite plural count noun (b) and (c).

Language Note:
We often use *any* and *some* before *more.*
Dad, I don't have enough money. I need **some more.**
Son, I'm not going to give you **any more.**

EXERCISE 14 A mother (M) is talking to her teenage daughter (D) about art school. Fill in the blanks with *one* or *it.*

M: I have some information about the state university. Do you want to look at ___it___ *(example)* with me?

D: I don't know, Mom. I don't know if I'm ready to go to college when I graduate.

M: Why not? We've been planning for ___it___ *(1)* since the day you were born.

D: College is not for everyone. I want to be an artist.

M: You can go to college and major in art. I checked out information about the art curriculum at the state university. It seems to have a very good program. Do you want to see information about ___it___ *(2)*?

D: I'm not really interested in college. To be an artist, I don't need a college degree.

Exercise 14 Variation

To provide practice with listening skills, have students close their books and listen to the audio. Repeat the audio as needed. Say: *In this conversation, a mother and her teenage daughter are talking about art school.* Ask comprehension questions, such as: *What does the mother want her daughter to do?* (look at information about the state university) *Why doesn't the daughter want to do it?* (She doesn't want to go to college. She wants to go to art school.) *What does the mother suggest she do?* (look at art schools) Then have students open their books and complete Exercise 14.

M: But it's good to have ___one___ anyway.
(3)

D: I don't know why. In college, I'll have to study general courses, too, like math and biology. You know I hate math. I'm not good at ___it___.
(4)

M: Well, maybe we should look at art schools. There's one downtown. Do you want to visit ___it___?
(5)

D: Yes, I'd like to. We can probably find information about ___it___ on the Web too.
(6)

(*looking at the art school's Web site*)

D: This school sounds great. Let's call and ask for an application.

M: I think you can get ___it___ online. Oh, yes, here it is.
(7)

D: Let's make a copy of ___it___.
(8)

M: You can fill ___it___ out online and submit ___it___ electronically.
(9) (10)

Expansion

Exercise 14 Have students practice the conversation in pairs. Ask volunteers to perform all or part of the conversation in front of the class.

EXERCISE 15

1. Have students read the direction line. Go over the examples.
2. Have students complete the exercise in pairs. Circulate to observe pair work. Give help as needed.
3. If necessary, review grammar chart **14.9** on page 458.

To save class time, have students do half of the exercise in class and complete the other half in writing for homework, answering the questions themselves. Or if students do not need speaking practice, the entire exercise may be skipped or done in writing.

EXERCISE 16

CD 4, Track 20

1. Say: *In this conversation, a mother and her daughter talk about the value of money.* Have students read the direction line. Go over the example.
2. Have students complete the exercise individually. Go over the answers as a class.
3. If necessary, review **Lesson 14.**

To save class time, have students do half of the exercise in class and complete the other half for homework. Or assign the entire exercise for homework.

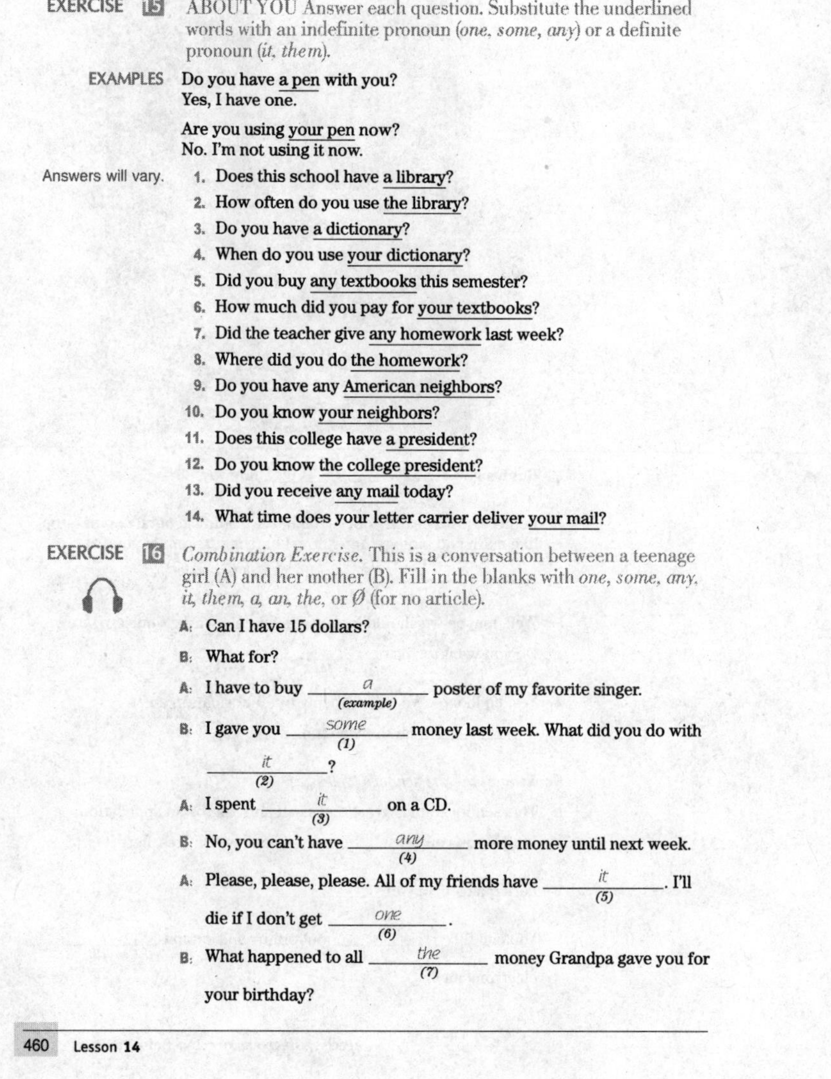

EXERCISE 15 ABOUT YOU Answer each question. Substitute the underlined words with an indefinite pronoun (*one, some, any*) or a definite pronoun (*it, them*).

EXAMPLES Do you have a pen with you?
Yes, I have one.

Are you using your pen now?
No. I'm not using it now.

Answers will vary.

1. Does this school have a library?
2. How often do you use the library?
3. Do you have a dictionary?
4. When do you use your dictionary?
5. Did you buy any textbooks this semester?
6. How much did you pay for your textbooks?
7. Did the teacher give any homework last week?
8. Where did you do the homework?
9. Do you have any American neighbors?
10. Do you know your neighbors?
11. Does this college have a president?
12. Do you know the college president?
13. Did you receive any mail today?
14. What time does your letter carrier deliver your mail?

EXERCISE 16 *Combination Exercise.* This is a conversation between a teenage girl (A) and her mother (B). Fill in the blanks with *one, some, any, it, them, a, an, the,* or *Ø* (for no article).

A: Can I have 15 dollars?

B: What for?

A: I have to buy ___*a*___ *(example)* poster of my favorite singer.

B: I gave you ___*some*___ *(1)* money last week. What did you do with ___*it*___ *(2)*?

A: I spent ___*it*___ *(3)* on a CD.

B: No, you can't have ___*any*___ *(4)* more money until next week.

A: Please, please, please. All of my friends have ___*it*___ *(5)*. I'll die if I don't get ___*one*___ *(6)*.

B: What happened to all ___*the*___ *(7)* money Grandpa gave you for your birthday?

460 Lesson 14

Expansion

Exercise 15 Take turns asking and answering the questions with a partner.

Exercise 16 Variation

To provide practice with listening skills, have students close their books and listen to the audio. Repeat the audio as needed. Say: *In this conversation, a mother and her daughter talk about the value of money.* Ask comprehension questions, such as: *Why does the daughter want money?* (She wants to buy a poster.) *What happened to all the money she received from graduation and her grandfather?* (She spent all of it.) *What does the mother suggest she do?* (She wants her daughter to work for the money.) Then have students open their books and complete Exercise 16.

A: I spent ___it___ (8).

B: What about ___the___ (9) money you put in the bank after your graduation?

A: I don't have ___any___ (10) more money in the bank.

B: You have to learn that ___ø___ (11) money doesn't grow on trees. If you want me to give you ___some___ (12), you'll have to work for it. You can start by cleaning your room.

A: But I cleaned ___it___ (13) two weeks ago.

B: Two weeks ago was two weeks ago. It's dirty again.

A: I don't have ___any___ (14) time. I have to meet my friends.

B: You can't go out. You need to do your homework.

A: I don't have ___any___ (15). Please let me have 15 dollars.

B: When I was your age, I had ___a___ (16) job. And I gave my parents half of ___the___ (17) money I earned. You kids today have ___an___ (18) easy life.

A: Why do ___ø___ (19) parents always say that to ___ø___ (20) kids?

B: Because it's true. It's time you learn that ___ø___ (21) life is hard.

A: I bet Grandpa said that to you when you were ___a___ (22) child.

B: And I bet you'll say it to your kids when you're ___an___ (23) adult.

Expansion

Exercise 16 Have students practice the conversation in pairs. Ask volunteers to perform all or part of the conversation in front of the class.

Exercise 16 Have students work in pairs to write similar conversations using their own information. Ask volunteers to perform all or part of the conversation in front of the class.

Summary of Lesson 14

1. **Articles** Have students cover up the Summary of Lesson 14. Create a fill-in exercise on the board:
   1. ________ child likes toys.
   2. I love ________ children.
   3. Everyone needs ________ money.
   4. I bought ________ toy.
   5. I bought ________ toys.
   6. I didn't buy ________ games.
   Say: *Fill in the blanks with* a/an, some, any, the, *or Ø if no article is needed.* If necessary, have students review:
   14.1 Articles—An Overview (p. 438)
   14.2 The Indefinite Article—Classifying or Identifying the Subject (p. 439)
   14.3 The Indefinite Article—Introducing a Noun (p. 440)
   14.4 The Definite Article (p. 443)
   14.5 Making Generalizations (p. 445).
2. ***Other/Another*** Have students cover up the summary on page 462. On one side of the board, reproduce the chart without the phrases. On the other side of the board, list the phrases in random order. For example:
   the other book
   other books
   my other books
   the other
   Ask: *Where does each phrase belong? Put the phrases in the correct box: singular/definite; plural/definite; singular/indefinite; plural/indefinite.* If necessary, have students review:
   14.7 *Another* and *Other* (p. 452)
   14.8 More About *Another* and *Other* (p. 453).
3. **Indefinite Pronouns** Have students cover up the summary on page 462. Write the following on the board:
   I need a quarter. Do you have ________?
   I need some pennies. You have ________.
   I don't have any change. Do you have ________?
   Say: *Fill in the blanks with the correct indefinite pronouns.*
   If necessary, have students review:
   14.9 Definite and Indefinite Pronouns (p. 458).

SUMMARY OF LESSON 14

1. Articles

	Count—Singular	Count—Plural	Noncount
General	*A/An* **A child** likes toys.	*Ø Article* **Children** like toys. I love **children.**	*Ø Article* **Money** can't buy happiness. Everyone needs **money.**
Indefinite	*A/An* I bought **a toy.**	*Some/Any* I bought **some toys.** I didn't buy **any games.**	*Some/Any* I spent **some money.** I didn't buy **any candy.**
Specific	*The* **The toy** on the floor is for the baby.	*The* **The toys** on the table are for you.	*The* **The money** on the table is mine.
Classification	*A/An* A toddler is **a young child.**	*Ø Article* Teenagers are **young adults.**	——

2. *Other / Another*

	Definite	Indefinite
Singular	the other book my other book the other one the other	another book some/any other book another one another
Plural	the other books my other books the other ones the others	other books some/any other books other ones others

3. Indefinite Pronouns—Use *one / some / any* to substitute for indefinite nouns.
   I need a quarter. Do you have **one?**
   I need some pennies. You have **some.**
   I don't have any change. Do you have **any?**

462 Lesson 14

EDITING ADVICE

1. Use *the* after a quantity word when the noun is definite.

   Most of ^the^ students in my class are from Romania.

2. Be careful with *most* and *almost*.

   ~~Almost~~ Most of my teachers are very patient.

3. Use a plural count noun after a quantity expression.

   A few of my friend^s^ live in Canada.

4. *Another* is always singular.

   Some teachers are strict. ~~Another~~ Other teachers are easy.

5. Use an indefinite pronoun to substitute for an indefinite noun.

   I need to borrow a pen. I didn't bring ~~it~~ one today.

6. *A* and *an* are always singular.

   She has ~~a~~ beautiful eyes.

7. Don't use *there* to introduce a unique, definite noun.

   ~~There's~~ The Statue of Liberty ^is^ in New York.

8. Use *a* or *an* for a definition or a classification of a singular count noun.

   The Statue of Liberty is ^a^ monument.

9. Don't use *the* with a possessive form.

   One of my sisters lives in New York. My ~~the~~ other sister lives in New Jersey.

Editing Advice

Have students close their books. Write the example sentences without editing marks or corrections on the board. For example:

1. *Most of students in my class are from Romania.*
2. *Almost my teachers are very patient.*

Ask students to correct each sentence and provide a rule or an explanation for each correction. This activity can be done individually, in pairs, or as a class. After students have corrected each sentence, tell them to turn to page 463. Say: *Now compare your work with the Editing Advice in the book.*

Lesson 14 Test/Review

For additional practice, review, and assessment materials, see Assessment CD-ROM with *ExamView Pro*, *More Grammar Practice* Workbook 2, Interactive CD-ROM, and Web site http://elt.thomson.com/gic

PART 1

1. Part 1 may be used as an in-class test to assess student performance, in addition to the Assessment CD-ROM with *ExamView Pro*. Have students read the direction line. Ask: *Do all sentences have a mistake?* (no) Go over the examples. Collect for assessment.
2. If necessary, have students review: **Lesson 14.**

PART 2

1. Part 2 may also be used as an in-class test to assess student performance, in addition to the Assessment CD-ROM with *ExamView Pro*. Have students read the direction line. Collect for assessment.
2. If necessary, have students review:
   14.3 The Indefinite Article—Introducing a Noun (p. 440)
   14.5 Making Generalizations (p. 445).

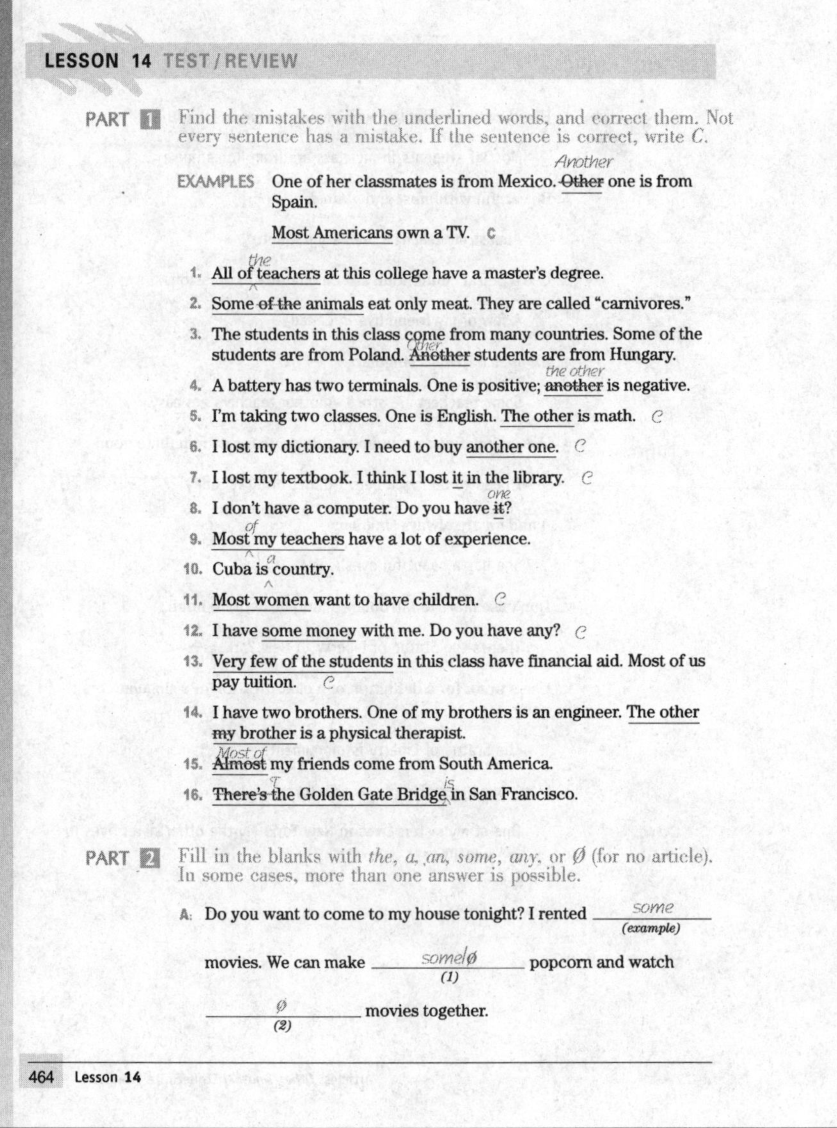

LESSON 14 TEST/REVIEW

PART 1 Find the mistakes with the underlined words, and correct them. Not every sentence has a mistake. If the sentence is correct, write *C*.

EXAMPLES One of her classmates is from Mexico. ~~Other~~ *Another* one is from Spain.

Most Americans own a TV. C

1. All of *the* teachers at this college have a master's degree.
2. Some ~~of the~~ animals eat only meat. They are called "carnivores."
3. The students in this class come from many countries. Some of the students are from Poland. ~~Another~~ *Other* students are from Hungary.
4. A battery has two terminals. One is positive; ~~another~~ *the other* is negative.
5. I'm taking two classes. One is English. The other is math. *C*
6. I lost my dictionary. I need to buy another one. *C*
7. I lost my textbook. I think I lost it in the library. *C*
8. I don't have a computer. Do you have ~~it~~ *one*?
9. Most *of* my teachers have a lot of experience.
10. Cuba is *a* country.
11. Most women want to have children. *C*
12. I have some money with me. Do you have any? *C*
13. Very few of the students in this class have financial aid. Most of us pay tuition. *C*
14. I have two brothers. One of my brothers is an engineer. The other ~~my brother~~ is a physical therapist.
15. ~~Almost~~ *Most of* my friends come from South America.
16. ~~There's~~ *T*he Golden Gate Bridge *is* in San Francisco.

PART 2 Fill in the blanks with *the, a, an, some, any,* or Ø (for no article). In some cases, more than one answer is possible.

A: Do you want to come to my house tonight? I rented *some* (example) movies. We can make *some/Ø* (1) popcorn and watch *Ø* (2) movies together.

464 Lesson 14

Lesson Review

To use Part 1 as a review, assign it as homework or use it as an in-class activity to be completed individually or in pairs. Check answers and review errors as a class. Reteach grammar points that students haven't mastered. Then student learning may be assessed using a test generated from the Assessment CD-ROM with *ExamView Pro*.

B: Thanks, but I'm going to ___a (3)___ party. Do you want to go with me?

A: Where's it going to be?

B: It's going to be at Michael's apartment.

A: Who's going to be at ___the (4)___ party?

B: Most of ___the (5)___ students in my English class will be there. Each student is going to bring ___some/ø (6)___ food.

A: ___ø (7)___ life in the U.S. is strange. In my country, ___ø (8)___ people don't have to bring ___ø (9)___ food to a party.

B: That's the way it is in my country, too. But we're in ___the (10)___ U.S. now. I'm going to bake ___a (11)___ cake. You can make ___a (12)___ special dish from your country.

A: You know I'm ___a (13)___ terrible cook.

B: Don't worry. You can buy something. My friend Max is going to buy ___some/ø (14)___ crackers and cheese. Why don't you bring ___ø/some (15)___ salami or roast beef?

A: But I don't eat ___ø (16)___ meat. I'm ___a (17)___ vegetarian.

B: Well, you can bring ___a (18)___ bowl of fruit.

A: That's ___a (19)___ good idea. What time does ___the (20)___ party start?

B: At 8 o'clock.

A: I have to take my brother to ___the (21)___ airport at 6:30. I don't know if I'll be back on time.

B: You don't have to arrive at 8 o'clock exactly. I'll give you ___the (22)___ address, and you can arrive any time you want.

Lesson Review

To use Part 2 as a review, assign it as homework or use it as an in-class activity to be completed individually or in pairs. Check answers and review errors as a class. Reteach grammar points that students haven't mastered. Then student learning may be assessed using a test generated from the Assessment CD-ROM with *ExamView Pro*.

PART 3

1. Part 3 may also be used as an in-class test to assess student performance, in addition to the Assessment CD-ROM with *ExamView Pro*. Have students read the direction line. Collect for assessment.
2. If necessary, have students review:
   14.7 *Another* and *Other* (p. 452)
   14.8 More About *Another* and *Other* (p. 453).

PART 4

1. Part 4 may also be used as an in-class test to assess student performance, in addition to the Assessment CD-ROM with *ExamView Pro*. Have students read the direction line. Collect for assessment.
2. If necessary, have students review:
   14.9 Definite and Indefinite Pronouns (p. 458).

PART 3 Fill in the blanks with *other, others, another, the other,* or *the others.*

A: I don't like my apartment.

B: Why not?

A: It's very small. It only has two closets. One is big, but *the other* (example) is very small.

B: That's not very serious. Is that the only problem? Are there *other* (1) problems?

A: There are many *others* (2).

B: Such as?

A: Well, the landlord doesn't provide enough heat in the winter.

B: Hmm. That's a real problem. Did you complain to him?

A: I did, but he says that all *the other* (3) tenants are happy.

B: Why don't you look for *another* (4) apartment?

A: I have two roommates. One wants to move, but *the other* (5) likes it here.

B: Well, if one wants to stay and *the other* (6) two want to move, why don't you move and look for *another* (7) roommate?

PART 4 Fill in the blanks with *one, some, any, it,* or *them.*

EXAMPLE I have a computer, but my roommate doesn't have *one*.

1. Do you want to use my bicycle? I won't need *it* this afternoon.
2. I rented a movie. We can watch *it* tonight.
3. My English teacher gives some homework every day, but she doesn't give *any* on the weekends.
4. My class has a lot of Mexican students. Does your class have *any*?

466 Lesson 14

Lesson Review

To use Part 3 as a review, assign it as homework or use it as an in-class activity to be completed individually or in pairs. Check answers and review errors as a class. Reteach grammar points that students haven't mastered. Then student learning may be assessed using a test generated from the Assessment CD-ROM with *ExamView Pro*.

5. I wrote two compositions last week, but I got bad grades because I wrote ___them___ very quickly.

6. I don't have any problems with English, but my roommate has ___some___.

7. I can't remember the teacher's name. Do you remember ___it___?

8. You won't need any paper for the test, but you'll need ___some___ for the composition.

9. I went to the library to find some books in my language, but I couldn't find ___any___.

EXPANSION ACTIVITIES

Classroom Activities

1. Fill in the blanks with *all, most, some, a few*, or *very few* to make a general statement about your native country or another country you know well. Find a partner from a different country, if possible, and compare your answers.

a. ______________ banks are safe places to put your money.

b. ______________ doctors make a lot of money.

c. ______________ teenagers work.

d. ______________ children work.

e. ______________ teachers are rich.

f. ______________ government officials are rich.

g. ______________ children get an allowance.

h. ______________ people work on Saturdays.

i. ______________ businesses are closed on Sundays.

j. ______________ families own a car.

k. ______________ women work outside the home.

l. ______________ people have a college education.

m. ______________ people have servants.

n. ______________ married couples have their own apartment.

o. ______________ old people live with their grown children.

p. ______________ people speak English.

q. ______________ children study English in school.

r. ______________ parents have more than five children.

Expansion Activities

These expansion activities provide opportunities for students to interact with one another and further develop their speaking and writing skills. Encourage students to use grammar from this lesson whenever possible.

To save class time, assign parts of the activities as homework. Then use class time for interaction and communication. If students do not need additional speaking practice, some of the activities may be assigned as writing activities for homework or skipped altogether.

CLASSROOM ACTIVITIES

1. First have students fill out the chart individually. Then have students compare charts in pairs.

Lesson Review

To use Part 4 as a review, assign it as homework or use it as an in-class activity to be completed individually or in pairs. Check answers and review errors as a class. Reteach grammar points that students haven't mastered. Then student learning may be assessed using a test generated from the Assessment CD-ROM with *ExamView Pro*.

CLASSROOM ACTIVITIES (*cont.*)

2. If possible, have coins and bills from various countries on hand in the event that some students forget theirs.

TALK ABOUT IT

1. Have students discuss each saying in pairs, in groups, or as a class.
2. Have students discuss this topic in small groups. Then have groups report to the class with suggestions for saving money.
3. Have students discuss the meaning of this saying, as well as whether they agree or disagree with it.

WRITE ABOUT IT

Before students begin writing, have a quick class discussion on the topic. Have students share their experiences and opinions. Write some important points from the discussion on the board.

INTERNET ACTIVITIES

Remind students that if they don't have Internet access, they can use Internet facilities at a public library, or they can use traditional research methods to find out information, including looking at encyclopedias, magazines, books, journals, and newspapers.

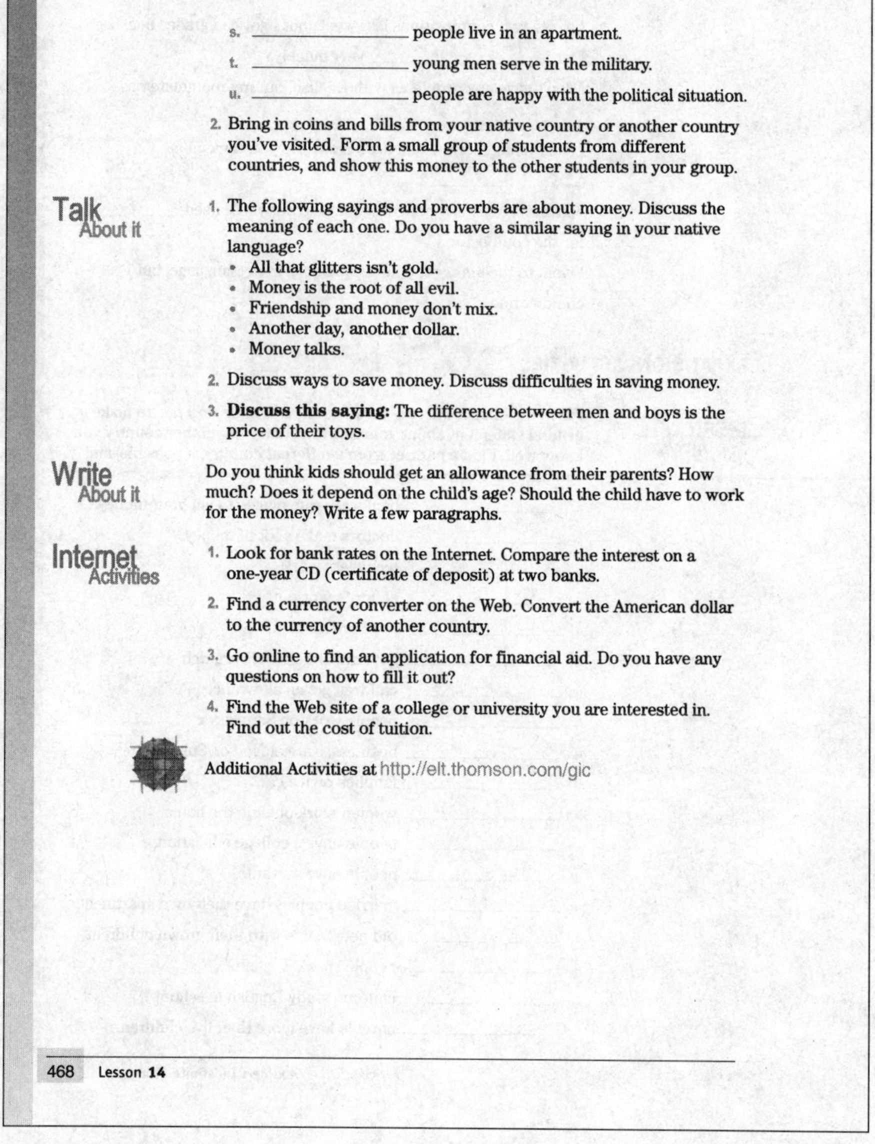

s. ______________ people live in an apartment.

t. ______________ young men serve in the military.

u. ______________ people are happy with the political situation.

2. Bring in coins and bills from your native country or another country you've visited. Form a small group of students from different countries, and show this money to the other students in your group.

Talk About it

1. The following sayings and proverbs are about money. Discuss the meaning of each one. Do you have a similar saying in your native language?
   - All that glitters isn't gold.
   - Money is the root of all evil.
   - Friendship and money don't mix.
   - Another day, another dollar.
   - Money talks.
2. Discuss ways to save money. Discuss difficulties in saving money.
3. **Discuss this saying:** The difference between men and boys is the price of their toys.

Write About it

Do you think kids should get an allowance from their parents? How much? Does it depend on the child's age? Should the child have to work for the money? Write a few paragraphs.

Internet Activities

1. Look for bank rates on the Internet. Compare the interest on a one-year CD (certificate of deposit) at two banks.
2. Find a currency converter on the Web. Convert the American dollar to the currency of another country.
3. Go online to find an application for financial aid. Do you have any questions on how to fill it out?
4. Find the Web site of a college or university you are interested in. Find out the cost of tuition.

Additional Activities at http://elt.thomson.com/gic

468 Lesson 14

Expansion

Write About it Have students exchange first drafts with a partner. Ask students to help their partners edit their drafts. Refer students to the Editing Advice on page 463.

Appendices

APPENDIX A

Spelling and Pronunciation of Verbs

Spelling of the *-s* Form of Verbs		
Rule	**Base Form**	***-s* Form**
Add *s* to most verbs to make the *-s* form.	hope eat	hopes eats
When the base form ends in *s, z, sh, ch,* or *x*, add *es* and pronounce an extra syllable, /əz/.	miss buzz wash catch fix	misses buzzes washes catches fixes
When the base form ends in a consonant + *y*, change the *y* to *i* and add *es*.	carry worry	carries worries
When the base form ends in a vowel + *y*, do not change the *y*.	pay obey	pays obeys
Add *es* to *go* and *do*.	go do	goes does

Three Pronunciations of the *-s* Form		
We pronounce **/s/** if the verb ends in these voiceless sounds: **/p t k f/**.	hope—hopes eat—eats	pick—picks laugh—laughs
We pronounce **/z/** if the verb ends in most voiced sounds.	live—lives grab—grabs read—reads	run—runs sing—sings borrow—borrows
When the base form ends in *s, z, sh, ch, x, se, ge,* or *ce,* we pronounce an extra syllable, /əz/.	miss—misses buzz—buzzes wash—washes watch—watches	fix—fixes use—uses change—changes dance—dances
These verbs have a change in the vowel sound.	do/**du**/—does/**dəz**/	say/**sei**/—says/**sez**/

Spelling of the *-ing* Form of Verbs

Rule	Base Form	-*s* Form
Add *-ing* to most verbs. **Note:** Do not remove the *y* for the *-ing* form.	eat go study	eating going studying
For a one-syllable verb that ends in a consonant + vowel + consonant (CVC), double the final consonant and add *-ing*.	p l a n (C V C) s t o p (C V C) s i t (C V C)	planning stopping sitting
Do not double the final *w*, *x*, or *y*.	show mix stay	showing mixing staying
For a two-syllable word that ends in CVC, double the final consonant only if the last syllable is stressed.	refér admít begín	referring admitting beginning
When the last syllable of a two-syllable word is not stressed, do not double the final consonant.	lísten ópen óffer	listening opening offering
If the word ends in a consonant + *e*, drop the *e* before adding *-ing*.	live take write	living taking writing

Spelling of the Past Tense of Regular Verbs

Rule	Base Form	*-ed* Form
Add *ed* to the base form to make the past tense of most regular verbs.	start kick	started kicked
When the base form ends in *e*, add *d* only.	die live	died lived
When the base form ends in a consonant + *y*, change the *y* to *i* and add *ed*.	carry worry	carried worried
When the base form ends in a vowel + *y*, do not change the *y*.	destroy stay	destroyed stayed
For a one-syllable word that ends in a consonant + vowel + consonant (CVC), double the final consonant and add *ed*.	s t o p C V C p l u g C V C	stopped plugged
Do not double the final *w* or *x*.	sew fix	sewed fixed
For a two-syllable word that ends in CVC, double the final consonant only if the last syllable is stressed.	occúr permít	occurred permitted
When the last syllable of a two-syllable word is not stressed, do not double the final consonant.	ópen háppen	opened happened

Pronunciation of Past Forms that End in *-ed*

The past tense with *-ed* has three pronunciations.			
We pronounce a /**t**/ if the base form ends in these voiceless sounds: /**p**, **k**, **f**, **s**, š, č/.	jump—jumped cook—cooked	cough—coughed kiss—kissed	wash—washed watch—watched
We pronounce a /**d**/ if the base form ends in most voiced sounds.	rub—rubbed drag—dragged love—loved bathe—bathed use—used	charge—charged glue—glued massage—massaged name—named learn—learned	bang—banged call—called fear—feared free—freed
We pronounce an extra syllable /ə**d**/ if the base form ends in a /**t**/ or /**d**/ sound.	wait—waited hate—hated	want—wanted add—added	need—needed decide—decided

APPENDIX B

Irregular Noun Plurals

Singular	Plural	Explanation
man woman mouse tooth foot goose	men women mice teeth feet geese	Vowel change (**Note:** The first vowel in *women* is pronounced /I/.)
sheep fish deer	sheep fish deer	No change
child person	children people (OR persons)	Different word form
	(eye)glasses belongings clothes goods groceries jeans pajamas pants/slacks scissors shorts	No singular form
alumnus cactus radius stimulus syllabus	alumni cacti OR cactuses radii stimuli syllabi OR syllabuses	*us* → *i*
analysis crisis hypothesis oasis parenthesis thesis	analyses crises hypotheses oases parentheses theses	*is* → *es*

Continued

Singular	Plural	Explanation
appendix index	appendices OR appendixes indices OR indexes	*ix* → *ices* OR → *ixes*
bacterium curriculum datum medium memorandum criterion phenomenon	bacteria curricula data media memoranda criteria phenomena	*um* → *a* *ion* → *a* *on* → *a*
alga formula vertebra	algae formulae OR formulas vertebrae	*a* → *ae*

APPENDIX C

Spelling Rules for Adverbs Ending in *-ly*

Adjective Ending	Examples	Adverb Ending	Adverb
Most endings	careful quiet serious	Add *-ly*.	carefully quietly seriously
-y	easy happy lucky	Change *y* to *i* and add *-ly*.	easily happily luckily
-e	nice free	Keep the *e* and add *-ly*.*	nicely freely
consonant + *le*	simple comfortable double	Drop the *e* and add *-ly*.	simply comfortably doubly
-ic	basic enthusiastic	Add *-ally*.**	basically enthusiastically

Exceptions:
*true—truly
**public—publicly

APPENDIX D

Metric Conversion Chart

LENGTH				
When You Know	**Symbol**	**Multiply by**	**To Find**	**Symbol**
inches	in	2.54	centimeters	cm
feet	ft	30.5	centimeters	cm
feet	ft	0.3	meters	m
yards	yd	0.91	meters	m
miles	mi	1.6	kilometers	km
Metric:				
centimeters	cm	0.39	inches	in
centimeters	cm	0.03	feet	ft
meters	m	3.28	feet	ft
meters	m	1.09	yards	yd
kilometers	km	0.62	miles	mi

Note:
1 foot = 12 inches; 1 yard = 3 feet or 36 inches

AREA				
When You Know	**Symbol**	**Multiply by**	**To Find**	**Symbol**
square inches	in^2	6.5	square centimeters	cm^2
square feet	ft^2	0.09	square meters	m^2
square yards	yd^2	0.8	square meters	m^2
square miles	mi^2	2.6	square kilometers	km^2
Metric:				
square centimeters	cm^2	0.16	square inches	in^2
square meters	m^2	10.76	square feet	ft^2
square meters	m^2	1.2	square yards	yd^2
square kilometers	km^2	0.39	square miles	mi^2

WEIGHT (Mass)

When You Know	Symbol	Multiply by	To Find	Symbol
ounces	oz	28.35	grams	g
pounds	lb	0.45	kilograms	kg
Metric:				
grams	g	0.04	ounces	oz
kilograms	kg	2.2	pounds	lb

Note:
16 ounces = 1 pound

VOLUME

When You Know	Symbol	Multiply by	To Find	Symbol
fluid ounces	fl oz	30.0	milliliters	ml
pints	pt	0.47	liters	l
quarts	qt	0.95	liters	l
gallons	gal	3.8	liters	l
Metric:				
milliliters	ml	0.03	fluid ounces	fl oz
liters	l	2.11	pints	pt
liters	l	1.05	quarts	qt
liters	l	0.26	gallons	gal

TEMPERATURE

When You Know	Symbol	Do This	To Find	Symbol
degrees Fahrenheit	°F	Subtract 32, then multiply by 5/9	degrees Celsius	°C
Metric:				
degrees Celsius	°C	Multiply by 9/5, then add 32	degrees Fahrenheit	°F

Sample temperatures:

Fahrenheit	Celsius	Fahrenheit	Celsius
0	−18	60	16
10	−12	70	21
20	−7	80	27
30	−1	90	32
40	4	100	38
50	10	212	100

APPENDIX E

The Verb *Get*

Get has many meanings. Here is a list of the most common ones:		
• get something = receive I got a letter from my father.		
• get + (to) place = arrive I got home at six. What time do you get to school?		
• get + object + infinitive = persuade She got him to wash the dishes.		
• get + past participle = become		
get acquainted get engaged get married get divorced get tired	get worried get lost get accustomed to get used to get dressed	get hurt get bored get confused get scared
They got married in 1989.		
• get + adjective = become		
get hungry get rich get nervous get well	get upset get sleepy get fat	get dark get angry get old
It gets dark at 6:30.		
• get an illness = catch While she was traveling, she got malaria.		
• get a joke or an idea = understand Everybody except Tom laughed at the joke. He didn't get it. The boss explained the project to us, but I didn't get it.		
• get ahead = advance He works very hard because he wants to get ahead in his job.		
• get along (well) (with someone) = have a good relationship She doesn't get along with her mother-in-law. Do you and your roommate get along well?		
• get around to something = find the time to do something I wanted to write my brother a letter yesterday, but I didn't get around to it.		
• get away = escape The police chased the thief, but he got away.		

• get away with something = escape punishment He cheated on his taxes and got away with it.
• get back = return He got back from his vacation last Saturday.
• get back at someone = get revenge My brother wants to get back at me for stealing his girlfriend.
• get back to someone = communicate with someone at a later time The boss can't talk to you today. Can she get back to you tomorrow?
• get by = have just enough but nothing more On her salary, she's just getting by. She can't afford a car or a vacation.
• get in trouble = be caught and punished for doing something wrong They got in trouble for cheating on the test.
• get in(to) = enter a car She got in the car and drove away quickly.
• get out (of) = leave a car When the taxi arrived at the theater, everyone got out.
• get on = seat oneself on a bicycle, motorcycle, horse She got on the motorcycle and left.
• get on = enter a train, bus, airplane She got on the bus and took a seat in the back.
• get off = leave a bicycle, motorcycle, horse, train, bus, airplane They will get off the train at the next stop.
• get out of something = escape responsibility My boss wants me to help him on Saturday, but I'm going to try to get out of it.
• get over something = recover from an illness or disappointment She has the flu this week. I hope she gets over it soon.
• get rid of someone or something = free oneself of someone or something undesirable My apartment has roaches, and I can't get rid of them.
• get through (to someone) = communicate, often by telephone She tried to explain the harm of eating fast food to her son, but she couldn't get through to him. I tried to call my mother many times, but her line was busy. I couldn't get through.
• get through with something = finish I can meet you after I get through with my homework.
• get together = meet with another person I'd like to see you again. When can we get together?
• get up = arise from bed He woke up at 6 o'clock, but he didn't get up until 6:30.

APPENDIX F

Make and *Do*

Some expressions use *make*. Others use *do*.

Make	Do
make a date/an appointment	do (the) homework
make a plan	do an exercise
make a decision	do the dishes
make a telephone call	do the cleaning, laundry, ironing, washing, etc.
make a reservation	do the shopping
make a mistake	do one's best
make an effort	do a favor
make an improvement	do the right/wrong thing
make a promise	do a job
make money	do business
make noise	What do you do for a living? (asks about a job)
make the bed	How do you do? (said when you meet someone for the first time)

APPENDIX G

Nouns That Can Be Both Count or Noncount

In the following cases, the same word can be a count or a noncount noun. The meaning is different, however.

Noncount	Count
I spent a lot of *time* on my project.	I go shopping two *times* a month.
I have a lot of *experience* with computers.	I had a lot of interesting *experiences* on my trip to Europe.

In the following cases, there is a small difference in meaning. We see a noncount noun as a whole unit. We see a count noun as something that can be divided into parts.

Noncount	Count
There is a lot of *crime* in a big city.	A lot of *crimes* are never solved.
There is a lot of *opportunity* to make money in the U.S.	There are a lot of job *opportunities* in my field.
She bought a lot of *fruit*.	Oranges and lemons are *fruits* that have a lot of Vitamin C.
I don't have much *food* in my refrigerator.	Milk and butter are *foods* that contain cholesterol.
I have a lot of *trouble* with my car.	He has many *troubles* in his life.

APPENDIX H

Verbs and Adjectives Followed by a Preposition

Many verbs and adjectives are followed by a preposition.

accuse someone of
(be) accustomed to
adjust to
(be) afraid of
agree with
(be) amazed at/by
(be) angry about
(be) angry at/with
apologize for
approve of
argue about
argue with
(be) ashamed of
(be) aware of
believe in
blame someone for
(be) bored with/by
(be) capable of
care about/for
compare to/with
complain about
(be) concerned about
concentrate on
consist of
count on
deal with
decide on
depend on/upon
(be) different from
disapprove of
(be) divorced from
dream about/of
(be) engaged to
(be) excited about
(be) familiar with
(be) famous for
feel like
(be) fond of
forget about
forgive someone for
(be) glad about
(be) good at
(be) grateful to someone for
(be) guilty of
(be) happy about
hear about
hear of
hope for
(be) incapable of
insist on/upon
(be) interested in
(be) involved in
(be) jealous of
(be) known for
(be) lazy about
listen to
look at
look for
look forward to
(be) mad about
(be) mad at
(be) made from/of
(be) married to
object to
(be) opposed to
participate in
plan on
pray to
pray for
(be) prepared for/to
prevent (someone) from
prohibit (someone) from
protect (someone) from
(be) proud of
recover from
(be) related to
rely on/upon
(be) responsible for
(be) sad about
(be) satisfied with
(be) scared of
(be) sick of
(be) sorry about
(be) sorry for
speak about
speak to/with
succeed in
(be) sure of/about
(be) surprised at
take care of
talk about
talk to/with
thank (someone) for
(be) thankful (to someone) for
think about/of
(be) tired of
(be) upset about
(be) upset with
(be) used to
wait for
warn (someone) about
(be) worried about
worry about

APPENDIX I

Direct and Indirect Objects

Word order with direct and indirect objects:
The order of direct and indirect objects depends on the verb you use. IO DO He told his friend the answer. DO IO He explained the answer to his friend.
The order of the objects sometimes depends on whether you use a noun or a pronoun object. S V IO DO He gave the woman the keys. S V DO IO He gave them to her.
In some cases, the connecting preposition is *to;* in some cases, *for*. In some cases, there is no connecting preposition. She'll serve lunch *to* her guests. She reserved a seat *for* you. I asked him a question.

The order of direct and indirect objects depends on the verb you use. It also can depend on whether you use a noun or a pronoun as the object.

Group 1 Pronouns affect word order. The preposition used is *to*.

Patterns:
He gave a present to his wife. (DO to IO)
He gave his wife a present. (IO / DO)
He gave it to his wife. (DO to IO)
He gave her a present. (IO / DO)
He gave it to her. (DO to IO)

Verbs:

bring	lend	pass	sell	show	teach
give	offer	pay	send	sing	tell
hand	owe	read	serve	take	write

Group 2 Pronouns affect word order. The preposition used is *for*.

Patterns:
He bought a car for his daughter. (DO for IO)
He bought his daughter a car. (IO / DO)
He bought it for his daughter. (DO for IO)
He bought her a car. (IO / DO)
He bought it for her. (DO for IO)

Verbs:

bake	buy	draw	get	make
build	do	find	knit	reserve

Group 3 Pronouns don' t affect word order. The preposition used is *to*.

Patterns:
He explained the problem to his friend. (DO to IO)
He explained it to her. (DO to IO)

Verbs:

admit	introduce	recommend	say
announce	mention	repeat	speak
describe	prove	report	suggest
explain			

Group 4 Pronouns don' t affect word order. The preposition used is *for*.

Patterns:
He cashed a check for his friend. (DO to IO)
He cashed it for her. (DO to IO)

Verbs:

answer	change	design	open	prescribe
cash	close	fix	prepare	pronounce

Group 5 Pronouns don' t affect word order. No preposition is used.

Patterns:
She asked the teacher a question. (IO / DO)
She asked him a question. (IO / DO)
It took me five minutes to answer the question. (IO / DO)

Verbs: ask charge cost wish take (with time)

APPENDIX J

Capitalization Rules

- The first word in a sentence: **M**y friends are helpful.
- The word "I": My sister and **I** took a trip together.
- Names of people: **M**ichael **J**ordan; **G**eorge **W**ashington
- Titles preceding names of people: **D**octor (**D**r.) **S**mith; **P**resident **L**incoln; **Q**ueen **E**lizabeth; **M**r. **R**ogers; **M**rs. **C**arter
- Geographic names: the **U**nited **S**tates; **L**ake **S**uperior; **C**alifornia; the **R**ocky **M**ountains; the **M**ississippi **R**iver

  NOTE: The word "the" in a geographic name is not capitalized.
- Street names: **P**ennsylvania **A**venue (**A**ve.); **W**all **S**treet (**S**t.); **A**bbey **R**oad (**R**d.)
- Names of organizations, companies, colleges, buildings, stores, hotels: the **R**epublican **P**arty; **T**homson **H**einle; **D**artmouth **C**ollege; the **U**niversity of **W**isconsin; the **W**hite **H**ouse; **B**loomingdale's; the **H**ilton **H**otel
- Nationalities and ethnic groups: **M**exicans; **C**anadians; **S**paniards; **A**mericans; **J**ews; **K**urds; **E**skimos
- Languages: **E**nglish; **S**panish; **P**olish; **V**ietnamese; **R**ussian
- Months: **J**anuary; **F**ebruary
- Days: **S**unday; **M**onday
- Holidays: **C**hristmas; **I**ndependence **D**ay
- Important words in a title: **G**rammar in **C**ontext; **T**he **O**ld **M**an and the **S**ea; **R**omeo and **J**uliet; **T**he **S**ound of **M**usic

  NOTE: Capitalize "the" as the first word of a title.

APPENDIX K

Glossary of Grammatical Terms

- **Adjective** An adjective gives a description of a noun.

  It's a *tall* tree. He's an *old* man. My neighbors are *nice*.
- **Adverb** An adverb describes the action of a sentence or an adjective or another adverb.

  She speaks English *fluently*. I drive *carefully*.

  She speaks English *extremely* well. She is *very* intelligent.
- **Adverb of Frequency** An adverb of frequency tells how often the action happens.

  I *never* drink coffee. They *usually* take the bus.

Affirmative means *yes.*

Apostrophe ' We use the apostrophe for possession and contractions.

My *sister's* friend is beautiful. Today *isn't* Sunday.

Article The definite article is *the.* The indefinite articles are *a* and *an.*

I have *a* cat. I ate *an* apple. *The* president was late.

Auxiliary Verb Some verbs have two parts: an auxiliary verb and a main verb.

He *can't* study. We *will* return.

Base Form The base form, sometimes called the "simple" form of the verb, has no tense. It has no ending (*-s* or *-ed*): *be, go, eat, take, write.*

He doesn't *know* the answer. I didn't *go* out.

You shouldn't *talk* loudly.

Capital Letter A B C D E F G . . .

Clause A clause is a group of words that has a subject and a verb. Some sentences have only one clause.

She found a good job.

Some sentences have a **main clause** and a **dependent clause.**

MAIN CLAUSE	DEPENDENT CLAUSE (reason clause)
She found a good job	because she has computer skills.
MAIN CLAUSE	**DEPENDENT CLAUSE (time clause)**
She'll turn off the light	before she goes to bed.
MAIN CLAUSE	**DEPENDENT CLAUSE (*if* clause)**
I'll take you to the doctor	if you don't have your car on Saturday.

Colon :

Comma ,

Comparative Form A comparative form of an adjective or adverb is used to compare two things.

My house is *bigger* than your house.

Her husband drives *faster* than she does.

Complement The complement of the sentence is the information after the verb. It completes the verb phrase.

He works *hard.* I slept *for five hours.* They are *late.*

Consonant The following letters are consonants: *b, c, d, f, g, h, j, k, l, m, n, p, q, r, s, t, v, w, x, y, z.*

NOTE: *y* is sometimes considered a vowel, as in the word *syllable.*

Contraction A contraction is made up of two words put together with an apostrophe.

He's my brother. *You're* late. They *won't* talk to me.

(*He's* =*He is*) (*You're* = *You are*) (*won't* = *will not*)

- **Count Noun** Count nouns are nouns that we can count. They have a singular and a plural form.

  1 pen — 3 pens   1 table — 4 tables

- **Dependent Clause** See **Clause.**

- **Direct Object** A direct object is a noun (phrase) or pronoun that receives the action of the verb.

  We saw *the movie.*   You have *a nice car.*   I love *you.*

- **Exclamation Mark !**

- **Frequency Words** Frequency words are *always, usually, often, sometimes, rarely, seldom,* and *never.*

  I *never* drink coffee.   We *always* do our homework.

- **Hyphen -**

- **Imperative** An imperative sentence gives a command or instructions. An imperative sentence omits the word *you.*

  Come here.   *Don't be* late.   Please *sit* down.

- **Indefinite Pronoun** An indefinite pronoun (*one, some, any*) takes the place of an indefinite noun.

  I have a cell phone. Do you have *one?*

  I didn't drink any coffee, but you drank *some.* Did he drink *any?*

- **Infinitive** An infinitive is *to* + base form.

  I want *to leave.*   You need *to be* here on time.

- **Linking Verb** A linking verb is a verb that links the subject to the noun or adjective after it. Linking verbs include *be, seem, feel, smell, sound, look, appear, taste.*

  She *is* a doctor.   She *seems* very intelligent.   She *looks* tired.

- **Modal** The modal verbs are *can, could, shall, should, will, would, may, might,* and *must.*

  They *should* leave.   I *must* go.

- **Negative** means *no.*

- **Nonaction Verb** A nonaction verb has no action. We do not use a continuous tense (*be* + verb *-ing*) with a nonaction verb. The nonaction verbs are: *believe, cost, care, have, hear, know, like, love, matter, mean, need, own, prefer, remember, see, seem, think, understand,* and *want.*

  She *has* a laptop.   We *love* our mother.

- **Noncount Noun** A noncount noun is a noun that we don't count. It has no plural form.

  She drank some *water.*   He prepared some *rice.*

  Do you need any *money?*

- **Noun** A noun is a person (*brother*), a place (*kitchen*), or a thing (*table*). Nouns can be either count (*1 table, 2 tables*) or noncount (*money, water*).

  My *brother* lives in California. My *sisters* live in New York.

  I get *mail* from my family.

- **Noun Modifier** A noun modifier makes a noun more specific.

  fire department *Independence* Day *can* opener

- **Noun Phrase** A noun phrase is a group of words that form the subject or object of the sentence.

  A very nice woman helped me at registration.

  I bought *a big box of candy.*

- **Object** The object of the sentence follows a verb. It receives the action of the verb.

  He bought *a car.* I saw *a movie.* I met *your brother.*

- **Object Pronoun** Use object pronouns (*me, you, him, her, it, us, them*) after the verb or preposition.

  He likes *her.* I saw the movie. Let's talk about *it.*

- **Paragraph** A paragraph is a group of sentences about one topic.

- **Parentheses ( )**

- **Participle, Present** The present participle is verb + *-ing.*

  She is *sleeping.* They were *laughing.*

- **Period .**

- **Phrase** A group of words that go together.

  Last month my sister came to visit.

  There is a strange car *in front of my house.*

- **Plural** Plural means more than one. A plural noun usually ends with *-s.*

  She has beautiful *eyes.*

- **Possessive Form** Possessive forms show ownership or relationship.

  Mary's coat is in the closet. *My* brother lives in Miami.

- **Preposition** A preposition is a short connecting word: *about, above, across, after, around, as, at, away, back, before, behind, below, by, down, for, from, in, into, like, of, off, on, out, over, to, under, up, with.*

  The book is *on* the table.

- **Pronoun** A pronoun takes the place of a noun.

  I have a new car. I bought *it* last week.

  John likes Mary, but *she* doesn't like *him.*

- **Punctuation** Period . Comma , Colon : Semicolon ; Question Mark ? Exclamation Mark !

- **Question Mark ?**

- **Quotation Marks " "**

- **Regular Verb** A regular verb forms its past tense with *-ed*.

  He *worked* yesterday.   I *laughed* at the joke.

- ***s* Form** A present tense verb that ends in *-s* or *-es*.

  He *lives* in New York.   She *watches* TV a lot.

- **Sense-Perception Verb** A sense-perception verb has no action. It describes a sense.

  She *feels* fine.   The coffee *smells* fresh.   The milk *tastes* sour.

- **Sentence** A sentence is a group of words that contains a subject[1] and a verb (at least) and gives a complete thought.

  SENTENCE: She came home.

  NOT A SENTENCE: When she came home

- **Simple Form of Verb** The simple form of the verb, also called the base form, has no tense; it never has an *-s*, *-ed*, or *-ing* ending.

  Did you *see* the movie?   I couldn't *find* your phone number.

- **Singular** Singular means one.

  She ate a *sandwich.*   I have one *television.*

- **Subject** The subject of the sentence tells who or what the sentence is about.

  My sister got married last April. *The wedding* was beautiful.

- **Subject Pronouns** Use subject pronouns (*I, you, he, she, it, we, you, they*) before a verb.

  They speak Japanese.   *We* speak Spanish.

- **Superlative Form** A superlative form of an adjective or adverb shows the number one item in a group of three or more.

  January is the *coldest* month of the year.

  My brother speaks English the *best* in my family.

- **Syllable** A syllable is a part of a word that has only one vowel sound. (Some words have only one syllable.)

  change (one syllable)   after (af·ter = two syllables)

  look (one syllable)   responsible (re·spon·si·ble = four syllables)

- **Tag Question** A tag question is a short question at the end of a sentence. It is used in conversation.

  You speak Spanish, *don't you*?   He's not happy, *is he*?

- **Tense** A verb has tense. Tense shows when the action of the sentence happened.

  SIMPLE PRESENT: She usually *works* hard.

  FUTURE: She *will work* tomorrow.

  PRESENT CONTINUOUS: She *is working* now.

  SIMPLE PAST: She *worked* yesterday.

[1] In an imperative sentence, the subject *you* is omitted: *Sit down. Come here.*

- **Verb** A verb is the action of the sentence.

  He *runs* fast.   I *speak* English.

  Some verbs have no action. They are linking verbs. They connect the subject to the rest of the sentence.

  He *is* tall.   She *looks* beautiful.   You *seem* tired.

- **Vowel** The following letters are vowels: *a, e, i, o, u. Y* is sometimes considered a vowel (for example, in the word *syllable*).

APPENDIX L

Special Uses of Articles

No Article	Article
Personal names: John Kennedy Michael Jordan	The whole family: the Kennedys the Jordans
Title and name: Queen Elizabeth Pope John Paul	Title without name: the Queen the Pope
Cities, states, countries, continents: Cleveland Ohio Mexico South America	Places that are considered a union: the United States the former Soviet Union the United Kingdom Place names: the ________ of ________ the People's Republic of China the District of Columbia
Mountains: Mount Everest Mount McKinley	Mountain ranges: the Himalayas the Rocky Mountains
Islands: Coney Island Staten Island	Collectives of islands: the Hawaiian Islands the Virgin Islands the Philippines
Lakes: Lake Superior Lake Michigan	Collectives of lakes: the Great Lakes the Finger Lakes

Continued

Beaches: Palm Beach Pebble Beach	Rivers, oceans, seas, canals: the Mississippi River the Atlantic Ocean the Dead Sea the Panama Canal
Streets and avenues: Madison Avenue Wall Street	Well-known buildings: the Sears Tower the Empire State Building
Parks: Central Park Hyde Park	Zoos: the San Diego Zoo the Milwaukee Zoo
Seasons: summer fall spring winter Summer is my favorite season. NOTE: After a preposition, *the* may be used. In (the) winter, my car runs badly.	Deserts: the Mojave Desert the Sahara Desert
Directions: north south east west	Sections of a piece of land: the Southwest (of the U.S.) the West Side (of New York)
School subjects: history math	Unique geographical points: the North Pole the Vatican
Name + *college* or *university:* Northwestern University Bradford College	The University (College) of ______: the University of Michigan the College of DuPage County
Magazines: *Time* *Sports Illustrated*	Newspapers: the *Tribune* the *Wall Street Journal*
Months and days: September Monday	Ships: the *Titanic* the *Queen Elizabeth*
Holidays and dates (Month + Day): Thanksgiving Mother's Day July 4	The day of (month): the Fourth of July the fifth of May
Diseases: cancer AIDS polio malaria	Ailments: a cold a toothache a headache the flu

Games and sports: poker soccer	Musical instruments, after *play:* the drums the piano NOTE: Sometimes *the* is omitted. She plays (the) drums.
Languages: French English	The ______ language: the French language the English language
Last month, year, week, etc. = the one before this one: I forgot to pay my rent last month. The teacher gave us a test last week.	The last month, the last year, the last week, etc. = the last in a series: December is the last month of the year. Summer vacation begins the last week in May.
In office = in an elected position: The president is in office for four years.	In the office = in a specific room: The teacher is in the office.
In back/front: She's in back of the car.	In the back/the front: He's in the back of the bus.

APPENDIX M

Alphabetical List of Irregular Verb Forms

Base Form	Past Form	Past Participle	Base Form	Past Form	Past Participle
be	was/were	been	bite	bit	bitten
bear	bore	born/borne	bleed	bled	bled
beat	beat	beaten	blow	blew	blown
become	became	become	break	broke	broken
begin	began	begun	breed	bred	bred
bend	bent	bent	bring	brought	brought
bet	bet	bet	broadcast	broadcast	broadcast
bid	bid	bid	build	built	built
bind	bound	bound	burst	burst	burst

Continued

Base Form	Past Form	Past Participle	Base Form	Past Form	Past Participle
buy	bought	bought	hide	hid	hidden
cast	cast	cast	hit	hit	hit
catch	caught	caught	hold	held	held
choose	chose	chosen	hurt	hurt	hurt
cling	clung	clung	keep	kept	kept
come	came	come	know	knew	known
cost	cost	cost	lay	laid	laid
creep	crept	crept	lead	led	led
cut	cut	cut	leave	left	left
deal	dealt	dealt	lend	loaned/lent	loaned/lent
dig	dug	dug	let	let	let
dive	dove/dived	dove/dived	lie	lay	lain
do	did	done	light	lit/lighted	lit/lighted
draw	drew	drawn	lose	lost	lost
drink	drank	drunk	make	made	made
drive	drove	driven	mean	meant	meant
eat	ate	eaten	meet	met	met
fall	fell	fallen	mistake	mistook	mistaken
feed	fed	fed	overcome	overcame	overcome
feel	felt	felt	overdo	overdid	overdone
fight	fought	fought	overtake	overtook	overtaken
find	found	found	overthrow	overthrew	overthrown
fit	fit	fit	pay	paid	paid
flee	fled	fled	plead	pled/pleaded	pled/pleaded
fly	flew	flown	prove	proved	proven/proved
forbid	forbade	forbidden	put	put	put
forget	forgot	forgotten	quit	quit	quit
forgive	forgave	forgiven	read	read	read
freeze	froze	frozen	ride	rode	ridden
get	got	gotten	ring	rang	rung
give	gave	given	rise	rose	risen
go	went	gone	run	ran	run
grind	ground	ground	say	said	said
grow	grew	grown	see	saw	seen
hang	hung	hung[2]	seek	sought	sought
have	had	had	sell	sold	sold
hear	heard	heard	send	sent	sent

[2] *Hanged* is used as the past form to refer to punishment by death. *Hung* is used in other situations: She *hung* the picture on the wall.

Base Form	Past Form	Past Participle
set	set	set
sew	sewed	sewed/sown
shake	shook	shaken
shed	shed	shed
shine	shone/shined	shone
shoot	shot	shot
show	showed	shown/showed
shrink	shrank/shrunk	shrunk/shrunked
shut	shut	shut
sing	sang	sung
sink	sank	sunk
sit	sat	sat
sleep	slept	slept
slide	slid	slid
slit	slit	slit
speak	spoke	spoken
speed	sped	sped
spend	spent	spent
spin	spun	spun
spit	spit	spit
split	split	split
spread	spread	spread
spring	sprang	sprung
stand	stood	stood
steal	stole	stolen
stick	stuck	stuck
sting	stung	stung
stink	stank	stunk
strike	struck	struck/stricken
strive	strove	striven
swear	swore	sworn
sweep	swept	swept
swell	swelled	swelled/swollen
swim	swam	swum

Base Form	Past Form	Past Participle
swing	swung	swung
take	took	taken
teach	taught	taught
tear	tore	torn
tell	told	told
think	thought	thought
throw	threw	thrown
understand	understood	understood
uphold	upheld	upheld
upset	upset	upset
wake	woke	woken
wear	wore	worn
weave	wove	woven
wed	wedded/wed	wedded/wed
weep	wept	wept
win	won	won
wind	wound	wound
withhold	withheld	withheld
withdraw	withdrew	withdrawn
withstand	withstood	withstood
wring	wrung	wrung
write	wrote	written

Note:

The past and past participle of some verbs can end in *-ed* or *-t*.

burn	burned or burnt
dream	dreamed or dreamt
kneel	kneeled or knelt
learn	learned or learnt
leap	leaped or leapt
spill	spilled or spilt
spoil	spoiled or spoilt

APPENDIX N

The United States of America: Major Cities

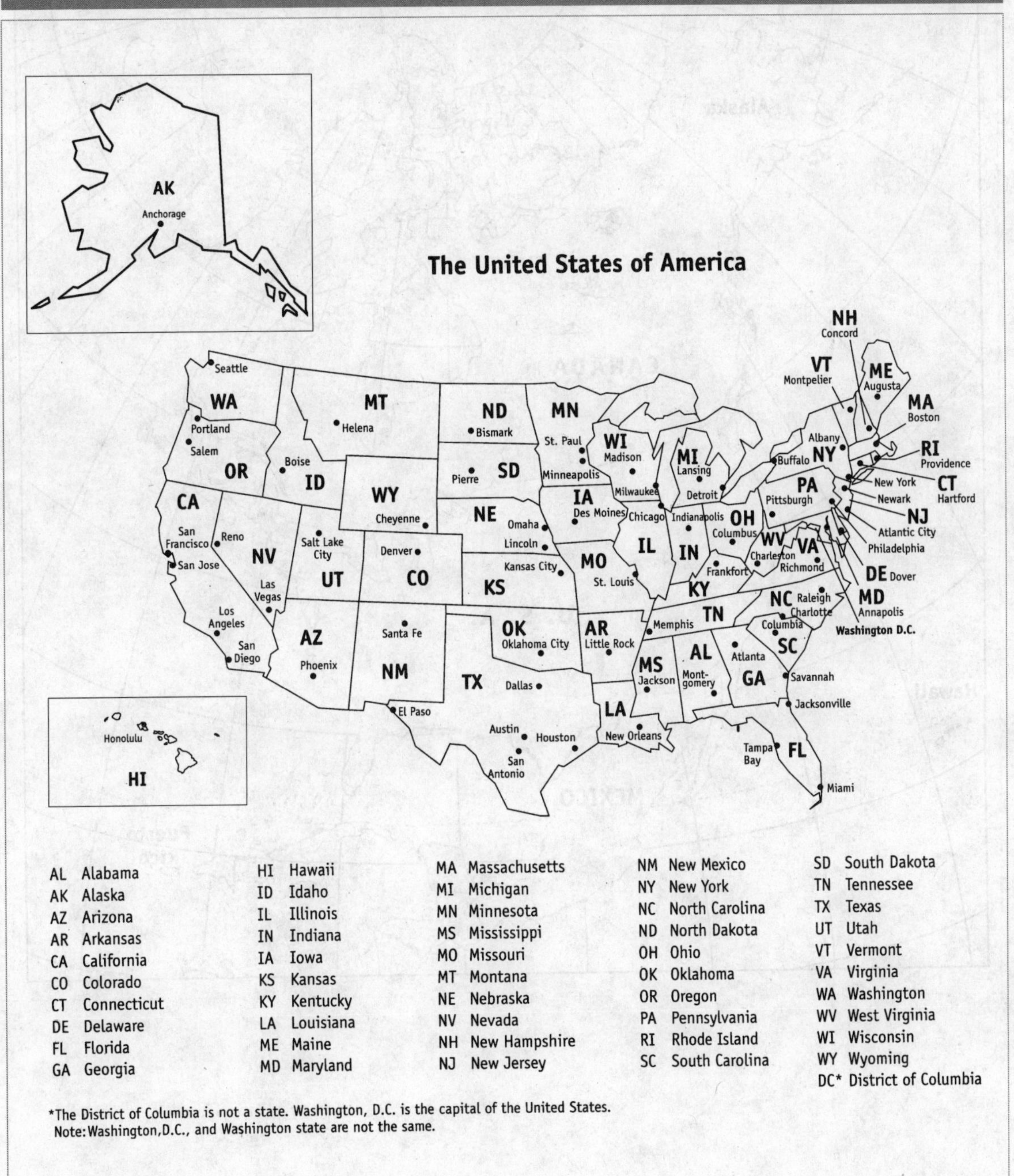

AL Alabama
AK Alaska
AZ Arizona
AR Arkansas
CA California
CO Colorado
CT Connecticut
DE Delaware
FL Florida
GA Georgia
HI Hawaii
ID Idaho
IL Illinois
IN Indiana
IA Iowa
KS Kansas
KY Kentucky
LA Louisiana
ME Maine
MD Maryland
MA Massachusetts
MI Michigan
MN Minnesota
MS Mississippi
MO Missouri
MT Montana
NE Nebraska
NV Nevada
NH New Hampshire
NJ New Jersey
NM New Mexico
NY New York
NC North Carolina
ND North Dakota
OH Ohio
OK Oklahoma
OR Oregon
PA Pennsylvania
RI Rhode Island
SC South Carolina
SD South Dakota
TN Tennessee
TX Texas
UT Utah
VT Vermont
VA Virginia
WA Washington
WV West Virginia
WI Wisconsin
WY Wyoming
DC* District of Columbia

*The District of Columbia is not a state. Washington, D.C. is the capital of the United States.
Note: Washington, D.C., and Washington state are not the same.

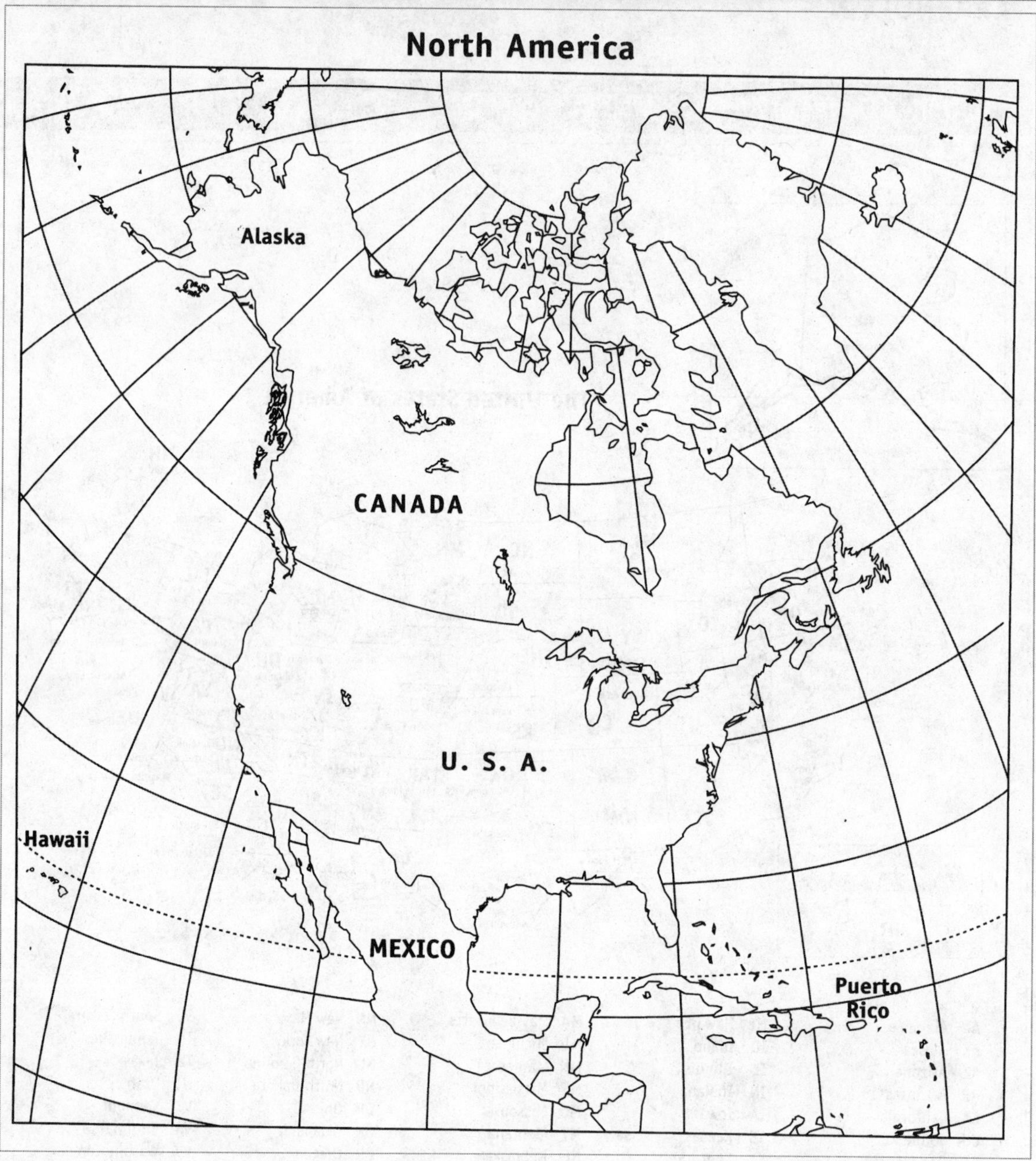
North America
Alaska
CANADA
U. S. A.
Hawaii
MEXICO
Puerto
Rico

Index

Photo Credits

2, left LWA-Dan Tardif/CORIBS, *right* Bill Truslow/Image Bank/Getty Images; *4*, Mary Kate Denny/Stone/Getty Images; *6*, Ann Marie Weber/Taxi/Getty Images; *14*, Stephen McBrady/PhotoEdit; *18*, Syracuse/Newspaper/David Lassman/The Image Works; *24*, Pam Gardner/Frank Lane Picture Agency/CORBIS; *25*, Michael Simpson/Taxi/Getty Images; *26*, Tim MacPherson/Stone/Getty Images; *43*, Tom and Dee Ann McCarthy/CORBIS; *44*, Ariel Skelley/CORBIS; *45*, Marty Heitner/The Image Works; *49*, Robin Sachs/PhotoEdit; *57*, Bonnie Kaufmann/CORBIS; *64*, Sandra Elbaum; *65*, Ariel Skelley/CORBIS; *68*, David Houser/CORBIS; *70*, Bonnie Kaufmann/CORBIS; *87*, *top*, Flip Schulke/CORBIS, *bottom*, William Philpott/Reuters/CORBIS; *88*, Bettmann/CORBIS; *89*, *left*, Duomo/CORBIS, *right*, Frank Trapper/CORBIS; *93*, Thomas Gilbert/AP/Wide World Photos; *97*, Bettmann/CORBIS; *100*, CORBIS; *115*, Rick Gomez/CORBIS; *126*, Steven Rothfeld/Stone/Getty Images; *127*, Brand X Pictures/Getty Images; *129*, Chuck Savage/CORBIS; *134*, Susan van Etten/PhotoEdit; *138*, Tony Freeman/PhotoEdit; *149*, Bob Daemmrich/The Image Works; *150*, Kelley Mooney Photography/CORBIS; *157*, Bruce Ayres/Stone/Getty Images; *166*, Ron Sachs/CORBIS; *168*, Tom Bean/CORBIS; *170*, Marty Heitner/The Image Works; *173*, Sandra Elbaum; *184*, Peter Turnley/CORBIS; *187*, *left*, Eric K.K. Yu/CORBIS, *right*, Royalty Free/CORBIS; *188*, Robert E. Daemmrich/Stone/Getty Images; *189*, ANA/The Image Works; *194*, Michael Newman/PhotoEdit; *195*, Dana White/PhotoEdit; *211*, CORBIS; *212*, Gail Mooney/CORBIS; *213*, Sandra Elbaum; *218*, Hulton Archive/Getty Images; *227*, Nancy Kaszerman/Zuma/CORBIS; *237*, Michael Newman/PhotoEdit; *239*, Shelley Gazin/The Image Works; *246*, David Young Wolff/PhotoEdit; *249*, Dwayne Newton/PhotoEdit; *252*, Bonnie Kamin/PhotoEdit; *257*, James Marshall/The Image Works; *262*, Willie Hill, Jr./The Image Works; *277*, Dex Images/CORBIS; *278*, Kim Kulshi/CORBIS; *289*, Aleata Evans; *292*, Images.com/CORBIS; *298*, Richard Lord/The Image Works; *315*, Ralf-Finn Hestoft/CORBIS; *316*, Royalty Free/CORBIS; *353*, Randy M. Ury/CORBIS; *354*, Tony Freeman/PhotoEdit; *361*, Aleata Evans; *364*, David Young Wolff/PhotoEdit; *375*, Duomo/CORBIS; *375*, Mike Segar/Reuters/CORBIS; *376*, Reuters/CORBIS; *377*, Reuters/CORBIS; *381*, Reuters/CORBIS; *382*, Reuters/CORBIS; *385*, Bob Daemmrich/The Image Works; *390*, Didrik Johnck/CORBIS; *397*, *left*, Albert Gea/Reuters/CORBIS, *right*, Robert Galbraith/Reuters/CORBIS; *413*, Jose Luis Pelaez, Inc./CORBIS; *414*, Billy E. Barnes/PhotoEdit; *422*, Michael Newman/PhotoEdit; *423*, Billy Aron/PhotoEdit; *437*, Susan van Etten/PhotoEdit; *438*, David Young Wolff/PhotoEdit; *442*, Mary Kate Denny/PhotoEdit; *444*, Jeff Greenberg/The Image Works; *451*, Michael Newman/PhotoEdit; *451*, Joseph Sohm/Visions of America/CORBIS; *456*, Dana White/PhotoEdit; *459*, David Young Wolff/PhotoEdit; *461*, Michele Birdwell/PhotoEdit.

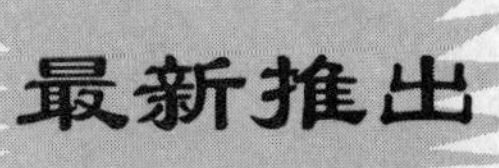

《英语语境语法》(第四版)系列丛书

尊敬的老师：

您好！

为了方便您更好地使用本套教材，获得最佳教学效果，我们特向使用该套丛书作为教材的教师赠送 CD-ROM 测试题库和教学录像。如有需要，请完整填写“教师联系表”，免费向出版社索取。

北京大学出版社

教师联系表

<table>
<tr><td>姓名：</td><td>性别：</td><td>职务：</td><td>职称：</td></tr>
<tr><td>E-mail：</td><td>联系电话：</td><td colspan="2">邮政编码：</td></tr>
<tr><td colspan="2">供职学校：</td><td colspan="2">所在院系：</td></tr>
<tr><td colspan="4">学校地址：</td></tr>
<tr><td colspan="2">教学科目与年级：</td><td colspan="2">班级人数：</td></tr>
<tr><td colspan="4">通信地址：</td></tr>
</table>

填写完毕后，请将此表邮寄或 EMAIL 给我们，我们将为您免费寄送 CD-ROM 测试题库及教学录像，谢谢！

北京市海淀区成府路 205 号
北京大学出版社外语编辑部负责人
邮政编码：100871
电子邮箱：zbing@pup.pku.edu.cn

邮购部电话：010-62534449
市场营销部电话：010-62750672
外语编辑部电话：010-62765014